WINDS OF LOVE

The Gunzburgs—Imperial Russia's foremost Jewish family, a banking dynasty raised to the nobility, cocooned in a world of Fabergé jewels and fabulous estates, united by blood and heritage, pulled asunder by clashing dreams.

WINDS OF PASSION

Baroness Sonia—the most beautiful Gunzburg, a woman men were willing to die for, torn between duty to her family and love for the handsome son of their deadliest enemy.

WINDS OF CHANGE

Against the gathering storm of war and revolution, they would struggle to survive in a collapsing world of violence and loss, heartbreak and betrayal.

WINDS OF DESTINY

Cast adrift in a turbulent era, Sonia would lead her family into bitter exile. But out of the ruins they will build a bold new life and a soaring monument to triumphant love in a brave new land.

THE FOUR WINDS OF HEAVEN

MONIQUE RAPHEL HIGH

THE
Four Winds
OF
Heaven

A DELL BOOK

Published by
Dell Publishing Co., Inc.
1 Dag Hammarskjold Plaza
New York, New York 10017

Dell ® TM 681510, Dell Publishing Co., Inc.

ISBN: 0-440-12566-9

Reprinted by arrangement with Delacorte Press
Printed in the United States of America
First Dell printing—January 1981

For my daughter, Nathalie Danielle, and my father, David Raphel. This is their history as well as mine.

*"I have spread you abroad
as the four winds of the heaven."*
—*Zechariah 2:6*

Foreword

In 1972, Baroness Sonia de Gunzburg died at the age of eighty-two. She was my grandmother. Several months later, three enormous crates arrived at my home, filled to the rim with her diaries and notebooks, covering a lifetime of thoughts and feelings. It was from these faded, dog-eared old books that I created *The Four Winds of Heaven*. This is, at heart, her story and that of her immediate family, the Gunzburgs of St. Petersburg. But this is not a biography: rather, it is a re-creation, a distillation of the characters and of the period through my own eyes, and written with poetic license.

This is a story of a Russia that no longer exists, except through the memory of those who lived there before the Revolution. I have attempted to capture its essence, its dialogue, its traditions. I must explain for readers unfamiliar with the latter that, in Russia, names possessed certain rules unparalleled in other languages. Certain last names received feminine endings, but not all. Diminutives often had no resemblance to the given, formal name. And, most important, only those on the most intimate terms could address each other without the patronym compound (formal first name followed by the father's first name and the ending meaning "son of" or "daughter of"—"-vitch" and "-vna" respectively). To give an example involving a single name, the Countess Natalia Tagantseva has an "a" added to the family name of Tagantsev; her diminutive, employed by those closest to her, is Natasha or Natashenka; and all but her family and intimate friends would call her Natalia Nicolaievna, because her father's name was Nicolai. I have kept the correct forms of address as they were used in Russian society, because one can sense formality and intimacy and all the layers in between through this convention, which does not exist in our less complex Western world.

This book would never have reached production had it not been for Linda Grey, my sponsor and first editor at Dell, who made this into a true labor of love; for valiant Andrea Cirillo, who handled a monumental task when she took over editorship upon Linda's promotion to Editor-in-Chief; for my agent and guardian angel, Dorris Halsey. Gracious help in the Russian language was given by Aliza Sverdlova and Serge Kourdoukoff. Good advice came from four fellow writers: Jean Sherman, Clancy Goode, Hubert Cornfield, and Patricia McCune Irvine. But most of all I want to thank Charlotte Hyde, who championed this book and is, in effect, its godmother.

Prologue

In that sprawling immensity that was all the Russias, from the steppes to the frozen woods of Siberia, a massive revolt had taken place, worse than any previous disaster that had threatened the land. When wars had come, when Tzars had died and been replaced by new ones, when the sun had baked the earth to a thin crust or when the snows had covered entire villages, Russia, like a sleeping giant, had but grumbled protest. But the Bolshevik Revolution in 1917 brought with it chaos; province lost touch with province, mothers lost trace of their children, and commanders of armies lost whole regiments fighting in the outlands for control of a government that was already established in the capital, Petrograd. At first the people of Russia sought to know who had won, who had been killed, what had been gained or lost on each side. But now, in April 1919, life had resumed its mechanical pace. Battles still raged. But for the peasants, only the crops mattered. No longer did they throw bouquets at passing squadrons. But then, no longer did these passing squadrons bear the regal attributes of shining saviors. Everyone had grown war-weary but the small children.

So it was that in a village in the south of Russia, a

motley group of soldiers, tired and muddied from their battles and endless marches, lined up to depart. Only a small, delicate young woman, holding a basket of fruit in her arms, appeared to be watching. She stood by the side of the road, her fine features drawn with tension, her large gray eyes haunting her emaciated face. She gripped her basket with hands once delicate, now bone-thin. The sun shone, a Tartar woman slapped her screaming child, an old crone with fresh produce pushed the young woman aside in an effort to cross the street rapidly. When the squadron commander called out, "Forward—march!" no one but the girl paid any attention.

That spring of 1919, the inhabitants of Stary Krym, a large Crimean village on the main route to Simferopol, thought little of the comings and goings of soldiers, whatever their flags. Simferopol was the provincial capital, less than sixty-five miles away. They knew that the city had been taken many times, but most of them were not certain who commanded the government in Petrograd. Their Russia was its fields, its cattle, its pigs, its fresh fruit and vegetables, and so they accommodated whatever army happened to arrive, Red or White, hoping only that the soldiers would not slaughter too much livestock, or ravage many young women. In Stary Krym, life went on.

Near the edge of the main road stood a small, low house. It belonged to a widow, Aspasia Vassilievna. But she had not resided there for some time, for it was rented. Instead, she now occupied the house of her late brother, who had been murdered during a Bolshevik looting several months before. She had taken a boarder in that residence as well, but the villagers hardly took notice of this woman. Stary Krym was composed of such diverse groups—Tartars, Armenians, Turks, and Jews—that newcomers did not attract attention.

Nighttime fell. No new garrison had come to commandeer sleeping quarters. Inside the low house by the edge of the road, the young woman who had watched the soldiers pulled down the window shades, then entered the tiny bedroom to the right of the living room. Another, older woman was sitting on the bed, and had already rolled back the rug between the cot and the wall. She handed the younger woman a rusted axe, and watched as her companion crouched on her haunches and attempted to pry the nails from the rough planks of the floor. The girl worked the edge of the axe under the heads of the nails until it was possible to extricate them, and then she handed them to the woman on the bed.

When she had removed a series of nails, she began to work on the wooden boards, lifting them slightly with her axe, then jamming the tool underneath as a lever, drops of perspiration beading her forehead with the effort. Only the sounds of her panting echoed in the room. She pulled up board after board, slowly, laboriously, so that no chunk of wood would break off and reveal a gap. Suddenly the woman said, "It is past midnight, Sonia. You have put in more than four hours tonight."

"Go to sleep, then," the girl replied.

The older woman nodded, removing her shoes. Her ungainly garments made her appear heavier than she was, but her face, oval and white, was remarkably unlined. Large sapphire eyes shone beneath thick brows, and her mass of hair was salt and pepper as she uncoiled it now. She did not speak, but her gaze of grave concern rested upon her daughter. How slender and frail she had become. Her tiny face seemed very young indeed. But the cool gray eyes set close together bespoke years of hardship. When at last Sonia fell upon the bed, fully clothed, the boards had been loosened and then lowered back into position, and the little carpet had been pushed back to cover her work.

Sonia was the first to hear the tramp of footsteps on the road, the loud knock on the door. The two women stood transfixed in the living room as the door burst open, revealing two soldiers. The first was young and scared-looking. His companion was more ominous. He was enormous, with shoulders so wide he had difficulty squeezing through the wooden door frame, and had a huge gut, taut like the belly of a pregnant woman. The young one said, "We are Igor Plotkin and Pavel Antonov, and our orders are to commandeer your house. We shall try to take up little space—"

But his thin voice was cut short by the other man. "Shut up, you ass! We'll sleep here," he announced, pointing to the living room. "Igor, take the floor. I'll have the sofa, and lots of food. Which of you cooks around here?"

Sonia remained erect, her gray eyes unflinching. "I do."

Suddenly the large soldier, Antonov, threw back his head and guffawed. "Splendid, splendid, my little turtle! I like the looks of you. A bit scrawny, but you'll do."

She brought them cooked millet. Antonov, his shirt coming unbuttoned to reveal his paunch, grabbed her by the wrist. She held his gaze. "Little pigeon. You are a strange bird, indeed," he said, and then took a swig from the vodka bottle he was holding with his free hand. "I have heard the villagers say that you are mad, for you do not smile like other girls. Come, make me laugh, right now!"

"Very well. Show me your palm, and I shall read it," Sonia said. She squirmed out of his grasp, rubbed her bruised wrist, and took the hand that had imprisoned her. She turned it over and nearly gasped in surprise and horror. But her gray eyes displayed no shock. She only shrugged. "I cannot read it. You have no clues to give me here." And with that, she departed to the bedroom.

Closing the door behind her, she stood leaning against it, her face ashen. Mathilde was making the bed. "What is wrong?" she demanded.

"Do you remember that fortune teller, Mama?" Sonia whispered. "I have just seen his palm—Antonov's—and it is smooth, totally lineless."

Mathilde de Gunzburg stopped her work and put a hand

to her mouth. "The gypsy said that only criminals have no lines."

But the rough voice of the big soldier interrupted them. "I want the little dove!" he was shouting. "Come, tell me about your life. Your love life. That should be amusing, eh, Igor?"

Plotkin, in distress, protested meekly: "Pavel. This is not one of your tavern whores."

"Shut up, Igor. What are you, child? An actress? Igor's an actor, but actresses . . . mmm . . . they are wanton and gay. I do not like women of mystery. You are too clean, and your accent is too pure. But then, my friend Igor speaks well, too, for his acting has taught him fine Russian. Me—my mother had no time to teach me a thing. She was too busy earning her living, doing what she knew best, using what lay between her legs. As for my father—he abandoned us when I was a boy, to go on to better things. A better life. You see, little one, he was hanged for killing a man."

"That's a nice tale," the girl said ironically. "Mine is far less spicy. I am merely the daughter of a schoolteacher, who is now deceased. He taught me to read and write when I was little, and if I speak like a *burshui*, it is because of him." She turned from Antonov and briskly removed the two plates.

"She's a pretty thing," Antonov commented as she moved toward the kitchen. "I like fragile women. I like them breakable. This one will shatter like a bubble of glass."

Several nights later, the women were alone in their bedroom when the front door squeaked open, and a feminine voice reached their ears. "Where are you?" someone said. A lean figure appeared in the doorway, her eyes shining with a kind of fever. "I have brought you bad news! Antonov knows who you are. He thinks you have money, and

—— • ——

jewels, and he is going to kill us for them! I could not stand to be away from you, to hide in my own house when I knew . . ."

"Then be quick, and shut yourself inside the armoire in the living room," Sonia cut in. Mathilde, seated beside her, opened her mouth, bewildered, and the girl squeezed her arm fiercely. "We shall hide here, in our own closet. Thank you for warning us." She could not help adding, "And when this is over, you must tell us how you learned of all this."

The lean woman turned quickly on her heels, and from the bedroom, Sonia heard the opening and closing of heavy doors. "She's inside," she whispered. "Now." Quickly she pushed aside the heavy carpet and began to lift the planks. "You first," she instructed. Mathilde hesitated, then climbed down into the darkness below the floor of the house. Sonia held up the planks and climbed in beside her almost at once. They huddled on dank ground, in a cramped area between the foundation stones. It was damp and very cold. Sonia was holding a knife in her hand, and when the boards had fallen back into place, she poked the knife above her, through a crack that revealed the light in the bedroom, moving her hand dexterously above their heads. Suddenly the light disappeared, and motes of dust came wafting down upon the two women. "I think the carpet is pulled over enough," she whispered tersely.

They crouched, huddling together, Sonia's hand on her mother's arm. Sounds were reaching their ears, at first distant, then clearer, sharper. A man was singing off-key. Sonia nodded, her grasp tightened on Mathilde's arm as the front door opened, then a scuffling sound by the living room sideboard announced Antonov and Plotkin's presence. "Drunk," the girl said in a warning whisper. "More dangerous."

"Well?" Antonov's voice was harsh. "Where are they? Look in the bedroom!"

Footsteps echoed barely inches over the women. Plotkin, surprised and meek, said: "Pavel—no one is here!"

The boards creaked as the heavier man entered the room. He pulled open the doors of the armoire. An animal roar resounded, and then the women heard the metal hinges of the dresser being torn off. "Bitches!" Antonov cried. "Where have they gone? If I get my hands on them . . ."

"Pavel. The militia," Plotkin reminded him.

"You goddamn ninny! If I find that goddamn waif, I'm going to have me a time! I haven't had a woman in ten days."

They heard him begin to throw open drawers. A grunt of disgust resounded. Cabinet doors were pulled out, their contents clattering to the floor. An eruption of blind frustration bellowed from Antonov: "Jewels? There's nothing here, nothing but these chipped cups, these blasted forks with the plating rubbed off."

They heard a door being yanked open, then sudden silence, followed by Antonov's disembodied shout: "You? What are you doing here, you whore? Where are they?"

Sonia's fingers were so cold that she could not feel their tips. Her hand was still gripping her mother's arm. They heard the female voice, pitched hysterically, crying, "The bedroom! They're in the bedroom!"

"And I'm in China!" Sounds broke out as Antonov dragged the woman from her hiding place, and her shrill cries pierced through the thin planking. "And what about their jewels? Was that a lie, too?" he shouted.

"No, no. Please, I beg you—there is a jewel. A crab, set in gold, encrusted with diamonds. I can show you where she keeps it—let me go, I can show you!" Their voices were clearer now, just above the heads of the two women. Sonia felt her mother sag against her, and realized that Mathilde had fainted; her weight pushed against her own frail body, crushing her against one of the foundation stones. Above her, Antonov was ripping open their mattress, and the shrill cries continued, "I know she has it! I have seen it, here, in this room!"

Underneath the planks, the weight of Mathilde's head had pulled Sonia's thick peasant blouse from her left shoulder. Just above the pointing of her breast, on her cloth chemise, gleamed a brooch of deep gold. In the blackness, its shimmering diamonds fired red and blue. Sonia's eyes, like magnets, sought the gem and held it. It was shaped like a crab.

Overhead, Antonov was slapping the woman, and, pinned against her mother, Sonia looked up to where the boards creaked, almost on top of her head. A sudden thud made the floor touch the coil of her braids. The woman was shrieking, "No, no! Please . . . please," but only thick male sounds followed as when a bulky man pushes his weight against something. The boards began to bend, creaking heavily, and Plotkin's reedy voice called out: "No, Pavel! The militia!"

"I don't give a damn!" Antonov shouted. His voice was directly above their hiding place. "I wanted the little one, d'you hear? So I'm going to get what I can, even if it's poor merchandise! You shut up, and guard the front door!"

The woman's cries were a continuous moan now, punctuated by sharp little shrieks. Sonia could barely breathe. Frozen, she felt the floor move up and down, in cadence to Antonov's grunts, then one piercing female sob rent the night. She huddled motionless against the cold, damp stone, waiting. Finally, the woman above her began to weep, groaning slightly. It was then that Antonov said, "Can't you ever shut up, you slimy bitch?" A single gunshot reverberated in the darkness, and the moaning was cut off; then footsteps, and Plotkin's voice mingling into the plaintive sounds of the Crimean night. Sonia recognized the litany he was chanting over and over to himself in hushed tones: it was the Lord's Prayer.

"Shut up," Antonov said, but he was no longer shouting. Sonia heard their footsteps leaving the room.

She smelled it before she felt it on her arm. But when she saw the drop of moisture seeping through a crack in the planks beneath the carpet, her mind did not work right away. She touched the spot of red on her white skin, rubbed her fingers together. She sniffed her fingers, licked them with the tip of her tongue—and for the first time since her early childhood, an animal terror coursed through her and she lost control of her muscles. A hot wetness flushed out of her down the insides of her thighs.

She felt her mother's weight crushing her, saw the salt and pepper hair pressed against her shoulder, yet all at once it was not gray, but a rich, raven black, and the bulky form that had collapsed against her was that of a young woman like herself, but clothed in fine mint-green silk, with pearls about her neck. And suddenly her own hair was no longer braided, it was flowing down her back, and she was running through a wheat field, her hand that of a small child, clutching a bouquet of primroses. She could feel the hot sun upon her shoulders, the wind in her face, and the voice that called out, "Look what I picked for you!" was her own, yet it was not her own, for it was the voice of a very little girl. And she could see the frilled pantalettes and her own blue pinafore . . .

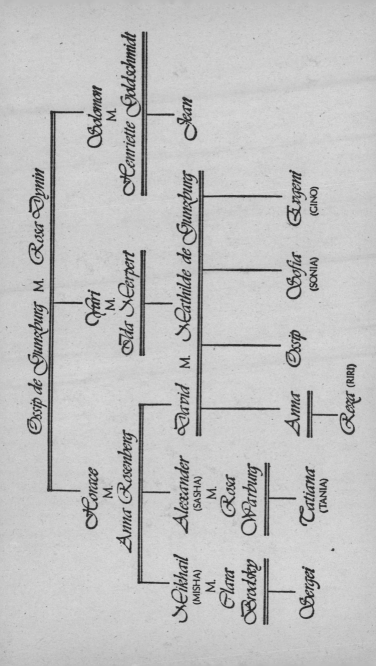

Book 1

One

In the mind of Sonia de Gunzburg, the summer of 1895 marked the end of an era and the beginning of another, for it was then that Gino was born, completing the family, that Ossip's illness abated sufficiently for him to reenter the mainstream of their lives, and the time when Anna had been her most mischievous self—or perhaps it only appeared that way in retrospect, because afterward the family had never again been together alone, and Anna, especially, had suffered from this.

The Gunzburgs were spending three months at their summer home, Mohilna, in the south Russian province of Podolia where Papa had been born in 1857. He had never forgotten the aroma of the sun-warmed grass of his boyhood. Years before Sonia was born he had purchased this estate of several thousand acres so far removed from civilization. Papa was a scholar and a member of the government in St. Petersburg, but in his heart he fancied being a country squire, and overlooked with interest the workings of his two sugar factories. One of his grandfathers had been the most important sugar producer in Kiev, and Papa, with a smile, enjoyed carrying on this family tradition. But the children loved Mohilna best because there, and only there, were they allowed to run barefoot and free. For the

Gunzburgs were isolated on their summer property; even Mama lived without formality there.

Sonia often heard stories about the Gunzburg family, and her sister Anna, who was ten, and her brother Ossip, eight, sometimes boasted to their friends that they belonged to the First Jewish Family of Russia. These words meant very little to Sonia, who would turn five at the end of June. The Jews were God's chosen people, her Papa had read to her from Bible stories, but did that not mean that everyone who lived in this world today was a Jew? For God had struck down Pharaoh, and surely he must have struck down all other nonbelievers by this advanced date. Sonia only knew that train controllers were very deferential to her Mama, that people in restaurants in Paris and Vienna always saved the best tables for the family, and that Papa, "the Baron David," was said to speak more languages than anyone in Petersburg. Yes, the Gunzburg family was well respected, and yet it was not until that summer that all the pieces began to fit together in the small girl's head.

Sonia, who loved a fairy tale beyond all childish joys, thought the emergence of the Gunzburg family from anonymity was the choicest one of all. She did not fully understand all the steps involved in the process, but that hardly mattered. Her imagination supplied her with sufficient pictures to delight her totally. She could not quite sketch the portrait of the family patriarch, Gabriel, who had come to southern Russia from the town of Gunzburg in Bavaria, adopting the name of his birthplace for himself. He had made this voyage in the late 1700s, and had set up a single-loom clothmaking shop in the village of Orsha, which had no sidewalks, only rough wooden planks, and where most people spoke only Yiddish and could neither read nor write. But Sonia had no trouble picturing her great-grandfather, Gabriel's son Ossip, who was born in 1812.

He was a comely boy, as she imagined him, lithe, with

thick black hair, and blue-gray eyes set close together, like Sonia's own. And he was a genius. First he set out to learn perfect Russian, and went to the public school. This took place during the reign of Tzar Nicholas I. Ossip helped his father make such a success of the shop that Gabriel moved to Simferopol, the beautiful capital of the Crimea. Sonia had visited his house, which was wide and comfortable, and stood at a busy crossroads.

Ossip fell in love with a girl from his village, Rosa Dynin, and he married her, even though she did not share his dreams of success and could speak no Russian. He also arranged for his two beautiful sisters to marry brilliantly. Bella was wed to Grigori Rosenberg, whose family owned the most prosperous sugar factories in Russia, and who was the most eligible Jew in Kiev. Louise did almost as well, marrying Vladimir Merpert, of Chernikhov, who worked in the provincial government. And then Ossip proceeded to stretch his business interests in all directions, providing supplies for the troops during the Crimean War, sponsoring the building of the Trans-Siberian railroad. Finally, with the special dispensation granted only to the wealthiest Jews, he moved to the capital, St. Petersburg, and set up the first private bank in the country.

Although he had bought a splendid house in the Russian capital, Ossip Gunzburg did not remain there for very long. Accompanied by his large family, and their entourage of servants and governesses, Ossip set off in ten horse carriages from Russia to Spa in Belgium to take the waters. It was 1861.

But it was Paris with which he fell in love, and where he decided to remain. He secured permission to construct his house near the Etoile where Napoleon I had erected his Arch of Triumph. His son Alexander settled in a different dwelling, but Horace, Yuri, and Solomon chose to live with their father.

Ossip was well received in Paris. His sons had learned

French as boys, for the Russian bourgeoisie and the nobility spoke French among themselves. Ossip had learned right along with them, from their tutors. Now a wealthy international banker, he was sought after in French society, and his own house was known for its excellent receptions. Rosa always sat at the head of the table, with the guest of honor on her right, even though she could understand no one, and missed the simplicity of her native Orsha. She did not follow the fashions, and always wore a bright red wig, as the village Rabbi had instructed her to do after her wedding, when her hair had been shorn in the Jewish Orthodox tradition.

Sonia thought that Ossip's love for his Rosa must have been strong and beautiful, for he had never failed in his respect for her. True, he asked Anna, Horace's wife, to plan his menus with him and to act as hostess for his dinners, but that was because Anna spoke French and knew all the ways of the world. And she possessed a rare beauty. She was milk-white of complexion, with dark hair and blue-gray eyes. Horace, small, elegant, with conservative good taste and his father's own business acumen, had found her perfect for him. Anna made Horace laugh, Horace the serious banker, and she gave him three children. Sonia's Papa, David, was the first son of their union.

In the meantime, Yuri had married also. Yuri looked much like his brother Horace and like his father, but he was flamboyant where Horace was sober, a spendthrift where Horace was a shrewd businessman. He was gay and handsome and selfish, and totally unsuited for the shy young girl whom he had married upon his father's request. Ida, in turn, looked much like her sister-in-law Anna, but she lacked Anna's tremendous capacity for enjoyment of life. There was not much laughter between her and Yuri, but they did have nine children, and Sonia's Mama, Mathilde, was their second daughter.

It was Papa's father, Horace, who had given the family

its title. For in 1875, the beautiful Anna had died, and, brokenhearted, Horace had returned to St. Petersburg and the Gunzburg banking dynasty there. He had been chosen by the government of Hesse-Darmstadt, a small German state, to represent its interests as its consul, and when the young Archduke Louis had come to Russia for a stint in the Guard, he had come to Horace for an important loan, which had been granted to him with the utmost discretion. As his reward, Horace had been made a Baron; a "de" had been added to his name, and the title had been extended to his father, brothers, and their heirs. The Tzar had permitted the title to stand in Russia as well. Anna had not lived to be a baroness, but old Ossip enjoyed the privilege for one year before his death.

Sonia knew that Papa had fallen in love with Mama during their childhood in Paris, when they had lived as cousins in their grandfather's house at the Etoile. But he had gone to Russia for his military duty, and had served with the Uhlans at Lomzha, and, like his father, he had felt the strong pull of his Russian roots. He had decided to live in St. Petersburg, not Paris, though Mama had felt totally French and had not shared his feelings. So, following their wedding in December 1883, Sonia's parents had come to the Russian capital. Now Papa served in the Ministries of Education and Foreign Affairs.

At the end of August, a new baby was expected, and Sonia, more than the other two children, was particularly excited. She had more reason to be. Anna, named after her Papa's mother, possessed so much verve and inner resourcefulness that she might even have been happy as an only child, and Ossip, who bore the name of his illustrious great-grandfather, had been confined to a special crib for nearly three years, so that now, frail and unable to participate in any physical game, he was barely capable of enjoying his boyhood. Both older children had been struck with illness at an early age, Anna as a baby with convulsions that had caused the left side of her face to sag, and Ossip with Pott's disease, which attacked the vertebrae and had kept him supine for almost half his life. But Sonia had been healthy, and she was tired of being the baby of the family.

She knew that babies, when the time came, were left in the fields to be picked like berries or wildflowers by their mothers. But, unlike the brilliant poppies that openly vied with sunny buttercups for the attention of their collectors, babies came one at a time, and the mother was forced to take home whatever child was left for her. Mama, of course, being a great lady, would be permitted to send another woman, a servant perhaps, into the fields in her stead. Still, when Sonia's birthday came in June, Papa asked her which she would prefer, a new sister or a brother. One Anna was sufficient, replete as this one was with wild schemes and projects, whereas Ossip was gentle and passive. Therefore, Sonia had said, "A brother, please."

That summer, Anna's imagination was more highly developed than ever. Sonia felt a fierce love for her sister, comprised of admiration, compassion, but also lack of understanding. She thought that no one was more daring than Anna, that every part of Anna was filled with a fiery spirit. She herself, diminutive and shy, was pushed to her heights of bravery only in order to please or placate her sister. She was angry that some people smirked behind Anna's back, or said unkind things about her "ugliness"— for how could they ignore the gleam of her flame-red hair, so like Papa's, and of her intelligent brown eyes? True, Anna's hair resisted the curling irons just as Anna herself resisted direction. But Sonia was baffled by Anna's wayward tastes: Anna much preferred the company of servants and peasants to that of Mama's friends, and she did not try, as Sonia did, to emulate Mama in each of her feminine perfections. She said, quite simply, that she did not plan to ever be a lady.

Anna was particularly fond of Eusebe, the water carrier,

a young man whose principal duty on the estate was to drive the cart upon which lay the enormous barrel in which water was brought to the various parts of Mohilna. She would rest her elbows on the windowsill of the bedroom, prop her chin upon the palms of her hands and stare out toward the vast courtyard and beyond it, to the woods that seemed to stretch forever toward the sugar factories. "There he goes," she would murmur, and then one morning she had added, her eyes ablaze, "I'm going to ask him to take me along!"

But later, when Sonia found her sister in the pantry, her bare feet tucked beneath her skirts as she sat on the floor, she realized that Eusebe had foiled Anna's plan. Anna, shaking her ornery red curls in anger, was saying, "But Eusebe, you aren't on Count Tuminsky's estate! Papa never whips his servants! You are being a ridiculous fool, and I thought otherwise of you. Why, I think you have the most important job I have ever heard of: so many people depend on you, for who can work and bathe and cook without water? In fact"—and her brown eyes glinted slyly—"if you were truly a brave man, I would choose your profession for myself. For I wish to perform great deeds, to help many people. But if you are a weakling, I shall not wish to imitate you at all." And her lower lip began to protrude forlornly.

The water carrier started to laugh. "Anna Davidovna! You must not even whisper such things. You, a baroness, with my job! Why, you will meet a handsome man, a count perhaps, and he shall give you a beautiful house like your Mama's. I have never heard such nonsense before."

Anna rose with dignity. "Laughs best who laughs last," she said. "But I shall bet you a kopek that I shall never marry, except maybe a man like you. But he would have to be more courageous, and not afraid of my Papa. And anyway, dear Eusebe, who would marry me, with my ugly face?"

Eusebe wrung his hands together. "Oh, my dear Anna Davidovna! To me you are a little flower, a wild one, but a sweet-smelling one, too. Do not say such dreadful things about yourself!"

"I speak only the truth. But I do not care if I am pretty or not. Pretty girls have debuts, and must go visiting with their mothers. I shall have more fun!" With that, Anna tossed her head defiantly, and ran out of the pantry, nearly knocking Sonia down in the process. Her small sister had been standing on the threshold, her tiny hands clenched together, her oval face alive with misery at her sister's words. Now she meekly took Anna's arm and walked with her into the courtyard. Her blue-gray eyes were filled with tears.

Sonia's mind was so crammed with conflicting emotions —pain for Anna because of her face, anger with her for not wanting to be like Mama, shock that Anna had expressed desire to hold Eusebe's job and perhaps marry a servant, when surely a man such as Papa fit the image of Prince Charming far more closely, that she did not object when her sister announced that they would hide behind the water barrel where it tilted in the cart. When Eusebe set off for the sugar factories, he would never know that two small passengers were coming along.

Sonia could see that Anna was determined. Briefly she thought of the time her sister had made a tent of the dining room curtains, and how Mama had withdrawn dessert privileges from her for two weeks. But then, grasping Anna's strong, sun-browned hand, she climbed into the cart and huddled beside her in the shadow of the large barrel. If only Ossip were able to come . . . She thought of her brother, who had become ill around the time of her own birth, and who, when he had finally emerged from his crib at age six, had begun to discover the world, step by step, almost at her own pace. Sonia and Ossip had been drawn together by circumstance. They were very close friends.

An unsuspecting Eusebe arrived shortly afterward. The ride was jostling for the girls, and they giggled in silence. But the view, as Anna had predicted, was magnificent—vast stretches of fresh-scented wheat fields as far as the eye could see, until the cart turned off through the forest, so emerald-dense the sun could hardly penetrate the leafy treetops. Wild birds called to one another, warbles and shrieks that awed Sonia. Soon they saw the Bug, the small river that crossed the Gunzburg property line. Finally, after numerous patches of sugar beets had dazzled the girls, Eusebe pulled up next to a low building, the first factory.

"He is going in to bring the workers out with pails and troughs," Anna whispered. "Quick! Let us climb down and explore. No one will see us. No one knows we're anywhere near here!" She hopped off the water wagon and lifted her sister down after her.

The two girls ran to the far side of the factory. Sonia had never been so bold in her entire life, but so great was her fear of being found by Eusebe and punished by her parents that she did not consider the new twist their escapade was taking. Anna, accustomed to punishment, had grown immune to it—for her, only the moment counted, and right now she wanted to see what lay beyond the bright green bushes a small distance from the factory. She took Sonia's hand and started to run. Mohilna was so enormous that never, perhaps, would the girls have the opportunity to see such a large part of it again; the formal gardens around their house encompassed twelve and a half acres by themselves.

Behind the bushes lay a field of tall grass, carpeted with breathtaking flowers. Wild iris and lilies and magnificent daisies with varicolored petals mingled with scarlet poppies and thousands of bluebells. Not even in the mountains of Switzerland had the children seen such a display, and they ran here and there, gathering bunches. They did not notice that the sun was descending to the west, nor did they know or care where they were going. Until, with a start, Anna's voice reached Sonia from among the tall stems. "There is a river here! I guess the Bug makes another turn, and we have found it again!"

Beyond the small knoll on which they stood, the brook gurgled. "Look!" Anna exclaimed. "There are some stones there, and we can walk across. The water isn't as deep or as wide as it was when we crossed it before." She scampered down to the rivulet. Sonia ran down behind her.

Very carefully, the two sisters skipped from rock to rock, avoiding the cascades of water. But the other side was not as pretty as their field had been, and now Sonia was sorry. She remembered her worries about Mama and Eusebe, and her eyes filled with tears. Suddenly she wanted to be home again, eating bread and jam with her parents and Ossip. She realized that she was very hungry; they had surely missed tea.

A group of people was marching toward them. Sonia and Anna, with their bare feet and disheveled hair, stood close together, their simple country pinafores splotched with mud and creased from the drive. There were two peasant men and one woman, her hair hidden by a kerchief, and ahead of them a tall, bony man brandishing a whip. His clothing was worn but it was not that of a field worker, and he held his head with an imperiousness that disconcerted Anna. "What are you doing here?" he demanded of them in Russian.

The Gunzburg children had been reared to speak French, not merely because they had spent most of their lives abroad, but also because people of their status spoke that language among themselves in Russia. They could converse in imperfect, but adequate Russian with their servants. Now Anna replied, "We are Sonia Davidovna and Anna Davidovna de Gunzburg, and we think we are lost. Who are you?"

The man laughed, an unpleasant, disbelieving sound.

"Who do you think I am? Count Tuminsky's chief overseer in the fields. And *you* are no Gunzburgs. Your Russian is too poor. And with no shoes, too. You are no doubt some of my workers who decided to sneak away from your duties. Tell me where you belong, and maybe I shall simply make you work over the usual time, instead of flogging you."

Anna shook her head stubbornly. "You do not understand! We are truly Baron David's daughters. Our Mama always lets us go barefoot in the summertime, and we were raised in the French language, so that our Russian is not yet perfect. But we are not liars. If you don't believe us, why not send one of your people on horseback to our parents, and they will come for us?" But even she was beginning to tremble, for Count Tuminsky, whom she had never seen, was a legendary figure of fear to the Gunzburg children.

The overseer displayed elongated yellow teeth in a rictus of a smile. "Horseback, no less! You're liars. Extra work would be too lenient a punishment for you!" He raised his whip. Sonia began to scream, but Anna stood still, and the cat-o'-nine-tails hit her full on the back. She fell forward, sobbing, the back of her dress torn, a streak of blood defined upon her pale skin. Sonia threw herself on top of her sister, smothering her head against Anna's legs, screaming incoherently. "That's what we do to vermin who don't obey," the man said, and raised his whip once more.

But he did not have a chance to bring it down. A rider on horseback was racing toward them, calling out at the top of his lungs. Through her tears, Sonia saw that it was Eusebe. The water carrier dismounted and ran to the two girls. Then, as his gentle fingers touched Anna's wound, he raised his tortured face to the overseer and whispered, "Man, what have you done? These are our misses, the Baron's daughters. You will be dismissed for this. I shall speak to the Baron myself, and show him Anna Davidovna's back. Poor sweethearts, such an innocent trick that they played on their faithful Eusebe, sneaking behind my water barrel." Eusebe was distraught. The moment he had found Sonia's lace handkerchief in the back of the cart, he had begun his frantic search for the children, but had never imagined they would wander off as far as the Count's property behind the brook. His voice broke, and tears spilled from his eyes. He stood up and carried each of the girls in his arms to his horse. Silence enveloped the group; the overseer's face had turned ashen.

"Come," Eusebe said. "I'll take you home."

When Anna's back had been bathed and bandaged, and the two white-faced sisters had received a dinner tray in their beds, Ossip came to see them. "Mama says you have been far more punished than you deserved, especially you, Annushka," he said soberly. "And Papa will have to go to the Count tomorrow. I was very frightened for you, and when no one could find you at teatime, I missed you so much! It was lucky for you that Eusebe came when he did, or you would have received a horrible whipping."

"That is really how they flog those children who work there, isn't it?" Anna said bitterly. She was still in great pain, but her eyes flashed brilliantly. "Oh, how unfair! They have no one to come running for them, as we did! Because they were born poor, and we weren't."

"I suppose what you say is true," her brother agreed. He sat down on Sonia's bed and stroked her hand. "If it weren't indecent, Annushka would become unbearable now and show everybody her back, like a badge of courage!" His eyes twinkled.

But downstairs, in the living room, David de Gunzburg was saying to his wife: "Tuminsky is without doubt embarrassed at this episode. But in his heart he must be amused. After all, has his man not degraded that annoying Jew who had the audacity to settle next to him?"

Two

———————————— • ————————————

David and Mathilde de Gunzburg, the squires of Mohilna, were undergoing quite different emotions that summer. For David, life was a simple matter which he thoroughly enjoyed. There were two sides to David: the driving force that had made his father, Baron Horace, an astute banker as well as the foremost advocate of the Jews of Russia; and the childlike passions which transported him to a bliss few mature men ever experience. With his first side, he was a dedicated scholar. He spoke over thirty languages and dialects with fluency, and he applied himself relentlessly to the mastering of each new tongue. Similarly, he found poetry a furious challenge, and often would sit up half the night attempting to place emotion within the narrow, precise boundaries prescribed by rules of prosody. He was dedicated to his religion in an almost Rabbinical manner.

His loves, however, were founts of pure fire, and they were few but constant. He had conceived a passion for Mathilde, his cousin, when he had been twelve years old, and she, five. He had loved the serene blue eyes, the beautiful black curls, the demure, well-mannered little girl. It had never occurred to him that perhaps she might have felt another kind of emotion for him, for once David loved, it was irrevocable. He did not know why, only the fact that she was there, in his grandfather's house, and that he would marry her someday. Having decided on Mathilde, he never even glanced at other girls, but channeled his furious energy into his studies instead. He had never followed his older friends to the fashionable brothels of Paris, nor did he bother to learn the art of courtship. Polite, well educated, he had known how to speak to his mother's friends, to girl cousins, to friends of friends. But he had never wanted to waste precious time making love to anyone but Mathilde, and to her he was sincere and not romantic. For, after all, did she not know of his devotion?

His father, for whom David had always felt respect and affinity, approved of his plan, although Baron Horace had made it clear to his agnostic brother Yuri, Mathilde's father, that religion was essential to all Horace's clan. And so David had become engaged to Mathilde. He wanted to be married as soon as he had finished his stint in the Uhlans, and had obtained his degree from the University of Göttingen in Hesse. But Uncle Yuri had delayed the wedding by six months. It was said that he was much in debt, and perhaps he had hoped to force his brother Horace to aid him more generously with his creditors. Poor David had been so frustrated, so dreadfully hurt by the delay, that he had run off to Russia, this time to Georgia so that he could lose himself in the learning of two new dialects, Georgian and Armenian. When he had returned, the marriage took place at last. He had already loved her for thirteen years.

In all that time, he had never wavered in his passion. It was for her that he composed his verses, and for her that he arose each morning to face the day. Unlike his brother Sasha and most of his friends, he never took a mistress, even though he saw Mathilde only during vacations. Since Ossip's illness, the family had moved from St. Petersburg's foul, miasmic climate. David alone remained in the capital. But his loyalty to Mathilde was total.

He also loved Russia, her grandeur and her vastness and

her untamed diversity. At Mohilna he felt complete, fulfilled. He would awaken at the first bleak streak of dawn and walk stealthily beneath his daughters' windows, calling to them to join him. Anna and Sonia, holding up their nightshirts, would slide their window up, and taking care not to disrupt the steady sonorous snoring of their nurse, Titine, would climb onto the outer ledge of the sill and wait for Papa to help them jump down from the second story. Then, together, they would go for a nature walk, David explaining why certain plants flourished where they did, and naming all the flowers. He loved Anna with a fierce protectiveness, for she was not beautiful, and he loved her bravery and her outspoken mischief because they were full of unbridled energy, like the horses he had loved to ride in Georgia. Sonia he loved for her precise, dainty beauty that recalled Mathilde to his mind, for her steadfast application, so like his own, and for her desire to make him proud. David's mornings alone with his daughters were sacred to all three. During the summer, his children grew to know this simple yet passionate man from whom they were separated for the remainder of the year.

The specialist who examined Ossip yearly in Paris had declared that perhaps at the start of 1896 the boy might be strong enough for the family to return to St. Petersburg, as long as his young patient was back at Mohilna by the time the spring thaws, with their accompanying diseases, wrought their havoc upon the capital. For when the great snows thawed, St. Petersburg once again became a swamp. Anna and Ossip could each remember their native city. Sonia did not. She had been born only three months before the family had been forced to leave its spires and cupolas. But because she adored David and could sense his patriotism, her soul wanted to reach out to his city and embrace it as her own. For she was a child of deep emotions, who sought the sublime and shuddered at baseness and ignored the ordinary.

Ossip, who had become observant as befits one who does

not participate in normal activities, was unduly mature for his age, somewhat of a cynic at eight years old. He had accepted his condition, but the true ebullience of childhood had passed him by, drying out some essential fonts of naiveté in the process. Anna provided him with a vicarious joie de vivre, and with her he could laugh and grow excited. His little sister, Sonia, filled him with all the tenderness of his being. He pitied her exalted emotions, yet also clung to her sweetness. She took care of him, almost as though he were younger than she, and in turn he wanted to shield her from her own vulnerability. Sometimes he thought that Sonia was much like their father, David, whom Ossip admired for his reputation as a statesman and a linguist, but whom he gently despised for his almost childlike passions. For Ossip was above all a small realist, who saw an excess of idealism as a barrier to the process of going from day to day. In this way Ossip most resembled his mother, Mathilde.

Mathilde, at thirty-one, did not like Mohilna. She did not like its rustic furniture, nor the isolation she felt when she was there. Her gay, elegant friends rarely passed through Podolia, and this summer, heavy with the new baby, she felt particularly languid and exhausted in the Russian heat. She looked forward to this new infant, but more for the relief it could bring to her life than for its own presence. She fervently hoped it would be a boy, for with Ossip's fragility, she knew that David yearned for the additional security of a second son. If it was a boy, then David's wish would be fulfilled, and she would no longer need to produce any more children. But she was resolute on one point: she would insist, whatever the baby's sex, that the family not expand any further. David might not agree, but she had ways of making sure, and she would use them, too.

With shivers of repulsion, Mathilde would think back on her father, Yuri, who, to amuse himself freely with his fancy ladies, had kept her mother, Ida, constantly with child. Ida had given life to nine children in less than thirteen years. Mathilde did not like anything to do with procreation, and sometimes was sorry that her husband kept himself so occupied with his work. Mistresses, she thought cynically, had their uses—so long as the man was discreet and did not publicly bring shame to his wife, as her father had done with his escapades.

She had married David for several reasons, but love had not been among them. As a child, she had grown up in a house of discord, for the debonair, flamboyant, charming Yuri had been anything but gentle in his home, terrifying the servants, cowing his wife, and making small Mathilde retreat within herself like a frightened snail. Mathilde had loved her mother, who was a true lady, who demonstrated control in every situation, whom she had never heard raise her voice. At one time she had also loved her father, for who would not succumb to the boyish charm of this man who made virtuous women lose their virtue with laughter? But she had witnessed the results of his rascality, had steeled herself against her love, and had condemned him. In David she saw an earnest man who worshiped her, who gave her blessed security and peace, something unknown in Yuri's household.

Mathilde knew that when David had first declared his intention to marry her, Uncle Horace had made some kind of arrangement with his brother. Mathilde had looked at her mother, at her sisters and brothers, and known that if she married David de Gunzburg, they would reap a part of Horace's bounty. Mathilde believed in duty, in honor. It was her duty to provide what she could for those she loved. And besides, if she had opposed the match, what possible excuse could she have given? That she would rather wait for someone who might never come? That David, who was tall, slender, and red-haired, was less handsome than his brother, that she disliked the color of his hair, that she disliked Biblical names? Yes, she might have preferred

Sasha, because he was handsome with glossy black hair, an erect posture, and brilliant blue eyes, whereas David stooped slightly from too much bending over books, and his eyes were paler than his brother's. But Sasha was arrogant, and arrogant men do not bring peace to their wives.

Mathilde had never loved a man, nor had she been courted in the usual fashion, for her fate had been sealed long before she attended her first ball. And who would spend time with someone else's betrothed, even though she was voluptuous and had soft white skin, sapphire eyes, and long, waving ebony hair? Her feelings for her cousin David included devotion and friendship, but certainly she did not understand him. Mathilde de Gunzburg was anything but emotional, and could not even comprehend David's deep love for her. Nor did she share his unquenchable need to learn. She enjoyed a yellow-backed love story far more than a well-formed sonnet. Least of all did she understand David's religious zeal. If she could have stated her life's philosophy, it would have been with these words: "Above all, I want peace. I dislike excess of any sort, for it disturbs my equilibrium."

David's religion was excessive. For that matter, Russia itself was excessive. Her mother, her sisters, her friends were all Parisians. But David said, "The Gunzburgs are not French, my sweet, but Russian. You will see, your own origins will come out in you once we are settled." She had bowed her head and accepted her duty, and then, in agony and fear, had allowed her husband to come to her bed and to enter her soft round body, which had, until now, been hers alone. She had borne this with wretched calm. Yet after their train was within the Russian borders she had finally cried out against him, and it was his religion that had pushed her to this.

One day as the sun went down and their train pulled into a small station, Mathilde had been wrenched out of her daydreams by the brisk entrance of the conductor, who had ordered some porters to remove the Baron and Baroness's luggage from their compartment. "David!" she exclaimed. "What is happening here? Where are we?"

He had placed a gentle hand on her shoulder, and replied, "Nothing is wrong, beloved. But the Sabbath has begun, and we must get off. One does not ride during the Sabbath."

"And you made reservations at a hotel here?" she asked.

He shook his head. "There are no hotels here. This is a very small village. We shall be forced to sleep on a bench in the waiting room."

Mathilde's emotions, so long kept hidden, had come flooding out of her in a humiliating torrent of tears, and she had cried out, her voice shrill with outrage and loneliness and horror: "No! I shall not get down! You may sleep wherever you wish, in the gutter if it appeals to you, but not I! You say you love me. How can you place a silly rule before me in your heart? I detest you, David, and I detest your religion, and I always shall! It is a religion for fools and fanatics!"

"But those rules help make our lives more sensible," he had replied with kindness. Yet inside his heart he was quaking, for never in the eighteen years of her life had he heard Mathilde lose her temper. She had wounded him, and though he pitied her, he also felt as though she had ripped something precious from their union. But he did not yield. In the end, holding up her heavy skirts, she had followed him off the train and had sat down on a hard bench in the station, facing him. All night long he had felt those hard blue eyes boring into him with their hatred, although Mathilde never said another word. Her cheeks glowed white with tension and he had been afraid, yet not certain why.

And she had thought: I have married a madman. But after that episode she never again tried to oppose his faith, although in other matters she learned that his love frequently changed his mind in favor of her own wishes.

Having children had been a special ordeal for her. There

had been two miscarriages before Anna was born in 1885. Anna, colicky and red-haired like David, was a disappointment to her. During Anna's first year, she had suffered convulsions so strong that the muscles on the left side of her face, still immature, had slackened. Mathilde, so beautiful, so fastidious, had wondered with horror what would become of this ugly daughter of hers. Who would ever marry her?

Worse, little Anna had early displayed the most remarkable temper, rolling herself on the floor and howling her fury. To Mathilde, who shuddered when a carriage drove too noisily in front of the house, her child could have committed no worse offense. Yet this spindly, unruly little individual was still her daughter. She did love her, though with misgivings and doubts—and with guilt at not surrendering herself to maternal love more wholeheartedly. It was David who rescued her from her bouts with guilt, for he, who loved all the unfortunate of the world, immediately formed a bond with his small daughter.

When Ossip arrived two years later, Mathilde felt as though finally her life had been justified. The baby was calm, with her own eyes and hair and an alabaster complexion. She took care not to favor the new child over her daughter, masking her genuine appreciation of the boy in quiet reserve. And then one day, when Ossip was three years old, David had entered the nursery and found his son doubled over.

"Come now, Ossip, straighten up like a little man," his father had said, teasing. The child had raised his limpid eyes, full of tears, and had frozen the smile on David's face with his own expression of pain. "I can't, Papa," he murmured. The specialist the Gunzburgs called in declared that Mathilde's sweet Ossip had Pott's disease. A special crib was fashioned for him, and for three years he was not allowed to rise from it. Then, slowly, he was permitted to stand, but not to sit, and finally to sit for short periods of time. He had been late starting his lessons, but had quickly caught up with Anna, who was too occupied with pranks to apply herself.

Mathilde had left St. Petersburg with her children when Ossip had fallen ill, and she had been too shocked, heart-sick, and weary to pay much attention at first to the second daughter who had been born only three months before. But then, traveling through Europe, resting at the homes of her mother, her cousins, and her friends, she had become numbed to the pain and the worry, and had awakened to the fact that her third child, Sofia Sara, was much worth considering. Sonia, as she was called, was tiny, well-formed, and gay. Not boisterous and spirited like Anna, but then again, not placid like Ossip. This baby gurgled and smiled and held out her rosy hands, and she seemed in perfect health. As she grew, people said that she was like a minia-ture of Mathilde, but her cheeks were pinker and her eyes a grayer shade. She followed Mathilde like a faithful puppy, and her mother would find her busily gathering bread-crumbs to the side of her plate, the way she herself did, unconsciously. Ossip was truly similar to Mathilde in his passive cynicism, but Sonia was serious-minded, with a studied calm. She enjoyed life, but thoughtfully, and tried to be brilliant like her father and feminine like her mother. Mathilde liked the presence of this child around her, and felt relief. Sonia, at least, would make the great marriage that Anna might never attain.

That summer, as Mathilde awaited the birth of her fourth child, she watched her children and was glad, for Ossip seemed healthier and Anna, for all her rebellious-ness, was obviously a favorite among the inhabitants of Mohilna. Sonia scampered about, making Mathilde smile. Still, she was tired. It was time to seriously consider obtain-ing a governess for the children, someone educated to please David, yet someone who would teach Anna to be a lady. The present girl, now taking her vacation, had been too young, though she would last out this year. But this winter, in Paris, Mathilde would begin her search, for if the family was indeed to return to Petersburg, she did not want to do it without an appropriate Mademoiselle for her children. Titine, the old nurse, would naturally have charge of the new baby, as she had had of Ida's nine and of Mathilde's first three. She sighed, a languorous exhaling of breath, and knew that at least this part was settled. Titine was a family fixture, unlettered but sturdily competent.

She blamed her pregnancy as well as the oppressive heat and isolation of Mohilna for the one recurring thought that would awaken her at night, sending tremors up her spine. Ossip's specialist, when he had first examined the boy, had said, "If he survives this attack, he will most probably suffer another one when he is twenty. Then, if he emerges once more, he will be struck again when he is forty-five. And then, my dear Baroness, his body will surely give up the good fight. But you must not take this prediction as the Lord's word. In cases such as these, patterns exist, and they guide our prognosis. Yet patterns are not blueprints. Keep the boy out of any situation where he might be jostled or pushed, and he will be able to lead an almost normal existence." Mathilde de Gunzburg said to herself: Do not be a fool. Ossip will not die, ever, and he shall not be sick again. And she upbraided herself for her emotions.

Toward the end of August, a woman arrived at Mohilna whom the children had not met before, and who filled them with excited wonder. She was middle-aged, with a plain, kind face, and her only attire consisted of a brown dress that hung in modest folds to her sturdy feet. Her name was Madame Gilina, and she took her meals neither with the family nor with the servants. Though they did not understand her presence, as the adults told them that it was not their business to know, the children liked her, for she spoke to everyone in her concerned voice and seemed equally at ease with their Papa as with their old nurse, Titine.

Anna and Sonia were not surprised when they entered their bedroom one evening and found Madame Gilina chatting amiably with the leathery, sinewy Célestine Varon. Titine, as always, was mending clothes, her bony fingers still agile. Madame Gilina was shaking her head and sighing, "Yes, they were being put out, and that house a mere hovel, no more."

"What are you speaking of?" Anna asked abruptly, coming to the women.

Madame Gilina softly ran her fingers through the girl's unruly hair, and said, "Never mind, Anna Davidovna, my dear."

But Anna shook herself free, her brown eyes blazing. "Please, you must tell, especially if an injustice has been done! I need to know!"

Unnerved by Anna's intensity, Madame Gilina said, "It was when I was being driven here from Uman. We passed a village—Rigevka?—and I saw a man and his servants putting a family out of their house. He was repeating over and over, 'If you cannot meet the rent, you have no business occupying my property.' But the father of the family, he looked so ill . . ." She wiped her eyes hastily on a sturdy white handkerchief.

Anna stood up, clenching her fists. "This story is as dreadful as what we learned about Count Tuminsky, when his man flogged me. If you are poor, you are a nobody, an absolute nothing! You can starve, and your body gets kicked aside! Oh, sometimes I wish that I were not a Gunzburg, that we did not possess Mohilna, or our fine carriages, and Mama's elegant dresses. They make me feel—ashamed."

"My little love, that is simply the way things are," Madame Gilina murmured gently.

"And your blessed Papa gives work and homes to all of us," Titine added reverently. "Oh, the Baron has never struck any of his people. But the Count, he has that reputation . . ." She motioned to Anna's back.

Sonia, standing behind her sister, had been listening thoughtfully. Now she took Anna's elbow and spoke softly. "Mama says that some people are born one way, and some another, and that one mustn't question, for that is the world. If we did not have Papa's money, then we would not be able to help the others."

"That's childish nonsense," her sister replied. "Why should we help them? Why can't they have enough money of their own to help themselves?"

"Mama says it is because we know what's best, and can help better. Look at our Papa—he is brilliant. He can help anyone who needs it. But Mama also says that we must have all kinds of people in the world, so that all kinds of work can get done. Titine knows how to take care of us, and Eusebe carries the water, and Papa does things in the government. And the Tzar is the Father of Russia."

Anna said roughly, "You are five years old, and you don't know how to think. You don't even understand any of this. But you do care about the family that was evicted, don't you?"

Sonia nodded solemnly. "It is so cruel. We must tell Papa. He will make it better. But if you yourself changed places with the father that was so ill, that wouldn't help anybody. Someone would still be without a home, just as your getting whipped didn't help any peasant child at the Count's."

Madame Gilina exchanged a sharp glance with the old Breton nurse. She smiled suddenly at Sonia, and sighed. Titine, under her breath, said, "Blessed Virgin, he must be another poor Jew. It is usually so."

Anna had already turned away, her mind aflame with plans to rescue the victims. But Sonia had heard Titine, and now her eyes grew larger. "But aren't all good people Jews?" she asked.

Madame Gilina was amused. "Did someone tell you that, my dear?"

"Well, the Bible says we are the chosen people. Surely all of us are chosen, aren't we?" Sonia was suddenly worried.

"It would be wise to ask your father, Sofia Davidovna," Madame Gilina said.

The next morning at breakfast, Sonia therefore took the problem to David. "Papa, I thought all good people, who believed in God, were Jews, like us," she began.

Her father put aside his jam and crumpet, and leaned forward. "And so we have come to that. No, Sonia, all the world is not Jewish. You see, the Jews came first. But there were other people who believed in God, only they chose to worship Him in different ways. Not better, not worse— simply different. God loves all who worship Him."

The older children already knew this, of course, but Ossip asked, "Then why is it important to light the candles on Friday? What does it matter, since God loves Titine just as much as us, and she eats fish on Fridays to make Him happy? You don't think Titine is any worse than we, yet you don't follow *her* rules. Why don't we all simply stop doing all these things and just believe?"

Mathilde, at the head of the table facing David, brought her fine linen napkin to her mouth to conceal a smile.

But David was not amused. "What you say makes sense," he said to Ossip. "Religions were built to strengthen faiths, however. You see, if my life is miserable, if I feel alone, merely thinking of God is sometimes not sufficient. Sometimes I need a ritual, something I do by habit, to make me realize how important my God is in my everyday existence. I feel good when Mama lights the candles. Titine feels pure when she does not eat meat on Friday. The Gunzburgs have always been Jews. We react to our traditions from our hearts. But that does not mean that God prefers our ways, necessarily."

Sonia said, "Titine was talking to Madame Gilina about the father of a family which was thrown out of their home because they had no money for the rent, and then she said that he was probably a Jew. Why did she say that, Papa?"

David's heart contracted, and he gazed with deep affection at his small daughter. "Because, my sweet, most people, especially here in Russia, are not Jewish. And to those who do not worship as we do, and who are not kind and intelligent people, something different means something bad. Many people think the Jews are bad, and so they hurt them."

"That is like the Jews of the Bible," Sonia said. Then she sat up brightly. "But why are *we* not being hurt?"

David sighed. "Because we have enough money to prevent hurt." For an instant his pale blue eyes flickered, and caught his wife's piercing sapphire ones. The memory of Anna's back loomed between them. "But it is our duty to help the Jews who have no money. Otherwise, people will keep on hurting them."

Mathilde was eating quietly. She was thinking of the double taxes, of the bribes to the police in St. Petersburg, and she murmured within: The wages of sin is death, but the wages of a Jew are measured in gold. She thought of the quotas, and wondered if even gold could stretch them. David was the first Jew to have been admitted to the Ministry of Foreign Affairs, and only because, in all the land, he alone could speak so many languages. There was another measure, then: intelligence. She was glad for her son, who was so sharp and who studied well. Had he been more like Anna, who never opened a book unless compelled to, no university would admit him when the time came. No, gold and brains worked in tandem, and without both, a Jew was lost indeed . . .

David was announcing, "I think it is time you children saw Hashchévato. We shall drive there this afternoon."

Mathilde parted her lips to cry out against her husband's

plan to go to the shtetl; to ask at least that Ossip, whose back was so fragile, might be spared the long ride which she remembered with quiet tremors. But an abrupt thought struck her before she could utter a word. She looked at Ossip's fine white profile, at Sonia's tiny, well-formed hands, at the contained energy that had brought fine coral hues to Anna's cheeks. Oh, my darlings, you will suffer, she said to them mutely. You will suffer, in spite of your status, your title, your intelligence. And there is no escape, for Gunzburgs do not escape from their duty. Mathilde knew that all too well. Gunzburgs do not choose, they accept with dignity. So go, go with your father, so that you will not be surprised when the pain comes to your own lives later. She rose, and with unusual swiftness for her condition, she left the room.

That afternoon, Ossip was strapped into a special back brace, and the three children and David were settled into the Gunzburg victoria. Sonia burned with curiosity. What was this Hashchévato that had made Mama turn so pale, that had shot pain into Papa's intense face? But she asked no questions. Anna had asked about Madame Gilina, and had been rebuked for her unseemly curiosity. So she sat quietly, gazing out the window at the immensity of Mohilna, her heart filling with joy when fields of fuchsia-colored flowers burst into view, when gold and orange butterflies rose in swoops above the wheat, and when the sun darted in and out of lamblike cloud formations.

After a drive of several hours, they left Mohilna behind them and entered county property. It was there, Papa explained, that Hashchévato was located. An old statute had forbidden the inhabitants of that village to extend their boundaries to accommodate increases in their population. As the victoria approached, Sonia saw a jagged cluster of houses, one-room shacks made of rough planks. Then the road ended, and was replaced by dirt. The carriage slowed, and now the children could see the village. The shacks were low and gray and sagging, huddled like cramped crates in an attic. But what struck Sonia most of all was the crowd. It seemed as though every inch of space was taken up by people—ragged people, screaming people, women with torn shawls and puling babies, bent old men with yarmulkes worn to shreds. She held her breath, shivers shaking her small frame, horror assailing her. It was as though all the tramps she had ever seen in the gutters of Paris had suddenly converged upon this miserable village.

The coachman stopped the victoria and she felt the door being pulled open. She heard, "Baron! Baron!" as Papa descended, and then someone lifted her from her seat and into the commotion. She was being passed like a small bundle from one pair of hands to another. Finally, a strong man heaved her up on his shoulders, and she felt the stench of pickles and garlic from his breath, the sour odor of poverty around her. The coachman, she saw, had kept frail Ossip beside him, and had lifted him to his own seat. Anna was somewhere in the air, as Sonia herself was, on another man's shoulders. Sonia was filled with wild terror. This multitude of evil-smelling, ill-clad people descending on Papa was beyond her comprehension. Then she caught sight of Anna's face, and saw the tears in her eyes, and how Anna was bending down to hear what was being said. Surely Anna did not understand, for these people spoke a strange dialect, but Anna was nodding, and Sonia saw her stroke the top of a baby's head. Sonia's fear melted then. Her sister had made friends among these people. Now, to her, they appeared no more harmful than the kindly servants Anna had befriended in the kitchens of Mohilna.

At long last she was placed on the ground, and found Papa and Anna beside her. Papa spoke to the people in their dialect, and then, to his daughters, explained that they spoke Yiddish, the only tongue that their own great-grandmother, Rosa Dynin, had ever learned to speak. He took his daughters' hands and led them into a small shop, where he purchased some greasy cakes, then into another where he bought thread, and down the entire length of the dirt highway, not bypassing a single store. When he was finished, he stood still, and now a wailing arose around him, which he stilled with his hand. He pointed to a thin man holding onto the tails of his baronial waistcoat. At once the man began to plead, bowing to David many times. David handed him a purse, and the man released David's coat and, still bowing, backed off into the crowd. "He needed ten rubles for his daughter's dowry," Papa told the girls. In the space of ten minutes, Papa had handed many purses and coins to the people surrounding him. Then, deftly, he removed from his coat pocket a sack of rock candies he had purchased only moments before, and distributed the sweets to the children. When the sack was empty, he walked back to the victoria. The coachman helped Ossip inside after his sisters, the door was closed, and the Gunzburgs turned back toward Mohilna.

For a long time the only sound came from the hooves of the horses. Then, her throat throbbing, Sonia said, "Oh, the poor Jews! To suffer so because they are the chosen people!"

Ossip said nothing, but his eyes, bright blue, rested with brief compassion upon his small sister. Anna cried out, "No! It is not because of that! It is because they are poor! They need money from us to live, if they can survive in those horrid houses." She burst into nervous tears. "Jews, or Eastern Orthodox, or Catholic! What does it matter? We are rich, and they are poor, and that is why they are reduced to needing our few rubles." Then, to her father: "How large is *my* dowry going to be, Papa?"

But Sonia exclaimed in shock: "Annushka! You know that we must never ask such questions! Papa will not answer you, he will punish you!" She gazed beseechingly at her older sister, who had trespassed into the world of grown-ups.

Anna said resentfully, "Well, then, never mind, Papa. I

am old enough to know a dowry for us would be hundreds of thousands of rubles. And that man was happy to have ten, for his own daughter!"

David was very grave. At length he spoke. "You are not entirely wrong, Anna. Of course we must help all poor people. But you see, there are so many wealthy Russians, and so few of them are Jews. That means that we must give first to those who are most frequently ignored. Do you understand?"

Anna said, "A poor man is a poor man. I still think you must help whichever poor man happens to be near you when your purse has money in it—even if I am still a child," she added petulantly.

But Sonia, her pure voice rising like the trill of a bird, said, "Yes, Papa, I understand. I shall do as you do when I am a lady, and have money of my own."

The horses' hooves continued to clop with even regularity, and Ossip said nothing. His eyes never left his father's face. When he finally spoke, it was barely a whisper. "Papa? In Russia the Jews have a worse life than anywhere else, don't they?"

David's face, with its gaunt intensity, was very somber. He regarded the small boy in his brace as though he were an equal, another man. "I cannot deny that, my observant one," he murmured.

"Then why are we here? Why are we not in Paris, with Grandfather Yuri and Grandmother Ida? What is the purpose?"

David said staunchly, "One day you will understand. The Gunzburgs have worked hard, since your grandfather's day, to build a reputation and a fortune, so that the powerful men of Russia have learned to respect us. Now we can speak for those who are weaker than we, for the other Jews. We have a duty to help them, to make those who hate all Jews accept the fact that we are human beings, too, as they are. We, my son, are here because it is our duty, and also because Russia is our home. We have no reason to run from it. One must do battle for those things that are most valuable to us."

Ossip was silent, and David thought: Now what have I done? I have voiced adult sentiments in adult phrases, and I have lost the lad. But suddenly Ossip said, "I don't see why people need suffer for methods of worship. Why not, instead, make the Russian Orthodox happy and change our way of worship?"

His father's lips parted and he paled. Ossip shrugged lightly and smiled his conciliatory gentle grin, the grin of a child, after all, and said softly, "But that is the sensible fashion, is it not, Papa?"

Sonia slept soundly that night; the visit to Hashchévato had drained her. By the time the victoria had pulled up to the residence at Mohilna, twilight had gathered and Mama was nowhere in sight. Mama, she observed to herself, was always exhausted. It was a good thing she had not come with them to the village.

When she awakened, the sky outside was filtering its white predawn glare into her bedroom. Soon Papa would be beneath the window, calling out to her and Anna for their walk. But when she searched for her sister's huddled form in the neighboring bed, she found it rumpled and empty. Sonia rose and looked for Titine. But the old nurse had disappeared as mysteriously as had her sister.

In a panic, she rushed to the connecting door that led to Ossip's room, and began to call out his name. Only silence replied. They have all gone away without me, and I shall never see my family again, she thought, and her heart constricted with a terrible loss. Tears spilled from her eyes. Why didn't someone wake me, so I could have gone along? she asked mutely. Then she sank to the floor and began to sob.

Suddenly someone was pulling her upright, and Titine's

rough voice echoed in her ear. "Well now, sobbing and throbbing! That's what they call you, you know, behind your back. And well they may! Crying on such a day, when the whole house is joyful!"

Joyful? Sonia felt as though someone had shaken her out of a nightmare, but she did not understand. The old woman took her hand and hurried her out of the room, up the staircase and across to the adjacent wing of the house where Papa and Mama slept. The door to her mother's room was opened wide. Titine placed a finger on her lips and tiptoed inside with Sonia, whose eyes had grown round with astonishment. Her entire family was gathered there.

In the large four-poster bed, on a mound of white pillows, Sonia saw Mama, pale and with her eyes closed. Her magnificent black hair lay all about her, like the locks of Snow White, the child thought. Papa, his thin red hair disheveled, was bending over her, her hand in his. Anna stood with Ossip, both in their nightshirts, at the foot of the bed, and, to Sonia's intense surprise, Madame Gilina, with a white smock thrown over her habitual brown dress, was in a corner, busying herself with what looked like a half dozen pots of still steaming water. "Look," Titine whispered softly, and Sonia watched as her leathery finger pointed to the large window. Just below it, Sonia saw the white wicker cradle, with its curtains and skirts of lace cascading down to the carpet. She held her breath with sudden ecstasy, and her gray eyes sparkled.

On the balls of her feet, she scampered across the room to the cradle, and then was struck with awe. Papa saw her, and came to her. "Yes," he said gently, "you may look between the curtains." And he lifted a corner of delicate lace for her. A small dark head, a round face, two tiny fists clenched on the coverlet. "You have that brother you had hoped for," Papa murmured softly. "We shall name him Eugene, Evgeni in Russian. It means 'well born,' as your name means 'wise one.' But we will call him Gino."

Sonia was radiant. Her eyes glided about the room, then rested on Madame Gilina, and she wondered again what she was doing here. And then the solution struck her: Why, of course! Kind, goodly Madame Gilina was the person Mama had sent into the fields to find Gino! All at once, Sonia understood a great many things. Papa must have told this good woman about Sonia's wish for a brother, and Madame Gilina must have searched extra hard to fulfill Sonia's hopes. Sonia left the marvelous white cradle with its tiny occupant, and resolutely directed her steps toward the woman in the corner. Without a word, she wrapped her small arms around Madame Gilina's legs and hugged her tightly.

Three

When the summer was over, David returned to St. Petersburg, and life was never again to be the same for the Gunzburg family. Mathilde took the children and Titine to France, to conduct a serious search for a proper governess. Fraulein Roggenhagen, the Prussian girl who had served in that capacity for nearly a year, and who had vacationed at home during the Gunzburgs' stay at Mohilna, was due to be married in November, and Mathilde had enlisted the aid of all her relatives in her search for someone more responsible, less youthful, and more polished than the Prussian miss. In the meantime, David was to find a suitable residence for his family, who would return to St. Petersburg in time to celebrate the Russian New Year.

St. Petersburg was a beautiful city, unlike any in the rest of Europe. It had been named after Peter the Great, who had wanted a "window on the world" and had resolved to build a city near the Baltic Sea. Peter had seen this marshland and declared that it would be dried out, and streets would be paved upon it, and it would replace Moscow as capital of all the Russias. Thousands of workers had died of diseases bred in the miasmic swamps, but they had been replaced by others, and finally, after some four years, the city was ready to welcome the Tzar and all his boyars. Splendid palaces with spires and rounded cupolas had risen, and the banks of the Neva River had been transformed into elegant quays with parapets of granite.

The Neva was short, only thirty-eight miles, beginning at Lake Ladoga and ending in the Gulf of Bothnia in the Baltic Sea; but it was fifteen hundred feet wide at its narrowest, as it ran through St. Petersburg itself, emerging finally into a delta from which several islands projected. Vassilievsky was the first and largest of these, and the only one on which people resided. Here stood the Academies of Arts and Sciences, the University, a military school, and the Exchange. It was connected to St. Petersburg by a wide bridge. The other isles were parklike, comprised of alleys and trees, and elegant society converged in their carriages to the last one, from which they watched the sun set over the sea during the summer. It was on Vassilievsky Island that David found a house for his family.

Before Ossip's illness, Mathilde, David, and the two small children had lived in an apartment in the vast residence of Baron Horace, David's father. He owned a building in the city proper, on one of the most distinguished quays where, further down, also lay the Tzar's Winter Palace. But now there were four children, more servants, and David, the scholar, had accumulated an enormous collection of books, so that new quarters were definitely in order. Because he wanted the third and top story of the house on Vassilievsky, and it was already rented out, he purchased the entire building and leased the two lower floors to other tenants.

Mathilde had always thought her husband a dreamer, impractical in day-to-day matters, and she was apprehensive when he wrote to her that he was furnishing their new, spacious apartment according to her tastes. But she failed to realize that in anything deeply concerning his wife, David's eye took in the smallest detail. He ordered their bedroom walls hung with the finest raw silk imported from Lyon, in her favorite shade of restful pale green, matching the exquisite bedspread and drapes from the four-posters. He chose all Louis XIII, with a fireplace of carved ebony, and the dining room, large enough for state dinners, had walls of tooled Cordova leather in three rich coppery shades, and molded ceilings of blue and gold. Above, magnificent chandeliers glistened, lit by electricity. Only in his study had David given vent to his own sturdier, simple tastes; here was leather and mahogany, and tall bookcases crammed with precious first editions. In every room gleamed a white enamel furnace.

It was already December when one of Mathilde's acquaintances in Paris told her of Johanna de Mey, who had been a lady's companion to a young American recently returned to her homeland. Feeling the pressure of time, Mathilde set up a meeting in a tea shop near the Luxembourg Gardens. She had been told that Mademoiselle de Mey was her own age, and of Dutch parents, but that she had been reared in France and educated in Switzerland. "It must be said, however, that she has never been a children's governess before," Mathilde's friend had added.

The woman who presented herself to Mathilde was tall, with a narrow waist, sloping shoulders, an oval face colored in light peach, and eyes of the purest aquamarine. Her hair, pulled into a modest chignon, was like fine threads of honey or Florentine gold. Her posture was erect, her attire fashionable. Why, this is a lady! Mathilde thought with true wonder. A lady fit for a salon, not a children's classroom. "Surely," she said with a smile, "my friend was in error. She told me I might, perhaps, offer you a . . . a . . . position . . . but you will have to forgive me, for you are certainly not searching for work." Mathilde, who was rarely ruffled, felt herself, to her own intense humiliation, turn red.

The other woman smiled back. "But yes, my dear

Baroness," she said gently, "I am in most desperate need of work. You see"—unbidden, she sat down, crossing her elegant, long legs—"I have a mother and two sisters to support, and have been working for several years."

Mathilde was moved, and again wondered. "It is most noble of you to carry this burden," she commented. "Your father is deceased?"

Johanna de Mey's long nose twitched slightly, and her head jerked up with a small spasm. She looked closely at Mathilde. "I may as well admit the truth." She hesitated slightly. "It is necessary for me to explain my . . . situation. My father was a gentleman in the Netherlands. When I was young, there was much money, and I received an impeccable education. But then"—and her eyes hardened perceptibly—"one day we heard a shot, and he was dead. He could not face us after having squandered all the family wealth. I was the oldest child, and the most educated one. I became a paid companion."

Mathilde, whose emotions were rarely summoned, felt as though something warm and soft had entered her heart. She saw the stiffness in the other woman, her dignity, her sense of pride. She thought, I respect her, for she is strong, but there is something more . . . Yes, she is a lady, my equal—that is it! My father, her father: two peas in a pod, selfish and careless and hurtful. For Papa there was always Uncle Horace, or I might be this woman, sitting in her place, earning a living . . . She felt little beads of perspiration gather at the base of her hairline, and darts of light painfully pushing at her eyes. She said, softly, "Thank you for explaining. I shall not betray this confidence." And then, once more, she wondered: why had she said that, when this was a mere interview for a position with the family, and David would surely have to be told? The other had not told her as a confidence, but as a matter of honesty.

"I hear that Petersburg is very beautiful," Miss de Mey was saying.

Mathilde said, "Yes, it has a charm all its own. But the climate in winter is dreadful. It is night for twenty hours, and the houses have double walls and windows that are filled with cotton to keep out the winds. You will not mind? Everyone of the nobility and the haute bourgeoisie speaks French."

"Are you offering me the position, Baroness?" Johanna de Mey was looking at her with amusement.

Impulsively, with only a moment's hesitation, Mathilde, for the first time in her entire life, plunged into an endeavor. "Yes, I am. Will you accept?"

A little smile formed on the perfect oval face of the Dutchwoman. She twinkled at Mathilde, then briskly nodded. "Yes, I accept," she replied, her aquamarine eyes resting on Mathilde's deep blue ones. She extended her long, elegant hand, and took Mathilde's small white one in her strong fingers. "Let us shake hands as men are wont to do," she said with humor.

Having taken this plunge, Mathilde relaxed. As she still had ten minutes before an appointment with a friend at the couturier Worth, she lingered for a moment with Johanna de Mey. She told her of the house David had purchased, and how her brother-in-law, Alexander de Gunzburg—David's brother, Sasha, who handled the family bank in St. Petersburg—and his wife had criticized the location, calling Vassilievsky "a mere suburb." Mathilde scoffed at their snobbery, and described how charmingly David had furnished their new home. She was relaxing, chatting with another woman of taste, as though she had known Johanna de Mey for many years and as though they were equals. Then, abruptly, she realized the time, and made a rapid departure out of the tea room. Johanna de Mey rested her fine, pointed chin on an upturned palm, and her eyes looked after the velvet-clad Mathilde with her thick black pompadour and her shapely figure. A half-smile appeared on her lips, and she nodded twice to herself.

But in the street, Mathilde suddenly stopped, a cold

tremor running through her. "You are a fool!" she exclaimed aloud, now aware that she had forgotten to discuss her children with this woman, that she had hired her without asking to see letters of reference, and that she had not seen proof of Mademoiselle de Mey's education, which was of such importance to David. Another thought struck her, too: If she had been careless enough not to mention the children, in her strange confusion, then why had the other, who had not been confused at all, not questioned her about her future charges, or the nature of the work?

A vision of Johanna de Mey, in her elegant tailored jacket, with her fine eyes and golden hair, interposed itself between Mathilde and her dreadful self-recrimination. She shook her head: No, Mathilde de Gunzburg never acted on impulse unless the right reasons motivated her. She resumed her brisk walk, putting out of her mind the fact that Mathilde de Gunzburg, to tell the exact truth, never acted on impulse at all.

Sonia was prepared to adore the woman, Ossip was perplexed, and Anna made an ungainly face, saying, "She will be a perfect lady—how boring for us!" None of them had yet met Johanna de Mey.

They first saw her in the Gard du Nord, where they stood by the luggage, waiting for the porters to load it into their reserved compartments. Sonia's small mouth fell open as a vision in sky blue, tall, erect, swanlike, approached. Johanna de Mey was wearing a two-piece ensemble that matched her remarkable eyes. Over a simple white blouse buttoned to her long, slender throat, she wore a jacket with sleeves that puffed below the sloping shoulders. The jacket terminated at her tiny waist, from which descended the simple folds of her blue skirt. Her hat was small, tilted at a saucy angle, with a single feather ornamenting it. Her golden hair was pulled away from her face. Sonia's heart rose on a note of pure admiration. Mama was the loveliest woman in the world, but Mama was real, even if she moved with grace and never raised her voice. This other woman was a finely chiseled piece of porcelain, as perfect as one of Grandmother's Dresden figurines, and beautiful in a totally different fashion.

Ossip grasped his sister's hand and squeezed it. "Yes," he whispered, "she is like a work of art." He thought of Madame Tussaud's wax replicas in London, and wondered why. After all, those were just waxen dolls, not real people.

But Anna, who had always possessed a gift for visual art, who had painted with feeling since her toddler days, thought of Switzerland. "A cool blue lake, in which we cannot swim because it is too cold; or the Mont Blanc, which rises so perfectly into the sky—and which the sun cannot thaw."

"You are crazy, Annushka," Ossip said gently, but he was amused.

Mama had gone to meet the vision in blue, and the three children, flanked by Titine with Gino in her arms, watched their heads draw together, saw the long, tapered hand rest for a moment on their mother's rich crimson jacket sleeve. Mama's figure was more womanly, rounded at the bustline and at the hips, and she was smaller than the blond woman. They came together to the children, and Mama said, "Mademoiselle, these are my daughters, Anna and Sonia, and my son, Ossip. And this is our faithful Titine—Célestine Varon—and the baby of the family, Gino."

Mademoiselle smiled. Her large aquamarine eyes shifted from Anna to Ossip, and finally rested on Sonia. She cocked her fine golden head to one side, and then said, "This one resembles you, my dear Baroness." She touched the top of Sonia's red hat. Sonia stared up into her face, her eyes round with adoration. The woman's smile twinkled. "You are a sweet thing," she said, and Sonia's cheeks turned bright with pleasure. "You will have to tell me the name of that splendid Spanish doll you are carrying, once our journey has begun. I am most intrigued."

"I call her Señorita, Mademoiselle," Sonia said proudly. She lifted the doll into Johanna de Mey's arms.

But the governess turned to Ossip. "That's a fine sailor suit you're wearing," she said. "And I have always appreciated elegant men. You are indeed an elegant little man, my Ossip." She regarded him with a straightforward expression, and he met the blue eyes with his own, gravely. He made a small bow and she inclined her head. Then she turned her full attention to Anna, who stood nervously next to her brother, her red hair already losing its precarious curl.

Anna's brown eyes appraised Johanna de Mey, and she felt a tremor at the base of her spine. The woman smiled at her, a wide smile revealing large white teeth, but still Anna regarded only the aquamarine eyes which did not shift from their unreadable expression.

"So," the woman finally said, "you are the oldest. I hope that you set a fine example, Anna. You should be the most responsible girl in the family. I know, for you see, I am an oldest child."

"I am afraid that our Annushka is not always the model child," Mathilde said softly, laughing. A sudden nervousness had invaded her. She pushed it out of her mind. But the governess was stroking Anna's red hair, feeling its springy texture in her fingers, and Mathilde admired the woman's ability to reach each child in a special manner. Anna was regarding the quay, tapping her foot restlessly. "Stand up and be a lady," Mathilde suddenly said to her daughter, and she was amazed at the sharpness in her tone. But Johanna de Mey continued to play with the girl's hair, and Mathilde, all at once, felt foolish.

Sonia, her eyes riveted to her beloved mother, saw her bite her lower lip and close her eyes momentarily, while Johanna de Mey examined Gino, the baby. The governess was stroking his cheek, then briskly patting it as Titine held him up proudly. But Anna saw the cursory glance the sylphlike Dutchwoman cast upon the Breton nurse, and heard the words, "That will be all," with which she dismissed her. A sudden, swift pain hit Sonia between the ribs, and she went to Titine and put her arms about her. But Mademoiselle turned her back to the children and was placing her fine fingers upon Mathilde's arm, and now her voice was rich, melodious.

"You are so weary," she said gently. "I fear that we are all too much for you. The holidays, bidding adieu to your parents—and now the return to this awesome city which you hope will not overwhelm you as once it did . . . You are a delicate spirit, Baroness, a spirit created for the boudoir and the salon, and not for train stations and baggage and restless children. Let me settle you in your compartment, with a pillow, and I shall handle the porters and our eager young family."

Ossip, watching from the side, smiled. But Sonia's mouth dropped open, her countenance falling. Mama would do as this lady suggested, and then they would not see her nor have her read stories to them when the train started.

"I'm sure that Mademoiselle can tell a brighter story than any of us have ever heard," Ossip whispered to his sister. She squeezed his hand, wondering at his capacity to read her thoughts. Dear Sonitchka, he was thinking, you are the most vulnerable of us three. For Anna has her anger to protect her, and you have only trust . . . And Mademoiselle, yes, could tell us all some stories.

Mathilde's ivory-tinted face grew bright at the cheekbones, and for an instant her calm face quickened. Her gloved hand touched Johanna's fingers, which were still resting on her arm. She nodded. "A small nap would do me a world of good," she said. "I don't know why, but I am truly exhausted. Thank you, Mademoiselle."

A half-smile flickered over the Dutchwoman's features. "This is presumptuous, and perhaps I shall offend you— but I would be honored if you called me by my given name.

None of my employers ever has, and with you, I feel almost as though—if life had been different, and we had met as . . . as . . ."

Mathilde, the controlled, whose key to her emotions was never out of sight, was stirred by a swift, unexpected compassion. "I understand," she murmured. Her voice was serene as always. But Johanna's own voice broke, and she pressed Mathilde's arm. "Nobody ever does," she said quickly, bending her lovely head and examining the ground. Mathilde, embarrassed, disengaged herself. But she said no more, and sailed toward the stairway to her compartment like an elegant liner moving calmly over the sea. She paused on the first step: "Johanna," she said, and smiled.

When the children had been settled comfortably in their own car, adjoining their mother's, Anna huddled near Titine but Sonia drew next to the beautiful lady who was their governess. Ossip, in his polite, well-modulated voice, so like his mother's, said, "Mademoiselle, in Russia people are not as they are in France. There is less formality. Friends say 'tu' at once, and instead of being called 'Madame' or 'Monsieur' or 'Mademoiselle,' well-bred people show respect simply by adding your father's name to your own given name. The servants call my sister Sonia, 'Sofia Davidovna,' which is perfectly proper. 'Sonia' is only for family, or Titine. But 'Sofia' is her given name, and 'Davidovna' means 'daughter of David.' What was your father's name? We shall need to know, for our servants at home, and for people who come to visit with their own Mademoiselles."

Johanna de Mey regarded the little boy with humor. "I see. But I thought everyone in Russia spoke French?"

"Oh no, Mademoiselle," Sonia piped up gravely. "Only those who are most refined, like my Mama. But Mama and Papa know many people, and unless they are very, very close to us, we, the children, and sometimes even our parents, call them by their patronyms. They say, 'Bonjour, Anna Davidovna,' or other things in French—but the names are the Russian way. Ossip is right. And I have learned all about that!" She beamed at Johanna, who patted her curls.

"In that case, I shall have to learn, too," the governess said. "My father's name was Johan. That is 'Jean' in French. What would it be in Russian?"

"It would be 'Ivan,' Mademoiselle," Ossip said, coloring slightly. "I heard Mama call out your name before— Johanna—so you would be 'Johanna Ivanovna.' That is very pretty," he added, to hide his confusion.

"And you are very pretty, Mademoiselle," Sonia stated.

Johanna de Mey began to laugh. "My, my, what have we here? My first lesson in Russian custom, *and* a fine compliment! I shall have to reward you both. Let me see, now . . . Perhaps you would like to call me by a special name, just among us?" She glanced at Anna and the baby. "Something only you four would call me. No more 'Mademoiselle,' for, as you say, everyone else has a Mademoiselle, too. 'Johanna' would be improper, for, after all, you are children and I am a lady, and it would seem disrespectful for you to call me by my name, the way you do Célestine, for example."

"But we don't call her that at all," Anna broke in, her voice clear and somewhat sharp. "We call her 'Titine,' because that is our love-name for her."

The eyes of blue crystal gleamed, but without warmth. "A love-name? Well then, Sonia, how about a love-name for me, something very different and exciting?" She pointed to the Spanish doll on the small girl's lap. "I have it! My name in Spain would be 'Juanita,' and I always preferred it to Johanna. You will call me Juanita, and you may even say 'tu' to me, since we are on our way to this great Russia, where formality seems to be out of fashion."

Sonia clapped her hands, and Ossip smiled. But Anna, her brown eyes solemn, commented softly: "Not out of fashion, Juanita. Just—different."

Sonia turned to her sister, and did not understand the sudden darkness which shadowed her face. Her own bright joy shook within her, and suddenly she missed her mother.

But she continued to smile, her hand on the Spanish doll, her eyes abstracted. She snuggled against her brother and fell asleep.

The patriarch of the Gunzburg clan, Baron Horace, had three sons: the youngest, Mikhail, who did not reside in the Russian capital, and his two other sons, David and Alexander, "Sasha" to his intimates. Horace, since the death of his beloved wife, Anna Rosenberg, was not given to much joie de vivre. It had been she whose liveliness and femininity had brightened his serious temperament. A stately man, his elegance was somber, and he occupied himself solely with matters of import. He was still the head of his bank, the Maison Gunzburg, which his father Ossip had founded in the late '50s; and he was also the most well-known *shtadlan* in Russia, a mediator between the government and the Jewish population. Horace was still Consul of Hesse, and now a Hessian princess, Alix, had become the Tzarina Alexandra Feodorovna; her father had granted the Gunzburgs their title. Horace, as his own father before him, found it his honored duty to attempt, little by little, to ease the burdens carried by his fellow Jews. He was proud of the fact that because of his intervention, St. Petersburg was now open to Jews of means and education, as well as to artisans contributing to the national economy. These were the members of the exalted First and most useful Second Guilds. When poorer men complained that he thought only of his own kind, he would reply: "Give the government time. Our Tzars have always been anti-Semitic. Now, at least, they have made a first step." The difference, he might have pointed out, lay between the Gunzburgs and the inhabitants of Hashchévato.

Between Horace and David, his first son, empathy existed. It was David who now took over the major part of Horace's charitable work. Passionate where his father was gloomy, sinewy where the older man was massive, David nevertheless believed in his heart that the Jews of Russia belonged in Russia, soon to obtain their deserved full citizenship, and should not escape to the haven promised by the growing number of Zionists. But Sasha, younger than David by seven years, was only amused by his kinsmen's zeal. His principal concerns were with his own position in the social circles of the capital, where he seconded his father at the bank.

Sasha, whose brooding good looks Mathilde had once so admired, was the most striking of the Gunzburgs. He was the tallest one, and sported a black beard and a large shoulder span. He possessed the Gunzburg eyes, set close together, and his were brilliant blue, like Mathilde's. But he had married a woman who was anything but his equal in looks, for, like some extraordinarily handsome men who are somewhat insecure at heart, he had chosen a wife who showed off his own splendor, and whom he need not fear would ever cease her adoration of him. Rosa Warburg de Gunzburg was all angles and bones, a small brown bird of a woman, and although she did indeed admire her husband beyond words, she was as shrewd as he, as snobbish, and as petty in her envies and social exhibitionism. But at heart she was a German Frau, protective of her family and always ready to advance their personal cause. They had a single daughter, Tatiana, a year younger than Sonia. No one ever understood how the little wren Rosa had produced such an exquisite porcelain doll with hair as fair as that of Rapunzel. Sasha and his wife found her the loveliest child in St. Petersburg. Few disagreed.

This, then, was the family that awaited the return of Mathilde and her four children to the capital. The children had only met their aunt and their cousin once, in Europe, and they did not quite remember either one. They were rather afraid of their paternal grandfather, for he was not gay and charming like Grandfather Yuri, his flamboyant brother in Paris, who told them incredible stories and made them laugh. But Mathilde had said to them: "How we feel is unimportant. Family is family. You, Sonia, will be good and kind to your cousin Tania."

Mathilde was enchanted with the house David had purchased on Vassilievsky Island, and which he had furnished so carefully. She was surprised, and touched. As they walked up the marble steps to the apartment on the top story, she noted with pleasure that enormous potted palms stood on each landing, and that a reproduction by David's friend, the sculptor Antokolsky, of his best work, the *Mephistopheles*, adorned the lowest landing. Antokolsky had been commissioned to make marble busts of Tzar Nicholas II and his wife and mother.

They had been greeted at the door by two familiar figures who had served the family when David and Mathilde had resided in Horace's own mansion. Stepan, tall, dignified, and well-dressed, was the maître d'hôtel. Alexei Fliederbaum, small and quick, had once been David's orderly in the Uhlans in Lomzha. Later he had served Sasha too in that regiment, until David had taken him out of the ranks and trained him as his bookkeeper and librarian. Their presence had made Mathilde smile through her exhaustion, and had enhanced her pleasure in the apartment. But the children had reacted with awe and suspended breath, for after the overwhelming spectacle of the spires and the Neva River, and the furious windswept drive across the bridge, they had been unprepared for so much magnificence inside their own home. And Stepan dwarfed even Papa, who was almost as tall as Uncle Sasha.

David had awaited his family's arrival with near-childlike exultation. He had been alone so long in this city, dining with sympathetic friends whose wives treated him with somewhat overt compassion, or poring over his work into the wee hours of the morning. He had frankly missed Mathilde in his bed. Now, for their first supper in his new home, she chose a gown of mint-green silk trimmed with ermine, and he was moved, knowing that this was her tacit signal of approval of the pale green bedroom. He had perhaps dreamed of greater effusion, but then Mathilde had never been effusive, not even on their wedding day. No, he considered, she is content, and she is glad to be here, with me. His pale blue eyes shone across the table, encountering hers.

His children were around him. Anna, her eyes rimmed with red after a long session with the curling irons; Ossip, quietly observant; and little Sonia, who appeared smaller even than Sasha's Tania, her little face rosy and ringed with bright black waves of hair. Between the two girls sat the new governess, Mademoiselle de Mey. David knit his brow, tasting his Madeira. He felt uneasy about Mademoiselle de Mey.

There she sat, erect and graceful, in a peach-colored gown, her golden hair glimmering beneath the chandelier. David had known many women in his life, some grand, like his wife, serenely beautiful in magnificent understatement. They were good listeners, they were kindhearted, they were true ladies. They did not shine by their wit, nor overwhelm by their jewels. They glowed with tranquility, and with them he felt comfortable. He classed his wife with these women, seeing her desire for peace as greatness of heart, judging her cool cynicism as penetrating, generous observation of others. He thought her wonderful, because she was never strident—and did not perceive that Mathilde's dream of peace was sometimes purchased at the price of true valor.

Then there was a second class of women, the gay, bright ones who tapped a gentleman on the arm with a flippant fan, who trilled with glee and made the naughtiest comments. They were always beautiful, but in their middle years they often grew brittle, and their wit hardened. These women generally adored David, for they thought him so teasable, and yet so kind. He found them pleasantly innocent, and did not mind them or their flirtatious jokes. Perhaps, in their way, they added a note of brilliance to the world. His tiny blond niece, Tania, might grow into this type of woman, he thought. She would make an amusing wife but a dreadful mother, jealous of any charm her daughters might accrue.

But there was a class of women who made David acutely uncomfortable—sharp-eyed, sharp-minded women whose every gesture proclaimed that they were better than men, that, in fact, they would be just as happy if that annoying sex would kindly disintegrate before their more intelligent eyes. And David, looking at the elegant blonde seated between his daughters, wondered if she were not one of them. She spoke to him with the utmost courtesy, but when he answered, her face remained rigid, as though it did not matter if she heard him or not. Nonsense, he told himself. The girl is Dutch, the Dutch are reserved, and she is in a new household with a new master. Yet, for all his chiding, the fine profile of Johanna de Mey caused him to cast aside his sherried veal after hardly a taste. It did not help that Mathilde refused to return his look of deep yearning, that she flushed only when addressing this outsider, this woman whose existence mattered so slightly to all their lives.

After supper, when Johanna went to put the children to bed, he said with unsuppressed annoyance to his wife, "How can this person afford such clothes? Why, her attire this evening seemed almost as expensive as your own."

But Mathilde, instead of smiling her indulgent smile and placing her hand on his arm, regarded him with a firm ridge between her black brows. "For a man who dedicates himself to the poor, you show a surprising lack of grace. Johanna is an excellent seamstress. She purchases the patterns, and makes the gowns herself. You should be pleased that such a 'person,' as you put it, will teach our daughters how to sew; they'll spend less of your money on their dresses."

He was abashed. "My dear, forgive me." He took her fingers and brought them to his lips. "Let us not quarrel over a governess. You are right: she will be perfect for the children. You and I have so much to make up for—so many months. Let's not be irritated with one another."

But she said, "David, I am tired. I should like to retire now. I feel a migraine coming on. We'll talk tomorrow." Before he could reply, she swept out of the room, a majestic figure in soft green. Tomorrow. He stood alone, aghast. Their first night together.

Suddenly, an irrepressible anger took hold of him, and he hurled a bronze paperweight against the mantelpiece. Then he fell into an armchair, and his head dropped into his hands. He did not hear Stepan enter the room and discreetly pick up the fallen object, nor did he hear him leave. He was far too upset.

Rosa de Gunzburg, wrapped from head to toe in astrakhan fur, shivered deeply as the gusts of icy wind flung themselves, moaning, against her elegant troika. She hugged her tiny daughter to her meager body. "Why do Uncle David and Aunt Mathilde live so far away?" Tania asked. She was herself enveloped in white ermine, with muff and cap to match, and her small face was red with cold.

"Heaven only knows, child," her mother sighed. Vassilievsky was a mere suburb, while her own house in the city dated from the days of the Tzarina Elisabeth, and was considered a landmark. The historic facade remained, but inside it had been remodeled, and it was full of clarity and open spaces, with a wrought iron bannister along the staircase and a living room all in blue silks. Rosa was most proud of her salon. She did not know that her friends sometimes made fun of her exclusively female help, however. "Rosa is a darling, but so German," the Russians would say. For the Warburgs of Hamburg had employed no male servants, and even now Rosa was afraid that her authority might be questioned by a man.

Now, when Stepan greeted her as they arrived at Mathilde's house, Rosa felt a pang of envy. He was such a fine specimen, and so excellently trained. She took Tania's hand and went into the Louis XIII living room, admiring it, in spite of herself. She adjusted the spray of lace at her throat, and mentally reviewed her appearance. Truly, the emerald afternoon gown from Worth was perfect, and Tania's pink pinafore was adorable.

Mathilde was rising to greet her, and Rosa noted with displeasure that Sonia, at her side, was a pretty child. Her eyes were smoky-gray, her features delicate, her hair raven black. But she looked so very Russian—men would find her attractive but . . . ordinary, unlike Tania, so golden, with her eyes such a bright blue.

Mathilde was also regarding Tania, and thinking, How absurd! A child in raw silk, which will stain when she plays. But she held out her arms and embraced her sister-in-law.

Sonia was staring at Tania, her eyes wide with admiration. "You are very beautiful," she said, taking her hand. "You are like a princess in a story."

"Yes, I know," Tania replied sweetly.

"But you're not supposed to answer that way," Sonia said with consternation. "Mama will be quite shocked, and so will your Mama."

"Oh, I don't think so," Tania explained. Her eyes twinkled. "Everybody compliments me. And Mama and Papa are very happy about it."

Sonia bit her lower lip. "You are very lucky," she said. "I guess I'm just not as pretty as you. Nobody tells me I am, except for Ossip."

Tania clapped her little hands together. "Ossip! Oh, where is he? I should like to see him again. He was a handsome boy when I saw him last. He gave me candy."

"You want to see my brother?" Sonia was hesitant. "Don't you want to go to my room and have cakes, and play with my dolls, and see Anna?"

But Tania made a wry face. "No. Anna is ugly. I don't like ugly people. But I like Ossip. He will play dolls with us."

"I'm not sure, for he is a boy," Sonia answered. "You will have to ask. And Anna is not ugly. You must promise never to say that again, or I shall not be friends with you." Her cheeks grew red with anger.

"Your Mama will force you to be my friend," Tania stated primly. "And Ossip will play what I want. They always do. Everybody."

"Ossip is not an everybody," Sonia replied, annoyed. Then she shrugged. "Come on," she said, and took her cousin's hand. She led the way out of the room.

Rosa commented to Mathilde: "They are so sweet together. Snow White and Rose Red."

A half-smile appeared on Mathilde's serene face. "Tania does get her own way, doesn't she? Someday she will be roundly spanked by an older and larger child. Or," she added, "by a sensitive mother."

But Rosa saw no irony in these words. "She charms the whole world," she said fatuously. "And besides, my dear, no one would dare to lay a hand on the daughter of Baron Alexander."

Mathilde poured some dark amber tea into tall Russian glasses. She sat back, annoyed at the irritation which disturbed her peace in this room which she loved. Rosa was like a fly, buzzing around her. Mathilde put a hand to her temple, and wondered if another migraine was about to begin. Her thick pompadour weighed on her head. She was vaguely pleased with Sonia, who had controlled her anger toward her cousin, and somewhat annoyed with Anna, who had refused to come to tea. Later she would enter, to kiss her aunt gingerly on the spare brown cheek, but that was hardly sufficient for the elder daughter in a family.

Still—she could imagine Anna sitting in surly resentment on the edge of the sofa, her red hair hopelessly disordered. Rosa would tell all of St. Petersburg about it. Mathilde sighed. The only bright point of this colorless afternoon would be when Johanna would join them, after making sure that the two older children were settled in their rooms with cake and tea.

"You have not met my Johanna," she said to Rosa, and her face quickened. "She is a jewel—not merely with the children, but also here, with me. She is literate and worldly and has traveled. And she has such a flair for fashion!"

"A hired woman? Come now, Mathilde, you exaggerate. Tania's governess is perfectly adequate—a Swiss girl—but I would no more discuss fashion with her than I would with your Stepan."

"You are so wrong! You, David—thinking in terms of pay. Johanna is a lady, I tell you. She comes from as fine a family as we do. Money is scarce. There is no dishonor in working." But she shivered at the thought, and her heart, so rarely touched, warmed with compassion for Johanna de Mey. She felt a surge of anger with Rosa that she had not felt when Tania had called Anna ugly.

Moments later, with a swishing of satin, Johanna de Mey entered the room. Her appearance alone made Rosa de Gunzburg shrink and darken in contrast, for she wore a gown of soft turquoise, and her hair fell in ringlets onto the nape of her neck. She said, "I am so sorry to be late for you, Mathilde." The smile that accompanied her speech was radiant. Rosa touched her breast with an intake of breath, and her black eyes rolled in their sockets. Mathilde repressed a smile.

"This is Johanna de Mey, Rosinka," she said, as the Dutchwoman took the small bony hand and made a slight but precise curtsy. Her willowy form hardly seemed to bow, so smooth and brief was the formality. "My sister-in-law, the Baroness Alexander de Gunzburg."

"I am pleased to make your acquaintance."

Mathilde patted the seat next to her on the sofa, and the governess sat down. Rosa watched, unable to speak. Smoothly, Mathilde poured a third glass of tea and handed it to the fair-haired woman beside her. Rosa thought, Mathilde has taken leave of her senses. But she could not regain her composure. Johanna de Mey, coolly sipping tea, was examining her with eyes of crystal blue. Rosa shivered. And then a tremendous envy welled up inside her, and she wanted to tear out Johanna's fine golden ringlets and spill tea over her elegant turquoise gown. She said, her birdlike face craned toward Mathilde, "I was planning to give a dinner in your honor, to celebrate your arrival. Sasha has discussed it with David."

Mathilde's eyebrows curved up. "Did you not wish to speak to me about it before the men discussed it?" she asked. Then, more kindly, she added, "But no, of course, they are brothers. When shall we come?"

"Two weeks from Thursday," Rosa replied, refusing to look at Johanna. Her hands were rigid in her lap. "We shall be only family. David was very touched," she emphasized.

"As am I, dear Rosa. So we shall be the Sashas, the Davids, Uncle Horace, and Johanna?" Mathilde made an effort to speak with gentleness, and her control jarred her sister-in-law's nerves. Rosa touched her forehead absently. "Did you hear me, Rosinka?" Mathilde inquired with solicitude.

Suddenly Rosa de Gunzburg came alive, with fury. Her hands clenched into fists. She half rose, and screamed, "No! You will not bring this woman to my house! You will not spoil my intimate supper! She is nothing, nothing at all, and I have not invited her. I also did not bother to include Stepan. What would Papa Horace say? Or Sasha? My God, Mathilde, it is uncivil enough for you to impose this creature on me alone, when I come to tea for the first time since your return. Are you trying to ruin me?" She burst into hysterical sobs, pressing her fists against her temples, her neat chignon coming undone.

Mathilde's eyes widened, but her expression of tranquil poise did not shift. She said calmly, "Let's be mature, Rosa. You have insulted me by insulting my friend. Johanna is my friend, and nobody will belittle her in my presence. You are my sister, and I value your good will. I would not think of including Johanna if she were not already precious to me. She is a lady, I have told you. But if you invite me to supper in front of Johanna, whom I have asked to join us for this tea, then it is only natural for me to assume that she is also invited. If she were not, you would have discussed the supper at another time, privately."

"But you gave me no chance!" Rosa cried out.

Johanna de Mey stood up. Her eyes had turned a strange opalescent hue, and her thin nose seemed pinched. She said, "Mathilde, it is clear that I am not wanted. The Baroness seems to think that I am a servant. It appears that I committed a grave error in accepting this position with the Gunzburg family. Your reputation is high, and I was told that I would fit into its aura of gentility and generosity. Yet now I am treated as a menial. I have not been invited, although a party has been discussed in my presence. That is the prerogative of the Baroness, but it is mine, nevertheless, to return to France. I have never accepted humiliation, and I never shall. If you seek a servant, then I am sorry, but you have made a mistake. My mother, in the Netherlands, was also a baroness." Even as Mathilde's hand reached out to touch her, she evaded it, moving aside with a swish of her satin skirt. She turned and left the room, where Rosa was still sobbing. All color had departed from Mathilde's cheeks. For the first time since her wedding trip, Mathilde de Gunzburg felt control slipping away from her, and remembered the ghastly night that David had forced her to spend in a train station. She thought of her father, pounding his fist upon the dinner table to roar insults at the cook for overheating the soup. Fear rose in her breast. She thought wildly: Johanna will go away, and she is the first person who has truly been my friend, the first person who has understood me since I left my sisters. She was in St. Petersburg, where she needed Johanna, needed someone with whom to share her feelings. She needed Johanna to act as buffer, to control the children, to help with the servants . . . to laugh about female things, to chat with idly. She could not let Johanna go, not now, not ever. A desperation such as Mathilde had never experienced in her thirty-one years overwhelmed her.

Fumbling wildly, she rang for Stepan. When he appeared, Mathilde said with a supreme effort at control, "Please help the Baroness. She is much distressed. She will need her coach, and her daughter. I must tend—to something." Without looking at Rosa, she hurried from the room, knowing but not caring that the maître d'hôtel was staring at her in shock and bewilderment. Only one thing mattered, and that was to convince Johanna not to leave.

If Johanna de Mey had made a lifelong enemy of Rosa de Gunzburg, it did not ruffle her in the least. Quite to the contrary, she smiled to herself, for the incident in the living room had, she knew, created a permanent, if unspoken, breach between Mathilde and her sister-in-law. And that was all to Johanna's advantage.

Mathilde had spoken to David about "Rosa's appalling lack of tact," and had indicated that she expected to receive a note of apology. As she lay upon her pillows, her face whiter than usual, a cautious David sat on the bed and held her hand soothingly. "It is a matter best forgotten, dearest," he said. "Rosa is a snob, and she behaved like an impudent child. But perhaps henceforth you had best refrain from asking Johanna to tea."

Mathilde, outraged, silenced his protests. She would not

go to supper unless he spoke to his brother about the apology. It was Johanna who had been cruelly wronged.

David, who was a diplomat in business affairs, felt acutely uncomfortable. Family was precious to him, even if Sasha was imperious and envious, and they had never been close. Surely Rosa, whom David privately disliked, deserved priority over his children's governess. But thoughts of Mathilde, distressed, flooded his mind. In an agony of embarrassment, David went to the bank to speak to his brother. Sasha laughed. Women were foolish creatures, though it amazed him that Mathilde, whom he had always admired for her regal beauty and elegant poise, would stoop to this sort of silliness. Had David, by the way, seen that little milliner whom Sasha now kept near the Nevsky Prospect? Imagine, renting an apartment there! The girl was a saucy piece, but costly, costly. David was wise not to indulge in passions of the flesh. David smiled, thinking of Mathilde. He had his passions; had they not driven him here against his better judgment?

After much deliberation, and a burst of anger from Sasha, the brothers had agreed that for the sake of family relations Rosa would send the note. At home, Sasha had to contend with his wife, who flew into a wild fury, throwing a precious vase against a wall and pummeling his chest. He had calmed her and repeated what he expected of her. Then, after she had rewritten the apology three times, he had taken her to bed. And so Mathilde had informed Johanna that her sister-in-law had begged forgiveness, that most certainly Mademoiselle de Mey was to be included in her dinner party. Johanna had known how to play this, too, to her own advantage.

"My dear Mathilde," she said, "I could not possibly attend. Rosa is doing this only for courtesy. Her heart is not in this invitation, and I do not wish to upset her further by being present where I am not truly a welcome guest."

Mathilde had agreed.

Johanna reflected upon all this as she munched daintily upon a crumpet. It was nine o'clock and she was partaking of breakfast in bed. The children had had their Hebrew lesson—what nonsense!—with their father at seven thirty, and now awaited her in the lesson room. But Baron David would be occupied in his study, receiving his daily petitioners and reviewing each of their cases before taking the carriage into town and the ministries where he worked. She pursed her lips with disgust. Never had she seen such an array of evil-smelling tatterdemalions as inhabited the waiting room outside the Baron's study. But then, it was just like this religious fanatic to work himself to death over supposed injustices committed against some poor Jews. Well, let him waste his time! It kept him from visiting the lesson room and discovering that she was not present. The children had their assignments: they were to learn a passage from the history book by memory, and that would take them a good hour. She would arrive at ten.

She remembered her own education. She had been the eldest daughter of Johan de Mey van Alkemade, of Utrecht. Her father, imperious, tall, and handsome, had possessed much noble blood, although her sweet, delicate mother came only from a bourgeois background. Her parents had bought a magnificent house on Lake Geneva during her childhood, and she had loved the blue-green, cool beauty of Switzerland. She had also loved her splendid, aristocratic father, after whom she had been named. She had vaguely despised her more common mother, always so gentle and kind. She herself had been authoritative from the start, and her father had said: "She is named for me, she resembles me, and she is strong-willed like me. I shall educate her well, not like these cream-puff females who adorn the world and are of no use to anybody."

His wife had blushed, knowing he was referring to her.

So Johanna had been sent to the best school for young ladies in Geneva, a boarding establishment run by two spinster ladies, the Frauleins Broun and Weichbrodt. They tolerated no nonsense, and were rigid disciplinarians. She had been the pet of the Frauleins; she followed discipline marvelously.

When she had completed her education, the Meys had moved to Neuilly, an elegant suburb of Paris. Not realizing that her husband was nearly ruined from mismanagement of his affairs, Lise de Mey had entertained lavishly. Her husband was too proud to admit his failures to her, and too stubborn to admit the extent of the damage to himself. Johanna, as beautiful and stately as an iris, had been courted by many wealthy young men. But compared to her father, they all seemed stupid and graceless. And Johan encouraged her dispassion, for it fed his own ego. He had reared his daughter to be brilliant, like a man. It did not matter to him that Lise was distressed.

And then, quite suddenly, catastrophe struck. Headstrong, vain, Johan de Mey continued to spend extravagant sums of money until one day there was nothing left. He had gone into his study, shut the door, and put a bullet through his left temple. Johanna had found him, slumped in a pool of blood, and her heart had ruptured. She was twenty-five. In her agony she had shaken her dead father, splattering his blood over her fine gown, screaming again and again, "Why have you done this to me?" Then, hardening herself, she had thought brutally: He never loved me, it was I who was a fool to think he did. He was a . . . nothing. I thought he was God, but he was nothing.

Lise was shattered and helpless, wracked by her pain, paralyzed by catastrophe. It was Johanna who took matters in hand. First, she paid off the servants with proceeds from the sale of the house, then she faced her father's creditors with rigid posture, meeting their cruel eyes with her own proud stare. It was she who auctioned off the paintings—beloved Vermeers and a small, treasured Rembrandt—the furnishings of buhl and rosewood and fine mahogany. Her heart did not stir with pain; it remained numb and cold inside her.

Johanna transferred the family to a small apartment in one of the less expensive areas of Paris, and raised her fine head as she took the degrading step of finding work for herself. She became a ladies' companion to a young American girl. She was well treated, for Americans felt insecure about their breeding, and hers, so properly European, had impressed the girl's family. But they had been ready, after several years, to return to America. It was a stroke of fortune that had allowed their return to coincide with Mathilde's need for a governess.

Mathilde. Johanna ran a finger down her nose, smiled, and touched a golden tendril on her forehead. She passed her hand over her chest, then parted the fine blue gauze of her nightdress and felt her small but well-formed breasts, like half-apples, and their hard nipples. A tremor of delight ran through her, and she shook herself out of it. Mathilde, in many ways, was like a child. She was an accomplished woman of the world, but innocent too, for it was clear that she had never been aroused. Certainly not by that sapless husband of hers. Mathilde tolerated him, but surely bore him little love and no passion. And had Mathilde not told her that they had been betrothed during her childhood? Certainly, then, no other man had stimulated Mathilde's imagination. Women, in truth, could only be appreciated by other women. Suddenly blood rushed through Johanna's body and she clasped her hands in blind yearning. For while her senses had known pleasure before, no one had ever possessed them in full save herself. Until now. But one had to be careful, to tread lightly—or all would be lost. She had to be more astute than ever before. Mathilde de Gunzburg was a proper woman, who would need to be deluded.

It was nearly ten o'clock. Johanna de Mey drank a last swallow of café au lait and wiped her delicate mouth with a linen napkin. Those damned children! She slipped out of bed and let the nightdress fall to the floor. The full-length mirror on the wall revealed her to herself, firm, pink, and sylphlike. She smiled, her ill humor dwindling. It was time for her to be with someone her own age. And Mathilde, at thirty-one, was exactly two weeks older than she.

After a month in St. Petersburg, Sonia's mind was filled with conflicting emotions. She loved the city. She thought the Neva splendid, and the drives along the Nevsky Prospect fairylike. And naturally, there was the apartment, which she admired in its every detail, though Anna had told her secretly that when she grew up her own house would be uncluttered with objets d'art, and that she herself intended to design each piece of furniture. But Sonia disagreed. Every inlay, every filament of gold was precious to her. Her Mama fit in here, with her calm grandeur. One day she, Sonia, would wear her thick black hair in a pompadour and sit amid antique furnishings too.

Tania was the single villain in Sonia's fairy tale. She was continually shocked by her cousin's lack of manners, and by her presumption. She particularly resented Tania's fondling of Ossip, who was her own treasured brother, and who politely bore the golden girl's attentions in quiet desolation. She did not like Tania's impudence toward Anna, who largely ignored her. But she did admire, with awe, her cousin's great beauty. How strange then that gloomy Grandfather Horace always asked her, Sonia, to perch on his lap! For the world seemed to grovel before Tania, especially the girl's own parents. Sonia also did not like her Aunt Rosa. Why was Aunt Rosa forever telling people about things that Tania performed better than Sonia? Whenever her aunt kissed her, Sonia felt ill at ease. She does not like me, and yet I have always been polite to her, Sonia would think.

But her confusion was even greater when she considered Juanita. What a lovely lady she was, so perfectly dressed and coiffed! And she was kind to Mama. Yet Sonia never knew when Juanita's temper might explode, or how to guard against it. During lessons, if one of the three children misrecited a single word Juanita's anger flared. A second error brought the textbook hurtling to the floor, and Juanita standing in fury over the head of the small criminal. Sonia sometimes made mistakes, and Anna made them constantly, but Ossip rarely did, for he had apparently learned that by doing exactly what Juanita required, furious tantrums were averted. But Ossip was brilliant. Sonia was not, and so even if she tried as hard as she could, until tears came, mistakes still happened. When they did, Juanita was merciless. "You are dishonoring me," the governess would say. "I was the best student at the Broun School, and I am doing my best to pound some knowledge into that stubborn brain of yours. You are a sore disappointment to me."

Poor Anna. She had never been good at lessons, only at drawing. She so disliked to sit at a desk and learn "all this useless nonsense" that she did not try very hard. She and Ossip, though two years apart, were at the same level. But it was almost as though Anna sought Juanita's anger, as though she were trying not to learn in order to show her active resentment of the governess. This was bewildering to Sonia, who thought that they were all indeed shaming poor Juanita and worthy of her anger and despair. "After all, she is so perfect," she would wail to her sister, who replied tartly: "Yes, she does tell us so each day, doesn't she?"

Gently, patiently, Ossip coached his sister, but Anna stalked impatiently away. "I'm going to the kitchen to talk to Cook," she would say. "He has fascinating things to show me. I don't care about geography anyway."

Sonia cried after her, "Don't go, Annushka! You will only get into trouble if Juanita finds you there! She says it's not your place to be with servants."

"Well, I refuse to go to tea with Mama," Anna declared. "Madame Warshavskaya is such a dreadful hypocrite, like Aunt Rosa, being sweet to me and yet knowing perfectly well that I know she dislikes me, as I dislike her."

"The secret is not to show it," Ossip said with a peculiar

smile. "Mama hates Aunt Rosa terribly. But Aunt Rosa doesn't know it."

"Then Mama is a hypocrite too. There, I've said it. I love her and I respect her but I don't want to be like her. It would *kill* me." And Anna ran off, her hair a shambles and her skirt wrinkled.

Johanna taught the children arithmetic and French grammar, French history, poetry by rote, geography, mythology, Roman history, and natural history. Their father taught them Hebrew, and a plump, intense young woman called Maria Sabatievna Komansky came twice a week to instruct them in Russian language and history. She was a learned person, having studied at the University, and at once she and Anna became friends. After the lesson, Ossip and Sonia would leave the two of them together to chat. This enraged Johanna, who would complain bitterly, "She is not a lady."

That was precisely why Anna fancied her. That, and the fact that Maria did not treat the eleven-year-old pupil as a child, but earnestly discussed with her the ideas that preoccupied her own University friends. She spoke of the evil of autocracy, of the wretched poverty of the peasants and the workers, of the unfairness of thoughtless, conscienceless wealth controlled by too few, and by the dissolute. Anna nodded in ardent admiration. She was confused by some of Maria's more exalted phrases, but basically she comprehended, and agreed. For the first time in her life, someone was expressing her own ideas.

"And one day soon, the masses will rule this nation, and the world!" Maria would cry, her eyes glowing. Anna would think of Stepan, and Eusebe, and nod. How much more wisdom such men could bring to the world than the Rosas and the Sashas. A life without frills, but with honesty, she thought hungrily, is all I want.

One afternoon, Johanna intercepted a servant girl carrying a tray of tea and cakes to the room Anna shared with her sister. "What's this?" she demanded.

"The Baroness said it would be all right for Maria Sabatievna to stay to tea with Anna Davidovna."

"Then allow me to bring this to them," Johanna said, taking the tray from the girl. She felt a tremor of excitement, although she did not know why. Her passion of hatred toward Anna bore its roots in a fact over which the girl had no control. Johanna loved beauty, and Anna was not beautiful. Her facial defect repulsed the immaculate Dutchwoman, and Anna's obvious dislike of her only intensified her constant virulence against the girl. Besides, she felt that Mathilde, in some measure, shared her sentiments, and was guilty about it. Poor Mathilde! She still let the girl have her own way—refusing to be dragged to teas, or inviting her Russian teacher to stay. Mathilde allowed all this in weariness, Johanna knew, for she simply did not wish to expend the necessary energy to compel Anna to change. Therefore Johanna, who certainly never lacked energy, took it upon herself to be Mathilde's avenging angel. But Anna defied her and this disturbed and irritated the Dutchwoman.

Now she opened Anna's door, without knocking. Maria Sabatievna was curled in a deep chair, her young pupil half lying on her bed. "Here is your treat, ladies," Juanita said. Her blue eyes searched the room and landed on a worn copy of a book by Anna's hand. "And what have we here?" she asked. She picked up the book and studied its title. "*The Communist Manifesto*, by Karl Marx. You don't mind if I read it, do you, Anna?"

The girl cried out, "It's mine, Juanita! Maria gave it to me. You have no right to take it away!"

Johanna regarded her with amusement, one eyebrow raised. "My, my, I'm not 'taking it away,' my rude little pussy cat. I merely wish to find out what fascinates you so. Perhaps I, too, wish to be fascinated." Before Anna could protest, Johanna sailed out of the room, the book in her hand.

Several days later, Johanna came to Mathilde in her boudoir, where she was writing notes to some Parisian friends. The face of the young Baroness brightened. "Johanna! It is nice to see you. I find that I have so little news to relate to my friends—have you any?"

But Johanna de Mey did not smile. She sat down, her hands folded in her lap. "My dear Mathilde, I have come about a serious matter. One over which I have no control. It concerns Anna."

"Oh?" Concern furrowed Mathilde's brow, and she turned in her chair to face Johanna.

Silently, the governess handed her the book she had taken from Anna. Mathilde felt its cover and frowned. "I don't know about this," she said doubtfully. "Is it . . . improper?"

Johanna concealed a half-smile. "It is subversive, my dear Mathilde. Karl Marx preaches revolt and revolution and a world without classes. And our Anna's mind is being spoiled by him and his followers—of which Maria Sabatievna Komansky is most assuredly an ardent one. The Baron must dismiss her. God only knows what other damage she has already wrought."

Mathilde felt a vague pang. "But Anna cares about her so much, and you know how few friends she has," she said softly. But Johanna's firm, elegant profile remained grave and condemning. Mathilde sighed. Johanna was wise, and Anna but a child. "I shall speak to David," she said, and took the book.

When Mathilde brought it to her husband, with Johanna's story, he shook his head. "Marx. I met the man when he was already old and I was still a student, visiting relatives in London. His work is flamboyant, even brilliant, and he does have a following." Then, considering: "Don't worry, my sweet, Anna will forget his wild predictions soon enough. And Maria is not an evil influence, as your Johanna says. She may be young, and somewhat misguided, but I am certain that at heart she is a loyal subject of the Tzar, just as we all are. Let us leave her be. Anna, as you say, is uncommonly fond of her, and that, in my eyes, makes her most useful."

"But Johanna has read the book. If we ignore her suggestion, she may be offended. She will feel useless, as though her word is not important. I cannot have that, David." Mathilde clasped her hands. "Surely you can hire a new Russian mistress?"

Sudden anger welled up inside him. His blue eyes blazed. "The girl is an excellent instructress. I do not send people away on whims."

His wife stood still, her beautiful face white as alabaster, her hands clasped, her posture erect. She said nothing. But when he looked at her, he saw the iron determination in her sapphire eyes, and he knew that he was defeated.

"I shall find some excuse," he said with disgust. His anger vied in his mind with the vision of Mathilde's closed door, and before this vision he was helpless and frustrated. Mathilde came to his side, and just as he was turning away in self-loathing and despair, she kissed his cheek. "I have work to attend to," he said harshly. Mathilde had not heard that tone since that time at the train station on their honeymoon.

When Anna learned that her book had been confiscated and that Maria Sabatievna would not be returning the following week, she broke into tears. She went to her bed and buried her face in the pillow, rocking back and forth in agony. It was thus that Titine found her, and it was not until nightfall that the girl ceased her wracking sobs and fell asleep in the arms of the old nurse. Ah, thought Johanna, so she is not made of granite. She can break, after all! And she turned her mind to the Breton nurse, who had rocked the child.

Sonia did not believe that Johanna had planned the firing of Maria, and she defended the governess to her sister.

"Annushka, she doesn't hate you!" she said. "It's only that she wants you to stop rebelling. If only you'd try to please her, things would be better between you."

"Wait until she does something to hurt you," Anna cried out. "Just wait! It's only Ossip, and the baby, that she'll let alone. But why?"

Ossip could not have told her. He saw the scheming in their governess, but he did not understand where it led or why. He felt relieved that she seemed to like him, and praised him. He did not guess that she was thinking: Men do not stay tied to their mothers; he will go his way. He had guessed that by being passive, he would prevent irritation from scratching her nerves. And so, carefully, he allowed her to slip over him, not touching him at all. She had not come to be aware of his cynicism, and found him sweet. She also thought him a coward.

Sonia's admiration clearly pleased Johanna, and when it was discovered how poor Anna was in music, Johanna was delighted. Only Sonia would therefore receive piano lessons. For a while she dallied with Ossip, but the boy was too busy to keep up with the daily routine of practicing. Johanna sat the small girl beside her on the piano bench, taught her how to place her hands on the keyboard, and started her on scales and in the deciphering of notes. Sonia loved music. She had always sat by her Mama's feet when Mathilde played Beethoven's *Pathétique*. But for some reason, since Johanna's arrival, Mathilde had ceased to play. Sonia did not know that Johanna de Mey's technical perfection had embarrassed Mathilde, who had always played for pleasure. Sonia wanted to excel, to please the two ladies in her life. But Johanna kept insisting that she could not play for her mother until she was far more experienced. Sonia was filled with sadness.

But in another area, the small girl knew that she was progressing. Her Papa allowed her to come to him each day before the Hebrew lesson to go over her rhymes. She admired Papa for being a great poet, and, all by herself, with no prompting from anyone, she had gone to his study during the summer at Mohilna to ask him to teach her to write poetry. Each morning they discussed a particular rhyme scheme, and he would correct her assignment of the previous day. She felt so unique, basking in Papa's learning! And to his life she brought joy, and pride, for neither of his elder children had cared much for the poetry that was so essential to his own existence.

Early one morning, her papers in hand, Sonia encountered a sleepy Johanna in the corridor. "Where are you going at this hour, so secretive?" the governess asked.

Sonia raised her oval face, her smoky-gray eyes alight with self-importance. "My Papa is going to help me with my rhymes," she replied, and glowed.

"Let me see." Johanna took the sheafs of verse from Sonia's hand and studied them. Then she shook her head. "What utter nonsense!" she said. "Surely, child, there are more useful ways to occupy your brain! Your father is an important and busy man. He cannot spare the time for this. Go back to your room."

"But Papa is waiting for me," Sonia insisted. She could picture him, seated at his great desk, ready for her arrival. He would smile at her and perch her on his lap. "I must go to him."

Impatiently, Johanna shook her head. "What a stubborn little fool you are. Why, your father is only humoring you! He laughs at you behind your back! Such childishness!"

But Sonia refused to budge. "Papa never laughs at anybody. He is proud of me. Please, Juanita, let me go now." A creeping sensation of despair enveloped her, and she bit her lip.

Neatly, meticulously, Johanna de Mey peered down at the small figure before her and tore each of the papers in half one by one. She watched as the little white face fell apart, as tears began to stream down her cheeks. Sonia bit her lip hard; she refused to cry out as Anna did, bringing down the wrath of this woman upon her time and again.

No, she would not. But she was bewildered and heart-broken. Then, Johanna reached into a side pocket and handed the girl a piece of chocolate. "There, there, none of this is worth your tears," she said calmly. Sonia stared at her beautiful governess, at the sweet, and was speechless with confusion.

"Let's leave poetry to Lamartine," Johanna said in a gentle voice. "And if you are truly excellent at your memorizing, I shall permit you to go to your father for help with your own verse, though only rarely. After all, he is more than just your Papa, he is a diplomat and linguist, and others have more pressing need of him."

Later, when the children entered the study for their Hebrew lesson, David called Sonia to his side. "You did not come for the verse correction," he chided her softly. "Didn't you have time to do any?" But his daughter merely gazed into his eyes, and shook her head. Inside, her heart was cracking. He is an important man, and I must not be selfish, she reminded herself. Juanita was right. But still, it was difficult to keep from crying in front of dear, self-sacrificing Papa, who had not truly found her gifted and who had merely been kind. Tania was also right, for she was constantly telling Sonia that she had no true talents. What a disaster she was, not good enough to play the piano for Mama, not good enough to learn poetry from Papa.

In her own room, Johanna de Mey was filing her nails, their perfect ovals shining with care. She pictured the Baron in his study, wondering at his daughter's defection. She imagined his feeling of loss. A radiant smile spread over her lips, and she sat back in her chaise longue, her blue eyes sparkling. She began to hum.

It was infuriating to Sasha that his brother David could enjoy such perfect understanding with their father. He had lived with that secret envy since his childhood, and more particularly since his return from the Uhlans at Lomzha, when he had joined his father's bank after his brother had set up his own household in St. Petersburg. As a boy, he had covertly admired Mathilde for her beauty, and had despised his studious, less attractive brother for his fatuous adoration of the girl, whom he thought he understood so much better than David. As a young man, elegant and courtly, he had frequently thought that she was bored by David and needed the sensual hungers of a man, a real man, like himself, to awaken her from her lethargy. Women such as Mathilde remained dead unless a man could transport them to the heights of physical passion. In this evaluation, Sasha was wrong. For Mathilde found in David's gentleness a peace-giving contrast to her lustful father. At least Yuri had known how to be a gentleman, but Mathilde saw Sasha as that feared breed of Russian men who were driven by personal greed and violence; her father might enchant duchesses and charm his way into their beds; Sasha, like the brutal, animalistic father in *The Brothers Karamazov,* would hardly bother with the amenities.

Sasha had been surprised at his father's approval of David's choice, for it was well known that Baron Horace despised his brother Yuri. In his superficiality, he did not think that perhaps Horace was smiling at David's total passion for his dark-haired, blue-eyed cousin and remembering another youth who had fallen under the spells of a sapphire-eyed beauty with hair of ebony—Horace's own Anna. Horace had watched the young couple, David and his niece, and agreed that Mathilde was a true lady of breeding, a "woman of character." For few knew her well enough to peer beneath her cool facade. But he had been disturbed by the lackadaisical manner with which she demonstrated her affection for her husband. His Anna had behaved quite differently, her face blooming with shy love and total admiration. And in seeing his father, Sasha was clever enough to gauge just where his disappointment was rooted.

If most had known of these matters, they would have been less surprised by Sasha's choice of a bride. He was terribly handsome, terribly rich, and though his intelligence was limited by a blunt narrow-mindedness, he was clever and no fool. He might have chosen any girl. He chose Rosa Warburg with utmost care and planning. She adored him, devouring him with her coal-black eyes and eager hands. To his own surprise, he found that she was shrewd, had good taste, and enjoyed the pleasures of bed with remarkable virtuosity. Best of all, she had produced Tatiana. But Sasha had planned wrong in that direction. For to Sasha's dismay, his father seemed to prefer that pale gray-eyed thing, Sonia, to his own exquisite daughter. Sasha was green at the thought. Was it not sufficient injury that David was independent, that his father had chosen him for the Jewish cause, whereas Sasha worked for him, almost as a boy, taking direction at the bank?

Not a religious man by choice, Sasha nevertheless attempted to please Baron Horace by having Rosa put out Sabbath meals as his mother Anna had. The old man came. That was a point in favor of the Sashas. Once Rosa, in her birdlike zeal, had cried, "Oh, Papa Horace, is it not a shame that our dear Mathilde does not take as much pleasure as I do in the Sabbath supper?" Sasha had seen his father's face darken. Baron Horace had replied to Rosa's gushings with his customary peremptory curtness, but his eyes had grown thoughtful. If Sasha judged right, Baron Horace would discuss the matter with David.

But when David, knowing that he would have to employ a great deal of tact, approached his wife to bring up the conversation he had had with his father, he did not know that another discussion had taken place that very day between Mathilde and Johanna de Mey. The governess had come to Mathilde while the children were resting after the noon meal.

"When our lessons begin, at nine in the morning, I have

frequently noticed how tired the children are," Johanna began. "Particularly Sonia. It has worried me, for the sake of their health, let alone the progress they should be making in their learning."

Mathilde's languid eyes had seemed troubled. "They do not sleep well?" she had asked.

"It isn't that. They sleep well. But it is embarrassing for me to give you the reason. You may, dear Mathilde, think me presumptuous again."

Mathilde had risen rapidly. "I never feel you are out of bounds, Johanna. Do not harbor such fears. Tell me what is on your mind."

"It is the Baron. He expects those babes to be in his study by seven thirty, alert and ready, for their Hebrew lesson. Hebrew is a most complex language. Could it not wait until they have a firmer grasp of French grammar, and Russian? In their teens, perhaps, their brains would be better disciplined. But then, I am not a Jewess. The Dutch Protestant faith is quite another story, and as a child I learned only its basics. I was fully able to comprehend them, because they were so simple."

She saw she had struck a nerve. Mathilde had digested this information with wrinkled brow, her hands nervously folding and refolding the edge of her sash. Then the clear, dark blue eyes rested on the fine profile of the governess. "What you say deserves consideration, surely." Mathilde fingered her cameo brooch abstractedly. "But my husband places great emphasis on conducting the children's religious upbringing. That aspect of their lives has never been within my control."

"Then you cannot speak to him? Not even of their exhaustion?"

Mathilde's eyes met Johanna's, and slowly, painfully, she shook her head. It was a gesture of total resignation.

Johanna placed her long, graceful hand upon Mathilde's sleeve, and said softly, "My dear. I am so sorry." Her expression became almost one of condolence. Then, briskly, it changed. She smiled brightly. "Well, then, the Baron must have his way. Let us make bedtime earlier, and solve the problem thus! Now why did I bother you about it, when I might have thought of this solution? So obvious!"

She left Mathilde still fingering her brooch, remembering Hashchévato.

Now, when David said to his wife, "Papa would be so pleased if we would make a more solemn occasion of the Sabbath," he saw her lovely calm face suddenly cloud. He was taken aback. "My sweetest love, Papa is so fond of you. You must not take this as a criticism of your efforts, but more as . . . an old man's whim?" He made his pale, gentle eyes sparkle with understanding.

She drew away from him, and began to pace their bedroom. Her features were distorted; her hair, ready to be brushed for bed, streamed down her back. All at once she whirled to face him. "You!" she cried out. "With your rituals and your dedication, with your accursed duties! Why do you not place your own children first, instead of your obsessions? Hebrew lessons when they are tired! And now this! What has brought this on, David? Has Rosa been making a case against me to your father? If I am such a heathen, then why does he love our children, the offspring of a heathen, more than that spoiled brat that Rosa brought into the world? Why, David, why?"

Mutely he stared at her, his tranquil goddess, and his own eyes shone with pleading and with misery. Then, all at once, they hardened. He saw the connection. He balled his hands into two fists, and said, "Why what, Mathilde? You are my wife. I saw fit to make a simple request on the part of a man I love, my own father. I thought you loved him too. And yes, I am a *shtadlan*, and proud to be one. Ossip and the baby, Gino, will follow in my footsteps. And as for their exhaustion, do you not think I would have brought that to your notice at once, if indeed it had existed? It wouldn't hurt you to come into the study once in a while, to watch your children learning their Hebrew. You would marvel at their aptitude, and at their quickness. They have never seemed too tired to me."

But his strong words only made the din in her head greater. She placed her hands over her ears, seeing her father yelling at the cook, hearing him roar at her mother. No, no. I have escaped all that, I am surrounded by peace, she repeated in her own head. But she felt only chaos and confusion. He rose quickly and came to her, and took firm hold of both her wrists. "This has to stop," he said calmly. "I love you, and it tears me apart to have to use harsh words to you. But that woman will cease her interfering or I shall boot her all the way back to France. Immediately."

Mathilde moaned, and backed away from him, hugging her sides. When he attempted to draw her to him she shook him off with uncharacteristic fierceness. Finally, he turned and left the room, slamming the door behind him. He went into his study and rang for Stepan, who, silently, presented him with a glass of Napoleon cognac. He downed it in a single swallow.

The commotion had been heard by more than the maître d'hôtel. Within minutes Célestine Varon, in her old slippers, clutching her shapeless bathrobe to her bony body, was opening the door to her mistress's bedroom. She found Mathilde, her hair disheveled, as she had found Anna after the dismissal of Maria Sabatievna. In her simple peasant's mind it was of no importance what had caused this disagreement between the kind Baron and his wife. It mattered only that her Mathilde, her little girl, whom she had reared from infancy, was in need of comfort. She kneeled on the floor and placed her sinewy arms around the soft body, and began to murmur an old Breton lullaby. Mathilde surrendered to the familiar sound so rooted in her childhood, and allowed warm tears to stream from her eyes. Later, when the tears had dried, Titine put the Baroness to bed. Then she returned to Gino in the nursery where she slept.

Several weeks later, in a daze of bewilderment, Célestine Varon found herself on her way to Brittany, with a nice pension to last her the remainder of her life. Mathilde had told her such strange things: that Gino was too big, that he was making her tired, that after all, she was not as young as she had once been, that surely no more children were to come. Yet if Mathilde had believed these words, why had she seemed so pained, and why had the children all cried, and why, especially, had the Baron angrily missed his breakfast and instead driven the coach himself to take her to the train station? Célestine Varon shook her gray head and thought with misgivings of the young Russian girl who had come from the steppes to take her place. "I may be old, but at least I have experience, and I know what is best for both babies and older Gunzburgs. That girl is a child, and will be useless," she said out loud.

Her sudden departure surprised all save one.

Four

Baron David, the scholar, was inwardly much pleased by
the presence of his older daughter, Anna, inside the sanc-
tum of his study. He knew that the girl, now fifteen years
of age this 1900, did not share his zest for learning, and
was often impatient with her studies. Johanna de Mey did
not tire of informing him of this state of events, knowing
the distress it caused him, as though Anna's indifference
were a rejection of David himself. Yet his heart would also
ache for Anna, for he knew that she lived an isolated life,
inspired only by her gift for painting and her tremendous
interest in political affairs.

She sat on the hassock by the fireplace, the red flames
reflected in her eyes. "We are going to have a war, aren't
we, Papa?" she asked suddenly, breaking the pleasant silence imposed by his quiet study of the legal papers on his
desk. Her hair, bright red, gleamed around her pale solemn
face. Suddenly, David thought it was no longer the face of
a child.

He laughed, gently. "I thought the size of this year's
ruffles would be more to your concern."

But her eyes, intense, did not smile back. "You know
that I have no use for Paris fashions," she replied, the hurt
coming through and seeming, all at once, like the hurt of a

very small girl. "I am thinking of our peasants. We have helped quell the Boxer Rebellion, and things are not as they should be with the East. I heard you speaking to Uncle Sasha last night, Papa."

"Were you listening at the door? Men—gentlemen—discuss politics after supper, when they retire from the ladies to the library. It is not like you to sneak, Anna." David, in spite of the vision of his wife instructing her daughters that good breeding entailed a healthy lack of knowledge of contemporary affairs of state, was mildly intrigued. He thought wryly that Johanna de Mey would find Anna's interest reprehensible, and would upbraid her in front of Mathilde at the first opportunity. He set aside his papers and regarded his daughter with renewed attention. "You were not sneaking, were you, love?" he questioned lightly.

Her eyes had filled with tears. "Of course not. I was on my way to bed. I—I could not—could not bear to remain with Aunt Rosa and Mama. You know I do not care what Worth and Lanvin are planning for their spring collections. Aunt Rosa does not like me, Papa. I wanted to come in and say good night to you. I had forgotten what you said, about the gentlemen retiring. And then, as I was coming toward the door, Stepan came out of your study—and I was taken aback. I heard you speak, for Stepan had opened the door—and when I realized what you were saying, I was disturbed, and I needed to think. I went to my room and—thought."

David said, "Are you still reading those pamphlets not destined for young ladies?" His tone was teasing, but his eyes rested upon Anna with compassion. He was not thinking of the problems with the East, which were peccadilloes at this point, despite what the doomsayers predicted. His mind was obsessed with the idea of his daughter hesitating on the threshold of his study, feeling unwanted. "Your mother would have liked for you to stay with her," he remarked.

Suddenly tears spilled from Anna's eyes. She brushed them savagely aside. "But—I could not, Papa. And Mama did not force me to." Then she said: "All this does not matter. Our peasants are slaving in the outlands, and the government does not care. It merely seeks to assert its imperialistic power. Japan is becoming modern, stretching to emulate Britain where a real Parliament exists and the people have their say. But we in Russia are stagnating, Papa, in feudalism. In your own way, you perpetuate this feudalism by working for the Ministries, which do not care about anyone outside the aristocracy and the wealthiest of the haute bourgeoisie. You are a scholar—but what does your scholarship bring to the illiterate peasants of Latvia or the Ukraine?"

"You invest the Russian peasants with a romance which they do not possess," her father remarked mildly. "Are you not being melodramatic, Annushka?"

"That is not so!" she cried. "I am not playing. I—I have read, and if there is a war, it is the peasants, who do not understand imperialism, and who care only about putting more bread into their mouths, who will be sent to fight. The Tzar is the last autocrat of Europe. While his peasants fight for him, he will delay resolving their problems. True problems, Papa. How can you not care, you who plead daily for the Jews?"

"I plead for the Jews because in some small measure I may be able to help them," he said. "Many men oppose me. Pobedonòstsev, who was Tzar Nicholas's tutor, is head of the Holy Synod, and he would like to bury the Jews once and for all. And there is a senator of the highest nobility, Count Tagantsev—he is like the Hydra, for if I succeed in modifying one law in favor of a group of Jews, he is certain to enact two new laws to countermand me. Yet I must continue, for even if the good I accomplish is slight, it is still something. I do not romanticize the plight of the Jews. No one is worse off than they in all of Russia."

"You plead for the Jews, as a diplomat will plead. But it is different with me, Papa. I wish that I could *be* a peasant, that I could till the soil. I do not like society, and never shall. And because I would be one of them, I fear for the peasants, and I follow their struggles. It is my nature, and not merely a romantic pastime. I despise what they call ladies' pastimes. Won't you please understand, Papa?"

The fire flickered on the hearth, and David sighed. No, he did not truly understand. But he was an optimist, and so, kindly, he tried to reassure his older daughter about the conflicts in the East. He did not believe that war would come, this war which brought her so much apprehension. But that evening, he said to Mathilde, in the privacy of their bedroom: "I wish that Anna could be more proud of who she is. The Gunzburgs are an enviable family." He did not mention the pamphlets he knew his daughter sometimes obtained, for he did not want Johanna de Mey ever to learn of their existence. This dissembling was the least he could do for this beloved daughter, who eluded him in spite of his honest efforts to reach her. For he could not comprehend Anna's desire to exchange places with those worse off than she.

Anna was viewed as an oddity among the Gunzburg family. Mathilde knew that her friends criticized the girl, and felt no more comfortable in her presence than she did in theirs; and so gently, with a kind of tired languor, she no longer fought her elder daughter's stubborn refusal to act as the young lady of the house on Mathilde's receiving day, when fashionable ladies of St. Petersburg paid visits to her drawing room. At first Johanna would bully the girl into appearing. The sight of Anna, sitting rigidly on the edge of a hassock and answering her mother's friends in terse phrases, brought a triumphant glow to her lovely aquamarine eyes. But soon the governess realized that her own interests would be better served by removing this painful source of embarrassment from Mathilde's sight.

Her brothers and sisters loved her, though they did not understand her any better than her parents. She had few friends, and those were girls who shunned society as much as she. But she had acquired a kind of bloom during her adolescence. She wore her hair braided into a macaroon coiled behind her right ear, so that the eye was drawn away from the sagging side of her face. She refused to dress as her mother would have liked, and once again, with a tightening in her chest, and a sigh, Mathilde permitted her to wear the simple clothing in which she felt comfortable—brightly colored mujik blouses or sometimes thick, flowered skirts commonly donned by peasant women in the provinces of the Ukraine. And because she was a fine artist with a flair for color, people would grudgingly concede that though the girl was pitifully out of fashion, she appeared to have found a style of her own. She spent her free time painting, and David had sent for an instructor from the Academy, much to Johanna de Mey's distress. The man praised the girl for her freedom of movement, for her landscapes as wild as her thoughts, for her magnificent shadings which went against all those precepts that a young lady was taught in the watercolor classes of the day, which emphasized pastels and prettiness. Anna's canvases were crimson and frog green and mauve and orange, and her lines were bold. She also immersed herself in the writings of a new author, Maxim Gorky, whose humble origins had made him the poet of the Russian people, and who had just recently come to St. Petersburg and its newspapers. But she carefully hid his works from her governess, who had already upbraided her sufficiently for her low-bred tastes.

At the other extreme of age stood Gino, the five-year-old. Like Anna, he was isolated from the mainstream of family life, but that was because of his youth. He did not yet take lessons with the other three children, and their pastimes were not his. Barely out of the nursery, he was still considered the baby of the family, and pleasantly permitted his two sisters to mother him. Of all the Gunzburgs, he was the child least capable of irritating others, he whose entrance caused the most smiles.

He was a comely boy, though not beautiful, as Sonia and Ossip were, with their mother's eyes and her jet-black hair and translucent complexion. Gino was a sturdy child with brown eyes like Anna's and chestnut hair to match an olive skin. Of the Gunzburg offspring he was the least brilliant, for he did not possess Anna's artistry nor Ossip's ability to grasp learning at a glance, nor Sonia's sensitivity which colored all her dealings with the world. But although his cousin Tania, who was eight, called him a dolt and a dullard, this was far from true.

He was of steady temperament, perhaps because he had never been hurt physically or emotionally, for even Johanna liked the boy. He was, after all, a boy, and therefore less of a threat than the girls. And also he was not, as was his older brother, Mathilde's secret favorite. He was not even David's favorite, which would have irritated the governess, for the Baron held each of his daughters in special regard for vastly different reasons. His brother and sisters all loved him, and he was not passive, as Ossip was in his calculated manner. No, he simply had no passions, no points of view as yet.

The two middle children, Ossip and Sonia, were thrown together a great deal of the time and developed an unusual closeness. They were thirteen and ten. They looked alike, for Sonia's figure had not yet begun to bud. Ossip was still very fragile, and beneath his specially tailored clothing bore a very small hump on his back from the vertebrae weakened by Pott's disease.

They were Mathilde's preferred children, but to Johanna, Sonia was still a child, too young to be thought of as a companion to her mother. True, she was frequently present during Mathilde's teas, but she sat modestly and passed around trays of petits fours. She was too young to be permitted to speak out of turn, and the governess had seen that her dress was simple, so that the ladies would not be drawn to her as they were to that bright bird of a cousin, Tatiana. In fact, Sonia, in awe of her splendid governess, regarded herself as plain, and had never been contradicted in this by the Dutchwoman. She knew that she learned well enough, that if she applied herself to the piano she could rise in rapture, though Johanna had frequently told her that she possessed only mediocre talent. She took ballet lessons at Aunt Rosa's house, where an instructress from the Imperial Ballet taught several girls three times a week, and she was well aware of her own agility. But her Aunt Rosa never praised her as much as she did Tania. One afternoon, a friend of her Mama had passed her hand over Sonia's sleek black hair and said, "You are a very pretty child." And Sonia had replied, "Oh, no! You have not seen my cousin!" Mathilde had set her glass down and calmly stated, "It is silly to compare people. You are fresh and gay, and that is most important in a person, Sonitchka." For she had not wished to make her favorite daughter vainglorious.

As for Ossip, mature beyond his years, he knew quite well how not to irk Johanna. Frequently, he and his mother would exchange looks that bespoke their kindred spirits, but almost by common accord they did this only when Johanna de Mey was otherwise occupied. When David became carried away by his Jewish causes, the governess would look upon the bland, expressionless face of the young boy, and would think: Indeed, I have an ally. She had guessed Ossip's feelings in that area, and so she did not hate him.

Each morning, now, David's two middle children helped him receive his many petitioners. For Sonia, this was a tremendous honor, a means of sharing a precious cause with her beloved Papa. But for Ossip, it was a duty to be executed with perfection, as all duties were. The men and women who came to beg for favors were of all kinds— wealthy businessmen with suede portfolios, and whining old men in rags reeking of pickle brine. Invariably, Alexei, David's librarian, would introduce each one into the Baron's study, to be greeted with a handshake and an offer to be seated. Ossip would draw the chair up, Sonia would remove shawls and excess baggage. The interview would begin.

Sometimes people came with grave problems that the Baron would then bring up with the proper minister or magistrate. There were questions involving stoppage of pogroms if news arrived ahead of time; removal from prison of an innocent Jew; permission to be granted for residence in the capital on behalf of someone who did not possess the proper credentials; or the assignment of an impartial lawyer to a Jew accused of a crime.

Other times the situation could not be brought to light, and was very serious. Widows of artisans, who had been members of the Second Guild and been allowed to dwell in St. Petersburg only because of their spouses' work, were, once husbandless, expected by law to remove themselves and their children to the Pale of Settlement, the only area where most Russian Jews were allowed to live. Many of these women had been daughters of artisans of St. Petersburg before they had become wives, and now were told to leave the only city they had ever known. David's most fervent wish was to obtain the abolishment of this law. But in the meantime, since the widows were expected to leave within twenty-four hours of their husbands' death, affairs had to be put in order for these bereaved people, and while this went on, shelter had to be granted them. Sonia and Ossip knew of the secret apartment at the back of the house where their father hid the widows and orphans, and although the police were well bribed, the risks were enormous each time. Sonia found these proceedings noble and adventuresome, but Ossip, a cynic, felt that no anti-Semitic government would ever change, that his father was tilting at windmills like Don Quixote.

The boy admired his father, who was accepted into the

inner chambers of noted diplomats because, so modest, he never came to plead for himself. But he had come to despise the man for not expending his vast and unique gifts in more selfish directions. Ossip was not a hardhearted egocentric like his Uncle Sasha, who only associated with those who could benefit him, but he did not believe in hopeless causes. Ossip believed that the Tzar and his entourage were possessed of an incurable disease, and that his father's hopes for an antidote or cure were vain and somewhat naive. The poor Jews whom Ossip helped tugged at his heartstrings, but also filled him with a sense of frustration and disgust. "Poor fools," he would murmur to himself, "their lot will never improve: they are such perfect scapegoats for the world!" And so he performed his duties with compassion, but also with lack of conviction, for he still believed that there was but a single solution to Jewish persecution. One quick conversion would eliminate all need for his work, and for that of his father and grandfather. Why didn't others, particularly David, see this point as clearly as he, a mere lad of thirteen?

He knew better than to share his feelings with Sonia. To her, the moments with the petitioners were a high point of the day. She fervently accepted their father's mission. And when Anna would tell her, "Your poor Jews will have all their problems solved once the government takes the entire peasant population into account, for theirs is part of a greater problem," little Sonia would deny it.

"I cannot hurt for those I do not see," she would counter. "At Mohilna, everyone seems happy. In Papa's study, I can see for myself many injustices. I can see the poor Jews, but I cannot see your beloved peasants."

"And so, after all, you are turning into a sweet-faced bourgeoise, like Mary Antoinette," Anna would say with bitterness.

Now and then a note of laughter would creep among the stern works of the Baron's study. One morning, a woman in shawls and a calico kerchief entered the room, and as she kissed David's hand, she wailed: "Dear messenger of God, you must help my son! We in our village know how you have financed so many young musicians, who started their careers at the Conservatory. That is where my son needs to go, and I have no money to send him there."

"Well then, what instruments does the boy play?" David asked easily.

Sonia, who loved her own music, listened eagerly, but the woman merely looked dumbstruck. "Instruments? He plays none. We cannot afford any."

David smiled indulgently. "But he has learned the rudiments of harmony and counterpoint, and he can read music? And now he wants to choose an instrument? Is that the problem?"

Tears arose in the woman's eyes. "Oh, no, my noble Baron! He cannot read music. But"—and now red patches of joy formed on her cheeks, and once more her eyes sparkled—"he can bang with two twigs on the old wine keg. And does it so sweetly!"

David did not smile, for he was keeping his face averted from his children's. Sonia had taken Ossip's hand and was squeezing it, and the boy was gazing at his shoes in order not to laugh. "My dear woman," their father said at length, "in order to send a boy to the Conservatory, he needs to be familiar with all the rudiments of music, and must play at least one instrument with talent." His face grew gentle. "What made you come to me, now?"

The woman said, "I have seen those men brandishing their little white sticks. And so I thought that it would be so easy for Misha to learn. Anyone can move a stick up and down and around, and look elegant. Is that not so?"

"I suggest that you think of another occupation for your Misha, for the conductor of an orchestra has the most difficult job of all," David said. And then he noted Sonia in the corner, bending over a frill on her skirt. He saw her small shoulders quivering. He rose, and the woman stood up too. Placing an arm around her, he led her to the door and remanded her to the care of Alexei. Then he returned alone to the study, and regarded his children with gravity. "Never laugh," he admonished them, "at the ignorance of others." And then, helplessly, he joined them in a paroxysm of soundless mirth.

In 1903, Anna's fascination with the bereaved peasants of Russia caused her some confusion. In her haphazard, unguided readings, she had at first embraced the ideals of the Narodnyki, the reform party of the '70s, because, unlike the Marxists, they focused their attentions on the tillers of the soil rather than on the workers of the cities. She felt uneasy about Lenin, this strange man who had been sent to Siberia in '95 for spreading Marxist doctrine to the factory workers of St. Petersburg, and who had now exiled himself to Switzerland, though his followers were still brewing plots in Anna's city. Just this year there had occurred a schism within Lenin's party, the Social Democrats, and now his followers called themselves Bolsheviks and favored revolution, while the milder elements went under the name of Mensheviks and sought first of all to turn Russian autocracy into a capitalistic state, to precede the onslaught of socialism. Anna thought: Well then, perhaps I am a Menshevik. But where have my Narodnyki gone? For Lenin, grim and unsmiling, filled her with a strange terror. He seemed so unflinching, so uncompromising. So inhuman.

The Narodnyki, it seemed, had turned quite violent. Now they bore the political name of Social Revolutionaries, and countered the Social Democrats by organizing fighting cells among the peasants. Anna found herself hopelessly alone, entangled in events that bewildered her, knowing only that she was a heartfelt socialist and that the Tzar had forgotten his people. She could no longer speak to her father, even in secret. She had discovered that he was a believer in class systems, that he truly did think that he, as a *shtadlan*, was better qualified to help the poor than they were of helping themselves. And in his blind patriotism, her father, furthermore, was wholeheartedly Tzarist.

Anna was eighteen, and a young woman, but she had refused to make her debut and enter society. She had lost her few girl friends to gay balls and parties. Her own figure had blossomed, and though she was thin, her breasts, beneath her rough mujik blouses, pushed roundly to the surface. Mathilde's despair had grown with her daughter: how would the girl make a good marriage, even with the dowry David would provide? She saw no young men, and besides, the sag was still quite evident on the left side of her face.

In St. Petersburg, young girls no longer were expected to bring their mothers to their parties as chaperones. It was sufficient for their brothers to accompany them. But generally, there was a companion at home with the girls, so that, when they drove into town, or went shopping, they were properly escorted. Anna went nowhere. But there was a banker, Aron Berson, with whom David was forced to transact family business, whose daughters went everywhere alone, and who gave parties the likes of which Petersburg had never witnessed. Aliza and Kazimira Berson were spoiled by their immensely wealthy father, and their mother, whose family had been prominent among Warsaw Jewry, allowed them total freedom. When dances were given, the parents were asked to leave, and unchaperoned, the young people would turn out the lights for a full fifteen minutes. Mathilde and her friends were so shocked that they refused to set foot within the Berson household, although they could not turn away the Berson girls if they chose to come by for a visit. "I do not understand," Mathilde would say to Johanna, "going to the home of someone who does not welcome you." But twice a year or so, Madame Berson and her two daughters, Alia and Kazia, would pay a visit to Mathilde's drawing room. The other ladies would make a hasty departure. Everyone knew that

Mathilde had to endure this family for the sake of business, but that did not mean that her more fortunate friends had to put up with them.

One morning, a messenger delivered a note to Mathilde. "It is that abominable Alia Berson," she wailed, having read the letter with increasing distress.

"She has written a novel. It has been published, with private funds of course, in Paris. Now she wants to come here and show it to me."

"You cannot refuse her hospitality, my love," David said with compassion. "The Bersons are one pill that I must force you to swallow. Alia's father controls a great many of our investments."

Mathilde nodded silently. A grim expression had set over her lovely ivory-toned features. She looked around the table, and her eyes rested on thirteen-year-old Sonia in her simple mint-green dress, her tiny, budding breasts appearing just above the Empire waistline. Her black curls hung innocently down her back, and she held her small, dainty hands demurely by the sides of her plate. "Sonia, you do not need to be present for tea. Why don't you and Ossip take it by yourselves, in your room? Anna will assist us in the drawing room." She looked directly at her older daughter, who had flushed with surprise and whose brown eyes flashed dismay. "It is a must, Anna, for today," Mathilde stressed severely.

Anna opened her mouth, then closed it again. The Berson girl. Sonia was too young to be "tainted." Ironic glints pierced yellow in Anna's pupils, and she nodded her comprehension. Then she resumed her breakfast, thinking that it might be interesting to listen to this wild girl about whom Petersburg smirked and gossiped. At least, she was not known to be a lady.

Anna had mixed emotions as she dressed for tea. Aliza, or Alia as her intimates called her, was petite and well endowed in the right places, and she dressed with elegance. Anna, in accordance, donned the very simplest of her blouses, a shapeless white peasant cotton affair. Then she thought of her mother, and relented. She selected her brightest flowered skirt, and slippers trimmed with gold that turned in a curl at the toe. She planted a yellow dahlia in the middle of the coil behind her right ear, and added a yellow belt to cinch her waist. The impression she created was arresting, if somewhat peculiar, and she was not unhappy with her reflection in the mirror. As an artist, she admired the colors.

As she entered the parlor, she wondered whether Madame Berson would be accompanying her older daughter. She straightened her shoulders, ready for an onslaught of critical looks. Even Madame Berson chose her clothing from Worth models in Paris. But as she looked toward the tea table, she was struck with surprise. Alia was there, trussed up like a small partridge, but next to her sat someone whom Anna had never seen before, a young man of about twenty with brilliant green eyes and blond hair that fell casually over his brow. A well-built young man with broad, sturdy shoulders and good strong hands folded in his lap. His clothing was as simple as Anna's blouse. He wore a brown suit of rough, well-worn corduroy. His shoes were scuffed. Then she recalled Alia's reputation, and remembered, blushing in spite of herself, that young men of breeding did not accept invitations to the Berson home any longer. He must be an impoverished student whom Alia had somehow taken as her lover. A sudden anger seized her and her face burned: How dare she do this to Mama! she thought furiously. Anna thought her mother a prude, but she deserved nonetheless to be respected within her own house! And yet, to her added dismay, her mother seemed more relaxed now than Anna had ever seen her around any of the Berson women.

Confused, and irritated by her own confusion, Anna coughed abruptly to indicate her presence. Juanita, thank heaven, was nowhere to be seen. Feeling more confident, Anna strode into the room. The young man rose, and

Anna thought he had more breeding than she expected. And then she was ashamed. If Alia had indeed picked a poor lover, perhaps she had more sense than any of Mama's snobbish friends gave her credit for. Eusebe, at Mohilna, would have been far more worthy of love than some of her father's wealthy cronies. She smiled at the young man.

"Anna," Mathilde said pleasantly, "Alia has brought us her brother, Ivan Aronovitch. Ivan Aronovitch, my daughter, Anna."

Anna's hand rose to her mouth, and Alia Berson began to giggle. "Oh, you are a naughty one!" she cried out. "Why, Mathilde Yureyevna, Anna must have thought that Vanya was my—"

"Whatever Anna Davidovna thought, it is not up to you to put into words, though you tell us that you have turned writer," her brother interrupted with a smile. He laughed, a low chuckle. "I am your effort at respectability, Alitchka. Do not ruin it by your habitual bad manners. I am sorry, Mathilde Yureyevna. My sister is incorrigible."

"Oh, but I am trying, trying!" Alia cried. She placed a pretty round hand on Mathilde's arm. "You know how much I love to come here. You are such a lady, Mathilde Yureyevna, and I want to feel accepted here. Vanya teases me, but I thought that you would approve if he escorted me. And then, there was the added incentive." She glanced meaningfully toward Anna. "Vanya does not go out much, unlike Kazia and me. He is the family recluse. He is reading law at the University, and spends all his time studying and . . . thinking, he says. Always about politics. So annoying, when I have so many charming friends for him to meet. And he never takes me to meet his own friends."

"They would hardly interest you," Ivan said. "We do not dance. We discuss matters of consequence, which are beyond you, my dear sister."

"How utterly boring."

"Will you be joining your father's enterprises, Ivan Aronovitch?" Mathilde asked, handing her daughter a glass of tea.

The young man hesitated. Then, resolutely, he looked into Mathilde's eyes and shook his head. He pointed to his clothing. "I do not think so. Somehow . . ."

Anna chimed in abruptly, "Somehow all your father's wealth makes you uncomfortable?"

And as Alia and Mathilde, shocked, stared at her, the young man nodded. "Yes, yes, Anna Davidovna. That is so! How well you have stated my feelings."

Anna was very red. She murmured, looking at her toes, "It was easy for me to say. I share those feelings." And then, overcome by embarrassment, she fell silent. Alia and Mathilde daintily chewed on coconut cream puffs. The silence was unbearable. Ivan Aronovitch was regarding Anna with keen appraisal.

Finally he said to his hostess: "Your daughter is by far the most attractively clothed young lady I have seen. I must apologize for mentioning personal appearance, which is such a delicate matter. But I am in love with color, and Anna Davidovna has arrested my imagination."

"Thank you," Anna replied. She wanted to be struck dead upon the spot.

"Yes. It is a pleasure to hear Anna's clothing complimented. She possesses a style quite her own, and refuses to go along with Paris," her mother commented. The young man's words had taken her aback, but she was glad for Anna, and thankful that Johanna was out of hearing range. Everyone, even her eccentric daughter, deserved a good word now and then to boost her morale.

"Still, Anna, Paris is a delight. You must try it soon. I shall give a ball and you must come," Alia said.

Mathilde's eyes registered shock, but Ivan said quickly: "Anyone who attires herself with such imagination has better ways to occupy her life, Alitchka. What do you like to do, Anna Davidovna? I am certain that you do not like dancing."

"Everyone is not a bear, like you, Vanya," Alia said peevishly.

"But Ivan Aronovitch is right," Anna replied. She looked up at him. His green eyes were riveted to her face. "I like to paint," she said shyly. "And to read."

"I should have guessed!" he cried joyfully. "A painter! I would be very honored if you would show me your work."

"It is only a hobby," Anna said.

"Yes, but my writing began as a hobby, and when I was in Paris Anatole France read my book, *Tamara*, and said that not a word should be changed. So now I have a career," Alia interposed.

"That is a formidable compliment," Mathilde said.

"Alia writes like a schoolgirl. But I am sure that Anna Davidovna paints like Cézanne. All brightness and light." Ivan Aronovitch was looking at Anna's skirt, and his green eyes glimmered. "And what do you read?"

Anna mumbled, almost to herself, "My favorite is Gorky."

The young man clapped his hands. "Mine, too! We must compare thoughts. Which was your favorite short story?"

"*Chelkash*," Anna murmured.

"Pah! Sentimental! If you go for sentiment, why not choose *Malva*? Ah, to be Seryozhka, retiring to the watch-place on the spur with that incredible woman! To live like that, unfettered, with a woman that would not be fettered!"

"That would indeed be a dream come true," Anna said. Her eyes glittered. "But old Chelkash had suffered, he was full of his past. And still he was a man. He did not need a woman."

"They are going to argue, and aren't they adorable?" Alia said. "I have never heard of such nonsense. Gorky! Whoever has heard of him?"

"He was elected to the Academy of Sciences," Anna said.

"And just as quickly ousted," her mother commented, having heard David speaking of it to a friend.

"By the Tzar! What does he know of writing?" Ivan scoffed. Then he bit his lip. "Oh, Mathilde Yureyevna, please forgive me. I did not mean to insult you."

"But you did," his sister said peevishly.

Ivan did not respond. He was standing in front of Mathilde, and his brow was knit. "Please," he begged. "Forgive what I have said. It was impulsive and thoughtless, and impolite."

Mathilde smiled. "We were all young once," she said kindly. "Never mind, Ivan Aronovitch. May I pour you another glass of tea?"

"I shall gladly take one," the young man answered, his relief spreading across his face in a smile. He turned from his hostess to her daughter. "But would you permit Anna Davidovna to do me this honor?"

Silently, Anna rose and took the glass that was handed to her. She filled it with tea from the small pot, then leveled it off with hot water from the samovar. At that moment, she saw Johanna enter the room. Abruptly, she passed the cup to Ivan without asking if he wanted cream, sugar, or lemon with his tea. Looking away from him, her face shining crimson, she said quickly. "Please excuse me," and, lifting her heavy flowered skirt, ran from the salon without further explanation. Her eyes had filled with tears, suddenly and illogically, and the others watched her flight with consternation.

It was Johanna de Mey who broke their silence. "Good afternoon," she said, and sat down.

The Gunzburg children were now eighteen, fifteen, thirteen, and eight, and apart from her art lessons Anna had ceased her education. But Ossip was still taking his lessons with Johanna. David had seen his work, and was proud of it, and because he was a boy, he had told Mathilde that he would have to supplement Ossip's learning with tutoring in mathematics by someone other than the Dutchwoman. Mathilde felt as though she had been hit in the stomach. "You will hurt Johanna's feelings," she said.

"A boy must know his mathematics," David replied. Mathilde passed her tongue over dry lips and remembered her father, Baron Yuri, who, instead of going to his own tutor as a child, had hidden in the fruit trees of his father's orchard. Now he could not compute his own gambling losses. She shivered, and straightened her back, and told her friend that her husband was sending for someone from the University to coach her older son in the more complex facets of calculus and solid geometry.

Johanna smiled, her lovely, illuminative smile which showed her perfect, large white teeth. She did not mind. Ossip, the favorite, was going to be one step removed toward the realms of manhood.

He was growing tall, and his appearance was poetic, for he was slight of build from his years of illness. Learning fascinated him. He did not care a fig for politics, but he was drawn to the Orient, and the trouble between his country and China and Japan disturbed him because he wished to study there one day. He knew that a dear friend of the family, Moise Mess, had settled in Nagasaki, and made a fortune in the coal industry. "What will happen to him?" he often asked.

"He is planning to transfer his enterprises to Port Arthur should the situation with Japan worsen," his father answered. "Why do you ask?"

"I am keeping track of those we know in the Orient," Ossip said. "Someday I shall go there."

Ossip did not set aside his dreams of the Orient. When he was not quite sixteen, he went into his father's study and meticulously shut the door. "Papa," he began, "I have been mulling over a plan these past months. I wish, more than anything else, to obtain my baccalaureate degree and go on to the Faculty of Far Eastern Studies at the University afterward."

David was pleased. "We shall have another linguist in the family then," he said, smiling.

But the elegant young boy with the waves of black hair and the blue eyes beneath their delicate brows remained disturbed, and intense. "I am not yet certain what I wish to do with my life, Papa. I only know that Oriental art, haiku poetry, all that breathes of those foreign cultures appeals to me. But I am not, like Annushka, an artist. In fact, I am not certain at all of my calling. You see, Papa, I have had absolutely no experience of the real world, of real life as other boys live it. I have lived secluded by my illness, and protected from ... well, normalcy."

David stroked his chin and reflected. Then he nodded. "That is so, my son. But I do not know how we could have avoided this, your mother and I. What have you in mind?"

Ossip leaned across the desk and searched his father's face. It was so dreadfully important, so essential, to convince his father, and to do so now. But he was scared. What if, instead, he threw a wall between the two of them, and his father refused ever to hear him through again? David possessed faith in him, but the boy was not built of the same material as his father. Ossip realized this more than did David, who only knew that in the presence of his smoothly polished son he felt a gnawing sadness, the sadness of the perennial optimist, of the devout, when faced with a true cynic. Ossip, who did not like to take risks, weighed the alternatives in his mind. No, he had to speak.

"Papa," he said, "I need to go to school, like other fellows. And then I will compete and obtain the marks that will gain me entry into the University. You know a Jew needs to score a 'five' in every subject, and that 'five' is the highest mark one can obtain. Here at home, no one will mark my work, and I shall not be admitted to the University, and will not receive my baccalaureate. I must attend a gymnasium."

David looked at his son, surprised at his intensity, his determination. Always it had been Ossip's easy-going passivity that bothered him. Aloud he replied, "But in gymnasia, there are forty boys to a form. Someone might push you, and if you fell, your back might be damaged for life. Worse—you could easily die. That is why your mother wants you to study here."

"But I want friends, Papa. I am not a fighter. I will provoke no one." The blue eyes shone with a strange brilliance that dazzled David.

"How many nations have spoken as you do, and been attacked by a greedy aggressor! It would be risking your life."

Ossip blushed. "My future depends on your decision, Papa," he said. "I do not want to be a houseplant where I fit into the scheme of things. Sonia can stay at home and visit with Mama, for one day she will marry and be a hostess, and a mother. But I shall be a man, and need to seek a direction. I need to know people, not merely my own family."

"You would be held back a form or two, because of your illness," David countered. "How would it feel to be sitting in class with people hardly older than Sonia?"

Ossip raised his head. "It would feel like living," he answered quietly. His eyes held his father's, and finally David looked away. Ossip took a deep breath. He knew that he had won, that he would soon be going to school. And David, his father, felt a tremor of pride that he had never experienced before in regard to this boy, whose scholarship had pleased him but whose essential soul had never come within his grasp. The lad has character, he caught himself reflecting. And then he felt a stab in his chest, and was ashamed at having doubted this handsome adolescent who was his flesh and blood.

Sonia had waited for her brother outside the study, and when he emerged, they embraced. She was glad that Ossip was going to have his freedom. Mathilde felt otherwise. She recalled the dreams that had haunted her before Gino's birth, when she had been pursued by visions of her son in the renewed throes of Pott's disease. She confronted her husband with contained arguments, but inwardly she was torn. She held back sobs and kept her lovely face immobile, only her eyes betraying her by their extraordinary wideness. Her son was going to be killed, and all for a whim! But with his mother Ossip stood his own ground, for he was meeting an opponent whom he knew as completely as he knew himself. "You must trust Papa," he told her. "He is going to find me a school of which even you will approve. But you must give him the opportunity to search for one. You would not have me hanging onto your skirts forever, would you now, Mama?"

David found a school. It was a private school, and so contained only twenty boys per form instead of the forty of public establishments. But it was accredited by the state, and would obtain for Ossip his baccalaureate degree. It was situated within walking distance from the Gunzburg home, on Vassilievsky Island itself, and only scions of important families were sent there to study. Ossip would meet other boys, and the high breeding of the pupils helped to reassure Mathilde. "Besides, my love, he will be close enough to return home for luncheon," David comforted his wife. And so Ossip was enrolled, and began his formal schooling just before his sixteenth birthday.

He did not mind, as he had predicted, being placed in a form where the other students were only fourteen. He had missed the companionship of other boys, and so, in this regard, Ossip was still immature. He realized that his illness had slowed down his learning at its onset, and he was not at all ashamed of being older than the others. On the first day of classes, the school director introduced him with an explanation. "This is Ossip Davidovitch de Gunzburg, your new comrade," the man told the assembled boys. "He has been ill, and cannot endure any rough physical contact. I trust that you will all watch your actions around him, although he insists on being treated as everyone else. But a single push, or a shove, can kill this youth at once."

Ossip never mentioned his ailment, and the other boys took a quick liking to him, for he was witty and bright, and so happy to be among his own kind that a newfound youthfulness seemed to emanate from him, where before he had appeared overly mature. At once, his marks proved as excellent as his father had hoped. He brought home only "fives" and "five-pluses," the highest honors in the class. He shared those top grades with a small group of fellow students who became his close friends. All came from distinguished families. Sergei Botkin was the nephew of the Tzar's private physician, Vassili Petri was the son of a famous geographer, and Vladimir, or Volodia, Tagantsev, was the second son of Count Nicolai Tagantsev, who sat in the Senate. It was Volodia who was Ossip's best and dearest friend, and about whom he spoke the most.

When Ossip first mentioned Volodia, at supper, David felt as though a sudden arrow had pierced his heart. He looked up quickly, his temples pounding, and saw that Mathilde's sapphire eyes were thoughtful and alert. She had caught the name, too. He cleared his throat. "Ossip," he said tentatively, "why are you so fond of this particular boy?"

His son's face, more pink than usual, stared back at him over the magnificent Limoges tureen the servant girl was holding between them. Ossip said, "Why, he is a marvelous fellow. He is strong, and has a fine, firm heart. He laughs well, but never at others. He—he—please do not laugh, Papa, but you know how much I love my Sonia, and Volodia, well, possesses the same kind of character as she. I enjoy his company and I respect him. I know that you will like him yourself."

David felt deeply troubled. Mathilde, across from him, bore a furrow between her black brows that indicated her own disturbance. Ossip's joy, his wholehearted enthusiasm in his first real friendship, hurt David, who knew that rarely was his son as purely innocent as in this new experience. But still . . . He said, "Does Volodia talk much about his father, Count Tagantsev?"

The boy shrugged lightly. "I suppose so. They are not as close a family as we are, and I gather that Volodia is not his father's favorite. There is an older brother, Nicolai, who is a law student, and the Count, I think, favors him. But I am not sure. His sister, Natalia, is Volodia's twin, and the two of them are the best of friends. We have spoken of you, Papa, and of Sonia, and of course of Mama. The way boys speak." He smiled as he said this, with some pride.

David ran his index finger over his nose and waved away the offerings from the servant girl's tray. "You have often helped me with the widows of Jewish artisans," he said. "You know of the law that banishes them from Petersburg twenty-four hours after the death of their husbands."

"Yes, Papa. But what has that to do with Volodia?" Impatience forced itself into Ossip's tone. He was irritated at the turn in conversation. Happy in his friend, he wanted to bask in the attention of his family, and not return to what he privately considered his father's obsession. There was time enough for that on another day.

But David continued. "This law is most ardently supported by two men, both highly influential. One of them, as you know, is Pobedonòstsev, head of the Holy Synod, who has been the Tzar's mentor for many years. The other advocate is your friend's father, who sits in the Senate. Did you know this, Ossip?"

Horror registered itself in Ossip's eyes. "Of course not, Papa! We do not discuss religion. And Volodia is not anti-Semitic. I am his best friend, and I know for a fact that he speaks of me in his home. Did you think I was betraying you behind your back, Papa?"

David sighed. He saw his son's anger and dismay. "I would never accuse you of betraying me," he said finally, weighing his words carefully. "I merely felt that you should know with whom you were dealing. Whether or not he is close to his son, Volodia's father is perhaps my most bitter opponent. Do with this what you will."

Johanna de Mey, who had daintily wiped the corners of her mouth, ventured to speak. "If the boy is as noble a creature as Ossip says, should we not allow this friendship to develop between them, as a private matter? After all, Ossip has never disappointed us. His judgment can be trusted. And if the boy were anti-Semitic, would he have picked a Jew for his best friend?"

"Johanna makes a valid point," Mathilde said softly. Her large eyes sought those of her friend, and she smiled. "Would we create a children's war by our own foibles? Perhaps this friendship is an omen of good things to come. Perhaps Nicolai Tagantsev will relent. In any case, let us not discredit his young son."

"I had no intention of showing prejudice in regard to the boy, Mathilde," David told her. "But Ossip is sixteen, and my successor. I felt he had to know about the boy's father, and be forewarned."

"Thank you, Papa," Ossip said. He picked up a piece of cake with his fork, and began to lift it to his mouth. Then he stopped, and regarded his father. "I may continue the friendship with no bad feelings?" he demanded.

"Of course, Ossip," David said. Ossip smiled, and plumped the morsel of cake into his mouth. His clear eyes looked around the table, and glimmered for an instant at Johanna. She was sitting with her long, elegant fingers steepled before her face, hiding her mouth from his sight. But he saw the answering glint in her own aquamarine pupils. He looked at his mother, whose placid coolness pleased him, and at Gino, his brother, who had not truly understood the conversation and was wide-eyed with bewilderment. Anna sat remotely withdrawn, and he passed over her to find Sonia, his beloved. But in her gray eyes he did not find what he was seeking. He saw something that shook him back to reality, away from his sense of victory over their father. Sonia's eyes, large and limpid, shone with a hard strength that bore no tender glow. Jolted, he was unable to meet the flintlike stare.

During the next months, the friendship between Ossip and Volodia Tagantsev deepened. Ossip spoke freely of the boy, and his mother would smile, listening with appreciation, knowing how precious it was for her child to have found so deep a friendship at long last. She understood even more than he realized, for she herself had found Johanna de Mey, and knew how much her own life had been transformed. She no longer felt alienated in a foreign land. And so she gently encouraged Ossip, a half-smile playing over her calm, poised features.

But Sonia sat rigid in her chair, on the edge of her seat, whenever Volodia was mentioned, her heart contracting with anger at this dreadful betrayal of their father. She was miserable, for she also wished to please her brother, her companion, who had chosen this friend in part because Volodia had reminded Ossip of herself. Without knowing him, Sonia felt strangely mingled emotions toward the son of the anti-Semitic Senator. She hated him on account of his parent's cruel bias, yet felt Mathilde's gratefulness on behalf of the child she loved most. The mere mention of Volodia Tagantsev's name would make her acutely uncomfortable, divided as she felt in her strong, ardent loyalties.

Ossip returned home at noon every day for luncheon. But Volodia Tagantsev, who did not reside on Vassilievsky Island, had too long a distance to travel, and was forced to eat at school. "It is so dreary there," Ossip told his mother. "Every four days the same meal is repeated, and there is no family cheer. I always feel so bad, leaving him behind." Mathilde merely nodded. It was unthinkable for her to proceed any further: she was not only Jewish but also the wife of the foremost *shtadlan* in St. Petersburg. The Counts Tagantsev were of the highest nobility, second only to the Imperial Grand Dukes, whereas the Gunzburgs were merely Barons knighted in Hesse. She could not have conceived of inviting the scion of the Tagantsev clan to join her son in the Gunzburg home for luncheon. In France, a Gunzburg, a Fould, or a Rothschild might aspire to heights inconceivable in Russia. A Fould had become Minister of Finance at the court of Napoleon III; his nephew had married Mathilde's own namesake aunt, and taken her to Court. Mathilde was a proud woman, a lady bred and born, but she was not one to defy tradition. Neither was her son. He did not hint at how happy an invitation to Volodia would have made him. Battling society was Anna's game, not his, nor his mother's. To some extent it was also David's, insofar as the Jews of Russia were concerned. But Ossip was not a fighter in any arena.

In every way, the Gunzburg children had been taught the sports of their social standing, but Ossip's condition had not permitted him to learn equestrian sports. At school, he played with his friends so long as strong physical contact was not part of the plan. There was only one boy who actively disliked Ossip. His name was Krinitsky, and he was a bad student, jealous of Ossip's facility with learning and his easy relationships with the other boys. One morning, during a recess break in the school courtyard, Krinitsky saw Ossip deep in conversation with another pupil and, taking a leap, jumped onto Ossip's back with limbs outstretched, bolting his legs around his waist and his arms around Ossip's torso. The shock momentarily threatened to send Ossip forward onto his knees, but with a supreme effort he tensed his muscles and withstood the assault. Then, calmly, he loosened Krinitsky's hands and legs and allowed him to slide down his back onto the ground. The entire class had stopped their games and talks, and, stupefied, watched entranced. When Krinitsky reached the ground, Ossip, his heart in his throat, collapsed into the arms of Volodia Tagantsev.

By this time, Sergei Botkin and Vassili Petri had rushed

to the scene, and were pummeling Krinitsky. Volodia made Ossip take a seat, and wiped his brow for him with his monogrammed handkerchief. But Ossip's faintness did not last long. "Stop!" he cried to Botkin and Petri, "It is not worth the effort to beat him so. Leave him alone."

"You must tell the headmaster," Volodia said to Ossip. "We were all warned that this sort of thing might kill you. He should be expelled."

"But I am not the sort who tells on people," Ossip said. "Besides, Vassya and Sergei have already punished him. I am grateful for your loyalty, all of you—but this matter will not go further."

"It certainly shall," Volodia said. He rose, and with a motion, gathered the rest of the class toward him. "We are going to go to the headmaster as a body, and it does not make any difference if you approve or not. What Krinitsky did was cowardly, and might have cost you your life. It was an unprovoked assault. Who will accompany me to the office, right this minute?"

Bewildered, short of breath, Ossip watched as not one student remained behind. Krinitsky looked at Ossip, his eyes bare with hatred. They were the only two left inside the courtyard. "You have made me lose my place at the gymnasium," Krinitsky said.

"No," Ossip murmured. "You did this yourself. I only care that I am still alive and well. I do not wish you harm. But you have lost your friends because of a stupid, thoughtless act. What did I ever do to hurt you?"

"You were simply yourself," the other replied. "I do not like sickly Jews too proud for their own good. You are an arrogant nobody, with a title you don't deserve."

"A man may be a Jew, a nobleman, a tramp, or a chimneysweep," Ossip said softly, "but as long as he is proud of his accomplishments, he will be honored to be called a man. Do you suppose, Krinitsky, that your accomplishments merit you that title?"

He was exceptionally tired, and the director sent him

home earlier than was customary. He entered the hallway just as Mathilde was making her way to the drawing room for tea. She was shocked by her son's pallor and by his untimely appearance. "What is the matter?" she cried, holding out her hands to him. He took them in his own, and told her what had happened. Mathilde's eyes grew hard, then moist, then hard again. She said, "So you were almost killed." Very gently, she pressed her lips to the boy's forehead and held him by the shoulders.

"But Krinitsky has been expelled, because of Volodia and the others," Ossip stated. "Now there is no one left to do me the slightest harm. Volodia saw to that."

"Yes," Mathilde echoed slowly, "Volodia saw to it. Tomorrow, I want you to do me a favor. You will ask Volodia to tell his parents that if they will not consider me impudent, I should be pleased if every day, instead of remaining at school, he would come home with you and share your noon meal. I cannot write them a note about it, for that would not be proper. But perhaps he will relay my message through you . . ."

"Oh, Mama, you are an angel from heaven!" Ossip cried. He kissed his mother on both cheeks and pressed her hands in his.

But she shook her head. "I am hardly that, my dear," she commented with a wry half-smile. "For angels belong to the Christians . . ."

For thirteen-year-old Sonia, Anna's absorption in her painting and reading, and Ossip's departure for the gymnasium, left a space that was like an oozing wound, not seriously dangerous but continually painful. Gino was too young to become a companion, and her father was too busy with pressing affairs. She adored her mother and felt at once terrified and fascinated by Johanna. Now, it seemed, she had become the focal point in the governess's field of observation, her primary pupil and the person with whom she most frequently spent time. Under this scrutiny, Sonia squirmed.

Moments with Mathilde were sheer ecstasy while they lasted, but Sonia could never fully enjoy them, for she knew that afterward, Johanna would have reprimands for her. "Why did you blush at tea when Vera Abramovna complimented you on the cushion you embroidered?" the girl would be asked.

"But you have taught me that flattery is undeserved, that young people should not receive praise," Sonia would answer, hesitating.

"If a lady is silly enough to offer praise to a mere child, then it behooves that child to accept it with grace, and not the awkwardness of a peasant. You are summoned to tea because you are supposed to be growing up. Yet there is always something that occurs to prove to me that you are just a child." The governess would dismiss her with a helpless wave of the hand. Sonia would emerge cowed, humiliated, yet also determined. No, I shall not let you take my heart away, nor my mind, she would silently vow. And then she would vacillate between her anger at her own inability to please the talented Johanna, and hurt at the injustice of never seeming to win, no matter what she did. I can play better than most of my friends, she would think in bewilderment after Johanna berated her lack of talent at the piano. I know that is so. But somehow, that knowledge was not sufficient.

Sonia was shy but only because Johanna de Mey, in her golden splendor, had repeatedly drummed into her signs of her own "weakness." Actually, she was a stalwart girl, a young person with tremendous inner pride combined with control, the control of her mother, the regal, poised Mathilde. Sonia was not cynical like Ossip, nor was she all reckless idealism like her sister. Sonia was thoughtful, and opinionated, in love with nobility of spirit and at war with baseness, as she had been even as a small child. But now, after years of Johanna, she had learned to face life, to realize when one had to employ control. She would not allow the governess to vanquish her strength of character, but at the same time she refused to grapple with her as did Anna, again and again. For Sonia despised ugliness, and found Anna's humiliations at the hands of Johanna de Mey ugly. Anna never won, and Johanna always employed tricks to make her lose.

Johanna still found Sonia difficult to handle. She was not weak, like Ossip, who allowed her to wreak her unfairness without stepping in. She was not foolhardy, like Anna, who foolishly stepped in every time. Sonia was vulnerable, but only to a point. She would not break, for there was an inner reserve that held her together. And the governess did not know how far she could push before the gray eyes would harden, and she, Johanna, would cease to exist. Sonia, at thirteen, presented Johanna with a strange challenge; sometimes the Dutchwoman prepared to enjoy it, while at other moments her resentment would propel her into hating the girl.

And then there was the added complication of Mathilde's role in this confrontation. Sonia was a balm for Mathilde. She was quiet, with a melodious voice. Her hair was glossy, and though not as thick as the golden locks of her cousin Tatiana, it hung in neat rolls down her virginal back. She was slim, with budding breasts that promised fullness like her mother's and sister's. Her eyes were blue-gray pools of clarity, the clarity of the just, and of the strong. And yet she was meek, and never violent, and never strident. She moved with the grace of a young nymph, her years of ballet lessons having taught her the art of elegant posture. She was an understatement, dressed simply in her soft pastels, and to Mathilde, who was the mistress of understatement, and to Ossip, who knew its value, she was a truly lovely thing, soft, like a nightingale, without the peacock glamor of Tatiana. "A man," David's friend, the sculptor Antokolsky, had said to him, "might commit murder on account of Tania. But for Sonia he would give his life."

Just as Mathilde's silent exchanges with Ossip took place behind Johanna's back, her approval of her second daughter lay hidden beneath her walled-in composure. Sonia did not know, for she did not possess her brother's sixth sense, developed as a child to cope with his lack of mobility, how central she was to Mathilde's well-being. She thought her mother perfect, and herself untalented, as Johanna had told her.

Johanna had begun to teach Sonia to sew, once a week. She herself created all her own clothes, mostly from remnants of costlier pieces of material, for only recently had ready-made gowns made their appearance in Paris. One day Johanna de Mey cut a pattern for a blouse, according to the fashion, high-necked and with long sleeves. It was to be made of wool, which was a difficult fabric with which to work, and the winter months were drawing to an end. "You are so slow," the governess complained, wiping her brow with a lace handkerchief. "At your age, Sonia, I could finish two of these in half the time it will take you to complete this one. But what else could I have expected of you? You are a plodder, child."

It was true; Sonia had been advancing slowly. Methodically, with precise stitches, she had sewn all but the cuffs on the sleeves. She listened to her governess, and her cheeks grew pink. "I have been doing my best," she said softly.

"It was a paltry best." Johanna shook her head. Then, with one swift movement, she seized the material from Sonia's hands and whisked it into the sewing basket. "That will be all for this week. Uninspiring, to say the least." She yawned, stretching her sylphlike arms and her elongated fingers in a gesture of dismissal.

Sonia stood up, smoothed her skirt, looked at the lithe stretching body with a slight shiver of revulsion, and walked out of the room. But her mind was determined. She would surprise Juanita, make her take back her words of disdain. She would prove her worth. She would complete the cuffs on the blouse in her own time, and Juanita would have to be proud. Softly, she closed the door behind her and returned to her own bedroom.

The following week, Sonia was waiting for her instructress when Johanna de Mey made her entrance. She was taken aback. Her pupil, eyes aglow, cheeks shining, was sitting quietly by the sewing table. In front of her was the blouse, completed down to the last detail. Sonia was smiling. "I wanted to surprise you," she said.

An overpowering rage seized hold of the governess at this sight. Blood came racing to her temples and began to pound behind her eyes. She clenched her fists and approached the girl, her fine features distorted into a mask of pure hatred. She began to scream, her nerves out of control. The shrill voice pierced the walls and reverberated around the room, so that Sonia, bewildered beyond belief, the smile disappearing from her lovely oval face, felt battered by the sight and sound.

"So you have gone behind my back, you sniveling little monster! So you have sneaked, and you have lied, and you have cheated! I thought of you as dull, as slow, but not as what you are—a weasel in girl's garb! How dare you not tell me what you do with the materials which I order for you, how dare you not consult me on the steps to take? What am I here for, if not to educate you, stupid, thoughtless, spoiled child? I shall tell your mother that I am returning to France, that no one wants me here, that no one needs me, that I am despised by her chit of a daughter—"

"But Juanita, it was you who complained about my being too slow. I thought you would be pleased if I finished. Why are you bringing Mama into this?" Sonia asked. She felt concern and shock. A strange dizziness had begun to make her head spin.

"Your mother needs to know what you do. She will punish you." Tears of anger welled from Johanna's eyes, and her nose looked pinched and pointed. She wanted to tear the blouse in front of Sonia, to violate her. But Sonia did not move. Johanna seized the material and rent it in half, and then, at last, the girl's eyes grew round and moist and her little hand, so white and delicate, rushed to cover her opened mouth. Johanna saw the expression and began to laugh, a wild, hysterical sound which made goosebumps appear on Sonia's arms and back. At that moment the door silently swung on its hinges, and Mathilde stood on the threshold of the sewing room, her beautiful creamy face a serene, poised counterpoint to Johanna's wrath. She glanced at her daughter; Sonia's face mirrored naked fear. Mathilde's resonant, even voice said, "What is all this?"

"She has gone behind my back, she has cheated and lied," Johanna cried. She pointed at Sonia and at the pile of torn material. "She has tried to make a mockery out of our sewing lessons."

Mathilde merely regarded her daughter, and her thick dark eyebrows shot up, questioningly. "I wanted to surprise Juanita by finishing my blouse, Mama," Sonia began. "I thought . . . she would be pleased."

"Well, evidently the surprise was too much for her. Pick up these rags, Sonia, and go to your room. We shall not discuss this matter further." Mathilde met her daughter's hurt expression with her usual face—calm, austere, even-tempered. Inside she ached for the girl and felt a surge of anger toward her friend. But she merely stood her ground, as Sonia gathered the remains of her blouse together and walked hurriedly from the scene. Then Mathilde sat down, and said to the sobbing Johanna, "It was a child's effort. No harm was meant. She would never try to sneak. Perhaps Sonia's problem in life is that her ways are too direct, too straight, too uncompromising. You must remember that."

"I know only that she has made me a fool in your estimation," Johanna murmured.

"That could never happen," Mathilde found herself saying. And as she did so, she felt a catch in her throat, and her hand shot out toward the other woman, whose blond hair had fallen out of its French twist and was tossing around her sloping shoulders. Johanna felt the hand on her shoulder, and one of her own hands found its way on top of it. She pressed Mathilde's fingers in her own trembling ones, and smiled through her tears. She could not understand what had caused her to lose her temper in this fashion, to want to kill this pretty, harmless girl as she had, substituting a piece of wool for the slender young body which she had wished to tear to shreds. She did not know, but nothing mattered any longer, for the girl had lost, her creation was ruined, and Mathilde had not sided with her own child. No, Mathilde had not sided with Sonia.

Sonia cried until she felt that there were no more tears remaining inside her body. But when she heard Anna's step outside their bedroom door, she covered her face with a damp washcloth and told her sister that she was suffering from a headache. No one guessed the extent of her hurt, of her wounded pride and sensibility, when she appeared for supper that evening. But in her mind, she had decided that never again would she permit Juanita to assault her emotions.

Johanna herself, looking somewhat pinched and haggard, noticed the girl's smooth posture, saw the firm young chin and the penetrating gray eyes, and thought to herself: Where is her self-respect? How can she face me as if nothing has happened? She could not comprehend that Sonia's self-respect lay in her sense of self, and that that sense of self would not allow its own destruction.

It was shortly after this episode that Sonia made the acquaintance of Nina Tobias. Mathilde's friend, Irina Tobias, had two children, Akim, a ten-year-old boy, and Nina, who was one year older than Sonia. Generally, when Sonia participated in her mother's teas, Madame Tobias came alone, although sometimes she would bring Akim under the pretext that the boy might play with Gino. Sonia frequently wondered why Akim's sister, who was supposed to be so close to her own age, never accompanied her mother. But she knew that such matters were not her business, and so she would sit quietly at her own mother's feet, on the ottoman, once in a while rising to pass the petits fours to the ladies. Akim, she thought, was pleasant enough—he was neither ugly nor handsome, neither bright nor stupid. But he was of a good disposition, and did not condescend to Gino who was younger by two years.

Yet one cold day in February, Stepan announced Madame Tobias and her daughter, Nina Mikhailovna. As Mathilde greeted her friend, Sonia walked over to the rather tall girl who stood shyly by the entrance to the drawing room, her nose red from the wind. Nina was not pretty, but she was attractive, Sonia thought, in a friendly fashion. She had auburn hair and brown eyes flecked with gold. Her chin was too strong and her nose too wide, but her figure had already started to develop, and, in her trim gray suit, she looked healthy and well bred. Sonia said, "I have heard much about you. You are Nina, aren't you? My name is Sonia—I am thirteen."

The girl smiled, and suddenly her face was bright, and she became pretty. "It is wonderful to meet you," she said, sounding breathless. "I have wanted to see you for a long time. As it happened, Mama was taking me shopping when she remembered that it was your Mama's receiving day— and that is why I'm here," she added, coloring with embarrassment.

"I am glad you are. Come, let us help Mama with the tea." Sonia took her new friend by the arm and gently propelled her into the room.

Madame Tobias did not seem to notice her daughter's entrance, but Mathilde looked kindly at the girl and said, "We have not seen you for a long time, my dear. How grown up you have become! You must be proud of her, Irina, for she is a girl in bloom."

"I had forgotten what day it was," Madame Tobias replied, "or I should have brought my Akim. He will be furious with me for letting him miss Gino. How he looks ahead to our visits! Besides, for me, they are also a treat. How often does a mother get to show off her heart's delight?"

Mathilde was embarrassed, and Sonia felt a surge of blood come into her cheeks. She looked quickly at Nina, but the girl was merely smiling. "Yes, Akim is a wonderful boy," she commented softly.

"You must not speak out of turn," her mother said sharply. And for the first time, Madame Tobias regarded her daughter. Sonia was dumbstruck, for in her eyes was the same hard glint that she had often caught in the aquamarine stare of her governess, Johanna de Mey. Nina bit her lip, and Sonia, impulsively, reached out and grasped her hand. The girl turned to her, and for an instant Sonia caught her expression of pure pain. She felt a sharp blow in her own stomach, and she squeezed Nina's cold little hand in her own. Suddenly, Sonia thought that she knew a blind hatred—and it was directed, she saw with horror at her own lack of justice, toward the absent Akim. At least, she said to herself, Juanita loves none of us. And then she was ashamed once more, and guilty about her evil thoughts concerning her governess. Juanita was bad tempered, that was a fact, but she did not dislike the children; no, she did not feel this lack of affection so apparent in Nina's mother toward Nina. And yet there was a similarity that insinuated itself into Sonia's thoughts, in spite of her good intentions.

When Nina Tobias left with her mother, Johanna had joined the group, and Mathilde, sipping a final glass of tea, said to her daughter, "You behaved nicely toward Nina."

"Too nicely, if you ask me," Johanna de Mey remarked. "The girl is vapid and empty. Her nose is too large, and she is awkward. Sonia bested her in every way."

But Sonia was not pleased at the compliment. She reddened, and looked at Mathilde. "Please, Mama, I should like to see more of Nina. Might I visit her sometime?" she asked.

Mathilde regarded the severe profile of her friend, and hesitated. But Sonia's eagerness touched her. "Naturally. Nina is charming, even if not yet as distinguished as Johanna would hope she will become . . . For after all, she is only fourteen, hardly out of childhood. I was quite pleased with her. She is well behaved, and of course her family is impeccable. There is no reason for you not to choose her as a friend."

Sonia's face shone with happiness. She had found a friend of her own. Since Ossip's friendship with Volodia Tagantsev, she had felt a lack in her life. True, she and her brother were as close as ever—but did not men also need men friends, and women, other women? Certainly this was apparent in the lives of her parents. "Ossip too will like Nina," she asserted.

Mathilde was gazing down at her, with the half-smile which gave her the expression of the Mona Lisa, or of a Renaissance Madonna. But Johanna de Mey cut in. "Is the Tobias family truly worthy of you, my dear?" Mathilde regarded her friend with a startled look. "Do not feel offended, my sweet," Johanna remarked soothingly. "But seriously, her father—Irina Markovna's—was a furrier from the Pale of Settlement. Sometimes I have found her to be . . . surely not coarse, for any friend of yours would never be that—but a little nouveau riche. Nina is not of Sonia's caliber. She is not fine, nor dainty."

Mathilde placed her hand over Johanna's. "Do not worry so, Johanna. You are always looking to protect me and my children, and that is why you are so precious to me. But please, do not be concerned. I was touched by little Nina. It is so clear that—" She glanced toward Sonia and was silent.

Sonia felt the silence and stood up. "Thank you for

letting me help with the tea," she said. She walked out of the room, and behind her, her mother's voice resumed its comforting tone directed at Johanna de-Mey. "Irina favors the boy far too much," Sonia caught as she stepped away from her range of hearing.

That evening, Sonia said excitedly to Ossip, "I have met a wonderful girl. You will like her, too. Her name is Nina Mikhailovna Tobias—Madame Tobias is her mother, and Akim is her little brother. She is not beautiful, but she is well groomed and is quite nice to look at, and she has the heart of a gracious queen. Why, her mother does not like her at all—but Nina looks at her with love, and speaks highly of Akim who is the mother's favorite. There is not a drop of jealousy inside her."

"I am glad for you, Sonitchka," Ossip said warmly.

Once a week, in the month that followed, the coachman would drive Sonia to visit Nina Tobias. They discovered that they enjoyed the same books, that they both played the same pieces on the piano. It was a dreadful shock to everyone when word came that little Akim had been struck with appendicitis. Then news arrived that he had died on the operating table. Sonia rushed to the home of her friend, and found Nina prostrate on her bed, unable to eat, her face haggard, and splotched with patches raw from tears. "Oh, Sonitchka, Sonitchka," she wailed. "I prayed to God to let me die instead. This is so unfair, so unfair to Papa and Mama, who adored him so. I wish, how I wish I had been the one to die."

Sonia, shocked, held Nina at arms' length and spoke to her solemnly. "How can you speak such blasphemy, Ninotchka? You? Why, now you are more needed than ever. Now that Akim is gone, you are the only comfort remaining to your Mama and Papa. Think a little through your grief: you are their only child, their only daughter. Now they will love you more than ever, for they have only you."

"But they do not care whether they have me or not," Nina said softly. "Papa also said that he was sorry it had been Akim. He was . . . special. I am just ordinary. My poor parents! How sad I am for them."

When Sonia returned to the Gunzburg residence, her face was white and drawn, and she refused to take supper with the family. She could not utter a single word. Silently, her body taut, she removed her gown and slipped into a flannel nightshirt, and combed her hair and braided it for bed. Then, in the dark, she slipped into her cot. But in the blackness she lay wide awake, her hands rigidly clutching the coverlet. When the door swung open and Johanna entered the room, she turned on her side to face the wall. The governess sat down at the foot of the bed, and for several moments neither spoke.

Then Johanna de Mey, in her clear, crisp tones, said, "You are causing us all to worry, and only because of that gawking girl, Nina Tobias. What is she to you that you should make her mourning your own? I shall not permit this to continue. What you are doing is tantamount to Anna's rebellions. Not coming to supper! From now on, you will limit your visits to that Tobias child. You see entirely too much of her, and she offers you nothing in return. Can she teach you any art? Can she teach you a language? Can she improve your deportment as a lady?"

"She is my friend, and I love her. She is lonely, and she needs me. I shall not stop my visits to her, no, not now and not ever. I shall not let those visits interfere in any way with my work, nor with my family life. You will not suffer from them. But I shall go each day, for right now Nina needs me more than I am afraid of you. Even if you punish me, I shall go. And Papa will not disapprove, for he has taught us to take care of those who depend on us for help."

Johanna de Mey allowed her mouth to form a speechless "o." She saw the slim form of the young girl outlined on the bed. She felt no anger, only total bereavement of her intellectual resources. Her mind, always so quick, was completely blank. Suddenly a vision of David passed through her memory, and she said, with amazement, "You have dared to insult me and threaten me. You—a child of thirteen!" But she could not continue, for she felt in her very bowels that Sonia had spoken the truth. In this case, she would dare to go to her father. And, this time, the Baron would support his daughter. A wave of rage and loathing filled her heart, and she left the room, banging the door shut behind her.

But the object of her hatred was not the young girl who had defied her. "That damned Jew!" she muttered, tears rising and stinging her lashes. "He will pay dearly for this." And she shut her eyes against a blinding vision of the Baron.

In her sorrow for her friend, Irina Tobias, Mathilde had all but forgotten her indirect invitation to Volodia Tagantsev. But less than a week after the incident with Krinitsky, while brushing out the long, thick coils of her black hair, Mathilde gave a sudden start. "David," she said, "we were all so relieved about Ossip, and so distressed for the Tobias family—that I did not remember to tell you what I said to our son." She turned to her husband, ready for the night, and told him what had occurred.

David ran his fingers through his thinning red hair and bit his lower lip.

"Let us hope that Volodia did not relay the message," he finally said. "Think what his father could make of it. He could voice it to his comrades. He could tell Ministers. What kind of *shtadlan* would I be then, Mathilde?"

But he caught her expression as she gazed at him through the gilded mirror on her vanity. At thirty-nine, she was still so lovely, even after four children. There was not a white thread in the blue-black mass of her hair, and not a wrinkle around her mouth or eyes. Not a glimmer of response. Her silence made a wave of anger crest inside him. "Are you never aware of my position, of what I believe in, of what I am attempting to achieve? For God's sweet sake, you are my wife!" he cried.

She lifted her chin a fraction of an inch higher, and her eyes shone with distaste. He shrugged. "They are only children," his wife said. "But I shall not renege, should the Tagantsevs accept my offer."

David came up to her and pressed her gently into his arms, burying his face in the cascade of raven hair, smelling her lavender scent. She may as well expect the Tzar himself to come to her bedside, he thought wryly, as the Tagantsevs to acknowledge her at all.

But the following day, when Ossip returned from the gymnasium, he could barely wait to greet his mother with his news: "Mama," he said, "Volodia has the most wonderful news! He told his mother of our offer, and she has sent you a reply. Not only do the Tagantsevs accept your luncheon invitations, but they wish you to know how grateful they are. You see, they have not liked for Volodia to have to stay at school for meals. They actually are relieved that you are going to have him here! He can start coming whenever you wish."

"Then he may as well come tomorrow. But I shall make arrangements for you boys to eat before the rest of us, since you are limited to an hour, and your father's business in the city makes it difficult for him to be here before half past twelve. The rest of us shall eat at one, when you leave. This will allow you both to take your time, to chat together at your leisure. I shall tell Cook about it tonight."

"Oh, Mama, thank you." Blue eyes held blue eyes and Ossip took his mother's hand and brought it to his lips. "You will like my choice of a best friend," he said eagerly.

But when David was told, the blood drained from his face. He rose from the supper table, gripping it with both hands. "Dear God," he whispered. "Tomorrow."

"What difference does it make if the boy comes then or another day?" his wife asked impatiently. Still, the Baron's pallor, the rigid tendons in his throat, alarmed her. It was not like David to give in to histrionics of any sort. She said, with some asperity, "What is the trouble?"

Her husband's light blue eyes rested upon her face, and she saw the eloquent exhaustion in him, and his eagerness, and a boyish appeal. "Tomorrow," he murmured across the table, "we shall be employing the small apartment at the back. We are to have a widow and her three small children here for several days, while the lawyers and I tie up their affairs. The presence of the Tagantsev boy could present a problem as bad as anything I had thought—including the unexpected visit of the chief of the Petersburg police. The police, at least, have been properly bribed. We cannot say the same of this fourteen-year-old boy."

"Volodia would never betray my father in our home," Ossip said.

"Volodia may be a gentleman, but he is bound to put loyalty to his family higher than loyalty to you." David sighed. "If he hears or sees one of the orphans, and tells the Senator—"

"Surely you can find a way to prevent that from happening," Mathilde cut in.

"I do not know how to battle against fate, my dear. But it is true, I alone must find a way. Perhaps"—his light blue eyes wandered round the table, and finally rested upon his younger daughter—"perhaps someone here can be of help. Sonitchka. You are Ossip's love, he must have discussed you with his friend. Ossip would wish for Volodia to meet you. You could make certain that the widow and the children are safe and under lock for the hour in question, and then you could come out and entertain our visitor. He will not be curious about the house if you are there, as he might be with Ossip alone, whom he knows well enough to question. With you he will be the attentive guest. Will you do this to help me?"

"I beg your pardon, Papa, but Volodia is too well brought up to ever ask questions regarding someone's home. If he heard a child cry, I would tell him before he asked that Cook had a visiting niece—or another such tale," Ossip stated. "Why should Sonia become involved?"

"But I want to be involved, Ossip," Sonia said firmly. She looked at her brother with large, passionate eyes. "Volodia Tagantsev may be your friend, but he is causing Papa problems that you are only too quick to overlook. The first day that I went to visit Nina, I was bold enough to ask her to show me her home. I was curious about their ballroom. I admit it, even though I know Juanita will reprimand me later. Who is to say that Volodia might not be as curious as I? I shall come, and speak to him. I am not afraid. What can this boy do to frighten me? Or is it that you find me too unworldly to meet this elegant friend of yours?"

"Forgive me, Sonitchka," Ossip murmured. He felt abashed. Never before had his sister spoken so to him. But he was also angered. "Do not place yourself above Volodia Tagantsev, Sofia Davidovna," he added defensively. "Your high opinion of yourself may not be so deserved after all. Who are you to dislike a person before meeting him, anyway? It is unjust."

"I cannot help the way I feel," Sonia replied stoutly. She folded her napkin and regarded her mother with pain distorting her young face. "Please, Mama," she whispered, "may I be excused from the table?"

Silently, Mathilde nodded. She was disgusted. David, and his obsessive causes, had come between her favorite children and caused them to quarrel and hurt each other. She had looked forward to Ossip's declaration at supper that the Tagantsevs had accepted with gratefulness. She had wanted to enjoy this triumph. And now no one was happy, and there was dissension among her kin, as there had always been dissension around the table of Baron Yuri, her father.

But Johanna de Mey smiled behind her embroidered napkin. Her heart soared with sheer pleasure.

Most days, after their lesson, Johanna would take Sonia and Gino for a long walk, but this time Gino went off with his governess by himself. Sonia closed the door of the lesson room gently, and then slipped to the opposite side of the Gunzburg apartment beyond the kitchen and pantry, to a large door. She turned the handle noiselessly and entered the rooms on the other side. A musty smell greeted her, and she thought: Alexei has been lax. For in the first room there was nothing but books, books of all sorts, bound in fine, ancient leathers with gold-trimmed pages, books of prints, books that unfolded into antique scrolls. They lay heaped upon four gigantic bookcases that were starting to sag in the middle.

She shook the dust out of her hair, and entered the room behind this. More bookcases heaved their burdens to the very ceiling, but in the center of the open space at the core of the room, a cot had been placed, and a small table. A young woman in a brown dress sat on the cot, her hair pulled into a simple knot. Cradled in her arms was an infant not more than four months old. "Good morning, Ekaterina Yakovlievna," Sonia said in a low voice. At once the woman started to her feet. Sonia held out a hand to restrain her. "We must be very silent, for this noon we are having a visitor who will come every day from now on. Were he to see you here today, he might take you for a new servant, but your children would shock him, and children can say things that are not for certain ears. If this were to be his only visit, we could explain your presence adequately, I'm sure. But soon he will know the ways of this house—who runs it, who visits at noontime. He is only a young boy, and will probably not pay the slightest bit of attention. But his father is a dangerous man, and if the son let slip the wrong description to his parents, we would all be in great trouble, and Papa would not be able to continue to harbor the widows. So I shall have to lock you in while he is here, and you will have to make certain that the baby, and the boys in the other room, do not utter a single cry. Then I shall unlock you, and all will be well."

The woman seemed frightened. She nodded several times, her face pale and her eyes wide. Sonia smiled. "Do not worry," she murmured. Then she went into a third room where, among more books, stood two smaller cots upon which two boys, one five and the other perhaps three years old, were playing. "Good morning, Shura and Mishka," Sonia said softly. The boys' clear faces looked up at her, and quickly, deftly, she placed each of her index fingers upon their parted lips. "We are going to play a game, with your Mama and the baby," she said. "We are going to see if all four of you can be absolutely silent for one entire hour. If you cannot stand it, then . . . well . . . we shall allow you to whisper. What do you say? Or rather—don't say it. Simply nod your heads. I shall bring you honey cakes from the kitchen when the hour is over. But not one crumb to anyone who utters a gasp. All right?"

They both nodded, bewildered, and she ruffled the top of each of their heads. Then, on tiptoe, she made her way back to the mother, gently touched her shoulder and squeezed it once, and came out through the third, book-filled storeroom. She closed the big door and locked it with a key which had been in the pocket of her pinafore. Resolutely, she returned to her own room.

Anna was not there. Sonia slid the pinafore from her shoulders and folded it neatly on her bed. She selected a simple woolen blouse, off-white with long sleeves that were cuffed with ivory lace, and a skirt of tan camel's hair. Thoughtfully, she pinned a single pearl flower to her breast, and combed her fine long hair. She took the two side panels up into a high, partial ponytail which she tied with a simple ribbon of ivory velvet. The tall mirror reflected back a small, slim person with large gray eyes and a straight firm nose, pink lips and white cheeks. Making a grimace, she pinched her cheeks for color, and thought: Tania and Juanita are right; I am a dim, pale thing, with no flair. Anna, despite her plainness, was thought by all to have flair. Sonia despaired. Volodia Tagantsev would not even want to talk to her—and then what would she do?

It was ten minutes past twelve when Sonia left the bedroom and walked quietly into the dining room. Stepan was the only person present and his dark eyes gleamed at her. "I was told that you would join the young men for luncheon, Sofia Davidovna," he said. "I took the liberty of placing a rose by your water goblet."

She blushed. "Oh, Stepan . . ." But her words were interrupted by the ringing doorbell and the maître d'hôtel strode off to open the front door. Gay voices of young men boomed through the paneling. Sonia stood very still and straight, wondering suddenly with a burning curiosity what this Tagantsev would be like, what he would say, how he would look. And then, side by side, Ossip and the stranger entered the dining room, and he, the intruder, the trouble causer, was before her.

He was fairly tall and rather stolid, and in his brown suit, she thought, he resembled a smooth brown nut. His hair was dark brown with glints of mahogany, and beneath thick brown brows were large brown eyes. Even his complexion was a creamy tan with ruddy cheekbones. He was not handsome, but he was pleasant looking enough, she told herself. And then he smiled, and she saw even, large teeth of a pure white, and she found herself making efforts not to stare at him. She had never liked pretty boys, she thought, only Ossip, and even in Ossip the prettiness denoted a weakness. This boy was strong, and looked older than fourteen. Suddenly, she was thinking how nice it would be to dance with him. And then she was ashamed. Never in a million years would she, Sonia de Gunzburg, accept even a single waltz with this . . . Tagantsev! Besides, there were still at least three years before her debut . . .

"Sofia Davidovna, it is a pleasure to meet you," he was saying.

"Vladimir Nicolaievitch," she replied, extending her hand quite primly. Ossip stood by, amused. Sonia seemed very ladylike in her camel's hair skirt, all thirteen years of her, and damned if Volodia was not turning red, like a schoolboy.

"I'm hungry," Ossip declared. "If you two aren't, all the better. I shall eat your portions."

"Please sit down, Vladimir Nicolaievitch," Sonia said. She motioned to the place next to Ossip, who was already seated. But Volodia came over to the opposite side of the table and pulled out her chair. "Allow me," he said. She sat down, and only then did he take his own place. Sonia was trying not to blush, but the red was burning her cheeks and she wished that Ossip would stop his idiotic smiling. "We are having sherried consommé," she announced, her voice clear.

"That will be delicious, I am certain," Volodia said.

"Our cook will be glad to hear it. Do you and Ossip share all the same courses at the gymnasium?"

"Unfortunately, yes," Ossip replied, and his friend laughed.

"Yes, we are partners in crime," Volodia added. His brown eyes twinkled. But the words "partners" and "crime" made a sudden chill creep up Sonia's backbone, and she thought of Ekaterina Yakovlievna hidden behind the door with the baby and her two sons. She shivered, the corner of her upper lip curling in spite of herself, in anger at the presence of this boy today. How dare he banter with her when matters of life and death were transpiring in this very house, and because of him?

"Ossip tells me that you play the piano exquisitely. I should like to hear you, Sofia Davidovna. The piano is my forte, too. Well—'forte' is an immodest word. I meant it is my greatest pleasure. We could try to do a piece for four hands some time."

Sonia allowed the servant girl to remove the empty dishes, and Stepan entered with a veal roast surrounded by new potatoes and baby peas. Then her clear gray eyes met the brown, frank gaze of their young guest. "I hardly think that we could accomplish much during the space of fifty minutes, Vladimir Nicolaievitch," she remarked with a note of irony. "And besides, I do not customarily take luncheon with my brother. Today was just . . . a special occasion."

"Ossip speaks most highly of you," Volodia said. He was serving himself a healthy helping of meat and vegetables.

"You, too, have a sister, don't you?" Sonia asked.

"My twin, Natalia. Natasha. We are not at all alike, actually. She is bright, and funny, and gay, and very beautiful, with thick black hair and bright blue eyes. In fact, she resembles Ossip here far more than she does me. I am the ordinary member of the family."

The word "family" reverberated through Sonia's mind, which momentarily froze. Volodia was looking at her across the table, and she thought: I hate him, but I also like him. He has a sense of humor, he is obviously kind and well mannered . . . but I hate him. He is the cause of Ekaterina's and Shura's and Mishka's discomfort, and because of him they must keep still as mice . . .

She said, "I know what you mean. I think the same myself. Ossip is brilliant, and our sister Anna is an artist, and our little brother, Gino, has the sweetest disposition I have ever encountered. It is only I who do not shine. But perhaps the world needs us to balance out the geniuses!" Her own eyes sparkled, and met those of her brother, and together they laughed. It felt so good to laugh. The young guest joined the merriment.

When the servant girl removed the main course and

Stepan had presented the platter of fruit, Sonia had all but forgotten the widow, and was enjoying the occasion, this meal with the two boys, without the hampering presence of Johanna. Perhaps she would never again be allowed to sit alone at a table with a strange young man and her favorite brother, but even Cinderella had enjoyed the Prince's ball. She said, "I see now why Ossip speaks about you each and every day, Vladimir Nicolaievitch. You are a good friend to him."

"And may I be a friend to you, Sofia Davidovna?" Volodia asked earnestly.

Sonia blushed. It was odd how many times she had blushed in the course of a single meal. "Any friend of Ossip is my friend," she replied. "Besides, it was through your effort that that dreadful Krinitsky was removed from Ossip's vicinity. We owe a lot to your loyalty."

With these words, she remembered her charges in the rooms behind the kitchen. The color drained from her cheeks. She lifted her young chin firmly, and regarded Ossip with coolness. "Please hurry," she said evenly. "You will both be late for class, and I shall be blamed."

Volodia stood up, and so did the two Gunzburgs. Sonia walked with the boys to the vestibule, where Stepan produced the fur-lined coats in which the two students had arrived. At the door, Ossip kissed his sister and Volodia Tagantsev took her hand and said, warmly, "I had a wonderful luncheon. I shall truly miss you tomorrow, Sofia Davidovna."

She remained in the hallway, uncertain, for several minutes. Hot flashes pulsed through her body, and she thought for a moment that she was ill. But the flashes were not unpleasant, and she shook off a sensation of fear and doom. Instead, resolute now, she walked to the kitchen and made up a tray of honey cakes. Then she unlocked the door and went to the widow and her children. "You are all winners," she announced. "Here is your reward."

Sonia saw the grateful expression on the face of the widow, Ekaterina. Something inside her rebelled at this sight: within a week, this woman and her two children would be sent away to the Pale of Settlement, a place where they had never been before, simply because the head of their family had died, and with him, permission to live in the capital. Sonia thought: Papa will make arrangements, will send her to live among kind people he knows. But her life is here, with friends! Would Volodia Tagantsev understand her own pain for these strangers? she wondered. Would he even know that an injustice had been done? But he was not a Jew! There was no earthly, no Godly way for him to understand this absurd situation, nor her own churned-up emotions concerning it.

When she returned to her room, Anna was there. "Tell me," the older girl demanded. "What is he like? Ossip's friend, I mean."

But Sonia shook her head. "I'm not sure," she replied, bewildered at her own words. "I can't really decide." She unpinned her brooch and sat down pensively on the edge of her cot. Anna put down her paint brush and looked at her, and flecks of gold shone in her brown eyes.

"We all meet someone like that," she commented gently. She herself was thinking of someone blond with green eyes. But her sister did not understand, and merely continued to peer dreamily into space, her small, girlish mouth slightly ajar.

Five

It was a bitter cold winter morning when David announced that Aron Berson, the banker, was sending someone over with papers for him to examine. Ossip had already left for school, and Sonia and Gino were in the lesson room, awaiting Johanna, who was lingering over a final cup of cocoa in her bed. Only Mathilde, huddled in her ermine-lined silk morning gown, saw Anna's face color deeply at her father's words. A slight frown appeared between Mathilde's brows. "That dreadful family," she said in spite of herself.

"There is nothing wrong with Ivan Aronovitch," Anna countered abruptly.

"He is a pleasant youth, to be sure," Mathilde said. She felt vaguely disquieted. "But one cannot separate a man from his origins. He resides in that tainted house, with his scatterbrained mother and his wanton sisters. We cannot be certain how this has affected him."

Anna merely bit her lip. But after Stepan carried away the remainder of the morning dishes, she did not go to her room. Instead, when her father proceeded to his study and her mother to her boudoir, she went into the drawing room and stood for a while before the long gilt mirror. Her bosom was ample, but her waist was slender, cinched by a belt of copper and rope. She wore a full-length skirt of Latvian design, and a coarse cotton mujik blouse with a multicolored woolen shawl in earth tones to protect her from the chill which penetrated even through the double walls of the house. Her red hair shone, unadorned, coiled over her right ear. But perhaps—no, even surely—Aron Berson would send a messenger from his bank. Ivan was a student, and besides, had he not declared himself uninterested in his father's work? Anna shuddered, and the pinpoints of her nipples quivered. He would have no reason to come.

But moments later, Stepan admitted someone into the vestibule, and Anna heard a gay, robust burst of young laughter. She could not restrain the impulse that propelled her toward that sound. Stepan, holding Ivan's astrakhan cape which bristled with particles of ice and snow, saw his young mistress, her cheeks ablaze, stride awkwardly toward the newcomer. Ivan Berson, his blond hair parted in the center, his frock coat of rumpled broadcloth unbuttoned, almost came to attention. "Anna Davidovna," he murmured.

She regarded him with a certain irony. "You? On banking business?"

His cheeks reddened. "I am not as impure as you think," he stated, and then took the briefcase that Stepan held for him. His green eyes looked eagerly around, and gave him confidence. He advanced a few steps, and at once Anna took the lead and left the vestibule. Near the drawing room, she halted. "My father?" she asked.

No one was near them. The young man's hand rose to his cravat, which was loosely tied. He stood over Anna, only barely taller than she. "I came, hoping to see you," he said. "You see, I am very bold. I hoped that you would be pleased to see me again. I thought—perhaps we could chat, for several minutes. You are not—too busy?"

She shook her head, motioning him to the sofa. She could not sit, herself, and kept her hands pressed nervously together. "I have made you uncomfortable," Ivan said gently. "I shall leave now, and bring the papers to your father. I was too abrupt, too presumptuous."

"No," she said. Her voice was rough because her throat was dry. Finally she took a seat. She became very red, and, examining her nails, murmured, "I wanted you to come, Ivan Aronovitch."

"I have never paid court to a young lady before," he told her frankly. "That is not to say I have no women friends. But my friends have all been fellow students, and in our discussion groups the atmosphere is informal, and we are all one, so to speak. So you may find my manners . . . wanting. I do not wish for you to regard me badly. I felt the need to explain."

"You have come to—pay court—to me?" Anna asked, her voice nearly inaudible. Tears seared her eyelids suddenly. "No, surely not."

"I am clumsy, but I needed to see you. I know—what people whisper about my sisters. I cannot help the way they are, any more than I can help my own disinclination for formality. You are a lady, and unaccustomed to this sort of familiarity. Have I shocked you, Anna Davidovna?"

"Yes, you have shocked me," she replied abruptly. She looked away, her embarrassment overwhelming her. "But not in the way you suppose. I am not a lady, Ivan Aronovitch. Not like my mother, or even my little sister. I was born into the wrong family, and have never felt at ease as a Gunzburg. I always wished that I had been born a peasant, in the heartland of our nation—where no one would notice me, and where I could act as I please. What shocks me is that you would have any desire to see me again, you who live surrounded by brilliant young University women, and pretty sisters. I am an oddity in this family—haven't Kazia and Alia told you that?"

Ivan Berson rose, and began to pace the room. Anna, in her shame, could not bear to look at him. She felt that the entire room had suddenly engulfed her, this room where ladies met for tea and where delicate antiques were placed in tasteful decor, a decor which she detested with all her heart. When the young man stopped, it was in front of her. He said: "Please, allow me to see one of your paintings. Baron David is not in a hurry this morning, for my father told me that he is not expected at the Ministry until later. I shall not depart until you have brought out a canvas, or a sketch—but I must see one."

Anna was very surprised. "Very well," she said. She was grateful for the opportunity to leave the room and this young man who made her chest burn and confused her thoughts. She went into her room and looked about. Her eyes rested upon her latest etching, a free-form rendition of her brother Gino seated on the floor by the piano. She took it in her hand, her mind a blur. She did not even catch sight of Johanna, on her way from the lesson room to her mother's boudoir. Anna walked, head bent, into the drawing room, and speechlessly deposited the small portrait in the lap of the young man. "This is unfinished," she stated. "I am going to add color next—blue glints on the piano surface, brown with gold highlights in my brother's hair, soft shadings of apricot on his cheeks. Gino is very healthy. His eyes will be nutlike, with points of orange and green. I do not know why I chose this one to show you, I've really only just started it."

Ivan Berson gazed at the picture, then at Anna. His green eyes gleamed. "I shall take you to meet my friends who paint for their living," he said. "You are as good as I had dreamed. For you see, I have dreamed of you. We were in a forest, hiding from the world, and then—" His hand reached out for hers, and in her total shock, she stepped back with an intake of breath. "Yes," he said, smiling, "you are a lady. In spite of yourself."

Anna's brown eyes suddenly filled with tears that spilled

over her lashes, and she turned away from Ivan with an abrupt sob. The sketch fell to the floor. Neither of them noticed. Ivan rose, and placed his fingers on her shoulder. Tremors began to shake her entire body, and she cried, "You must go away! You are mocking me, and I shall not bear it. Go back to your student friends and leave me alone, or I shall scream, and Stepan will come."

But Ivan's fingers tightened on her shoulder, and with force he wheeled her around to face him. She squirmed, turning her head to the right so that her deformity was hidden. She was sobbing convulsively. His hand stroked her shoulder, then moved up to her hair. Softly, he ran caressing fingers through the red coils. She shivered again and again, uncontrollably. He tilted her chin up with his index finger, and her eyes, with their hunted expression, shone their fear at him like those of a deer in flight. He bent down and touched her lips with his, and drew her toward him with a powerful movement of his arm. She could not budge. Stiff, she received his kiss, then gave a small animal cry and parted her lips, responding. He released her then and she stood before him, red and ashamed. "I did not come to mock you," he said gravely. "And I shall find other opportunities to return."

Her hand touched her left cheek. "But why?" she whispered.

"If I were a romantic, I might tell you that I was falling in love with you. If I were a peasant, I would merely tell you that I want you. What would you have me say, Anna Davidovna? I like you very much."

"You are a madman," she breathed. Then, incongruously, she began to laugh, a high, uncontrolled laugh. She shook her head, turned, and ran out of the drawing room, still laughing. In the hallway she stopped, and touched her lips with wonder. She did not see Johanna watching her from the depths of the corridor. But she heard Stepan's soft knock on David's study, and his announcement that Ivan Aronovitch Berson had arrived. Once more Anna laughed, but this time without hysteria. Her laughter was soft and low and gentle.

Sonia noticed that in the days preceding the New Year her sister seemed to unbend, to melt her hard resistance to the outer world. Often she would catch Anna with a softness in her eyes, a dreamy look which made her almost beautiful. If Sonia, at thirteen, became aware of this, then David did all the more. David's heart held an ache for his older daughter. But the Baron did not know enough about women to associate this ripening of womanhood in Anna with the quite frequent appearances of Aron Berson's son, who would deliver messages at all hours of the day, sometimes appearing at tea time and remaining with the younger members of the Gunzburg household. "It is strange, we had never seen much of Ivan," he said one evening to his wife. "Now he is always around, for some reason or other."

"Yes," Mathilde said. She was not sure whether she should be glad or angry. A Berson, in her home, was an affront. Yet, if he were truly paying court to Anna, if she could only be sure that his intentions were indeed those of a respectable young man toward the girl of his choice, then she would have to allow it. After all, Anna deserved happiness, and lately she had even consented to taking tea with her Aunt Rosa, another sign of her softening toward the world. Would Anna ever be wooed again? Mathilde, the anxious mother, would worry. But still—a Berson as son-in-law would be dreadful. Her friends would never understand. Or would Anna's marriage restore her to the realm of normalcy in the eyes of people who thought her such an oddity?

"But he has never come calling, as young men do," she said to Johanna de Mey with a troubled expression. "He merely slips in and out of the house, running errands for his father. Could I be mistaken? Perhaps Ivan wants nothing of Anna?"

The governess smoothed her fine golden pompadour. "Mathilde," she finally said, "I am afraid that you are simply too naive to realize the truth. Some young men are indeed interested in girls—but not necessarily to wed them. Your Ivan Berson would soil Anna. If I were you, I would stop these visits. They are making the girl hope, where nothing will ensue. He is having fun at her expense. I have—observed them together."

Mathilde paled. "You have seen them—behave improperly?"

Johanna bit her lower lip and cast her lovely blue eyes upon a speck of dust on the carpet. "They thought they were alone," she murmured.

Mathilde recoiled, and her features grew slack. "My God," she moaned. She remembered her father with one of the kitchen maids in Paris one day, when he had thought himself similarly alone. She closed her eyes to the vision. "Not Anna," she finally stated. There was an element of despair in her voice. Johanna de Mey placed a cool hand upon Mathilde's clenched fingers, and softly stroked them. "I shall speak to Anna myself," Mathilde said. "David will have to deal with the boy." Johanna de Mey smiled.

But when she stood before her in the boudoir, Anna did not flinch. She regarded her mother with wide-open eyes, and stood erect. "There is nothing for me to hide," she said. "Ivan Aronovitch has done absolutely nothing wrong. He is not the sort to come courting. He is not social, nor am I. We understand each other. I am happy with him. I have never been happy before, except when I paint. He is nothing like his stupid, vapid sisters. If he has offended your sense of propriety, Mama, we are both sorry—he will tell you so himself, if you give him the chance. Neither one of us would feel comfortable in a formal courtship."

"Will he speak for you to your father?" Mathilde demanded.

Anna flushed a deep scarlet. Her eyes blazed. "I would

never ask him to," she said with pride. "Perhaps one day
he would marry me, but in the meantime there is much we
wish to accomplish. He is still a student. I would never
wish for him to be forced into a formal engagement, simply to make a good impression. I could not bear it, myself.
I could not stand to have Papa humiliate us both by asking
Ivan questions about his intentions. Why should our lives
be so important to anybody? We are hurting no one, nor
have we done . . . any unseemly acts."

"You have seen him alone, unchaperoned."

"But we still did no harm. He sat with me in the drawing
room, but anyone could have walked in."

"Still, I shall not have this sort of behavior taking place
in my household. You have set a fine example for Sonia! I
would not mind if Ivan spoke for you, even though you
know I would have preferred another son-in-law. But not
this stealthy visiting, without permission. You are a woman
now, Anna, and capable of compromising yourself. I shall
not permit you to do this."

Mother and daughter stared at each other, Mathilde's
blue eyes proud and haughty, Anna's brown ones shining
with pain and anger. "If you really loved me, Mama, you
would understand!" she finally cried out. "You gave me
life. If I am deformed, part of the reason must lie in you. I
know how much you are ashamed of me, of my face.
Ivan—Vanya—does not care. He sees me as a whole person. He does not care, either, that Papa has set aside a
dowry for me. You needn't be afraid of that. Besides, his
own father is a wealthy man. Vanya would like me even if
I were poor, and a nobody."

Mathilde's right temple began to throb. A migraine was
coming on. She clasped the arms of her chair, thinking:
Johanna, why have you deserted me now, of all times?
And then she recalled that it had been her own decision to
instigate this talk with Anna. She had never been physical,
nor had she ever struck one of her children. The nurse-

maids had seen to spankings. Now she rose on an unaccustomed wave of passion and slapped her daughter fully across the face. At once, she collapsed back upon her pillows, nausea gripping her. She, Mathilde, the poised, the calm, the nonviolent, had done this. She regarded Anna with eyes that the girl could not decipher. "I always honored my own mother," Mathilde said finally.

But Anna stood her ground. "I am only speaking what I have been feeling for years. I love you, Mama. I do not like to hurt you by my words. But I do not wish to spend my life as you do. I know that Vanya likes me, that I like him. I do not wish to be married. Marriage has never seemed, to my eyes, the wondrous thing that it is held to be. Women marry, and their husbands forget them; or they marry and forget their own dreams. Or each leads a life apart, while very respectably sharing the same children and the same roof. I want to paint, and to help people poorer than myself. I do not want to live in St. Petersburg, or Paris, or Vienna, or any other 'civilized' city. I simply want to be left alone, and perhaps that is what Vanya wants also. I have not discussed it with him. But it would be wrong to involve Papa, and Monsieur Berson, in Vanya's life. Right now we enjoy each other, and that is sufficient to make us happy. If, one day, we find that there is more, perhaps I shall change my mind about marriage." Anna paused. She was trembling. "But I shall not be regarded as an old maid, who needs to be bound into matrimony at the first sign of male interest. I may not be beautiful, but I am not a crushed hat in the basement of Worth's milliner . . . something to be disposed of."

Mathilde looked at her daughter, whose sagging face was now streaked with red from her own fingers. An impulse ran through her, to touch the girl and apologize. But hardness replaced the impulse at Anna's words. "You are a Gunzburg, and have obligations," she said coldly. She wanted to add: What you say is not untrue, my little one.

For what is my life? What was my mother's life? We married the men we were told to marry. At least Mama loved Papa, but what did her love bring her, save shame and misery? And what of my emptiness of feeling for David? Compassion, yes, friendship, yes again. But I could have felt this way about him simply as my cousin, without making him my husband for life. "It is not for us to question the mores of society," she said, more gently.

But Anna did not know what her mother had been thinking in her silence. Her shoulders hunched forward, she resembled a broken marionette. A pang of pity shot through Mathilde, but Anna, once again, was not aware of it. She lifted her brown eyes to her mother, and they were filled with tears. "I should like to go to my room, Mama," she murmured.

Mathilde's lips parted, but no sound emerged. She felt as though, somehow, she herself had been the one slapped. She found that she did not possess the strength to rise from her chair. Her daughter turned around, swishing her long skirt of crocheted wool around her ankles, and nearly ran into her own bedroom, grateful that Sonia was not there. Her face contorted with grief, Anna sat down at the small secretary and brought out a sheet of paper, a quilled pen, and an inkwell. She began to write:

Vanya—What can I say except that I do not wish for you to visit me here, in my home, any longer? I cannot explain to you the reasons why. They have nothing, my dear, to do with you, or what I think of you. Please believe me. Anna.

She began to cry. What a dry note, how devoid of sentiment! But this was how things had to be. Vanya wanted to change the government. He did not have time to love her. It was not right to ask it of him, to demand any commitments. Besides—she wanted to help, too. What did her personal feelings matter in the grander scale of their ideals?

Anna rang for the little maid who took care of her and Sonia. "Marfa," she said, "please see that somehow, soon, this message is brought to Ivan Aronovitch Berson. But please, be discreet. I do not want Mademoiselle de Mey to learn of this."

When Marfa had departed, Anna's head fell forward onto the blotter, and her shoulders began to shake with dry sobs.

In St. Petersburg, matters requiring the highest political finesse were handled by the Secret Police, and the more routine problems of crime and disorder by the local police. Baron David and his father, Baron Horace, had established a pattern of bribing all levels of officials. As Jews, this was the only way that they could hope for the same measure of justice granted to Christian citizens. If a pogrom was brewing, the local police chief would warn David in advance; and in the case of the women and children illegally harbored by the Gunzburgs after the death of the head of the family, the police pretended ignorance. Corruption was rampant.

One of the few truly honest men in the city was Alexei Alexandrovitch Lopukhin. David had first encountered him socially many years before, for the Lopukhins were an old, established Russian family who, for an unknown reason, had shown themselves too proud to accept a title from the Tzars. Lopukhin's wife was also a member of the highest aristocracy. David and Mathilde saw them frequently, and their children also were acquainted with one another. And so, when Alexei Alexandrovitch had been named Chief of the Secret Police, David had felt that at last God had justified his faith in the Russian government. Here was a man above bribery, above manipulation of any sort.

That night, at supper, Alexei Alexandrovitch was seated at Mathilde's right, and on his own right sat Johanna de Mey, resplendent in a mauve taffeta gown, daring in its ruffled bateau collar which displayed her long neck and collarbone usually covered by laces and jabots. Madame Lopukhin was ill, and had not come. The chandelier's refractions bounced off Johanna's golden hair, and Mathilde thought: What infinite style she has, my good, my dear friend. She herself wore a gown of ivory-colored silk, but with a more modest neckline than Johanna's. She sported a "dog collar," five rows of pearls wound tightly about her throat in the new fashion. With gentle amusement, David had compared her to an elegant poodle. The dinner was small, tinged with the intimacy of friendship and good food.

Johanna de Mey liked Alexei Alexandrovitch. She professed to be fascinated by his work, about which he was discreet. She teased him coyly: "There are rumors of disturbances, of arrests. Is the Tzar truly concerned?"

"My dear, I could be sent to Siberia for discussing matters of state. If the Tzar didn't, the Tzarina would, to punish me for being political in front of you ladies."

David smiled. "Come now, Johanna, Mathilde is firm about the subjects we are not permitted to approach at her table. Think of it this way: if Alexei were to suggest an after-dinner game of cards, would you not become offended, knowing that at the Gunzburgs no games of chance ever take place?"

"Yes, we all know of your austerity, my dear Baron," Johanna replied somewhat tartly. Then, ignoring him, she turned once again to the guest of honor. "But tell us simply this—who is stirring up the trouble?"

Alexei Alexandrovitch Lopukhin scratched his dark beard. "You need not be frightened, Johanna Ivanovna. Some students have formed *besedas*, informal conversation groups. They speak of Maxim Gorky, who has inflamed their hearts. We do not like this, but after all, they are merely young people, in the throes of their idealism. Once in a while, reprisals occur, and our police make an arrest. But these arrests are more to scare the youths than to punish them. We do not like secret organizations, especially organizations that believe the Tzar is guilty of mismanagement. But surely, he has nothing to fear from these young dreamers."

"But the young can be unruly, and need to be stopped before they start to do wrong. Do you not agree?" Johanna said.

"That is a precept for rearing children," Mathilde inserted with a smile.

"Perhaps. I am not in a position to pass judgment on what I am commanded to do," Lopukhin said.

David looked kindly at his friend. "For if you were, Alexei, you might be more indulgent. Is that not also a fact? Our young people are an impulsive lot. But hardly evil."

"The Baron sees innocence everywhere," Johanna commented.

But David merely shook his head and took a bite of poached salmon *en gelée*. The governess regarded him with her aquamarine eyes, and he caught the expression of brittle disdain which flashed over them. He thought: She truly detests me! and was amazed. Then, as he ate, he came to a second realization: She is the least ingenuous person I know. He wondered why he had never before seen the reptilian form of her slim body. A serpent in our garden.

But Mathilde was gazing lovingly at the golden-haired Dutchwoman, who had evidently finished a clever anecdote. "David and I have been so lucky," she was saying to their friend, "to be graced by Johanna. A true gem."

And hard as a diamond, David added in his thoughts. In the face of Mathilde's relaxed air, her tranquil joy, he had a searing realization: He was helpless in his own home, at his own table. "The Baron appears to have lost his appetite," Johanna de Mey remarked, with teasing concern.

"I intend to finish the last morsel," David stated. He smiled.

"Ivan Aronovitch is here to see you, Sofia Davidovna," Stepan announced after luncheon. Sonia was alone. Johanna had taken a tray into Mathilde's boudoir, for Mathilde was suffering from an acute attack of migraine. Anna had refused to eat, her eyes rimmed with red, and Ossip with his friend Volodia Tagantsev had taken his meal earlier, as usual. Sonia remembered the pounding in her temples when she had crossed the dining room and found Volodia at the table, peeling his apple. He had risen quickly, coloring, and extended his hand. "Good day, Sofia Davidovna," he had said brightly, shining his smile at her, and she had felt momentarily weak. Yet she had returned his greeting with cool composure. Afterward, she had shared her own meal with her father and brother Gino, but now Papa was being driven back to the city, to one of the Ministries, and Gino was taking his afternoon nap, burying himself surreptitiously in an adventure story.

"Me?" the girl repeated, with disbelief, and tucked a tendril of black hair behind her ear. She began to wonder. Ivan was Anna's special friend, and hardly knew her, Sonia. She liked him, for he was direct and frank, and made her sister's face glow. Anna's acute discomfort in the presence of others always seemed to fade when Ivan stayed to tea. He would tease Sonia, kindly, the way Ossip did. But still, they were not exactly friends. He was seven or eight years older, a law student. What business had he with her? And then she recalled her sister's ghastly appearance that day, her refusal to discuss anything, her silence in the face of gentle looks of inquiry. He has done something offensive, Sonia thought, and her little face stiffened. It is he who has caused Annushka to suffer. And now he is too cowardly to apologize to her directly.

Still, her good breeding made her go to the drawing room to greet him. He stood still, hatless, his blond hair falling into his green eyes, his black broadcloth suit creased and worn to a satiny finish. He had forgotten to button his jacket. She frowned at the ill-matched brown waistcoat. Her single objection to Ivan had always been his total lack of care in his personal appearance. She gave him her small white hand, which he gripped firmly. "Ivan Aronovitch," she greeted him simply.

She did not ask him to be seated, and he made no move to do so. His face appeared as haggard as her sister's, she observed. Suddenly she felt a pang of sympathy for him. "What is wrong?" she asked.

"You are very young," he said doubtfully. "I myself do not truly understand, and I shall not try to tangle you into it. Evidently, Anna has been frightened out of seeing me here, in your home. She did not explain. But I cannot accept this. I do not know to whom to turn, and so, because you are so kind, I am turning to you. I must see Anna. If she will not allow me to come here openly, then—"

"Surely you do not propose to see her in secret, unchaperoned?" Sonia cried.

Ivan smiled slightly. "Anna is my friend. I would like to talk to her. Tonight some other friends of mine, whom I have wanted her to meet, are gathering near here, on Vassilievsky Island. I shall send my carriage for her at nine o'clock this evening. If she wishes to come, let her meet me downstairs. I shall not be alone, Sofia Davidovna. There will be another young man, and another girl. I would not hurt your sister's reputation. Please believe me. I can read the shock in your eyes, but Anna is not a child anymore. There will be older people at the meeting, too—even a professor from the University. I am not suggesting anything improper. Do not worry. My scandalous sisters will certainly not be around, I assure you. They would find my friends too stuffy."

Sonia stood speechless before him. She gazed absently at the neat frills of her shirtwaist blouse, with its delicate bishop sleeves that belled out just above the cuff. Waves of blood flowed into her face. For an instant her embarrassment was so overwhelming that she could not breathe. Then, rearing her head up, she met his teasing green eyes with her fine gray ones. "If my sister has cut you off, then she must have good reasons," she said.

"Ah, you are a sweet child," Ivan countered. "Anna does not despise me. Would it upset you terribly to know that she loves me?"

"When decent people love each other, they meet openly and declare an engagement, if their parents do not disapprove," Sonia said hotly. "If Anna loved you, you would have spoken for her, instead of asking to meet her behind everyone's back. Love is sacred. My mother and father love each other. You are impudent, Ivan Aronovitch. I do not like you any longer, for you don't speak of my sister with respect."

"This is 1903, Sofia Davidovna," Ivan said softly. "This may surprise you even more, but I would never speak to Baron David Goratsievitch without first having obtained Anna's permission. That is because I do respect her. I respect her judgment. It is not up to your father whether or not Anna should marry; it is, I think, only up to Anna. I would never love a woman who allowed conventions to rule her decisions. I would love only someone capable of knowing her own mind. I have come to love your sister, because she is strong and sometimes stubborn and rebellious. My own sisters want to be carried off on white stallions, and to spend the rest of their lives giving parties and balls and suppers, and ordering gowns from Poiret and Worth. Anna is unique and I will not give her up so easily. I want her to see me. She deserves to make her own decision about tonight. You must give her this opportunity. I could have sent one of our servants, or given Marfa a message—but servants talk. You are loyal, and devoted to your sister. Do her this favor. I can promise you—I shall never tarnish that proud spirit of hers, for it is far too dear to me. Beyond that, my conscience will guide me."

Sonia's thoughts were spinning: If I turn him away, what will become of Anna? If he were to hurt her, Papa would ruin his father. Ivan would not risk that. He must truly love her. But she knew that she herself could not be a part of this . . . this *assignation*. She raised her eyes and encountered Ivan's pleading ones. A fleeting image crossed her mind: Volodia, this noon, peeling his apple. "I shall give Anna your message," she said.

Ivan Berson reached for her hand and impulsively brought it to his lips. "Thank you, little one," he said. Then, unable to meet her eyes, he turned on his heel and disappeared. Sonia, angry, watched him depart, and then she too turned away. She walked briskly to the corridor which led to the room she shared with Anna. If she were to tell Anna she must do it now, before her sense of honor returned in full force. She felt a surge of hatred well up within her for Ivan Berson. He had compromised her self-respect by involving her in this dreadful thing.

Suddenly, she realized that if her sister were afraid to receive Ivan in this house, it must be, it had to be, because of Juanita. She opened the bedroom door resolutely, grimly recalling Nina Tobias and her own conflict with the governess. After all, she told her worried conscience, Ivan and Anna were merely good friends, as she and Nina were. If there were more to it, Sonia felt confident that Anna, the pure, the just, would ask her friend to speak to their father. Her sister might not love society, but she did possess regard for her family and her own good name.

Johanna de Mey, whose sixth sense always reached out, like a tentacle, to those emotions which, in others, were momentarily out of kilter, felt a keen excitement at supper that evening. Her large slanted eyes moved from person to person, dismissing Mathilde first, for her friend was pale and still struggling with the after effects of her headache; then glossing over Gino, whose ruddy face displayed only enjoyment of his food; passing by Baron David, who was speaking of his meeting that afternoon with a friend of the family, and finally encountering Ossip's deep blue eyes. He was smiling slightly to himself as if he too had caught something in the air, but like Johanna, was uncertain what it was. She looked at Sonia. The girl was terribly white, and her small round mouth was bloodless. She was looking only at her plate, though occasionally, the Dutchwoman observed, she would steal a glance of pure pain at her mother and father. When she raised her gray eyes to her sister, she winced. Had these two argued? No, Johanna had heard no angry voices from the girls' room. Anna sat hunched over her food, her eyes abstracted, thin lines around her lips. Her face flushed when Sonia's bright eyes encountered hers, but that was all. Johanna bit lustily into the succulent lamb. "What a marvelous meal, my dear," she said to Mathilde. "Cook must be congratulated."

When supper was over, Johanna de Mey allowed Mathilde to be whisked to her room by a concerned David, who had expected to be followed by his wife's friend. To his relief, the governess merely touched Mathilde's arm with solicitude, and bade him a very agreeable good night. Then, she packed Gino hurriedly into his bed, and watched Ossip enter his father's study, where he always did his homework. She went into her own chamber but left the door ajar, listening . . .

Anna was sitting on her bed, lacing her sealskin boots with a buttonhook. Suddenly Sonia said, "You are really going?" Her heart was in her trembling voice, full of supplication. Anna rose, and her thick wool skirts fell to her ankles. She looked around, past Sonia's eyes, and saw her cape, lined with dark fur. She threw it over her shoulders with a wild motion. "Yes," she replied. Her brown eyes, shooting sparks of fire, flew to her sister's. "Do not be angry with me," she added.

Sonia ran to her and wrapped her arms about Anna's caped body. "I love you, 'Nushka," she cried. "Be careful." Then she released the older girl, who opened the door and peered quickly up and down the corridor. Gay laughter echoed thinly from the kitchen quarters, but that was all. Anna slipped noiselessly out of the room and made her way toward the vestibule. Stepan was eating his own supper with the servants. She opened the wide front door and shut it soundlessly behind her. Sonia had remained by her own bedroom door, her ear cocked for anything unexpected. Tension gripped every muscle in her small body, and she remained behind the door like a rigid guard.

It was not long before her vigil was rewarded. Suddenly, Johanna appeared, fully clothed for the outdoors, and made a dash for the stairs. On tiptoes, her heart in her throat, Sonia followed her. If Johanna had seen Anna, then why had she not cried out to her, stopped her then and there? Something terrible was going to happen, Sonia knew. In her slippers, she followed the governess until Johanna disappeared out the front door, moments after Anna.

Sonia rushed to the drawing room windows. The street was dark under a clouded moon. She saw a carriage pull away, and then, to her amazement, she watched as the slender figure that was Johanna sprang into the coachman's seat of the Baron's victoria, which had not yet been put away for the night. The victoria took off after the first carriage. Sonia stood by the large bay window, her mouth open. Pure agony shot through her, and she bent over, grasping her stomach with pain. My God, my God! she thought, Juanita is going to expose Anna in front of Ivan and his friends. Her sister would be dishonored forever in St. Petersburg. But Sonia could not move, for there was nothing she could do to come to Anna's aid.

Slowly, she pulled herself up and returned to her room,

where she tossed herself upon her bed, her heart pounding erratically. Minutes passed. She dared not think, but she bit her lower lip so violently that it began to bleed. Then, she heard the front door open. She threw ajar her own door just in time to see Johanna darting by. Several moments later, the governess reappeared, magnificent in a silken dressing gown, her hair undone and flowing down her back. Sonia was bewildered. Where was Anna? What had been the point of this chase in the bitter cold winter night, if not to bring home a humiliated Anna? Once again, she slipped out of her room and followed the governess.

Johanna was in the hallway between the drawing and dining rooms, under a small light which flickered over a tiny rosewood stand upon which rested a new contraption, the telephone, of which David was so very proud. Sonia watched in mounting dismay as Johanna flipped through the pages of a leather notebook. The Dutchwoman picked up the receiver and spoke softly, asking for a number. There was something dreadfully familiar about this number, Sonia thought, but her mind could not connect it. It did not belong to her Grandfather Horace, nor to her Uncle Sasha. Then to whom would Juanita be speaking?

When she heard the governess speak, she was seized with ghastly awareness. Johanna's well-modulated, crisp inflections were gone. Sonia listened, astounded as the elegant blond woman addressed the receiver in nasal tones, with a distinct Yiddish intonation reminiscent of so many of the pleaders who came to visit David in the mornings. She was saying, "Tell Alexei Alexandrovitch that there is a *beseda* at the address I have just given you, on Vassilievsky Island. Never mind who I am. I am a friend of the Tzar. I tell you, I am certain that this meeting is more than simple talk. Plots and plans. The Tzar does not like for his people to plot and plan." And then, rapidly, she put down the instrument and closed the leather notebook. Her oval face, under the small flickering lamp, appeared to glow.

She did not see Sonia crouching in the dark, for she was

concentrating upon her remarkable coup as she walked back to her own bedroom with a slow, gliding step. But the girl had heard the entire conversation. A violent nausea overpowered her so that, for a few minutes, she had to hold her head between her legs until her vision cleared. She trembled, chilled, and tears streamed down her cheeks. Alexei Alexandrovitch Lopukhin, the Chief of the Secret Police. Juanita had set him after Anna, her sister, and Ivan Berson. Sonia could not believe what she had witnessed. Surely, surely Juanita had not meant to bring Anna to harm, to have her jailed. She, Sonia, must have mistaken her intentions. For no one could hate someone that much, especially not Anna, the innocent. She wanted to cry out, to rush into her parents' bedroom and explain—but no, she could not, for that would be compromising Anna, too.

All at once, in her desperation, Sonia seized upon the one person who might come to Anna's rescue. Blinded by tears, she ran to the servants' quarters where stupefied faces looked up from the kitchen table into her own. She saw only Stepan, who rose and came to her, bending his tall, elegant form to take her hands into his, concern overriding the fact that she was his young mistress. "You must drive me to a certain address," she sobbed, "and you must do it now, without a word to my parents or Johanna Ivanovna. It is a matter of the utmost importance. We must go to my sister."

"But Sofia Davidovna, surely Vova will drive you?" the maître d'hôtel said gently.

She threw him off, shaking her head wildly. "No! It must be you. I know that you are not a coachman, but I can trust you, Stepan. Only you. And right away, please!" She took his hand, and began to pull at him like a small child tugging at its mother. He dropped his dinner napkin to the floor, and followed her, leaving bewilderment in his wake. Suddenly he turned to the assembled servants: "You have heard the young Baroness," he said harshly. "Not one word out of you."

In haste and silence Sonia allowed Stepan to wrap her in several layers of servants' coats. Her eyes continued to brim with tears, but her sobbing had ceased. Stepan took her in his arms and carried her into the waiting victoria. One horse, tired of unexpected nocturnal rides, neighed into the darkness. Stepan jumped onto the coachman's seat and cracked the whip. The carriage began to roll. Whatever thoughts coursed through the mind of the maître d'hôtel, he did not voice them even to the wind.

Stepan stopped the carriage in front of a neat three-story building. Lights glimmered from the large windows on the top floor. When Sonia emerged from the carriage, she had no idea what part of the island she had reached. She looked at Stepan and thought briefly that if he came upstairs with her, he would find Anna with Ivan Aronovitch Berson, and that would not do. For no matter how devoted he was to the Gunzburgs and to Anna himself, Anna would be unable to face him if he had seen too much. "I shall go alone," she said to him.

Her black hair disheveled, her eyes red-rimmed, wrapped in bundles of thick servants' clothes, Sonia opened the large door which led to the main staircase of the apartment house. She walked up the steep steps until she reached the third landing, and could hear the sounds of gaiety inside. Young voices laughed, someone was singing in a languid gypsy voice. She stood on the threshold, trembling with fear and cold. Then, resolutely, she knocked. Her small white knuckles rapped hard upon the oak door, harder and harder until finally it swung on its hinges and a blast of heat almost toppled her. A bearded man in his mid-thirties, with a glass of vodka in one hand and a thick sheaf of papers in the other, stood facing her, grinning widely. "What have we here?" His voice was merry. "A babe in arms?"

Suddenly, there were many people near the door, peering at her. Girls in woolen gowns, their hair gold and black and auburn, men who had evidently removed their frock coats in the stuffy room. Cigarette smoke assailed her nostrils and made her gag. "I have come for my sister," she whispered, and then, gaining strength, her gray eyes meeting those of the bearded man with all the Gunzburg hauteur, "Please take me to Anna Davidovna de Gunzburg. It is urgent."

Someone's arms were about her. She heard Anna's voice and could feel Anna's hands upon her hair. "Sonitchka, Sonitchka, what has happened? Why are you not in bed, at home? How did you know where I was?"

She blurted out: "Juanita knows. She telephoned Alexei Alexandrovitch. The police will be here any moment. Nobody knows I came, only the servants. Stepan is waiting downstairs, with the carriage—"

But all at once she was roughly pushed away from Anna, and she saw a group of men enter the apartment. One of them said: "In the name of the Tzar, we arrest you for conspiring against the government. Stand against the wall, all of you. Pull out identification papers."

She cried out, her voice shrill with fear: "No!" One of the men approached her, and her heart leaped into her throat. "A child!" he said. He looked her up and down in her bundles of clothing, and Sonia's mind began to reel, recalling the episode with Count Tuminsky's men at Mohilna when she had been five and the overseer had not believed that she and Anna were Gunzburgs. "We are Gunzburgs," she murmured, almost inaudibly. "We are the daughters of Baron David de Gunzburg. Our grandfather is Baron Horace."

"It is true," a cultured voice asserted behind her. She recognized familiar tones, but could not place them. The horror of the overheated room, of finding Anna with these men and women, of the Secret Police appearing on the premises, was making her ill. The room, the people began to twirl about her head, like dancing dervishes, until she turned away and vomited. Strong hands were on her shoulders. The cultured voice was speaking. "It's all right, Sonia. I'm going to take you home, and Anna too. I don't want to hear any explanations, except that this was a mistake." As her eyes began to focus, she made out the features of her father's friend, Alexei Alexandrovitch Lopukhin.

"I am not going home, if you are going to arrest these people," Anna said in crisp tones.

"Stepan is downstairs, waiting," Sonia said, not understanding.

"I have seen him." Lopukhin's voice was stern. "I have also sent him back. I shall take you girls home, right now."

"No." Anna's eyes combed the room and rested with expressive longing upon a young man pressed against a far wall. "I did not come alone, and I shall not flee like a coward. Please, Alexei Alexandrovitch, take my sister home."

The Chief of the Secret Police followed her look, then addressed one of his men. "This is a fine mess, indeed," he said. "There, in back, with the mop of yellow hair: the son of Aron Berson, the banker. Bring him here, Popov."

"If you arrest Vanya, you must take me, too," Anna remarked calmly.

"Do not be a fool, Anna Davidovna," Lopukhin replied. "Your father is one of my dearest friends. He is in business with Berson. We shall not arrest either one of you. There are ways of stifling the entire matter. The rest will spend a night or two in jail, and then will be let go. No one will ever know about your presence here—or for that matter, of the involvement of your young friend. He will go home, and I shall find a story to tell your parents about the two of you wandering around unchaperoned in the streets of Vassilievsky. But do not push me to the brink with your foolishness, Anna Davidovna. I have no time for that."

Sonia opened her mouth, but no sound emerged. Pinpoints of painful red light erupted upon her field of vision, and she fell forward. She thought that she had uttered a loud, strident shriek, but nobody heard her. She had fainted in the arms of Alexei Alexandrovitch Lopukhin.

While the doctor gave Sonia an injection and put her to bed, David de Gunzburg sat in front of his haggard older daughter, his friend Lopukhin, and his maître d'hôtel. It was four in the morning. "You know that I do not believe you, any of you," he said. "What kind of story is this, that Anna felt restless and asked Stepan to drive her around to gaze at the stars, in the middle of a subzero St. Petersburg winter? Where was Vova? In all my years I have never heard such a pack of obvious lies. Anna is not crazy, and neither is Stepan. And then the rest! You would have me believe, Alexei—you, a man of responsibility—that Sonia, my thirteen-year-old, was so concerned about her sister's disappearance from their room that instead of coming to me, or her mother, or one of our other servants, she telephoned you in the middle of the night, and that you found her shivering downstairs, searching for Anna? Am I dreaming?"

"We ask you to believe us, Baron," Stepan said with the utmost respect. "I know that I deserve to be dismissed on the spot for allowing Anna Davidovna to talk me into such foolishness."

"But you will not dismiss Stepan, will you, Papa?" Anna pleaded. "He knew that I was upset, that I had not been sleeping well these past few nights. If I had asked Vova, he would have refused. I was at fault, asking Stepan, who is so devoted . . ."

"So devoted that he is willing to risk his position to swear to a pack of lies." David was trembling with rage. "I shall not tell Mathilde. And you, Alexei, I know that if you are involved, a catastrophe must have been narrowly averted. I thank you. What else can I do? I have no conception of what is going on, of what we have escaped. Only that I am in your debt. And Stepan—there is a purse of gold on that table. It is for you. See to it that you don't usurp the place of my coachman again! My daughter—my two daughters—have lied to me. Yet I cannot disprove them. Sonia is terribly ill. The doctor fears pneumonia. Whatever else has occurred tonight, this is of uppermost concern. Pneumonia! That is sufficient worry for her mother. Alexei—"

The Baron opened his arms, and his friend embraced him. Lopukhin felt the hot tears that had welled from David's eyes, and he released him. "Go," he said gently, "go to Sonia. She needs you. And you need to be with her. She is a valiant little lass."

Anna placed an arm about her father, and in her face the Baron read pain and anguish beyond words. Together they entered the corridor. They were met by the doctor and Johanna de Mey in her silk dressing gown. "She will be all right, I think," the physician said. "Mathilde Yureyevna is with her now. Do not stay too long, or she will hear you and awaken. She is half delirious. Let her ramble, it does no harm."

Johanna de Mey's steel-like gaze encountered Anna's brown eyes. "Have you made heads or tails out of what she is saying in her sleep, Juanita?" the girl asked. Her father felt her body stiffen as she held him, and he heard the sharp, contained hatred in the girl's words.

"You have heard the doctor: she is delirious," the Dutchwoman replied. For a brief instant, David saw a flash of fear pass over her features. He cleared his throat. "Anna," he said distinctly, "the next time you cannot sleep, do not ask Stepan to show you the moonlight. We are extremely lucky that only one of our girls has fallen ill. These are not the tropics, my child."

"Your father speaks sense," the governess said. Once again, her almond-shaped eyes bored into Anna's.

"My father always speaks sense," Anna replied. She began to walk again, holding David, in the direction of her room where Sonia lay.

Six

In Russia, the height of the social season was always the winter months. But this November of 1904, Sonia was midway between her fourteenth and fifteenth birthdays, too young to participate in the swirl of events which rendered giddy those young girls who made their debut at the age of seventeen; and Anna, who was nineteen, had no interest in masked balls and soirées at the theater. For war with Japan had erupted in February, and the Russians had taken tremendous losses.

While Mathilde and Johanna de Mey organized their social calendar, David and his two older children watched the war unfold from afar. Ossip was fascinated by the scene of the drama, the Far East. David had a friend, a Russian Jew, who had made his fortune in the production of coal in Japan. His name was Moise Mess, and early on Ossip had begun asking questions about this man. When war broke out, Mess had transferred his enterprise to Port Arthur as David had predicted. There, he was able to come to the rescue of the Russian navy, which had calculated the amount of coal necessary to get their ships to the Far East, and neatly forgotten that a return voyage would have to be undertaken. But Moise Mess salvaged the situation by putting his own coal at the disposal of his countrymen. David was deeply distressed by the government's mistakes; but for Ossip, the war meant only an intriguing game, in which he chose to involve himself as one does in a chess tournament. Besides, he wanted to make certain that his own plans to one day travel to the East would not be ruined by the present situation. And he admired Moise Mess, whom he considered a true adventurer à la Marco Polo.

Anna, however, was concerned with the war's effect upon the Russian people. She continued to meet Ivan Berson and his friends, with whom she found she could speak freely. But she was more careful now. She always made sure to be accompanied openly by one of the University girls, and to return at a decent hour. "You see, Anna can make friends," her mother would say, smiling. Her smiles were somewhat forced. Anna's friends were plainly clothed and never came to tea to chat with normal girlish relish. Still, she would think, they are young girls her own age, and if they attend the University, they are certainly not stupid.

"Women scholars are either terribly rich and terribly eccentric, or of modest means and in search of a suitable profession," Johanna had told her. Uncertain which category best described Anna's female companions, Mathilde said nothing. She had never forgotten Anna's words to her about marriage, and although she did not see Ivan Berson any longer in her house, she wondered at times if her daughter had truly put him out of her mind. And if so, whether that was a good sign, or whether it meant that Anna had shunted aside the one man who might have made her his wife.

The Russian defeats had done nothing to strengthen the faith of the people in their government. To David's shock, a group of professional, liberal men, many of whom were known to him personally, formed the first union in the country, calling it the Union of Unions. Men of letters came to him, wanting to know what he thought, if he would join them. And Anna, almost beautiful with her ardent, passionate look, waited by his side for his answer. "It is too soon," he said. "The Tzar will grant us a constitution. I have faith in his vision for his people." That night Anna cried herself bitterly to sleep.

But Sonia was too young to understand, and her mother, Mathilde, kept her well sheltered. Then an invitation came which, Mathilde thought, could not have arrived at a better moment. For with Anna and David silently at odds, with Ossip's unhealthy interest in this war, and with the dreadful cold of winter which made Mathilde remember Sonia's pneumonia of the previous year, a time away from the capital would provide Sonia with proper distraction.

The invitation was from Kiev, which had, centuries before, been the capital of Russia. It was still called the Mother City of all the Russias, and it was the center of the prosperous manufacturing of sugar from beets. Years ago, David's grandfather, Grigori Rosenberg, had been the most important sugar producer of Kiev, but now another family, the Brodskys, had surpassed Grigori's descendants, and were the foremost Jews of the area. David and Sasha had a younger brother, Mikhail, Misha to his intimates, who had married one of the Brodsky heiresses and taken over the management of her father's sugar factories. It was Clara, Misha de Gunzburg's young wife, who was inviting Sonia to spend the New Year with them in Kiev.

Misha de Gunzburg was seventeen years younger than David. In 1904 he was barely thirty, and his wife, Clara, twenty-four. He was the golden boy of Horace's sons, handsome and light where Sasha was dark and somewhat primeval. He had obtained a degree from the University of St. Petersburg in the Faculty of Mathematics, and had not known what to do with himself, until he had met Clara Lazarevna Brodsky. She, too, had been gifted in mathematics, and could play the piano more than adequately while Misha sang. But he had married her because of her colossal dowry, and because her father wanted him to supervise his sugar factories. For Clara was tall and thin, and in spite of the finery she affected, was nothing short of ugly.

Misha de Gunzburg had built a magnificent town house in Kiev. One entered his home through a large hallway, two stories high, and topped by a panel of glass. Adjacent to this hall, and equally tall, were a study and a dining room, and farther back, behind the staircase, a vast drawing room. The bedrooms and guest apartments were off a gallery that circled the hall on three sides, as a balcony at a theater. Throughout this mansion were strewn ancient Persian carpets, and on the walls hung paintings by the Old Masters. Misha had selected everything, while Clara, openmouthed and filled with love, had simply watched. Her husband, a Russian and German baron, had ordered their china from England, and unlike Sasha's and David's, which was ornamented with a coronet of seven pearls as befitted barons of the German states, his bore the French coronet of four pearls—to which he was not entitled. But so fine was this china that if a demitasse were laid upon a marble table without first being placed upon a saucer, it would shatter at once.

Mathilde liked her cousin Misha, of whom she had grown fond during the early years of her marriage, when David had first brought her to his father's house in St. Petersburg. Misha was ten years younger than she, and she had watched him grow. Unlike Sasha, Misha loved beauty for its own sake, and if he had made a marriage of convenience, he had done so without malice, but with the simple ease that characterized all his gestures and deeds. He was genuinely fond of Clara, and most discreet in his choice of mistresses. Certainly his cousin and sister-in-law, Mathilde, was not aware of them. He was not a snob like Sasha. He enjoyed his life, and indeed had no need to improve his position: for with his father's name and title, with his father-in-law's business, and with his own charm and good looks, he was unrivaled in Kiev society.

Rosa de Gunzburg, when she heard of Clara's invitation to her niece Sonia, became hysterical. Facing Mathilde with fury and clenching her small brown fists against her temples where the curling irons had been busy making fine tendrils, she cried out, "But this cannot be borne! What does she mean, that upstart, that provincial nobody, excluding Tania? Why only Sonia? Tania would delight all of Kiev, and Misha would love her. I shall write to Clara, and tell her of my indignation, and of my hurt. Tania is her niece also, and deserves equal treatment. And," she added irrelevantly, "Kiev is farther removed from this horrid war, too."

"I doubt very much, Rosinka, that Japan shall invade our capital tomorrow," Mathilde replied, a half-smile playing over her full lips. But her sister-in-law merely regarded her with a malevolent expression.

The upshot of the matter was that Tania, now nearly thirteen, was bundled off to Kiev for the holidays, along with her cousin Sonia. Both girls were diminutive, but Sonia was slimmer, more delicate, with milk-white porcelain hands and an oval face surrounded by thick dark hair which she wore parted in the center and held up by two ivory combs with pearl studs.

Tania was already endowed with feminine curves, more pronounced than Sonia's. She sported a tiny waist, a small, plump bosom, and magnificent golden curls which she wore gathered at the neck in sausage loops. Her eyes were a periwinkle blue, and twinkled constantly. She ate lustily, and did not gain weight, and when she spoke her curls danced about her. She found Sonia too quiet, and Sonia found her too self-centered. Indeed, although her precocious ways had made her a favorite at her mother's teas, Tania de Gunzburg was not much appreciated by her cousins on Vassilievsky Island.

Marfa, the little maid who served Anna and Sonia, accompanied the two girls to Kiev in a private compartment which had been reserved for them. The conductor had been well paid to take special care of the young Baronesses, and he acquitted himself admirably. Kiev was only one day's travel from Mohilna, and thus, much of the countryside was familiar to Sonia. But the gentleman who met them at the terminal at Kiev was a complete stranger. Had he not possessed thick black hair and blue-gray eyes set close together, and had Misha's coachman not been next to him awaiting the guests, the two girls and Marfa would not have looked at him a second time. But Tania, placing her plump little hand to her lips, cried out: "That young man! He resembles Papa, and our grandfather! And even Aunt Mathilde . . ."

The young man was twenty, tall and elegant in gray broadcloth and fine silk shirt. He greeted the girls with a charming smile. "I do not know which of you is Sonia, and which one Tania," he stated, "but then again, you do not know me, either. I am your cousin, Jean de Gunzburg, and I too am a guest at Clara and Misha's. I have recently come from Paris."

"Jean? But how can you be our cousin?" Tania demanded, archly raising her brows. "Whose son are you?"

"I am Solomon's son." Solomon, Barons Horace and Yuri's youngest brother, had died years before, the girls knew. "So," Jean continued, "I am only your second cousin." He looked pleased with his explanation. "This is my first trip to Russia," he said, "but long ago, when you were in Paris, you visited my mother. I was a small boy, and you were both babies. We probably ignored one another." He smiled brightly and Tania opened her mouth to reveal her tiny well-formed teeth and proceeded to seat herself next to the handsome French cousin in Uncle Misha's carriage.

Sonia said softly; "Yes, I remember Aunt Henriette. She is one of the most beautiful women I have ever seen. I shall never forget her."

"I do not remember her at all," Tania said regretfully, gazing deeply into the face of Jean de Gunzburg. She remembered quite well, however, the tales her mother had told her about the infamous Henriette de Gunzburg, and she could not repress a giggle. Jean stared at her, wrinkling his brow. Henriette, it was whispered, had had a scandalous number of lovers, including—and here, voices always lowered and eyebrows raised—King Edward VII when he had still been the Prince of Wales. (People still suspected Jean's younger brother of having been fathered by Queen Victoria's heir.) When Solomon committed suicide it was generally agreed that his wife's amours were the cause of this dreadful tragedy. Tania now regarded the Frenchman with her full blue gaze, and dimpled at him. How terribly exciting. Mama would simply have *expired* to know that Aunt Henriette's son was a guest at Uncle Misha's.

But Sonia was smiling her pure, fresh smile, for she did not know anything of the family scandal. Mathilde and David had been most careful to refrain from any mention of it in her presence. But Tania had overheard much, and read her mother's yellow-backed romances in secret. Tania knew what a mistress was.

Clara and Misha greeted their nieces effusively and settled them into adjoining rooms. Sonia was delighted by the mansion and by her Uncle Misha and cousin Jean. When the two men were together, one so dark, the other so blond, it hardly appeared that ten years separated them. It was strange, Sonia realized with a start, that she and her Aunt Clara were also a mere ten years apart. She thought with compassion of this ugly young aunt who had been sheltered all her life, and who, in spite of her father's tremendous fortune, had traveled little and received so few social graces. Clara was shy, and reminded Sonia somewhat of Anna, for in her shyness she was abrupt. But as the wife of Mikhail de Gunzburg, who possessed the most sumptuous townhouse in the city, her social duties were ceaseless. They must weigh heavily upon her, Sonia thought.

During the first week of the girls' stay it became clear that Jean had not come to Russia merely to visit relatives and amuse himself. Long ago, when the first Ossip, great-grandfather to Sonia and Tania, had established himself in Paris, he had told his children that under no circumstances would he tolerate their becoming French citizens. He had purchased a great number of military exemptions for his children and grandchildren, for only the oldest or only sons in Russian families were exempt from military service. David, Sonia's father, had chosen to serve in the Uhlans at Lomzha, as had Sasha, Tania's father. But Misha had taken advantage of one of the family exemptions to escape bearing arms. For Jean, who had been raised in France, and who did not even speak Russian, there had never been the slightest question as to whether or not he should serve in a Russian regiment. But he was a second son. He had searched through his dead father's papers for the needed exemption notice, but he had found nothing. In terror, he had gone to his Uncle Yuri, and to other relatives, but no one could help him. And so, in desperation, he decided, before his twenty-first birthday, to come to Russia to learn its language. In that way, when the time came the following year, he would be able to do his duty.

Jean spent much time poring over textbooks of Russian grammar and vocabulary, for he had found to his dismay that the upper classes whom he frequented spoke French among themselves. Sonia and Tania would keep him company, helping him rehearse his verb forms. Sometimes Tania would bounce upon his knee, like an overgrown child, and Sonia, scandalized, would pull her down. But Jean would only laugh.

There were many gay events at the Mikhail de Gunzburg mansion. Young people came to meet Clara and Misha's nieces. Many of Clara's relations came, and some members of the sugar industry, with their offspring. One evening, the Zlatopolsky family came to supper, and Sonia was placed at the table between Shoshana, the daughter, a large girl slightly her elder, and her brother, Mossia. He was not a handsome youth, but even though he was not yet fifteen, Sonia's own age, she found him compelling to look at. He was very tall, very well built, and had the square face of a lion, with green-tinted blue eyes and strong features. He did not resemble his parents in the least, for his father was a small distinguished man with a Vandyke beard, and his mother, less elegant, was also quite short. Where had Mossia and Shoshana acquired their largeness, attractive in the boy but quite ungraceful in his sister?

Sonia considered Mossia Zlatopolsky brilliant. That year, he was to take his entrance exams for the University of Moscow. His father had begun as a small sugar manufacturer, and was now almost as wealthy as Uncle Misha and Aunt Clara's father. "I am starting to learn my father's business," Mossia said, and Sonia thought: How extraordinary, when Ossip still has more than two years of gymnasium left! But, as though sensing her wonder, Mossia laughed, a frank, hardy chuckle. "I am a quick learner," he confessed, "but if I am in a hurry, it's because I am hungry. I want to experience life, to work with Papa, to dance, to sing, to travel. I cannot do these things if I am trapped in school." Listening to him, Sonia felt momentarily frightened of the big leonine face, on which lust for the world had appeared. How unlike Ossip, her beautiful brother, who watched the world go by for fear of being crushed to death in its embrace. The boy would risk everything for a breath of new, fresh air.

But his sister, Shoshana, was not gay and lusty. She sat stiffly, and answered Sonia's query as to her unusual name with quick haughtiness: "You may know that 'Shoshana' means 'rose' in Hebrew," she said. "I was born Rosa, but I have changed my name."

Sonia, blushing, asked, "But your parents? Were they not hurt when you did that?"

Shoshana merely shrugged. "Papa was very proud," she said. "He is an ardent Zionist, and has been purchasing land in Palestine on behalf of several active Jewish groups. Someday, all the Jews of Russia and other oppressive nations will once again possess a home."

"But my father says that we must struggle to attain full citizenship here, in Russia. He says that Russia is our *home*, and that Judaism is our *faith*." Sonia regarded Shoshana with her gray eyes, unafraid of the other's domineering attitude.

"I have heard of your father, the famous Baron David," Shoshana said, and suddenly Sonia felt chilled. "He is a *shtadlan*." Shoshana spoke this as though she were spitting out an insult.

"You must not mind my sister," Mossia said at once, seeing the younger girl turn very pale, and her eyes fill with outraged tears. "You see, she has recently undergone a dreadful experience. She used to attend one of the best schools for young ladies, here in Kiev. One day, she had an argument with a friend. The girl turned on her and called her a 'dirty Jew.' Shoshana slapped her, and was dismissed from the school."

Sonia was appalled. "But that girl was in the wrong!" she cried.

"The Jew in Russia is always in the wrong," Shoshana said tersely.

After that, Sonia found it very difficult to enjoy her supper. She wanted to cry, and to return to the warmth of her father's arms in St. Petersburg. Never before had she thought that his own people, other Jews, would turn against Baron David and what he stood for the way Shoshana had. Her wonderful father, who worked so hard for the Jews! A bitter hatred came into her young heart for Shoshana Zlatopolskaya.

After coffee, the young people retired to a corner of the drawing room to play games. Jean, though somewhat old to join in, was good-humored enough to allow his little cousin Tania to drag him boldly by the hand into the circle. They began by pushing the delicate furniture against the walls. First came a boisterous blind man's bluff. Then, laughing, panting, they sat down upon Misha's ancient carpet and started a series of word games. "We shall do something novel, for the sake of Jean!" Tania announced brightly. "We shall play this game in Russian, instead of French!" And she threw a knotted handkerchief into the circle, calling out a syllable. The handkerchief fell closest to Jean, who closed his eyes with effort and then added a second syllable, so that a word had been formed. The group applauded. He threw the handkerchief toward Sonia, and called out a new syllable, for her to complete. When several more of these games had been played, it was Tania once again who made a suggestion: "We shall play charades, in Russian!" she cried, her golden hair cascading down her back, her small breasts bouncing saucily. After that, Clara brought in the tea table, laden with cakes and biscuits. It was Tania, naturally, who devoured the most, without a wince of heartburn. And then it was she who ran to her Uncle Misha, and who threw her small round arms about his neck and begged, "Please, let us roll up the carpet, and allow Sonia to sit at the piano so that we can dance!"

"No, my love, that would not be fair," her uncle said. "Your aunt shall play. I shall dance with Sonitchka." Misha had seen Sonia's look of loneliness and desolation during supper, and his heart had been moved.

"I am not jealous," Tania said pertly. "Sonia may have you, but I shall have Jean!"

She did not see the look of amusement which passed between her uncle and her French cousin. She was too busy tossing her curls and showing off her perfect white teeth.

The crowd had gathered in the small, gritty square in the center of Kiev's poorest neighborhood, where the streets were unpaved and haphazardly strewn with uneven planks of wood from which brown slush oozed. Men in tattered clothing, their faces red and perspiring in spite of the winter ice, were muttering shouts in response to the thin young man who had hoisted himself upon an overturned beer keg.

A man shouted, "The Tzar says he is our little Father. But he is killing off our brothers and making their wives starve, that's what he's doing to take care of us!" Women with babies in their arms were wailing, their hands balled into fists. "Where is my Petrushka?" one cried. "He is dead in a faraway land that does not concern him, and his children are orphans!"

The thin man on the beer keg waved back their angry words. His voice, high and shrill, penetrated through the thickening mob like a sliver of thin steel into a fat man's gut. "It is not the Tzar who should be blamed, my friends," he spat. "It is the Jews. The sugar barons who refuse us employment, the ones who live in their fine houses with their well-bred servants and their sleek carriages. It is the Jew who has infested our country with problems, who is bleeding us all to death. Brothers and sisters, shall we allow the heathen pigs to suck our nation dry? Or are we going to fight back, to give them a piece of what is coming to them, the arrogant bastards!"

Slowly, one red face turned to another. A murmur spread through the crowd and swelled. Fists were raised. Somebody entered a hovel nearby and returned with a knife, another made a hasty exit and brought back the sturdy leg of an old chair. "Yes, yes, the Jews!" The cry was taken up. The thin man smiled. "This way, my friends!" he called out, swinging his arm toward a hill behind him.

Then, as hundreds of feet began to move, he slipped down from his perch and ducked into an alley. He was met by a well-dressed man waiting with a small buggy. "Get in," the man said. "You have done good work and shall be well rewarded by the governor."

Tea had just been served in Mikhail de Gunzburg's drawing room. Misha was seated on a Louis XV sofa with his French cousin, Jean, at his side. Clara was pouring amber liquid into fine crystal goblets, and the two girls, Sonia and Tania, were adding slices of lemon and sugar cubes as they were requested by their elders. Suddenly the maître d'hôtel entered the room, his hair disheveled and his black frock coat unbuttoned. Clara's mouth opened in silence, and the man cried, "Baron! Baroness! There is a mob on its way, and word has spread of a pogrom—"

Misha rose instantly. "Pogrom? But no one would come here! After all, we are friends with the police, we are known to all in power—"

"We must act with haste, honored Baron. The servants await your orders."

Clara finally succeeded in uttering a wail, and fell back upon her pillows. Sonia and Tania huddled together, their faces white. Then Misha, running an absent hand through his fine golden hair, exclaimed; "Have the back doors unlocked. Clara, get your case of jewels from the safe. We are going to go over the hedge to the British Consulate. Lord Latimer is a friend, he will grant us asylum. But move at once, and take nothing unnecessary. We must hurry."

In the moments that followed, Sonia's mind did not have time to sort anything out. She squeezed Tania's hand, for the younger girl had begun to shriek. The maître d'hôtel pushed the two girls unceremoniously to the servants' wing, where Marfa joined them, holding two small purses in which each girl kept several gems of value. Running out the kitchen doors, Sonia could hear shouting coming closer to the house, and her heart nearly failed her. But she strengthened her grip upon Tania's hand, dragging the other girl almost bodily behind her. They were in the garden. Their Aunt Clara, looking more gaunt and sallow than ever, stood huddled by a ladder which the maître d'hôtel was clumsily pushing against the wall that separated the Gunzburg property from the British Consulate. A roar could be heard from the street. Misha ran out, holding one small painting by Vermeer and a small case. "Where the devil is Jean?" he demanded.

"I shall find him, honored Baron," the maître d'hôtel replied. "But the ladies must go over this instant." He gave his hand to his mistress, who struggled onto the ladder. Sonia followed and Misha came behind her, supporting Tania between them. "Jump!" he ordered his wife. There was no ladder on the other side but the British Consul had heard the commotion and sent several servants, who now extended their arms to the frightened Clara. Shutting her eyes, bumping her jewelry case against her chest, she jumped, and was caught by a sturdy coachman. Sonia took a deep breath and followed, then Misha, holding his second niece by the waist, for she had begun to kick with hysteria. Last of all came little Marfa.

Jean, who had run out of the house empty-handed, had suddenly realized that he had forgotten something inside his cousin's mansion. In spite of the warning, he had made his way back to his room, then stopped in a panic. Horrid yells were now reverberating from inside the house, and he saw a red face in the hall, then a knife slashing through a Rembrandt. Broken china shattered from below. He thought: Dear God, what have I come for? And then, seeing his silk top hat, he grabbed it with relief. At that instant he had run out, and now, barely twenty feet ahead of the looters and murderers, he reached the ladder in the garden. Clutching at his hat, he climbed the rungs and jumped over the wall to the other side. The maître d'hôtel, behind him, was hacking at the ladder to destroy it.

Lady Anne Latimer, the Consul's wife, was tending to the Gunzburgs in her sitting room, administering smelling salts and distributing brandy. She came to Jean, her hands outstretched in sympathy, and said, "You had left something dear to you in the house, Jean Solomonovitch? Was it of great price, or of personal import?"

Gazing with wonder at his hat and turning it over in his trembling fingers, the young man shook his head, dazed. "I don't know!" he exclaimed. His knees buckled under him quite suddenly.

Not long afterward, on January 22, 1905, an event occurred that convinced Jean de Gunzburg not to visit his cousins in St. Petersburg. Several hundred workers, under the guidance of a priest, Father Gapon, marched peacefully to petition the Tzar for reforms while the sovereign was at his Winter Palace, only blocks away from the residence of Baron Horace de Gunzburg. They were received with volleys of open fire, and this massive slaughter was given the name of Bloody Sunday. Anna, prostrate with tears, demanded of David during the days that followed: "Are you not sorry now that you did not join the Union of Unions, Papa? What will happen next?"

David took her by the shoulders, but she stiffened defensively. "My beloved," he replied, his own face reflecting deep grief, "what happened to Sonia, what has occurred so recently here, are demonstrations of violence that defy comprehension. Surely the Tzar cannot be blamed for the actions of some of his soldiers. I am not so naive as you think. There are of course agents provocateurs who stir up trouble. But as a member of two Ministries, I know more than men such as Pavel Milyukov who have formed this Union. I know, for example, that the Tzar has plans to instigate a Duma, a kind of Parliament. He is attempting to face his problems. Do not lose your faith in your country."

But Anna regarded him with ill-hidden contempt. "I possess a strong faith in my country, Papa," she said. "In its healthy peasants. But the Tzar frightens me, and you frighten me with your blindness. I share a room with Sonia. Since her experience in Kiev, she cannot sleep properly. She cries out. Somehow the pogroms are tied into this Bloody Sunday, although I cannot quite see how. But the people are being deluded. Of that I am certain."

Sonia was not so certain. Unlike her sister, she accepted David's explanations of the massacre of Bloody Sunday. Horrified, she believed, nevertheless, as he did, that the Tzar could not be held responsible. But she could not rationalize Kiev. Over and over, she kept hearing Shoshana's mocking voice. Finally, she took her anguish to her father. Her small face was white, and purple circles puffed beneath her eyes when she appeared in David's study.

"Maybe we are wrong," she said gently. "Perhaps it is the Zionists who are correct, for if the Russian mob can turn against members of their own nation, then perhaps we are truly citizens of nowhere."

His heart filling with love and a deep pain, David tilted the small, firm chin upward, and gazed into Sonia's face. "Never, my sweet," he said. "We shall never cry defeat. This is our country, and should you or Anna happen to marry a foreigner, my last request would be that you might never forget that you are Russians."

Sonia threw her arms around his neck, and pressed her cool cheek against his, which had grown gaunt. For the moment, she was comforted.

But Ossip, who was eighteen, regarded all this with irony in his deep blue eyes. He said nothing at all, but he was thinking: We could so easily convert. Then nobody would harm us, and the Tzar would have to find proper means to deal with his peasants, rather than taking the easy way out by making scapegoats of the Jews. Ossip did not believe in God. It did not matter to him how, or whether, he worshiped.

Mathilde, however, had lost patience with philosophy. Her fine black hair piled into a thick chignon, her hands pressed against her alabaster cheeks, she came to her husband and stated calmly: "I have borne all I can. We could all be murdered! If you will not accompany me, because of your work, then I shall take Johanna and the children back to France."

David's heart contracted. He took her hands in his, but she withdrew them angrily. "I know all about your duties. Duty to the government, duty to the Jews. What about duty to us, your family? Ossip could be hurt."

"You will not stand by me?" he whispered.

"No, it is you who will not stand by us! Tomorrow. We are leaving tomorrow! Was it not sufficient that your daughter and your niece nearly lost their lives in Kiev, that your brother Misha has had to settle his wife in Paris, that he intends to come to Kiev only during the months of the sugar campaign? He, at least, is a man who cares for his wife."

"But he is not a man of purpose," David said with distress. "I would lose my honor if I abandoned my country, my Jews. Even Sasha, who has only the bank to think of, is not departing."

"He probably has some seamstress hidden away in a garret!" Mathilde declared. "Besides, he is not my husband."

The following morning, Anna came to her mother in her boudoir. She stood erect, in an embroidered blouse over a multicolored skirt that ballooned from her waist. There was a look of fierce determination on her face. She said, "Mama, I am twenty. I do not want to leave during this crisis, as the others must. I have my landscape work, with the artist Kuindji. Besides, the only friends I have are in Petersburg. I would like to remain here, keep house for Papa. If there is anything, Aunt Rosa will be here, and Grandfather Horace. I am not a child, to be sheltered."

A wave of despair washed over Mathilde. She saw the pride in her daughter, the burning resolve. Suddenly she was tired. Forcing Anna to go would make the trip unbearable for everyone, especially for Mathilde herself. Johanna would quarrel with the girl, there would be shouting and sullennness. "I am leaving to escape from havoc, not to create more of it," she sighed. "You are stubborn and selfish, traits which seem to run in this family. All right, Anna, stay. But remember that you are a lady, and a Gunzburg."

"I am never allowed to forget it," the girl murmured. But a glimmer of joy flickered in her deep brown eyes.

Sonia had grown thinner during the months since the pogrom in Kiev. It was her last morning in St. Petersburg before leaving for Paris with her mother. Ossip had gone to the gymnasium, and she had had her lesson with Johanna. They had not taken their customary stroll afterward, for with the strikes, people were afraid to be on the streets unless they had to. She sat at the piano, the gray skies beyond the house penetrating to her soul, which felt inexplicably mournful. Her fingers traveled absently over the keys and she began to play an ineffably sad melody, a Schubert composition to which she could not place a name. She sat erect and the delicate bones of her back could be seen beneath the batiste of her shirtwaist. Suddenly she felt tears upon her eyelids.

A young male voice echoed behind her. "Ah, Sofia Davidovna. Why are you so sad?" Someone placed a strong, firm hand on her shoulder. She was dumbstruck, for she had thought herself completely alone, and then furious at the intrusion. She wheeled about on the piano stool and found her gray eyes directly confronting the chestnut gaze of Volodia Tagantsev, Ossip's friend. He had grown, for he was now sixteen, and sported a light mustache on his frank, tan face. She had opened her mouth, but now found herself totally speechless.

"The weather was so dreary that our master let us out early for the noon break," he explained. Then, conscious of his hand still upon her shoulder, he reddened and removed it. "You are going away," he added.

"Only for a little while, until the disturbances end. My Mama is very concerned."

"Mine, too," he said, and smiled, revealing his large white teeth. "I suppose that is the nature of motherhood, don't you think?" His tone was pleasantly casual.

But all at once Sonia felt her anger rising. "Your mother has much to fear, for your family is close to the Tzar," she said, and something in her voice made him start.

"You are not exactly members of an unknown clan, yourselves," Volodia replied, continuing to smile. "We all have much to safeguard from the seething masses."

His words made her feel ridiculed. She shrugged lightly, and regarded him with a stern expression. He was so compact, so trim and well dressed in his dark suit, and his hands, which he now held clasped together, were excellently shaped for a musician. She remembered his fondness for the piano. Impulsively, she said: "It is such a gloomy day, Vladimir Nicolaievitch. Why not sit with me for a while, and play this exercise for four hands?" She showed him some sheets of music.

He looked about for another stool, or for a low chair to place next to hers, but there was none. Apologetically, he said, "You shall have to permit me to share your stool, Sofia Davidovna." When she blushed violently, his smile reappeared. He sat close to her, and she felt the smooth muscles of his thigh touching hers beneath the fine broadcloth. A shiver ran through her. "Are you ready?" he asked.

They began to play, their fingers first stumbling, then dancing from ivory to black and back to ivory. The still room reverberated with their noise, which pealed in trills, in waves of sudden joy. And then they became conscious of the presence of someone else within the room. Volodia stopped playing. "Ossip," he said.

Sonia started, and pink spots touched her cheekbones. She lifted her eyes to her brother's, which sparkled like dark blue gems. "I was saying good-bye to this piano, for these few months," she said lamely.

"We were saying 'see you soon' to each other," Volodia added. Ossip smiled. But his sister gave their guest a hard look, and a line formed between her brows.

"I have packing to do," she declared. Then she rose and rushed from the room.

Ossip raised his brows and remarked, with amusement, "Strange that she did not bid you good-bye. Sonia is usually a most correct young lady . . ."

In May, when the streets of St. Petersburg were starting to dry from their overflow of thawed, dirty snow, Anna wrapped herself in a velvet cape and secured her feet in thick sealskin boots. It was early afternoon, and her father was at one of his Ministries. She saw dim sunlight peeking through a hazy sky, and resolutely walked out of the apartment, down the stairs, and into the open air. Then, breathing deeply, she directed her footsteps toward the University. Now and then she peeked out from the hood of her cape at the houses she passed, but she did not truly see them. At length she reached a small, somewhat dirty side street. There, in front of a brick building, she stopped. The building was not unlike the one in which Sonia had found her the night of her escapade almost eighteen months before. Anna bit her lower lip and entered the house. She ascended the staircase and stopped before a small wooden door on the second landing. She knocked, and waited.

Ivan Aronovitch Berson opened the door. His blond hair was more tumbled than usual, and he wore no coat and no vest, only a plain cotton shirt, open at the collar. When he saw the hooded figure on his threshold, he stared with embarrassment. "Annushka," he said. And then: "You have never come here, to my students' quarters."

"I have come today," she said. She stepped into the room and saw the unmade bed and the lawbooks scattered haphazardly on the floor and piled on the single chair. "I wished to see how you lived, since you moved from your parents' home," she said.

"It is very different. Alia came yesterday, and nearly fainted." He was smiling at her, extending his hands.

She seized them with sudden ardor. "I do not care what Alia did. I care about you, Vanya—oh, how much I care!" She closed the door with the back of her heel, and gazed at him with her wide brown eyes until he felt that he was swimming in them.

"Vanya," she said, "Vanya, I have come to you because I love you, and because we are free. Free to love each other."

He pulled her down upon the sofa, and carelessly brushed off the handwritten pages which had been strewn there. Without hurry, she unfastened her cape and removed it. Then she began to unpin the coil of red hair to the right of her face, letting the brilliant red mane surround her shoulders. She bent over and removed her boots, and then stood up, in her simple skirt and blouse, and faced him. Her brown eyes glowed. She moved her hands behind her back and unfastened the hooks on her skirt, which fell like a collapsed bell by her toes. Then she unbuttoned her blouse and dropped it to the floor. She stood, uncorseted, in her drawers and chemise. But she said nothing.

Vanya's mouth had fallen open, and the blood had drained from his cheeks. Now he looked at her, his serious green eyes going to her brown ones and then to the clothes she had discarded. "You may touch me, Vanya," she said gently. "I am real." And now it was she who smiled. "There has always been my face—but there is the rest. Most people would stop at the face." She winced, a hurt expression passing over her features. She brushed a wave of red hair over her left cheek, as though to hide it.

But he was rising to envelop her in his arms, and she buried her face in his chest. Softly he tangled his fingers through her hair. "I had thought—of asking your permission to speak to your father," he told her in a muffled voice.

She reared her head and became rigid. "You do not have it!" she cried. "I do not wish to be bound to you by law, or by religion. If I came here today, it is because I thought that you would want my love, offered freely. Please, Vanya. You must not humiliate me. I do not wish to become someone's wife, not even yours."

"But Annushka. We could buy a small farm, work it together. You could paint. I do not want to dishonor you."

"You could never do that." She touched his face with her fingertips. "If you love me, then what is the meaning of honor?"

He pressed her fiercely against him, crushing her parted lips with his own. He lifted her in his arms to the bed, and it was there that they discovered each other for the first time, the girl of twenty and the man of twenty-two.

When they had lain together and fallen asleep, their hair entwined, a sudden brilliant shaft of sunlight filtered through the glass pane of the window. He awakened abruptly, and touched her arm. "Annushka," he whispered, "I want you to stay with me forever."

Anna raised herself upon one elbow and regarded him gravely. "I am happy now," she murmured. "I had never been happy before. Do not frighten me with talk of tomorrow, when we have this moment." Slowly, she kissed his nose, his chin, his eyelids. "Go to sleep, my Vanya. I must go home."

Seven

On September 5, 1905, the Peace of Portsmouth was signed, marking the termination of the war with Japan. For the aristocracy, this peace was a blessing, after the waste of lives and materials which had drained their powerful nation and made it, at length, bow in abject defeat. Baron Horace de Gunzburg said to his son David: "Now we can turn the page upon our national shame." But for the Russian people, peace was a meaningless word; war had sharpened their senses, rubbed their nerve endings raw. Its end was hardly noticed in the rising crest of their grievances.

Autumn had come to St. Petersburg. In Ivan Berson's small apartment, Anna heated a pot of water on top of the old cast-iron stove in the corner. In another part of the room, several young people were engaged in animated conversation. Some were seated on the sofa, others on the floor, still others stood, their backs to the wall. She could hear Ivan calmly telling a thin, nervous girl with her hair falling in strands down her back: "Of course I am not in favor of the October Manifesto. Who in his right mind would not understand that the Tzar's Duma will never equate with the British system of Parliament? There's going to be a hitch of some sort, wait and see. Still, the idea of gaining what we want through terrorism goes against my moral code."

"You are a fool, Vanya!" the girl cried. Her voice was shrill. She was wearing a shapeless gown of corduroy, belted at the waist, and rimless spectacles. Anna knew that she was a schoolteacher, and very poor. "One can see that underneath all your good will lies the soul of a *burshui*—a true burgher. We have been forming fighting groups in the countryside since 1903, in order to educate the peasantry. Yes, there is bloodshed! How else are we going to show the aristocracy that we mean what we say? The first strike was not sufficient. Living without electricity, water, and railroads did not terrify those in power, as we'd planned. The Soviet may be divided but they are real Social Democrats, who are concerned with the workers. We Social Revolutionaries have grown out of the Narodnyk party, and are going to obtain what we want through the people of the Russian soil . . . our peasants. We need your help. You are almost a lawyer. Educate the ignorant, Vanya, in the laws, so they may find out how inadequate these laws are to them. And then help them to formulate proposals for new legislation! But we shall not be granted a single new freedom without some fighting."

Anna poured the boiling water into a large pot of thick porcelain into which she had put black tea leaves. She left the brew standing, and hastily came to Vanya and placed a light hand on his arm. "Lolya," she said, "you are a mistress of rhetoric, but so are all our friends. You have made a grave mistake in calling Vanya a *burshui*. His father—and mine—are wealthy men, but we do not espouse their ways of life. Vanya lives as meagerly as you, and it is his life I have been sharing far more than that of my family. Vanya is reading law in order to become a legislator, in order to educate, as you say. But not with hot words that incite to murder. What about the agents provocateurs who tell the angry peasants that the Jews are responsible for their unjust standard of living, rather than the Tzar? I am frightened of violence, but if the workers can obtain reforms by striking I am all for it. I myself would much prefer to live in the country and work the land, and not be bothered with electricity or railway systems. But the fighting cells which you organize among the peasants are not formed to bring facts to them, only to use them, and the force of their numbers. I'm against this infighting among Social Democrats, Social Revolutionaries; workers, peasants; Mensheviks and Bolsheviks; Trotsky and Lenin. All that is meaningless. What is important is the goal of getting the right of vote for everyone, and seeing that the men and women who vote know whom they are electing, and why."

Lolya's face reddened fiercely. "You say that you do not live like your father. Do you know what the poor Jews of the Pale call him and your honored grandfather, and their fine friends? The Council of Notables! Count Witte, our new Prime Minister, drinks his afternoon tea with Baron Horace de Gunzburg, and comes to his home to bring him the Tzar's most distinguished decoration, second only to the one granted to the Imperial family: Evident State Councillor! Among the wealthy, prejudices seem to disappear. And while they sip their tea, Baron Horace's protégés, the poor Jews of the Pale, die slow deaths of starvation. You are for gentle teaching of the peasants? Very well, Anna Davidovna, my elegant demoiselle. Go out there yourself and test the climate. The peasants are ready for blood, not school desks!"

"You think I am afraid to go, don't you?" Anna accused her. Her voice was low, and trembled slightly, but her fingers on Ivan's arm did not tighten. She said, "Send us there, then, Lolya. And do not boast so of your own parentage, for it makes me ill. We all know that your mother was a prostitute, and your father unknown. We are all bored of it, too."

Lolya rose from the sofa and stood before Anna with a

fierce expression on her face. She raised her hand into a fist and held it out toward Anna. Ivan smiled ironically. "We have had sufficient drama from Bizet's score sheets for a single evening," he declared. "Come, Annushka. Let us serve tea to our friends."

"Always the perfect gentleman," Lolya said derisively. But she lowered her fist. Then, as Anna turned her back to her and began to move toward the stove, she called out: "But don't forget! The fighting cells shall have two new members. I'll hold you to your word. The Gunzburg word is gold, is it not? Rubles and rubles of gold . . ."

"I for one am glad that Mathilde and the three little ones are out of the country, my son," Horace de Gunzburg said, resting his back against the comfortable leather cushions lining the armchair in David's study. "I wish Sasha had sent Rose away with Tania. And that Anna had accompanied her mother, as she should have. Why didn't you and Mathilde insist upon it?"

David said, "I do not seem to understand my daughter these days. She is so quiet, my little ball of fire. And she is angry with me. She would have me join unions, and Lord knows what else. When I pointed out to her that Pavel Milyukov was encouraging a renewal of the general strike, she said, 'He is wiser than I thought.' It is good that Mathilde does not hear such talk. But Anna frightens me."

"At least she is no Milquetoast, David," his father said. He shifted his weight in the armchair, and stroked his whiskers. They were nearly white now, barely tinged with gray. But still his blue eyes shone with keenness. "Anna has character, even if she is misguided. Which leads me to the point: why do you not guide her properly, David? Sasha tells me that two years ago there may have been something with the Berson boy. Heaven knows, I do not approve of the Berson girls, but Aron, their father, is a man with whom to side, financially. His enemies fear him. Why did the boy not come to you to propose?"

"We do not know that it was ever serious between them. I rather liked Ivan. He used to come to tea. I must say, I did . . . entertain hopes. But Mathilde told me that she had spoken to Anna. Anna said they were merely friends. I do not want my daughters to marry men of *my* choice. Times have changed, and young girls now marry for love. I did the same. How could I try to force Anna, when I myself made such a definite choice, even as a child? I would not trade my Mathilde for any other woman."

The old gentleman regarded his son with a strange, bemused expression. But David pressed him suddenly: "You and Mama were my examples. You loved each other from the very first. Why should Anna not have the same opportunity?"

But Horace was thinking of a transaction that had occurred in Paris almost a quarter of a century earlier. He recalled his father's house on the Barrière de l'Etoile, where he and his brother Yuri had each possessed an apartment for their respective families. He saw himself once more, a rather somber, elegant man of early middle age, seated at his secretary; his brother, slightly younger and clothed with flamboyant good taste, his flowered waistcoat barely touching his growing embonpoint, smiling, smiling. That damned smile that had created so much scandal. He had sat—he, Horace—composing the financial agreement that would bind his young niece, Mathilde, to his son, David, and all the while he had felt pangs of conscience. Had he not noticed how this calm, serene young girl, with her slim waist and thick hair, had looked with longing at Sasha? Had she not sat one day at her window, dreamily ignoring David who sat entranced by her side? Horace had been in the street below, about to climb into his carriage, and he had seen the two young people and caught their expressions. Space, empty space, seemed more romantic to his niece than his own favorite son. For a brief moment, then and there, Horace had felt a stab of pity, and then once more, when he had signed the agreement. But Yuri had merely looked triumphant. "They say I breed beautiful daughters," he had said, to goad his brother. But Horace had ignored the lewd implication. He had thrust the paper into Yuri's waiting hand, all the time telling himself that David would love Mathilde, that David was his own child, that every man must learn to make certain compromises. Now he wondered, permitting doubt to play with his thoughts.

"I miss her," David was saying. "I miss her scent, I miss her silly way of gathering her breadcrumbs to the side of her plate. Do you know that Sonia has picked up this habit? I miss Sonia, too. And the boys. Ossip will have so much to catch up on for his classes. I wonder how the Tagantsev boy is doing, without my son? They have become so inseparable."

"I do not approve of this friendship," Horace said abruptly.

"I am not totally in favor of it myself, Papa," David sighed. "But Mathilde is happy. She feels that Ossip needed a truly good friend, a soul-brother, and that Volodia just happens to be the one."

"And that Dutchwoman, Johanna de Mey? Is that what she has become for your wife, David? A soul-sister?" Horace de Gunzburg watched as his son's features began to tighten.

In the house at Saint-Germain-en-Laye, the elegant Parisian suburb where Baron Yuri de Gunzburg resided with his wife, Ida, Mathilde sat by the window of her bedroom, looking out at the gardens below. Her father, now sixty-five, was walking with his grandchildren. Ossip, delicate for his eighteen years, slim in contrast to the portly Baron, held his sister's small hand. Sonia, in her Russian furs, reminded Mathilde touchingly of a Dresden figurine. She said aloud, to Johanna: "I hope that such frailty will not cause her difficulties in bearing children. Look, she has no hips to speak of."

"She is not yet sixteen," Johanna said comfortingly. The two women held their embroidery in their laps as Mathilde continued her examination of her children. Little Gino, ruddy and healthy, was running ahead, now and then turning on his heels and making his sister throw back her head and laugh. Mathilde, through the windowpane, could not hear the tinkling sound, but she imagined it. "Anna has not written me," she said abruptly. "It has been weeks."

"Anna is keeping house for her Papa."

"Still . . . I felt disquiet in David's letters. But if there were a problem, surely he would let me know? We have had our differences, but she is my daughter, too."

"You are allowing worry to cloud your mind," Johanna declared. "There: see how Gino and Sonia are each taking their grandfather's hand. He is so delighted with them!"

"Papa is growing old," Mathilde sighed. She turned to her friend, and Johanna saw that tears had begun to fall. Mathilde's face, so lovely and unlined, resembled a Raphaelite portrait of an infinitely sad Madonna. "Papa is old. I had always thought, as children do, that he would never age. And, seeing him grow old now, I am aware of the passing of time in my own life."

Johanna de Mey rose then, and gently pulled the curtain cord to hide the view of the garden. The pale blue draperies veiled the window, and she lit a standing lamp in the corner of the room. Apricot hues shone softly around them. She said, "But my darling, you are anything but old. I have yet to see a single white hair on your head. It is the children who grow, but we"—and there, she smiled—"we remain static, do we not?"

"Perhaps I remain static because the world proceeds, and I am withdrawn from its growing pains. When I think of St. Petersburg I am torn. Half of me feels tremendous relief to have escaped an unbearable life there without electricity or water. How does David manage? Or Uncle Horace, who is even older than Papa? And my daughter? But the thought of them brings guilt with it. A city without the basic comforts of civilization is no place for a young girl."

"She has her father," Johanna declared. She gazed at her friend, and Mathilde looked up and met her aquamarine eyes. They did not speak. Mathilde saw the fine golden pompadour, the slim, lithe figure in its gown of cerise silk. She said, "It is you who have not aged, Johanna. Sometimes, when I look at you, I become filled with fear. You are going to marry one day, and I shall lose you. At least, my hope is that you will marry a gentleman of Petersburg, so that we may continue to see each other. But it would not be the same—oh no, it would never be the same! I could not face the day without consulting you. You are my buffer, my warrior's shield. Without you I am lost, or worse, overwhelmed."

"Most women would be speaking such words to their husbands," Johanna said. "Surely the Baron would take care of you, my sweet, if, as you say, I should decide to wed." She bit her lower lip and did not look up into Mathilde's face, which had fallen as though she had been slapped. She embroidered with steadfast motions, counting time with her needle's thrust.

Mathilde cried out, but in the muffled tone of someone horror-struck: "But Johanna! If you have indeed—found someone you care for—why have you said nothing to me? Why have you kept this hidden?"

Very calmly, Johanna de Mey said, "We are not schoolgirls, that we should run to each other with every detail of our lives. Yes, I have received a proposal of marriage. I shall not tell you—no, do not stare at me so with your enormous eyes—I shall not tell you his name." Then, her own eyes softening, filling with moisture, she turned to her friend and seized her cold fingertips. "I shall not tell you, so that you may face him in society and not blush at his discomfort. For you see, I shall refuse his kind offer. I have no intention of becoming his wife." She smiled, but Mathilde's face was still a ghastly white, her lips still parted in fear. Johanna de Mey rubbed her friend's fingers, then brought them to her lips and kissed them. "I am cruel to you," she said. "For I should not have told you. Will you forgive me for my thoughtlessness? Will you, Mathilde?" And her voice began to rise with emotion.

Mathilde de Gunzburg nodded silently. And then it was Johanna who began to cry, sobbing aloud: "I am ashamed, so ashamed!" she cried. "Oh, please, forgive me!"

Surprised, and again serene after the reassurance, Mathilde stared blankly at Johanna. She placed a shy hand upon the other's shoulder. "No, it was I who have not been discreet," she said. "There is nothing to forgive. Let us forget this discussion. You are not leaving. What else is important?"

"And that truly matters to you?" Johanna's beautiful oval face was bathed with tears.

Mathilde lifted her friend's chin in her own palm, and smiled with infinite tenderness at her. "Yes," she murmured. "More than all else. I mean this with my whole heart."

Suddenly, in a girlishly impulsive movement, Johanna stood and threw her arms about Mathilde's neck, covering her cheeks, her hair, her shoulders with hot, tremulous kisses. "Then all is well, all is well," she murmured to the amazed Mathilde, who began to laugh, unused to displays of great emotion.

"Yes, of course," Mathilde said, but she was pink with embarrassment and confusion. Then she gazed at the other woman, and her eyes shone with relief. "I am so glad," she stated. "For if you were to leave—" And then she shook her head. "But I am supremely selfish! What have I to offer you, compared with marriage, position, and wealth? I love you, my dear friend, and I wish for your happiness. If you should meet another man, then you must not think of me. Think only of your own life. Life is too short. Look at my father, who is old today . . . You must never grow old, Johanna."

Inexplicably, she turned away, her eyes filling anew with tears. It was then that Johanna de Mey placed her arms about Mathilde's waist, and held her close, not saying a word. The two women remained, embracing, for several minutes, until loud knocks broke into their silence, and Gino's voice came through the thick door: "Mama! We have stories to tell you!"

Johanna de Mey watched as her friend opened the door to the children, and sparks of triumph glinted in her pupils. I have nearly won, she thought.

"Come, Gino," she said briskly, "take off your overshoes before you soil your mother's fine carpet. There are some cakes here, for all of you."

It was now the beginning of December. A second railroad strike had isolated St. Petersburg from the world, and the rest of Russia. Lolya Raffalovitch, the young schoolteacher, stood in her small apartment wearing men's trousers made of coarse peasant cloth. She brandished papers in her bony fist. "Witte has bowed to the landowners!" she cried, her eyes rimmed with red behind her spectacles. "You see? The peasants were to represent a large electorate, to vote in March for members of the Duma. And your precious Count Witte was going to present land grants. Now what? The gentry speaks, and suddenly it is their interests that are put first, and to hell with the peasants! Do you think that education will help them now?"

"We have agreed to go out," Ivan cut in tersely. "When are we to leave?"

The schoolteacher regarded him and Anna, seated beside him, and thrust her chin out at them. "How soon can you be ready?" she asked.

"We do not need to take much with us." Anna reached for Ivan's hand, and he squeezed it. "Give us twenty-four hours."

Lolya smiled. "Good. We shall be going in small groups —cells. There is no railroad so we shall go in carts and buggies. There will be four in our group: you two, myself, and Petya Orlov the printer. We shall leave in the morning; that way, no one will miss your fine ladyship until nightfall. And you are not to know where we are headed." She grimaced sardonically. "Who can tell, you might have a sudden attack of fear, and warn the Chief of the Secret Police . . . Or are you still friends with him, Anna?"

"You know very well that Lopukhin has been replaced," Anna answered angrily.

"I warn you—we shall be transporting munitions for the peasants. Just so you two don't think this is a pleasure trip for lovers. Petya is to be our leader. Don't cross him, Anna. He isn't an intellectual, like our Vanya here."

"Lolitchka," Ivan remarked with iron, "you need your reserves to fight the *burshuis*, remember, love?"

The girl ignored him. She said, "Bring a bag filled with woolens, it will be cold during the trip. And food. Anything will do: bread, cheese, vegetables. So we won't have to stop all the time to fill our bellies."

"We shall be here then, tomorrow," Ivan acquiesced.

"At ten. By then Anna's father will have left for work." She looked at them again, and extended her hand, grudgingly. "Good luck," she said more softly. Then her eyes bored into Anna's: "I must say, I expected you to back down," she commented.

"I am not a coward," Anna replied.

But outside, she took hold of Ivan's lapels and huddled close to him. "Vanya, I'm scared," she whispered. "Scared of not doing the right thing, scared of being caught, scared of execution. Scared—of leaving my home, my father."

"I know," he murmured back. "I am thinking of the

small farm we could still have if I go to him—your father —and ask him for your hand in marriage. It is not too late, Annushka."

She shivered. "It is too late, Vanya. We have forgotten ourselves for a greater movement. How could we go back to our small comforts?"

"We shall be together," he said, holding her.

She remained muffled in his coat, her red hair blowing in the December wind.

Anna's small bundle lay hidden beneath her bed, crammed with all the warm things she could assemble in a small bag, and some foodstuffs she had stolen from the pantry. She had gone into Ossip's room and taken some of his trousers, for it would be cold, and men and women dressed alike in the fighting cells. But now the dinner bell had sounded, and she thought: This is my last civilized meal, my last meal with Papa. Her bright brown eyes filled with sudden tears. Oh, Papa, she thought, and wrung her hands together. What am I doing? What will this do to you—and to the others? She suddenly felt like a very small girl again.

She hurried to the dining room, and all at once she was sorry that he would be there alone with her. For he would be the most hurt of all when he discovered her departure. He would never guess where she had gone. That was a relief, for her heart ached at the idea of his distress. He believed in the Tzar, in the promised Duma. She did not; but still, she could understand his loyalty in a way that she would never understand the Victorian prudery of her mother. Anna felt that she had always been a gaping sore in Mathilde's life, but that her father had respected and cherished her. Now he waited politely by the table for his twenty-year-old daughter to take her seat first. In his mahogany-colored coat of thick velvet, his thinning red hair looked dull, and his face was etched in tired lines.

"Good evening, Papa," she said softly, as Stepan held the chair for her across from him. "You seem weary tonight."

"We are attempting to take back control of the railroad, my little dove," he replied, smiling at her. His pale blue eyes were filled with tenderness for her, and she felt as though a knife had been thrust into her stomach. "Not only the Ministries—also your grandfather, and his interests. You know that your great-grandfather was one of the foremost promoters of the railroads in Russia?"

"I had not forgotten," she said.

"I have been thinking, Annushka," David said after a pause. "I have heard that there are some specialists in Sweden who are working on ways to remodel burned areas of the face and body. I would like to see if perhaps one of them might not take a look at you."

She turned very red. "That is silly, Papa," she stated.

"No. If it is possible to help burn victims, then surely muscles—"

"You would be wasting your money, Papa," Anna said abruptly.

"Think about it, my love. I am not at all certain that they could help, and it was cruel of me to raise your hopes—but I want to do all I can, the way we did for Ossip, when he fell ill."

"But I am not ill," Anna countered gently. "I am who I am. When I was a little girl, I would have given the world to be pretty, as Sonia is, or Tania, or Mama. But now that I am a woman, I find that there are more important things than how one looks in the mirror, or even to others. If a doctor could change my entire face, he still would find it impossible to erase what I have become, *because* of my face. He would be too late; and it would be meaningless to me now. I am happier than I have ever been, Papa."

"Are you, little one? What do you do with your days?

What do you dream of? There was a time when you would tell me, but lately . . ."

"Perhaps it is better this way," Anna said. Her large brown eyes held her father's warm blue ones. "But promise me that you won't worry about me, not any more?"

Puzzled, he smiled at her across the table. "I shall not raise the issue of the Swedish doctors, if it brings you discomfort," he said.

"No, Papa. I want more than that. No worries, about anything to do with me. Remember what I have told you, about my happiness. I am very happy."

He sighed. "While your mother is gone, I've had a lot to think about. I should like to give a ball, in your honor, on your twenty-first birthday, to show the world that I am terribly proud of my older daughter. Now what do you have to say to that idea?"

He smiled, and was shocked when Anna burst into tears and ran from the table. He heard her sobs as she fled, and was utterly amazed. And then, he felt very guilty. Poor girl, he thought, she does not enjoy society. A ball would be an ordeal for her. I have thought only of myself, wanting to show her off, forgetting how uncomfortable she would be. He thought once more of the Swedish physicians, then dismissed the notion with anger at himself. Women were still mysterious to David, and these days, added to his wife's sometimes confusing attitudes, there was his daughter, Anna, now a woman too. He sighed deeply. He would have to think of a way to apologize to her, but it would be best if he let a little time go by. Morning would be better. He did not know that morning would be too late.

The house in Saint-Germain, where Mathilde and her children were spending the holidays, had been purchased by Baron Yuri's father, the original Ossip, founder of the Gunzburg dynasty. He had wanted a suburban home. He had already built a large mansion on the Barrière de l'Etoile in Paris itself, but, a true Russian, he had also yearned for the country, and had bought a marvelous château in the Beaune region, which was famous for its wines. For this suburban estate, his third French home, he had considered first the Malmaison, where Napoleon I had resided; but it had been too damp. Next he had considered the château of Maisons-Laffitte, with its vast acres for horse racing; but Baron Ossip had not liked the work of Mansard, the sixteenth-century architect who had constructed it. Instead, he had become enamored with Napoleon III's officers' mess hall.

Mathilde, who had profoundly loved her Grandfather Ossip, could understand the emotions that had drawn him to this far smaller house. She could feel the peace that bathed the small town of Saint Germain, with its palace where Louis XIV had been born. Mathilde found repose in this château's neat straight walkways, in the glistening stone that was centuries old. In the French garden there were chestnut trees and oaks to provide shade, a loving shade, she thought, like the cool hand of a mother on a child's feverish brow. The English garden, which the children preferred for its cheer and freer lines, was inside the forest. Mathilde adored the forest, for though it was wild, it was also majestic and peaceful, unlike the threatening Russian woodlands. She liked to walk along its paths, which were safe and wide. But best of all, she enjoyed ambling along the Terrasse, a large, straight avenue nearly two miles long, which bordered the parks and the forest.

In contrast to the winters of St. Petersburg, this winter seemed mild to Mathilde. Wrapped in white ermine, with a matching muff and bonnet, she walked arm-in-arm with Johanna. "Look," she said softly, "today the Seine is calm and gray." The great river stretched far below them, winding its lazy way. She regarded her friend, glad that Johanna seemed so happy here, too and smiled. "You are Dutch, and I am Russian," she said, "but are we not both French? There is something so civilized about this country, about its land and even its rivers. Something controlled and tamed. I am never afraid here, never gasping for breath. David, you know, has never been fond of Saint-Germain. Perhaps that shows the essential difference between us: he is a true Russian."

Johanna squeezed Mathilde's fingers through her muff. "My dear, your heart has ached for this moment. If that silly revolution had not broken out, you would only have dreamed of this, and a place in your heart would have died. I do not think the Baron knows what sacrifices you have made for him. You have given up your own self for his wishes. But then, you are far too good to think in such terms."

Mathilde said, "No, I am not good. I know myself well enough to be aware of that. I am lazy, and uncommitted. David is passionate, and a believer. It is true, though, that living in Russia erased part of my very being. Right now, I wish—" But she stopped, her teeth on her lower lip.

"You wish you never had to return." Johanna de Mey, her fine eyes compassionate, did not allow Mathilde to look away. She began to whisper, with a strange urgency: "Yes. And you also wish that you could forget. All the problems. Anna and her pain. The Baron and his love, which you do not reciprocate. I know all these things, for I know you, the Mathilde that lies beneath that surface of regal dignity and serene composure. You detest your life."

"Johanna!" Mathilde cried, appalled. Her face turned whiter than ever, then bright red, then white again. She attempted to withdraw her fingers from the other's grasp, but Johanna only tightened her own over them. Mathilde began to shudder, and Johanna said, "You are furious with me, because you believe you have been violated in the deepest privacy of your thoughts. But I am not an intruder, my dear Mathilde. I belong there. I am the only human being who has completely understood you, and that is because my love for you is undivided. Even the Baron has his children, his father, his Jews, his Russia. The children each have their father, one another, their grandparents, their friends. But I have only you, Mathilde. Only you. I think of you when I awaken in the morning, when I turn out the lamp at night. I yearn to be with you, to comfort and love you. You are my life."

For a moment Mathilde could not speak. Then, shaking her head vehemently from side to side, she cried, "But no! That cannot be! You have your own mother, your sisters . . ."

Very softly Johanna said, "No, I have only you. And you have me, for I shall never turn my love away from you. I shall never disappoint you as others have. Isn't it good to know that there is someone who will love you no matter what happens?"

Mathilde was silent, and let Johanna's steps guide her back toward the gardens. As they walked, Johanna kept her fingers over Mathilde's muff, not pressing, merely holding. Snow began to fall gently about them. It was then that she saw that Mathilde's bowed face was bathed in tears.

During the night, when she heard Baron Yuri, always the last to retire, mount the stairs to his chambers, Johanna de Mey, clad in her nightdress of lavender silk, left her room with a candle, and made her way to Mathilde's door. She turned the handle. The door yielded silently. The room was dark. Mathilde sat by the bed, her hands clasped, her magnificent black hair flowing over her shoulders and back. She whispered, "Johanna? I could not sleep tonight." Her voice trembled.

"I could not, either." The Dutchwoman kneeled by Mathilde's feet, took the clasped hands, and kissed them. "Come to bed," she murmured. She pulled back the sheet and made Mathilde lie down on her side. Then she began to massage her neck, her back, her arms. Tears flowed from her eyes, and she let them fall upon Mathilde's pale skin. She bent down and kissed the shoulders, the arms, the neck, and then her long, elegant fingers became entangled in Mathilde's dark hair. She caught the soft strands and curled them about her hands, kissing the curls. Then all at once Johanna slid beneath the sheet and pressed her body against Mathilde's back. She encircled her waist and held her powerfully, but Mathilde did not, could not, move.

"Only I know how to love you," Johanna said at length, burying her face in Mathilde's hair. "Only I, and that is good, for you can trust me. Trust me, Mathilde, my darling, my sweet, my beloved . . ."

The lone candle flickered on the nightstand.

Alia Berson, with her customary frivolity, had ordered, several years before, a magnificent covered troika, so that she and her sister could take drives through the snow without fear of the elements. The landau, a kind of brougham drawn by two horses, seemed too staid to her, and because the victoria was open it was therefore unsuitable—and entirely too connected with the despised British queen. Only a troika would do: it was a totally Russian mode of transport, designed for Russian snows and ice, for it was a sleigh and not a wheeled carriage. It was drawn by a team of three horses, which pleased Alia. The only problem was that most troikas were not enclosed, and Alia Berson, novelist laureate, would not risk uncurling a single tendril in the wind. She had cajoled her father into ordering hers covered.

But Alia was not one to persevere in any area of life. Suitors were soon found boring, novels were also discovered to require a surfeit of imagination and diligence; she abandoned her efforts with a trilling laugh. And so, when her brother Ivan showed interest in her troika, she had given it to him as a present for his twenty-first birthday. "A lawyer must ride in style," she had stated with a flourish. Ivan had protested, somewhat outraged, that he would not accept such a costly, useless present. Alia knew that his way of life was simple, that he would never use this extravagant toy of hers. But she had patted his cheek and burst into giggles. "I want my brother to be a gentleman," she had declared. "Whether you use it or not, the troika is yours, forever. And if you continue to reject it, then *I* shall feel rejected, and pout. My brother does not love me sufficiently to receive tokens of my affection."

Now it was Petya Orlov, the dour-faced little printer, who sat on the driver's stoop of the troika and guided the three thoroughbreds through the Russian countryside. He was wearing three overcoats, the last one made of sheepskin with a fleece lining, and high felt boots. Covering his knees was a heavy blanket from Mathilde de Gunzburg's closets. Inside the carriage sat Anna, with Ivan's arm around her to keep her warmer, and on the seat facing them, the thin schoolteacher, Lolya, and the sacks containing their food and the arms destined for the peasants. Now she gave a small, harsh chuckle at the thought that during these times of strike and crisis, no one had stopped the elegant vehicle. "You are useful after all," she said to Ivan. "It is not I alone who take you for a *burshui*."

It was only the middle of December, and winter had not yet attacked in full force. But the winds were like small tornadoes, and the horses, terrified, reared more than once as they were blinded by snowdrifts. The roads were bad, sometimes mere tracks. But Petya Orlov knew them well. He headed south toward Novgorod, stopping frequently in small hamlets along the way to distribute arms, shoe the horses, and let them rest, and pausing for nights at larger villages, where one hut would open its doors to him and Lolya, and another to Ivan and Anna. The huts were always alike: one room for an entire family, with a big square earthenware oven to keep them warm.

Past Tsarskoe Selo, where the Tzar had his Summer Palace, and Pavlosk, where his uncle, the Grand Duke Konstantin Konstantinovitch, had a magnificent residence, the countryside became farmland, now white with snow. Each day, Petya found that he could drive nine miles, even though at times he had to make detours because of bad weather conditions. Anna, her face stinging with cold, huddled near Ivan, who would draw her head upon his shoulder. Nobody spoke much during the drives. Perhaps Lolya was thinking of the peasants, and of their mission, but Anna was so weary and chilled that her mind was as numb as her body.

When they stopped in the villages, they consumed bowls of potato soup and raw onions with black bread, and Ivan introduced her as his wife. Once, in Lyuban, she whispered to him, "Why does Lolya jeer at us, and detest me so?"

He shrugged lightly, and pressed her fingertips. "It is an old story, my sweet. Of no importance. Lolya is a very bitter girl, and vindictive."

"But why? Have you ever done anything to hurt her?" Anna cried.

A half-smile passed over his face. "It was very simple, really. Long ago, before I ever met you, she and I were students together, and we shared a few . . . lonely moments. That is all. Maybe she believes that nothing came of our relationship because she was poor, and I was a Berson. She is wrong. I never pretended to love her, nor she me. But she is angry that I have found another to love, and that you belie your origins and feel a true commitment to our cause. She would prefer to fling your aristocracy in my face—but she cannot, and is galled."

Anna's face whitened, then reddened abruptly. "I cannot understand jealousy," she said. "If Lolya loved you, she would have found happiness in your joy, even if that joy is shared with another woman. If I lost you, I still would wish for you to have joy. We do not own one another in this world, and love is a selfless emotion."

His eyes filled with tears, and softly, she kissed his eyelids and his cheeks. "You are truly my wife," he murmured.

And so, in the cold and the worry caused by their grim duties, this journey, with Lolya facing them and Petya as their driver, was their honeymoon. The peasants were kind to them, and smiled upon their clasped hands and whispered words of love, seeming to understand the look in their eyes far more than they did Petya's dry instructions regarding the revolution, and Lolya's exhortations against the Tzar. They stared with glazed expressions when the little printer distributed weapons and demonstrated how to make them work. "We are cold, our crops lie beneath blankets of snow," they said with wonder to Anna and Ivan. "What need do we have of weapons, or even of this Duma your companions have discussed?"

With infinite patience, Ivan explained that the way to a fuller stomach was through elected officials, that Russia's peasants made up a large majority which needed to be represented, that they possessed the right to demand laws to better their living conditions. "But why the arms?" they asked him tentatively.

Stiffening himself against his natural peace-loving disposition, he replied, "The workers in our capitals have made their requests known by going on strike. Now the government is afraid not to listen to them. It is your turn. If you accept your lot, and allow yourselves to become dulled with hunger and fatigue, you will never accomplish anything to give yourselves an easier life. The government wanted to issue land grants to you but the gentry has persuaded it to rescind this decision. You must display your strength to turn the tide once more in your direction."

But Anna murmured to him, "Your words are those of a University scholar. You must simplify your expressions, my Vanya." And then, sitting upon the surface of the ovens, her legs crossed beneath her thick skirts, she began to talk, the way that she had spoken as a child to Eusebe the water carrier and to the other peasants of Mohilna. It was not rhetoric, not exhortation. She spoke calmly, sometimes flaring into momentary anger, but she was not self-righteous or political. The peasants knew that she was one of them.

Sometimes, during the first nights of their journey, she cried in her sleep, dreaming of her father. Ivan held her tightly against him then.

Although it seemed to her that they had left St. Petersburg months before, they crossed the frozen Volkhna River in ten days. "We shall be in Novgorod in a day or two," Petya announced to them. "And then we shall meet up with other groups, and with the Novgorod leaders."

But Anna thought: Is that all the distance we have traveled? When the railroads were running, it took only a single day to go from the capital to Novgorod. She shivered, and looked out the window of the troika. An immensity of whiteness faced her, flat and bleak. And she thought: I love you, my Russia, I love all of you, your spaces and your forests alike. Papa loved you too. Why is it then that we oppose each other on your behalf? She felt cold and unwashed, and drained of emotion.

The telegram was delivered to a startled Mathilde during the midday meal. When she opened it, her fingers trembled. As she read David's message, her face blanched, and she fell back into her chair. The piece of paper fell to the floor, and Gino squirmed near her, his eager young features scrutinizing her. "Who's it from, who's it from?" he demanded in his boyish tones. Yuri rose, and placed strong arms around Mathilde's shoulders. "What is it?" he asked.

But she could not reply. Only Ossip saw Johanna de Mey pick up the telegram and run her eyes over its contents, then pocket it noiselessly. It was she whose voice now came, crisp and decisive: "Come, children. We must all begin to pack at once. We are returning to Petersburg."

In the bedlam that followed, Sonia clung to her older brother, and when Johanna ushered them from their mother's presence, Ossip spoke to Sonia in his calm voice, quieting her fears with little jokes. She did as she was told, packing her clothes, and helping Gino. But all the while her restless gaze ran back to Ossip, and she did not hear the smaller boy's exclamations. Her heart constricted in the fear that their father had died. Nothing could dispel this vision from her mind.

Anna did not know that the majority of Russian liberals had accepted the Tzar's manifesto of October 30, and his further explanation as to the formation of a Duma. She had not realized that their backing would give the Tzar sufficient strength to finally control the second railroad strike that had placed St. Petersburg in virtual isolation from the end of November to the middle of December. She believed, as did her companions, that the city would exist without rails at least until the New Year. But her grandfather, Baron Horace de Gunzburg, was one of the first to learn of the strike's end. He was still a major investor in the Russian railways, and possessed a network of intelligence that could supply him with information almost upon demand.

Dulled by the wintry journey south, Ivan had not thought that his troika might have been noticed. When Baron Horace began his inquiries concerning the disappearance of his granddaughter, it was not long before he put together the fact that Alia's brother possessed certain revolutionary connections. But the railroad was still out, and the old Baron, above all, wished to avoid alerting the Secret Police to anything that might cause harm to his oldest granddaughter. He sat with his son David, and the two men smoked their pipes, sharing a tense silence. The old man was astute enough to know how tortured David felt, how he blamed himself for Anna's disappearance. Though he would never have voiced this to his son, the patriarch blamed the absent Mathilde.

When the trains began to move once more, it was only a matter of days before several of Baron Horace's agents picked up the trail of the fugitives. Aron Berson had come to him, his face ashen. "Perhaps they have eloped," he suggested, wringing his hands. But Horace's blue eyes silenced him with their icy disdain. Berson did not dare approach David. But even more than he feared Horace or David, Berson feared Mathilde. He knew that she would return soon, and he dreaded facing her.

Horace's agents took the first available train to Novgorod, then doubled back to the small village of Netylskiy. They came upon Ivan and Anna as the two were about to head south for the final few miles to the larger city. They seized Anna as gently as possible, but she cried out, kicking them, and called for Vanya. "Your grandfather sent us, Baroness," they told her respectfully. "You have nothing to fear. But we shall not leave without you."

"Then I shall come, too, and we shall stop somewhere and be married," Ivan stated firmly.

Anna burst into tears, and kissed his hands. "It does not matter about me," she said, shaking her head wildly. "But I will not have your life ruined. If you return, they will change you, Vanya! They will make us live *their* lives! If I return alone—what else can they do but send me away? I would not wish it otherwise. I shall not remain on Russian land enslaved by their ways! In another country, perhaps there will be some peace for me . . ."

His arms were about her, and he would not let her go. "You cannot leave my life," he murmured. Tears streamed down his cheeks, but he was unmindful of them. "I have always wanted you to be my wife! These men will allow us to be married. That is the life I want: a life with you!"

"But I do not want that! I have told you many times—I shall not marry you, especially not like this, almost by force, to please my family. Nor even to please you, my darling. For one day you would hate me! I would rather go, and have you love me, than cling, and cause you to turn from me later. A banker's life is not for you. Please, Vanya! Stay here, do what you must—but don't ever return to St. Petersburg. No, no—don't talk any more!"

She hurled herself away from him, catapulting herself into the arms of one of Horace's men. They took her by the shoulders and led her toward their carriage, and Ivan followed, screaming incoherently and attempting to grab her from behind. But they kept him from her. He could hear her muffled sobs, which rang pathetically in his ears. A frenzied anger seized him, and he began to shout, but the doors of the carriage were closing. He beat his fists against them. Her tiny face appeared in the window, the brown eyes dilated, her mouth parted, and he felt his face contort with grief, uncomprehending. Then the carriage started off, and he stood in the snow, his tears slowly freezing upon his cheeks, his face numbed with cold.

He felt someone put thin arms about his body, and a harsh, yet strangely warm female voice murmured, "Come, Vanya. The troika is ready." Lolya's face, with its angular nose and chin, and its beady eyes behind their rimless spectacles, took shape before his eyes. He heard her sigh. "When Russians suffer, their pain is like a roar in the wilderness," she said softly. And then, pressing his arm: "You don't have time to suffer. She knew it, too."

Sonia thought that she had never spent a stranger New Year's Eve, waiting in her room for Anna. Johanna had not allowed her to wait in the sitting room, with Mama, Papa, Uncle Sasha, and Grandfather Horace. So she sat on her bed, twisting her handkerchief. Gino had been sent to bed, but Ossip was beside her, stroking her small hand. "I don't understand at all," she murmured.

"Anna was never happy here," Ossip stated. "Perhaps she could not stand it. We never really knew what she went through, did we?"

Her sister shook her head mutely. "Vanya Berson must

have loved her after all," Ossip murmured pensively. But Sonia stood up, rejecting him with a jerk of the hand.

"No!" she cried. "Once I believed him, when he said he loved Anna! But when you love someone, you do not bring shame to that person, you do not tear a family apart. Ossip, have you no honor?"

He began to chuckle gently. "Oh, Sonitchka, Sonitchka. Will nothing ever make you see the way things really are? You are my little Joan of Arc, my little Bernadette, my Esther. Anna is made of flesh and blood. As for poor Ivan—I myself will not condemn him as everyone else seems to be doing. He simply had ideas of his own."

When Anna appeared inside the threshold of her home, she saw the adult members of her family awaiting her. Her grandfather, somewhat stooped, surveyed her from beneath his severe brows, and swiftly, she felt a hatred for him swell within her. She dismissed her uncle as unimportant, with his derisive look that said: The children of my favored brother are not so pure. Her brown eyes, angry and shot with small red veins, moved to her mother, who stood carved in alabaster, her face bloodless, her eyes proud and hurt and haughty. Anna shivered, then turned to her father who stood slightly apart from the rest, his face gray, his cheeks sunken, his eyes filled with sadness and defeat.

"Oh, Papa!" she burst out, and suddenly she ran to him, and he enveloped her in his long, thin arms and rocked her back and forth. She cried hot tears of relief and pain and intense humiliation, while he held her.

"You have brought shame on our family," her grandfather said roughly. "I shall not dwell upon it. But you have torn apart a good man, your father. About that I cannot keep silent. You are my flesh and blood, Anna. I was proud of you. Have you nothing to say?"

"No," she answered. Her father released her, and she looked tentatively at her mother. But Mathilde turned her face away, and a hot red flash passed over Anna's face. "I am sorry, Papa. But only for you. I shall find work somewhere, and you can all forget me, for I do not wish to remain a member of this family. I shall go away—"

But all at once she saw her younger sister running toward her from the corridor, and as Mathilde's hand flew to her mouth and Sasha turned with shock to his father, Sonia threw her arms savagely about her sister's neck. "Anna! You're back!" Sonia cried, and she began to sob aloud. "Oh, Annushka, don't ever leave again! Stay with us, love us—" Anna felt hot kisses upon her cheeks, and she held the small girl in her embrace, something hard and painful dissolving inside her. She began to cry with Sonia.

A firm hand came between the two sisters, as Johanna de Mey, who had followed Sonia into the room, separated Anna from Sonia. "That is a sufficient display of hysteria," she declared. "Sonia, you were to remain in your room. As for you"—and her mouth became a sneer as she regarded the crumpled, disheveled Anna—"you have caused enough trouble for a lifetime, let alone one night. I have ordered Marfa to set up a cot in one of the storage rooms. You will sleep there." She took Sonia's elbow in her hard fingers and propelled her from the sitting room. Not even Baron Horace had breathed so much as a syllable.

Without a word, Anna stood up and walked in the direction of the kitchens. She opened the door to the area where her father's books were kept, then closed it noiselessly behind her. She saw the small iron cot in the middle of the first room, and suddenly threw herself upon it. "Oh Vanya, Vanya!" she cried softly.

But she was alone, all alone. She was home.

On New Year's morning, 1906, Sonia awakened early. She had barely slept between her bouts of heavy tears. She had thought only of her sister, and of the people gathered to meet her in the sitting room. Now she sat up, shivering in her white satin nightdress this cold winter morning. She shook her thick black hair behind her, and covered herself in an incongruously childish flannel bathrobe. Then she tiptoed out of the room.

She went first to her father's study. The night light still burned through the crack in the door. She hesitated, then set her face in grim lines, her gray eyes hard. She had wanted to go to Anna, to sit with her, to bring her some of the New Year sweets that had been given to her in France. But the hushed sounds that came from the study told her that David was speaking to Anna at that very moment. She had never eavesdropped before. But now, her heart pounding, she could not help giving into this abominable sin.

"Switzerland will do you good," Baron David was saying. "It contains marvelous landscapes to paint, and good teachers. The boarding house we have selected is fine, decent, and quite luxurious. When you return home, everyone shall have forgotten all this nonsense. Nobody knows about this business with the youth group, and as for the Berson boy—"

"Papa, do not speak of him. Please!"

"Then I shall not. Aron Berson does not know the whereabouts of his son. After your grandfather's agents took you home, he lost track of the boy. He plans to disinherit him. But that is Ivan's disgrace, not yours. Nobody we know is aware that you two were in the same group, not even Berson's wife and daughters. They cannot be trusted to be discreet. But he can: he needs our business as much as we need his."

"Yes, business. Always business," Anna said ironically.

"I am afraid we cannot overlook our interests," her father replied. "But you needn't worry as far as we are concerned. We all know that it was a coincidence that you and the Berson boy were thrown together in the same group. There is no scandal."

"It is to Mama that you should speak those reassuring

words," Anna said. "She is concerned with scandal in her household, not I."

"Your mother is a saint, to have borne all this. I shall not permit you to speak of her that way. We are all concerned with our good name, but as it is connected to *you*. This whole dismal affair could have ruined you."

"And now I am being sent away to avoid damaging the reputation of my sister and brothers," Anna said.

"I shall miss you, Anna. I love you very much. If I have taken this step, it is for all of us, you included. This revolution bred strange thoughts in you—the good fresh Swiss air of Zurich will restore you to healthy thinking. Do not look at me with such disdain. It was not easy for us to decide what to do."

"You might have continued to hide me with your extra books, and no one would ever have guessed I had returned to my baronial home," Anna said with unconcealed bitterness. "But do not worry, Papa, I also realize that you were not the one who wished me gone. That is sufficient comfort. I would not remain here, anyway. But—"

Sonia heard a sudden muffled sob, a scraping of chairs. She felt the hot blood rush to her cheeks, and quickly, before the door was flung open, she hid in the hallway. Anna came bursting forth, disheveled and weeping. Sonia, her face now very pale, could not move as a faintness overwhelmed her.

When she felt sufficiently strong, she went determinedly to her mother's boudoir. It was so early, Mathilde would surely still be sleeping. Sonia thought of her mother's wan, white face, of the small lines of worry at the corners of her beautiful eyes, and pity filled her. Still, there was Anna. Her mother needed sleep, but Anna needed . . . She needs to be saved, Sonia thought with sudden passion, and in this passion, her gray eyes glowing, she knocked on her mother's door. "Mama," she called in her girlish voice; then, when there was no answer: "Mamatchka! Please, it is important!"

She heard soft steps, then her mother appeared at the door. Her face was drawn, but she was fully awake. She stood in her green silk nightdress and instinctively she brought her hand to her breast to hide her bared collarbone from her daughter. "What is it, at this hour, Sonia?" she asked with impatience.

"It is about Anna. Please, Mama, let me speak with you—" Tears welled up once more in the gray eyes, spilled onto the young cheeks.

Mathilde regarded her with the expression of a startled doe, uncertain as to where to flee. Her face was ghastly white. At length, another, stronger voice emerged from behind her in the boudoir. "Mathilde, I can continue this massage while Sonia speaks to you. Come inside, or you shall freeze!"

Mathilde, her hand on her breast, opened the door completely, and Sonia saw Johanna sitting on the bed, a rose satin bathrobe trimmed with fox fur flowing about her like a gentle wind. She came to Mathilde with infinite gentleness, brought her back to bed. Then she dazzled Sonia with a splendid smile. "Your poor Mama has had a difficult night," she said. "I was giving her a soothing massage. What was it you wanted, child?"

"I wished to speak to Mama alone, please, Juanita," Sonia said.

"Your mother is too weak to sustain much conversation," the governess said, a line forming between her brows. "You must not be insensitive."

Sonia, clenching her fists, turned from the Dutchwoman to her mother, and her small, dainty features were constricted with frustrated anger. She lifted her frail shoulders, dropped them, looked all around the room at the beautiful objets d'art and remembered how her sister had once told her that one day she, Anna, would design her own home, that it would be simple and uncluttered and functional. Sonia had not agreed: antiques appealed most strongly to her own sense of beauty. But now it did not matter, nothing mattered but Anna and her dreadful misery, her impending departure. She flung her hands into the air in an uncharacteristic gesture, and her mother sat up, alarmed.

"Don't you love Annushka any more? Is that it?" she cried. Before anyone could respond, she ran out of the room, her sobs resounding in the corridor.

"Oh, my God!" Mathilde wailed, and she began to rock back and forth, her hands over her face. Standing beside her, Johanna de Mey, her golden locks cascading over her shoulders, resembled a statue chiseled in rose-colored marble. She did not say a word.

Eight

After Anna left, Sonia, though outwardly poised and cool, became very depressed. She was nearing her sixteenth birthday, and her figure had filled out, though not like her mother's and sister's, which were full of hip and bust and slim of waist. Sonia was a small girl, and her breasts were small, too, but round and firm; and though her hips were not broad, now they were softer and more apparent than before. She did not wear the outfits made famous in America by Charles Dana Gibson, for they were geared to more womanly shapes than hers. But a revival of the Empire look, with its simple high-waisted gowns that clung to the hips, were perfect for her delicate slenderness. She now wore her hair up, loosely pulled into a demure topknot, for her mother had tried to cheer her with this gift of adulthood. "You are spoiling her," Johanna had warned Mathilde, but on this point Sonia's mother remained firm. The haunted expression in the girl's gray eyes reminded Mathilde too painfully of her failures in rearing Anna, and of the hatred and disdain her older daughter had displayed toward her during their last months together.

After her lessons, when Ossip was at school, Sonia would retire to practice her piano. Mathilde heard the doleful sounds as the young fingers attacked the keyboard, and again she was reminded of Anna. Mathilde tried not to allow her mind to dwell on Anna, on the situation with Ivan Berson, on the escapade with the youth group. She smiled upon Sonia, and found this daughter infinitely sweet; and so Sonia's mournful playing was upsetting to her. There was a small room off the main sitting room, actually an alcove, and Mathilde ordered the piano moved there, so that she would not have to pass her daughter when she went into the sitting room. And the sounds were farther removed from the rest of the apartment. "This way, you will not be disturbed, and Gino will not burst in upon you," she had told Sonia.

Sometimes Ossip would join her after supper in what was now called the piano room, and then the sounds would be gayer. They spent all their free time together, and he would tell her stories of school and make her laugh. "My bedroom is so empty now," she said at times. "For you and I are the quiet ones. Gino is boisterous, but Anna—"

"Anna is what some people call 'spirited,'" her brother stated. "And you are right: we are a most decorous house, but not a spirited one anymore."

One noon, Ossip came home with Volodia Tagantsev, his face aglow. He was nearly nineteen now, Volodia seventeen, and the two young men still lunched at the Gunzburg home every day. Sonia would finish her walk with Johanna and Gino just as the boys were eating their dessert. She had to pass through the dining room on her way to her room. Each time, Volodia, dapper in his padded jacket which emphasized his athletic physique, would rise from his chair and extend his hand, shaking hers, and saying, "Did you have a pleasant walk, Sofia Davidovna?" or: "I hope that you were not too chilled today, Sofia Davidovna." Sonia would smile and blush, and reply in her quiet voice whatever suited the occasion.

This time Ossip called out to her: "Sonitchka! I have

exciting news! Come, I want to tell you all about it." Sonia raised her fine eyebrows, and smiled, and spots of color appeared on her cheekbones. She hurried to the table.

Volodia had already risen. "Let me tell her," he said. She turned to him, her small face tilted upward, shining from the bracing walk and from anticipation. "My mother has sent a message, Sofia Davidovna, inviting Ossip to supper at our home next Thursday."

Suddenly Sonia turned her face aside, paling. She breathed deeply. "Vladimir Nicolaievitch," she whispered, "what you say is impossible!"

But the young man shook his head, joy sparkling over his tan face like ripples of refracted sunlight. "No, it is true! My parents want to meet this best friend of mine—and so does Natasha, my sister."

"But our father will never allow Ossip to accept," Sonia said simply.

Her brother stood up now, his slender form taller than hers, his dark blue eyes boring into her. She took a step back, startled. "Mama will allow it," he said. For the first time in her entire life, Sonia felt as though her brother had abused her. Tears filled her eyes, but she swallowed, and raised her head proudly.

"You are so confident," she said.

But now Ossip had changed into his habitual laughing expression, and he reached for her hand. "I am *fairly* confident," he replied. "I know our mother. But of course I cannot be certain. I can only hope. But after all, I am nearly a man now."

"Perhaps, but a real man would think of his family first, and only then of himself," Sonia said coldly.

Now Volodia interrupted, his color rising: "But Sofia Davidovna, I come here every day. What difference would it make if it were Ossip who visited my home?"

But Sonia shook her head. "I cannot explain it," she said. "Perhaps it is simply that our father has never attempted to hurt your father's way of life, whereas yours has come between ours and the goals dearest to his existence. You will surely not understand. Ossip, clearly, does not either. But Papa will be hurt."

"I am sorry, Sofia Davidovna. I only meant to convey an invitation," Volodia said defensively. Then he added: "Ossip is closer to my heart than my own brother. Whatever you may think of my parents, they do love me, and by knowing Ossip they will feel that they know me better, too. Do not think of them, if it is painful to you. Think, instead, of me."

Surprised, Sonia regarded him with parted lips. She began to say: But who are you that I should think of you, Vladimir Nicolaievitch, when my father is also concerned? The words remained unformed in her throat. All at once, gazing into Volodia's rich brown eyes, Sonia was overcome with a strange emotion that choked her, and she brought her hand to her throat. In the silence that followed, Ossip saw her wide gray eyes blending into Volodia's brown ones, and it was not haughty familial loyalty which he read in those eyes. It was something beyond words, something primeval. Ossip had never seen such an expression on his sister's face, had never guessed at its potential—and he was as amazed as she was at her own reaction.

And then the objects in the room took focus again, and she blinked, and bit her lip. She looked away from Volodia Tagantsev. Suddenly she seemed younger, smaller, a child in a woman's hairstyle. She stammered, "I hope that no one will be disappointed," and Ossip wondered whether she meant him and Volodia, or their father. She bowed her head politely to Volodia and walked away toward her room with tiny footsteps.

Sonia felt confused about Ossip's dinner plans at the Tagantsev palace, for at first she had refused to speak about it, averting her eyes whenever he came near her;

then, seeing his high color, she had warmed somewhat to his excitement. Ossip had been to suppers and balls before, for he was nineteen, and much in demand as an excellent dancer and gay addition to the social events of the younger generation. But the Tagantsevs . . . He was without doubt the first Jew ever to set his dancing pumps within their walls. And it was to be a formal dinner, too.

When she saw her brother, Sonia started, for never, to her eyes, had he seemed so magnificent. His slim form was encased in a black tuxedo, and he wore a white vest encrusted with buttons of lapis lazuli that matched the cuffs to his shirt, which was stiff with fine pleating. His pumps were black patent leather, and he sported new pearl-gray evening spats. On his right hand he wore the gold signet ring etched with the family emblem given to him by his grandfather for his eighteenth birthday. Ossip's waving black hair was brushed back into a pompadour, unparted. His dark-blue eyes were more dazzling than the lapis as he stood before his sister. Sonia cried: "You are absolutely splendid!" And he bowed and pirouetted before her. Mathilde came to him from the doorway, her eyes filled with tears, and pressed his hands, quickly. Little Gino ran around his older brother, shouting war cries. Only David was nowhere in sight.

Stepan held Ossip's caped black evening coat for him. Downstairs the landau was waiting. The Swiss doorman, a skilled liveried servant who stood guard by the house, helped him inside, and laid a quilt upon his knees. Vova, the coachman, took his seat, as did the uniformed footman, for this was a formal occasion. Then the carriage departed. From the window, Sonia saw the horses trot off in the direction of the bridge connecting Vassilievsky Island with the city itself. Suddenly she felt a pang in her chest: a vision of Volodia dressed like her brother passed before her eyes, and she imagined him bowing before her, inviting her onto the dance floor. She felt like Cinderella here at home. This was Ossip's evening.

The coachman took off for the Quays, crossing the Nicolai Bridge and turning onto the Quai Français, which bordered the Neva River. It was a long, elegant block which Ossip knew, for many Gunzburg friends resided there. They passed the Quai de l'Amirauté and Alexander Square with its equestrian statue of Peter the Great; then, the Quai du Palais upon which stood the Winter Palace and the Hermitage Museum. Ossip's eyes glowed, seeing these sights as if for the first time. There was a hiatus of greenery as they passed by the immense municipal Summer Garden, and at last the Quai Anglais, where the mansions of the high aristocracy loomed like palaces. The horses stopped before one of them, and the footman delivered Ossip to the massive door.

From that moment on, Ossip was unable to keep track of events. Once inside the Tagantsev palace, where the Countess herself greeted him with gentle courtesy, Volodia seized him by the arm and brought him into a group of young people. Ossip, who had not mixed with children in the early years of his life, had nevertheless observed them well, and now he was comfortable with others, a witty speaker. He knew what to expect of people, how to be with them. His school friends, Botkin, Sokolov, and Petri, were all present, as were many older fellows whom he did not know. But he hardly noticed them, for at a distance he had seen a vision of utter loveliness to which his eyes, magnetized, were riveted.

She was almost as tall as he, her waist slim, her soft young bust round below a ruffled bateau neckline which revealed pink shoulders and exquisite long arms and tapering fingers. Her hips flowed with her long skirt, and around her neck she wore a collar of rubies and diamonds. Her gown was red, ruby red, as were her full, laughing lips below a tiny, uptilted nose. Even at a distance he could tell that her eyes were deep blue, rimmed with curling black lashes, and her cheeks were a glowing pink. Her hair was clearly as mischievous as she, for already this early in the evening tendrils were escaping from her diamond-studded pompadour at her forehead and her neck. Ossip stood, his eyes widened, marveling. And then the girl came running, with long, graceful steps, toward the group. "Volodia," she exclaimed, "I have met all your friends but this one!" And she regarded Ossip, who stood dumbfounded.

"This is—" the young host began. But the girl burst out laughing, and placed light fingers on Ossip's arm: "No, let me guess! You are Ossip Davidovitch de Gunzburg. Why is it that I have not met you till now? I made my debut this year, you know. Volodia might have invited you! Instead Papa chose the dullest boys in Petersburg. Papa does not understand *la jeunesse!*"

"Then," Ossip stated, bowing, "you are Natalia Nicolaievna. I am most honored."

"I hope that you will not feel too honorable to twirl me in a spirited waltz!" she said gaily.

"It would be dishonorable to do otherwise," Ossip countered.

Natalia brightened. "Volodia! Did Mama tell you who was to escort me to supper tonight? I should like to change him for Ossip Davidovitch. Could you speak to her about it? This is such a special night for us, my angel, and if there were a young girl who made your heart patter, I would do you the same favor. Is there one? You blush, Volodia."

Vassili Petri bowed to her. "I was to be your escort, Natalia Nicolaievna. But before my friend's success, I shall step aside. Not for long, however," he added.

Volodia laughed. "I shall see if Mama agrees. You have the worst manners in the city, Natasha." To himself, he thought: If only *she* could have come with Ossip . . . But he steeled his mind against the intrusive notion. Yet, as he moved toward his mother, he could not help seeing the gray eyes in front of him, the firm little chin, the fine black hair. I cannot put her out of my mind, he thought with frustration.

It was to be a supper for thirty, of which only half were young people; afterward, more of Natalia and Volodia's friends were to appear for the ball. Count Nicolai Tagantsev had made the rounds, pausing to be introduced to Ossip, and he had shaken his hand. He was a tall, massive, elegant man, and his handshake was warm. "You have brought joy into my son's life," he had told Ossip. Then he had gone to another group.

Now the Countess inclined her head, and the Count took the arm of Princess Trepanova, the most important female guest, and began the march into the dining room. Every man found the lady he was to escort, and followed suit. Closing the ranks came the Countess with the guest of honor, her own cousin, General Prince Andrei Kurdukov; he was a handsome man, tall and strong, with auburn hair and whiskers, who had been pointed out before by Volodia. Prince Kurdukov looked every bit the part of a guest of honor: he was already in his prime, self-assured and successful. One could easily imagine him at Court. Ossip, somewhere in the middle of this procession which reminded him of the formation of a quadrille, felt Natasha's fingers upon his sleeve, and his heart raced. She tilted her head at him, regarding him frankly, and he smiled. "No painter could capture your lively charms, Natalia Nicolaievna," he murmured in spite of himself, and she laughed, a low, intimate ripple of music.

The guests did not go to the large table in the center of the room, but instead to the smaller one set against the wall. This was the *zakouski*, hors d'oeuvre table, laden with a large white fish, the traditional *sig*, which was boiled and cold; smoked mackerel; herring in wine sauce; fine slices of smoked salmon; stuffed green olives; marinated mushrooms; two kinds of caviar, one black and one gray; and tiny meatballs covered with tomato sauce. On both sides of the table were piles of small dishes and rows of silver forks and knives, and in silver baskets were the breads, white and rye, thinly sliced. Against the wall stood bottles of vodka, with liqueur glasses before them for the older gentlemen.

"I am starved," Natasha whispered.

Ossip chose the most enticing delicacies for her and brought them to her on a plate. They stood together by the large window, eating and talking excitedly. He was hardly conscious of their friends around them, only of Natasha's eyes and of her delightful dabbing with her napkin on her lower lip.

After a while the Countess took the arm of her escort, and everyone followed to the large damasked table. Ossip found his name card, which Volodia had repositioned so that he would be seated to Natasha's right. Near each principal plate was a smaller dish with a slice of white and a slice of black bread, to accompany the meal. Natasha picked up the orchid on her plate, and Ossip pinned it to her shoulder. In the center of the table was a large basket of red roses; flanked on both sides by crystal bowls, one filled with fruits and the other with sweets. Here and there upon the table were small bouquets of baby red roses, and at every third place setting was a French menu in the finest calligraphy.

The first course was the soup, a clear consommé. Along with this, the servants passed a platter of *pirojkis*, fine pastries filled with meats and eggs. Ossip observed the customary silence, but he gazed surreptitiously at his companion, noting her aristocratic profile and her lovely hair. Then an enormous trout with hollandaise sauce was served to each of the gentlemen at the table, and it was their duty to help the ladies. Ossip served Natasha a dainty portion, wondering what would follow. It was a loin of veal with tiny sautéed potatoes, green beans, and a salad of beets and Belgian endives. The servants filled the glasses with Bordeaux wine.

Ossip said, "You and Volodia have always been especially close, haven't you?" and Natasha grew gay, extolling her brother.

"I do not know if he will choose to enter the Senate, like Papa, and like our older brother, Nicolai," she said. "Volodia is somewhat of a solid person, reliable, good, honest. But far more fun-loving than Papa and Kolya. I should be happy to marry a man like my brother someday. Oh, I am in love with my father—what young girl isn't? But I have been sweet and proper for too long. I want more laughter and less gloom!"

"Yes," Ossip agreed. "My grandfather is a gloomy sort, too. And Papa—Papa is an idealist. I am not. I see life as it is, and do not waste time wishing it were more golden. We must adjust to reality."

They had been eating the vegetables, asparagus spears, and drinking Madeira wine. Now came a roast goose stuffed with chestnuts and surrounded by baked baby apples. "I cannot eat another bite," Natasha murmured. "If I do, I shall split my corset on the dance floor, and you will be too embarrassed to dance with me again."

"Nothing in this universe would embarrass me that much."

The flat glasses were now filled with champagne, and when it had been downed by all the guests, dessert was brought in, a sumptuous bombe of chocolate and raspberry ices. Tiny wafer fingers filled with chocolate accompanied the bombe. Then the servants passed around the two crystal bowls, and the guests helped themselves to pears imported from France, Calville apples, and other exotic fruits and sweets. They rinsed their fingertips in bowls of warm water with slices of lemon. When the Countess rose, the guests followed suit and, taking the arm of her escort, each lady came to the hostess and thanked her as she stood by her chair. Natasha kissed her mother, and cried: "You are a love, Mamatchka! Will you come watch us dance?" Ossip brought the Countess's hand to his lips, bowing. The Countess watched them depart, an indulgent smile upon her face. There was a note of benign envy in her gaze as it followed Natasha. She was thinking: How lucky we are when we have youth . . .

Natasha took Ossip into the drawing room, where, as the young lady of the house, it was her duty to pour the coffee, which was brought in at the same time as the liqueurs. The young people who had been invited only to the dance began to arrive. Ossip looked on as Volodia and his sister greeted these people, and suddenly he realized that he was jealously watching Natasha's expression as she spoke to each young man who arrived. He felt himself sigh inwardly with relief when her lovely hand did not touch their arms, when after a slight cocking of her pretty head and a brief trill of laughter she would comb the room for him, and smile her warm engaging smile for him alone.

The younger generation, at Volodia's command, went into the enormous ballroom. He said to Natasha, "I'm tonight's master of ceremonies," and when she cried, "But then, you won't enjoy my friends!" he silenced her with a composed look. He thought: If she is not here, half the pleasure is gone, in any case. And it is amusing to invent orders for the cotillion. It is a challenge to the imagination. He had voluntarily replaced a young banker who was frequently chosen to direct the special movements of the dancers during the evening. There were many who hoped for this privilege.

Ossip was a supple dancer, and he held Natasha with the ease of true grace. She was light, despite her tallness, and she exuded a fragrance of wisteria. They waltzed and they joined in the quadrille and they executed the Cracovienne and the elaborate Polonaise, and when other young men arrived to beg for dances Ossip stood perplexed, not knowing which of the many girls to invite, for he felt that it hardly mattered, that all would be equally dull compared to the vivacious Natasha.

Between formal numbers Volodia would call out: "Large circle!" and everyone would hold hands. "Ladies' circle, gentlemen's circle!" he would say, and the girls would all hold hands inside the wider ring of young men. When he called out *"Corbeille!"* two youths would hold hands and lower their linked arms about a girl, and take several dancing steps with her imprisoned between them. Then his directions became more complex, and the younger people would laugh, attempting to follow his orders.

At midnight the maître d'hôtel announced that a light supper was ready in the dining room. Natasha, the hostess, started this procession, demurely holding Ossip's arm. There were small tables spread out about the room, the large one having been removed. Volodia and Natasha sat on either side of Ossip as they feasted on tea and cakes, while the servants aired out the ballroom for the spirited, breath-stopping mazurka.

But now came the moment for the intricate figures of the cotillion. Volodia chose his sister for the first number, and she stood upon a chair, a lighted candle in her hand, and raised this hand high above her head while the young men massed about her, attempting to blow out the flame. The candlelight played over her features, which, to Ossip, seemed to emerge from a gypsy fairyland. When another young man succeeded in blowing out the candle and won the prize of dancing with Natasha, a profound dejection settled upon Ossip.

When the ball came to a close, Volodia escorted his friend to the door, but Natasha followed, her blue eyes mournful. Her hand took hold of his forearm, and she whispered, "Come back, Ossip Davidovitch. It is not fair: my brother has you all to himself, and sees your family every day. Twins are supposed to share, are they not?"

He found himself unable to answer. He took her hand, bowed over it, and brought it to his lips. Murmuring his good-byes, he exited, a caped black figure in the wind.

"I do not give a damn about what Papa says," Natasha

said to her brother as they watched him depart. Volodia turned to her, startled. But her blue eyes were hard, and small flashes of fire illuminated them. "Come on," she added with impatience, "let's say good night to the rest of these cardboard figures!"

When Ossip slipped into the Gunzburg apartment, he was amazed to find Sonia, clad in her woolen bathrobe, waiting in the drawing room. She had never greeted him after other soirées. She said softly, "I could not sleep. How was it? Was Volodia's father polite to you? What is their home like?"

Suddenly her brother grabbed her by the waist and twirled her into the air. "She is wonderful!" he sang. "Wonderful, wonderful! I have never encountered anyone like her, and I never shall! She is perfect, perfect!" And humming the notes of Strauss's Waltz of the Blue Danube, he held her above the ground and began to dance.

When her slippered feet touched the floor once more, Sonia suddenly burst into tears. She left her brother standing in the empty drawing room, bewilderment painted upon his face as she hurried to her bedroom and leaned against the door, sobbing aloud. She could not understand her own tearful display, and when it was over, she wiped her tears and went to bed. But she could not sleep. Next door, her brother Ossip too lay awake, but his was the insomnia of effervescence, while hers was uneasy restlessness. It would not have occurred to her to wonder whether the Tagantsev twins were asleep or not in their palace on the Quai Anglais.

From family friends in Zurich Anna had learned that a landscape artist of great repute, Herr Bader, was teaching his craft in the picturesque town of Darmstadt, in the German province of Hesse. "I plan to join his group of students," she wrote her parents. "This will further my talents, and you need not worry, for the pupils are all of the very best families." Mathilde winced upon reading this. She felt again as though her daughter, from afar, were throwing sarcasm in her face like vinegar on an open wound. But Anna was safe at last, and productive. "And perhaps she is finally coming to her senses," Johanna reassured her gently.

But there was no one to reassure Anna. The young woman was wracked by loneliness, greater loneliness than she had ever experienced before. For this time she had known love, and had been wrenched from Ivan before her relationship with him had fully blossomed. Within her family she had encountered moments of strangeness, of alienation—but not like the searing pain which she now felt at the thought of Ivan. She had loved him so! And her grandfather's men had not even allowed her to say good-bye to him, to kiss his sweetness one last time before dragging her away. Sometimes she was afraid that the anger which consumed her, the sheer misery, would not let her continue living. She was grateful only to her art, for without it to sustain her interest in herself, she might have died.

David had arranged for a bank in Zurich to add monthly installments to the account which he had had established there for her. And when Anna turned twenty-one, a trust fund formed by her Grandfather Horace was made available to her. She went to the bank and made plans for checks to be forwarded to her in Darmstadt. But just as she was preparing to leave Switzerland, strange signs of illness began to assail her.

She would awaken in the morning, and before swallowing the slightest morsel, her stomach would turn. She felt dizzy at odd moments. One afternoon, in a tea room, she nearly fainted. It was at that instant that a young woman three or four years older than Anna came to her and helped her to the restroom. She was dark-haired with a deep beige complexion and enormous chocolate eyes. "I do not know what could be wrong with me," Anna murmured helplessly, as the woman pressed a damp cloth to her temples. "I am not the sickly type . . . but lately . . ."

The other smiled. "Perhaps this is a mystery to you, my dear, but not to me. I have only too recently suffered the same symptoms. Let me relieve your mind: you are merely expecting a happy event. It is your first time, is it not?"

Mute horror took possession of Anna. She recoiled from the other woman and clutched the towel rack in panic. "It can't be," she whispered.

"You are not pleased?" the young woman asked, a look of surprise on her face. "You must tell your husband. Where is he? I can telephone him to pick you up here—or perhaps you were waiting for him . . ."

"No, no!" Anna cried wildly. She regarded the other woman, and noticed that she was extremely well dressed, but that below her breasts was a small, unconcealed bulge.

"It is not so frightening," the woman said gently. "For me, the scare lies not in birth, but in miscarriage. I have already lost one baby. This would be my second, had I carried the first to term. Switzerland has the best physicians, Madame. Madame . . . ?"

"You do not understand," Anna said. "It is not Madame. It is Mademoiselle. And there is no husband."

The dark woman cocked her head and appraised Anna. She took in her green suit trimmed with sable, which Mathilde had insisted upon ordering for Anna before her departure, the elegant black boots, the fiery hair coiled in the strange macaroon to the right of her face. She noticed the emerald brooch, the matching earrings, and the youth of this strange woman whom she had never seen before and who had told her such shocking facts. "My dear," she said, "these are not matters to discuss in public. Let us go to my hotel. We shall order our tea there, and we can rest, together. Both of us need to take care of ourselves."

"But we are not acquainted," Anna remarked in bewilderment.

"My name is Dalia Hadjani. I am from Teheran, in Persia. I am here in Switzerland to have my baby, for my country is not as advanced in these matters as the Swiss. Actually, my physician is in Lausanne, but I have not met him yet. My husband made all the arrangements when he learned that I was expecting. We had already lost one child—and we wished so much for a successful birth this time. But first I wanted to visit Zurich, and some of the other parts of the country, during the early months—that is why I am here right now." As she spoke, her voice soothing and rhythmic, she was helping Anna to her feet, and gently guiding her out of the restroom and to the door of the tea room, where she hailed a passing coach.

In the luxurious hotel where Dalia Hadjani took her, Anna seemed oblivious to everything until she reached the woman's suite. All at once Anna burst into tears. "Oh, my God, my God!" she cried, sobs shaking her. Dalia ordered tea, and sat down beside her, taking one of her hands. Suddenly Anna turned to her, her cries abating. "Why are you helping me?" she asked abruptly.

"I have no friends here," Dalia said simply. "When a woman is in this condition, she looks for a friend. Maybe I have found one who is also alone?"

Anna smiled for the first time. "Yes," she admitted, "I am here alone. My name is Anna de Gunzburg, and my home is in St. Petersburg. *Was* in St. Petersburg. I shall never return there."

The vehemence of her tone startled Dalia. "Because . . . of the father?" she questioned softly.

"Oh, no!" Anna cried. Tears welling anew in her eyes. "He is . . . was . . . a wonderful man. He is the only person who ever truly loved me, or understood me. He wanted to marry me. But I wouldn't tie him to me—you wouldn't see why, but I cannot explain. Things are too difficult to explain. He must never learn of . . . of this. Then he would find me, and force me to marry him—and—"

"If you love each other?"

"I would never bind him to me with his child. Our love was an act of freedom . . . But why am I telling you all this? How could you understand? You are a married woman."

"Yes," Dalia said, "I am married. I have a good life. And I love my husband. I do not have to understand, Anna. If you feel that you cannot return to him . . . then will you have the child?" She blushed and looked away. "You are evidently a person of means and distinction. There are . . . ways . . ."

Anna did not speak. She was thinking of Vanya, of his blond hair falling into his eyes, those brilliant green eyes that laughed, that danced, that wept. "I shall have the baby," she whispered. "I do not care what anyone says. I shall have the baby, and love it, and rear it the way I wish I had been reared, in simplicity and joy, and freedom."

"That is fine," Dalia said. "But do not say you do not care about the world. For your child will have to bear the brunt of its whispers."

There was a knock at the door, and Dalia rose to open it. A waiter wheeled in a cart with tea and cakes. He set it before the women, and Dalia waved him away. "That will do," she told him. "We shall serve ourselves." When he had left, she poured the hot liquid into fine china cups. Offering one to Anna, she asked, "Will you remain in Zurich? Are you known here?"

Anna was startled. "Yes, I know people here. I had planned to go to Darmstadt, to study painting. I was going to leave in a few days. Now . . . I don't know anymore. Suddenly I am two people—everything is happening so quickly!"

But Dalia's face had brightened. "You are a painter?" she cried. "How extraordinary! I am a dabbler, but that is my fondest hobby. In Teheran I belonged to a small class. We painted still lives, or garden scenes. Tell me, Anna, do they know you in Darmstadt?"

Anna shook her head. She felt too confused to comprehend what was happening around her. She felt dizzy again as though seeing things in slow motion. Dalia turned to her, a look of determination on her face. "We shall go together, my friend," she stated. "You shall find a name—any name —that is not yours. Madame . . . Madame Kussova! A good Russian name, is it not? You shall be Madame Kussova, a widow, and we shall travel together to Darmstadt. I shall send my husband a telegram. He will be so happy that I have found a friend, and that I shall paint once more! And we will help each other. I am glad to have discovered you in that tea room, Anna de Gunzburg."

Anna regarded the beige face, the heavy mass of black hair, and nodded in silence.

"Come now," Dalia said, passing her a chocolate éclair, "we must celebrate our meeting by fortifying our constitutions! Eat, Anna de Gunzburg. Eat, Anna Kussova!"

Dazed, Anna picked up her fork and speared a bit of the éclair with it. All at once she was very hungry. She said, "I like you," and her brown eyes caught the other's darker ones and held their gaze. The colors of the room had sharpened, and Anna thought: I am still alive! It was the first time the numbness had departed from her mind and body since her arrival in Switzerland. "Let me tell you about Herr Bader," she began.

A year before, Ossip's physician had announced that as long as the family took frequent small trips to such resort areas as Imatra, in Finland, he would not have to interrupt his studies to leave St. Petersburg during the spring. This had always meant that the young man's work load upon his return was prodigious, and had he not been a brilliant student, he would never have succeeded in passing his exams. Now that he was completing his next to the last year at the gymnasium, Ossip was relieved to be allowed to proceed on schedule. But he had yet another reason not to wish to absent himself from the capital.

In March 1906, he could think of nothing but Natasha

Tagantseva. He wandered about the apartment, singing, waltzing by himself, holding her dream form in his arms, and whispering into her invisible ear. At night he would compose poems to her, and sometimes, in reckless folly, he showed his poems to Volodia. His friend read them, smiling, and then with irony he said, "You did not think that our friendship alone was sufficiently dangerous?"

"Since my earliest childhood I have lived in fear of life itself, or rather, of losing it," Ossip told him solemnly. "Would our fathers alone frighten me? For the first time in my existence I have someone for whom to risk my security. Is she not worth it? Tell me, does she ever think of me, Volodia?"

His friend sighed. "She thinks of you. You two have placed me in a damned awkward position. You speak to me of her, she speaks to me of you. But what good will that do except to cause you both unhappiness? I have no one dearer to me than the two of you. That is why I blame myself. I shall not give this poem to her, Ossip. It will only serve to feed useless fantasies."

Angrily, Ossip cried, "And you are too self-assured to entertain fantasies?"

Volodia looked away. A searing pain tore his chest. He said, coldly, "I am less of a fool than you, or than Natasha. But that does not make me impervious to your feelings. All right. I shall give her the poem. But for the last time, Ossip."

"Someday I shall repay you," his friend said fervently. But Volodia turned his back to him.

"You cannot," he stated grimly. But he took the ode and pocketed it.

Not long afterward, Mathilde received a small envelope, bearing an unusual crest, in the morning mail, and when she opened it, she could not speak. She merely passed the note, on the finest of vellums, to David. Johanna de Mey opened her mouth in bewilderment and exasperation that she had been passed over. David exclaimed: "That family baffles me more than ever! I am impressed by this gesture of the Countess. Surely her husband is unaware of it."

"The Countess? Who?" Johanna cried.

"Countess Tagantseva. She writes to me that she wishes to come to tea on Thursday next, if it is convenient for me. It is a most gracious note," Mathilde stated.

Ossip's face flushed quickly. "She is a gracious lady," he commented.

"I am certain that this will be the first time Countess Tagantseva will ever pay a visit to a Jew," David said.

"After all, my dear, the Prime Minister set the pace with Uncle Horace," Mathilde commented softly. "Perhaps the Tagantsevs are learning to accept our humanity." She looked with gentle irony on her older son, whose blue eyes matched hers. "Ossip is very human, and he has been to their palace."

But David was annoyed. "That's beside the point, Mathilde! If the Countess learns to accept you, or even my son, in however small a measure, that has no bearing on the larger question. Her husband may accept one Jew, as a great exception—but is that progress?"

"You are picking lint from a clean carpet," his wife replied.

It was Sonia who spoke up, her voice high and young, but firm: "Whatever passes between the Tagantsev children and us, or between Mama and the Countess, must not weaken your own position, Papa. Perhaps the Count does know of this proposed visit— and perhaps also he encourages it, to mollify you. You are the one man, besides Grandfather who has grown old, who can speak on behalf of the Jews. If you can be stilled, the Count's purpose will have been achieved that much faster."

The family sat in stunned silence. Then Johanna de Mey, cords standing out in her long neck, rose in her chair and, leaning across the breakfast table, said shrilly, "You impudent chit of a girl! Go to your room at once!"

But her voice died in her throat. David also was standing, facing her, his jaw pushed forward, his eyes blazing, his fists clenched on the table. "Sonia will remain where she is," he declared, and he saw his wife's lips part and the color leave her face. Johanna de Mey staggered, then fell back into her seat. But the Baron remained standing, regarding his family one by one until his eyes fell upon Sonia's, her fragile face childlike beneath the heavy pompadour, her chin quivering.

"This is the house of Gunzburg," he said, "but only Sonia seems to have remembered that. Henceforth, no one shall forget it. Countess Tagantseva is welcome here, and I applaud her excellent breeding and her sense of justice in choosing to visit those who have made her son feel comfortable. We have had Christian friends before, and hope to have many more. But there will never be a bridging of the gap with the Tagantsevs until the Senator changes his position on the Jews of Russia. That is all."

Ossip looked at his sister for a moment in silence. He had seen the quick flood of color upon her cheekbones when their father had spoken, saw her chin stop quivering. He met her cool gray eyes and murmured, so that no one could hear but her, "I thought you had come to like Volodia! Have you now turned against him for his father's sins?"

Sonia looked aside, fumbled with her napkin. "No," she answered simply. Caught up in her sudden anguish, she did not notice Johanna's glance of interest in her direction. The governess no longer appeared cowed, and a glint of brightness shone in her aquamarine eyes. She bit into a piece of toast, and dabbed at her lips. Behind her napkin she was smiling.

On Thursday afternoon Sonia came to her mother in a soft blue-gray gown that was the exact hue of her eyes, and which was singular in its austere simplicity. The high ruffled collar and the trim on the long sleeves were of the finest lace, and they provided the only ornamentation on the outfit. In her pompadour Sonia had placed a comb encrusted with gray pearls. She wore no other gem.

Mathilde awaited their guest in a day gown of deep sapphire, which outlined her full figure. Johanna de Mey, in peach-colored muslin, was by far the most exuberant of the three women. Mathilde had sensed that this meeting meant a great deal to Ossip, and although she did not understand that more was involved than his friendship with Volodia, he had wordlessly communicated his message to his mother. Now she sat regally upon the sofa, wondering. Sonia, by her side, stood erect, almost protective of her family, thinking at once of her father's fierce expression during that breakfast several days before, and of Volodia's nut-brown features, so honest and unabashed. Super-imposed upon their faces was Ossip's, flushed as though with fever, as it had been the night of the Tagantsev ball. He had cried with such rapture, "She is perfect!" and Sonia felt herself stiffen against this mysterious "she" of whom her brother had not spoken since, but whom she instinctively felt to be a threat. She waited, her throat constricted.

When Stepan entered, he announced, "Countess Maria Efimovna Tagantseva, and her daughter, Countess Natalia Nicolaievna." Mathilde exchanged glances with her daughter: that was Volodia's twin. Mathilde's brows rose on a note of inquiry. And Sonia thought: Is this the "she"? When the women entered, and her mother stood to welcome them, Sonia's heart leaped with recognition: there could be no other "she" than this tall, willowy girl who had just appeared.

The Countess, who was in her middle forties, was elegant in a matronly way, with a high-crowned hat trimmed with flowers. She wore a gown of red silk with a high-necked overblouse and a skirt ending in three rows of ruffles. But her daughter, Natasha, gleamed beside her, her tall, slender form sheathed in a simple tailored dress of green cotton and a shorter jacket trimmed with astrakhan. Her straw hat was wide-brimmed and tilted up over her forehead, and her magnificent color radiated health. Sonia was taken aback. Sparkling blue eyes sought hers, and a warm hand pressed hers, and Natasha was saying, "So you are Ossip Davidovitch's sister!"

"You remember my brother . . . ?" Sonia asked, her voice small. But the young woman was already sitting down beside her, and the face she turned to Sonia was almost mocking in its happiness.

"How could I forget him?" she said. "I had so hoped he would be here . . ."

Sonia passed the girl a platter of delicate tea cakes, and replied: "But Ossip is in school. With Vladimir Nicolaievitch."

Natasha's lips parted, and she nodded. "Yes, naturally, you are right! So you are the one who sees my own twin brother more than I do! It is most intriguing to meet you at last. Ossip is the most charming man I know. Volodia speaks of him constantly! And he has described you to me in great detail. I could have recognized you anywhere! Would you have known me, too?"

Sonia passed Natasha a glass of hot tea with a slice of lemon. "I—I am sorry," she answered, "but I seldom see Vladimir Nicolaievitch for more than a few minutes a day. Unless, of course, it was Ossip you were talking about—" She blushed, and lowered her eyes. "Whom do you mean, Natalia Nicolaievna?"

The other girl tilted back her head and laughed. "I see why I have confused you!" she cried. "Although—to tell you the truth—I had been thinking of both. It is Volodia who described you for me, but I had wondered if perhaps Ossip Davidovitch had paid me a similar compliment. Or has he forgotten the dance?"

Sonia's hand went to her throat. She stammered, "I am certain he hasn't." Inside, she was thinking: He has told her of me! Of me! And I am not even pretty! Then she regarded Natasha, and saw that the color had left her cheeks and that her mouth had fallen open in an expression of dejection. She looked more closely at the beautiful girl, Ossip's mysterious "she," and suddenly she felt compassion. Impulsively she said, "He finds you 'perfect!' " And then horror assailed her. What had she said? Her father's face loomed before her, and she hid her confusion by sipping her tea.

But Natasha Tagantsev had tears in her eyes. " 'Perfect' . . ." she repeated. Then she leaned over and touched her mother's sleeve. "I beg your pardon, Mama, but did Volodia not say that he would meet us here after the gymnasium, with Ossip Davidovitch?"

Natalia had interrupted an agreeable conversation about Worth, Poiret, and the changing fashions, a genteel and matronly conversation, and now both mothers and Johanna looked at her. Natasha's frank blue gaze disarmed them.

"Yes, he did," her mother said, and then, apologetically, to Mathilde: "I hope that this was not yet another presumption on our part . . . ?"

"Not at all, Maria Efimovna. Vladimir Nicolaievitch is always welcome."

But Sonia, dismayed, whispered: "Ossip told me nothing of this plan!" And her hand flew to the comb in her pompadour, which she readjusted. Natasha smiled. "You have lovely fine hair," she stated gently.

They began to talk, unconscious really of the subject matter, for each was most acutely aware of the time. The young men would be arriving at any moment. Sonia stood straight-backed, like a figurine of porcelain and lace, and kept her voice controlled, pleasant, and neutral. Natasha relaxed against the soft cushions, her form elastic, her eyes expectant. She was older than Sonia by a year, and had officially come out into society, whereas Sonia was less sophisticated but more apt at hiding her emotions. She did not know how she felt about Natasha, only that she was greatly perturbed by this lanky, elegant girl who was Volodia's sister. She would think things through at a later, more private time.

When the young men's voices, joyful and deep, resounded from the hallway, instinctively both girls rose. Sonia felt frozen in position. She saw her brother's beautiful, fine face flush as he exchanged one intense look with Natasha, and that look disturbed her, as though she had seen something private. Both young men were greeting the ladies, bowing, kissing hands. Sonia saw Volodia's muscular form, his trim mustache, his waving brown hair parted in the center. She tried to avoid the magnetism of his chestnut eyes, but when he came to her, her heart began to pound in her temples. He said, "How good it is to see you when you are not rushing off to your room during our luncheons!" She smiled, and replied something inane. He had his sister's smile, open, totally disarming.

It was Johanna who called out to the young people, suggesting that they move to the piano room. Ossip, more lively than Sonia had ever seen him, led the way. "We shall play something for four hands," Volodia announced. Before Sonia could protest, he had drawn up the piano bench and was looking over her music sheets. Finally he sat down, for she had daintily taken her place, and Ossip and Natasha had moved farther back, by the window. She felt him take his seat, felt his leg again as she had felt it that day before her departure for Paris during the revolution. Their fingers stood poised above the keys, and they began to play. It was almost as if they were dancing with their fingertips. Neither of them spoke.

But Ossip was saying to Natasha, "I could not concentrate in class, thinking of you. It kills me not to see you. You look wonderful."

"And you," she said, unabashed, "are Apollo wading by a stream. I would be a naiad, if you would but have me!"

He could not touch her, so he gazed upon her, and she met his eyes. "I think of you when I go to sleep, Ossip Davidovitch," she said.

"And I do not sleep at all, thinking of you." He moistened his lips. "Natalia Nicolaievna—you wouldn't tease me, would you?"

Mutely, she shook her head. And then, surreptitiously, he seized her elegant tapered fingers and brought them to his lips. No one saw the gesture, for Sonia and Volodia were playing the piano, their music speaking for them. From the drawing room behind, the low laughter of the Countess with Mathilde and Johanna trickled through the halls.

Then, tentatively, Volodia spoke. "Your brother likes my sister," he declared; his words had a cadence in rhythm with the music.

"You would know more than I," Sonia said.

"Is Ossip afraid of your disapproval?"

Sonia blushed. She looked sideways at her companion. "It is the way of the world to like other people," she said.

"But Sofia Davidovna, liking is not the same as . . . loving."

She started, visibly. "We are all very young," she said, her voice high and strong. "Love is something too exalted for us to grasp."

His eyebrows rose. "We were speaking of them, not us," he said softly.

"Naturally," Sonia retorted angrily. Her fingers pranced over the keys, avoiding his. "I was merely explaining that Ossip and your sister cannot be taken seriously . . . and . . ."

"You are your brother's keeper?"

Sonia stopped playing. "Vladimir Nicolaievitch," she whispered furiously, "you know as well as I that they will only hurt each other! Do you wish to encourage what cannot be?"

His brown eyes bored into her level gray ones. "No," he said sadly, "I do not encourage them, though I wish I could. I know of no finer individuals than Natasha and Ossip. I respect their feelings, though you do not. That is because you have not learned to love my sister. But no, I do not encourage them. I don't, however, discourage them too much. It would be cruel to throw water upon their fire. Life will do it in time."

"And our fathers," she stated.

"It will never go that far," Volodia countered. Then he gazed at her, and his mournful expression surprised her. "This is a cruel life," he said with bitterness.

Her young profile shone like an etching next to him, and all at once his hand moved upward as if to touch her cheek. She felt rather than saw his intention, and turned to face him. Her gray eyes opened wide, like those of a frightened doe, and her bloodless lips were parted, aghast, yet yearning. "No!" she said, but she could not move, and so his fingers reached out and rested for a second upon the softness of her cheek. They sat in numbed, shocked silence, his fingertips upon her cheek, her lips parted, her eyes afraid. And then his hand fell away, and she watched it fall, entranced, electrified. "I envy Ossip his facility with words," Volodia murmured, and once again he began to play. But this time there was no fire to his music, only a restless imprecision.

"It is time to return home, my children," the Countess was calling.

Although the First Duma, composed of officials elected by the Russian people, had opened in early March 1906, the Tzar's Council, or Senate, still acted as the upper house of this effort at parliamentarianism. The elite, selected by the Tzar himself, and those chosen by the aristocracy, belonged to the Senate. Count Nicolai Tagantsev was a distinguished member.

On the evening following the Countess's visit to the Gunzburg home, David faced his family and announced gravely: "I have been asked to accomplish a tremendous task, for which I have prepared, it seems, all my life. Our attorneys, my father, and I have drawn up a proposal which comes before the Council tomorrow, and I must argue for its adoption. If I win, then the law that now banishes widows and orphans of Jewish artisans and members of the Second Guild to the Pale of Settlement within twenty-four hours of the death of their provider, will finally be abolished. But if I fail in convincing the Council members, then I am afraid that the law will be here to stay . . ."

Mathilde said: "And who will support you, David?"

Her husband sighed. "Since Witte's dismissal from before the opening of the Duma, we have lost our sta est supporter. Pobedonòstsev will oppose us with all might, as will Count Tagantsev, who can sway others with his eloquence. I am afraid, my love."

"But you needn't be, about the Count!" Mathilde exclaimed. "The Countess was telling me that he is ill with influenza, and has had a raging fever. It is a stroke of pure luck, isn't it?"

"Oh, Papa, you shall win!" Sonia cried. She raised bright eyes to her father. "Please, Papa, I should like to hear you plead. Would Grandfather take me?"

But Johanna replied at once: "Young ladies do not belong in politics. Have you not sufficiently learned from Anna's mistakes? Do you wish to cause your family renewed embarrassment?"

David's mild blue eyes went from the governess to his daughter. Coolly he declared: "Sonia is a lady, Johanna. In my father's presence not one tongue would wag. In fact, I should be proud to know that she is there, in the gallery. And no one," he added, gently regarding his wife, "looks to the gallery during speeches. Do not be concerned, Mathilde."

"I think that you are embroiling the children in matters that should not involve them," she replied coldly.

"Papa is old. The presence of his young granddaughter would do him infinite good. I would think of your approval as a blessing, Mathilde."

"But what an outrage . . . !" Johanna murmured, rolling her eyes in their sockets. "A little girl—"

Mathilde closed her eyes and pressed her fingers to her temples. Her husband insisted, softly: "This is the most important task of my life as a Russian Jew. Would you deprive me of my children? Ossip will be in school, and Gino is too young. That leaves me Sonitchka."

No one spoke for several minutes. Then Gino, who had perked up at the mention of his name, looked brightly at his mother. He was a tousle-haired boy of eleven, with apple cheeks and glowing eyes. Now he asked: "Mama, when will the Countess invite you to her home? Do you want to see it?"

Mathilde opened her eyes and said evenly, "But I shall never visit Maria Efimovna. It would not be proper. She paid us a great compliment by coming here, but she made me understand that it would be impossible for her to receive me. Her husband would never allow it. Ossip is a young boy, and for him an exception can be made. But our socializing has ended with the Countess's visit."

Johanna de Mey lifted a corner of her mouth in disdain, and looked at David with unconcealed dislike. Only Sonia saw her, and for a few minutes blazing hatred filled the young girl's heart. "Oh, Mama, please!" she cried. "I promise never again to mingle where I do not belong! You know that I am not the least concerned with politics—"

Mathilde stood up, shaking. She brought her linen napkin to her lips, and steadied herself by holding onto the table with her other hand. "I cannot bear this chaotic discussion," she whispered, and pushed back her chair. She began to walk away, and was caught by Johanna, who placed her thin arm strongly about Mathilde's body. The two women left the room, leaning upon each other.

"Do not worry, Papa," Sonia said, and her pure young voice was fresh with confidence. "We shall win this battle."

Sonia sat beside her grandfather, frail and petite in this grandiose gallery where, below her, the most important personages of the nation were assembled. She wore a bonnet trimmed with white ermine and a matching woolen suit and kept her tiny hands encased within her fur muff. Baron Horace, more somber than ever, breathed heavily next to her, following the reactions on the faces of the Senators as his own son pleaded in the arena.

Sonia's cheeks were bright, and she thought: Papa has never spoken such moving, passionate words! How can one remain dry-eyed before him? She listened to the closing message, which David's voice conveyed with strength and urgency. He walked slowly before the members, clothed in his most elegant black suit with tiny white pinstripes, and Sonia's heart swelled with pride that he was hers.

"Honored Senators, I lay before you the plight of these impoverished women and children, most of whom were born in this capital, most of whom have never left it for a day in their lives. I place before you this image: torn with grief, bewildered and lost, a young woman and her babies arrive in the Pale, without means of livelihood, without knowing a single soul to whom to turn. Would you banish this woman, for the mere reason that she lights Sabbath candles instead of crossing herself before the Icon of Jesus? I think that your hearts would not allow you to continue this immorality, for you are good men, one and all, and each of you knows the true meaning of compassion. Justice, gentlemen. Justice to these unfortunates, to these insignificant women who can hurt no one, who are burdens to no one. I beg of you—"

All at once a commotion interrupted David's words, and

Sonia squirmed in her seat to see where the noise had come from. Two men and a young boy were entering the hall, bearing a stretcher upon which lay a fourth man. They laid the stretcher down and helped the ailing one to a seat. There was something disquietingly familiar in this picture, Sonia thought. She stared below, fear gripping her. Her father had stopped speaking, and now the sick man rose, steadying himself upon the shoulder of the boy, and his voice, enormous and infuriated, filled the chamber:

"Fellow Senators! Will you be harangued by Baron Gunzburg, whose golden tongue buys him our top officials, whose honeyed images fall like a veil between you and reality? I heard about this proposal, and although I am weak and ill, I could not let you down. I came, disobeying the orders of my physician. I risk my life, dear friends, to oppose this man's folly: he seeks to fill this holy capital with Jews, who bring their pestilence and their meanness to our cities, who envelop us with disease, who foment trouble between our peasants and the government. Would we fall like other empires to the hands of the Jews? Would we be Prussians? Or French? Would we succumb to the rule of these Disraelis? No, for we are members of Holy Russia, and Jesus Christ protects us from the scum of the earth who seek to destroy us with their wiles and their hypocrisies! Let not the Baron take this first step into your souls—for with him come the hordes of Antichrist, to swallow us!"

Sonia sat immobile, her mouth white, her eyes wide with horror. She saw her father, tall and spare, and before him the massive sick man brandishing his gold-studded cane. She was so horrified that for a few seconds this face, distorted with red hatred, blotted out everything else in the auditorium. Then she glanced down and saw the young man upon whose shoulder her father's attacker leaned. She froze, and shivers passed over and over her spine as she made out the stocky, muscular form of Volodia Tagantsev,

his brown hair waving, his brown eyes large and serious. A
scream died in her throat, and she remembered the touch
of his fingertips upon her cheek. A faintness overpowered
her.

She began to breathe in small gasps, to regain her
strength, and when at length the room came back into
focus she sat still. Then, to her horror, Volodia turned his
face toward the gallery, and she saw his glance encounter
her and witnessed his momentary trembling at the sight of
her. Their eyes held. But in hers was such a complete,
unadulterated rage and hatred that he took a half-step
back, as though stricken. She rose from her seat and
turned quickly upon her heel, her grandfather's shocked
gaze upon her back. Before Baron Horace could utter a
word to hold her there, she had run from the gallery, down
the stairs, and toward the majestic doors of the Senate.
There she halted, breathless, and let her face sink into her
hands.

Dry sobs shook her. She heard rapid footsteps approaching but did not look up. Nothing mattered now, her father
had lost, and life would never be the same. A male voice
said, "Sofia Davidovna! It is not as you think! He is my
father, and an ill man. I did not come here to support his
views, only to support his body, which is failing. You must
believe me—"

Her hands dropped to her side, and she stared into
Volodia's earnest face. Her own features were drawn into a
grimace of pure horror. "Don't ever speak to me again!"
she cried at last.

"But I have done nothing!" Volodia replied, his voice
strong and defensive.

"You? You have the gall to come to me, after your
father has destroyed mine, after he has crushed his heart?
You are a worm, Vladimir Nicolaievitch. I hope that Ossip
bars you from our home!"

"You are being melodramatic, and childish," Volodia

argued. "This is but a single battle of many. Each of our fathers has won some, lost others. But why should you turn away from me, when I am your avowed friend?"

Hot tears streamed down Sonia's cheeks. "Go away," she pleaded, the harshness leaving her. She resembled a very small girl. Her frail body trembled uncontrollably. In desperation and frenzy, Volodia took a step toward her, and waited. She appeared not to notice him anymore, so wracking was her grief, so alone did she feel. She wept, and wrung her hands, and her pathetic face wrinkled and reddened. He took a second step, firmly placed his arms about her shaking form, holding her against him. When she did not protest, his hand reached to her hair, and he smoothed it with calm fingers. "Don't break your heart, little one," he whispered, "there must be a solution . . ."

When she looked up into his face, he nodded, and repeated, his words stronger now, and more determined: "There must be a solution!"

Book 2

Nine

Dearest Sonitchka [the letter began],

You are nearing your sixteenth birthday, and are able to understand certain matters now as an adult. You write me of your wish to come to see me, to arrange for Mama and you to come to Darmstadt during the summer. Please—it would be a grave error, and would prove disastrous!

What can I say to explain my tremendous reluctance to see any member of our family? "Reluctance" is hardly the word: I would, quite literally, make another escape, this time without leaving a single trace of my whereabouts. I cannot face any of you—no, my love, not even your sweetness, for I have my own pain to bear and I am not prepared to share it with anyone from the past. I love you dearly. You must remember that I think most of you, then of Gino and Papa, for you are all in my heart. But my life these recent years was most important to me, and to see you without dredging up bitter memories would be impossible. And *not* to discuss what happened would be hypocrisy.

So please, Sonia, tell Mama that I shall not see her this year. I am of age, and shall stand by my feelings.

Next year the wounds will have begun to heal, and I will want to be with you all, even Mama. But not now.

You can tell everyone that life in Darmstadt continues to be productive and peacefully charming: in other words, *gemütlich,* as they say here. I work with Herr Bader on my landscapes, and he is most pleased with my progress in oils. He says that aquarelle is too soft a medium for my stormy nature! I am also taking sculpting lessons from a Herr Habig. I have finished a statuette called "Despair," which fitted the moods of previous months. But do not be concerned: my next work is to be a profile medallion of you, sweet sister, from memory. You can see how I think of you!

My friend, Dalia Hadjani, is still with me all the time, and a more interesting, compassionate human being could hardly exist. A terrible tragedy recently befell her, which has knocked the breath from me and which has also placed all my own "problems" in perspective. Her husband died in Teheran, quite suddenly. We did not learn of it at once. First, the money he was sending stopped coming. Then news arrived. He had died of an infection, for Dalia tells me that Persia is not quite the hygienic paradise to which we are accustomed in Europe. He did not leave her the fortune she expected, for it seems that business was worse than he had led her to understand. She does not wish to return to Persia. First of all, there is the physician in Lausanne who must deliver her baby. Then, there is the sadness of returning to a country where her beloved is no more—and Dalia cannot bear the idea. Her parents are both deceased.

Therefore, she will remain with me. We are grateful for each other's company, and we share our passion for our art. She is really quite better than she had thought, and Herr Bader has praised her a good deal. We shall lick our wounds and proceed, and perhaps we shall grow wiser in the process! I do not guarantee it—who can? But we shall try, in our own way. And there will be a baby soon. Babies offer their own opinions on the world. I am looking forward to Dalia's child.

Take care, Sonitchka. Take care of Papa, and my Gino, and Ossip, who must be quite splendid from the way you described him in your last letter. Give Mama my regards. I hug you to my heart, little one, for I love you tenderly.

Sonia felt a pain in her chest from the scrawled signature, "Anna," as she put the letter down on her secretary. She stood still, her mind disquieted. Her sister did not want to see her, but was constantly in the company of a stranger, the Persian woman. Anna did not appear to love Mama any longer. Anna was bitter; Anna tried to be funny—Anna's mood could not be gauged. Yet she had a friend, and was involved in a life that brought her peace. She, Sonia, was selfish to be jealous of this friend, for Annushka had only made one other friend in her life, and that had been Ivan. Now she had a new friend, and this time she seemed to have chosen well. Anna had sent a portrait she had made of Dalia Hadjani, and everybody, even Johanna, had declared that she looked distinguished and well bred. Now this woman had undergone a tragedy, and Anna was helping her. It always felt good to help, Sonia thought.

Yet there was a strange note to this letter, Sonia mused, though she could not explain her anxiety. She put the letter away to be answered later that week, after she had read it to her Papa and spoken to him about Anna's adamant refusal to see them. She had an odd sensation that Johanna would, for once, take Anna's side. For with Anna removed, the vocal opposition had been drastically reduced in the Gunzburg household, and the governess appeared much happier.

"No, thank you, Marfa," she told the young servant who had come to the door. "I am truly not hungry for tea today."

"You do not seem to realize the danger into which you are placing yourself," Volodia said to his sister. "If Papa—or Mama, for that matter—so much as suspected that there was the slightest courtship between you and Ossip, he would send you away. Every time he comes to supper, I am afraid for you. You are both so reckless, Natasha!"

She tossed her head and shrugged impatiently. "But you are so solid, my love! Ossip is like quicksilver, and so am I. I shall not do without him. We belong together. We laugh at the same silly things, we like the same plays and are bored by the same people. You must convince Papa to invite him for the summer to the Tambov. I could not bear to be away from him for two and a half months! Papa likes him—he really does! He does not think of Ossip as a Jew, but as your friend!"

"As my friend, perhaps. But never, never as your lover! And life is not merely a matter of plays and people, and silly jokes, Natasha—you are not a child! You are nearly eighteen! Puppy love is fun, but don't play at Romeo and Juliet with someone who would give his lifeblood for you at the least encouragement—and Ossip would, I know. He would defy his family if you would let him!"

"Then I shall let him! You belittle me, Volodia. I love Ossip. I would leave all of you, even you, even Mama, to spend my days with him forever! And you would begrudge me two and a half months? Papa would not refuse you your friend. And I promise you to behave, and not give away my feelings for him. I swear it to you, Volodia."

"Even if Papa allowed me to invite Ossip, do you think his father would allow him to accept? It was not amusing in the Senate, Natasha."

His sister was sprawled elegantly on her chaise longue,

regarding him with her deep blue eyes. Suddenly she sat up, her face quickening. "Volodia!" she cried. "I have the most wonderful idea—an idea to foil the suspicions of a veritable spy! What if Mama were to make this a family invitation? You don't dislike Sofia Davidovna, do you? I like her very much, although I don't think she approves of my love for her brother. But if she were invited along—she is to have her debut soon, isn't she?—then no one would think to watch me and Ossip! The group would be larger, and you and Sonia would both be our chaperones. Don't you see?"

Volodia had gone chalk white. His hand, on the side of her chaise, gripped the soft silk more tightly. He said, "I suppose that is a possibility. But Sofia Davidovna is a willful girl. She won't want to go."

"Ossip will convince her," Natasha said. "They are close, aren't they? I am convincing you, am I not?"

Volodia smiled grimly. "You have your ways, Natasha. I shall broach the subject to Mama, then. She liked the Baroness very much. Perhaps she will succeed in persuading Papa. After all, Ossip has come to supper several times, and he does know him now."

Natasha clapped her hands, and then, impulsively, threw her arms around her brother's neck. He began to laugh sheepishly. "No wonder Ossip is a besotted fool!" he declared. Then he stood still, remembering the feel of Sonia's young, frail body in his arms. Now he did not laugh. Perhaps it was dishonorable to try to trap her this way, through Natasha and Ossip . . . He thought for a moment of her grieving face, turned to him in fury—and then he made up his mind.

"I am tired of being used," Sonia said to her brother. "First there is Anna, who does not want to see me, but who wishes instead that I find ways of persuading Mama not to go to her this summer. And now you, Ossip! I shall not tell Mama that I would like to go with you to the Tagantsevs. The fact is that your behavior over Natasha is shameful! The daughter of that dreadful man—"

"It is always Papa, isn't it, Sonia?" Ossip shot back, his eyes flashing angrily. "What about me? Don't I have feelings? I have a heart, and Papa has a cause. How can you place his damned cause above my feelings?"

"You are selfish in your indulgence. Papa thinks of the Jews," Sonia replied. "You were not at the Senate. You didn't even care! You would much rather not be a Jew at all, wouldn't you?"

Clenching his fists, Ossip nodded, his face flooded with color. "That's right!" he cried. "I don't believe in God, or why would he have allowed me to be crippled as a baby, or Anna to be deformed? If I believed, then I might choose the faith that suited me. But I am stuck in a religion that excludes me from what I want in this world. If Papa accepts the Jewish way, it is because he is strengthened by a firm belief. I am not. It's as simple as that. I'm as good as the next man, but because of a religion in which I do not believe, I am barred from certain privileges, and, what's more important, from openly courting the woman I love, and who loves me! Is that fair? Tell me, is it?"

Sonia's small face constricted with pain. "I wish that you believed," she whispered.

"So do I. It is far easier to live when one's faith is intact. But you are perfect, Sonia, untouched by hurt. You have reason to cling to a God. I stopped listening to Papa's litanies when I was still tied to my special crib. Mama does not believe, either. She was not happy as a child, and so she, too, had reason to doubt the existence of a fair-minded God. Only those who are unscathed can still believe."

"I am not so unscathed," his sister murmured. "You don't know me so well."

"I would like to," Ossip said. "You are a secretive person, Sonia. I share myself with you, but you only take, you do not return confidences. Sometimes I am ready to give up with you. And sometimes you make me furious, for you are rigid as an oak tree, when you should be a willow." He looked at her closely. "What is wrong with Natasha?"

"Natasha has everything, and I believe she would share it all with you. I see no harm in her intentions. But it's impossible! Don't you see? You are not realistic, Ossip. Is any woman worth hurting so many people? If Natasha were Jewish—or even if she weren't, but was the daughter of another man—then I would be happy for you, and would do anything to help you. Don't you *see*?"

Ossip passed his tongue over his dry lips. "All right, Sonia," he said. "Why don't you give me the chance to see? Come with me to the Tambov, then she and I will see if we truly do love each other, seeing each other in the same house day after day. Perhaps you're right, and we are merely being children, playing at love. There is attraction in forbidden fruit. There is also attraction in memory, from visit to visit. We have never been together sufficiently long, or sufficiently frequently, to see whether our feelings would survive the test of a life together. Won't you help me make up my mind? Then, if I reject her, you will feel that you helped set me free of this obsession; and if I don't— you will feel that I gave myself every chance, that I was not an impulsive adolescent!" His blue eyes pleaded with her. "Won't you do this for me, Sonitchka?"

She stood before him, her hands together as in prayer. She nodded slowly. "All right," she replied. But her voice was almost inaudible. She cleared her throat. "You are a weakling, Ossip. I love you more than anyone on earth, but you are weak. I will do this for you, but in your place I would not have to ask. It is good that Natasha has spirit, for you lack it."

His mouth opened, then closed without making a sound. The color had drained from his face.

It was the Countess Tagantseva who convinced Mathilde before anyone else. She made her invitation by telephone, telling Mathilde that her children had grown much attached to Ossip, and were becoming quite fond of Sonia. "During our visit, the four of them enjoyed one another, did they not?" she asked, in her gentle, cultured voice. "We always fill our summer residence in the Tambov with young people. If you would permit Sonia and Ossip to come, my children would be delighted. The twins will soon be grown. I shall not be able to give them these pleasures when they are married and away from me . . . Friendships are wonderful, don't you agree, Mathilde Yureyevna?"

"Yes," Mathilde replied. "Volodia was Ossip's first friend, and Sonia is very shy. Our summer plans have changed. We had first thought to visit my older daughter in Darmstadt." Her voice faltered, then regained its strength. "And now that Ossip and Sonia are older, Mohilna, our estate in Podolia, has become somewhat boring to them. There are so few young people around them . . ."

But when she entered David's study that evening, Mathilde hesitated. She remembered the few times during their marriage when David had been intractable, and she flinched at the memories. He had been reserved, almost removed from family concerns since that day in the Senate, and now she was suddenly afraid of the gaunt pale face that turned to greet her. But she stood before him and calmly explained that Countess Tagantseva had invited the children to spend the summer at their family estate in the Tambov. "Think how much the Senator must love his children, to bend so to their desires," she concluded.

David's blue eyes narrowed. Then, slowly, grimly, he nodded. She saw that he had not even looked at her. "They shall go," he declared. "Nicolai Tagantsev will assume that the Gunzburgs won't dare face him. He shall be proven wrong. My children will go, and will be good guests. He will be compelled to see them for two and a half months, day in and day out. Sonia will charm him. Yes, Mathilde. They will go to the Tambov."

* * *

Ossip had never been able to participate in too many sports, and when Count Tagantsev and his older son, Nicolai, took their male guests hunting through their magnificent forest, he remained behind, rowing across the lake to the small island where the young people spread out white linen cloths to eat their lunch. He took special care not to look at Natasha too much when her parents were present, was cautious when guests arrived from neighboring estates for a game of croquet on the green lawns, or to play the newfangled sport, tennis, from which he was excluded because a hard ball might hit him on the back. But during the picnics on the island, he would sit with her beneath a large tree, and while they distractedly nibbled finger sandwiches, their eyes, of a twin blue that was like a darkened summer sky, would devour each other's faces with unabashed hunger and the wonder of discovery. Then, in hushed tones, they would talk, and everyone else would melt into the lush background.

Ossip had never spent such marvelous days. His entire body suddenly felt tense and virile, and he noticed the wind on his skin, the sunlight on his face, the rain on his shoulders. He had always observed the world, detached and aloof and somewhat cynical, but now he participated, with a child's delight. Before, he had questioned everything; now he accepted all, most of all Natasha, whose voice, throaty and somewhat husky, haunted him at night as he tossed in his bed. He imagined her nude, and was unashamed and happy at his own reaction. Sometimes he would burst into wild laughter, and nobody knew why, except Natasha, who would join in. They laughed at their togetherness, at their great beauty, at the novelty of being in love.

While Ossip and Natalia danced on the grass in their bare feet, Sonia and Volodia watched them intently. Volodia, who loved them both, was immensely sad, and Sonia, who loved her father and her brother and who did not quite understand the impulsive, winsome abandon of a

Natalia Tagantseva, was disquieted. There was something offensive to her in Ossip's capacity for laughter and fun and love, when the reason was this girl, so unlike herself in appearance and temperament. Yet she could not dislike Natasha; she was a fountain of goodness as well as of mirth, and she showed her vulnerability in her eyes, which stated, openly, her love for Ossip.

Sonia was so watchful of her brother that she did not notice a pattern developing. While Ossip and Natasha paired off, she would walk slowly behind them, Volodia at her side, having conversations that never quite began and never quite left off from the previous one. She knew that the young man was near her, and she accepted his reassuring words, his staunchness. It was as though she sought his support in an unspoken way, and was rewarded by his invariable presence, quietly strong. She admired his lack of drama, so different from both Natasha's and Ossip's. Yet she was aware of his body, of his solidity, of his good smell of cologne and health. She was aware of his thighs beneath their broadcloth, of his brown hands. And most of all, she discovered how comfortable she felt when they spoke together. Yet, under all this comfort, there was a tautness inside her that frightened her, a kind of expectancy.

He was very careful with her. Although he was not quite eighteen, he seemed older, for he possessed the maturity of the strong, an inward calm. "My little brother, Gino, will grow up like you," she said to him one day. "He is simple, uncomplicated, and perfectly at ease within himself."

"You make us both sound like cuts of roast beef," he replied, smiling.

She blushed. "I did not intend it that way, Vladimir Nicolaievitch. It is just that I detest histrionics. They make me uncomfortable."

"You mean that Natasha and Ossip make you uncomfortable," he said.

She started. Then, looking at him, she nodded. "I suppose

so. My mother is very calm, very serene. Our governess is just the opposite. Juanita is hysterical and grandiose and strident, and when I am near her every nerve in my body is on edge. I could not sleep in the same room with her."

"Mademoiselle de Mey? But she seems very different from my sister, or Ossip. High strung, nervous, like a jack-rabbit by the side of the road. Natasha and Ossip, on the other hand, are alive, and able to release their nervous energies. I envy them. I am so calm, so 'wise,' my mother says"—and an ironic smile lit his tanned face—"so uniform, that I do wonder why more lively people do not shy away from me."

"I find you peaceful," Sonia stated simply. Her large gray eyes sought his, and he was deeply moved by the innocent trust that glowed there.

"Another man might be dismayed if a lovely lady called him 'peaceful,' " he said. "We men wish to excite, don't we? But I cannot be what I'm not. And so . . . I am flattered."

She smiled at him, and he saw the perfect teeth, the tilted chin, the small fine nose. He wished all at once to crush her against him. He was a boulder, and she was a tiny edelweiss, rare and dainty. He knew that he was already a man, but what was she? His sister was unquestionably a woman; Sonia was still part child. And it was this strange mixture that sent his blood coursing hotly through his veins. He gazed at the tiny hand, milk white, and wanted to hold it. But he did not. Instead, he resumed his steps, and she went along beside him.

One afternoon, on the island, they saw Ossip and Natasha near the edge of the water. Sonia had remained by the baskets of food, and Volodia sat beside her, folding the linen. At the water's edge, Natasha raised her arms as though to hug the skies, and twirled on her toes. Ossip, facing her, threw back his head, and they heard his laughter. Natalia was like a daffodil, extending her fingers upward and out, and suddenly she fell back, and was caught by the laughing boy. Then she turned her face to him, and their lips met. Sonia's mouth parted, the glass fell from her hand. Ossip's dark curls had bent toward Natasha, and now their kiss was fierce. Sonia could not see Natasha's face, only her shining hair. Her own eyes grew wide, and she turned around and looked at Volodia.

His face had not changed. He met her gaze, and reassured her with the steadiness of his own. She bit her lower lip. He looked away, and saw the tiny hand motionless upon the white linen cloth. Her face was ashen. Without a word, he reached for her hand, and before she could remove it, he pressed it quickly, once. Then he let it go. She sat speechless by his side, confused and shocked and yet relieved.

It was Volodia who rowed back under a copper sun. Sonia sat still, numbed by the hypnotic motion of his muscular arms. A strange thrill ran through her. She felt warm, moist. Beside her, Ossip was saying, "No, I do not agree. The Knights of the Round Table are not dead. They dwell somewhere in the woods, with Robin Hood's merry men, and they continue to inspire gallant youths pursuing fair maidens. Why should they have died?"

"I would like to agree with you, but really, our own times are far less romantic than you say," Natasha replied.

"What do you think, Volodia?" Ossip asked.

"Oh, I don't know . . . We Russians do have a romantic spirit, Natasha. Ossip here is a perfect example. He is Sir Galahad incarnate. I am more reasonable—but for a fair maiden, even I might be moved." He smiled at them, continuing to row.

His sister laughed. "What is your opinion, Sofia Davidovna?"

"It depends," Sonia declared. "I think that Vladimir Nicolaievitch can dance admirably. But I do not imagine him in an atmosphere such as that of the Round Table. You are probably right, Natalia Nicolaievna. Our time does not lend itself to grand gestures, such as fighting a war over a woman."

"Helen of Troy, or Guenevere? What did they possess, dear heart, that you do not?" Ossip cried, striking a dramatic pose and gazing at Natasha. Everyone laughed. "Come now," he continued, "put me to the test. I would fight a war for you!"

Sonia was suddenly silent, but Natasha cocked her head to one side and examined him impishly. "A war. That's nice. But hardly likely. How easy it is for you to promise me the moon! What if, instead, I were to ask you to jump overboard as a pledge of devotion?"

The sun was gleaming upon the lake, casting copper lights upon its smooth surface. Volodia rowed, smiling. Even Sonia sat smiling. Natasha's head, dark and curled, tilted up toward Ossip. All at once, he bowed deeply from the waist, and tossed his legs over the side of the boat.

"Ossip!" Sonia cried. "You can't swim!" But he had jumped into the water, and his arms flailed wildly about him. Natasha stood up, breathless, her smile gone, and Volodia pushed the oars back and bent over the rim of the boat. He stretched his hand out and grabbed Ossip's arm. Straining, he pulled his friend to him, until Ossip could grab the side and be hoisted up, dripping wet.

"Oh, Ossip, you fool!" his sister cried. But Natasha was throwing a tablecloth from the baskets over his shoulders. Ossip shivered and laughed.

"Sir Galahad always was a fool," he admitted. "But it was all for a worthy cause!" His eyes sought Natasha's, which gleamed with unspilled tears. He sat, huddled under the white linen cloth, his hair matted, but there was a radiance in his face that made his ludicrous appearance seem almost noble. He held out his wet palm, and silently Natasha placed her slender fingers upon it. Sonia stared at them, her heart beating erratically. She opened her mouth but could not speak, and her embarrassment was so great that she turned her face aside.

Volodia was rowing once more. "Don't worry," he told her gently, "he will not have time to catch cold. We shall tell my mother that the boat tipped and Ossip was caught off balance and fell out. All this is quite harmless, I assure you!"

But her gray eyes met his and he fell silent. A strong pain gripped his heart, forcing him to look away. The oars dipped into the calm waters, dipped again. In the boat, the four young people sat wordlessly. Natasha's hand remained inside Ossip's, motionless. A soft breeze began to blow in the amber sunlight.

"I don't know," Mathilde repeated, shaking her head. "Sixteen is very young, Irina . . . Do not forget that Nina is a full year older than Sonia."

"But Sonia is more mature," Irina Markovna Tobias countered pettishly. She poured her friend a glassful of strong tea, and deposited a slice of lemon into it. "Come now . . . I shall not give a ball to introduce Nina into Petersburg society if you refuse to allow your own daughter to make her debut at my party!"

"I suppose that since they are such good friends, Nina would miss Sonia," Mathilde said.

"No, it isn't that, really. The ball will be one big bother, to tell you the truth, Mathilde. I would not go through with it merely for Nina. She's such a plain little thing. But if it were known that Baroness David de Gunzburg's daughter were also making a debut, then my efforts would seem more worthwhile. You would not mind? If Sonia came out at my ball, rather than at one of your own?"

Mathilde sat still, shocked. "I do not mind if she comes out at your ball, Irina," she replied. "She is actually too young, but you are right, she is poised for her age. It was Anna's lack of involvement with my friends . . . However, one should not give a party for someone else's child. Sonia would be honored to attend Nina's ball—but it cannot be a ball in both their names. That would be improper, and I could not be a part of it."

"As long as she and Ossip attend, I shall be happy," Irina Markovna said. She twinkled at her friend: "You needn't come, if you don't want to! Society these days is so permissive! Can you imagine what it would have been like, to be allowed to go to balls with one's brother, instead of one's Mama? Yet today the mothers do not want to bother entertaining one another, and the girls come with their brothers. Poor Nina! She has no brother."

"I am sorry, Irina," Mathilde said gently. But she thought ironically: Now I see your need for Sonia! If my daughter comes out at the same time as yours, then you shall not have to trouble yourself to accompany her to future engagements! My son will serve as a suitable escort for both girls. She said, "David may not agree with me about Sonia. But I shall let you know next week."

"Yes. Be a lamb, and convince him," Irina Markovna cooed. She plumped a cushion and reclined upon it, sighing with contentment. Mathilde thought: I shall let Sonia go! But for Nina's sake, not yours. Nina needs a friend . . .

Nina's ball was to be in costume, and Tatiana de Gunzburg, who was fifteen, was red with rage. It was November 1906, and she stood in her aunt's sitting room, her pretty hands on her round hips, her blue eyes flashing, her golden curls falling out of their knot. "It simply isn't fair!" she cried, and real tears appeared on the edge of her long lashes.

"It will be your turn next year, Tania," Ossip said, smiling. He was amused. His mother and Johanna were finishing the last details of his costume, which was quite unusual. They had dripped candle wax in circles and polka dots and straight lines, all over the large silk trimmings of his oldest tuxedo, and over the back of his jacket. The hardened wax had formed a strange design, in different colors, from different candles. Johanna had cut the pant legs at midcalf and had sewn green lace ruffles at the edges. He wore white stockings and black patent leather dancing pumps, and in his green silk cravat knot was a crystal decanter stopper. His cufflinks had been concocted out of wine corks, and on his head sat a green straw basket, upside down, in which a friend of the family had sent candied figs for somebody's birthday. Johanna stood on her tiptoes, pinning a hat brush with an ivory handle to the front of this inverted basket, "So that your hat will have its trim," she announced.

"No one will dance with you," Tatiana said peevishly. But her blue eyes widened as she watched, admiring his supple body in its strange disguise.

"Perhaps not," he chuckled. He did not really care about this ball, and did not mind humoring Tania. He thought: If they only hadn't spoiled her so, she would actually be beguiling. She had grown quite beautiful, though she was not Ossip's type. Suddenly he was sad, remembering the ball at which he had met Natasha, who would of course not be present this evening. "I am going in order to please Sonia, and that is all," he said out loud.

"And do you have a name, you selfless man?" Tania demanded.

In reply, he handed her a round green card engraved with the words "Knight Mare of Dread." She burst into laughter. "Do break a few hearts," she said. "That will help to eliminate the competition!"

But he was lost in thought, and her words caught him off guard. "For whom?" he asked.

Johanna stood back, surveying her work, and her sharp aquamarine eyes sought his. She said, sharply, "You are a child, Tatiana Alexandrovna. Your cousin does not take you seriously." But she was still regarding Ossip. He has something on his mind, that one, she thought, and it has no bearing on that little minx. But she said nothing more, and her terse statement seemed to dismiss Tatiana, whose eyes began to flash with true hatred.

Sonia's outfit was not at all bizarre. She wore the traditional peasant garb of the Ukraine, which had been sewn for her by the servants of Mohilna. It was a holiday outfit, fancier than the everyday dress which Anna had often worn at home. As Sonia entered the room, her mother said, "You look charming, my love," but she was thinking: When I was sixteen, I had already been betrothed.

Sonia's shirt was of white linen, embroidered in red and black above the puffy sleeves and in two strips down the front, as well as on the tight cuffs and the straight low collar. Instead of a skirt, she wore a *plakhta*, a square of woven red and black wool held together at the waist by a large pin, and opening slightly at the front. A woolen belt cinched her slim waist. Her black hair fell loosely about her dainty shoulders and was crowned by a braid of dried flowers, bluebells, daisies, pansies, and interwoven sprigs of wheat. Around her neck were eight rows of glass beads, each row a different color and a different size, tied at the back with multicolored ribbons that cascaded down her back to her knees. Her feet were encased in red moccasin boots adorned with a golden acorn on each foot. She sought Ossip's eyes and read his approval.

"Don't be frightened, little one," he said softly. "This is a grand occasion, for you are now a woman in the eyes of the world!" But he did not know that behind her apprehension and mingled with her excitement, was the wrenching pain of knowing that someone special would not be there, as he had been during the summer. She pushed the memory resolutely from her mind, as if it were a wisp of recalcitrant hair, and she said to her brother, "You will dance often with Nina?"

"Naturally. She is to be my hostess," he replied, amused.

"He may even find better," Johanna commented. "Your Nina is too unassuming for a splendid boy like Ossip."

"Nina is a lady, and does not promote herself in flamboyant ways," Sonia stated coolly. She thought of Ossip, dripping water into the boat, holding Natasha's hand as though they were married already. Nina, she said to herself, and inwardly she smiled, a warm glow spreading through her.

Soon it was time for Ossip and Sonia to leave for the ball, while a sulking Tania stayed behind. Ossip held his sister's hand as they rode in the landau. His feelings toward her had gone through several rather drastic changes over the past months, for he had felt outraged at her apparent lack of enthusiasm for Natasha, but had also sensed her own despair. At that moment he loved her more than ever; she was beautiful, and he felt that once he announced his plans regarding Natasha, she would have to accept, and take the other girl into her heart. He was prepared to love everyone, for he was loved in return by Natalia Tagantseva herself.

Nina Tobias greeted them with quiet joy. She was clothed as a Roman, in a piece of red cloth draped toga-fashion about her strong young body with its pleasant curves. Her brown hair rippled down her neck in coils, and a crown of laurel leaves sat upon them. Her hazel eyes gleamed like polished bronze, and her cheeks were red with anticipation. She did not know Ossip well, but when she saw him her eyelids fluttered shyly, and she accepted his compliments with warm graciousness.

Sonia had always loved to dance, and now, sparkling with vitality, she found herself besieged by admirers. There was another guest sporting the garb of the Ukrainian, but Sonia noted that her outfit was not genuine, but made in a city store. Her *plakhta* was of velvet squares, and her shirt of silk, and her boots had heels, which were not worn by peasant women. Sonia scoffed at her from afar, and was pleased at her own simplicity. But she did not distinguish the faces of her dancing partners, for she did not care about any of them. She was glad to be with young people, glad to be liked, glad to be waltzing. But she did not know how truly close she had come to her mother's feelings upon Mathilde's first ball, in Paris, in 1880. Mathilde had been betrothed, and so her admirers had not really sought her out. Sonia, for her part, was being sought out, but by the wrong young men. Their situation represented opposite sides of the coin.

At midnight, it was time for supper, and the dancers moved to the dining room where numerous little tables had been arranged. Sonia found her brother, and Nina. She sat between them, and remarked, "Ninotchka, you are more lovely than a princess tonight! Is that not so, Ossip?" Her gray eyes rested eagerly upon her brother.

"Indeed, my sister is right, Nina Mikhailovna," he murmured, embarrassed by Sonia's effusiveness. He was not accustomed to her in this mood, and attributed it to the thrill of her first ball. He smiled conspiratorially at the brown-haired girl with the rather flat nose and ruddy color, this pleasant girl with the good posture and amusing costume, which suited her sturdy nature. She reminded him somewhat of Volodia, solid, loyal, dependable. He decided that he liked her. "Sonia is not herself this evening," he teased.

"We are both novices at this," Nina replied. "I love Sonia so. She brings kindness itself into the house with her."

"She can be hard, when she wants to be," her brother countered.

"Oh, Ossip!" Sonia protested. But she was not offended in the least. Ossip and Nina were smiling at each other, and she felt heady with anticipation. She bit into her marinated mushrooms with gusto.

"How is it that I have not come to know you better?" Ossip was asking Nina. "I used to be on friendly terms with all my sister's friends. Yet you are her favorite, and we hardly know each other."

"That would be remedied, if you were not so busy with your studies," Sonia inserted between bites.

"You are to pass your examinations this spring?" Nina questioned in her low, soft voice.

"We hope so. I need a gold medal, Nina Mikhailovna. A Jew cannot enter the University unless he has a gold medal. One mark below 'five,' and my medal will be silver and I shall be done for."

"You will have your gold, I am certain," Nina replied. Her hazel eyes rested on Ossip's handsome features, so finely chiseled, and she shivered slightly. "And then?" Nina went on. "What will you do?"

Ossip blushed. "I am not sure," he answered with reserve. Then he added, more kindly, "The Faculty for Far Eastern Studies, perhaps. But enough about me! Your caviar is delectable, Nina Mikhailovna. I am spending a delightful evening. As for Sonia, I have rarely watched her consume so much food at one time. Have you?" He twinkled at his sister.

"He is not always so unbearable," Sonia said to Nina. "Sometimes he can be positively gallant. But not tonight!"

"I find your brother charming," Nina replied. And she blushed. "Charm runs in your family, Sonitchka. You have it, and Mathilde Yureyevna—"

But it was time to return to the ballroom. A young man, dressed in violet silk as Henri III of France, bowed before Sonia, and she accepted his arm. Ossip turned to Nina. "I should appreciate another dance with you," he declared.

Demurely, Nina Tobias laid her hand upon his sleeve. When the piano struck up a frenzied mazurka, Ossip noticed her high color, and her beautiful eyes. She is most agreeable, he thought. At once he felt a sharp pang of loss. *Agreeable*, whereas Natasha was lovely, spirited, magnificent—and his own. How could one possibly compare a healthy apple to an exotic passion fruit? He looked into Nina Tobias's eyes, and he saw kindness, gentleness, meekness. He smiled, inclining his head. But it was merely the smile of politeness.

When the guests were preparing to leave, Sonia took her friend aside and asked, "Do you like my brother? I so wanted him to truly make your acquaintance!"

Nina bowed her head, and nodded. "I like him very much," she replied.

"Really? You are not saying it to please me, Ninotchka?"

"Oh, no!" her friend cried. Then, whispering, "He is heavenly. But do not humiliate me by telling him I think so. Perhaps someday he will notice me, on his own. I hope he shall."

Sonia pressed her friend's arm, and her gray eyes shone. "Of course he shall!" she declared. "He has excellent taste!"

On the way home Sonia chattered, but her brother was mostly quiet. He kissed her lightly on the cheek, and listened to her with an amused expression. But his thoughts were not of the ball, or of Nina Tobias. They were not even of his sister's debut.

Anna's letter was postmarked "Lausanne, Switzerland."

I have been lax in corresponding [she wrote her sister], but so much has happened. Dalia has given birth to a baby boy, whom she named "Reza" after her husband. We have taken to calling him "Riri," and so he probably shall remain. I have never seen such beauty in a child—he is so fair, and so smooth, and I feel he is a miracle in our lives. Yes, he is partly mine, too, for Dalia has gone to work for the Persian Consulate, and I am taking care of the baby. We both attend a studio for artists, and take turns with Riri at home. Our life is simple; we subsist on my money and Dalia's salary, and most of the friends we have made are fellow painters and sculptors. We have purchased a small house, so that the baby may have a garden. I shall send you the medallion for the New Year, and I am quite proud of it. Meanwhile, it makes me think of you.

Do not worry, this year I shall see you. I am far less shy than I was, and have put the past in perspective. Or at least I keep attempting to do so; for I miss Vanya more than anyone on this earth will ever know, believe me: however, I cannot allow such thoughts to kill me. I have a life to live for myself, and also for that little being who needs me, ever so slightly: Dalia's child. I am also trying my hand at new modes of painting: my most recent venture is the painting of glass. I do not think I am meant to join ranks with Leonardo and Michelangelo and Rosa Bonheur, and this realization has cost me a good deal of pride. But I am good at modest projects, and I cannot survive without my paint pots. Dalia and I have but a single servant, who does the heavy cleaning chores. We cook together and I have learned how to impose a yogurt crust upon Persian rice. You would be impressed by my prowess! But mostly I puree vegetables and fruits for Riri, and have become a veritable expert!

Sonia thought: This isn't Anna! Calm, happy, busy with a baby—where are the sour grapes? She was bewildered, and then, pleased. Her sister was leading a life that she, Sonia, would find simplistic. A life devoid of waltzes, of plays at the Mariinsky Theater, of elegant furnishings. Sonia thought: Am I becoming as vapid and frivolous as Tania? She was angry with herself. A good life with intelligent, artistic friends: that was Anna's existence, and it was a worthy one, befitting her sister's straightforward, independent nature. Anna was truly made for the small, clean, uncomplicated charms of Switzerland. Russia, her mother country, had threatened to destroy her. But still . . .

"We are Russian," Sonia said to Ossip, "and now I know what bothered me about Anna's new life. It is totally un-Russian—and Anna, with her angers and her passions and her idealism, was the most Russian of us all!"

"Something of the old intensity has been burned out of her," Ossip commented. "Yes, it is a shame. But she is happy this way, and that is more than she was here . . . Maybe her Russia was like a bad passion, the kind that can warp."

Sonia regarded him with a bemused expression. A bad passion! That's Natasha, who is so wrong for you. Kind, gentle Nina will be a balm to you, my brother, as Lausanne is to Anna. Stubbornly, she refused to face her brother's joy, which had sprung from the vibrancy of Natalia Tagantseva, and which had set him free from passivity for the first time in his life. She closed her heart to Natasha's appreciation of her brother, an appreciation composed of true and total understanding. For she, Sonia, did not possess Natalia's fine perception of Ossip's needs and potentialities.

Her own life was divided into two aspects, and revolved simultaneously around both. There was her overriding concern for Ossip, whom she watched constantly. And then there were the evenings toward which she found her whole self turning, like a sunflower seeking the light. Volodia had made it a practice to come twice a week after supper, to visit Ossip and play the piano with Sonia. The three would sit and chat, and then Sonia would bring the sheafs of music to Volodia, and together, animatedly, they would select their pieces for the evening. Ossip would sit behind them in the piano room for a while, and then, somewhat listlessly, would move into the sitting room to speak with his mother or to read a book while awaiting the reappearance of his friend and sister. Volodia and Sonia would be alone, their fingers dancing minuets on the black and ivory keys.

If Sonia had certain blind spots where her brother was concerned, he, usually so astute, was so immersed in his newfound world, in himself as a man, and in Natasha, that he did not think twice about his sister's feelings. He thought only that it was good that Sonia and Volodia had become friends. It would make it easier when he told her. But he did not find it strange that Volodia came so regularly, and that so little of those evenings were actually spent with him. He also heard Sonia's voice, calm, composed, courteous, but caught no emotion struggling beneath the controlled phrases. Their words were commonplace, almost like those which Ossip exchanged with Nina when he encountered her taking tea with Sonia. They spoke of Chekhov, of the ballet, of an amusing story that someone had related. Volodia's compliments were gallant, but impersonal, as indeed were Ossip's toward Nina. Ossip never thought to question his friend, nor his sister, and in that he was not alone, for even Mathilde saw nothing more than vague friendship between the two young people. No, Ossip was in love, and he knew what a young man did when he was prey to his emotions. Volodia was surely not in love.

He was grateful for the frequency of his encounters with Nina Tobias, for he had grave matters on his mind, and found her refreshing to talk to, and a good excuse for eluding the questions of his elders. He was seen at balls escorting Sonia and her friend, and when in passing he heard someone's mother say, in an undertone, "That little Nina has found herself an admirer of distinction," he merely smiled with amusement. Nina did not seem to mind this supposed courtship, which was lifeless, and which he never imagined could be taken seriously. Nina, he had discovered, was intelligent, though not quick like Natasha. She was too intelligent, he reassured himself, to believe that his few gallantries were something more.

But Sonia watched them. Once, that winter, at a tea, she saw Nina's quick, not unbecoming blush when Ossip entered the room, and saw the pulse beat in her throat as he bowed to all the ladies and slowly made his way to her. "Ossip Davidovitch," she said softly, making room for him on the love seat, "may I tempt you with a cream puff?" She passed him a platter of cakes, smiling when he took two, an indulgent smile.

"Cream puffs . . . You arc not at all a cream puff, are you, Nina Mikhailovna?" Ossip bantered lightly. "They say that women are like sweets. What kind of sweet are you?"

She blushed, and her eyelids fluttered. "I'm not sure," she demurred. "What do you think?" And her eyes, flecked with fine gold specks, fastened upon his blue ones.

He laughed. "An apple tart. With a good rich crust."

"Do you like them?" she asked, almost whispering.

He cocked his head to one side and examined her with easy affection. "Indeed I do. Our people make the best at Mohilna, where the fruit is hardy and flavorful. I much prefer a robust dessert to a cream puff. My cousin, Tatiana, is a cream puff, and she has spoiled my appreciation of the real thing!"

"Oh, Ossip Davidovitch, how unkind! Tatiana Alexandrovna is gay and golden. She is only fifteen! Do not be irritated by her, give her a chance . . ." Nina's gentle hand fell upon his arm. How different those fingers felt from Natasha's electric touch. He gazed at this young girl, who was only a few months younger than Natasha, and found her sweetness suddenly cloying.

"You are a kind little thing," he said to her, and rose quickly. He wanted to pat the top of her pompadour, and smiled to himself. "Do not worry, I shall be a good boy, and not detest my cousin. For I am sure that my aunt would find out, and make life impossible for Mama!" And bowing, he departed, seeking Sonia.

He found his sister in a corner, discussing Chopin. "Will you come with me out on the balcony?" he asked her. She stood up, small and delicate in a soft silk gown. Her eyes sought Nina and her pulse quickened when she saw the flush on her brother's cheeks. "Excuse me," she said to her friends, and took her brother's arm.

They walked sedately out of the French doors and onto a large balcony, overlooking some neatly trimmed gardens. Sonia said, "You have left Nina! You didn't quarrel with her, did you?"

"No, of course not. How could anyone quarrel with little Nina? I merely needed a breath of fresh air."

Sonia passed her tongue quickly over her lips. "I am sorry," she began, "but I am about to question you on a matter that does not concern me. At least not entirely. But I cannot help myself. I have watched you with her, and cannot help wondering—have you spoken to her about your feelings?"

The color drained from Ossip's face. He dropped his sister's hand. "Spoken? To whom?" he cried.

"Why, to Nina, naturally. She cares deeply about you, my love. You are only twenty, and about to enter the University, and she is seventeen. That is too soon to speak for her to her father. But she deserves to know, don't you think? To know that you would like her to save herself for you, to wait until you have your degree—"

"Sonia, you must be mad!" he exclaimed, his eyes flashing. "I am not in love with Nina Tobias! Whatever gave you such a preposterous idea?"

Her cheeks sunken, Sonia stammered, "But I'm not the only one! Other people have remarked upon your interest in her! Why, Ossip—at every ball you dance with her more than with the other girls, and you are always most attentive, and, and—"

"And I did these things for you, you little goose! As you sit with my best friend, Volodia, and play four-handed sonatas on the piano! What has possessed you?" He stood, outraged, regarding his sister with glaring eyes.

She took a step back. "Ossip. You do not have to pay

court to my friend for my sake. I should be asking you, 'What on earth has possessed *you*?' Nina cares for you, and mostly because you have led everyone around us to believe that you are not indifferent toward her! Now you tell me that she means nothing to you. I do not under-stand."

"That is because you have never wished to understand, to understand *me*!" he cried, a curl falling into his eyes, his nostrils distending. He appeared wild, maddened, and she brought one hand protectively to her throat. "You do not love me at all, Sonia! If you did, you would stop being so selfish and care about what I want, *I*, Ossip—not you, not Papa, not Grandfather! Nina is very nice. I like her. She is a good friend. But I am going to marry Natalia Tagantseva, and nothing that you say or do is going to stop me! Do you, finally, after all these months, understand the truth?"

Sonia's body began to tremble, and she felt numb. Her lips parted, and her teeth began to chatter. Her hair fell to one side, over one ear, and hung lopsided. She dropped her bag. The trembling increased, and now she breathed in small, hysterical gasps. Her gray eyes were wide with hor-ror, but no tears came, only little moans, sharp and dread-ful. Ossip stood transfixed before her, the savagery gone from his expression now. He reached for her hand, but she withdrew it with a scream. "Sonia," he pleaded, "this is my life! Not anybody else's!"

But she was already running back into the salon. He followed helplessly, calling for their wraps and their foot-man. Nina Tobias, her brown eyes perplexed, caught his attention. Quickly he looked away from those flecks of gold, so gentle and warm. Great shivers were creeping up his spine, and he thought wildly: It was the wrong timing. I should never have told her now. Now I am going to have to face Mama . . . He made hurried attempts at a courte-ous farewell to his hostess, mumbling incoherently that Sonia was ill, and darted out the door behind his frenzied young sister. His temples were pounding painfully, and he felt nauseous.

Mathilde heard a tap on her boudoir door, and when she said, "Come in!" Ossip's slender form appeared in the doorway. She had been reading in her chaise longue, and on the hassock at her feet sat Sonia, diminutive and pale this morning. Johanna had awakened with stomach troubles, and so Mathilde, knowing the girl would not have her lesson, had sent for her. She had recalled her ghastly appearance the previous night at supper, and wished to be reassured that her daughter was not about to develop another case of pneumonia.

Sonia, on the footstool, stiffened at the sight of her brother, and Mathilde eyed him with bewilderment. "Do not tell me that you are ill too," she said. "Why are you not at school?"

Ossip hovered in the doorway, his features drawn, his eyes seeming larger than usual. He licked his lips and darted a quick look at his sister, but she turned her head aside. "Mama," he began, "I have a matter of the gravest importance to discuss with you. And no, it is not necessary for you to leave, Sonia. I wish for you to hear me, too."

He advanced into the room, and straightened his back. He closed the door, then regarded the two women with an even, clear gaze. He inhaled, locked his fingers together, and said, "I have only insisted about my life in a single instance, when I wanted to attend a normal school. This concerns something far more essential to me, and to my future. I have found a girl I wish to marry, Mama. She wants that, too. But there are . . . problems."

Mathilde clasped her hands upon her lap. "Problems? Is she of the wrong sort of background?"

Ossip's face contracted into a tight smile. "In a way, yes, Mama. But not in the way you think. She is, first of all, a girl of total charm, total goodness, total understanding and intelligence. Her personal qualities do not stop there. As far as her breeding is concerned, it is impeccable. She is of noble birth, of refined culture."

Mathilde relaxed upon the pillows. "Then what could be wrong?" she asked gently. "Is she too young? You are not yet twenty, my son. Perhaps it's too soon . . ."

"That, yes, of course. But we intend to marry, and I wish to declare my intentions now. Neither one of us is a child. It is not that, Mama."

To his intense discomfort his sister rose, and wringing her hands, cried, "I cannot bear this, Mama! I must go now."

Mathilde's eyes widened. "What drama, Sonia. Your brother wished for you to remain. Sit down." She looked at her daughter with severity. "You are not to interrupt again. What, then, could we possibly hold against this girl, if she is so perfect, Ossip? Do we know her?"

She heard Sonia's sharp intake of breath, and a frown appeared between her own black brows. Ossip, pale and erect, advanced a step. "Yes," he replied, and his eyes met his mother's without flinching. "You know her, and have openly admired her. The only one who doesn't is Sonia—"

"That is unfair, Ossip! I never claimed not to admire her! You are twisting my feelings—"

"Who is she?" Mathilde demanded.

"Natalia Tagantseva."

He did not remove his eyes from his mother's face. Her hands flew to her throat, but then she sat up straight and sighed. "Natalia. I had no idea. And you, Sonia—you knew of this, and—"

"Sonia has fought me on this for months! But she had no notion of the seriousness of my intentions. In fact, she wanted me to pay court to Nina Tobias." He paused, then: "Mama, I have never begged you before. Now I ask that you listen, for what I am about to say will surely shock you. You know that I do not believe in God. You also know that here, in Russia, civil weddings do not exist. I am going to convert in order to marry Natalia. She is the only thing that has meaning in my life—I could never love another woman! If you oppose me, I shall go to the Count, and I shall arrange for immediate religious training. And if he does not accept my suit, Natalia and I shall elope. It is as simple as that. No one can stop us."

Mathilde sat, still and white, on her chaise. She saw the splotches of red on her son's face, his fists clenched by his side. She had never seen her calm, cynical, passive son this way. Then she looked at her daughter, and saw her distorted features, her horrified expression. "I see," Mathilde stated. No one spoke, and the room echoed with the gentle ticking of a golden clock upon the mantelpiece.

"Ossip," she said at last, "Count Tagantsev would reject you at once. As a convert, he might accept you—even as David's son. Perhaps even more readily as your father's son, to gloat over him. But you have not thought this through. David would disinherit you, as would your grandfather. As for me—you know that I brought no dowry into my marriage. You would have your title, but the Count's is a more important one. You would be destitute, Jew or not, and he would laugh in your face. I doubt that Natasha would defy her entire family for a boy with nothing behind his name."

"We have discussed it," he replied. "Natasha wants me as much as I want her. And you said so yourself—Papa took you without benefit of dowry. Love is stronger than money!"

His mother smiled. "Maybe. In certain instances. Where the man is wealthy, if his bride adds nothing to his fortune he may overlook her poverty. But not in the opposite case, my dear. How would you and Natasha live? You'd have nothing. Nothing! A man needs a fortune if he is young and without profession, and if the girl he desires comes from a family of great standing. Natalia's love for you would not survive abject poverty."

"And you, Mama, would allow us to starve?"

Mathilde sighed. "Ossip. There are small things that I can do for my children, on my own. There are things in which I can convince your father to see life my way. But you know as well as I that religion is not one of those things. And in this your Grandfather Horace would have his say, and it would outweigh mine. Do not think like a child."

"But Natasha has a fortune in her own right—"

"Which is dependent upon the good nature of her father. If David disinherited you, the Count would do the same to his daughter."

"I do not think so," Ossip said staunchly. "Papa and I have never seen eye to eye. But Count Tagantsev adores Natasha. He could not bear to lose her! And besides—we do not care. Money, no money—no matter what, I shall convert, and then we shall be married! I merely wished to give my mother the courtesy of advance warning."

"You are most considerate," Mathilde said with irony.

"No, you are immoral!" Sonia shouted suddenly, rising. She stood before her brother, her gray eyes blazing. "You would kill Papa with no remorse! What do you mean, 'never seen eye to eye'? Papa loves you, and has hopes for you. You are his heir! Your duty is to take over the Jewish community of Petersburg, as Papa did for Grandfather. Duty, Ossip! Your honor as a Gunzburg demands this, requires it! Have you no feelings for the family that has reared you, given you its title and name?"

"You think nothing of sacrificing my happiness for Papa's causes!" Ossip cried. "I speak to you of my love, of my marriage. Would you have me live without Natasha, simply to honor Papa's religion, which is not mine?"

"Yes!" his sister answered.

"Sonia. Be quiet," Mathilde declared. "I understand your feelings, Ossip. I am very sorry. I think that I can sense your plight, my son. But your sister is not wrong. I do not feel that you must support the Jewish cause, if you do not have your heart in it. But you cannot, as a Gunzburg, shame the family. You cannot openly convert. Do not celebrate the Jewish holidays, reject the Jewish God—but in your soul, Ossip, not for all the world to see. It is a question of noblesse oblige."

A tremor of fury passed through the young man. He looked at his mother, and his eyes were shot with red veins. His lips were drawn into a tight, bloodless line. "Thank you," he said, in a clipped tone. "At least, Madame, you gave me ten minutes of your time. That was more graciousness than I received from my sister."

He turned on his heel, and Mathilde lifted her hand and called, "Ossip!" He wheeled about by the door, and his face, white and withdrawn, suddenly became vulnerable, pleading. She gazed at him, her eyes full of unspoken sympathy, remembering her own betrothal. But she said nothing, and a spasm of pain constricted his features again. He opened the door and walked rapidly out.

Mathilde's eyes filled with tears, and she murmured softly, "I have done this to him. Dear Lord—"

"No, Mama," Sonia said. "He has done this to himself!"

But all at once her mother's eyes were cold. "Go to your room, Sonia," she said. And then, more sharply, "Send Johanna to me. I need Johanna!"

Sonia could hardly bear the estrangement from her brother. He took care, during the first few months of the new year, 1907, not to mention Natalia Tagantseva to his sister. Their mother watched him, but he did not speak of his love. Toward his father he remained courteous and agreeable, but toward Mathilde he displayed an ironic detachment. She ached from this rejection by her favorite child, but she did not show him her wounds. Instead, she returned irony with irony. They would speak to each other in tones laced with hidden meanings. To others, this seemed strange and disquieting, but inexplicable, for there had always been an understanding between mother and son. But it was Sonia who suffered the most cruelly, for Ossip behaved as though she were a stranger.

She felt as if her life were torn apart. There was no Anna, fiercely loyal; no Ossip; and worst of all, there *was* Volodia Tagantsev, who continued to visit, but whom Ossip spirited away to his bedroom. She sometimes caught his eye, and he would raise his brows in question. But he knew what had happened between Sonia and Ossip, and he was Natalia's brother. In certain ways he must have found Sonia despicable too, for she had caused the rift by not offering her support. Volodia felt compassion for her, but Sonia did not know that. She was certain that he hated her now, that Ossip and Natasha had seen to it that their friendship was destroyed. And that was almost too hard to bear. She lost weight, and refused invitations to balls and teas. At night, she sobbed silently into her pillow. But she did not apologize to Ossip, nor did she attempt to explain herself to Volodia.

One evening in early spring, Ossip burst in upon her in her room. His face was ashen, and there were deep purple circles beneath his eyes. Without warning, he threw himself upon her bed, wracked with sobs. Sonia could not see his face, but she dropped her embroidery and rushed to him, propelled by love. She wrapped her arms about his trembling body, and tears sprang to her eyes, spilling over her lashes. She held him, and they cried together without a word. Never had she encountered such despair, except the night of Anna's return, when her sister had been sent to the widows' room to sleep. Yet somehow, Ossip's pain reached even more deeply within her.

Finally, he sat up, and whispered, "Natasha and her mother have left the country. It's over, Sonia."

"She refused you?" his sister asked gently. But now she was outraged. "I thought that she had promised herself to you!"

"She made only one error, and that was to speak to her father. We warned her not to—both Volodia and I. But she did not want to wait or hide. He has sent her to South America, with her mother. He would not let Volodia know where they are, for fear that he would tell me."

"But she will be back, Ossip! She will return, and then you can arrange matters between you! Papa is not made of stone! Papa will arrange things with Count Tagantsev! As long as Natasha still loves you, there is no reason to lose hope, Ossip! No reason!"

He shook his head and turned aside. "It's even worse than I said, Sonitchka. The Count has arranged a marriage for her when she does return. There is no way for me to reach her in time. There is a Prince Kurdukov, who is vaguely related to the Tagantsevs, who wants to marry her. The Count has sealed an agreement with him today—"

"But that is medieval! And Natasha does not have to marry him! Come now, Ossip! You will be at the University, and will have a brilliant career ahead of you. The Count will not turn you away, and Papa will help you. Grandfather, too! All you need now is hope, and courage. And hard work, for you must soon pass your entrance examinations, and receive your gold medal! Think of the future, Ossip! This will work itself out. I believe in that. I do!"

"Life does not work out for Jews," Ossip muttered, his mouth twisted in a bitter grimace. "You used to say, when you were a child, that we were the chosen people. Yes, I suppose that's correct enough: chosen to be despised, and beaten. I would like to give up, and die, Sonia. There is no reason to continue. Yet I am too much of a coward to kill myself. Isn't that ludicrous?"

He began to laugh, hysterically, falling on his back upon the bed, tears rolling heedlessly down his cheeks. It was the most horrible sound Sonia had ever heard. She began to shiver. "I shall call Mama," she whispered. "Maybe a sedative . . . a glass of Papa's brandy . . ."

But Ossip reached out and grabbed her by the arm. "I do not need my mother," he said ironically. "Right now, there is too much hatred in my heart for her. Why did she allow me to be born?"

"Ossip!" Sonia cried. But he had started to laugh again, and shocked, she took a step back.

"You may as well bring the entire bottle!" he said. "Papa's brandy, remember? But not Mama. She isn't any fun: she is too serious, and we need to joke, and to laugh! Bring a servant or two—Marfa, and the little wench, Katia! That one looks like a nice healthy girl, who could take on ten men at once! Don't you think so, Sonitchka?"

His sister backed away from his maniacal laughter, horrified, nearly paralyzed. She reached the door, but she could not leave the room, nor utter a word.

In May, Ossip and Volodia were to take their examinations, and so few weeks remained till then that Volodia, under pretext of studying, ceased his evening visits to the Gunzburg apartment. No one spoke of Natasha. Sonia had told Mathilde what had occurred, but no words were exchanged between mother and son. Ossip, gaunt and white, shut himself in his quarters and attacked his books. Mute pain was evident in his eyes, which were forever rimmed with red. Sonia brought him tidbits at night, and sat by his bed, embroidering. But they did not break the silence between them. She sat and ran her needle expertly over the linen, and she thought of the Tagantsev twins who had entered her life and Ossip's, and who had wrought havoc there, like a sandstorm in the steppes. She saw Volodia's quiet strength, his solid body, his dexterous fingers upon the piano, and she bent her face over her work, berating herself for dwelling on an impossible situation.

Then the qualifying examinations began. The great thaws had come to the capital, and Ossip studied. He alone among his friends felt the pressure. For Volodia, Petri, Botkin, and Sokolov were Eastern Orthodox and did not need to enter the University on a quota. The first three days of examinations went well, and Ossip returned home with "fives" and "five pluses." Not a single "four" to mar his record. Only one day was left. He was confident, for he was fluent in French and German, the languages on which he was to receive final questioning. But during the evening, he knocked on his sister's door, and when he entered Sonia gasped in fear. His skin was flushed, there were bags beneath his feverish eyes, and his teeth chattered.

"I am ill, Sonia," he whispered. He lowered his collar, and turned his head so that the nape of his neck was exposed. An enormous abscess stood out like a yellow mountain below his hair. He sat down beside her, and she pressed her small cool hand upon his brow. She withdrew it quickly.

"You have a high fever," she said. "You must go to bed, and let us telephone the doctor. Here—lie down at once."

"No, I cannot," he replied. "Tomorrow I must pass the last tests. I cannot fail. After all this work—I cannot put them off or I shall lose an entire year, and have to repeat the exams next spring. You must promise me—not a word to Mama! Not until tomorrow afternoon, when the examinations are over!" he said, adding, as she started to protest, "You cannot let me lose that gold medal. I beg you, Sonia. Keep quiet about this."

She took him back to his room, and settled him into bed with warm milk and honey. She sat by his side and asked him questions about German literature, and when he closed his eyes with fever and exhaustion, she quietly tiptoed out of the room. She was assailed by doubts. The abscess— what did it mean? She hovered by her mother's bedroom, thinking: He may die . . . and then, bravely, she returned to her room. She had given her sacred word. Natasha was no longer his. Could she remove the hope of a gold medal from her brother?

Throughout the next day she was so anxious she could not eat. Her mother thought it strange that every time she tried to speak to her, Sonia found an excuse to leave the room, gazing at the floor. Then, when Ossip returned from school, Sonia bolted frantically toward the door crying, "Well, Ossip?"

Ossip stumbled into the sitting room, his hair matted with perspiration, his eyes bulging with fever. Mathilde rose, her hand to her breast. "My God," she breathed.

Ossip swayed, and his sister pushed a chair under him. But he was smiling. "I have my gold," he said. "Can you believe it? This fall, I can enter the Faculty of Far Eastern Studies. Papa . . . will be . . . pleased . . ." His voice trailed off, and he fell against the side of the chair in a faint.

"Telephone the doctor, Mama," Sonia said immediately. "He has an abscess the size of a fist on his neck."

It was the middle of the afternoon. Mathilde and Sonia took Ossip in the landau to the best surgeon in St. Petersburg. Ossip's face was green, and when the horses missed a cobblestone he groaned with pain. Mathilde held his hand, Sonia had his head on her shoulder.

When the surgeon had examined Ossip, he turned to Mathilde. "I shall have to admit him to my clinic tomorrow to remove the abscess. But this is far more serious than it may seem. What is your son's medical history, my dear Baroness?"

Mathilde regarded the man, her eyes enormous in her white face. "My God," she murmured, "it was the doctor's prediction! He is twenty—maybe he will die this time!"

"What prediction, Mama?" Sonia questioned anxiously. She faced her mother and held her by the shoulders. "Mama! Tell us!"

As though in a dream, Mathilde began to weep. "The physician who diagnosed Ossip's illness seventeen years ago," she mumbled. "My son had Pott's disease. The doctor said it would recur, when he turned twenty . . ."

"We shall hospitalize him at once, without a moment's delay," the surgeon stated. He rang for his nurse.

Sonia and Mathilde looked at each other, and silently they fell into each other's arms. "I have let him kill himself," Sonia said with dazed wonder.

The surgeon operated upon Ossip, but the wound would not close. Ossip hovered between life and death, his sister and his mother waiting outside his door, his father and brother coming each morning and each evening. Finally he was able to sit up, and three weeks later, to leave the clinic. But, to his chagrin, he was ordered away from St. Petersburg, where the air was miasmic.

"We can send him to my sister's summer house, in Normandy," Johanna suggested to Mathilde, who sat in rigid silence by her son. "I can go with him. You are not strong enough to take care of him, but I am an accomplished nurse. Let us go, tomorrow! He will be by the seashore, and will grow stronger. And then, you and the Baron can decide upon his future!"

"Your sister?" Mathilde echoed, in a trance.

"Yes! The one who has recently married. My family will help me to care for him."

Mathilde shook her head. "No," she said firmly. "I will go with him. If it becomes too arduous, I shall hire a professional nurse. Thank you, Johanna. Ossip will go to Normandy, but I must be with him, every day. I must see to him, watch over his improvement with my own eyes. Please. Help me to pack, and write to your sister. I shall be forever grateful."

Johanna de Mey placed a firm arm upon Mathilde's shoulder. "We shall go together," she asserted. "I could not allow you to go through this alone.You need my strength."

So, together, the women took Ossip to Normandy. After several weeks, he wrote his sister: "I shall return by fall, to enter the University. Have you seen Volodia?"

Sonia read between the lines. He wants to come home in time to find Natasha, she thought. She would have come back by then from her voyage . . . Perhaps, perhaps, something might be arranged, before she married Prince Kurdukov. . . . Ossip was holding onto that thought with all his might, she knew. It was his reason for staying alive.

But Mathilde had written David: "The wound will not heal. He will not be able to come home for a long, long time. The doctor here has told me, in confidence, that he will need bracing sea air for at least two years. What are we to do?"

And so, in early June, David said to his daughter, "This fall your brother will remain with Johanna's family. Then, I have arranged for him to travel to Yokohama, where my friend, Moise Mess, runs his coal enterprise. Moise needs an assistant, and Ossip has always wanted to visit Japan. He will go by cargo ship, starting in Odessa and going through the Black Sea, the Red Sea, the Indian Ocean, and along China's coast. He will be at sea for two whole months, and will work in Yokohama, which is itself a port. The voyage will do him good, and he will enjoy his job. He will return having mastered the intricacies of the Japanese language, and that will place him at the head of his class at the Faculty for Far Eastern Studies."

"But then, we shall not see him for several years!" Sonia exclaimed.

"It is the price that we must pay for your brother's good health," David replied.

Sonia was overwhelmed with despair. Life without Ossip . . . It seemed impossible. Then, a week later, her friend Nina came to visit her. As the two girls sat drinking tea and munching on crumpets, Nina said, "I have news, Sonia. An important society wedding has taken place. I thought that it would interest you, for it concerns that family with whom you spent last summer."

"The Tagantsevs?" Sonia cried. Her pulse begn to race. "Nicolai. The older brother. Correct?"

Nina smiled sweetly. "No. It was the young girl. What

did you tell me her name was? You never did seem to take to her, actually. What was her name?"

"Natasha," Sonia said softly.

"Yes! Natalia. They say it was a splendid ceremony. The Tzar and Tzarina were present. She married a much older man—a Prince Somebody. I am not very good at names, Sonitchka."

But Sonia sat staring at the wall, all color drained from her face. She began to weep.

"Sonitchka! Have I hurt your feelings?" Nina asked anxiously.

"No," Sonia murmured, "it was not you. I was merely thinking of . . . of . . ." But she could not proceed. Her cheeks were flooded with tears, and she held her handkerchief to her lips. "However will I tell him?" she whispered.

"Tell him? Tell whom?" Nina demanded.

"It does not matter," Sonia said brokenly. "But I shall not give him the news. He would not survive it now!"

He will go to Japan, and get well, she thought grimly. Then, when he returns, I shall tell him the news. Perhaps by then he will have met someone else in Japan. Moise Mess has a niece . . . She turned to Nina and suddenly brightened. "Ninotchka!" she cried. "I had not thought to ask you—but Ossip will be going to Japan, and he will be homesick. Will you write to him while he is gone?"

Her friend blushed. "But he has not asked me to," she said.

"He was too ill! And before that he worried so about his gold medal! I am certain—certain!—that if he had remained healthy he would now be asking you to wait for him until his studies are over. I am not asking you in his stead. When he returns, he can do so in person. But if you care for him, you must let him understand, by writing . . . Or else he will think you interested in someone else, and will not press his suit when he comes home!"

"All right," Nina assented.

Sonia brought her friend's hands to her lips, and kissed them. "You are so good," she declared, and poured them a new glass of tea. But her hand was still shaking.

Ossip had been sent to Normandy so quickly, his health so precarious, that his friends from the gymnasium had been unable to see him off. Now, one by one, Petri, Botkin, and Sokolov arrived at the Gunzburg apartment, and Sonia and David greeted them and received the good-byes that were meant for Ossip. All were planning to enter the University in the autumn: Petri to the Faculty of Letters, Botkin to History; Sokolov planned to become a chemist. Only Sokolov had been granted a silver medal; the others, like Ossip, had received gold ones, as had their companion, Volodia Tagantsev. David congratulated them warmly, for he was a profound admirer of scholarship and academic excellence. It hurt him to think of Ossip's disappointment in being held back once again because of illness.

The three young men expressed sympathy for their friend, and wrote down his address. When Botkin came, he was carrying a small flat package, and he took Sonia aside in the sitting room and bade her open it. She unwrapped it and stood back, tears coming to her eyes. It was a portrait of the five friends, Ossip, Volodia, Sokolov, Petri, and Botkin. "My father painted it from memory," the young man said. "It was to be my graduation present. Now I want Ossip to have it, so that we may remain at his side even in Normandy and Japan." Sergei Botkin, nephew of the Tzar's physician, was also the son of Mikhail Botkin, an artist of great repute. His name was signed in the bottom left corner.

After the news of Natasha's wedding, Sonia hesitated, and held back from sending the painting. She took it to her bedroom, and propped it by her secretary, near the etching of Gino that Anna had left there when she had gone to Switzerland. She would try not to look upon those faces, for she did not want to stare into the velvet brown eyes of Volodia, who had not come with the others. And yet she did not blame him. She understood his reasons. He had no way of knowing that she had not written to her brother about Prince Kurdukov.

Now and then, as though drawn by a magnet, her gray eyes would seek Volodia's face in its frame, and she would feel a surge of blood rising to her temples. But she raised her chin, and forced herself to distract her troubled thoughts. She was determined to put him out of her existence.

Then Mathilde and Johanna returned. Ossip was sufficiently recovered that he no longer needed constant care and nursing, and Johanna's family planned to remain in Normandy for the rest of the summer, until Ossip departed for the Far East. Mathilde had not wished to stay away from her two younger children. Summer vacation plans had been delayed because of Ossip's critical condition but now, in July, Mathilde wanted to take Sonia and Gino to see her parents, and their sister, Anna. She also intended to take them for a short farewell visit to Normandy.

The remainder of the summer went quickly by. Baron Yuri and his wife, Ida, had rented a mansion in the Black Forest of Austria, and it was there that Sonia saw her sister, Anna, for the first time since their separation. Had Johanna not been absent, visiting her own family in Normandy, Anna would clearly not have come. She had brought along her friend, Dalia Hadjani, to meet the Gunzburgs.

When Mathilde first saw her daughter standing in front of her, in a suit of rich brown linen in the fashion of the day, she was somehow surprised. There was an awkward moment while they looked at each other mutely. Anna's eyes seemed to be asking whether she would now be unquestionably accepted, while for Mathilde there was the fear of rejection and, at the same time, refusal to be cowed into submission by her own child. It was Dalia Hadjani, the outsider, who broke the silence. She stepped toward Mathilde and took her hands, forcing her to look away from Anna to herself. Mathilde saw the black mourning clothes, the elegance, the handsome exotic face, and then she heard the gentle, well-modulated voice of the Persian saying to her: "Madame de Gunzburg, it is so kind of you to receive me on such short notice."

"Not at all," Mathilde replied. She felt drugged by Dalia's quiet presence, which forced politeness to the forefront of her own consciousness. If she allowed herself to go through the right motions, then she would not have to deal with Anna. "It is we who are delighted that you have come," she remarked, and smiled. "Please sit down, Madame Hadjani."

"No, you must call me 'Dalia.' For you see, Anna has grown to be as my own sister—my own family, except for my son. In fact—Anna's help has been indispensable to me with him, too."

Mathilde sat down and indicated some comfortable chairs for Dalia and Anna. She wondered where her daughter would sit; Anna chose a seat near her beautiful dark-haired friend. "And your baby?" Mathilde asked. "Is he well?"

"Riri is fine. Our little maid is taking care of him during our absence. But naturally, we are uncomfortable about having left him."

"Of course. It must be so difficult for you, my dear. After the tragedy . . . alone with a child."

"But I am not alone," Dalia smiled. "I have Anna."

"Yes, Mama. I am always there for Dalia and Riri." Mathilde looked at her daughter, and saw a glow of defiance in the fine brown eyes. What have I said to offend her now? she thought. "You look very well, Mama," Anna remarked in her stilted tone.

"And you." Mathilde gazed at the simple garnet earrings and the gold watch pinned upon Anna's breast. There were no feathers or ribbons on her hat, no exotic belt—as a matter of fact Anna wore no bizarre accoutrements at all. She looked sedate. Subdued. The warm brown color of her suit was pleasing to the eye without crying out for attention. Had her daughter changed so much in so short a time?

Then Sonia entered, with Gino. Anna's features lost their stiffness, and became tender as she took them both into her arms. But even in her pleasure she was not the boisterous, exuberant girl of before. Sonia went to sit on an ottoman at her feet, but Gino went to Dalia. "You must tell me all about Persia, if you please," he said, and sat next to her, his young face full of questions.

"Very well," Dalia replied. She laughed, and her voice became conspiratorial. "What would you like to know? About the veils that the women wear?"

Anna and her friend remained in the Black Forest for two weeks. Dalia made an excellent impression upon the family. Baron Yuri found her a receptive listener to his colorful tales. Baroness Ida liked her poised manner, her clean coiled black hair, her smooth creamy complexion which demonstrated a solid background of gentility. Dalia talked with Ida about her life in Persia, about her husband's business, about her upbringing. And while Dalia was thus entertaining their grandparents, Anna, Sonia, and Gino attempted to regain lost ground to make up for the time together they had lost. But Sonia could not quite grasp this new Anna. She wrote to Ossip: "Anna is afraid to be close to me, as she once was. And there is something else, something difficult to explain. It is almost as if she were trying to negate those very qualities that made her unique." Sonia attempted to hide her sadness from Anna, but their reunion was a great disappointment to her.

After a fortnight, it was Anna who announced one morning that she would have to end her visit. "We have been away from Riri for too long," she explained. "We have never gone anywhere without him, and it is time we returned."

"You should have brought him, Dalia," Baroness Ida remonstrated.

But Anna answered first: "Trains are not good for babies, Grandmother."

"You all traveled during infancy," Mathilde contested. "Nobody became ill."

"Nevertheless, we did not want to take any risks with him," Anna said. Her face had become strangely animated.

"It was I who insisted," Dalia cut in pleasantly. "You know how nervous a first-time mother can be . . ." She smiled wistfully: "And . . . I shall probably never have another little one . . ."

After their departure, Mathilde said to Ida, "At least she came, even if she did refuse to have us visit her in Lausanne. Maybe the time will come when we will be comfortable together again. I must hope so."

"She is your own child," her mother answered. "And I must say she has become a lady. One day she will be grateful that you stepped in to stop her eccentric behavior."

"I don't know, Mama," Mathilde sighed wearily. "With Anna, who can tell? I least of all."

At the end of July, Mathilde took Gino and Sonia to Normandy. Johanna de Mey's younger sister had a summer residence in the beach town of Arromanches, and Mathilde took several rooms at the local hotel so that she and her children might visit Ossip each day. He had grown stronger, but still appeared drained of energy, his skin ashen, his eyes enormous in his gaunt face. Even his hair hung limp, the crisp curls gone. Sonia found him a pathetic semblance of his former self, as she sat near him on the beach. They spoke of Petri and Botkin and Sokolov, but not a word was spoken of the Tagantsevs. Sonia did not mention Mikhail Botkin's portrait.

The day before Sonia's departure, a letter arrived, and

Ossip's eyes glowed when he began to read it. "Imagine!" he cried. "It is from Nina Mikhailovna Tobias! She says that they are in Imatra, in Finland, for the summer. Did you know that she planned to write to me?"

"She spoke of it in passing," his sister replied softly.

Mathilde took the family home early, for Ossip had grown tired from too many visits. In the train, Sonia thought with infinite sadness of her brother's face, of Natasha in the boat, of her own loneliness in St. Petersburg. Her entire life had been tied to Ossip. Even her feelings for Volodia . . . She saw the spires and onion-shaped cupolas of her city and for the first time they did not make her heart rise on a crest of emotion. A numbness had taken possession of her senses.

When, one mid-August afternoon, Stepan entered the sitting room where she was serving tea for her mother and Johanna, Sonia hardly lifted her head until he said, "Vladimir Nicolaievitch Tagantsev is here to see you, Baroness."

"Volodia? Please, show him in!" Mathilde said. She exchanged looks with Johanna.

The young man strode into the room, clad in rich chocolate wool and a neatly starched shirt. As always, he struck Sonia as appearing older than his not-quite-nineteen years, and her pulse began to pound blindly in her temples. She could hardly breathe. When she raised her clear gray eyes to his face, he colored slightly.

He came to Mathilde, bowed over her hand, and did the same with Johanna. "Mathilde Yureyevna," he began, "I wanted to come, long before this. Circumstances prevented me. I have written to Ossip, and plan to do so every week. Now I came to learn of his progress from you, and to apologize for not coming . . . sooner."

"I understand, Vladimir Nicolaievitch," Mathilde replied. She regarded the young man with indulgence. She had always liked him. "How is your mother?"

"Mama is fine, thank you. But Ossip?"

"Sit down, and Sonia will pour you some tea, and you can try some of these éclairs," Mathilde said. He looked at Sonia and sat upon the sofa next to her, so that his leg touched hers under her pink skirt. She was silent as she poured from the magnificent silver pot, her tiny hand clutching the scrolled handle. Her mother began to speak of Ossip, and Volodia sat attentive, his brow knit, his face pensive. Once in a while he took a discreet bite of cake, or a sip of tea. But he did not interrupt. Mathilde was grateful to be speaking of her favorite, who was gone, and h allowed her this pleasure with unvoiced compassion.

Finally, Mathilde stopped speaking and Volodia made some comments, not once looking at Sonia beside him.

Johanna de Mey said, "Mathilde and I would enjoy some music. You always played so well, Vladimir Nicolaievitch. Sonia has been neglecting her practice these days —why not play some four-hand pieces for us, to encourage her?"

"It would be my pleasure, Johanna Ivanovna," Volodia said. Sonia rose, and silently preceded him into the piano room. She sat down, holding some music sheets out to him. Still without a word, he made a selection and took a seat beside her. They began to play.

"I have not yet congratulated you upon winning your gold medal," Sonia murmured.

"Thank you, Sofia Davidovna. That is very gracious of you. The chief honors belong to Ossip, though, who succeeded under such dreadful circumstances."

"And what will you do now?"

"I am scheduled to begin classes at the Faculty of Law," he replied.

"A family tradition?" she said with slight irony.

"Yes, it was my father's wish. But I do not always comply with his desires. I like the law. I would not do what did not please me."

"I find that difficult to believe," Sonia stated.

"You are being unnecessarily cruel, Sofia Davidovna. My sister is very unhappy. I would give the world to relieve her of her misery. But she is a woman. I am not, and my will is my own."

"Your father is one of the most powerful men in the nation. Would you really defy him?" she asked, and this time, beneath her sarcasm, a soft note lingered. She raised her gray eyes to his brown ones, and then lowered them again with a blush.

"I would defy him in a minute," he whispered. "I need but one word of encouragement."

She stopped playing, and his fingers continued, by themselves, while she stared at him in wonder. He struck up a furious tempo, attacking the keyboard with frenzy. "Sofia Davidovna," he said, "it should hardly be a secret to you that I love you. I have been mad about you since you were thirteen. Surely you knew?"

"You dare to say that, after what has happened?" she asked, in a hushed voice.

"No. I dare to speak *because* of what has happened. I swear—it will not happen to us! I never thought, all these years, that we could make it work. I thought Ossip and Natasha senseless fools. I thought they were romantic and silly. You shared my opinion. But now I am a man, and I realize that Ossip was right. It was his timing, and his sense of drama, which were wrong. I shall not take 'no' for an answer, Sofia Davidovna. Two lives have been ruined. I shall not stand for two more."

She said, aghast, "But I had no idea you felt so strongly! It occurred to me, once or twice, that I might have—appealed to you. But never this! I did not think you cared . . ."

"I have never been more serious in my life. I beg of you—do not turn me away. I love you. I could make you happy!"

"But I thought—and Ossip too—that you were being kind to me for his sake, out of friendship for him!"

"Please continue playing, while I talk to you," he pleaded. "I never shared my feelings with Ossip. He might have revealed them to you, and I was certain that you did not care. Now that I am about to enter the University, I had to learn the truth. Tell me, Sofia Davidovna," he whispered, "do you care for me at all? Could you spend your life with me? Do you love me?"

She opened her mouth and wanted to cry out: Of course I care! I too have always cared! But she could not speak. He read the answer in her eyes. Her fingers played from memory, without feeling, and her face, turned to his, was completely open, as though her entire being was pouring out to him through her pupils. He bent toward her and she lifted her lips, but before he could touch them with his own, he drew back and asked, in a trembling, husky voice, "Tell me aloud, Sofia Davidovna. I need to hear the words."

She turned away. Then, in a detached monotone: "No, Vladimir Nicolaievitch. You are my sworn friend, but I do not love you. I am sorry."

He stared at her in disbelief. This time it was she who kept playing. He said, "But——"

"You misunderstood me, Vladimir Nicolaievich. It was sympathy, and companionship. But not love."

"I cannot believe you," he stammered. The healthy color had fled from his cheeks. "You did not lie to me with your eyes."

"I am telling you the truth now. Please, do not hurt your pride! I have told you: I care, but not as you would have me care! And I am not even worthy of such caring! I am an average girl, Vladimir Nicolaievitch. You deserve someone far more exquisite, far more intelligent. Someone who could return your wondrous love. I—I cannot. I wish I could, for my own sake. But feelings occur when they occur—I cannot force them."

He stood up then, his legs shaking. "My God," he said. She looked at him, and for a second her eyes lit again, and her hands reached to him; and then she shook her head, mutely. Without looking at her he walked out of the room, and he saw nothing of the undisguised adoration on her face as she watched him go. She heard his hasty farewell to her mother, and Johanna's surprised exclamation. She even heard Stepan in the vestibule calling for Volodia's footman. Her head came down upon the keys, and she began to weep, her arms outstretched upon the piano. Heavy sobs shook her and drowned out the other noises in the house.

It surprised her when no one came to rouse her. She lifted her head and dried her tears, and realized that it was completely dark in the piano room. Her mother and Johanna had long since left the sitting room, which was bathed in gentle evening light. She stood and smoothed out her hair. When she went into her room, she saw a tray on the bed. Beneath a glass dome was a breast of chicken with new potatoes and asparagus spears, a croissant, a dollop of butter, and a baked apple swimming in raisins and rum. There was a note by the tray, and to her amazement, it was written in Johanna's angular handwriting: "I thought that you might not feel up to supper," it read.

Sonia was shaken. This was the first time her governess had performed an act of kindness toward her. Had she guessed? But Sonia had never spoken of her feelings. Not even Ossip, who loved and understood her better than anyone else, had known. In dazed bewilderment, she took the dome off the platter. A rich aroma reached her nostrils. She replaced the glass, nauseated, and once again began to cry.

The following week, her Aunt Rosa said, as she sat munching a honey cake, "I have heard the most extraordinary news! It seems that Ossip's young friend, Vladimir, has joined one of the regiments fighting the British for control of interests in Persia! Surely the son of Tagantsev would not be required to join. David says there is to be a settlement of this conflict any day now. So his enlistment can make little difference in the outcome of the fighting. It would seem like the act of a desperate man!"

"I thought he was about to enter the Faculty of Law," Mathilde stated. "He was always so solid, so stable. I wonder what on earth possessed him?"

Early one morning, after the peace agreement had been made, Johanna entered Sonia's room. Sonia was doubly surprised, because it was Johanna's custom to awaken late. She sat up on her pillows, half asleep, while the older woman came to the side of her bed. "I did not want to wake you last night," she stated. "We heard the news from a friend, by telephone. It seems that the fighting was bloody just before the peace. Volodia was killed."

Sonia opened her mouth and jammed her fist into it between her teeth, biting fiercely on her knuckles. Johanna said, evenly, "He died at once. It was painless."

The girl's eyes, huge and staring, repelled the governess. Sonia said nothing but remained upright, her hand in her mouth, her face white.

"Sonia?" Johanna de Mey regarded her with concern, but turned away when she saw the nakedness of the girl's pain. She tiptoed out of the room, closing the door gently behind her.

Sonia did not weep. She bit with all her might into her flesh, until the blood came spurting onto the clean sheet. It was cold, but she did not feel the chill. Her gray eyes sought the small portrait upon her secretary, and she stared at it with horror.

Then she rose and went to the painting, taking the small frame in her hands. She brought it to her lips, and kissed the nut-brown face, so small and perfectly etched. But when she replaced it, it faced the wall. She closed her eyes and clenched her teeth, and brought the fist of one hand into the palm of the other, so that it hurt. She was still standing there when Marfa's knock announced breakfast.

Ten

David and Mathilde never knew what ended their second daughter's childhood and turned her so suddenly into a woman. Had he known of Volodia's last moments with Sonia, David would have recalled the words of his friend, the sculptor Antokolsky, who had since passed away. The artist had said, contrasting the two cousins, "A man might commit murder on account of Tania. But for Sonia he would give his life." Sonia had never heard Antokolsky's pronouncement; but her guilt was tremendous, and she carried it silently within her, not even writing Ossip about it. For where she knew her own ability to endure grief, she also suspected a weakness in her brother. She did not write him of Volodia's death until 1908, when she felt that he had sufficiently recovered his health to stand up to the loss of his dearest friend.

Sonia had decided to write to her brother about Natasha's wedding at the same time. "I know what you are feeling, reading this," she had told him. "I feel it with you. Today I know you loved these two more than anyone, except perhaps Mama, and me. Volodia will never return, and Natasha's life will surely never be the same because of this loss. Think of me a little in your grief: for your health and happiness are the only hope I have that my fate will be different from Natasha's. Do not allow the life and love inside you to perish." Her brother would never know what writing these phrases cost her, or what a sacrifice she had made to try to ease his grief while letting her own resurface.

Only Johanna de Mey knew what Sonia was feeling. She had said to Mathilde, "The Baron is stifling the life out of his children one by one," but her friend had not understood, and Johanna had thought better of explaining it, now that the Tagantsev twins, by death and marriage, could no longer influence David's relationship with his wife. She had allowed the matter to drop, and with it her sympathy for Sonia, so brief and incomprehensible to the girl, had ceased. Johanna sensed that Sonia had grown, had hardened from Volodia's death. And in this newly matured young woman Johanna de Mey saw an adversary.

The government of Switzerland had decided to send an ambassador to St. Petersburg, and had selected a Monsieur Odier, whose wife Mathilde had met on one of her vacations with her parents. Madame Odier, who had never traveled, had been afraid to come to a country so distant from her own. And so, to make her life easier, David had set up the bottom floor of the house on Vassilievsky Island for the new Minister and his family. Now the Swiss flag hung from a long pole outside the front door.

Sonia was mostly an observer during these months. Her father had opened a school of Oriental languages, for being a Jew, he was not allowed to teach at the University. He was also busy making speeches before the Duma and the Senate. But Sonia thought that there was a new sadness in his eyes when he looked at her mother: could it be that something was not going well between them? she wondered. The idea was too disturbing, and she fought against it with all her might. Mathilde's behavior toward her husband could not have been more courteous. Still, Sonia watched for signs of ill feeling to explain the look in David's eyes.

She was also observing Johanna. How odd this friendship was between her governess and her mother. Sonia's studies were nearly complete, and Gino, at thirteen, was attending the gymnasium where Ossip had gone before him. In spite of this, Johanna was around more than ever, and acted primarily as a companion to Mathilde, a companion who never left Mathilde alone with her daughter. Johanna was a wedge between them and the constant devotion and attention she paid Sonia's mother made the young girl most uncomfortable. Yet she herself was devoted to her own friend Nina, whom she loved very much; why, then, was this friendship different? And why did she always feel as if Johanna, in her dealings with David, behaved as the winner in a game that he had never chosen to play with her?

Baron David gave a reception for the Minister of Education late in the winter season. His niece, Tania, was nearly seventeen, and had made an early debut to emulate Sonia. Now she stood in the drawing room, tossing back her golden locks, her small, well-shaped body draped in yellow satin. The young men flocked to her, even Minister Fedorov's assistants, who were considerably older than she. Sonia sat at the piano, admiring her cousin, who was speaking to a group of three young men dressed in the elegant fashion of Savile Row. "I love London," she was saying. "Do you know that Adeline Genée, the ballerina from Copenhagen, dances there? And they have wonderful vaudeville comedy at the Alhambra!" Sonia began to play a piece by Scarlatti, thinking to herself, Tania is so beautiful, so comfortable in company. But these reflections were untinged by envy. Sonia knew she and Tania were two very different people, and each could only be herself.

When Minister Fedorov said to her, "Sofia Davidovna,

your fingers are like lightning! Do you realize that Scarlatti is almost impossible to play correctly and with feeling?" she could only shake her head and blush, charmingly. Surely the great man had not heard her governess, Johanna de Mey . . .

During that summer of 1908, Mathilde took the two children who still remained at home with her to France. Baron David took them to the train station, and once more Sonia felt, in her own body, the pathetic sadness on his face. It was the face of a man who was bewildered: he knew there was not another man in his wife's life, and yet he also knew, deep within, that she was somehow not truly his own. It made no sense. He could only flail about helplessly, searching for the answer, prey to attacks of migraine and indigestion.

The day before Mathilde's scheduled return on the Berlin express with Sonia and Gino, David awakened to Stepan's knock with a dreadful migraine. "The Baron has an important appointment today, Alexei tells me," the maître d'hôtel reminded him, while applying a compress of ice water to David's left temple.

"Appointment? I am too ill to move," David groaned.

"But the Baron must go to the island of Yelaghin, to confer with Prime Minister Stolypin," Stepan insisted.

"Tell him to go to the devil," David said. He fell back against his pillows, wracked by waves of nausea and the pounding pain at his temples.

"Yes, sir," Stepan answered. He backed away into the dressing room, and noiselessly selected David's clothing. He laid it out for him, meticulously, and then stepped out of the room. David sat up, cursing under his breath. Everything was prepared, down to the diamond pin for his cravat. Stepan knew him well . . .

He rose, shaking slightly, and went to wash and dress. When he emerged, the only tell-tale sign of illness was his half-shut left eye. He smiled at the tall maître d'hôtel. "Is Vova ready to drive me?"

"He is in front, with the footman. Alexei has given me this briefcase for the interview with the Prime Minister." Stepan knew that on mornings when David suffered migraines, the mere suggestion of breakfast was enough to upset David's stomach. He held out his master's cape, and helped him to the door.

Inside the landau, David closed his eyes and attempted to go over his proposed speech to Pyotr Stolypin. The drive was a long, jarring one. The plaid cover on his knees fell to the floor, but David was too weak to pick it up. He began to shiver, though the sun shone brightly. He was accustomed to working in spite of the headaches, but this time he could hardly turn his head without feeling alarmingly dizzy. The Prime Minister had a sumptuous villa on Yelaghin, and once Vova had reached the island, David, from his seat, began to tap violently upon the windowpane. The footman signaled to Vova, who reined in the horses. From where the landau was parked, David could see the silhouette of Stolypin's house. "I must rest here," he said. "The audience is scheduled for ten thirty. I have never been late in my life. This time, I shall arrive five minutes late—but that cannot be helped."

He pressed his fingers against his aching temples, and looked out idly over the countryside. All at once, his vision was filled with flying debris. A loud explosion resounded. The horses neighed and reared. The carriage shook; David, holding onto the sides of the landau in shock, forgot his pain. He saw a wall collapsing, an entire house, parapets included, mushrooming into a cloud of smoke and brick. His pale blue eyes protruded incredulously as the earth beneath him trembled, and one of the horses jumped forward. Vova fell from his seat, and one of the wheels of the landau rolled off. David felt himself swaying as the footman grasped for the reins, and soon Vova was tugging at the door, trying to help David from the damaged carriage. "Oh, my God," David murmured, pointing to the scene before him. "That was the Prime Minister's home. He must be dead. They must all be dead inside." Only a crater remained.

Later that evening, when the newspapers arrived at the Gunzburg house, David read about the bomb that had been planted in Stolypin's residence. But it seemed that the Prime Minister had been detained at a previous conference somewhere else and had escaped harm. When David met his family at the station the following day, they had not yet seen a newspaper, and were horrified by his account. Mathilde clung to his arm. "It was the migraine that saved you," she stammered. "Thank heavens!" He thought, gratefully, that whatever might have separated them in the past, this incident had drawn his wife closer to him.

"Let us move to Paris," Mathilde entreated.

But David shook his head. "Perhaps our country is besieged by demons and madmen," he stated, "but it is still our country, and I shall never abandon it."

Mathilde said nothing more. But several nights later, a new crisis occurred to further jolt the household. David's old friend, Alexei Alexandrovitch Lopukhin, came to call, ashen-faced and disheveled. For several years Lopukhin had been retired from politics. Now his older daughter had been mysteriously kidnapped during a visit to London. David did not hesitate: over Mathilde's fearful protests, he packed his bag and accompanied his friend to the British capital. They suspected that Evzo Azev, an agent provocateur against whom Lopukhin had worked during the revolution of 1905, might somehow have engineered the kidnapping. But once in London, they found the girl with her sister and governess at the hotel: she had been brought back, with as little explanation as when she had been taken. Mathilde said, "I wish that you had kept out of this matter, David. You are a Jew, and I am afraid of reprisals."

He was moved by the concern in her wide blue eyes, and he touched his finger to her lips. "I know, my love. But in the matter of daughters, I owed Alexei a debt." He did not elaborate, and Mathilde remained perplexed by his comment.

That December, Mathilde gave David a lavish formal dinner and ball as a silver anniversary present. Sonia played the piano, and noted poets, scholars, and diplomats were in attendance. Mathilde wore a simple gown of blue velvet, and her *kokoshnik*, the jeweled tiara her husband had had made for her to commemorate the Tzar's coronation in 1896. Johanna de Mey watched the couple as they prepared to initiate the dancing, and Mathilde's smile chilled her. It was not that she melted into her husband's arms, for Mathilde had never done that; but the way she listened to his whispered words, her head tilted to the side, suggested quiet contentment. She was forty-three years of age and still beautiful. The Dutchwoman clasped her hands together and thought: Let me not lose her. Let me not upset the delicate balance by some foolish act. . . .

When the evening was over, Johanna de Mey tiptoed to the master bedroom, and listened at the door. She heard only the rustle of David's pen upon the page of his diary. Then she moved to Mathilde's boudoir and hesitated, her heart pounding. She smelled Mathilde's scent, felt rather than heard the soft silk of her nightclothes brushing against the vanity. She tapped quickly, and turned the handle. The door swung open. Mathilde, combing her masses of raven hair, faced the intruder. She shook her head and extended her hands: "Come," she murmured quietly.

"You did not go to the Baron?" Johanna asked.

Mathilde's eyes fastened upon the Dutchwoman. Slowly, she made a gesture of infinite weariness. Then she smiled, and her features came alive like those of a small child awakened to a new sensation. Johanna shut the door behind her, and sighed with inward relief. Her lips tilted upward at the corners.

In 1909, Ossip returned from Japan, healthy and anxious to see his loving family. He had learned a good deal about the coal industry, under the tutelage of his employer, Moise Mess, and had mastered the Japanese language. Sonia felt as though her life had stopped that spring two years past when Ossip had left, and that her hopes and dreams, which had lingered on, ghostlike, after his departure, had been banished by Volodia's death that September. Now, at nineteen, she greeted her twenty-two-year-old brother with enormous relief, as though by his return he had given her life again. But she refused to share her personal grief with him, and kept it locked within her. He was perceptive enough, now that love no longer blinded him, to see that she had suffered deeply, that her laughter was perfunctory where once it had been spontaneous, full of joy and life. But he did not intrude. Not even Ossip could intrude with Sonia.

She, for her part, noticed that the brief surge of vitality that had characterized her brother during his love affair with Natasha had been drained out of him. He was the old Ossip, her friend and ally, the one who had watched others live and never dared to live himself. Natalia had transformed him, with her power to bring courage, daring, and drama to her brother. Sonia had found Ossip foolish then, histrionic, and disloyal to their father. Now she was sorry, for the young man who returned from the Orient had lost his zest for life. What is it that love does? she thought with bitterness. It had turned her sister into a recluse, her brother into his former passive self—and she herself would never again trust her own impulses toward a man. For if she had said yes to Volodia, he would not have died. But what would their future have been?

Soon after his return, Ossip began attending classes at

the Faculty of Far Eastern Studies, and because he had already learned to speak Japanese, he was also able, in the afternoons, to take a part-time position at his grandfather's bank, the Maison Gunzburg, which was managed by his Uncle Sasha. Sasha had always cast a favorable eye upon his oldest nephew, and now that Ossip had returned with some knowledge of business, Sasha was anxious to introduce him to the family enterprise.

In the evenings, Ossip found himself attending endless soirées, for he had returned to discover himself topping the list of eligible young bachelors of the capital, and was therefore deluged with invitations. He would escort his sister and almost always his eighteen-year-old cousin Tania, as Sasha and Rosa would not hear of Sonia's attendance at any ball or dinner to which their own daughter had not been invited.

Tatiana Alexandrovna de Gunzburg, at eighteen, had completed her studies at the French girls' school, the Ecole Lebourdet-Caprenier, and had spent a final year in a gymnasium in order to pass her baccalaureate examinations. She was by no means stupid, but her desire to play far exceeded any desire to learn. She had attended this exclusive institution in order to possess yet another desirable attribute with which to catch a husband. She spoke perfect French and Russian, and also her mother's language, German; and she was familiar with the Hermitage Museum and the Museum of Alexander III, for it was considered detrimental to a young lady's personality to appear ignorant of certain works of art. But museums bored her. She had stopped reading serious literature, and had ceased attending lectures with the advent of her diploma. She now awakened after ten, took a leisurely walk before luncheon, and in the afternoon she went visiting or received her friends in her mother's house. Evenings were spent at the theater, at dinners and balls; or there would be a reception in her home.

For Sonia, life was different. She had studied without fanfare under the coaching of Johanna, and she still practiced the piano at least two hours a day. Early in 1909 Sonia and Nina Tobias asked a young English girl, Miss Maxwell, to come to them twice a week, and they would take turns reading aloud from books while Miss Maxwell corrected their pronunciation. The evenings would end with a three-way conversation in English. In the fall, Baron David arranged for his daughter and her friends to take some philosophy courses. Nina, who was a rather serious person, was always present. The two girls also attended many lectures: they heard an avant-garde poet recite his works, a professor of Greek speak of his travels, and an explorer recount his adventures on the North Pole. Since on Saturday night there was always a ball or a reception, Sonia made a point of going to the matinée rehearsal of the symphony, which was open to the public; symphony nights coincided with dances, and she wished to miss no concerts or recitals. There was no chance of encountering Tania at any of these events, except when Ossip was known to be accompanying his sister.

Tania was a constant irritant to Sonia, but she amused Ossip. Nina Tobias, quiet and reserved, danced with her gold-flecked eyes upon him, her soft-voiced questions probing his work, his interests, his stay in Japan. He liked her a great deal, and thought that during the two years of his absence she had acquired a calm grace somewhat like his mother's. But she was not regal, as Mathilde was. She was like a soft flower in bloom, a soft but sturdy flower, a pansy or a poppy. She was well read, and Ossip enjoyed her conversation. But it was Tania who made him laugh.

Tania had heard whispers about a dark, forbidden love affair in Ossip's past. She had guessed, quite accurately, that the young man must have been seduced by verve, by exuberance, by total sensuousness. She did not think that to conquer Ossip it was necessary to understand him. She saw the slender, sensitive man, and did not guess how terror gripped at his insides in the face of risk, of involvement; she knew only that life had long withheld its pleasures from him, and that he had stood enviously on the sidelines. Life, to Ossip, was the forbidden fruit, desired as well as shunned in fear. Natasha had conquered his fear and shown him that together they might bite harmlessly into the apple. But since losing Natasha his fear had returned with even greater strength. Tania's small efforts at bringing him laughter caught him off guard, for they were truly harmless. He was amused rather than delighted, when only delight might have caused him to risk his regained security.

There was an easy carelessness about Ossip now, as though nothing were important anymore. He laughed with Tania and went off with his male friends to the Aquarium, the nightclub where the privileged youth of Petersburg spent their rubles on the gypsies who entertained them. Sonia had never set foot inside the club. It was considered off-limits to unmarried girls; even married women went there only accompanied by their husbands. Ossip craved the fun, the mindless gaiety, and sometimes ended the evening with a feverish gypsy upon his lap, and a bottle of Dom Perignon on the table. But he seldom finished the champagne, for halfway through he would grow bored and restless. Not much captured his attention these days.

"I do not know what to make of your brother," Nina once said to Sonia. "He spends time with me, sometimes his eyes sparkle when we discuss a play, or a new ballet. But then, the next time I see him, he treats me like a stranger. What am I to believe?"

"You must give him time," Sonia replied. More and more frequently, when Nina went into society, a young man of their acquaintance, Zenia Abelson, was proffering his attentions upon her; but Sonia was not concerned, for she knew that Nina's feelings were for Ossip. She grew anxious over her brother's shiftlessness, however, over his lack of perseverance in anything but his University work. Even his job went well solely because of his good mind, not because he relished what he was accomplishing in the service of his grandfather and uncle. He continued to work only because there was no reason to stop.

Sasha and Rosa frequently invited him and Sonia to supper. For Sonia these evenings were an unpleasant chore. Rosa usually ignored her. But she fussed over Ossip, and he permitted it, not bothering to discourage her. She would serve him his favorite foods, all the time drawing attention to Tania and her charms. Ossip would smile. His cousin had grown into a superb young lioness with a golden mane, an apricot complexion, and blue eyes rimmed with black lashes. Her figure was round and pleasant, though she was petite, like her cousin Sonia. And she dressed in the latest Paris fashions, in warm colors to match the tones of her skin and hair. "If she were less egotistical, Tania might fool a man into believing he was in the presence of a sensualist," Ossip told his mother with amusement. "She bites into an apple with such relish, and her bosom palpitates with excitement. But it is not life that moves her: it is only the prospect of grabbing something from it for her selfish pleasure—preferably a husband."

"You must keep your shocking thoughts to yourself, young man," his mother said; but she could not help smiling at him with her eyes. She was as fond of her niece as her daughter was.

"I have never been interested in Russian men," Tania said to Ossip one evening at her parents' dinner table. "They bore me. I want the civilization of Paris, or Rome, or London. Russian men are peasants at heart."

"She is being foolish," Sasha said fondly. "All Russians are not like that. Have I made you afraid of your countrymen, little one?"

Tania giggled. "Oh, Papa! I know all about you. No, I

would not marry you, if you were mine to choose. But Ossip is an exception. He is delicate, like Aunt Mathilde, who is, after all, Parisian. I am certain that if Ossip marries he could easily be transferred to the Paris branch of the bank."

"But I am perfectly happy in Petersburg," Ossip declared.

"Is it Nina Mikhailovna? She is a tadpole, Ossip! No spirit whatsoever. If you married her, boredom would overcome you within minutes of breaking the nuptial glass beneath your slipper!"

"I am not committing myself, Tanitchka," Ossip said, bursting into laughter. "Perhaps you are forgetting that I am a prince among men, and that one kiss might turn a tadpole into a princess!"

"I have the society bulletins, Ossip," his aunt interposed. "Come, look them over with me. See if you can find something interesting to which to escort Tania after supper. She has been so lethargic today!" Rosa held out the bulletins which had arrived in the morning mail. "There is nothing tonight," Rosa sighed. "It is Saturday, and so there is ballet instead of opera at the Mariinsky Theater, with the prima ballerina Karsavina. But Tania has already seen her twice in *Sleeping Beauty*. At the Alexandrinsky Theater there is some Chekhov; but Tania has read all his works, and it is stupid to waste time to see what has been read. At the French Theater . . . Well! That is unsuitable! There is the weekly concert—but how boring! No ice skating upon the Neva River tonight, and two lectures, but such dull ones. The Grand Duchess Vladimir is giving a Charity Sale—but Tania would know very few people there. Oh—what shall we do?"

"You have invited us, Aunt Rosa," Sonia declared. "We can keep Tania company at home."

Her aunt started. She laid aside the papers and said, "Sonia, I had forgotten all about you, so quiet in your corner! But you, now that I think of it, the three of you, could talk. Tania has received some delicate embroidered handkerchiefs which she can show you, and then you can play dominoes, or *halma etiha.* Better yet, you can play the piano while Ossip and Tania waltz!"

"What a pity," Ossip said softly, his tone tinged with irony, "that you did not invite one of those boring young Russians, to waltz with Sonia. She likes to dance, as well as Tania. And she is less choosy. Her countrymen will do, in a pinch."

"That is why Sonia will be married later than Tatiana," Aunt Rosa stated. "She is so unparticular! But then, perhaps she is just being a realist about her possibilities. Tania has received five proposals since her debut."

"But I want my foreigner!" Tania cried. Then, blushing, "Or one who is half and half. . . ."

In the fall of 1909, David was introduced to a young Indian man of small stature and delicate fingers. His name was Naraian Kershaw, and he was the son of the deposed Maharaja of Baroda. He had come to St. Petersburg to arouse sympathy against the British colonialists, who had deposed his father. His slanting almond-shaped eyes glittered like rare Oriental gems, and Mathilde did not trust him. Nevertheless, David was intrigued by what Naraian Kershaw could offer him. The young man spoke an Indian tongue which the Baron had wished to learn for a long time. David proposed to Kershaw that he move into one of the apartments rented out by the Gunzburgs in the building where they lived, and in return David would come to him for lessons in the Marathi dialect.

In spite of her distaste for "the young serpent," Mathilde was above all a woman of impeccable manners and form. As his hostess, she took Kershaw into society. He began to receive invitations from prominent people, and after supper he would launch into his plea for political support. St.

Petersburg responded to his earnestness and his excellent breeding, and he was soon regarded as a rare bird to be displayed for effect. Ossip often spoke with him in Japanese, and Sonia, forever curious to learn, sometimes asked the young Indian prince to translate a word here and there for her into Chinese; she recorded his answers carefully into a notebook. And every day, Kershaw would hold telephone conversations in Japanese; no one paid them the slightest attention.

That summer, Alexei Lopukhin had gone to Paris, and had encountered his old opponent, the agent provocateur and double agent Azev. More than four years had passed since the events of the revolution, and the two men had walked through the Luxembourg Gardens companionably. Azev had said, "Now that these troubled times have gone by, and we have both become private citizens once again, will you not tell me what transpired on your side, and why you opposed me?" Lopukhin, smiling, had demurred: his orders had been secret. "But what does it matter, today?" Azev had insisted. Lopukhin had shrugged, and related his part in the matter. Upon his return to St. Petersburg, the Tzar's Secret Police, of which he was no longer the head, arrested him on the charge of high treason. Alexei Alexandrovitch was sent to the Pyotrpavlovsky Fortress, the most rigorous prison for political enemies, and at last Baron David understood that the kidnapping of the Lopukhin girl had been a form of blackmail—and that his friend had told Azev about his involvement only to prevent a second attempt to harm his family.

David was very frightened. What times were these, that an honest man had been coerced in the vilest, most inhuman manner into betraying his honor? He rushed to Lopukhin's apartment to seize his papers and burn them, to protect his friend. At this same time, Naraian Kershaw was making more and more frequent calls in Japanese on the Gunzburg telephone, but David was in no frame of mind to notice, or care. Lopukhin's trial was taking place, and his friend, who had helped to save Anna, was about to be condemned and sent with his family to Siberia as a political criminal. David's entire being, all his principles, bristled at this blatant injustice. But he was powerless to help Alexei Alexandrovitch.

Then, one day, Naraian Kershaw announced that he was leaving Russia to continue his trip. David gave him the address of friends in Vienna, which Kershaw planned to visit next, and courteously accompanied him to the train station. Shortly after the Prince's departure, Ossip stumbled upon Sonia's notation of Kershaw's Chinese interpretations. "What's this?" he cried. "Surely he fooled you! If this is Chinese, then I am King of England!" Nobody knew what to make of this oddity, and Sonia threw away the meaningless words.

A week elapsed. One evening, after supper, Stepan announced that a police official had arrived to confer with David. Bewildered, the Baron got up and received the man in his study. He was a policeman with whom David was not acquainted, and he spoke somewhat awkwardly. "Baron Gunzburg, I am afraid that I have orders to arrest you," he announced. He coughed, to hide his confusion: Baron Gunzburg was a man with a reputation, and he was hardly accustomed to arresting notables.

"What does this mean?" David exclaimed, rising with alarm. The Lopukhin matter rushed into his mind and nearly blinded him: had someone discovered that he had burned his friend's papers? But the police official said: "I must arrest you for harboring a Japanese spy in your home. Naraian Kershaw."

"Japanese spy? But the man is an Indian prince! And besides, I registered him at once as my guest with the authorities. Look to the records, my dear man."

"We have had many problems since the war with Japan,"

the policeman explained. "Spies have entered our country on a steady basis. Many of them have been Indians; the Japanese wish to come steadily west, and these spies are, in a sense, attempting to pry open a gate for them into our country. You are an honorable man, Baron; had you no suspicions?"

"I am hardly the sort who meddles in the affairs of his guests. But, look here: does the Chief of Police know you are here? He would not, I am certain, permit you to arrest me."

The other considered. Baron David was a wealthy Jew, and men such as he paid well for their freedom. He said cautiously, "Let me call the Chief on your line, if you please. I shall discuss it with him."

When the two men emerged from the study an hour later, David was white-faced and his hair lay matted upon his temples. The policeman was smiling broadly and bowing. Stepan let him out as David returned to the drawing room. Mathilde stood up, her lips parted in concern. "It's all right," he reassured her quietly. "I have paid him well. And his superiors, too. But I shall not be able to sleep for many nights after this. Perhaps I shall never be able to sleep again." When a little cry escaped her, he shook his head. "No," he stated, "we are not going to leave the country. We have done no wrong."

Eleven

---•---

Before the New Year, Baron Horace passed away at the age of seventy-six. He had caught a chill, which had developed into pneumonia and later pleurisy. David began to notice that his father was seriously ill toward Hanukkah: the old Baron was red with fever, and did not allow his grandchildren to enter his bedroom to visit him. He lay upon his pillows, pathetically attempting to gulp air which his tired lungs could not absorb. When David sat next to him, he shook his head, and even that effort seemed too much for him. David kissed him and left the room precipitously. In the landau he wept soundlessly. If Mathilde was the muse of his life, his father was the strength and the example.

In the days that followed, David and his brother Sasha spent nearly every hour at the dying man's bedside. But it was only when finally he lost consciousness that the rest of the family was allowed in. Sonia, Gino, and Ossip sat together on the small sofa, their faces drawn, each with his own precious memories. Ossip had not shared the ideals of Horace's life, his religious beliefs; but he had found his grandfather a great man, and as such, unique. Gino and Sonia had truly loved him, and had always tried to please him, so that some of his sternness might dissipate in momentary joy. Tania came too, although she had not really loved Horace. He had been the only man to escape her charms. But the occasion was momentous, and she shared it with her cousins. This was the first death that would have a profound effect on all their lives.

Mathilde grieved for her husband. Her Uncle Horace had represented so many conflicting emotions for her. He had "bought" her from Yuri, and she had resented him at first. Later, she had accepted the deed as less humiliating and more an unspoken compliment. After all, most women came endowed to the marriage dais: her father-in-law had instead reversed the situation, and he had been too much the gentleman to ever make her feel the oddness of what had taken place. She knew what to expect from her Uncle Horace. Perhaps she too, like Ossip, had never entered into his world of piety, but at least she had grasped the real man. He had been decent, and good, unlike her own father, Yuri. She knew, most of all, what Horace meant to David. As she watched the old man die, as she heard his final death rattle slow down to silence, compassion flowed through her toward David, compassion so strong that it was almost like love. And the only one who noticed it was Johanna de Mey.

During the long vigil nobody spoke, nobody looked into any of the other faces in the room. Sasha and Rosa, Tania, Mathilde, her three children, David—each sat quietly, waiting. At five in the morning the erratic breathing stopped. Then Mathilde quickly ushered her children from the room, and Rosa led Tania away too. Only the sons remained.

The cemetery was eight miles from Vassilievsky Island, out of the city, which had to be crossed to reach it. David had built there the small gray synagogue where the last rites could be administered.

It was the end of December. The road was paved with ice, and the wind howled dismally on the day of the funeral. But Baron Horace had been the most respected *shtadlan* in St. Petersburg, perhaps even in all of Russia. The procession was therefore very long. Carriages bearing innumerable friends and fellow statesmen lined up behind the coffin. Sonia, Ossip, Gino, and Tania decided to join the younger people on foot, in order to pay in full their final respects toward their grandfather. Mathilde had never been able to walk long distances, and she and Rosa rode together. The two sons of the old Baron headed the procession, and walked the entire eight miles; David's own sons accompanied them. But the two young girls, exhausted and emotionally drained, had to stop their mothers' car at the confines of the city, to be driven the last few miles. They had made a valiant effort.

Sonia's memory of the burial was unclear. She knew that they carried the coffin to the small gray synagogue, and that the Rabbi said a prayer. Then they brought her grandfather's remains to the relatively empty third section of the cemetery. Horace had asked to be placed in the third section, among the petty artisans and small businessmen, hoping to show his peers that there was no dishonor in sharing the space of death with poorer men than he.

The Neva flowed close by, and here the swamps were worse than anywhere else in the city: when Baron Horace's coffin was lowered below the ground, Sonia heard the most undignified sound in the world. *Ploof*, said the water as it lapped around the cedar box. She put her gloved fist to her mouth and stifled a sob.

After David recited the Kaddish, Sonia took her brothers' arms to return to the carriage. But the mourners were not leaving the cemetery. One by one, old men and women in black shawls lined up in front of them, facing Baron David. Sonia and Ossip and Gino were pushed aside in the melee, but it was not a mob that was forming: rather a neat, organized procession toward their father. David appeared surprised when the first person kissed his hand, and he made a motion for him to stop—but then another came, and a third. The Jews of St. Petersburg were coming to pay homage to the new head of their community, their new leader. Soon Sonia and her brothers saw that their father was weeping freely. And they, too, wept.

Sonia and Ossip began their year of mourning for their grandfather in hard work, and even the bright, blond Tania did not dance at the start of 1910, when Petersburg was alive with joy. Mathilde slept in her husband's arms many times during the days that followed Horace's death. She mopped his fevered brow and stayed awake to soothe his anxieties, never guessing that behind the door Johanna de Mey was clenching her fist so hard that her sharp nails cut into the delicate flesh of her palms. Mathilde de Gunzburg believed in the Gunzburg family and knew that as others had sacrificed for its welfare, so too must she; this was David's time of need.

Ossip had resolved to accelerate his education at the Faculty of Far Eastern Studies, and was to obtain his degree in the spring of 1911. Gino, at the gymnasium, struggled to maintain a good average and, at fifteen, was one year ahead scholastically. His father, who knew that his second son did not possess the brilliance of the first, had started Gino one year before the usual age so that, if he needed to repeat a level, he would not feel humiliated. Ossip had been physically disabled, and had never felt awkward about his age; but Gino had no excuses for failure. His father was proud that his precautions had been taken in vain, and that Gino was a solid student, if not a distinguished one. He was to take his baccalaureate examinations in the spring of 1912, and that, David knew, would represent a considerably more difficult hurdle to surmount.

Baron David was a scholar of repute, and his particular field of interest was the languages of the Middle East. He was so well respected that when University professors happened across students of special merit in the Arabic and Semitic tongues, they would send them to the Baron. In 1909, David found that his small study could no longer hold these eager young people, for now there were more than fifteen of them, so with two associates he formed a School of Mid-Eastern Languages, for which he rented an apartment near their house on Vassilievsky Island. Sonia, when not at work on the piano, was most frequently found at the back of her father's classroom, notebook in hand. She was one of a few young women among the men, and was the only one who had not passed her baccalaureate examinations or been a member of the University. The year 1910 was a year of introspection for her; she ruminated about Volodia, and about her father. She did not appear to miss society gatherings, although Nina visited her frequently, as before.

With the death of Horace, the patriarch, David became head of the Jewish community of Petersburg, and Sasha of the Maison Gunzburg. Ossip, at twenty-three, was still working for his uncle, and was being groomed for a more important position after the granting of his University degree. He was neither pleased nor unhappy about this turn of events; even his passion for the Far East had diminished, and he received his uncle's praise with due courtesy and gratitude, but no enthusiasm. It did not escape him that his uncle encouraged Tania's flirtations, nor that his sister found ways of placing him near her friend, Nina Tobias. He was amused by these maneuvers, but not inspired to act beyond the blandest of courtships.

But with the New Year, the period of mourning came to an end, and the Gunzburgs learned that their French cousin Jean was arriving to spend the social season in St. Petersburg. Tania ran into her aunt's sitting room, her blue eyes sparkling, and declared, "Jean is going to inject some life into this dull city! Don't you remember him, Sonia? From our visit to Uncle Misha in Kiev?"

"Yes," Sonia replied. "The handsome young man who had been unable to find a military exemption among the family papers in Paris! Why didn't he ever return to serve his tour of duty?"

"He was extremely lucky," Mathilde explained. "My father was able to locate one last exemption. Papa is not always careful in business affairs, and had failed to check one of his safes. Jean, therefore, did not have to come here to serve. And I understand his reluctance—he is a Frenchman, by everything but passport!"

"Yes, he is a Parisian—and I do so love foreigners!" Tania cried.

Her Uncle David ignored her. "Jean was all the more lucky, for by 1905 new restrictions had been imposed, regulations that did not exist when I was in the Uhlans at Lomzha. I was, as the British say, an officer and a gentleman. So was your father, Tania. But Jean, because he is a Jew and would have served after the new ruling, could not have received a commission. Gino, as a second son, will have to be a simple soldier."

Mathilde shivered. "He is still a child," she said stiffly.

"And children are uninteresting," Tania added, nodding conspiratorially at her aunt. "Let us talk of how we shall entertain Jean. Was he not to have visited us once before?"

"The pogrom curtailed his trip," Mathilde said quietly, looking at Sonia as Tania blushed and bit her lip. "Now he is making up for lost time. At twenty-six he will fit right into your group of young people, although he is our first cousin—mine, and your father's, and your Uncle Sasha's. He is only three years older than Ossip." Mathilde smiled at her daughter, hoping to see a spark of excitement light up her features. But Sonia's expression did not change.

"Sonia is far too serious for a man like Jean," Tania interposed. "He was my pet in Kiev. I wonder if he remembers me at all?"

"My love, you would clout the man that might forget

-you," Ossip stated. His cousin threw an embroidered cushion at him, and he deftly avoided it by moving his head out of the way, and the cushion landed only inches away from the tea tray. Mathilde regarded her niece severely, and Tania looked away, playing with a ruby ring upon one of her slender fingers. "Poor Jean . . ." Ossip moaned.

Jean de Gunzburg, tall, elegant, his black hair waving and his blue eyes alert, was to divide his stay in the Russian capital between the homes of his two cousins, David and Sasha. He was warmly welcomed by Mathilde, but when he saw Sonia, his face became gentle with remembrance. "Jean," she said, and held out her hands to him. He thought: She has become as lovely as a porcelain figurine, delicate and fine—but who has robbed her of her gaiety? He kissed her, as one would kiss a favored young sister. When he saw Ossip, who matched him in sartorial good taste, he could not help feeling the same letdown. Here was a young man, laughing, telling amusing stories, complimenting the ladies, yet without excitement, without life. What had taken the joy from these two beautiful young people?

Although the first part of his stay was to be with David and Mathilde, Rosa de Gunzburg gave a splendid dinner in his honor shortly after his arrival. He entered with his cousins, and there, on the threshold, stood Tatiana, her hair a mass of golden ringlets, her throat aglow with rubies, her gown crimson to match. He sucked in his breath.

"Well?" she cried, and pirouetted for him. "Have I changed?"

"You are a woman now," Jean declared. He could not remove his eyes from her lush figure.

During dinner they sat side by side, and she spoke to him in small gulps, gazing at him over the rim of her champagne glass through half-closed eyes. He thought: She is spoiled and a damned nuisance. But he could not take his eyes from her. His own body felt alive with desire. A nineteen-year-old brat, and he with Mademoiselle Singer and Madeleine Hirsch each awaiting marriage proposals in Paris . . . He did not need an entanglement such as this, for he knew women like Tania. His mother, Henriette de Gunzburg, had been one of them—splendid to behold, avaricious in the extreme, and with only financial interest at heart. She had arrived in Paris an orphan from Vienna without benefit of dowry. His father, Baron Solomon de Gunzburg, had married her, wild with love. But once she had acquired his name and fortune, Henriette had abandoned him for a string of lovers. Jean de Gunzburg did not like his mother, and he admitted to himself that he did not like Tania either. He had not even liked her as a child, in Kiev. Why then did he have this sudden uncontrollable urge to crush her against him here and now, before all the guests in attendance?

During the days that followed, Jean discovered that Tania haunted his thoughts. David and Mathilde took him with their three children to the Mariinsky Theater, which was hung with blue and silver velvet, to hear Rimsky-Korsakov's opera, *Sadko*. They occupied a private box, with six chairs and a small hallway at the back, where their capes and boots were deposited, and where refreshments were served when ordered. When the first act was over, David handed Jean his opera glasses, and the young man looked around the theater, admiring the elegance of the ladies. All at once he saw Tania, a small tiara of pearls in her pompadour, her shoulders daringly bare, diamonds at the throat. He began to quiver.

"We often run across the street to Dumas', the French sweet shop, during the intermission, to buy boxes of sweetmeats for the ladies," Ossip murmured to him. "Will you accompany me? I have just spotted Nina Mikhailovna Tobias, Sonia's friend."

"I have seen someone, too," the young Frenchman said.

They rose, bowed to Mathilde and Sonia, and dashed out with their top hats. When they had purchased their gifts, Ossip asked, "Shall I go with you? Or would you prefer to go alone?"

"Go to Nina Mikhailovna, Ossip," Jean declared. He directed his footsteps toward the opposite side of the theater, where he had noticed Tania. He entered her box and heard gay laughter. She was surrounded by young men, and was holding five boxes of French sweets in her lap. He was about to leave, feeling foolish, but she had spotted him. She jumped up, upsetting the candies on the floor. "Jean!" she exclaimed, and ran to him in tiny doelike steps. "I hoped you would come. What have you brought me?"

"My heart," he said lightly, and she cocked her head to one side and examined him shrewdly. Then she began to laugh.

"My Mama always told me that one cannot survive on love and rosewater," she said. "I shall keep your heart, but now I am hungry. I prefer your bonbons!"

The bell sounded, and Jean turned red, feeling like a child caught in a foolish act. "It was nice to see you, Tania," he said. Impulsively, he took one of her hands and raised it to his lips. "Tomorrow evening Sonia and Ossip have planned a drive. Would you join us?"

In answer, she merely fluttered her eyelashes. He left the box, his temples pounding, angry with himself for his reaction.

The following evening, in the snow, Jean de Gunzburg held little Tania's hand as the troika glided over the Nevsky Prospect. And when Sonia and Ossip were engaged in a conversation of their own, she turned her pert face to him and offered him her lips, full and red. He kissed her quickly but with passion, and when the kiss was over he felt like a prisoner, and did not know whether to be happy or sad about this golden girl who was captivating his senses.

A week later, Rosa de Gunzburg said to Mathilde, "I

shall not be able to ask Jean to stay with us. I think that he has fallen in love with Tania. If it's true, he must declare himself before I can allow them to sleep under the same roof. It would be improper. Will you keep him?"

"Certainly," Mathilde replied. "He is charming, and would make her a fine husband. But I do not think he would propose before speaking to his mother first."

"I suppose not," Rosa sighed. But her cheeks were abnormally red, and her raven eyes glimmered with unusual life.

Tania's eyes were even brighter these days. She threw herself on Sonia's bed one afternoon, sighing. "I am so afraid of losing him," she whispered, and tears came to her eyes. "I love him so, my heart cannot bear our moments apart. Have you ever felt this way about anyone, Sonia? But no, of course you haven't! If you had, we would have heard of it, would we not?"

Her cousin stiffened. "Yes," she murmured, "you would have heard of it. But I am glad for you, Tania. Jean is trustworthy, and good, and already part of our family. You will be happy with him, always."

Tania sat up abruptly and smiled at Sonia. "I have been a fool all my life!" she cried. "Wanting fortune, and glitter. Not reading the books I should. Being rude to you. You are an angel, Sonia, and now that I am happy, I want to share it with you! Jean and I are going to be married, I am sure of it—and you will be my bridesmaid, won't you?"

"Of course," Sonia said. She placed her slender arms about her cousin and hugged her. Yet she felt a pang of unbearable pain, and she bit her lower lip to keep a sob from rising from her chest.

Toward the end of Jean's visit, Mathilde and her daughter conferred.

"I am amazed at Tatiana," Sonia said. "She has been transformed. Perhaps Ossip and I never really gave her a chance. Jean has been truly remarkable for her. Today, when she ripped her gown and Marfa repaired it during tea, Tania gave her several kopeks without having to be reminded, and she didn't ask Aunt Rosa for the money. It is as though he has opened a dam, and goodness is flowing through her."

"We must encourage them," Mathilde agreed. "Let's give a ball in Jean's honor. All of Petersburg whispers of the oncoming engagement . . . and Jean has not yet attended a ball here."

Jean was dazzled by the intricate figures of the mazurka and the cotillion. After he had fulfilled his social obligations to the other ladies, he monopolized Tania until the early morning hours. She is so lucky, Sonia thought. Ossip was slightly jealous, for his cousin Tania seemed to have virtually forgotten his existence, and had not once tossed a frivolous remark in his direction. Instead, she whispered to the young Frenchman, "I am hopelessly enthralled with you. Everybody knows it. Are you pleased with your conquest?"

Jean was taken aback. He stammered something, then looked at Tania's small full figure, at her apricot complexion, and her blue eyes fringed with curling lashes. He was speechless. He felt her tremble in his arms. "I am more than pleased," he murmured, beside himself with emotion. At twenty-six, he was an experienced man of the world, acccustomed to the demimondaines of Paris nightclubs. Yet the desire he felt for Tania overwhelmed his sense of reality.

Mathilde invited her niece to accompany her, Johanna de Mey, Sonia, Ossip, and Jean to the ballet, for before Jean's departure he had to witness this wonderful Russian display of grace. In Paris, during the intermission at the opera, a group of twenty girls would execute a dance, but nobody bothered to watch them. Diaghilev, it was true, had made a successful tour in France, but his dancers had been clad in full costume, and Jean had heard that in St. Petersburg the Imperial troupe wore tutus.

At intermission, Jean took Tania aside. "I have a gift for you," he said.

While she opened the elongated satin box he watched her, wetting his lips. She made an "o" with her red mouth, and removed a watch bracelet of blue enamel, with diamonds all around the face. "It was made by Fabergé, the Tzar's jeweler," he said softly. She threw her arms about his neck, and in the box her aunt, cousins, and Johanna de Mey watched her uninhibited display of enthusiasm. Tatiana showed them her present and exclaimed; "I have never received anything like it! I shall wear it always, Jean! Oh—I do love you!"

When he departed from St. Petersburg, Jean de Gunzburg carried away the memory of the small girl with the golden hair, waving to him from the station. During the long trip home, he could not rid himself of the restless passion which this memory evoked in him. He would have to speak to his mother, Baroness Henriette. Girls such as Tania, once awakened, never fade in their ardor, and he was certain that to possess such a girl for life would be like feasting upon delicacies until his dying day.

In St. Petersburg, girls came to Baron Alexander de Gunzburg's sumptuous apartment to help Tania pass the time until Jean's first letter arrived. And, in the meantime, Jean reached Paris and went to see his mother.

He saw his mother, and as he perfunctorily kissed her cheek, a chill pervaded him. He felt numb with dislike, then nauseated. To have considered a wife like her . . . How could he thus have taken leave of his senses? That evening he called upon Mademoiselle Singer, and brought her red roses.

When Mikhail de Gunzburg, his cousin who had moved to Paris after that terrible day in Kiev, asked him how his trip had been, Jean shrugged lightly and smiled. "I saw the ballet and rode in a troika, and kissed a pretty girl. What else is there to add, Misha? I am back, for good. And I am glad."

After a while, the girls stopped asking Tatiana about the mail. She hurled the enamel watch against her mother's china cabinet. The undercook retrieved it for herself, and wore it each Sunday, though it no longer kept time. Sonia, in her own bed, cried, thinking of broken things that could not be mended.

In the spring, Ossip was granted his diploma, and received his official post in his uncle's bank. Nobody spoke of Jean, or of his visit, and Sasha and Rosa made a great fuss over Ossip's future and his prospects. One evening, when the weather was balmy, Ossip knocked on his sister's door, and found her reading and eating fruit. Biting into a plum, he announced; "You have won, Sonitchka! I am tired of this aimless existence. Tomorrow, I shall ask Nina Mikhailovna for her hand in marriage."

"Oh, Ossip!" his sister cried. Then, reddening, she stammered, "But I am not the one who is supposed to win! In this you must think of yourself. Nina is my best friend, but anyone you choose would be my friend, too."

"You did not always say that," he commented tersely.

"It is useless to dredge up the past," she flung back at him. "But if you really want Nina—then I am certain that you shall be happy."

But when Ossip returned home the following day, he encountered Nina with Sonia and Mathilde, in the sitting room. Irina Markovna Tobias, Nina's mother, was sitting beside the girl in a rare moment of affection. Ossip regarded his sister, and saw her look of pain and embarrassment. He was mystified, and came into the room, smiling. He bowed over Irina Markovna's bony hand, kissed his mother's cheek, his sister's forehead, and finally came to Nina, who sat blushing. Taking her hand in his, he declared; "You look very happy today, Nina Mikhailovna. And very lovely."

"She has good reason," his mother stated. "Ossip—Nina has come to us to announce her engagement, to Zenia

Abelson. They are to be married this fall! Is that not wonderful news, darling?"

"Zenia Abelson? Why, I had no idea you even knew him!" Ossip burst out, turning pale. "Sonia never told me!"

"It was only a casual courtship, Ossip Davidovitch," the young girl replied. "I am twenty-two, and ready for marriage. Zenia is a good man."

"And that is enough to make you become Madame Abelson?" he cried, outraged.

"Ossip!" his mother interposed, blushing.

"If he were a prince, or a count, I could read your ambition!" the young man said bitterly. "But simply Zenia Abelson . . ."

"He will be a good, decent husband," Nina replied, looking away. "And he truly loves me." Her brown eyes, with their flecks of gold, fell upon his bright blue ones. Their eloquence shook him. He ran his fingers through his hair, scratched his chin, and then adjusted his cravat and bowed before her.

"Forgive me, Nina Mikhailovna," he stated, his poise resumed. "I wish you all the luck, and all the love. You deserve more than some could offer, and I hope that Zenia will come to you with filled heart."

"He came last week," she said simply.

"He was most well timed," Ossip replied.

Several evenings later, Ossip came to supper at his aunt and uncle's house, and immediately noticed Tania's absence. Rosa turned red. "She has not been well recently," she said. "But perhaps if you would visit her . . . You might cheer her up. She needs good cheer, my dear."

"I need it, too," the young man stated. When they finished dessert, he made his way to the upper floor where Tatiana's rooms were. It was warm but he could see a fire burning in the hearth of her sitting room. He knocked on the opened door, and heard her mournful reply. Then he saw her, lying on embroidered pillows near the fire, her blond hair in disarray, her unexpectedly drab gown wrinkled around her legs. "Tanitchka," he murmured.

"I did not want to be seen," she stated. But he moved toward her, and took a seat next to her upon the floor. She held her hands out toward the flames, and there were blue circles under her eyes. A surge of compassion flooded him. He took her frigid fingers in his warm hands and began to rub them.

"It's no good, no good, Tanitchka," he remonstrated gently. "No one is worth this self-destruction. Not you, sweetheart. For you are our bright bird, our peacock!"

But she shook her head. "Once," she remarked in a dull voice. "I thought I loved you, Ossip."

"And it was very nice, that pretense of love. I enjoyed the attention. But I knew it was not serious."

"Was your heart ever broken, Ossip?" she queried.

He gazed deeply into her small pale face. "Yes," he answered.

"And you have not loved since?"

"No," he said, continuing to rub her fingers. "But then, I am a fool. I am afraid of life, afraid of hurts. Do not spend your days like me, Tania."

She searched his face, and her eyes brightened slightly. "You all thought I was nothing but a selfish child," she commented. "I am sure you were all correct in your estimation. Is that why he left me, Ossip?"

He shrugged. "Sweet, I do not know. In all honesty. Sometimes people think they feel one way, because of the magic of the occasion. Then they return to their natural habitat, and decide it was an illusion. I am certain that he did care, and that if he left, if he did this to you, it was only because he found himself lacking, and did not want you to feel cheated someday."

They sat silently by the fire. Ossip suddenly turned to her, and she to him. He took her face in his hands, and kissed her lips. Her arms went round his neck and then dropped. He moved away. "It's not right," he murmured. "But it's up to you. If you want me to marry you, I shall."

She began to cry. "No," she said. "We are both in love with other people, and we are too different. You are easy, I am driving. I would turn into a shrew, and you would grow more passive. Soon we would hate each other, always at odds. I need a dominating husband, and you need a girl who can live sufficiently for two, to bring you out of yourself. We are strange people, you and I."

He caressed her cheek, and smiled sadly. "Jean was a very stupid man," he said, and gazed into the fire.

They sat together for a long time, listening to the crackling logs, until their bodies grew numb. When he returned home, Ossip stopped to say good night to his sister, Sonia. Her door stood ajar, and as he raised his hand to knock, he saw her turned away from him, gazing toward her secretary. In her hands was a small framed painting, and he could not help straining to make out its subject. Even at a distance he could distinguish the five young faces etched upon the canvas, Volodia's, Sokolov's, Petri's, Botkin's, and his own. Ossip started. Where had it come from? He had never seen this painting before. He stood in the doorway of his sister's room, wondering why she had the portrait, thinking of the young companions one by one. Sonia had hardly known Sokolov, Petri, and Botkin. But Volodia—

All at once, he understood. He longed to enter the room and hold Sonia, as he had held Tania, but she sat mutely, turned away from him, thinking she was alone. Her sorrow was all the more eloquent for its privacy. Abashed, Ossip tiptoed away. But he could not forget the delicate milk-white hands holding the painting of his dear friend.

Twelve

In the spring of 1912, Gino, who was nearly seventeen, received several marks of "four" on his baccalaureate examinations, and obtained only a silver medal upon finishing the gymnasium. He would therefore not be granted entry into the University, but David, who had sensed a very healthy practical mind in his second son, decided to send him to a commercial school in Hanover, where Gino would be able to perfect his German. Since he was younger than most gymnasium graduates, this extra year could only benefit him, and afterward he might once again attempt the baccalaureate examinations in St. Petersburg.

Gino was not displeased with the situation. "I have done my best," he stated, in his clear, strong voice. It was resolved that he would board with a family whom the Gunzburgs knew in Hanover. He was not afraid to leave the sheltered atmosphere of his own family life, and as he had not yet made his entrance into society he was not leaving behind any tearful young girls.

During the summer, Gino, Sonia, and Mathilde made the voyage to Hanover, and settled him into his new place of residence. Before returning home, Mathilde took her daughter to Paris. It was there that she said to Clara, her sister-in-law, Misha de Gunzburg's wife, "Something must be done about Sonia. I cannot penetrate her facade of composure, but I know something is wrong, Clara. She does not seem to be able to laugh anymore, to enjoy."

"I have a marvelous idea!" Clara cried. "You know how, every autumn, Misha returns to Kiev to supervise the sugar campaign on our estates. Toward the end of November, I plan to join him there, and I should like to invite Sonia to come along with me. Would you permit it, Mathilde?"

Mathilde nodded, and her features lightened. "How kind of you, Clara!" she exclaimed. "A change of atmosphere would do her infinite good. She could meet new people in Kiev, where your family knows everyone. I can stretch my stay in Paris until November, and when you and Misha return to your home here after the season, I can send a maid to fetch Sonia and bring her back to Petersburg."

After the pogrom of 1904 had completely destroyed Misha and Clara's mansion in Kiev, they had moved to Paris where the two of them spent most of the year. Clara had given birth to a son, Sergei, in 1910. But Misha had inherited his father-in-law's sugar factories, and, like the other sugar manufacturers of Kiev, he liked to be present during the harvest each year. Usually the factories ceased their work by the New Year, and the Gunzburgs could return to France with their minds at ease.

This year, Misha departed for Kiev in September as he had planned, and when Mathilde left Paris in November Sonia and her Aunt Clara made the final preparations for their trip. Clara examined Sonia's wardrobe, which consisted of both simple and embroidered blouses, one morning suit of navy blue, two afternoon gowns, two evening gowns, and one ballroom outfit. Clara thought that a second suit could be added, and took her niece to Creed's, where they selected a dark-green corduroy with a matching toque brightened with a pink ribbon. Clara furthermore decided to order for Sonia a pair of slippers from Hellstern, the finest ladies' bootmaker in Paris.

In Kiev, Misha spent most of the day at the office, and Clara was grateful for the company of her niece, only ten years her junior. Sonia found the Mother City of all the Russias quite charming. Her mood was lighter than it had been for months, and she stood before the full-length mirror in the guest room of her uncle's apartment and examined her reflection with mounting pleasure. There was no Tania to contrast with her now, and Sonia approved of her slenderness, her daintiness, her small feet and hands, her oval face with its large, almond-shaped gray eyes, her high cheekbones and thick, raven hair. Her breasts had grown fuller, her complexion translucent. She was not as beautiful as her cousin, but she was certainly not unpleasant to behold, she decided. It was the first time in years that she had actually given thought to her appearance. Sonia was not vain, but now she touched her topknot and smoothed out a tendril, and began to laugh. It was a shame that Ossip was not with her.

The day following Sonia's arrival in Kiev, there was an inauguration ceremony for a new dormitory at the Jewish Children's Hospital. The entire upper crust of Jewish society, of which Clara's family, the Brodskys, ranked foremost, was congregated in a large hall, and Sonia was introduced to some forty ladies and gentlemen, whose names she desperately tried to remember. When the champagne was passed around, after the Rabbi's blessing, a sturdy male voice resounded near Sonia, and made her start. "Sofia Davidovna de Gunzburg!" she heard, and when she wheeled about, a tall massive young man stood behind her. She had seen that face before, somewhere, the mane of black hair and the blue-green eyes that sparkled intelligently in the square face. She smiled uncertainly.

"You do not remember me," he said, and shook his head with mock reprobation. "Moissei Gillelovitch Zlatopolsky— 'Mossia'! We sat together at your aunt's dinner party years ago, when we were barely out of childhood," he explained. Sonia brightened. "My sister Shoshana was most rude to you," he added. "My sister, the ardent Zionist. You cannot have obliterated her from your memory!"

"It was just before the pogrom," Sonia said. "Later, I often thought of what your sister had told me."

"Come," Mossia said. "Let me show you our hospital. We can catch up on each other's lives as we walk along." She accepted his arm. They began to walk out of the reception hall, and Mossia took her to a large room where little children lay in iron beds, convalescent children, sick children, dying children. Mossia said nothing, and Sonia too was silent, until they reached a tiny room with three cots, two of which were empty. In the third rested a toddler with a sallow complexion, whose breath was labored.

"Why is no one with him?" Sonia whispered. She sat down on the edge of the cot, and took one of the boy's tiny hands in her own. It was icy.

"He is two and a half years old, and will not live till tomorrow," Mossia said. He stood behind Sonia, and placed a solid hand upon her shoulder. She turned her face to him, and he saw the unspoken grief. "At least we have the best physicians, and all has been done that could possibly be accomplished," he said. She stood and took his arm, her eyes full of tears.

On their way back to Clara and Misha, Mossia spoke to Sonia of his work. He had obtained two degrees from the University of Moscow, in literature and in law. Now he was his father's chief manager. His father was one of Kiev's most important sugar manufacturers and headed other businesses as well. "And you have no wife yet, no children?" Sonia asked. It struck her that this solid, compassionate man should be protecting a woman and a family. Perhaps the vision of the child dying alone in the stark white hospital bed had raised this thought in her mind.

He began to laugh. "Oh, no, and I have no intention of acquiring any at the moment!" he said. "You see, I work long hours, and when my duties are over, I play. My father trusts me, and pays me a tremendous salary to run his vast enterprises. I have invested some of it, but since I am only twenty-two, the rest I spend as I see fit, and that is for my pleasure. Kiev is a gay town. Someday I shall surely take a wife, and treat her like a queen. But for now I propose to enjoy my youth. I am not an exemplary person, Sofia Davidovna. But at least I spend only what I earn, and first I give my all to my duties."

"You are very honest, and that is rare," Sonia declared. She smiled at him. "I have known many young men in Petersburg, and most spend their fathers' rubles, not their own, and think nothing of it. My brother is twenty-five, and I should not have assumed that you would be already wed. Twenty-two is still very young to be married."

Sonia was amused by Mossia Zlatopolsky, and felt comfortable in his presence. So many new faces, such pressure to greet strangers by name! His familiarity reassured her. He brought her back to her aunt and uncle, bowed, and departed. He had work to do. "He is a brilliant young man," Misha said. "I would not say the same of the one who is coming toward us now. Solomon Moisseievitch Halperin. A weasel in man's garb."

"That is true," Clara said to her niece in an undertone. "The Halperin family is very wealthy. In fact they are the guests of honor here tonight, as they financed the new dormitory. But they are crass, nouveau riche. They have donated funds not out of goodness, but in order to ingratiate themselves with their betters. It is said that Solomon—Sioma—the third son, wishes to marry a Baroness Gunzburg, so that his status may be elevated. And he has spotted you, my dear."

A lanky, pockmarked young man with reddish hair was approaching. "Baron, Baroness," he crooned, bowing. Misha greeted him stiffly, Clara barely allowed his lips to skim the top of her hand. A shiver of revulsion passed over Sonia. Just as Mossia Zlatopolsky had inspired her with confidence, this man filled her with distaste. He was standing before her, his watery eyes upon her, and she reddened.

"The city of Kiev speaks only of your arrival," he said to her, and she tried desperately to summon the courtesy not to draw away from him. His breath was sour. She made a perfunctory half-smile in response. "We shall most certainly encounter one another at a soirée or an afternoon tea," he added. She felt as though he were undressing her with his stare, and she inclined her head. He clicked his heels in military fashion, and wheeled about. Sonia turned to Clara and Misha, and her uncle began to chuckle. "He will not eat you," he said softly. But she could not suppress the feeling of revulsion from the very pit of her stomach.

During the days that followed, Sonia managed to sort out all the Brodsky relations, and cousins of cousins. There were Clara's two brothers, Alexander and Aron. Alexander had seven children, one of which, a daughter, Moussia, was married to a rather stern young man named Ilya Saxe. Both Brodsky brothers and their wives and children entertained often, and made Sonia welcome. There was also Aunt Guitele, the widow Augustine Feodorovna Brodsky, quite elderly and half blind, but of great heart and intelligence. Clara was most fond of her, and visited her frequently.

Aunt Guitele had been widowed for a long time, and lived with her only son, Max, who was thirty-three and a bachelor. Max was small, thin, with fiery red hair and sharp features. His nose was aquiline and pinched, his lips thin, adorned with a red mustache; his ears were large, and his blue eyes pale, far paler than those of Baron David. There was an aura of ill health around him, although he was actually quite healthy. Each time that she saw him, Sonia was struck anew with the shock of his almost ludicrous physical defects. She had never witnessed so much ugliness concentrated in a single individual. But he was touching to watch interacting with his mother, never allowing her to cross the street by herself because of her poor eyesight, bringing her small gifts, always showing his respect and affection for her.

Max was extremely talented. He played the piano beautifully and composed his own pieces, but he never wrote them down, always improvised anew. His mind was crammed with extraordinary inventions: mechanical objects, household products, ideas for women's fashions. In his head, he would improve his inventions and perfect them. He often spoke of his creations but never submitted any of them for patenting, or had them constructed once he had worked them out. As soon as one was completed, his thoughts would jump to another, and disregard the first.

He was immensely wealthy, and did not work. He did not play cards, or chase women, or spend nights drinking with his men friends. He read, played the piano, thought about his inventions, and escorted his mother around Kiev. His cousins all liked him and had nicknamed him Maxik the Red.

Clara Lazarevna de Gunzburg admired Aunt Guitele Brodsky and frequently took Sonia to visit her. But most of the time, Maxik, after a few courtesies, would lead Sonia toward the piano, and begin to improvise. "What beautiful melodies!" the young woman would exclaim. "But why don't you write them down?"

"Oh, I am far too lazy," he laughed.

"But it is criminal to let go of tunes that are so lovely!" she cried in dismay. "All that emotion! And the expertise!" He teased her about her intensity, and they would launch into other discussions, for he was full to the brim of opinions, and was well read, if somewhat stubborn.

Clara's niece, Moussia, her brother Alexander's daughter, had married the older son of the Saxe family, sugar plantation owners like most of the Gunzburgs' acquaintances in Kiev. Clara was very friendly with Moussia's

mother- and father-in-law, Svetlana and Maxim Saxe. He
was a tall and slender man with white hair and a distinguished manner, and though his wife was small, plump,
and more provincial in appearance, her quiet good nature
endeared her to many. As Maxim Saxe was growing old,
he no longer managed his prosperous business. But it was
not Moussia's husband, Ilya, who had taken it over, for
Ilya was too indolent; it was Ilya's younger brother, Karl,
who was known to his familiars as Kolya.

Kolya Saxe was thirty-three years of age, like Maxik
Brodsky. Unlike his brother, he put in long hours administering the sugar refineries, and sometimes, when Sonia and
Clara came to tea, he was not there. He came in later, his
footsteps resounding in the hallway outside, quickening as
they approached the drawing room. When she heard them,
Sonia would feel a flush spreading over her face and into
the roots of her hair. He was tall, imposing of stature while
slim of hip, and his hair was black and wavy. His mouth
was full-lipped and his large teeth were white and perfect,
but above all his eyes magnetized her, for they were fluid
black, the irises indistinguishable from their pupils. Sonia,
who loved true beauty, was enchanted by him: he was
surely the most pleasing man she had ever seen. She followed his movements with her eyes, enjoying his slightest
gesture as though she were watching a thoroughbred horse
cavorting around a field, or a ballerina executing steps of
remarkable difficulty in the most graceful and unaffected
manner.

Kolya was aware of the impression which he was creat-
ing. He sensed her admiration, yet could see that it was his
physical being and not his true self which caused it. Sometimes their eyes met as she laughed, and she would remain
staring at him for several seconds, as if unable to bring
herself to look away from him.

He allowed this to go on for a period of days, chatting to
her all the while no more nor less than he spoke to her

aunt or to his mother. But if she demonstrated an interest in a particular subject he would, the next afternoon, find something to tell her about it. At a ball he was the first in line to ask her to dance, and when he took her tiny form into his capable arms, he saw that her gray eyes lit with joy. He danced in silence then, knowing that she was basking in the pleasure of movement and his grace. But she said, "I am amazed, Karl Maximovitch. A man so busy as you, who finds time to waltz with such agility!"

The comment was rather inane and therefore unlike Sonia, but he seemed pleased with it. "Papa needs my help," he said seriously. "I work because it is a challenge, but also because there is little choice. However, I do take time for amusement. Since your arrival, I have taken more time than ever."

She gazed at him and smiled. "Thank you," she replied. And that was all. But when Sonia went home, she said to her Aunt Clara, "I am impressed with Karl Maximovitch. He takes his duties seriously. Why is he not married?"

"Perhaps because he has never found the right mixture of laughter and honor in a woman," Clara answered. Sonia pondered the notion and found it odd. "No, think about it," her aunt said. "Tania, for instance, is full of mirth. But she would bristle at the thought of Kolya's long working hours. Another girl might be kind and good to his parents, a dutiful wife—but not one who would stimulate his intellect, or make him laugh." Sonia winced; she had known one woman like that, but had seen only the joy in her. Natasha Tagantseva. Yet perhaps Ossip had found in her just such a combination. Sonia went to sleep intrigued, and curious about Kolya Saxe.

More than anyone else, the Gunzburgs visited Aunt Guitele and the Saxe family. But Sonia also attended other teas, and there were theatrical presentations and concerts. She found her days filled with pleasant activities, and her evenings bright and animated. She loved Kiev. Her single point of irritation concerned Sioma Halperin, the social upstart, who crossed her path whenever he could. She could not stand him, and cringed at the mere sight of him. Sometimes she would see Mossia Zlatopolsky, and would think: I have made a friend that will last. Someday a woman will be pleased to be his wife. She did not know that in his mind, he thought: Too bad she is twenty-two, the perfect age for marriage. I envy the man who will possess her, for one will certainly come before I am ready to pledge my faith to any woman.

One morning, Clara knocked on Sonia's door, and when she entered, her thin face was grave. "What is it, Aunt Clara?" Sonia asked. She rose and nervously smoothed out a wrinkle in her blouse. Never since the day of the pogrom eight years before had she seen the older woman with such a serious expression. "Have I offended you?" she asked anxiously.

"No, my love, of course not," her aunt replied. She sat down, a strange glow in her eyes. "But I come bearing news. You have two suitors for your hand in marriage. Aunt Guitele has told me that Maxik wishes you to be his wife, and Madame Saxe came to me yesterday, announcing that Kolya is very much in love with you and also wishes to marry you. What do you think? Have you thought about either of them, Sonitchka?"

The young woman sat down abruptly, the blood rushing to her cheeks. "It did occur to me that Kolya was most gracious at the last ball, and that Maxik enjoys talking with me," she said slowly. "But somehow, I did not think that they were serious. I like them both. Each one possesses unique qualities, each surely has his faults. Frankly—I am quite speechless, Aunt Clara."

"But you are not leaving Kiev for two weeks," her aunt replied. "Nobody will press you for your decision until the moment of your departure. You will have time to reflect, and to decide. Each one is a good match, in your uncle's and my opinion. Of course, I need not tell you that Sioma

Halperin has made a similar proposal. But I have only to look at you when I mention his name to gauge your reaction. Your uncle has already politely discouraged him."

"Oh, thank God!" Sonia cried. "Now perhaps he will leave me alone!"

Sonia felt dizzy. With Volodia she had felt something new, something actually quite terrible, something forbidden and yet sweet. She had respected him, but hated his family. Never had the idea of a union truly entered her mind. She had wanted to kiss him, yes, but had in fact wished mostly for the security of knowing his love—just that. Because she had not allowed herself the freedom of candidly loving in return, she had never resolved her emotions after his death. Now she was suddenly presented with two mature young men of good standing who could offer her an entire life of which no one close to her could disapprove. She could decide, and permit her emotions to influence her decision. She could acknowledge her womanhood! Finally, after all the years, she could place Volodia in a special niche, a treasured and beloved niche, but nonetheless remove him from the mainstream of her existence. She could hope to live in joy again, and put away her guilt.

But after the first breath of happiness, sobriety returned. Sonia had always been logical, and now she sat in the quiet of her room, thinking about her future. She could not select a husband for his attractiveness alone, for she knew so many who had, disastrously. There must also be emotional, financial, physical balance. Max was a good son, faithful, affectionate, and therefore would indubitably be an attentive husband. He was a very talented musician, and that was an important point they had in common. He dressed well and had received an impeccable education. He was original, which was both good and bad, but at least she could be sure that he would not bore her through their days together.

However, Max possessed two enormous defects. For

one, he was excessively ugly. If his children, particularly a daughter, were to resemble him, what a disaster that would be! But, and this was more serious, he did not work and did not wish to work. Certainly he had no need of additional income—but Sonia wished he would do something, no matter what, even collect rare coins or stamps! How could Sonia, so industrious by nature, live with a man of total leisure and no dedication?

Kolya Saxe, on the other hand, was extremely handsome, yet not in the pretty manner that she despised in so many dandies of her generation. He was more refined, more worldly than Max, and was a driven worker. But there was something indefinable which kept her from unhesitatingly going to him, guided by her physical attraction for him and her respect. Was it the slight drooping motion of his lips, was it the bright glitter of his black eyes that were so difficult to penetrate? She thought: Perhaps he would fall in love with another, and one day be unfaithful. With Max, I would never have to fear that . . .

Since Aunt Clara had told her of the two proposals, Sonia no longer felt the same toward the two young men. At Aunt Guitele's, Maxik would dispense with an excess of formality and whisk her toward the piano more rapidly than before, and at the Saxes', she was placed next to Kolya for tea. But now, when Kolya's black spaniel came between them under the table, begging for scraps, Sonia would lower her hand to comb her fingers through its fur, and would encounter Kolya's fingers performing the same caress from his side. It was their only intimate gesture, but it filled the young woman with feverish chills so that she could hardly speak. Yet she was almost afraid of her magnetic pull toward the tall, dark man. She had never realized that she, cool and poised like her mother, possessed such emotions urging her to do forbidden, impulsive things. She wondered if she were quite normal, quite healthy, when she sat beside Kolya and felt his fingertips brush past her own, electrifying her entire body.

Time continued to pass, inexorably bringing Sonia's day of reckoning closer. One afternoon, when Kolya was taking tea at Aunt Clara's apartment, she asked him softly, "Will you be at the Horowitz concert tomorrow?"

He started. "Is it tomorrow?" he cried. "I had certainly intended to be present, but work piled up and I forgot the date." He gazed at her, and his black eyes bored intensely into her delicate face. "If you go, I must go, absolutely. When I return home, I shall send someone to purchase me a ticket."

She blushed, and regarded her glass. "I doubt that you will find one, Karl Maximovitch," she stated. "Uncle Misha purchased ours three days ago, and few remained even then."

"But I shall try, nevertheless," he asserted. She raised her gray eyes and saw his longing, and shuddered. She was both delighted and afraid.

The next day the Gunzburgs arrived early at the concert hall, which was still nearly empty. On the stage, the piano had been pushed against the right wall, and in the open space, seven or eight rows of chairs had been set up. The first row was barely six feet from Horowitz's stool. It would be difficult for him to play with people crowding behind him, and for the listeners it would be no less disagreeable, for the balance of the music would be wrong. But undoubtedly those seated on the stage would be students of the Conservatory, and to hear the Master from too close was better than to miss him altogether.

The public began to stream in. Sonia turned in her seat and stared at the front door, straining to discern all who passed through it. Kolya was not among them. The flow of patrons became a flood, and she could no longer make out each individual. She turned back nervously and adjusted the folds of her skirt. Kolya had not come. Evidently he had been unable to purchase a ticket.

Horowitz entered, greeted by thunderous applause, although he was only at the start of his career. As he bowed and sat down silence fell upon the hall. He began his first piece, and when he had finished it, the audience applauded and the ushers opened the doors to let the latecomers into the hall. Five or six people entered, but not Kolya. He would definitely not come. Sonia regarded the program on her lap. But all at once, a deep electric shock rushed through her body, and she raised her eyes. Horowitz had patiently awaited silence, was raising both hands above the keyboard to attack the second piece. At that instant, Sonia saw Kolya upon the stage, about to take one of the student seats at the back. One second later, the people in front of him hid him from her sight. She had just had time to make him out. He would come to her at intermission.

She closed her eyes, and warmth flooded her being. Now she knew! If she had suddenly felt his presence so strongly, it must be because she truly loved him. She allowed the nape of her neck to touch the back of her chair, and thought: My mind is made up. But when he sought her out between numbers, and bowed over her hand, she did not betray her decision. Nor did she breathe a word of it to her aunt and uncle.

The following morning, at breakfast, she announced, "I would like to accept Kolya's suit, Aunt Clara, Uncle Misha. But how can we announce this to Aunt Guitele without offending her?"

"There shall not be a problem," Misha declared. "Guitele always knew about Kolya's proposal. She is aware that Max is not a man to turn the head of a pretty girl. Clara will go to her at tea, without you, and tonight I shall go to the Saxes. We shall telegraph your parents. Your father can meet us in Warsaw, for we too must leave Kiev and head back to Paris. Then I shall be able to discuss the details with him, matters which would not interest you but which must be settled. This is not a time for a lady's maid to escort you home."

When the Gunzburgs departed from Kiev, their many

friends and relatives flocked to the train station to see them off. Maxik came to Sonia and said, "We shall see you again, Sofia Davidovna. Kiev is in need of you." But he did not linger, and she was swept up in good-byes, from new friends who she knew would be hers for life, since she would be returning soon as Madame Karl Maximovitch Saxe.

Most of those present had come to kiss Misha and Clara good-bye, as they would not see them again until the next sugar campaign, so they did not fuss too much over the visiting niece. No one but Max and his mother knew of the impending wedding plans, and so they did not notice that Kolya's parents, and Moussia and Ilya, took Sonia aside and kissed her, or that she blushed when she was momentarily left alone with the second son, Karl. He did not kiss her. But his black eyes did not leave her face, and he whispered, "You will return as my bride, and the next time I shall see you, we shall be betrothed before the world."

At the Hotel Bristol in Warsaw, Baron David met his brother, his sister-in-law, and his daughter. He declared that he did not need to meet Kolya in order to grant his consent, after the glowing report he heard from Misha. Mathilde would write the Saxes, and would invite them to spend the New Year in St. Petersburg, where they would formulate an official marriage proposal. It would be two weeks hence. Until then, only Ossip and Johanna would be told.

On December 30, Kolya and his parents arrived at the Hôtel de l'Europe in the capital. Mathilde and Sonia went to greet them, and Mathilde thought: This young man is everything I myself would have liked in a husband. She looked at her daughter and admired the rosy glow upon her cheeks, the sparkle in her eyes. The two young people were never alone, but they spoke to one another with their faces. Mathilde felt a twinge of regret, witnessing this younger, lither version of herself in the throes of a fulfilling love. But she was glad for her daughter, and relieved, too, after her years of worry concerning Sonia's withdrawn moods. She invited the Saxes to spend New Year's Eve with the Gunzburgs and also asked them to come to luncheon the next day, in order to make their first official visit to the parents of their son's intended.

Baron David had recently begun to suffer acute attacks of angina pectoris, and was in bed. But waiting for Sonia and Mathilde was Johanna de Mey, very excited, the cords standing out in her neck, her hands dry as she rubbed them over and over each other. Her eyes gleamed unhealthily. "Add '1912,' " she said to Sonia when she returned from the hotel with her mother.

"I beg your pardon?"

"Add all the digits. They make up the number 13. And the year that is about to start will be 1913. A most unlucky circumstance. You shall have to celebrate your engagement on New Year's Eve, on the stroke of midnight. That way you can dispel ill omens, for you will be pledging your troth between two most unpromising years."

Sonia cleared her throat. "But I am not the least superstitious," she declared calmly.

Johanna placed her hands upon her hips, and cried, "You are ungrateful! I, in any event, shall take no part in this ill-fated celebration, unless you do it according to my plan! I, who have sacrificed my youth for you, will not even appear otherwise. Do you wish to insult me?"

"Sonia—" Mathilde interposed.

"Mama, you know how I feel about New Year's Eves! I have always spent them in quiet intimacy. My engagement is another matter altogether. That is one of the most important moments of my life! It is a public celebration! I do not want to mix the two events."

"Then I shall return to France, where my family needs me. Here, my advice is repudiated by a mere girl— Mathilde, I am useless!" And Johanna burst into loud sobs, her thin shoulders shaking. Mathilde regarded her daughter, who stood erect and firm, and then her own eyes widened with sudden fear. Sonia sighed and turned away as Mathilde placed a gentle, hesitant hand upon her friend's arm, and murmured something inaudible. The Dutchwoman lifted her hands from her face, and encountered Sonia's cold, disdainful eyes. Her own, bloodshot, were full of hatred. She said, "Your mother, at least, is wise. You will be affianced between the years."

Silently, Sonia squared her shoulders and stuck out her chin, and she stared with bitterness at her one-time governess. Then her face fell. "It is as Mama wants, of course," she whispered. A flicker of a smile flashed across Johanna's tight features, and Sonia wheeled about and ran out of the room, feeling utterly defeated, dejected. Take me to Kiev! she thought pleadingly, speaking to the image of Kolya. She did not see her mother's distressed face, where fear mingled with anger and distaste and abject love.

The luncheon was cordial. David was feeling better and joined his daughter's future in-laws for a light repast, but Sonia noticed that although Johanna de Mey spoke with deference to Maxim Saxe, she as much as ignored his petite, round wife. Kolya was sitting at the table with Sonia, and the sheer excitement of his presence, with his marvelous black eyes and majestic deportment, was sufficient to send little prickles of delight up and down her spine.

The Saxes returned to their hotel, and reappeared for the evening's celebrations. After a light meal, the young couple was left alone for the first time ever. It was eleven o'clock, one hour before the moment of their official engagement. Kolya took hold of Sonia's hands, and pressed them in his larger, stronger ones. "Never in my life have I known such joy!" he said. "My love for you will never cease, my darling. It has grown from the instant of our encounter. I do not deserve you."

Sonia raised her eyes to him, and the blood flowed into her cheeks. She murmured candidly, "I shall do anything to make you happy. I love you so!"

"Then," he declared, "you must kiss me now. I have dreamed of this kiss, of this magic moment, since the evening when I was told that you had accepted my suit. Do you not wish to kiss me now, beloved, while we are alone?"

She hesitated thoughtfully. "I told my governess that I am not superstitious, Kolya," she said. "But in one hour we shall be engaged. I have always wanted you to kiss me, that is true—but it would mean so much more if I were your declared fiancée . . . Can we not wait until the New Year?"

"Others will share that moment, which I wish to be a private one," he countered gently.

Tears welled into her eyes. "Oh, Kolya, you think me silly, and old-fashioned . . . My cousin Tania kisses English fashion, in empty landaus and troikas that are parked outside ballrooms, when the coachmen have gathered together for a chat! I know that things have changed! It is not that. When I was much younger, my brother Ossip fell in love with a beautiful girl, and one day I saw them kiss. She was . . . wrong for him. He still suffers from the loss of her. I do not wish to cloud any part of our future. I do not wish to lose you, as Ossip lost Natasha! Can you understand?"

He reached out and touched her chin, and said, "You are a silly little doe, my Sonia. Whatever could come between us? We shall be married in 1913, and you will bear my children. I would like to tell those children that their mother and I shared a private festivity, before the public kiss. You are mine, and what I ask of you is hardly improper. Grant me my wish, Sonia."

She shivered. But he lifted her small oval face, and he grasped it in both hands, and bent his head toward her. She closed her eyes, feeling queasy, and suddenly his lips were upon hers, his tongue had entered her mouth, and she abandoned herself to the delicious pleasure of this kiss, her very first. Her arms went round his neck, and she could hear buzzing in her ears, and pinpoints of red flashed from her closed eyelids. Then he drew away, and she laughed lightly, touching her hair in an embarrassed gesture. He laughed with her, seizing her hands. "It wasn't such a dreadful thing, was it, darling?" he teased her softly.

"It was wonderful. But it was not what I wanted. You are stronger than I, and have proved it. Are you always so willful, Kolya?"

A flicker of unexplained emotion passed like a film over his eyes. "I am not willful," he declared. "It is my love for you that is so."

Shortly before midnight, the Gunzburgs and Saxes passed into the dining room where a cold supper had been laid out. When midnight struck, champagne glasses clinked around the table and David stood up, magnificent in his dinner jacket with the decoration of State Councillor pinned to the lapel. "I toast the fiancés, my daughter Sonia and the man she has chosen, Kolya Saxe!" he stated. All through the room gay voices echoed: "To Sonia and Kolya! To Kolya and Sonia!" Kolya placed his glass before Sonia's lips, and she took a sip, while her family clapped. Then, gently, she reciprocated the gesture and made him drink from the glass. His eyes glittered over the rim, and she inhaled deeply. The bubbles tickled her chin and nose. But somewhere deep inside, she felt mournful. This was the New Year, and now people were toasting it along with her engagement to Kolya. She had not planned to share her celebration with anything else.

Now Kolya pulled out of his pocket the small box which held the ring. He had ordered it from Marshak, the most renowned jeweler in Kiev. In all the Russias, only Fabergé was held in higher repute than this jeweler. The ring was set in platinum, and was composed of an emerald and a diamond of the same size, placed side by side. Kolya placed it upon Sonia's slender finger, and the two families gathered around her to admire and kiss her. Johanna stood back, watching, and a vague glimmer of distaste shadowed her eyes. But she too approached the young woman and raised her fine eyebrows at the lovely gems. Sonia smiled and thanked her brother and parents and future mother- and father-in-law for their blessings, and thanked Johanna, too. She smiled and she smiled until lines of exhaustion began to form around her eyes. And then, under the magnificent chandelier, with its unique set of light bulbs, she fainted.

It was January 1, 1913.

On New Year's Day the gentlemen of St. Petersburg went calling upon their acquaintances. Baron David and his son put on their jackets and their pinstriped pants, and filled their pockets with pieces of ten or twenty kopeks to tip all the Swiss doormen and the maîtres d'hôtel whom they would encounter that day. In the Gunzburg apartment Mathilde, Sonia, and Johanna, clad in their finery, awaited their own callers. And Kolya Saxe, unknown in the capital, tall, dark, and extremely elegant, stood by his fiancée's side. Sonia, her gray eyes twinkling, took mischievous pleasure in introducing him to everyone as her husband-to-be. For no one had suspected an impending engagement in the Gunzburg family.

Svetlana Yakovlievna made a special present to the woman who was to become her son's wife. She had seen the love that shone in Sonia's face, a quality of enraptured passion that was close to idolatry. And Svetlana approved, for she herself considered her son greater than life. Ilya, her elder, was a normal man; but Kolya's character, so upright, strong, and commanding, made him in his mother's eyes worthy of unquestioned devotion. Consequently, she was pleased by Sonia's attitude, and took her aside. "My dear, I had this made for you," she said, and handed the young woman a gold locket. When Sonia opened it, she saw, finely painted in enamel, her fiancé's handsome face, laughing into her eyes. Touched, she pressed Svetlana's hand and kissed Kolya's portrait gratefully. Only a man's mother could truly release him to his beloved—and Svetlana had graciously made that gesture.

Kolya's parents had to return to Kiev on the third of January, although their son could remain two days longer. Accordingly, Sonia said to her mother, "Let us have an intimate supper for the Saxes and our immediate family tomorrow night. Even if Aunt Rosa is busy, we shall have made the gesture. You see, Kolya told me that he and Papa discussed where to hold the wedding, and it will go as you and I had anticipated, Mama. We are to be married closer to Grandmother Ida and Grandfather Yuri, who are too old to travel to Petersburg. They had thought perhaps in Belgium, to avoid the long residency requirements of France. The Saxes shall therefore not meet the Russian Gunzburgs unless we organize something now."

"Madame Saxe is too provincial to introduce to your Uncle Sasha," Johanna interposed.

"That is not so!" Sonia retorted at once. "And besides, she is Kolya's mother, and will be the grandmother of my children. I am not ashamed of her—so why should you be?"

"The Saxes are fine people, Johanna," Mathilde said. "The family stands high in Kiev society, and is related by marriage to my sister-in-law, Clara. What do you have against Svetlana Yakovlievna? Has she offended you?"

Johanna de Mey clenched her fists and unclenched them, then ran her fingers through the blond strands of hair gathered into an elaborate coiffure on top of her head. She grew quickly red, then white. "Svetlana Yakovlievna! Have you no taste, Mathilde? I am shocked at you. The woman dresses badly. I am certain that if you listened carefully, you would even detect . . . an accent of sorts. All she needs is the scent of pickle brine to complete the picture. How could you humiliate yourself by introducing such a person to your most intimate relations? Rosa is a snob. She would mock you."

"Juanita means that Svetlana Yakovlievna is too obviously a Jewess," Sonia declared. Her eyes were like hard pebbles. Her mother turned to her, her lips parted in surprise. But Sonia continued, adamantly: "She is to be my mother-in-law. I, too, am Jewish, and I do not care how provincial she looks. My great-grandmother, Rosa Dynin Gunzburg, spoke only the Yiddish dialect, and ministers of France sat on her right. She wore a red wig, and yes, she made her own pickles, too, in the magnificent house where my mother was born, on the Barrière de l'Etoile in Paris! Svetlana Yakovlievna is in good company!"

"All Petersburg will laugh at you, after Rosa describes her," Johanna said. Her aquamarine eyes flashed. "Maxim Saxe is a gentleman, and looks the part. But his wife is not presentable to a Baroness Gunzburg. However—I need not be present. I may as well take a long trip now, and visit my mother in France. There I shall be listened to."

"Johanna!" Mathilde cried. "You would not do this, merely on account of a family dinner?"

"I could not bear to have you be the laughing stock of Petersburg, my dear," the Dutchwoman declared. Her pupils contracted, and her eyelids narrowed. She turned her face and regarded Sonia pointedly.

"It really does not matter," Mathilde sighed. She said to her daughter, "After you are married, when everyone knows our distinguished Kolya, your mother- and father-in-law will surely come for a visit to the capital. We shall entertain them properly at that time. Right now, your Papa is not well, and the excitement of such a celebration might be unwise. Kolya will understand. He knows of David's condition."

"The only conditions I feel restricted by are those imposed upon us by Juanita," Sonia declared. Her face was very red, and she was breathing rapidly, hoarsely. For a moment she remained where she had been standing, a diminutive figure of barely controlled anger; then she turned and exited, her skirts swishing noisily. Mathilde sank upon the sofa, and fanned herself with the back of her hand. But Johanna de Mey arched her back like a proud cat observing a dismembered canary.

When Mathilde gently explained to Svetlana and Maxim Saxe that it would be impossible to organize even a small family dinner in a single day, and that her husband, Baron David, had not been well, the Kiev couple nodded, and Svetlana Yakovlievna murmured, "But of course, Mathilde Yureyevna. Do not concern yourself on our account. We have met you, and David Goratsievitch, and Ossip. That was the point of our coming." But Sonia saw the proud rearing of Kolya's dark head, the flash in his eyes. She felt the tension inside him as he came to his mother and took her hand, stroking it. It was evident to the young woman that all three Saxes knew that her mother had not told the truth, and that they were somewhat stunned by the slight. Sonia was more embarrassed than she had ever been, and for the first time in her entire life her great admiration for Mathilde was rattled. She quickly concentrated her fury upon Johanna, who was its cause. It was unbearable to blame Mama.

On the fourth of January, Kolya fell ill with the grippe and was confined to his bed. His parents had departed the previous day without meeting Sasha, Rosa, and Tania, and now Kolya was forced to put off his leaving. Taking Ossip with her as chaperone, Sonia spent as much time as possible by her fiancé's bedside, reading to him, caressing his long, strong fingers, mopping his fevered brow. But on the third day the fever abated, and Kolya could no longer hold off his return. On the platform at the train station, while Mathilde and David stood at a discreet distance, he enveloped her tiny form in his arms, and kissed her lips. "I shall write you each day," he promised, and she melted into his eyes, her body flowing like honey, magnetized by his look of passion. Anxiety seized her, and she held his lapels with a kind of frenzy. "I shall be back soon," he reassured her, guessing her thoughts. "For the Carnival, in February—remember, sweetest?"

She nodded, but her eyes were full of inexplicable tears. Her father had decided that, since Kolya could get away from the sugar works for a few days then, the formal engagement festivities would be held at the time of the Carnival. Then, in April, the young couple would meet in Brussels and be married.

After Passover, weddings were forbidden for forty-nine days until the feast of Shabuoth, the Pentecost. Russians did not like to marry in May, for the saying went that those who did would quarrel ceaselessly thereafter. But on the fifteenth and the thirty-third days of the religious hiatus, weddings were permitted, and so David had selected April twenty-third as the date when his daughter would become Kolya's wife. The Belgian authorities required only that one of the parties have resided there for six weeks, rather than the six months demanded by French law, and so Sonia and Mathilde planned to leave St. Petersburg during the first week of March. Now Sonia clung to her fiancé, tremulous, and whispered, "You are everything to me. My life, my love. I have never known such happiness as now, basking in your love. Promise me never to leave me again!"

"You are mad to think that I would ever want to," he replied. "We shall travel together, and I shall carry you everywhere upon my arm like my most prized possession. No, Sonitchka, I shall never be apart from you after our wedding. It is I who would not bear it." He detached himself from her and took a long velvet box from his coat pocket. He opened it himself, removing from it a long chain of gold. Her mouth opened in wonder, and he smiled. From the chain hung a small plaque of solid gold, and from that two smaller chains of unequal lengths. Each of these was weighted by an emerald in the shape of a tear, surrounded by diamond chips. Kolya placed the necklace around Sonia's throat, and clasped it at the back. "Think of these as my tears, each day that I am separated from you," he murmured. She turned, and her gray eyes held him, more expressive than any words.

He returned to Kiev with the mission of finding a suitable apartment for his bride and himself. She had told him that she trusted his taste, and insisted only upon a Louis XVI salon and an Empire dining room. He had promised to send her detailed accounts of what he had found, and what he was proposing to purchase. She would hire a cook and a chambermaid in Kiev, but Mathilde would give her Stepan and would find another maître d'hôtel for the Gunzburg household in St. Petersburg. It was a family tradition for the Gunzburg daughters to be married in gowns made to order from Worth's in Paris, and Sonia would purchase her trousseau in Brussels, renowned for its fine laces and linens. And so, matters were set.

Kolya liked for a woman to be perfumed, but Sonia had never been able to bear more than the most diluted of cologne waters. A tremendous disgust took hold of her upon smelling the heady scent of perfume, and nausea soon followed. But for Kolya she wished to overcome this aversion, and so, during the weeks before the Carnival, she carried a small vial of perfume from lilies of the valley in her hand at all times, and every so often she uncorked it and inhaled its odor. Her repugnance did not decrease. She panicked, thinking herself condemned to a lifetime of perfume, for the idea of depriving Kolya of his pleasure did not occur to her. She must please him, and endurance of the hated odor would be bound to arrive.

During their separation, Sonia received a letter from

Kolya every day. The missives, for the most part, were passionate and tender: he missed her each minute of each day. Sometimes the notes were short, containing but one sentence: "My beloved, I am so busy that I have not a second to myself, but I do not want the mail to leave without taking with it my daily kiss to you." She saved each piece of his handwriting, kissing the paper which bore its imprint. And her eyes glowed, and filled with tears of unbearable joy.

She did not feel that she deserved the exhilaration which touched her every nerve ending. So that was how Ossip had felt about Natasha! She had never allowed her emotions full rein before, not even in the privacy of her thoughts. With a pang of quick pain she thought: Volodia, I did love you. But I never felt this way with you, as though each moment were a new adventure. Then guilt would cloud her spirits, momentarily eclipsing her joy. Volodia had died, and if he had not loved her he would still be alive. Yet had he not died, would she have had the opportunity to meet Kolya? Selfish enthusiasm would seize her soul, and the guilt would subside. She was young, and the world was hers!

Then came the Carnival. In St. Petersburg there was no procession of chariots or of lights, no celebrations in the streets. Long ago it had been the custom to hold costume balls during these eight days, but now, during the entire winter season, such dances were given at the drop of a hat. However, this was the last opportunity for the fashionable to give balls of any kind before the end of the brilliant social season, for next would come the seven weeks of Lent, during which the Christian Orthodox did not dance, then Easter, and then preparations for the summer holidays. But the Carnival of St. Petersburg was characterized by three things: the *blinys*, the *verbys*, and the *veikis*, and Sonia wanted Kolya to enjoy each of these.

The *blinys* were small, thin pancakes of buckwheat and

wheat, which were eaten before each meal, with melted butter atop them, and with sour cream inside. They were only made during Carnival week. The *verbys* were pussy-willows, the first vegetation after winter's barrenness. Their name was given to the small fair which took place on the Boulevard de la Garde à Cheval. Stands were set up alongside it, and artisans sold their wares: bowls, spoons, pitchers of varnished wood adorned with red or black or gold designs, paper flowers, simple toys, porcelain knickknacks, linen tablecloths and doilies, and, of course, branches of the proverbial *verbys*, with which the ladies garnished their salons. The entire city, rich and poor, converged upon the *verbys* fair, and the children were allowed to purchase what they pleased. Tatiana had once, as a little girl, been reprimanded by Rosa, and had declared in retaliation that she would find herself a new mother at the *verbys* fair. "For one finds everything there," she had announced triumphantly.

The *veikis* were small sleighs drawn by a single horse, a tiny long-haired pony, and led by a small, bearded man. They came from Finland and were allowed to drive throughout the city for the duration of Carnival week. The coverlet of the sleigh was richly embroidered and the pony was bedecked with brightly colored ribbons. The only problem was that the drivers did not know much Russian, nor the streets of the city. And so, at each corner, local gentlemen would have to tap them on the shoulder and, amid much laughter, attempt to redirect them toward their destination. The city coachmen were enraged by the *veikis*, which stole all their usual customers. But the young people immensely enjoyed the colorful chaos they caused.

Kolya arrived. Because the Gunzburgs had friends of all religions, they had not wished to celebrate Sonia's engagement at a time when their Christian Orthodox friends would be unable to partake of festive meals, because of the Lenten restrictions. Mathilde had planned three dinners.

The first evening was the official supper for the family and their most aristocratic acquaintances. The following evening she had organized a less formal dinner for the Gunzburg lawyers and doctor, and their children: they were less wealthy, and their daughters would have felt uncomfortable among Petersburg high society. Then, on the last evening, Sonia's intimate friends would come, and she counted upon having a truly good time among them.

But from the moment of his arrival, Sonia noticed that Kolya appeared preoccupied. His black eyes did not dance, he did not burst into effusive laughter. When her own gray eyes sought his face, he would turn aside. Sometimes, when people spoke to him, he seemed abstracted, even dazed. Finally Sonia took him aside, a nameless anxiety rising in her throat, and she asked, "What has happened, Kolya, my darling? What is so wrong that you have not told me?"

"It is only my work," he replied, and tenderness softened his features. He took her hand and caressed it. But he did not raise it passionately to his lips, as he had once done. She trembled, and bit her lip. "It is nothing important," he reassured her.

He brought with him another gift, from the jeweler Marshak: a purse of gold mail, with a clasp composed of square sapphires. She admired it, and wore it the first evening for the formal dinner, but her heart was heavy and she was pale, smiling perfunctorily when her parents' friends congratulated her and Kolya. He stood by her side, elegant and stately, but stiff. She thought: Before, we were separated by half a continent, yet we were one. Now that we are together, it is as though we were more apart than ever . . . And that night, when she fell into bed, she sobbed into her pillow, overwhelmed by a sensation of dread.

Sonia began receiving wedding gifts. The first was several yards of lace, handmade centuries ago. There was also a small handkerchief of finest batiste, embroidered as if by fairy hands. Last came a lace fan with trimmings of enamel and studded gold. She held them up for Kolya, and he marveled at the handiwork. But if she had expected founts of enthusiasm, she was sadly disappointed.

The last evening, after supper, the young people rolled back the carpet of the sitting room. Someone went to the piano, and dancing began, gaily, informally. But Sonia thought: Kolya is not happy. Only my friends rejoice. What is bothering him? Why won't he share it with me? But as even Ossip failed to comment upon Kolya's mood, she thought: No one but I has seen his misery. Could it be that I see shadows where there are none? Yet when he held her in his arms, she felt none of the urgent pressure of his passion, and inside, she froze. She went to bed and did not sleep at all. A raging headache kept her awake throughout the night.

The following day Kolya left for Kiev. At the station, she took his hand, and said, "Only a few more weeks, and I shall leave for Brussels. And then I shall be your bride. Will you count the days with me?"

"Of course," he replied. But his eyes did not lock with hers, and his voice lacked the emotion that had characterized their last good-bye. She pressed his hand. A flicker of pain passed over his features, and she stood back, perplexed. "I detest farewells," he murmured, and looked away.

"It is *au revoir* and not *adieu*," she said gently. "Won't you kiss me, Kolya?"

He held her finally in his arms, and his lips felt hers, like velvet roses. But something was missing from this kiss, and she left her fiancé with a hole where her heart had been. She could not see for the tears that blinded her, and her mother chided her, saying, "He is not going to be gone for long, and you are a goose to carry on so." Sonia merely nodded, mutely, for she could not explain her misgivings.

He wrote to her, as before. But now the letters were newsy, not loving. She was shocked. Where were the love words, the gentle names that he had made up in her honor? Where was the breathless anticipation? She stored these letters with the rest, but she could not eat, for doubt gnawed at her stomach. Her mother thought that she was experiencing girlish jitters at the idea of marriage, and the wedding night. Mathilde's heart contracted in silent sympathy. She did not know that before the Carnival her daughter had looked forward to her first night with Kolya. Now she did not think about it at all. She could not concentrate on anything but the pit inside her stomach, the fear.

Two days before Sonia and Mathilde were to leave for Brussels, Misha de Gunzburg telephoned, and announced that he was in St. Petersburg, having made a detour on his way home from a business visit to Kiev. When Mathilde casually invited him to supper, he refused, saying that he preferred to come afterward. Sonia went into the vestibule to greet him when he arrived, but his face was pale, and he averted it from her searching eyes. "I must speak to David," he declared, and was led to his brother's study. Sonia saw her mother join them and close the door after herself, and she stood outside, her heart pounding. She leaned against a wall and closed her eyes.

Then her uncle emerged, alone. "I must say a few things to you," he said softly, and then she saw his blue eyes, full of compassion. She could not bear their expression, and turned away. "Sit down," he said. But she shook her head, mutely. "I have something sad to tell you," he stated.

And at that point she wheeled about and cried, "Is Kolya dead?"

"No," he answered. "Sweetheart . . . He is all right, but he has decided not to marry you. He does not wish for your reputation to suffer from this, and he has asked me to tell you to give any reason you please, to invent anything you like, to explain this to your friends. He is at fault, and will take the blame."

Her eyes wide and unmoving, her face drained of color, she stammered, "But I have nothing to hold against him. What has happened?"

"He does not wish for you to know," Misha replied.

"It is my right!" she countered, and her lips trembled. But no tears came to her clear eyes, and Misha felt a spasm of horror at that face.

"Very well," he assented. "Kolya has a mistress, who is energetic and authoritarian. To avoid any unpleasant scenes, he did not speak to her of his impending engagement, wishing to tell her about it only after the fact. But when he announced to her his wedding plans, she cried out against you, and threatened to cause a scandal. He took fear, and gave in."

So, she thought, he did not have the strength to stand up for his feelings . . . He cares more for her than for me. "When did he give her the news?" she asked, controlling her voice.

"Just before coming for the Carnival," Misha said.

Sonia clasped her hands together. Poor Kolya! How he must have suffered during those three days of rejoicing! But she was the one who was supposed to be wounded. She was silent. Misha regarded her quizzically, and then asked, "Well?"

"Well, nothing," Sonia answered. "Since Kolya will not have me, I shall not marry him, and that is all. Thank you for taking it upon yourself to bring me this painful announcement. I know how much it must have cost you." She extended her hands to him, and he took them, grateful for her lack of hysteria, but haunted by the large, distended gray eyes that stood out in her tiny bloodless face. She turned around and darted out of the room.

When she entered her bedroom, she latched the door and went to her secretary. She took out the pile of Kolya's letters, and opened the first one. No tears would come. She read the first, then the second, and one by one went through the entire pile. Her fingers began to tremble. Her teeth began to chatter. The candle on the secretary dimmed. She remained in the near darkness, immobile, gaunt, shivering. Someone knocked on her door. She did not answer. Her eyelids stung. But no tears came.

The next morning her mother came to her, and this time Sonia opened the door. The two women faced each other in silence. Sonia cleared her throat, and said, "Let us leave as planned, Mama. This way, no one shall know, and there will be no one to face. We can write Aunt Rosa from France, and tell her to make the announcement."

"We shall do whatever you want," Mathilde replied. "Sonia—"

"I just want to get out of here," the young woman said in a low, tense voice. She regarded her mother, whose beautiful face reflected compassion and unspoken grief. Sonia's face became a grimace. "Nothing else," she muttered. "Only to be left alone, and to leave this city!"

"Very well," Mathilde replied. Her hands reached for her daughter, but Sonia stiffened and shook her head. Mathilde stepped back, repelled by this vision of naked pain. Sonia went to the door, opened it, and held it for her mother. On the threshold, Mathilde hesitated. But Sonia sucked in her breath, and her whole body seemed to shy away from the proffered sympathy. She stood alone, watching her mother leave, her face white, her hair black, her gown a muted gray like her enormous eyes. Sonia closed the door and returned to her secretary. She had placed the ring, the necklace and the purse upon it side by side, and now she stared at them, for hours.

Still the tears would not rise, but she refused food and tea for two days until it was time to leave. At the train station, her friends had congregated with boxes of sweets to wish her farewell, and to congratulate her on her upcoming wedding, to which most of them had not planned to come, for it would be too far away. She smiled at them, and accepted the wishes with graciousness. She answered their excited queries. Then the bell rang, and rang again, and she said her last good-byes and followed her mother into their compartment. When the train pulled away, her face was ashen. She could hardly breathe. But she kept repeating over and over to herself: There must be a reason, there must be a reason. If God killed Volodia and took him from me, it was so that I might meet Kolya. Surely, surely, he has taken Kolya from me for a reason, too! But she could think of none, and remained awake at night, wondering.

The tears never came. She and Mathilde went to France, for they had no reason to go to Brussels now. When Sonia arrived at her grandmother's house, she had neither spoken nor eaten since her departure from St. Petersburg. Her cheekbones stood out in her small face, her hands trembled. But her eyes were dry.

Thirteen

———————————•———————————

Sonia and Mathilde remained in France for some time, in the suburban manor that belonged to Baron Yuri in Saint-Germain-en-Laye. It had never been intended for Johanna de Mey to accompany them to Brussels, before the wedding: now, since her daughter remained locked inside her grief, Mathilde wrote to her friend that it would be better for her to take a vacation in Normandy, with her own family. For with Gino in Hanover, it seemed pointless for Johanna to wait in St. Petersburg alone with David and Ossip. Mathilde might suffer from the separation, but she was mother enough to know that Johanna's mere presence would kill whatever chance existed for Sonia's recovery.

Sonia dressed herself meticulously, arranged her raven hair into coils and twists, and replied courteously to her grandfather's bantering and her grandmother's concerned demands; but she hardly touched a morsel, for vivid nausea overpowered her almost as soon as she lifted a spoon to her lips. She greeted her grandmother's guests with ceremony, but excused herself almost at once. When she was alone with her mother, she did not speak at all. Mathilde had never witnessed such intense suffering, and felt helpless in its presence.

Sonia refused to take the coach to Paris, and would not face her Aunt Clara and her Uncle Misha at all. During the day she would go out into the garden with a book, and stare at its pages unseeingly. She thought only of Kolya, of his black eyes, of his kisses, and of her bereavement. But though she tortured herself with memories, she did not bask in self-pity. She did not think of her fiancé with anger, or with blame, nor did she see herself as cruelly wronged. She simply thought of him, and of the happiness they had shared. Still, the searing pain that accompanied her thoughts burned inside her without bringing the relief of tears. There was no outlet for her grief, for she was hard with herself, allowing none.

She had always been petite and slender. Now she lost weight until her clothes hung limply over her, and her bones showed everywhere. Her breasts had flattened, and her ribs gave the effect of a xylophone on display. She did not complain, but Mathilde noticed with growing alarm her sallow color, and her expression of physical agony. When Baron Yuri's physician came for his bimonthly visit, Mathilde drew him aside and begged him to examine Sonia. He discovered that she had developed a floating kidney.

It was nearly summer, and Mathilde resolved to take her daughter to Switzerland, to consult a specialist of great repute, Dr. Roux of Lausanne, where Anna lived too. She came to Sonia with a certain amount of apprehension, for the young woman had read her father's expressive letters, addressed to his "Little Dove," with a stony silence, and had not even been moved by Ossip's lengthy missives to his beloved sister. Yet Ossip, too, had known a great sorrow, and Sonia had always accepted her father's devotion before. How would she take the notion of facing Anna? But Sonia regarded her mother with a quickened look. "Yes," she said softly, "I do wish to see her. We have not seen her for a long time, and we have never visited her home. Will she let us stay with her, Mama?"

"I think that her wounds have healed by now," Mathilde sighed. "And Dalia likes us. The . . . news . . . upset your sister, Sonitchka. She wanted to come here, to you. I wrote her that you did not seem to want company."

"But I do want to see Anna. Of all people—yes, I want to be with my sister."

Mathilde ordered the maids to pack their bags, and she thought, with bitterness: But the situations were different. Yes, I can see where Sonia now feels drawn toward Anna. But Anna caused her own misfortune. Sonia was wronged. Anna acted foolishly, brazenly. Sonia merely trusted, and was deceived. But Mathilde was relieved that her younger daughter seemed willing to visit Anna, and that the thought of seeing Dr. Roux did not frighten her.

The weather was warm in Switzerland. The sun shone through the blue-green pines and Lake Geneva gleamed placidly beneath them. Anna met her mother and Sonia at the train station, and Mathilde was struck by the composure of her older daughter. Anna stood before them, her red hair coiled behind her right ear, a feather in her chignon. She appeared young, and wore a necklace of colored beads she had made herself. She was neither the vibrant young artist of St. Petersburg, nor the severe, remote woman who had visited her family in the Black Forest after the debacle. Mathilde gave Anna her cheek, and Anna kissed it; yet there was a diffident quality to her kiss, and Mathilde stiffened inwardly. Anna wrapped her arms strongly about the frail, emaciated body of her little sister, and rocked her wordlessly in her embrace. If Anna could only bring solace to Sonia . . .

In the carriage that took them to Anna's house, the sisters were mostly silent. Anna had never been a talkative person, and since the shock of Kolya's abandonment, Sonia had preferred quiet to conversation. Mathilde cleared her throat and said, "Our old friend, Alexei Alexandrovitch Lopukhin, was pardoned earlier this year. Had Papa written you about it?"

Anna shrugged. "All the prisoners were pardoned when the Tzar celebrated the three hundred years of the Romanov dynasty in February. I assumed that Alexei Alexandrovitch would be granted similar treatment."

Mathilde held up her head with its heavy topknot. "But he was pardoned before the others. And his was not, actually, a pardon. It was an exoneration."

"Then he must now be a most happy man," her daughter concluded tersely. She passed a hand through the hair at the left side of her face. "He was one of the Tzar's own men; I wonder if he has forgiven the Tzar for what he was forced to undergo . . . But then, these days, political matters do not touch me. Here in Switzerland I am concerned with my art, and with the friends that I have made."

"Alexei Alexandrovitch moved his family to Moscow," Mathilde stated. "We have not seen them since."

"That is too bad," Anna murmured. "I know how fond Papa was of his friend. Papa has not been very well, has he?"

The carriage was drawing up to a gate, a small white gate in front of a green-grassed garden, not at all in the tradition of meticulous lawns and flowerbeds that characterized the landscaping trend of the day. Anna stepped out and gave her strong hand to her sister to help her down before the coachman offered his arm. She was smiling with anticipation.

When they had paid the coachman, and the horses had pulled away, Anna unlocked the gate and led Mathilde and Sonia toward a rather small brick house set behind the garden. Before they even reached the front door, it was opened from the inside, and Dalia Hadjani appeared on the threshold, her dark skin glowing, her ebony tresses piled high on top of her head. A boy of some six years stood beside her, and it was evident that it was he, in his eagerness to greet the guests, who had opened the door so impulsively. "Welcome, my dear Baroness, dear Sonia," Dalia said, extending her hands to them. They stepped into the house. "Riri could not contain himself. He was wondering what our Russian visitors looked like. I'm afraid he had in mind ladies of a far more exotic nature!"

Anna was sitting on her haunches, close to the boy. "I told you that Russia was a civilized country, pussy cat," she said laughingly. Then her hand reached out and mussed the boy's hair. He threw his arms about her and nearly toppled her over in the exuberance of his hug. She laughed and kissed him. "This is our Riri, Mama, Sonitchka," she said. Her eyes sparkled. "Let us be proper, shall we, young man? This is Reza Hadjani."

"But I don't like my name," the lad said to the ladies. "Aunt Anna says that I must use it later, to please Mama. But I prefer the names in your family: Ossip, David, Gino. Did they not travel with you?"

"I am afraid not, sweetheart," Sonia said. She smiled at him, and her mother thought: How extraordinary! This child has conquered one daughter, and now he is working on the second. But truly, he is a beautiful child.

Sonia was looking at the little boy, and something inexplicable stirred within her. It was as though she had met him before, yet she knew that she had not, ever. He had a fair complexion and bright green eyes beneath a shock of yellow hair, and his body was frail and slender, so that he appeared younger than his six years. Silently she placed her fingers upon the fine tow head. But as Dalia took them through the house, and the boy chattered on, her sensation of déjà vu increased. "Why have you never sent us a photograph of Riri?" she asked Anna. "He is such a handsome young fellow."

"Photographs are for well-organized ladies, and Aunt Anna is not organized," the boy piped up. Sonia began to laugh and twinkled at her sister. "But Aunt Anna speaks a great deal about you. Could I call you Sonia, or must I say 'Baroness'?"

"You may certainly call me Sonia," she replied. She took

his hand and allowed him to lead her ahead of the others into a large gallery enclosed with glass, in which pots were hanging and two easels had been set up. The pots were all hand-painted in gay, bright colors. Sonia wandered up and down, examining the various canvases which were stacked up by the sides of the room. "Your Mama and Auntie work here?" she asked.

"Oh, yes. But Aunt Anna is a better painter than my Mama. And when I am just a little more grown-up they will both teach me how to do still lifes, and landscapes. But I want to do people. Here, let me show you. Aunt Anna did a portrait of me, and it is to be my birthday present this August!" He scampered like an elf to a canvas that had been turned to face the wall, and held it up triumphantly to Sonia. "See how grown-up Aunt Anna has made me?"

When Sonia looked from his eager face to that of the portrait, she sucked in her breath with shock. Her hand flew to her throat and her gray eyes widened, for the face that was regarding her from the canvas possessed the gift of life. "You do indeed look older," she murmured. She stood mesmerized by the green eyes of the portrait, by the nose, by the thin sensuous lips and the line of intensity between the fair brows. This was not the reproduction of this child. It was a rendering of someone else, someone from the past, someone forbidden and expelled . . .

But Anna was coming into the room, and when she saw Riri and Sonia she shook her head abruptly, and turned the canvas back toward the wall. "Now Riri, that was impertinent of you, before your birthday!" she admonished. Sonia saw that quick color had jumped to Anna's cheekbones, that she was not looking at her. The little boy replied something in his defense, and Sonia moved away, lost in thought.

"You have not yet seen my bedroom," Dalia said, holding her elbow. "Anna has made such lovely curtains for me. Come, I'll show you." Sonia allowed herself to be led away, although her eyes were unseeing and her breath was short. She went down the stairs behind Dalia, and entered a sunny room with a large bed and curtains of gay cotton, upon which had been painted three children picking a bouquet of posies from an antique garden. But Sonia's eyes were drawn to the photographs which had been placed in silver frames upon Dalia's dresser. Without a word, she walked up to them and held each up to the light. There were three. One represented a very young Dalia, her hair loose about her shoulders. The second was clearly of Riri, his face aglow with laughter and good humor. And the last showed a handsome man in his thirties, with features that reminded Sonia of Dalia herself. He had dark hair, black eyes, and thick dark lashes. "You are admiring my late husband," the hostess said softly. "He was very striking, don't you think?"

"Yes, indeed," Sonia murmured. Her eyes had filled with tears and suddenly one spilled from her lower lid. She pressed it away with the back of her hand in a gesture of embarrassment. But Dalia came to her, and placed an arm about her shoulders. "I, too, lost someone dear to me. I understand," Dalia declared. Inexplicably, Sonia shook her head. It was the first time since losing Kolya that she had cried, but he was not the reason.

Sonia excused herself early from supper that evening. Nobody thought to question her, for Dalia and Anna had heard from Mathilde about Sonia's condition, and understood that she needed to rest. Visible signs of strain had appeared around her mouth and eyes, and she had eaten little, Mathilde thought. Thank heaven, tomorrow we shall see the specialist, and he will know what to do about her kidney.

The next several days were taken up with visits to Dr. Roux, who placed Sonia under strict observation and on a rigid diet. Mathilde wished now that she had allowed Johanna to accompany them, for the latter was an able nurse and had boundless energy. But Dalia and Anna took Sonia in hand. She spent her days reclining on a padded chaise longue in the painting gallery, watching the two artists and the small boy who played at their feet. There was an expression of deep pain in her gray eyes when she looked at him. Maybe I made a mistake, Mathilde thought. Perhaps Sonia was not ready to face Anna after all. They hardly seem to spend any time alone. Dalia is always there, as though to shield them from each other. I do not like this at all. But she said nothing.

It was not until a few weeks after their arrival in Lausanne that Dalia took the boy into town one afternoon, leaving Sonia with her sister in the gallery. Mathilde was reading outside in the garden, under the warming sun, and the fresh scent of Anna's wildflowers filled the air. The two sisters were silent, Anna busy at her easel, Sonia writing notes in her diary. Suddenly, Anna could stand it no longer. She turned her face to her sister and cried out; "You are holding something against me! For God's sake, what have I done? I want to help, but you won't let me near you!"

Sonia turned very pale, and clenched her fists in her lap. "It is nothing," she whispered hoarsely.

"You are lying!" Anna stated. Their eyes met and locked, hers brown with spots of molten copper, Sonia's gray with points of fiery blue. It was Anna who looked away first, fumbling with her brush.

"He is yours, isn't he?" Sonia said. Her voice was low and steady, cutting through the silence like lightning in the dark. Anna wheeled about, her painter's smock splotched with reds and blues, her face flushed. Her eyes appeared enormous in her face. "I don't understand," Sonia added.

"What is there to understand?" Anna said with disdain. She bit her lower lip and applied herself to her work. All at once she hurled her brush to the ground, where it splashed bright purple. "What is it you want?" she cried. "Confessions of guilt?"

"No," Sonia answered. Her eyes were limpid with tears.

"But it's true, isn't it? Then why does he think he is Dalia's son? How can you stand it when he calls her 'Mama'?"

"It is very simple," Anna said suddenly, quiet. She sat down at Sonia's feet, and folded her hands in her lap. "Dalia came to Switzerland to have her baby, because she had already miscarried once. She miscarried again. I was pregnant. I had my child in the clinic that was expecting Dalia, and since they had not met her, I registered in her name. The boy was born with her name as mother, and her deceased husband's as father. Nobody ever thought to question us. Why you? I believed you were the last of the innocents, that the truth would never occur to you—or I would never have allowed you to come here."

"I am not a fool," Sonia said. "He looks like Ivan. And I would not betray you. Do you take me for a heartless prude?"

"A prude, yes. But not a heartless one." Anna's eyes sparkled for a moment, and she smiled briefly. "That is why I never wanted the family to come here. Papa and Mama would not have guessed. It is not their nature. But Ossip—even Gino—and of all people, Juanita! I could not permit it. Because Riri must never know! Dalia convinced me, for his sake! Do you think it has been easy all these years, rearing him as hers, when he is mine? She is an admirable mother, but it is I who take care of him more. I changed his diapers when he was a baby—she did too, but I got up at night to feed him at my breast—and I have taught him so much, Sonia, so much! He is all that matters in my life. I did not even mind rearing him a Moslem—for what difference does religion make? Life is love, and care. Riri is my life and my love. I wanted him and I had him. And I gave him up out of love. Can you understand that? For I loved his father, Vanya, and once I gave him up too, because my love was stronger than convention. He—Riri—is happier here, freer, with Dalia and me, than he would have been as the grandson of Baron David de Gunzburg and the banker Aron Berson. And I could not have survived Petersburg, married to Vanya and tied to a life such as Mama leads."

"That is beyond my comprehension," Sonia said. "Because, you see, I want to be married, to run a household, to go to the theater with my husband, to entertain our friends. Kolya—it was so difficult, letting go of the dream. I wanted to wake up beside him every morning. I wanted to face him at breakfast. I even wanted to wear perfume, to go out into the world with him. If Ivan wanted you—I cannot understand why you felt you had to give him up. I had no choice!"

"We are different people," Anna said. "I do not mock your dream. I can understand it."

"But not share it?"

"No." She laid her hand over the left side of her face. The gesture was eloquent and clear. The sisters sat side by side on the chaise longue, and they were silent now. Sonia's small oval face reflected misery. It was pinched and drawn. Anna's was flushed, and her eyes were deep and mellow, like brown velvet. Then Anna raised her face and asked, "How does it feel to be an aunt? For I am glad that you know. I am proud of him."

"I am proud of him, also," Sonia replied quietly. Her hand stretched toward her sister, and pulled her to herself. Their arms went about each other, and Anna drew Sonia's head to her chest, stroking the soft black hair. Sonia began to weep, then to sob. Anna rocked her, singing, and the words formed an old Russian peasant lullaby from their childhood at Mohilna. Her own eyes filled with tears, which flowed easily from her lids down her cheeks, and onto Sonia's head. They remained like this for several minutes, while the dusk set outside the glass panes of the gallery.

Neither knew that Mathilde, frozen in horror, stood on the other side of the door, where she had come to join her daughters after a gust of wind had disturbed her reading in the garden. Revulsion overcame her. She clutched at the wall. My God, it is my fault, she said to herself. All this is my fault. I allowed this to happen to my own child, my daughter! Then she listened to the soft melody from Anna's lips and made out Sonia's sobs—the first since Misha's visit—and a sort of relief came to her.

It is not true, not true, Mathilde told herself over and over. She stood still, her eyes clenched shut, denying what she'd heard. Not Anna. Not true. Not Anna. And then she heard sounds of childish laughter, and knew that Dalia and Riri had arrived downstairs. "Aunt Anna!" the little boy was crying. "Look, Mama has bought you some paints!" Aunt Anna, Mama. Pretend. Pretend not to have heard. Pretend not to know. Her daughter was Aunt Anna, that was all. She turned and faced the boy as he ran up the steps. "Well," she declared, "it seems that you had quite a day, young man!"

His large green eyes looked up at her, and she touched his cheek. It was going to be all right. All right. As long as she forgot Ivan Berson. Something tugged at her insides. She bent down and kissed the boy.

"I like you," he said. "You are a nice lady, and you smell good. Will you let me come to Russia to visit you one day, when I am older?"

Mathilde felt her eyes fill with tears. She turned aside. "That would be fun," she replied. "But it is up to your mother." She bit her lip and clasped her hands together wretchedly. But the child had not noticed, for he had opened the door and was calling out to the two young women within.

Sonia's cure took a long time, and so, during the summer, when Gino had passed his examinations and obtained his diploma from the school of commerce in Hanover, Mathilde went alone to see him. He had become a stalwart young man, no longer a boy, and his broad shoulders, his vivid brown eyes, his ruddy complexion, somewhat startled his mother, who had not seen him for a year. Her baby was no more. Gino was eighteen, fluent in German, and confident about his future. It was he who took her around the city, dining in its more elegant restaurants. He was tall, and tipped his hat to some of the young girls who passed his way in horse carriages. But he was not entirely sure about the direction he wished his life to take. "I have received several offers from good firms here," he told his mother. "But the truth is, I miss the family." She pressed his hand and smiled at his words, so reassuring to her ears.

Then, unexpectedly, a letter came from David, and the young man read it over breakfast one morning, his features lightening into a broad smile when he scanned its contents. "Oh, Mama!" he cried. "Papa has found a way to get me into the University in Petersburg! I don't know how he went around my silver medal, but I don't care. I shall have to pack, and return home at once." His eyes gleamed with pleasure and excitement, and she breathed deeply with the relief that her younger son would be following in the steps of his brother, that he would assume the position which should be his as a Gunzburg Baron.

Mathilde sent her son off, and left her daughter in Anna's care while she joined Johanna de Mey in France for several months. From Normandy, Mathilde had received pleading letters from the Dutchwoman. Could she not join her now at Anna's? Hadn't her exile lasted long enough? But Mathilde had not allowed her friend to come to Switzerland. She had feared that Johanna would see traces of Ivan Berson in Riri Hadjani; and she did not want to impede Sonia's progress, which depended so heavily upon Anna's frame of mind. The easy atmosphere of the house where the two women painted and sculpted, where the boy played and cavorted, seemed to bring peace to Sonia. Johanna's presence would only create havoc, and, with a pinch at her heart, Mathilde was forced to admit that her friend had worsened her own relationship with Anna, and had not allowed Sonia's brief engagement the smooth course that it might have had.

Later in the year, when Sonia was suitably recovered and her kidney was once more functioning properly, she came to her mother in France and they traveled together. Sonia was still vehement about not wanting to return to the city of her birth. They took a health cure at Vichy, where the baths restored them. They visited the Scandinavian countries. There was an exhibition in Malmö featuring handicrafts, arts, costumes, and furniture from Norway, Denmark, Finland, and Sweden. Then while Johanna stayed with her own mother, Sonia and Mathilde spent some time with Baron Yuri, who was not well, and with Baroness Ida. In spite of his many years of philandering, Yuri had given his wife more than fifty years of marriage, and the elderly couple seemed more united now than ever. Ida's bitterness had abated with her husband's age, and his lust for the fairer sex had likewise been toned down by ill health. And so, 1913 became 1914, and the months wove into one another like a tapestry.

In St. Petersburg, Tatiana de Gunzburg, the belle of her society, was growing frenzied. She had not found the foreign husband of her choice. Her heart still ached for Jean, but she would toss her head in defiance and dance the more frantically to prove that she no longer cared. Ossip would watch her, his blue eyes perceptive, and he merely shrugged when friends told him that his cousin claimed that he had proposed marriage to her, and that she had rejected him. "He is too Russian," she would say, and he smiled and shook his head at the words when they were reported to him. There were others who said that Tatiana Alexandrovna had alluded to Ossip's dark moods of previous years, widely attributed to the conclusion of a secret romance; and she had raised her fine golden brows, adding, "But of course, I would not humiliate him by revealing the name of his beloved. I know it well, as I know my own name." Ossip frankly laughed at this but he said nothing to Tania about it. He did not care about anything at all.

In the summer of 1913, Sioma Halperin, who had so importuned Sonia during her visit to Kiev several months before, arrived in St. Petersburg. He was over thirty, and had heard that there was another Baroness Gunzburg in the capital, with whom he might try his luck. He saw Tania at a reception just before her departure for the holidays, where she would again seek a match abroad. He had only to see the golden girl before his palms began to perspire, and he came to her with flowers and sweets, his watery eyes aglow with love. Yes, he had wished to take a Gunzburg as wife in order to enhance his position in Kiev society, which shunned his family as nouveau riche. But now he was in love with Tania, and the proposal he made was from the heart.

She laughed, her head flung back attractively, her pink throat exposed, her bright eyes half-closed. It was always agreeable to be courted, even by this country bumpkin with his pockmarked skin and his sour breath. She did not shrink from him as Sonia had, for he was very rich, and among the boxes of kirsch-filled chocolates he brought baubles of pearls and rubies. Rosa and Sasha were somewhat appalled, but they were not the sort to interfere. Let the girl amuse herself!

Sioma returned to St. Petersburg after the sugar campaign was over in January 1914. By June, she had not refused him. He would come to her with his small gifts and she would feverishly tear open the wrapping. Ah . . . another enamel brooch. Another Calville apple. She accepted his compliments but laughed at him. "Surely you don't suppose I shall marry the boor?" she said to one of her friends. But her mother and father began to feel uneasy. Too many baubles, too many visits. Tania would have to resolve the situation one way or another, for she was twenty-three and no longer a girl. At her age, in her position, she could only tease a man so long before her reputation would begin to suffer.

In July, Sonia and Mathilde returned to Switzerland, and this time Johanna de Mey came along, for they were not visiting Anna but going to Grindelwald, a lovely resort area. Baron Yuri de Gunzburg, whose strength had left him, called for his physician, who ordered that he travel to the German spa of Badenweiler for a water cure. He and his wife lived frugally in their manor in Saint-Germain-en-Laye. The old Baroness scrimped and saved, while her husband continued his extravagances, but only when his health permitted the appreciation of a luxury. He had squandered his fortune years ago, and lived mostly on a stipend from his son-in-law, David. Now, at the thought of traveling to the elegant resort of Badenweiler, Baron Yuri called for his tailor and ordered twelve new silk shirts to dazzle the ladies taking the waters. In spite of his paunch and his seventy-four years, he liked to be noticed for his dapper dress. Baroness Ida quaked at the cost, but could only protest. He had long since ceased to hear her.

Rumors of war had come, faint rumblings about mobilization. Baron Yuri and his plump wife sat together on the train in their private compartment, and she held his hand and stroked it. The train moved with infinite slowness and the heat was suffocating. Many times Ida rang for water compresses for her husband. She too was exhausted when at last they pulled into the station at Badenweiler. The old man was leaning heavily upon his wife.

But no sooner had they descended, when a German official directed them to the waiting room. A small straight-backed officer stood before a large group of people, and Ida asked, "What is going on? Why are we here?"

"You are not German citizens," someone near her replied. She appeared dazed, and a young man took pity and rose from his seat so that the Baron might have it. Ida stood by his side, for she was too tired to rouse one of the younger people and insist upon a seat for herself.

The officer began to speak, in clipped, harsh tones. "War has been declared," he announced. "As neutrals and enemies, you who are gathered here shall be allowed to do the following things." He proceeded to list numerous activities which were lost upon Ida, whose head had begun to spin. Sitting in the chair, Yuri's face had sunk and his color was ashen. Finally, the German clicked his heels and shouted, "You may now go to your hotels!"

Distraught, Ida found the young man who had kindly given up his seat for her husband. She had never been a woman given to tears, but now they peeked from the corners of her magnificent blue eyes beneath their white brows. "Please," she begged, "find us a hansom cab. My husband is ill." The young man took her hand and called to her when the coach was ready. Then he helped Yuri to the carriage. They were deposited at their hotel, and Yuri went to sleep at once. Ida watched over him silently.

The very next day, Ida and Yuri de Gunzburg were roused at dawn and told to go to Baden-Baden, where all foreigners were being collected. When they arrived there and found a hotel, Yuri could hardly open his eyes. Four days later, holding the hand of his wife, he breathed his last sigh, and died. Ida was alone in a hostile land, and she knew that Mathilde, in Switzerland, would not be able to come to her. Mathilde was a Russian citizen and would not be granted a visa, as Russia was at war with Germany. But what was happening to Mathilde and to Sonia and Anna? Were they all right? The old woman, bewildered and sick and alone, decided to go to Stuttgart, where she collapsed in a sanatorium.

In Grindelwald, the peaceful mountains seemed to belie the political news. Mathilde, Sonia, and Johanna de Mey proceeded with their easy summer existence, took walks in the woods and feasted on hot chocolate and crumpets in their favorite tea room. On the morning of August 2, Sonia came to her mother and said, frowning, "The newspaper is not here." When she rang for the bellboy, he arrived with his cap on backward and burst out, "Baroness! They say that war has broken out!"

No further news reached the three women, and in the afternoon, because they were tired of their idleness, and because the sky was the color of cornflowers, they decided to go out for a stroll to an inn, the Little Scheidegg, which was higher on the hill than their hotel. They arrived in time for tea, and ordered it on the terrace. But the owner came to them, her face red, her clothes awry, and shook her head. "We can give you only bread and butter, my ladies," she said. "For war has come, and the cakes have not been delivered."

Sonia and Mathilde looked at each other, all color leaving their cheeks. War? They hardly knew the meaning of the word! Mathilde had been a mere child at the time of the war of 1870, and she and her mother had fled Paris for Switzerland. And the conflict with Japan in '04 had been so far away . . . Now they had to believe that war had actually reached them, in remote Grindelwald, this charming resort of pines and winding trails.

For the next two weeks, chaos reigned. Switzerland was neutral, and sought to remain so, surrounded as it was by fighting nations: France, Germany, Italy, Austria. The Swiss sent their soldiers to the borders, to prevent invasion at all cost. The Gunzburgs and Johanna remained as prisoners in Grindelwald, where the hotels were full but the banks were closed. Nervous, without news, the vacationers clustered together, and an American businessman, seeing the beginnings of mass panic, called a meeting in Mathilde's hotel. Hundreds crowded into the dining room, and the American stood on a dais and spoke out, his voice calm and serene:

"I shall attempt to reach Bern, and there charter a train to take the American guests to Paris, and then to Le Havre, and from there to the United States. If there is room, I shall accept foreign citizens, too. The journey to Paris will last about three days, and we shall have to bring our own food, plenty of raisins and other dried fruits for energy. Lemons, too, for lemon juice can make any water drinkable." His words sounded reassuring to his audience, for he was a natural leader.

He was gone the next day, no one knew how, and when he returned on the third day he had chartered a long train. But by then the tracks were occupied with special military trains, and the Americans had to wait. He had promised to take Mathilde, Sonia, and Johanna along as far as Paris with his convoy.

Then, slowly, life began to resume. Banks reopened. The tracks cleared. Mathilde changed her mind. "We shall go to Geneva," she stated. "I have a special bank account there with some emergency funds. Why should we go to St. Germain and bother Mama and Papa?"

In Geneva, the Gunzburgs found a pension, a simple boarding house in a pleasant neighborhood, where all the guests were French and Russian refugees. Mathilde managed to wire her husband and sons in St. Petersburg, and her parents at their manor on the outskirts of Paris. Several days passed, and then a telegram from David arrived, announcing the death of Baron Yuri. Mathilde sat down, her hand trembling. She regarded her daughter and cleared her throat. "Your grandfather is dead," she declared. She felt numb and tired.

Softly, Sonia began to weep. "Poor Grandmother," she whispered.

"I don't know," Mathilde sighed. "The world is a shambles. Papa is gone, and perhaps he left just in time. He was never a man to face his problems." To her amazement, tears came to her eyes for the man who had shamed and frightened her in her youth, who had belittled her mother. She remembered how she had loved him as a small girl, when he had delighted her with his stories. "One of the world's great entertainers has died," she said.

Fourteen

Although Mathilde, Sonia, and Johanna felt somewhat isolated in Geneva, the common route back to Russia entailed crossing Germany, an enemy nation. Mail took five weeks to reach them from David, Ossip, and Gino, but in each communiqué her husband reiterated his hope that they would remain safely in neutral territory. Besides, Mathilde possessed a bank account in Geneva, and as they could hardly trust the mail to furnish them with their living expenses, they attempted to rely upon Mathilde's reserve funds. The Pension de la Grande Bretagne was comfortable, its occupants genteel, and in these days of war it was hardly the moment to live lavishly. The Gunzburgs and their companion felt that they might manage quite adequately there, and rented an extra sitting room where Mathilde had a piano installed for her daughter. Then she purchased a tea set, a copper kettle, and a kerosene lamp, so that they would not have to take their midafternoon tea in pastry shops and tea rooms.

Life had slowed down. Young men and those of healthy middle age had all been mobilized, and now scout organizations, the old, the sick, and the women attempted to take over wherever they could. Sonia had heard that in Russia the people were united in their realization of the need for this war. The Duma and the district governments all backed the government in its decree for Slavic emancipation from the Germans and Austrians. David wrote that pro-Serb, pro-Polish sentiments had risen to such a pitch that St. Petersburg had been renamed "Petrograd," so that it would sound less Germanic.

Sonia had loved Kolya Saxe with all the idealism, all the strength of her convictions, and now she felt the same commitment to helping the Allies. Issues mattered not at all to this young woman, who, though intelligent, never questioned those things she idolized. She had never formed a criticism of her mother, even though she sometimes noted Mathilde's fretful need of Johanna, a person who seemed altogether unworthy of her mother's devotion. She had never questioned the dictates of the Jewish religion. She would never have questioned Kolya's love, after their engagement, had he not betrayed her trust. And Russia, her homeland, was almost like her God, a holy entity higher even than her earthly idols. If Russia was at war, then war was honorable, and she, a patriot, wanted to serve her country's allies in any way possible.

But to her intense disappointment and self-directed annoyance, her senses failed her at the wrong moment. Johanna had declared, with a glint in her magnificent aquamarine eyes, that though she was fifty years of age, it was not too late for her to serve as a nurse for the convoys of wounded soldiers that passed through the train station each night. There the men were rebandaged, fed, and given hot drinks. Sonia agreed with Johanna. She would become a nurse, too. But on her first day of training she was asked to give an injection, and the sight of the soldier's bloodied arm, half mangled, made her faint on the spot. She resolutely returned to duty, but once again, although she clenched her teeth and took a deep breath, she became faint. The doctor took her aside and gently reprimanded

her: "My dear young Baroness, we waste precious moments reviving you, while these men are dying. I should
think that there might be more suitable ways for you to
serve your country."

Her shame was profound—and Johanna's triumph all
the greater. She made a great production of her nightly
journeys to the station, causing Mathilde to clasp her
hands together with worry over the icy drafts that buffeted
her friend about as she distributed chocolates and cigarettes to the wounded, and sometimes changed a messy
dressing. Sonia was mortified. But she had not fully recuperated from her bout with the kidney ailment, and was
still weak. Yet pride was not at stake here. It was, Sonia
thought, a mere matter of doing what needed to be done,
and although nursing was covered with a veil of glory,
other tasks too needed to be performed.

So she signed up with the committee headed by the wife
of the Russian Consul, who had opened a workshop in her
house. Two afternoons a week ladies gathered to sew flannel shirts and pajama bottoms for the wounded. Wagons
full of garments were sent back to Russia, and Sonia was
an accomplished seamstress, after her years of training
with Johanna. But the young woman was annoyed. The
ladies arrived on time, for the most part, their hair elaborately coiffed and their nails polished, and arranged themselves comfortably so that their taffeta and silk skirts were
not creased. But during the sewing, they would sip from
china teacups and then they would laugh together and
gossip. An elderly plain woman next to her whispered to
Sonia, seeing the fine line that had drawn between the
young woman's gray eyes: "Indeed! One cannot work
while visiting." And Sonia noticed that at the end of the
session, calmly and without fanfare, this woman, a
Countess Benckendorff, took some of the unfinished pieces
home with her. Sonia, her face lighting up, did likewise,
and soon she was spending all her free hours at the pension
sewing busily.

There was another job which Sonia performed in addition to her sewing for the Russian Consul's wife. Near the pension was a milk cooperative, where working mothers were able to drop off their babies' empty milk bottles in the morning, and where young girls would fill them anew according to each baby's specified formula during the day. Everybody vied for this work, so that there was no one to perform the equally necessary task of washing the three hundred bottles and drying them upside down in a strainer. Sonia undertook this job, and for approximately three hours a day she stood all alone in the vast kitchen of the cooperative, interrupted only when the bottles were brought in and later picked up. She never saw the young girls in the next rooms, pouring out the babies' formulas. But she had time to think, to compose poetry and fairy tales, to remember. Where was Kolya now? she wondered. She still hurt, but now the pain was less acute, less personal. And she would think about her brothers.

Gino, at nineteen, had become a man. He was tall and broad, not unlike his Uncle Sasha, but in his coloring he resembled neither of his parents, nor, for that matter, his four grandparents, all of whom had possessed black hair and blue-gray eyes. He was "bold and brown," as his father put it, and with the mahogany of his large frank eyes he had inherited a measure of his great-grandmother Rosa Dynin's sturdy peasant stock. But he did not seem plain. There was a nobility to his carriage, a simple elegance that did not even attempt to challenge the more flamboyant style sported by his brother Ossip, eight years his senior. He had entered the University the previous year, and was specializing in the reading of law, not because of any particular fascination on his part, but rather because that seemed to be the most practical of disciplines, short of the natural sciences for which he felt no affinity. Like Sonia, he was diligent and possessed a sound memory. He would laughingly acknowledge his lack of imagination. Unlike Ossip, he could not pay court to a young girl with a quick wit; he was charming in his honesty, in his lack of pretense. Had he been older, he might have loved Nina Tobias, now comfortably married to Zenia Abelson, a wealthy young burgher of Petrograd. Natasha Tagantseva would have been too bright, too dramatic for his tastes.

His father had long since stopped hoping that Gino might become a scholar. He had, early on, given up on Anna, and recognized the artist's temperament in her. Ossip had performed exceptionally at the University, but Ossip, the Baron realized, with his usual pinch of annoyance whenever he thought more than cursorily about his older son, lacked something essential—something called "nerve" or "backbone." He would keep working for Sasha for lack of other motivation; he was not ambitious, and let challenge slip by with a careless smile. A disturbing thought pierced David's mind: Could it be that Ossip was a coward, refusing to meet life head on? But no; his childhood illness had merely weakened him, and that was all. Sonia? Yes, she might yet be the family scholar, but only if she did not marry. For, once married, Baron David envisioned his daughter more than ever emulating her mother. And she would marry, even if that young fool from Kiev had seen fit to humiliate her. But Gino was not an intellectual, any more than Anna had been.

Sometimes, David would speak to him about Henri Sliosberg, a dear friend, the family attorney, and a great *shtadlan* in the cause of the emancipation of the Jews of Russia. "Yes, maybe I shall train with him," the young man would nod gravely. And then he would smile, with his whole soul, that marvelous childlike smile that revealed large white teeth, and say with love, "But I am best at commerce, Papa. And I am most at ease in the country." And what could David say? Love of the land was more Russian than tea. David himself possessed it.

David was undergoing a unique experience, living with both his grown sons under the same roof. He missed his wife, missed her intensely, and often he did not feel well, his bouts with angina pectoris more frequent than before. His hair had thinned, his expression was more gaunt, his posture somewhat more stooped. Mathilde was now fifty, with an ampler figure than before and some strands of gray in her thick black hair. But still, he desired her, and though their years together had been interspersed with moments of withdrawal and bitterness on her part, he could not help but feel how much her presence brightened his existence. He also missed his daughters, who had adored him each in her own way. Yet there was something appealing about this enforced male cloister in his house, for he was a man much like most, and proud of his sons. They were his scions, they would carry on his genes if not his work. Sonia alone seemed ready to take his duties upon her frail shoulders, but it was hardly fitting. She was a woman, and would soon be too busy bearing sons of her own. No, his sons would pass on his name, but without the tradition with which he had taken it from his own father. They would not continue his mission, they would not be *shtadlanim* for the Jews of Russia.

David knew, without ever having discussed the matter with his older son, that Ossip shared his mother's agnosticism and derision of the intricacies of the Hebrew faith so dear to himself. Ossip accompanied his father to the synagogue when David asked it of him, but lately the Baron had not asked, for Ossip's presence, though outwardly unmarred by disrespect, brought David disquiet and a sense of shame. It was as though he felt Ossip's profound indifference, as well as something else, something indistinct that David preferred not to explore: it was as though Ossip actually found his Judaism a bother, an impediment, as one would a wooden leg. Anna had been impervious to her faith, for she had been concerned with the poor, the downtrodden; like most idealists she had not cared about such matters as the Sabbath. But Sonia cared, and of this David was certain. In his own way, Gino too cared, though not at all like Sonia. In Gino's simple way he revered God, and the God he revered happened to be the God revered by his father, for Gino loved and respected David. So when it came time to go to the synagogue, David turned to his younger son, who had the soul of a child but the stalwartness of a man. Yet Gino would never be a *shtadlan*. He was too robust, too vital, and not patient or unselfish enough. He was the most totally Russian of all David's children, and his love of God was as simple as that of a peasant.

With sadness, David had told his sons that he could not foresee either of them needing his Judaica library, as neither was a scholar or a devout Jew. This Judaica consisted of some thirteen thousand erudite volumes of Jewish law and lore, and David had collected it with intense love. "But if you will not use them, these books will be dead after I am gone," he said to his sons. "I would rather have strangers consult them, than let them sit upon your shelves, gathering dust. Perhaps a university would purchase them."

"We need not speak of this now, Papa," Ossip said. "You are alive, and well. You use them."

"But I am suffering more each day. The pains in my chest grow more acute all the time. Should the moment come, then I would not wish this burden to rest upon your shoulders. I will sell the books, with the arrangement that I keep them until I die," he said. "Do not look so glum; my affairs must be in order, and your dear mother must not be troubled. I am not preparing to lie down and expire, my sons. But I want to know where this beloved collection will go."

Only days before the outbreak of the war, the Baron received a letter from the University of Pennsylvania, asking to purchase his Judaica collection. As a scholar, he was overjoyed. But when the war came, communications were cut off. David sighed, and went about his business. With the world in turmoil, it was hardly the moment to worry about his books. He was a statesman, and concerned with matters of more far-reaching import. And, not long afterward, a personal matter came up that caused him conflicting emotional reactions.

With war came mobilization for all youths of twenty-one years or more, except for those who had a physical ailment, such as Ossip, or who managed important businesses, such as Sioma Halperin, who still pursued Tania with his ardor. Ossip easily obtained his white exemption paper. Mathilde, in Geneva, was relieved, for with one son out of danger due to a previous infirmity, and another too young to be called up, she had no personal maternal worries. She knew Ossip well enough to imagine his thoughts, as did his cousin, Tania. On the day that he received his white paper, the young woman came to see him at her father's bank, and removing her ermine-trimmed silk cape she flung her graceful legs over his desk and sat among his papers. "You, at least, are not a hero, my pet," she announced.

He laughed. "I must admit that I would not relish risking my life," he assented.

"It hardly seems worth the bother. You are too European. The Russians nauseate me, with their mujik mentality. Kill the Hun! And why? There are very civilized Huns, I am told, who are as loath to die as you or I."

"You really have your heart set on a continental wedding," he said. "Most unpatriotic."

She made an unpleasant face, and turned from him. She did not like his mocking eyes, which said too much. He had once offered to marry her, and now she sometimes regretted her refusal. So many of the young men were being called to arms, so many would die . . . And who would be left? Sioma Halperin, who was pockmarked and whose offspring would bear the patronym "Solomonovitch." Should she instead have married her cousin? Ossip was elegant, appealing, worldly, and hardly the religious fanatic Sioma was reputed to be. But he knew her altogether too well and did not adore her. He did not even love her. They would amuse each other—and then? "You are really a coward, my darling," she commented, half-closing her cornflower-blue eyes and regarding him malevolently.

He stirred in his seat. His face was pale, drawn, serious. "Perhaps," he murmured. "But I shall never need to test myself, shall I?"

"Don't you care—about anything?" she cried. "Anything at all?"

He looked at the soft pastel shade of her gown, at her apricot complexion, at her parted lips. Slowly, very slowly, he shook his head. "If I did, I might care enough about my life to risk losing it, wouldn't I? How I envy those who do! And you, Tanitchka? Do you care enough to refuse Solomon Moisseievitch Halperin?"

She tossed her head with a fierce movement. "I can't stand him! But what else lies in store for me? To be a spinster, because of this absurd war, which threatens to kill off all the Frenchmen, the British, the Russians, and yes, the Austrians and the Germans? I don't want to be a spinster, to live at home, in Mama's house, following her around like a faithful mouse—like Sonia! Oh, Ossip, what choice do I have?"

"You don't have much respect for my sister, do you?" he said tersely.

"Do you? She couldn't keep him, and that's the truth. A country boy, and she couldn't hold on to him! What is there to respect?" Tania's color was rising.

Ossip's blue eyes, like piercing sapphires, glimmered at her. "At least she had a marriage proposal, my love," he replied, his words almost a whisper. Her head jerked up, her eyes widened, her lips pulled back from her small pearly teeth. He shrugged. A cynical smile played over his features. "Don't ask for trouble, and you won't get it," he said amiably.

In her haste to leave Ossip's office, Tania nearly collided with Gino, who was opening the door, his face red with excitement. He stepped back, startled, to make way for his cousin, whom he knew to despise him. She looked, he thought, like a lioness on the rampage, and had he not possessed such tremendous news he would have been amused to learn what Ossip had done to upset Tania. Politely, he made a small bow, but she shrugged her shoulders at him and raised her eyebrows. "Russian boor," was her only comment, and it left Gino openmouthed with bewilderment. He did not know whether to laugh or to protest.

"Don't worry about it," Ossip told him when she had departed, and he had closed the door upon her. "You merely exemplify all that she is angry with. Uncle Sasha told me this morning that he has given her two weeks—two weeks!—in which to make up her mind about Sioma Halperin. She is furious with Sioma, with her father, with the Tzar for making war—and with me, of course, for not being more heroic and sweeping her off her feet. All this makes her angrier than ever with Mother Russia, but don't ask why. She finds you the epitome of what she calls 'the Russian spirit'—hence, my chap, you're it!"

"I see—only of course, I don't!" his brother replied, sitting down. Sliding a thin cigarette forward in the gold monogrammed case which he now carried everywhere in his waistcoat pocket, Ossip held it toward Gino, who somewhat shyly and clumsily extracted the long white cylinder from the pack. Bending over his desk, Ossip lit it for him, then repeated the process for himself. Finally, he sat back, expectant. The two brothers were on the best of terms, for they were of such different temperaments that they did not have to compete upon a single point.

"So," Ossip stated, blowing smoke in delicate rings above his head. "Do you come from a class?"

"Better," Gino replied. He leaned forward in his chair. "I have quit the University. No, no, let me finish, it is too important! I have just enlisted! My only fear is that the damned war will be over too soon, before my training is complete and I can accomplish something. But I'm in. I'm in!"

Ossip's lips parted, and he paled. Then, on a quick intake of breath, he rose and crossed the short distance between him and his brother. Gino stood up and they embraced, their arms tight around each other. "Congratulations, old chum," Ossip stammered. "But Mama? She so hoped the war would be over before you turned twenty-one!"

"This is not the time to be thinking of our mother," Gino said quietly. "Tania is right: all I can think of is Russia, and her success!"

When, five weeks later, Mathilde learned of her younger son's enlistment in the Russian army, Gino was already training for the cavalry at the garrison of Pskov. She fell back against the cushions of her sofa, her eyes full of tears. "The Baron has failed you," Johanna said, bringing over the sachet of smelling salts. "He should have seen to it that the boy listen to reason, and not break your heart."

But Sonia, thin and white, turned upon her erstwhile governess, and spoke through clenched teeth: "No, Juanita," she said. "It was you who helped to take the manhood away from my older brother. But this time you were gone, and God protected Gino. He is in God's hands, and no place outranks that."

She did not feel that this was the right time to divulge the news which she herself had received by the same post: Tania had written to announce her engagement to Solomon Moisseievitch Halperin, the same Sioma who had once filled her with revulsion. While Sonia's heart pounded rapidly with mingled pride and concern for Gino, with pathos for her mother, and with rage toward Johanna, a strange sense of being in a dream-world was taking hold of her senses. I must be unwell, she thought, and touched her temple. There is war, my brother has enlisted—and Tania is marrying that unhealthy upstart from Kiev? To her dismay, she began to laugh, a high-pitched, uncontrolled titter. Tania, for whom Petersburg was démodé, for whom only Paris or London would do, Tania who had so mocked her when she had pledged her troth to Kolya, a mere provincial?

"She can't continue like this," Mathilde was saying over her head, and Sonia realized that she had fallen across the bed. "The sewing, the long hours at the milk cooperative— and she doesn't eat sufficiently . . ."

Still Sonia laughed, though tears were streaming down her face. In the same town as he, in the same town: she, Tania, will be in his city, Kiev, she thought. Her heart constricted with pride for Gino, and with numbing fear. She fell into a troubled sleep, and did not know that she was being undressed and laid in bed.

While General Pavel Rennenkampf attempted his sally against West Prussia on behalf of the Tzar, Baron David, head of the Jewish community of Petrograd, pondered the Russian Pan-Slavic feeling and determined that it had merit both for the Russian people as a nation, and for the Jews of Poland. No matter how constrained the Jews were in Russia, they could not help but fare better than under German and Austrian domination. The Baron gathered his cohorts in his study, and spoke to them of an idea. Russia was already evacuating refugees from the fighting areas. He proposed to send special trains to Poland, to bring the Jews of that country to a better environment. "Once they are here, it will be up to our community to find work and housing for them," he declared.

While the discussions took place, Ossip sat quietly in the background. The capital was rapidly emptying of all the men he knew, and business was slow. When David said that he would need leaders to escort the refugees on the trains, he felt his father's pale blue eyes resting upon him, and he chewed the tip of his fountain pen. An ironic smile glittered on his face. "Yes, I shall go," he answered. "I may as well make myself useful. Somehow, there is little glamor in being the only available bachelor remaining in town." But his father did not laugh. He merely nodded, and addressed another aspect of the problem.

So, while Ludendorff drove the Russian soldiers from

East Prussia, Ossip took several days off from the bank. He
did not relish his task, and in his heart he did not even find
it necessary. The Jews were always being maligned; how
would Russia, with its inherent anti-Semitism, help them?
The economy was going downhill: it would be no easy job
to feed these new mouths, to find work for these displaced
people. But he was past caring, and certainly did not care
enough to oppose his father. He flicked an ash with a
measure of bitterness, and was surprised at his own emotion.

He was lonely. He had always preferred the company of
women to that of men, perhaps out of an inbred fear that
men might hurt him physically. The single exception had
been Volodia, whose loss he had deeply mourned. Now,
during the early part of the war, Ossip frequently found
himself wondering what might have impelled his stolid,
reflective young friend to enlist in such a rash expedition.
Volodia had never confided in him affairs of the heart:
Could it be that a woman had hurt him by sending him
away? His own sister, Sonia? No, thought Ossip: impossible! For while he had seen Sonia with the painting of his
schoolmates, and wondered about her feelings for Volodia,
surely she would have kept her feelings secret. It was inconceivable to think that Volodia would have returned
such a love, to the point of risking his life . . . Yet, Ossip
now recalled certain fleeting glimpses of his friend, which
in hindsight were like a revelation. At the time they had
occurred, Ossip had been too engrossed in his own problems with Natasha to notice. He remembered the summer
at the Tagantsev estate, the piano sessions. His sister's lum-
inous gray eyes, Volodia's soft words. No, it was all too
fantastic!

Perhaps it was Gino's resemblance to Volodia, both
physical and mental, that had drawn Ossip to his young
brother now that he was a man. Ossip missed Gino. His
good nature, his unthreatening manhood, were gone from
the Gunzburg house. Ossip worried about his trusting

young brother. He truly was touched by him, as few individuals touched his cynical soul. He did not feel, as Gino did, that Russia had a mission, that its citizens should accept war simply to be patriotic. In fact, he was totally opposed to violence of any kind. And Tania was right, he thought. The Germans were no worse than anyone else. This war was absurd, as were all wars and all prejudices. Gino's problem, thought Ossip, was that he never questioned anything or anyone he loved; whereas his own problem was that he questioned altogether too much, and accepted nothing whatsoever on faith.

David's librarian and private secretary, Alexei Fliederbaum, who had served the Baron in the Uhlans at Lomzha, had a son, Dmitri, known to all as Mitya, and whom David had sent to the Conservatory of Music. Sometimes this amusing young man accompanied Ossip on the convoy trains. They would sit together on the way to Poland, smoking elongated cigarettes and speaking of the arts. Ossip found Mitya cultured and agreeable, although his emulation of Ossip was obvious. It seemed ludicrous that these two calm young men in their fitted coats discussed literature and opera on their way to gather hundreds of ill-clad, frightened refugees in a blighted, warring territory. But Ossip had few people with whom to speak, and although Mitya was not of his class, Ossip accepted him in an easy manner.

It was not so when Mitya's older brother, Shura, accompanied him. Shura was an embittered, sour-faced man, for whom the world was a place of evil. Ossip kept his distance from him, and Shura stared down his long, thin nose at this young master with his dandified airs.

Because he was unhampered by pity or anything more than a vague compassion, Ossip's feelings hardly came into play during the organization of the refugees, and so he managed his job quite well and with expediency. He was a gentleman, and treated his charges with quiet if sometimes urgent courtesy. He was like a conscientious shepherd with a flock that he intended to deliver promptly and without mishap, but which did not trouble his state of mind. What would happen to these people afterward was not part of his concern.

One rainy morning his train arrived in Poland, and after he had organized the mob awaiting him at the station into compartments, he sighed and ordered coffee from an attendant. He watched as Shura herded the men and women roughly into their boxcars, and saw how some old men, bedraggled and tired, could hardly lift their battered luggage. Suddenly he felt a tug at his sleeve, and when he looked down he was startled to find a small girl, her impish face circled with black hair, her cheeks pale with hunger. "Please," she said in Yiddish, "would you buy me a sweet? I am very hungry."

"But where are your parents?" he asked.

She pointed to the train with her head. "In there. Mama is going to have a baby when we get to Petrograd."

"Let's hope not till then, please God," Ossip murmured. "But you?" he asked again of the little girl. "Why are you begging?"

"Mama doesn't feel well, and Papa has no kopecks to spare. You look like someone who might have money—lots of money, even!"

"Such as maybe a whole ruble?" he said, and squatted beside her. His face broke into a smile. He fished for his wallet, and removed a bill. "There now, it isn't polite to beg things of strangers, so perhaps we'd better introduce ourselves." He motioned for the attendant who had brought him coffee, and ordered a sweet roll with butter on it. He gave the man his bill and turned back to the small girl. "My name is Ossip," he announced.

"I'm Verotchka. Pleased to meet you." She bobbed a quick curtsy. He took her small hand and brought it elaborately to his lips, kissing it. She began to giggle. The attendant returned with change, a napkin, and the roll. Ossip handed it to the girl, who sank her small white teeth into it with moans of pleasure. Butter dripped down her chin. Ossip dabbed at it with the napkin.

All at once he heard a rough male voice, and Shura was standing above them, his hands upon his hips. "For God's sake!" he cried with ill-concealed annoyance.

Ossip rose. Placing one hand on Verotchka's head, he regarded the other man coldly. "You don't believe in God, my friend," he stated with infinite contempt. Then he shoved the coins into the small girl's coat pocket. "Keep these for another roll, little swallow," he murmured gently, and he pushed her ahead of him onto the train.

As he stared at the dismal countryside, Ossip experienced a strange emotion as he thought of Vcrotchka. Some day, he said to himself, I shall have a daughter. But I should like for her to be a child already, and not a mere baby, so that I may know her as a person . . . Then he shook his head with scorn.

In November, Gino wrote his brother to invite him to visit him in Pskov, where he was in military training, and so Ossip packed a bag and was careful to include his new camera, so that he might snap pictures of Gino for his mother and sister. He found Gino sporting a mustache, which made him look dashing, as did his khaki uniform. Together, they walked around the city, talking. Gino was full of stories about garrison life, but more than anything, he wanted to fight. He had become, he said with naive pride as he tapped his rifle, quite an expert marksman.

As they talked, Ossip snapped photographs of Gino near a fountain, in front of a store, on a busy street. After a while, a policeman came up to them and stopped Ossip. "This is a military zone, sir," he explained. "Did you realize that you are not permitted to take pictures of public buildings or bridges?"

"Oh, I am well aware of that," Ossip replied. "My brother here has already informed me. I have taken no illegal photographs, I can assure you."

"Nevertheless, I shall have to confiscate your camera," the policeman stated. Ossip shrugged and handed over his apparatus, but he was annoyed. What if it were not returned? It was an expensive new model.

But he was able to reach Petrograd with news of Gino for his father, and wrote his mother and sister a long letter describing how impressed he had been with his brother, the young soldier. Soon after, Ossip received a package from Pskov, in which he found not only his undamaged camera, but also his film, fully developed for him. "We deeply apologize for your inconvenience," wrote the Chief of Police. Ossip mailed the choicest photographs to his mother and his sister.

Almost at once after Ossip's pleasant visit, Gino was commissioned as lieutenant in a cavalry regiment of the Guard, and was sent to the Baltic provinces. The weary Russian troops had lost the fight for Silesia and Poznan. Now new forces were being sent out, of which Gino was a part, as he had so ardently wished.

Gino found that he quite enjoyed military life on the front. The other officers with whom he bivouacked were pleasant enough, and although he was younger than most, they accepted him. He was tall, strong, and on his right hand he wore a massive gold ring with the Gunzburg crest. He had inherited this ring from his Grandfather Yuri, and his mother had received it in a package from her mother in Stuttgart, and had mailed it to him shortly before his departure for Pskov. He wore the ring unselfconsciously, and thought nothing of it. He was a soldier as were all the men, and his title was immaterial.

One morning before the New Year a letter came for him. He had been resting in his tent, reading, when another lieutenant, Tomasov, entered, holding the letter. "Baron

Evgeni de Gunzburg," he declaimed. "I did not know you had a title, Gino."

"It is not important," smiled the young man, accepting his missive. "It's from my sister, Sonia, in Geneva," he said. "I wonder how my mother is."

"It is amusing, that," Tomasov commented, raising his eyebrows. "You must be a rare bird. I have never before encountered Jewish nobility."

"The Rothschilds started it all long before us," Gino replied mildly. He tore open his envelope and began to read.

But Tomasov would not be deterred. "Seriously," he continued, "I am amazed that they gave you a commission. I understood that that was no longer a practice."

"My religious convictions will not be called upon when it is time to shoot the Hun," Gino replied somewhat testily.

"No, of course not," the other said.

But near them sat a captain whose surly disposition was well known. "Nevertheless, Tomasov has a point," he inserted. "How bizarre that none of us noticed how unusual the presence of our fine young Yid here is—"

Gino flushed brightly, and stood up. "It is not necessary to be insulting," he declared. "I was hiding nothing. Anyone who cared to find out would have learned my religion. Tomasov did, not long ago. And as for my title, there is no need to parade it here in the army—our ranks suffice."

"Indeed," the captain said, and turned away.

Gino found that he could not resume his reading of Sonia's letter. His heart was beating fiercely and his temples were wet. But he calmed himself with silent exhortation.

A week later, he was called to his colonel's tent, and there he was stripped of his lieutenant's insignia. To his unspoken query, evident in his brown eyes liquid with humiliation, the colonel shook his head sadly, and sighed. "We knew of your religion when you enlisted, and we chose not to make an issue of it, hoping that you would have sufficient sense to be discreet. Now we have no choice but to demote you. We need good officers, and for me that was more important than your religious beliefs. But the regulations are clear: no Jew can hold a commission in the Tzar's army. If you had said nothing, you would have offended no one. You would have made an excellent officer."

"My father was," Gino said.

"Ah, yes, but that was long ago. That was when the army was composed of gentlemen. This one is composed of ruffians in the garb of gentlemen, my dear Gunzburg. Anyway—good luck to you in your new unit."

Red with anger and frustration, his eyes smarting, Gino exited from the colonel's tent a simple soldier. But they don't have me yet! he thought with fierceness. I am a Russian, and my country needs me. I shall show them, when the time comes for battle. He gritted his teeth and clenched his fists, wishing that he could cry as he had as a child. His heart, he thought, would not break, for valor was necessary to save his country.

In speaking of her daughter Tatiana's impending marriage, Baroness Rosa de Gunzburg told an acquaintance in Petrograd: "No, they are not at all distingué, my dear, and there's no doubt that Tanitchka will add luster to their family tree. But don't forget that they provide sugar to our army, and stand to make a considerable profit from this. I have heard it mentioned in high circles that in this sugar campaign alone they will sell seven million rubles' worth to the troops. Seven million rubles!"

"But surely you will not have a grand wedding, because of the state of our nation?" the acquaintance asked.

Rosa arched her fine black eyebrows. "We have but one daughter," she declared. "Would you have me give her away wearing beggar's rags?"

Fifteen

———————————•———————————

In the Baltic Provinces, bone-tired troops engaged in valiant battles as well as flustered skirmishes with the enemy,
sometimes winning a fort, more frequently losing their
hold over some ground that they had gained the day before. Gino was strangely exhilarated by this experience, for
he was young and at the heart of the action. It no longer
embittered him that he had lost his insignia. Starting out as
a simple soldier, he had discovered that the sturdy young
peasants who shouldered their rifles next to him were more
like him than his mother had educated him to assume.
Soon he was promoted to corporal, then rapidly to sergeant. He knew that he would rise no further, but he
accepted this now with equanimity. Let it be, he thought,
there is much that I can accomplish as a noncommissioned
warrior. Perhaps more, with these few good people.

He now had eight men under him, all peasants. They
called him "Baron," for Evgeni Davidovitch seemed too
complex, and a more familiar appellation, though frequently used in army ranks, seemed to them out of place.
And yet, if he felt superior at all, it was only in respect to
his learning. Often in the evenings he would gather his men
around a campfire and while they ate their meager ration

of wheat and onions, he would teach them geography and history. They, in turn, told him about their wives and sisters, their farms, their crops, their gripes against their district governments, the Zemstvos. But when they talked about defeat, or the futility of this war, he would become fierce, and would cow them. Yet he could not explain why this war was so necessary, only that it was.

The men were tired, and supplies were not always adequate. Frequently Gino noticed that the enemy was better furnished, that their guns were more recent models, that a strange, burning gas could decimate the Russians in one swift release. Nevertheless, he urged his small band to action. He was fascinated by his colonel, a deeply religious man, who would give the call to battle and then, as he applied the spurs to his horse, would cross himself and murmur a prayer, sometimes in the midst of flying debris and under the roar of a cannon. The colonel was never wounded. "There must be something to his faith," Gino said to one of the young men under his command, Vassya, a cowherd from the Crimea.

"But your God is not the same as his," Vassya retorted with bewilderment.

Gino smiled. "I think that under fire, God, the God of all of us, forgets these details."

In the spring of 1915, Russia was attempting to hold on to Poland, Lithuania, and Courland, and was even threatened in its own Byelorussia, and in the Ukraine, which wanted independence from the rest of the nation. The Germans were everywhere, giving encouragement to the separatists in the Ukraine. One of Gino's soldiers was from that province and in the trenches he would moan, returning fire with slow movements that threatened his life and that of his companions. Gino upbraided him. "That's it, Gorik!" he shouted, his eyes flashing. "No rations tonight if you aren't with us all the way. Do a job well, or don't do it at all. If you want to leave, then choose outright the path of desertion!" But the youth trembled, and looked away from his sergeant. The idea of being deprived of food was more overwhelming than his feelings of provincial loyalty.

One morning, Gino was instructed by his captain to attempt to locate the enemy headquarters, which were known to be nearby. He took Vassya with him, and in the scarred countryside they proceeded with caution. The captain had chosen Gino because of his extraordinary capacity for long walks, an endurance that he had developed during his year in Hanover. He also knew that Gino spoke fluent German, and could bring back essential information. The two young men slid from bush to stump, pausing each time fire rang out in the distance.

All at once, pinpricks of alertness arose along Gino's spine, and he reached out and touched his companion without turning to look at him. To their right stood what appeared to be an abandoned farmhouse. Gino bit the nail of his index finger, and breathed as silently as he knew how. Something was not quite as it should have been. Very slowly, he crawled on his belly, camouflaging his khaki uniform between bits of underbrush. He could sense Vassya's progress behind him as they moved like slithering snakes, perspiring in fear.

Suddenly they saw a slim figure emerge from the farmhouse, look about, adjust his helmet, and walk to the small well in front of the barn. Gino looked at Vassya, and the young man nodded: the figure in the distance was wearing a German helmet. They waited as the enemy soldier pumped some water into a can, and walked back to the farmhouse. They heard voices, crisp and merry, as the door opened to readmit him. There were at least a handful of men inside, but maybe more, maybe as many as two dozen. Gino and Vassya made their way back to their own camp, and Gino told the captain about the farmhouse.

"I want you to return there, with your squad, and approach with caution. If there is only a handful—then you can take them. But if there are too many, send one of the men back to me and we shall reinforce you," the captain ordered. Gino saluted and gathered his group together. He explained the situation quickly. Then he took the lead, and sandwiched his men between himself and Vassya, who brought up the rear. They duplicated their previous trip, keeping themselves well hidden. Now and then Gino's arm would reach out to forcibly put down a head, to silence a whine or a whisper. They reached the farmhouse at noon, with a blazing sun above their heads. Gino made a motion with his arm, signaling the men to spread themselves out around the farmhouse, covering a side and a back entrance. Then he threw a hand grenade toward the main door.

From the moment he released the weapon, Gino's mind was filled with conflicting sensations. He experienced a total, gut-contracting fear, and for an instant he did not know what to do. Then, calm emerged, the fear receded, and excitement began to penetrate his veins. "Keep hidden!" he called out, as a volley of rifle shots was aimed from the farmhouse. A machine gun protruded from an attic window, and faces appeared surrounding it. Gino shouldered his gun and fired, and glass shattered. A figure toppled like a dismembered scarecrow from an upper story. His men followed suit, aiming from their hiding places. He thought, licking his dry lips: Anna was right, it is the Russian peasant who is most underestimated. They are not losing their heads, not even the simplest of them. He fired again, carefully.

How long the skirmish lasted he could not tell, but suddenly Vassya was by his side, whispering, "We're giving out. Shall I go back for the captain?"

Gino thought of his group, of the eight men who trusted him with their lives. He nodded tersely, and Vassya slithered off like a desert animal, quick and noiseless. Gino threw a grenade toward a window, and heard a cry. Someone had been hit. But what about his own men? Were they hurt? Were they dead? Fire came from his left, and he sighed. At least one of them was all right.

They held out until the captain arrived with two other sergeants and their fresh mounted squads, and with them they brought the field artillery drawn by very tired horses. The captain crouched by Gino's side and placed a hand upon his shoulder. "This is good," he muttered. "Very good indeed." He ordered the cannon to be fired. But as Gino turned, he saw the men gingerly carry Kostya away.

Within minutes of the first cannonfire, the front door was opened, and a white flag, suspended from a rifle butt, was held out toward the Russians. "Come out, those that are alive!" the captain shouted. He turned to Gino and asked him to translate the message. The young man cleared his throat, found it constricted, and began to deliver the words.

To his great surprise, the door creaked, and one youth, tall, blond, and very pale, appeared in the archway. He was bareheaded, and clutched his stomach. A surge of compassion knotted Gino's nerves. He half-stepped toward the apparition but his captain stopped him. "How many are you?" he demanded, and repeated the question in halting German.

The pale young man fell to his knees, and whispered something. Gino moved to him, put a hand on his arm, and said gently, "How many?"

"I am the lieutenant of record," the young wounded soldier replied, and a light flickered in his blue eyes as he regarded Gino. "There were . . . two dozen of us. Took us . . . by surprise. Headquarters for the day, about to move on, awaiting orders . . ." He made the feeblest of motions toward the farmhouse: "Inside . . . six wounded . . ." he whispered, and gagged on a flow of bile.

The captain had reached them, and now requested Gino's translation. But all at once feverish hands seized Gino, and the young wounded soldier, blood trickling from his parted lips, spoke urgently. "You—" he said to Gino, "you speak . . . excellent German. You . . . are a gentleman. I am going to die. Please, help me. I want . . . to send a message to my parents . . ."

Gino did not even search his captain's face for approval. He reached inside his coat and removed a crumpled and soiled strip of paper, and a pencil stub. "I shall be glad to write the words for you," he answered. "My name is Evgeni—Eugene—de Gunzburg, and I shall forward your letter."

"Thank you," the German mumbled. Gino sat down beside him and placed the boy's head upon his lap. The young soldier murmured, "I am the only son of General von Falkenhayn, and I am nineteen. My father is fighting somewhere in Russia, I am not certain exactly where. You will have to send this to my mother, in Germany." He gave Gino an address, then began the dictation of his message. Gino bent his face toward the paper and wrote rapidly: "My dear parents, I am fatally wounded and shall die in a short while. Please do not allow this to break your hearts, for I am dying for the fatherland, and love you dearly." The page blurred before Gino's eyes, and he placed the pencil in the limp fingers of the young man. Closing his own strong fingers over that cold hand, he guided it in a final signature.

The blue eyes gleamed toward Gino. A smile cracked the young face. "You have been good to me," the dying man murmured. He gasped painfully on Gino's lap. "I . . . thank you . . . with all my heart." And his hand fell away from Gino's. The brilliant blue of his eyes stared at the Russian, and Gino drew the lids down over them and slowly removed the boy's head from his knees, placing it carefully upon the moist farm earth. He folded the paper in his hands, putting it in his coat pocket. Then he dropped his head into his upturned palms and began to sob.

It was Vassya who came to him and touched his arm. "That was a kind thing you did, Baron," he said tentatively.

But Gino pushed him roughly aside. "What 'kind thing'?"

he cried. "He was nineteen years old, the same as I—and I have no idea if it was my own bullet that killed him!"

"If not him, Baron, then you," Vassya replied. He shook his head mournfully. Gino gazed at him, stunned, dazed, then followed his resolute steps back to the remainder of the troop. Gurneys were being sent into the farmhouse for the German wounded. Gino's mind flashed with the vision of little Kostya.

"I shall recommend you for the Cross of St. George," the captain told him. "What you accomplished was of utmost bravery and resourcefulness."

"Vassya stated it better than I, sir," Gino answered with bitterness. "It was my men against the enemy. There was little choice in what I could have done."

"Nevertheless, it was a splendid display of action," the captain retorted.

But Gino, head bent, was thinking of something else. He would have to send that letter, somehow, to the boy's mother, the wife of one of the top Prussian generals. How could he, a Russian soldier on the battlefront, achieve this miracle?

In Geneva, Sonia had been contacted by a young woman from the Red Cross who received and sent letters to and from the occupied territories where no other mail was permitted. Now that she had become an expert in the sewing of pajamas, she did this at night until the dawn's pink rays pierced the sky. She only worked at the milk cooperative once a week, and began going to help at the Red Cross. It was more important, she thought, for her to help transcribe letters for the sensitive eyes of the censors, than for her to wash bottles. Any young woman might do that, whereas she had been approached because of her fluency in Russian, French, English, and German. She might accomplish more work than someone who knew fewer languages, and therefore she felt duty-bound to perform this task.

She would mount the steps to a large hall where long tables were spaced about, with seven or eight chairs around each table. Young girls and old women sat diligently copying missives destined for those in Poland or the east of France, leaving out lines that might be considered compromising. She also did the reverse, checking through letters written by those living under enemy domination. Sonia had a clear, even script, and day in and day out she would sit at her place, her posture erect, her right hand racing across pages and pages of words that she copied and edited, eventually without even comprehending them. Like her sewing, the work had become a routine to her.

Sonia had no free time, and therefore no time to think, as she had done in the kitchen of the milk cooperative. She merely labored, under the fearful gaze of Mathilde. Whenever her mother would offer her tea and biscuits, she would shake her head with its coiled black tresses, and reply, "It's all right, Mama. I'm not hungry." Sometimes she would sit at her rented piano, but her mother knew that she was doing so out of a sense of obligation toward her, and not from any inner joy or desire. Clasping her hands to her breast, Mathilde cried out one day, "How like your father you have become! Duty, duty. Is there no life for the likes of you?"

Sonia merely smiled, and arched her brows. She was hardly accustomed to bursts of emotion from her placid mother. She looked into her mother's eyes and said gently, "During such times the world has need of people like Papa and me. Or at least like me. Papa is a brilliant man, a linguist, a scholar, a diplomat, and his talents are always in demand. I am simply a worker, who does what needs to be done. There is no time now for joy, or even for a life of my own. Later, when the war is over, I shall dance, and sing duets, and eat delicacies. But now I cannot. I suppose you are right, that I am obsessed by duty. But I am what I am." She thought wryly of her beloved brother, Ossip. How like their mother he was! Ossip, so gay and charming, would now have found his Sonitchka an unbearable bore, as Mathilde probably did. But it could not be helped.

If Sonia spent so much time away from the Pension de la Grande Bretagne, a small part of her reason was selfish. Johanna's nervousness was making life even more unpleasant than the circumstances warranted. With age, Mathilde had grown plumper, more gray, but her skin was still smooth, her figure agreeable. Johanna, on the other hand, had lost that marvelous supple slenderness, the full breast, and had become thinner with the years, so that she now resembled a high voltage wire, taut and sinewy. Her eyes were the same, almond-shaped and aquamarine, and her hair was still gold, but now it, too, was thin. She made a big to-do over her nursing duties, and complained endlessly of fatigue each morning. If she noticed Sonia's loss of weight or her pallor, she failed to mention them to Mathilde. In fact, she spent her time with Mathilde fretting, sighing, pacing the carpeted sitting room, picking up a book and then thrusting it down impatiently.

One day at breakfast, Mathilde broached a familiar subject with her friend: she wanted to leave Switzerland to return to Russia where she belonged. But Johanna flew into a rage. She berated Mathilde, who sat eating her meal: "You think that you could do some good by merely being in the same country as Gino—that's nonsense! As for Ossip, you moan about missing him, but a young man such as he has better things to do than spend time with his mother. And then, the way you carry on about Sonia! She is strong, and willing. One thing I have noticed about Sonia —she only does what she wants, the selfish girl, and to the devil with other people! Aren't you at all happy to be here with me—away from your household worries?"

Mathilde carefully swallowed, then dabbed at her lower lip with a lace napkin. "I long to return home, Johanna," she stated. Dear God, she added silently, now I would even welcome David and his obsessions, his religious and patriotic fervor . . . She sighed and said, "These are strenuous times. You do not need to accompany me if the voyage will upset you."

But at the idea of such a trip without her, Johanna shrieked with anger and terror. Mathilde took her calmly into the bathroom and sponged her forehead with cold water. "It was only for your sake that I suggested it," she murmured, her sapphire eyes gleaming with tears. "You are now in a neutral nation. Clearly you have less reason than I to wish to return to Petersburg—Petrograd."

Some days later, the pension bellboy delivered a letter from the Russian front, which Mathilde tore open with trembling fingers. Her mouth, as she read the news, formed a small circle. "This is extraordinary, indeed," she commented. Turning to her daughter, she said, "Gino sends me a letter dictated to him by the dying son of a Prussian general, von Falkenhayn. He writes: 'Mama dear, Upon my honor I promised this boy that I would make this message reach his mother, in Germany. No one can help me but you, who are in a neutral zone and can send mail anywhere. Here is the address of Frau von Falkenhayn.' But I can't write to this woman, can I? I, who am not only an enemy but a Jewess as well? I fear she would find me indelicate, and her grief would be all the greater, wouldn't it?"

"Gino is a sensitive person, Mama," Sonia answered pensively. "He must have considered his alternatives at length before appealing to you. And how can you even think that any woman might find you lacking in taste or propriety? You must write to her, and you will find the proper words. For, after all, she is—or was—a mother like you, with a beloved child at the front. She will not find your compassion offensive."

Mathilde sat down at her secretary, and composed a short letter for this lady unknown to her, whose husband's name was familiar in wartime news, this grand Prussian lady who had lost a son, but who was now residing at the estate of her daughter, the Countess von Bismarck. She wrote in German, which she had learned during her childhood in Paris under the tutelage of a German governess. Thinking of Gino and of her own terror, she selected her words with sparing care. Then she slipped her note as well as the one dictated to Gino into a heavy vellum envelope embossed with the family "G." "And that is the end of this episode," she sighed. "She will not deign to answer me."

But six weeks later, Sonia handed her mother a sealed envelope, and when Mathilde had opened it and scanned its contents, tears came to her eyes. She handed her daughter the sheet of note paper.

My dear, gentle Baroness [the letter read],

Only you, a mother, can understand how the news of my loss has affected me. At night, when I remember Hans as a baby, and when I think that morning will never come, there is but one thought to assuage my sorrow. And that is that your son befriended him, and helped him in that most arduous task, to face his death. Thank you for your kind words, and for having borne such a son as Eugene, who must be a joy to you, in spite of the distance that separates you from him. When this dismal war is over, I should like to meet you in person.

The signature read: "Lina von Falkenhayn."
"It is time for us to return home, Mama," Sonia said, and there was an urgent note to her voice. "You and Papa need each other now, more than ever."

Anna de Gunzburg, in Lausanne, played with the little boy, Riri, who was nine years old. She painted and gardened; but she was nonetheless aware of the presence of Lenin in Switzerland, and of the ideas which he was propagating in his native country, which was also hers. She knew that the Bolshevik members of the Duma had spoken out in behalf of abandoning the war effort, that they fa-

vored defeat, and that because of this they had been arrested that very spring of 1915. Anna sat in her bedroom,
gazing out toward the blue-green hills, and thought: I am
not certain anymore, of many things. Gino and Sonia want
to crush the Triple Entente and Turkey; Mama and Ossip
only want life to return to what it was before. And Papa?
He too is uncertain. Oh, not about the war, for he supports
his government loyally; but is he fearful for the people, for
their stirred-up emotions? And what about Lenin? Is he so
single-minded that he does not care about the peasants, or
the poor, so long as he can rule? Is it right to forego one
system for another that is equally oppressive? Anna wondered what Vanya would say.

Oh, Vanya, Vanya, she would cry out, her heart suddenly aching fiercely. She would squeeze shut her eyelids
and shake her red mass of hair, and say aloud, "No, I must
not try to learn what has become of him, or wonder if he
still cares! But wherever he is, I am certain that he is a
leader among men. And I shall always love him, and the
memory of our time together."

In the spring, she went to Stuttgart to retrieve her grandmother, Baroness Ida, who had been in a sanatorium.
"After all," she had written her mother, "Grandmother
cannot live comfortably with you in your pension, but she
will have a garden here, and Riri. There is no one like a
child to lighten the atmosphere." Mathilde was glad. At
least her mother would be out of Germany and in neutral
territory, and Anna and Dalia were strong and would care
for her. As for Riri . . . Mathilde was grateful that her
mother had always resided in France, and had never met
the Bersons.

When she and Sonia went to Lausanne to see Baroness
Ida, she refused to allow Johanna de Mey to accompany
them. "You and Anna have never gotten on, and you have
nursing duties here," she had stated. Johanna had been
startled at her tone, insistent and almost hard in its urgency. Mathilde had sensed her friend's shock, and had

placed a hand upon her arm, adding, "Don't you see? Mama has just recovered from a great loss, and a debilitating illness. Any sort of disharmony would be most upsetting to her nerves."

When Mathilde and Sonia returned to Geneva after their brief trip, Sonia did not look well. She hardly touched her plate at mealtimes, and was white, with blue circles under her eyes. Often, during the night, the bathroom door remained locked, until both Mathilde and Johanna realized that something was seriously wrong with her. They had no need to take her to a specialist, for an excellent Geneva physician declared without the slightest doubt that Sonia was suffering from enteritis, a bad form of colitis. Her mother took her to the Ballaigues, in the Jura Mountains, and there she remained for the summer, restricted to a special diet once again. She was exhausted from her war relief work. Now, she breathed the crisp mountain air and allowed the children of her hotel to surround her chaise longue on the open porch, where she would tell them fantastic stories that she invented on the spur of the moment.

In the fall, when Sonia had recovered, Mathilde knew that she could no longer delay their return to Petrograd. God only knew what conditions were like in Russia, but David was not healthy, and the boys . . . Encouraged by Johanna, she proposed that Sonia remain with Anna and their grandmother in Switzerland.

But Sonia was outraged. "Mama, have you gone mad?" she cried passionately, her gray eyes darting blue sparks of fire.

Mathilde stood back, shocked at the way her daughter had spoken to her. "But my dear, you have been sick . . ." she stammered.

"And Papa suffers from angina pectoris! He is no longer his strong self. God knows, Ossip is unreliable, much as we love him dearly. I would entrust you to Gino, but he is at the front. Don't you see? I must go with you. You will need me!"

"Your mother has me," Johanna cut in.

"But you are not her family!"

The two of them stared at each other, Sonia's hatred at last showing as nakedly as Johanna's. Mathilde trembled, wishing that somehow peace might be restored, tempers calmed. This was more dreadful than she had ever feared. At length she spoke up: "Very well, Sonia. There is no need to create such a scene. We only meant that the voyage will be dangerous and that we shall not have an easy time. In your condition this is hardly safe. But if you insist, I cannot stop you from coming."

"Not even God could stop me," her daughter replied with a steady look of steel gray.

Because of Johanna de Mey's sullen ill humor, it was Sonia who organized the trip. They would go via Paris, London, and Norway, and from the north of Norway travel the whole length of Finland until they reached Petrograd. It was the only way to circumvent enemy territory. They would travel by train and ship, and as there were no longer any porters at the stations, Anna had painted green and yellow circles on their luggage, so that they might pick it out right away and not risk losing part of it. The week before their departure, Russian refugees clustered round them at the pension, begging them to deliver messages to beloved members of their families, to sons and husbands at the front. "You know that we are not supposed to bring any written material with us," Mathilde gently reproached them. But Sonia stood forward, and allowed each person, one by one, to give her his message. And each day she endeavored to memorize them.

"It is really quite a straightforward method," Sonia explained to her mother. "I have Papa's good memory. Each morning, before breakfast, and each night in bed, I have been enumerating the messages and counting them off on my fingers. To these poor people this represents a sacred mission, and I could not let them down, any more than you could have let Gino down in the matter of the Falken-hayns."

"But how many messages do you have?" Mathilde asked.

"Forty, exactly. Eight hands' worth."

"All this wasted energy for people we shall never see again!" Johanna sniffed disdainfully. But Sonia regarded her levelly, and she turned away.

It was October, and a cold, frosty one. The train ride to Paris went smoothly, but there it was discovered that the necessary papers had not been prepared for them as planned. Johanna de Mey openly cursed Sonia, and set out for the Dutch Consulate to prod along the officials of her country. Sonia went to the Russian Consulate and waited patiently in line, a trim figure in muted gray, her small hat perched demurely on the coils of black hair, one egret feather its single ornament. In the meantime, Mathilde went to the home of her brother-in-law, Misha de Gunz-burg, and visited his wife, Clara, and their five-year-old son, Sergei.

After a fortnight, they were able to obtain their traveling papers, and they took a train to Calais, a boat to Dover, and another train to London, which lay shrouded in folds of bleak fog. But because of wartime emergencies, the consulates there too had become tangled in webs of paper-work, and the necessary visas and passports were not ready. Mathilde remained in their hotel, holding her fingers out toward the overworked radiator for warmth, while her daughter stood in line once more, her bones chilled to the marrow.

Ten days later, consumed with impatience, worries concerning Gino, and sensations of infuriating impotence, the three women, papers in hand, took yet another train to Hull, a British port on the North Sea. It had been decided that they would travel to Bergen, in Norway, on the only available passenger ship, a small Norwegian cruiser that could hold some forty people comfortably. When they ar-

rived in Hull, it was evening. The *Haakon VII* stood before
them on the pier, high upon the waves, so high, in fact,
that Sonia was troubled at the sight of it. But she looked
about her and shivered, dismayed. At least sixty people,
indistinct in the mist and the oncoming night, were waiting
to board the *Haakon VII*. "Come on, Mama," she urged
gently, and pushed her mother before her onto the deck.
Johanna de Mey, her back erect and dignified, her features
tightly drawn, climbed on behind Sonia.

The ship began to crowd, and soon Mathilde, Sonia, and
Johanna were pushed against a rail, from which they could
see the sea. The vessel pulled up its anchors, and took off,
dancing like a nutshell over the waters. Sonia was an excellent sailor who had traveled by boat many times, and never
felt too ill to take an interest in the sailing process. Now
she winced. But she said nothing as she gazed at the swirl-
ing gray waters that threatened to upset the hull of the ship
itself.

Before the hour was out they were caught in a tremendous storm, and passengers gathered in small groups that
could hardly be perceived in the blackness. Many fell prey
to seasickness. Mathilde retched, as Sonia held her by the
waist and helped her to lean over the railing. Next to them,
a girl with a Swiss accent kept repeating in French, "This is
exactly like home! Exactly like it! Why do they have foreign countries if everything remains the same everywhere?"
Sonia smiled grimly, clenching her teeth as the deck swayed
back and forth and her feet slipped. Like everyone else,
she was entirely drenched by the spray.

A surge of unquenchable frustration had taken hold of
her, and the more the ship wavered, the less she could
quiet her need to do something. "Please take care of
Mama," she asked Johanna. "I am going to find someone,
if I can." She did not explain, for she hardly knew what
she would do in the raging storm, on this tossing deck. But
she needed to move.

This was hardly easy. The young woman, holding on to her hat with one hand, and to her muff with the other, slid between groups of shrieking people whom she could barely make out, nearly falling on the slippery planks. And then, in the distance, toward the prow, she discerned a white figure moving about, and went toward it, hoping. She saw, as she grew closer, that the figure was indeed one of the ship's officers, giving orders to some sailors. A sudden gust of salt spray threw her against him, and she gasped with shock. "I beg your pardon!" the man cried in English. "You must look for something to hold onto, Madam."

"I wanted to speak with you," she stated evenly. She saw his look of polite annoyance, but nevertheless he took her arm and led her to the nearest railing. "I'm sorry to trouble you," she said humbly. "But—doesn't the ship carry any cargo in its hold? We seem to be buffeted about as if we were inside a floating eggshell!"

An expression of alarm, for one small moment, appeared upon his face, and she began to tremble. "Madam," he said, "leave the sailing to our captain. This is no time for chitchat. We are not rowing for Oxford, or taking a pleasure cruise to the Americas. Don't you have any friends on board?"

She jerked her arm from his patronizing hold and faced him, her gray eyes alive with anger. "I have asked you a simple question. You have evaded an answer. Why?" she asked.

"You are taking up my time," he said gently, turning aside.

But she grabbed his sleeve. "All right," she said tersely, looking around her at the little groups of people crowding the deck. "I shall yell, at the top of my voice, that there is something wrong with the ship! Or," she continued matter-of-factly, "we can speak together as two adults, for five minutes, after which you will no longer be troubled by my presence."

Reluctantly, he turned to her. "God and the captain forgive me," he said in a low voice, in clipped tones. "But even before we pulled into Hull, we spotted an enemy submarine following us. The captain refused to accept any freight, and drastically reduced the ballast, so that we would float high and free above our shadow. In this storm, he could not plot a zigzagging course, so we have proceeded north, to the far north of Norway, in order to throw off our pursuer. There will be no submarines on the lookout there, and then we can make our way back to Bergen, and let the passengers off. Now I beg of you—"

"But," Sonia interrupted indignantly, "how could you have accepted passengers, and endangered all our lives by sailing at all, if you knew you had already been trailed to Hull?"

He sighed. "It was not an easy decision, Madam. But during the war, nations prevail over mere human beings. There is an important diplomatic courier on board. He needed to leave today, and we were his only means."

"Well." Sonia stood numbly in front of him, overwhelmed. She had requested information, but had not expected anything such as this. Now she only nodded. "You have been most kind and courteous," she stated. "I was a nuisance. Forgive me. And God be with you—and with us all!"

She left him by the railing, and made her way back to her mother. How she found her footing, how she wound through the clusters of people in the slippery darkness, she never knew. She did not have time to ponder over the officer's words. It was only when she found herself holding Mathilde by the shoulders that a wave of pure fear, as well as relief that she was no longer lost among strangers, exploded within her. She held her mother and thought: Dear Lord, if I so much as breathe wrong, she will know that there is danger . . . And she started to talk, loudly, incoherently, her phrases jumbling together. Mathilde nodded, nodded again, reassured not by the words, which she could hardly make out, but by the sound of her daughter's strong voice.

Thirty-six hours later scores of bedraggled passengers disembarked from the *Haakon VII*. Once safely ashore, Sonia considered, then rejected, the notion of telling the others about their near-confrontation with the submarine. The Gunzburgs and Johanna then took the train to Oslo, which had been named Christiana when they had been there last, then proceeded far north to the border of Finland, at Hammerfest. At the border they changed to a Russian train, for Finland was part of the Russian Empire, but to reach it they had to travel a mile on foot, between the two customs stations. The snow lay deep, and Sonia could feel her toes tingling with the slush and ice that penetrated through her leather boots. Thankfully, the luggage was being driven from one train to another on sleighs. The three women, Sonia and Johanna sandwiching Mathilde in her sealskin coat, crossed a long bridge, and at length passed through the Russian customs booths. They were on home soil!

The next day they arrived in Petrograd, where David and Ossip and Vova, the coachman, were waiting for them with the landau. David! How pale he looks, Mathilde thought with a surge of emotion as she allowed her husband to clasp her tenderly to him. And he was thinking: How gray she has become in two years! Sonia was rocking back and forth in Ossip's arms, crying and laughing with exhaustion and joy. Only Johanna remained apart, seemingly forgotten in this reunion. "You will be cold if you don't climb in, Johanna Ivanovna," Vova chided her with deference. He and the other servants had always feared her.

There was no blackout, no soldiers on leave in the streets, and because of the immensity of the population, and of the dispensation of the precious white exemption papers, there were still young men around, doffing their hats at ladies. It was almost as if there were no war at all, it was so far away. A welcome numbness spread over Mathilde and Sonia in the landau. But it did not last long. "How is Gino?" they demanded, almost simultaneously.

"He will be here soon," David smiled. "He has a leave coming up, and he saved it till after your return. How is Aunt Ida? And my Annushka?"

As soon as they had unpacked their most essential bags, Sonia left her mother, father, and brother talking animatedly in the sitting room, in front of a roaring fire, with hot tea and cakes. She went into her room, closed the door, unpinned her hair, and let it fall loosely about her frail sloping shoulders. She sat at her secretary and dipped her favorite quill into the inkwell. Her notepaper, a muted gray, lay before her. She pressed her left hand over her aching forehead, then resolutely began to write. She had forty messages to compose for forty Russians scattered all over the nation, and she knew that she must do this now, before she rested and forgot.

Many hours later, she opened her door, and found to her surprise that it was twilight. She tiptoed into the drawing room but it was empty. She halted before her father's study, and heard him cough. She smiled. Her hand was raised to knock, but she reconsidered, and resolved to allow him uninterrupted work. As she was about to walk away she heard a joyful laugh from inside, and a smile spread over her features: Mama was in there, with him. She turned to leave.

In the corridor she passed her mother's boudoir, and saw the flicker of a handheld candle from the room within. The door had been left ajar, and Sonia saw a form huddled upon the bed. She bit her lower lip, uneasily. Soft moaning reached her ears. She ground one fist into the other, and clenched her teeth. Resolutely, she headed back toward her bedroom.

Sonia lay upon her pillows, and an absurd thought entered her mind. What would her father say if he learned that he had a grandson? She wept softly, then stood and dried her eyes. She went to her secretary, which she opened to find the small painting by Mikhail Botkin, and she took it in her hands. Silent tears flowed down her thin cheeks. Volodia . . . She thought of Ossip kissing Natasha, of his hurling himself from the rowboat into the lake, of Volodia holding her in the hallway of the Senate, where his father was arguing against hers. Then she reached farther back into the secretary and brought out a gold locket, which she opened. A young man, painted in enamels, laughed back at her with brilliant eyes. His hair was black and waved elegantly. Kolya . . .

Perhaps Riri is the only grandchild that Papa will ever have, she thought. A piercing doubt filled her chest: Maybe he would, after all, have preferred the fruit of his enemy's own children, rather than this barrenness.

She fell asleep, her mind tortured by recriminations, by wavering faith and loneliness. The homecoming had not been sweet; it had reopened wounds the rawness of which had not softened, as she had thought they had during the long months away. She was twenty-five now, the age at which her mother had been carrying her inside her own body. She fell into uneasy slumber with her fingers clutching her flat belly.

Sixteen

———————————•————————————

As soon as Sonia had become settled once again in her
native city, she went to see her friend, Nina Abelson. Although it was fall, fast turning to winter, the normal brilliance of the social season was quite subdued. Apart from
the few young girls who had turned seventeen or eighteen
that year, and whose mothers gave them a small ball to
allow them entry into a society from which most eligible
young men had vanished, nobody organized social events.
Most families had at least one member at the front, and
could not consider dancing away the hours while their men
were fighting for their lives.

But, Nina said, there was a new fashion, and that was
for girls to turn themselves into angels of mercy—nurses.
"Everyone we know has become one," she stated. "Naturally, there are those of us who are truly dedicated, and
who are willing to go to the front, where the critically
wounded are. Those soldiers who are able to withstand the
trip to Petrograd are not badly off, some even convales-
cing. And many of the girls feel that the uniforms are
flattering, and they enjoy flirting with handsome officers,
bringing them flowers and goodies, writing letters for
them." She smiled and blushed, looking at her hands with
sudden embarrassment. "But I am being cruel. After all,

Sonitchka, they do perform helpful tasks. The men are glad to see a pretty face: it brightens their day. And perhaps I'm jealous. If I were not married, and tied to my home, would I not have joined their ranks?"

"Perhaps not," her friend replied, patting her hand. "I wish I could go to the front. But I tried nursing and I was a dismal failure. I faint when I see a bad wound, and so I cannot be useful. No, Ninotchka, I shall have to discover other means of helping in this wretched war. Are you doing . . . anything else?"

Nina's brown eyes flashed. "Yes," she murmured swiftly. "But it's against the law . . . so maybe you wouldn't be interested."

Sonia began to laugh. "Something illegal? You, Nina? I can't believe it!"

"It's true," the other replied earnestly. She took a swallow of tea. "You know that the government considers all prisoners of war to be traitors. 'One gives up one's life, but one does not give oneself up,' is the motto. And in the camps our poor prisoners watch their French and British comrades receive packages from their homes, to supplement the food—but they receive nothing. So certain ladies have formed a committee to find out the number of Russian prisoners in each camp, and to obtain foodstuffs to be sent every month. There is an office to take care of administrative duties, and to purchase the items to be mailed. And centers have sprung up throughout the city where ladies go to make up packages and wrap them. The Baroness Sokolova chairs our committee, and we are shorthanded. If you could join us, Sonitchka—"

"Oh, but there is no question about it! I shall join tomorrow, of course!" Sonia exclaimed. Her gray eyes sparkled. "You see, my sweet, who is to predict that Gino might not, one day, be a prisoner too? I could not bear to think him forgotten, dismissed as worse than dead by our government. What an unspeakable injustice!"

"I know," Nina echoed gently. "I had similar thoughts.

For if my Akim were alive today, he would be at the front, with your Gino . . ." Her eyes filled with tears at the memory of her dead brother. Her husband possessed a white paper.

Sonia went to work for the prisoners of war. She helped for three hours each morning and three or four hours in the afternoon. With the old Baroness Sokolova and Nina, she weighed white beans, barley grains, rice, flour, and sugar, and placed them into individual bags; they would add tea, tobacco, and cigarette paper, chocolate bars, a bar of soap, and made as many packages as there were names on the list for a specified camp. A hired boy placed these parcels into huge cases and when a case was filled he would nail it shut and surround it with metal strips. The ladies would then inscribe the name and address of the camp in red paint on each of the four sides of the case.

Sonia also gave time to another cause. On Thursday afternoons, she would accompany Baroness Sokolova to the Winter Palace, where the Tzarina had transformed an immense hall into an area for the production of gauze bandages. Against the wall stood machines of different sizes which men operated with hand cranks, unrolling gauze bands of all widths and lengths. They would bring them to the long tables where five or six women sat with readied scissors, to snip off the loose threads on both ends. Nina would stay home those afternoons, for she had a household to run, but Sonia respected the old Baroness who thought first of her duty and last of herself.

One evening, when the young woman returned from her work for the prisoners of war, she felt particularly exhausted as Stepan helped her to remove her boots and cape in the foyer. Her tired gaze landed upon two hats and overcoats which looked unfamiliar to her. "These are not Papa's and Ossip Davidovitch's wraps?" she asked the maître d'hôtel, to check her assumption.

He blushed, which was an unusual reaction for Stepan.

"I beg your pardon, but these belong to two of the Baron's guests . . . from Kiev, Sofia Davidovna."

"From Kiev? Not my uncle Mikhail Goratsievitch?" But the breath had stopped in her throat, and she thought wildly: He has reconsidered. He is coming to me, to beg forgiveness, to ask if I will marry him in spite of everything . . . Oh, God is indeed wonderful. He is merciful . . .

She turned her face, radiant, tendrils falling about her forehead, grateful to Stepan for being the harbinger of such good news. But he averted his eyes, and the smile, so pure, so loving, died upon her lips. Her heart beat out of control, inside her throat. When she lifted her misty eyes, she saw the young man before her, the one who was not Kolya. She stood, in her war outfit of black velvet, her eyes wide and dazed, as he took her pallid hand in his and kissed the cold fingertips. "Sofia Davidovna," the strong voice said, with evident cheer. "What a pleasure to see you!"

She blinked, and took in the tall stature of this young man, the one who simply registered in her mind as "not he," and saw his massive shoulder span, his thick crest of black hair, virile and untamed, and his blue-green eyes. "This time, I deserve a recognition," he murmured, gently deprecating.

"Mossia Gillelovitch Zlatopolsky?" she asked, with hesitation.

"None other. Your father has been telling us of your noble effort for the war. I wanted to enlist, myself——"

"Then why didn't you?" she asked pointedly, regarding him with eyes that shone feverishly, and removing her hand. She turned red, but continued to stare boldly at him, daring him to answer.

He replied softly, "I am of greater use to my country this way, Sofia Davidovna. You see, I am second in command, so to speak, in Papa's enterprises. We provide the army with metal for weapons. Papa now owns several metal works—and sugar, and even textiles, which will make blankets—"

"How comfortable for you!" she commented. "For one million rubles a year, you work for your father, who in turn makes a profit of many millions. And how you will be remembered, at dinners and luncheons! While my brother merely offers one insignificant life. You are a hero, Mossia Gillelovitch. I admire you."

"Sonia!" It was her father, Baron David, coming toward them, his face bewildered and angry. He turned to the young man, and stopped in his tracks.

"I beg your pardon," he said. "My daughter—is not herself, it seems. Sonia! Mossia Gillelovitch and his father, who are in the process of transferring the headquarters of their enterprises to Moscow, have come to see me about the Judaica books. They are our honored guests. They have made me an offer, on behalf of the University of Jerusalem, which has not yet been constructed but is in the offing. Their presence is an honor to us and you will please treat them with respect."

"There has been no problem, my dear Baron," Mossia stated. "Your daughter is correct in her appraisal of my situation. I am certainly getting off more lightly than your son, who is in the army. But it was not I who decided to stay, it was our government who decided for me. As for my salary, it is large, doubtless. But I do earn it. My hours are long and arduous, and business is good." He said to Sonia, "Is the precise amount of my earnings truly that well known about the nation, Sofia Davidovna?" His eyes twinkled merrily.

Had her father not been present, she would have turned aside in embarrassment and fury. But now, calmly, she met his gaze and replied, "My cousin, Tania Halperina, resides in Kiev, you know. She has always . . . paid attention to such matters. I believe it was from her letters that I learned this fact, which is neither my business nor hers."

"But Tania is not one to notice such details," Mossia stated with a wide smile.

All at once, Sonia laughed. "That is true," she commented. "And Sioma, her husband, is only a third son, and tightly supervised by his father. You, however, are trusted by yours, and given free rein. The Halperins are not unduly fond of you."

"Probably not. My father is my friend. In that, and in many things, I am a lucky man. Although the beautiful Tatiana is a lucky asset for her husband that cannot be equaled in rubles."

Sonia's eyes crinkled with mischief. "But you, Mossia Gillelovitch, would not part with your rubles for a wife—correct?"

Once again, a shocked David exclaimed: "Sonia! What has gotten into you?"

Mossia Zlatopolsky was laughing, his head thrown back. "I am pleased," he said, "that your daughter has remembered one of our last conversations in the Jewish hospital of Kiev, three years ago. It was to that she was referring."

Sonia left her father with their guest and went into her room to prepare for dinner. Her dreadful misery had seeped away with the immense good humor of young Mossia Gillelovitch. Yes, she thought as she repinned her hair, he is charming in his way. He is truly a man. And she thought, suddenly blanching: He reminds me of Gino, and of Volodia. For, like them, he exudes self-liking, which is most different from arrogance. He is comfortable with himself. She clasped a string of pearls modestly about her neck, pinched her pale cheeks for color, and went into the sitting room.

Supper was simple, but it was animated by the presence of the two men from Kiev. Hillel Zlatopolsky sat on Mathilde's right, stroking his dapper Vandyke beard. His suit was elegant but subdued. His son sat between Sonia and Ossip, dominating them with his largeness and his sonorous laughter. Only Johanna de Mey seemed distracted, her eyes shifting from point to point along the table, picking at her food with ill-concealed nervous tension. She did not like the fact that Baron David, at the head of the table, was the focal point of the visitors' attention.

"What has happened to your sister, Shoshana?" Sonia asked of Mossia.

"It is because of her that we are transferring our business to Moscow," he answered. "After she was expelled from school—when you met her—she insisted upon studying for her baccalaureate examinations at home, on her own, without even the benefit of a tutor. Papa gave in, and she passed with brilliant marks. But not too much later she met Yosif Persitz, of Moscow, and became his wife. Or, should I say, he became her husband! Shoshana does things her own way. Her household is the first in that large city in which they speak Hebrew night and day. We spoke Russian at home."

"What? Not French?" Johanna cried.

Mossia smiled. "No, Johanna Ivanovna. My mother, in particular, is very modest. Her family was bourgeois, not aristocratic."

"And yet, Russian as you feel, you are a Zionist, Hillel Israelovitch," David remarked. He took a second helping of parsleyed potatoes. "I must admit that I cannot understand that. If you love your country—and I can see that you do—then why are you at the head of so many Zionist organizations that are purchasing land in Palestine? Why prepare to leave a beloved country?"

"Ah, but times are bad, my friend," Hillel Zlatopolsky replied, smiling. "I am a Russian, yes. But Palestine is for all Jews, not merely Russian ones. The German Jew is persecuted, so is the French. One day, these Jews will have a choice: either to stay and fight for their freedom, as you would advocate, or to leave for a land composed of their own kind, where they will be able to sleep nights without fear of pogroms. Palestine constitutes a necessity for the poor Jews, the ones who cannot buy privileges as, you will admit, we can. I am not even certain that I would leave Russia myself—but I would want to have such an option left if my businesses floundered. My daughter will go, I am certain, for she believes the Jews have suffered so much that they deserve to live in a country where they are the majority. Can you blame her?"

"But Papa cannot believe in the need for a Palestine, when he is spending his life trying to better Russia herself for the Jewish citizen," Sonia interposed. "We must have a nationality. What if all the Catholics demanded their own state, or the Orthodox?"

"Dear Sofia Davidovna, the Catholics can turn to Rome to resolve their crises. At least you can agree with me on this point," Hillel Zlatopolsky said with a smile. "I am attempting to convince your father to sell us the Judaica, rather than let it go to the University of Pennsylvania, for one important reason. Many scholars in America will read the marvelous collection of works in Chaldean, Aramaic, Assyrian, Arabic, and of course Hebrew; many will peruse your father's Bibles and Talmuds, his rarest of manuscripts. But a Jewish state *needs* his books. It needs them the way a house needs its foundation. In Pennsylvania, young people will use it as research. But in Palestine—what can I say except that the most intricate and ancient masterpieces of the Saints' works, handcrafted by medieval monks, belong to the Vatican, and I would like to see the works of our faith in the homeland of our faith."

"And your wife does not feel slighted by the amount of time you spend on behalf of Palestine?" Mathilde asked.

"Oh, no," her guest replied. He rested his gaze upon her lovely, full face with compassion.

After supper, Ossip and Sonia served tea to Mossia on one side of the sitting room while Johanna, Mathilde, the Baron, and Hillel Zlatopolsky sat on the other. Sonia was amused, watching her brother and the young man from Kiev. They represented such opposites that it was funny just to watch them—one so slender and elegant, the other so massive and strong. But she could not help feeling embarrassed in the presence of this man who must, surely, know of her humiliation. When Ossip had to leave them to dress for a ball, to which, in these lean times, he was rarely invited, she turned to Mossia, her eyes wide, and murmured, "I am sorry for my behavior earlier. There was no excuse. But"—and she blushed deeply—"the maître d'hôtel said that we had visitors from Kiev, and . . .Tania is not the only person I know there."

His greenish-blue eyes, surrounded by short but thick black lashes, gazed deeply into her own. "I understand," he answered. Then, as he saw her mortification, he continued: "It would be better for me to be honest, Sofia Davidovna. Yes, I am painfully aware of what happened to your life— and worse than that, I know the reason. But you have no need ever to feel ashamed, either in front of me or in front of anyone from Kiev. Kolya Saxe—yes, I shall be insensitive and mention his name—did himself a grave disservice by not marrying you. His reputation suffered enormously. Besides, women like that never follow through. This one— forgive me. I shall not continue to torture you with matters better left unsaid."

"No, no, you must tell me," she pleaded, her face drained of color. "What happened to the girl?"

"First of all, Sofia Davidovna, she was hardly a girl. She was a married woman. Her husband learned of the . . . liaison . . . and left town with her. She had far more to lose than Kolya. Kolya, I am sorry to say, was a coward."

"So now—why . . . *why*?" she asked in a whisper, leaving her thought unfinished. She could not restate what she had thought earlier, that now he could return, make up for the time they'd lost . . . She could not, for he had rejected her in favor of someone else, a married mistress, an older woman who was no longer even a part of his life.

She felt someone gently seize her hand and say, "He could not, after what he had done. Not because you would not have forgiven him, but because he was doubly a coward, and could never have faced you, knowing that you knew. He . . . married someone, last year. I do not think he ever loved her as he loved you. But she was a widow, and needed a father for her little girl. Maybe he married her to help atone for his disgraceful behavior."

She fell forward, and he caught her, and eased her back upon the sofa. "No," he murmured, "this will not do at all, Sofia Davidovna. You are ten times the person he is. But you had to know. Sooner or later, someone else—Tania—would have told you. Come on."

"I could have forgiven him everything, if he had not married," she said, her eyes shut tight to stem the tears. "Oh, no, he couldn't have done this! Not—marriage."

"You are being a sentimental child," Mossia Zlatopolsky said harshly. "He may love you forever, but he is a man, a person. You could hardly expect him to spend his life as a monk, loving only the memory of you. Surely such is the nonsense of novels."

She stopped moaning and regarded him, aghast. He broke into a smile. "Good, good!" he cried. "You are reacting like a strong individual, winning back your pride. Come now, be my hostess and allow me the pleasure of another glass of tea."

Sonia nodded, mutely, and when she returned to his side, Ossip was there, and not long afterward the Zlatopolskys asked for a carriage to their hotel. Before leaving, however, Mossia fetched a small package from the foyer, and handed it to Sonia. "Tatiana Alexandrovna knew that we would see you," he said, "and she asked me to give you this book. It is, it seems, a novel by the daughter of the British Ambassador, Miss Buchanan. Your cousin told me to tell you that the plot amused her, and will quite take your fancy. I hope that I have accomplished my mission adequately."

"It was kind of you to undertake it," she said, and gave him her hand. "In return, you will give Tania my love?"

"Most certainly. I shall endear myself to the Halperins by kissing the new Madame on both cheeks and the third, and shock them all. After all, is Tania not . . . expecting?"

She closed the door upon his tall, broad form, and stood in the foyer, lost in thoughts that were too jumbled to make sense. But as she went to bed, after kissing her parents good night, she felt queerly drained of all emotion. Her last waking thought was: Since when has Tania started to read books?

In the carriage that was taking them to the Hôtel de l'Europe, Mossia and Hillel Zlatopolsky smoked in companionable silence. Finally, it was Mossia who drew his father's attention from thoughts of the Judaica and the rich supper at the Gunzburg home. "You are quite taken with the young Baroness, Papa," he chuckled.

"She is a lovely, delicate child," the older man mused.

"Hardly a child. She must be my own age. But she is one of those women who will always be childlike, don't you think?"

"I'm not certain," Hillel replied. "There is a hardness about her that isn't childlike at all. And it is that which draws me to her; it saddens me to see it."

"Why?" Mossia asked. "A little toughness in a girl isn't always bad. As long as she doesn't become a woman of iron—such as that Dutch governess. I prefer them soft, but zestful."

"Like Lialia."

Father and son regarded each other seriously in the darkness of the coach. The hooves of the horses clopped on the cobbles of Petrograd, and still neither would lower his gaze. Lialia was a sore point between them, though never discussed beyond this. She was a singer in a Muscovite café-concert, and was kept by Mossia. As long as the young man paid for his gypsy from his own earnings, Hillel felt that it was not his business to interfere. He loved Mossia, respected his brilliant business sense, but did not easily understand his immense appetites, which included women such as Lialia.

"Like Lialia," Mossia assented lightly. But he recalled the instance when his father had quelled him, the single time, and how searing a humiliation that had been. Mossia was a passionate aficionado of billiards, but in Kiev and Moscow, billiard halls were found only in the most disreputable neighborhoods. Hillel had strongly disapproved of his son's presence among blackguards and thieves, although he had never been an interfering parent in regard to Mossia's private activities. Mossia had chosen to overlook Hillel's objection, and one night, in the midst of a tense game in the back room of a shanty in the slums of Kiev, he had seen his father, elegantly clad in tuxedo and top hat, a black pearl pin resplendent in his cravat, push open the door. Hillel had merely looked at the young man from his small, piercing eyes, and Mossia had dropped his cue in the corner and followed him home. Not a word had been exchanged between them; but the humiliation still rankled.

"It was a generous deed, to give Lialia the money for her mother's operation," Hillel now stated gently. "Oh, don't look so peeved! Your friend Pierre told me about it."

"It was not his affair," Mossia replied offhandedly. Then, his eyes shining, he turned to his father with animation: "Papa, while we are here, shall we go to the Opera? I have become good friends with Fedya Chaliapin, and I should like to have you hear him in *Boris Godunov*."

"I have already had the pleasure of listening to Chaliapin. He's a genius. When he comes next to Kiev, bring him to the house, Mossia."

"Thank you, I shall. Now, tell me, do you suppose the Baron will sell the Judaica?"

Hillel Zlatopolsky shrewdly narrowed his eyes. "I am not sure," he replied. "He will want to wait, and weigh his options."

"But you will win, Papa," Mossia stated. "You never fail." He smiled, thinking of the sugar plantations in Kiev, the banks in Moscow, the shipping companies on the Volga, the tramways in Odessa, the mills, the mines, the pastures. "Still, I wish that you and Baron Gunzburg were on the same side."

"But we are, Mossia, we are," his father replied, his small eyes twinkling. Then he sighed, and huddled comfortably beneath the plaid blanket in the landau. His son scrutinized him, but this time Hillel had no desire to share his thoughts with his son.

Sonia was brutally awakened by loud voices in the foyer, and she peered at the elegant glass dome which held her clock upon her mantelpiece. It was after midnight. She turned on the small lamp by her bedside, and rose, her throat constricted. Her black hair cascaded down her back and over her shoulders, and she shuddered, slipping into her bathrobe which was at the foot of her bed. Then she ran out of her room toward the noise.

Two men were arguing with Stepan, tall and stern, his hair tinged with strands of regal white. "What is it?" she asked, joining them.

"I beg your pardon, Baroness," one of the men said, and bowed. His attire was nondescript, his face sallow but intelligent. "We are searching for Baron Ossip de Gunzburg. This man says that—"

"Ossip Davidovitch has gone to a ball," Stepan articulated with disdain.

"Who are you?" Sonia demanded. Goosebumps had spread over her arms, and although she examined the men carefully, she could figure nothing out. "Our maître d'hôtel speaks the truth," she added, moving toward Stepan.

"We are with the Secret Police," the second man stated. "It seems unlikely to us that your brother would pick this one of all nights to attend a dance. Where is he?"

Sonia's head jerked up, and she straightened her sloping shoulders. "My brother is at the Abelmans' home. Mademoiselle Abelman has turned eighteen, and because of the war there are few escorts available. My brother was asked to attend—although we do not believe in socializing during the war," she could not help adding with displeasure, having argued this point many times with Ossip. She thought: If only he had listened to reason he would be here, and no one would make him sound like some kind of criminal! Thank God, she thought with a surge of relief, that he has no interest in politics. Thank God, for now they cannot arrest him! She nearly swooned with suppressed emotion. "Why is it you want him?" she asked.

The first man shrugged. "We must search his room. Can you lead us to it?"

Stepan cried out, "No, indeed, we shall not! The young master has done nothing wrong."

But Sonia turned to the maître d'hôtel. "Stepan," she said quietly, "we must summon my father at once. He would not allow such an indignity to take place in his own house. Although," she added, a small but proud figure in her bathrobe trimmed with Brussels lace, "my brother has nothing to hide. You may as well begin your search, and see for yourself. But waken Papa, please, Stepan."

The two men entered the room then, and opened all the drawers and cabinets, and removed Ossip's clothing to check the pockets and hems. Sonia stood erect by their side. "There," she said finally. "You see? Nothing!"

At this point, Stepan returned with a disheveled Baron David. In the commotion Mathilde and Johanna had awakened too, and they entered Ossip's room on David's heel. Mathilde seized her husband's arm, and cried, "Stop them! You must call the minister at once!"

But David shook his head. "Let us first find out what this is about," he stated. "Calm yourself, my dear." But the pain in his chest grew worse, and blue lines showed around his lips. Sonia rang for tea, but fetched her father a shot of Napoleon brandy.

She returned to her own room bewildered. In the distance, she could hear Johanna's strident tone as she attempted to lead Mathilde to her room and back to bed. She heard her father, politely offering tea to the policemen, who accepted gingerly. Finally, she pushed her hair from her temples and lay back upon her pillows. She could not even think of sleeping. She reached for the book that Mossia had brought her, Tania's gift, hoping that it might relax her. It was entitled: *The Emeralds.* She flipped through the pages, then opened to the first chapter, adjusting her lamp so that she might read more clearly. All the while, she kept one ear cocked for the sound of Ossip's key at the back door, off their hallway.

Strange, she thought, as she began to read. Tania has never given me a book before. Pregnancy must do odd things to a woman. The story, a bit farfetched but still enjoyable, concerned a young woman, ambitious and selfish, who wished to wed a young man of ancient and noble lineage, who was deeply in love with her as well. As always in such novels, Sonia reflected with a wry smile, the heroine was named Clarissa. (Sometimes they were Vanessa or Alicia.) The lover had given Clarissa a lovely emerald engagement ring, and also a family jewel composed similarly of emeralds, a necklace which was passed from generation to generation. Therefore, the necklace did not rightly belong to the lady who wore it; it constituted a loan until her own son's wedding. She received it upon her engagement, but was not permitted to wear it until after the wedding. The vain Clarissa, however, insisted upon wearing the emeralds to a ball several days before her marriage, in spite of the supplications of her fiancé and his mother.

The clasp was old and fragile, and during a mazurka, it opened, and the necklace fell to the ground. But in the time it took for her dancing partner to wheel about to pick it up, the crowd of dancers had moved, and it was nowhere to be seen. Someone had cleverly seized it. The young man, in a rage, broke the engagement.

Sonia could not continue. She flung the book aside, tears stinging her eyes and pressing through her long, curling lashes. Her breast rose and fell rapidly, her cheeks burned. How had Tania dared? Why had she been so cruel? She thought wildly: My ring, my betrothal necklace, were emeralds, too, and I wore them for three months before Kolya refused me. All of Petersburg knew these jewels. And now she lives in Kiev, and knows that he has married another woman! Why, Tania, why? She wept bitterly, as she had wanted to but had not done in front of Mossia Zlatopolsky. She would write Tania, she would accuse her angrily—she would have young Zlatopolsky return the book. And then she thought: No, of course not. I shall not give her the satisfaction. I shall even thank her for her present.

As she nodded resolutely to herself, tears upon her cheeks, she heard a vague scraping noise and rose quickly. Ossip! She dashed from her room, barely noticing that it was after three in the morning, and in her delicate slippered feet arrived at the back door, which no one but Ossip used, and he only after balls now when the rest of the household had retired early. She swung open the door before his key had unlocked it. Bewildered, he faced her in his top hat and tails. "Sonitchka! What is it?"

"Ossip! There are two policemen here searching your room, waiting to arrest you. You must go to a friend's house, and tomorrow I shall pack a bag for you and deliver it," she whispered urgently.

For a flicker of an instant, he hesitated on the doorstep. Then, shaking his head, he pushed past her. "Sonitchka, my love," he declared, "it can only be a mistake. I have done absolutely nothing. There is no cause for alarm—or cowardice. I shall go to them."

Hat in hand, he strode elegantly into his bedroom and stood in the doorway, appraising his disarranged clothing strewn about the floor. "Come now, gentlemen, state secrets or no, you must improve your housekeeping," he chided them lightly. "But what's all this about?"

Respectfully, the men stood up, and one of them said, "Please, Baron. Change into your daytime attire. We beg your pardon. We did not believe that you were attending a dance, but evidently we were wrong, as we can see by your clothing. But you will have to accompany us to the station. Take along your toilet articles."

"Toilet articles? Where are they taking you, Ossip?" Sonia cried.

"Don't worry, we shall clear it up," David said, putting an arm around his son's shoulders. He was glad Mathilde had gone to her room.

Ossip shrugged lightly. "Try to sleep, Papa," he said soothingly.

Ossip excused himself, and returned dressed as for a day at the bank. He touched his sister's cheek with lingering softness. "Cheer up," he murmured. "I cannot be sent to a worse place than Gino."

Sonia's terrified face was the last thing he saw before leaving the room, between the two men. But when he had left, Sonia went at once to her father, and pulled his head onto her narrow shoulder. "It's going to be all right, beloved," she whispered. "All right."

Baron David was up at dawn, and his secretary, Alexei Fliederbaum, made many telephone calls. Sonia went to her Uncle Sasha, and explained the situation, begging him to round up all those who might help them locate Ossip and help him. Because of the havoc created by the war, they had no idea where Ossip had been taken. David recalled with anxiety how his friend Lopukhin had been sent to Siberia on charges of high treason, only to be pardoned after years of suffering when the case had been reviewed by the Tzar. If only Lopukhin were still Chief of Police, he might have been able to help, but David's friend had retired to Moscow after his release from exile. Now David's ministers were absent on war business or could learn nothing. What confusing times! Sasha's colleagues did little better. Even an aged general, on leave in the capital, was barely able to learn that Ossip had been taken to the most dreaded of prisons, the Pyotrpavlovsky Fortress. But he was not able to gain admittance to see him, nor to discover what the young man might have been charged with.

It is my fault, my fault, Sonia repeated to herself endlessly that day, as well as the next. It is because of my illegal work for the prisoners of war . . .

But six days later she was struck by an idea. Nervously turning an opal ring around on her slender finger, she went into her mother's boudoir and there faced Mathilde, her face frozen with fear and bewilderment. She kneeled before her, took her mother's cold fingers between her own, and gazed beseechingly into her eyes. "Mama," she stated, "there is someone we had not thought to call upon."

"Well?" her mother cried.

"It is . . . Senator Count Tagantsev. I know Papa would hate it, and hate me for even suggesting it. But you, Mama, you could write to the Countess, Maria Efimovna. It is worth a try, is it not?"

Mathilde sat back and regarded her daughter with a brilliant stare. "I do not care whether your father approves or not," she declared at length. "Thank you, Sonia. I shall write to the Countess. If she ignores my plea, I shall have lost little but my pride. And Ossip's safety is worth that risk, isn't it?"

She quickly composed a note, and gave it to her maid

with the order that it be hand-delivered to the Countess Tagantseva at her mansion, and, she added, "Tell the footman to await a reply." Then she lay back and closed her eyes, not daring to hope. Her Ossip, in the Fortress! It was as ludicrous as that unspeakably immoral peasant, Rasputin, in the Winter Palace. Yet there they were, both of them, incontestably. She began to wait.

In the Tagantsev palace, the Count and Countess were finishing a late breakfast when a footman was announced from the Gunzburg house. "The Baron David de Gunzburg?" the Count exclaimed, and his hirsute eyebrows lifted. "Give me the note, Anton."

"It is actually for the Countess, from the Baroness," his servant interposed with deference. The Count regarded his wife with shock, and Maria Efimovna blushed. She took the note and quickly looked away from her husband's angry face.

"Oh, Nicolai, this is dreadful!" she finally cried. "Poor Mathilde Yureyevna! It seems that—"

"It seems only that my wife has gone behind my back to make the acquaintance of that Jewess!" the Count exploded, oblivious to the servant shrinking timidly against the paneling.

"Oh, Nicolai, that was . . . years ago. I visited her once, out of courtesy. You must remember how kind the Gunzburgs were toward Volodia." Her eyes filled with tears. "She is a lady, Nicolai. And her children . . . were perfect. Do you not remember them, that summer?"

"I remember only . . . afterward." The husband and wife locked eyes, the specter of Natasha between them, while he thought of the shame his daughter had escaped, and she thought only of the girl's abject distress.

"But, they were so young, it was such a meaningless flirtation," Maria Efimovna finally said. "You rather liked Ossip. Didn't you?"

"Not that way! Never that way!" the Count cried.

"No, naturally, Nicolai, my dear. But as a human being. And, you must admit, a fine gentleman." Her hand reached toward her husband's, across the embroidered tablecloth. "My dear," she said, "the young man has been arrested, and the Gunzburgs are beside themselves with worry. No one knows why, but he has been incarcerated at the Fortress. Would you—for the sake of the son we both cherished—would you go to see him, help him in his trouble? He must be innocent, Nicolai."

The Count withdrew his hand, and his eyes flashed malevolently at his wife. Now another specter hung between them, that of Volodia. A sudden quick pain constricted the Count's heart. He turned aside. "For his sake—not yours!" he shouted hoarsely. Tears of gratitude and relief moistened his wife's eyelids. She sighed, and beckoned the servant for some paper upon which to write her answer to Mathilde.

In the vestibule, Anton, the servant, nearly collided with a tall, elegant young woman in a plumed hat, who was saying with a burst of gaiety to the small girl behind her, "Oh, come now, Larissa! You will not, will not beg Grandmother for anything, not so much as a sweet—" But she halted by the open front door when she saw the servant with his note. "Anton!" she exclaimed in surprise. "You look somewhat in shock! What is this paper? Is anything wrong?"

The servant bowed his head. "It is not my business, Princess," he replied.

"Then give me that!" she said, extending her pretty hand with its elongated fingers. She laughed, and he passed her the note from her mother to the Baroness. She read the few lines, her color fading, put a hand to her throat, and blinked several times. Then, grabbing Anton by the arm, she began to shake him. "He is at the Fortress?" she demanded. "You are certain of this?"

"Yes, Princess. The Countess spoke of it."

Now the little girl, tossing back her black curls, tugged insistently upon the jacket of her mother's suit. "I can smell jam, Mama," she said.

The young woman said to the servant, "Tell my coachman to wait, Anton. I have an errand I must run." Then, straightening her hat upon her head, she took a deep breath and followed the child into the breakfast room.

Ossip sat in the dank cell, his hands crossed behind him, and thought for the hundredth time: This is insane. Did I, while in Poland, stay at the home of someone suspect to the government? He chewed on the inside of his lower lip, perplexed.

Outside, the turnkey, at heart a jovial workman who was quite taken by this elegant, slender man of twenty-nine, with his gentleman's attire, came to the door and said, through the grill panel, "There is somebody of great importance nosing around your business, Excellency. Do you know a Senator Count Something-or-Other?"

Ossip grew very pale. "Senator Count Tagantsev, perhaps?" he asked.

"Yes, yes, that's it! Gentleman wouldn't see you, though. But he sits in the Senate, doesn't he? Friend of the Tzar?"

"He is admitted at Court. What did he want?"

"Well, here's what's odd, if you'll pardon me, Excellency. He wanted to know, same as you, why you were here. Said he wanted to . . . help. But then, why d'you suppose he didn't come to see you? Seems many's the ones who tried to, starting with your own father. And the Minister of Education himself. But this Count—they allowed him to see the records, but he didn't want to see you in person. Strange, no?"

"Not really," Ossip replied. He smiled sardonically. "The Count particularly detests me, and the feeling is quite mutual, I assure you, Popov. In fact, if he does succeed in getting me out, I shall be at pains what do do. Going to thank him would cause us both unbearable embarrassment. But then again, he wouldn't receive me."

"Then why is he helping?"

Ossip shrugged. "His God may know; mine doesn't," he said lightly. But he thought: Mama! He was filled at once with incredible bitterness and with a glimmer of hope. Oh, to get out of here, to return home! But to have to owe a debt to her father, to the man who had ruined their lives . . . It was like handing a glass of vinegar to a man dying of thirst.

It was not long, however, before a prison official arrived, and Popov unlocked the door of Ossip's cell. The young man nearly jumped to his feet. His clothing was rumpled and he had a six days' growth of beard upon his face. But his eyes, sapphires above their mauve circles, shone with anticipation. "Well?" he breathed.

"You may leave, Baron," the official stated. "Now, if you wish. There have been many calls about you—"

"But what was the problem?" Ossip cried.

"I am not at liberty to disclose this," the other replied. "Now, if you'll follow me . . ."

In his exhilaration at being released, in his frustration at still not learning what had occurred to bring him to this wretched place, Ossip nearly tripped as he walked out to freedom. The sunlight made him blink with pain, for he had been in near darkness for six days. All at once, before the gates, a footman in red and gold livery approached him, and he stepped back instinctively, afraid of once again being captured. But the man bowed and Ossip frowned. He could not remember this uniform. Besides, his family would not yet have learned of his sudden release. "You are Baron Gunzburg?" the footman demanded.

When Ossip nodded, dazed, the man said, "Then, if you please, the Princess is waiting in the carriage." Ossip followed his gaze and saw an English tilbury parked to his left. It was a tiny, open carriage drawn by a single horse, and inside sat a lady wrapped in white furs, with an elegant plumed hat set pertly upon her black hair. She held up one gloved hand. He could not move. His hand touched his unkempt beard, his limp collar. His eyes were full of tears, and he did not discern, through the blur, whether she had smiled or not. "The Princess has been out in the cold for two hours, Baron," the footman said with polite concern. "Please come inside."

It was not yet springtime, in 1916, and a chilly wind blew around the tilbury. The footman opened the door for him, and he sat down, bewildered in the passenger seat beside the lady. She said, clearly; "Drive anywhere, Ivan! Oh! Not on the Nevsky, please. Just—around." The footman tucked Ossip's knees under a silk and fur coverlet, and the coachman cracked his whip. The carriage began to move, swaying slightly in the wind.

"I do not understand, not at all, not any of this," Ossip said, without looking at her. The footman stood behind them, but neither he nor the coachman could hear because of the wind and the tapping of the horse's hooves.

"It was nothing but a silly mistake. You took some pictures of your young brother, in Pskov, and the police confiscated your equipment. Later, it was returned. But then, you see, a new chief of police was named in Pskov, and in an excess of zeal, to please his superiors, he re-opened all the old cases. It was those silly pictures they were searching for in your room. They didn't know that they were harmless family photographs. But it's all right now, everything's been cleared up—"

"I'm grateful. Your father will be thanked, as is proper." Ossip sat stiffly, his face impassive. Suddenly he turned to her, and asked, "What on earth are we doing here, you and I?"

Her beautiful face, he thought, had hardly changed in eight years, although it was a bit leaner, and her great blue eyes seemed deeper and yet less merry. Her lips parted, she tried to speak and shook her head with self-annoyance. "For God's sake!" she cried. "Words! I—I haven't seen you for—for half a lifetime, and you've been in prison, and you ask me—nonsense! Not how I am, or how I've managed, without you."

"I'm sorry," he said rapidly, "but this is all so unreal! First the arrest—and now you! One minute I am a criminal, the next minute I am mysteriously released, and then you, of all people, are here to greet me, in what can only be called the most ridiculous of carriages, in wintertime, in public!"

"I was out with my daughter, Larissa," she said defensively, tears coming to her magnificent eyes. "She's only five, and the tilbury is not ridiculous, it's British, and Lara wanted a ride! How was I to know that you were in prison, and that I'd have to take this contraption all the way out here, to wait for you?"

"I beg your pardon?"

"Oh, Ossip, look at me! Did I come here for nothing, after all?"

Soft gloved fingers touched his face, and turned it so that he was looking at the pert nose, the red cheeks, the smooth forehead with tendrils curling about it underneath the hat. "It was you who married," he said cruelly.

"You could have found a way to come to me."

"Nobody forced you to say 'yes' beneath the icons."

"I—I had lost all hope. For any sort of life for myself."

"Then why—now? Eight years later! Why not simply have pretended to forget?"

"Because that's all it was: pretense! A vast self-deception. When I read the notes between our mothers—when I learned you were at the Fortress—it all came back, and I had to come. My . . . husband . . . is a general on the Northwestern front, where we are planning an attack on the center of the German front. I went into the Fortress and told them I was . . . his wife, and Papa's daughter.

They told me that Papa had helped you, and how. That way, I did not have to ask him, personally. Then, I simply waited."

"But it was dangerous for you," he said, suddenly gentle. "You are a married woman. This tilbury—it's open—"

"Oh, it's all right! That's why I told Ivan to avoid the Prospect. You are a family friend—my poor brother's best friend. It is natural that I should try to help you—even to socialize with you."

He peered at her, and swallowed. "You say . . . you have a child? Or is it children?"

"One daughter, Lara. And you, Ossip? You are not married?"

Brusquely, he turned away. He could no longer bear her presence, smell her perfume, listen to her voice. But she whispered, "I still love you, Ossip." He faced her, and took her hands, squeezing them beneath the coverlet, so that the footman might not see. As he said nothing, she began to weep, softly. "He . . . is a kind enough man, much older than I. Once I hated him. But he gave me Larissa, and now he's away, and . . ." She stopped, and their eyes met. She became red with shame as their thoughts coincided about her husband. "He is Lara's father," she said staunchly, to dispel her own wishes.

"Yes." But he continued to stare at her, and thought: Uriah too died at the front, and then David took Bathsheba. What does hope cost me?

"He is very valiant and patriotic," she said emptily.

"Of course," he assented. He had heard of General Prince Kurdukov. Did she take him for an illiterate fool?

"I still grieve for Volodia, every day," she continued changing the topic. "More now than ever."

"I, too," he murmured. Would this never stop? Would she not go and leave him in peace?

All at once she said, fiercely, "It was your sister who killed him! I could not forgive her—or you! Did you know that, Ossip?"

Again his eyes filled with tears. "I suspected it," he said. "But she did not kill him, Natasha. She loved him. You must believe me."

"How can I? My darling brother, my twin? She sent him away! And he would have fought to keep her, more than you ever did on my behalf, Ossip Davidovitch!" Now it was she who turned away, her face distorted with pain. "You both left me at the same time! Was I truly such a worthless, evil person?"

She began to sob, her shoulders shaking, and he grabbed them and held them, stroking her back. All at once she sighed, and regarded him with enormous eyes. "You are twenty-nine now," she stated in a low, trembling voice. "You earn a living. Rent a discreet apartment in the city, Ossip. Then I shall come to you. You cannot come to me. My home is near Mama's. But so long as he is . . . away . . . we are both free, aren't we?"

Aghast, he released her, unable to think clearly. "You will do it?" she asked urgently. "Soon?"

"Yes, my life, my love, soon," he said, and knew that he had made a commitment greater than marriage, greater than God or country. The tears flowed freely from his tired eyes beneath the cold clouds of Petrograd.

"You may now drive the Baron home, to Vassilievsky Island," Natasha said, tapping her coachman on the back and raising her voice above the wind. She smiled at Ossip, and touched his hand beneath the cover. "It's all right," she said, her eyes full of love. "Remember our Volodia. He would have waited six days in the cold, not two hours, and would have personally bundled you home. I am merely carrying out his wishes." The old mischief sparkled in her eyes, but there was also pain, naked and vulnerable.

When he appeared in the foyer of his parents' home, Stepan nearly kissed him. His mother, his father, his sister, even his former governess clustered about him, asking so many questions that he could not begin to answer them.

The cook unceremoniously brought out hot soup, even before Ossip could change his clothing. He laughed out loud, and there was a hysterical note to the laughter that alarmed his mother and vaguely disquieted his sister. But his father stated, "The boy is famished, and tired, and happy, and angry, and dirty. What he needs is some peace and quiet . . ."

"And this, Baron, if you please," Stepan said, offering a glass of brandy to the young master.

During the week that followed, Sonia noticed Ossip's high color, his quick jokes, his good humor. She watched him when his mother carefully sent a basket of exotic fruit, set in bowls of silver and crystal, to Countess Tagantseva. He marveled over the selection, his eyes dancing with merriment. Something was strange here, Sonia thought. But she could not figure out what had happened to the broken remnant of her brother's spirit during his stay at the Fortress. She watched him surreptitiously, with concern. But he would tell her nothing, and she was too respectful of his privacy to intrude.

In the spring, Tania and her husband came for a visit to Petrograd. Tania was heavy with child, and in a delicate condition. Rosa, birdlike and excited, said to Mathilde, "The dear child is so sentimental! She insists upon delivering the baby in our home. She, who used to complain so about Russia, is now more Russian than all of us. She says that she knows she will have a son, and hesitates between the names 'Horace,' like her grandfather, or 'Boris.' I do not know whether to embroider the layette with an 'H' or a 'B.'"

"I should think you would have more pressing concerns," Mathilde commented. She thought of her strong-headed niece, who was being treated for a difficult pregnancy with complications of the liver, and whose doctor in Kiev had forbidden her to undertake a voyage at that time. Rosa reproached her with her eyes. Mathilde said, "But if she feels up to it, David and I should like to give her and Sioma a dinner. We have not entertained at all, so to speak, since the war."

"Tanitchka will be so pleased!" Rosa cried.

The Halperins arrived, and Sonia was forced to pay them a visit almost at once. She was annoyed with Ossip for being unable to accompany her—in fact, he seemed forever occupied these days with his own affairs. She wished she could confide in her parents concerning the book which had so turned her against her cousin Tania, but she had determined not to speak of it. So, resolutely, she dressed herself simply, as became a wartime lady, in an afternoon suit of blue. Her distaste was coupled with dread at once again seeing Sioma, for whom she felt such revulsion. But she stepped into her aunt's Elizabethan house, and breathed in as if to steel herself, handing her cloak to the maid who admitted her. "Tatiana Alexandrovna is expecting you," she was told.

Sonia braced herself for her first encounter with her married cousin, but the woman who appeared before her took her breath away. It was Tania, the blond, cornflower-eyed Tania, but with sunken cheeks, pale lips, and bone-thin arms, a Tania carrying her child in front, with nothing, it seemed, on the hips. Sonia's set lips, her erect back, slackened. She opened her arms and closed them about her poor cousin, and wanted to cry. Instead, she said, "I have missed you, my love. Tell me all about yourself. Letters, you know, are never sufficient."

Tania sighed, and this heartfelt sigh pierced Sonia's flesh like an arrow. They sat down together in the sitting room, and Tania ordered tea. It was Sonia who poured it, and while she did so, Tania's eyes jumped all about the room, taking in its elegant blue upholstery, its oil canvases. She came alive. "I could not stand the idea of giving birth anywhere but here!" she cried.

"But your home—surely you like it?" Sonia asked with care.

"Oh, that! Sioma's mother changed it all during our honeymoon. If you thought that Svetlana Yakovlievna was a tasteless provincial, you never met my—" Tania clapped her hand to her mouth, and blushed a deep, unhealthy crimson. "I'm sorry," she said.

Sonia smiled, and regarded her cousin levelly. "There is nothing to feel sorry about. First of all, I never thought anything of the kind. Let us be clear on this point. I admired and respected Kolya's mother. It was Juanita who felt that she was . . . shall we say, not quite the cosmopolitan gem she wished to display to our society. I was staunchly opposed to her treatment of Svetlana Yakovlievna. If she felt insulted, I cannot blame her. Living in Kiev, it is normal that you would hear things there that are passed around as gossip. But I do not wish to hear them. I know that Kolya has a wife, and stepdaughter, too. I am pleased for him. As for me—if I am to remain a spinster, don't worry, I shan't be a bored one. Now tell me more about you."

Tania seemed subdued. "Sioma spends much time at his mother's. He wishes me to come there often, too. But I don't like her, Sonia. She is . . . vulgar, and possessive. A young married man should spend his evenings with his wife, shouldn't he? Shouldn't he?"

"He can spend time with both," Sonia said gently. She passed her cousin a cake, but Tania pushed the silver platter aside. At that moment, a tall man entered the room, and Sonia turned to face him pleasantly. It was Sioma, stooped, pockmarked, with watery eyes. He, at least, was little changed. He bowed over Sonia's hand, then sat and gulped down a glass of tea, his Adam's apple making vulgar throat noises. Tania watched him with wide-eyed dismay, and Sonia's compassion grew. They spoke about little things, about the trip, about the child that was about to come. Sioma's eyes brightened in anticipation, but Tania's grew fearful. Sonia squeezed her hand. "June will come and go before we know it," she said with too much cheer. And thought: But what do I know of childbirth?

That evening, at supper, Sonia said to her brother, "You must make it a point of duty to go there and tell her your jokes—you could always reach her better than the rest of us. Please, Ossip! Whatever takes up your precious time, you must set some aside for Tania."

"You will cease your insinuations," he replied tartly. She looked at him, surprised and hurt, but his face registered only aloofness.

A week later, Mathilde gave a formal dinner for the Halperins. As it was the custom to place fiancés next to each other at the table but not married couples, Sioma and Tania were seated far apart, across an expanse of table-cloth and silver. In 1908, Mathilde and David had cele-brated their twenty-fifth wedding anniversary, and her mother, Baroness Ida, had given her a magnificent set of floral-painted dishes from Saxony. The flat plates lay be-fore each guest, and the servants were placing filled soup bowls on top of them, when suddenly Sioma raised his flat dish and examined it carefully, reading the back label. His face quickened, and, leaning forward, he cried out, "Tania! Did you see? It's real! Genuine Meissen!" A stunned si-lence answered him, as guest turned to guest in consterna-tion. But Ossip said brightly, "Let us pray that the food, too, will be genuine!" Whereupon Tania began to laugh, a high-pitched, tense laughter which spread to the other guests. Sonia smiled at her brother, and bit her lip.

After supper, they moved to the sitting room for coffee. Now that she was not only a married woman, but an expectant mother, Tania sank gratefully into an armchair, for it was unseemly for a mere girl to take up so much room. Lovingly, Sioma went to her, and sat on the arm of her chair. He slipped his arm around the back of his wife's shoulders, but Tania, with a grimace, bent slightly forward so that his arm should not touch her. Nobody but Sonia noticed this gesture, as the guests were busy turning their spoons in their fine cups, and watching the sugar dissolve and the cream blend in.

In June, Tania was put to bed with labor pains, and all the Gunzburgs congregated at the home of Rosa and Sasha. The delivery was delayed by hours of pain and complications; three doctors and a midwife sat in attendance upon the mother-to-be. At long length, a boy was born to Tania and Sioma, and the exhausted mother announced that he would be known as "Horace Boris."

To Sonia's relief, Gorik, as the boy was surnamed (for the name "Horace" in Russian was "Goratsy"), resembled his beautiful mother. His healthy cries filled the nursery where once Tania's own cries had resounded, but she could not feed him. In fact, she hovered between life and death for several weeks, during which her cousins came frequently to hold her hand. One afternoon, thinking she would surely soon die, she whispered to Sonia, "It is better this way. You will take Gorik? I do not want Sioma's mother to have him, ever! And this way, you see, I shan't have to return to Kiev at all!" A horrified Sonia could find nothing to reply, but she nodded dumbly.

Tatiana, however, did grow stronger, and after almost three weeks was even permitted to take her baby to bed with her, where she held him tenderly. Sonia thought: If she does love the child, she cannot hate its father . . . And in fact, though she was still convinced of their mismatch, Tania's period of illness had persuaded her of Sioma's total devotion toward his beautiful young wife.

Book 3

Seventeen

---•---

After Tania's confinement and recovery, the Gunzburgs faced one another, drained and tired, and decided that this was no time for going abroad. Besides, having summoned any extra energy she might have possessed after her grueling schedule by the side of Baroness Ivanov, and having employed this energy to aid in the nursing of Tania, Sonia was showing signs of exhaustion which distressed Mathilde. And Gino was in Russia, Gino for whom they had braved the *Haakon VII*, Gino who had put off his leave for so long, in order that he might prepare for the onslaught against the Austrians on the Southwestern front.

"I shall take Sonia to Pavlovsk," Mathilde declared. This was the resort closest to Tsarskoe Selo, where the Imperial family resided during the summer. It was very lovely, with parks and outdoor concerts, and was also near the capital, so that Gino might visit his mother and sister there just as easily as in Petrograd. And Mathilde would be able to keep her eye on her husband, whose heart problem was not improving. Rosa, Tania, and Gorik joined them, but Sioma returned to his sugar plantations in Kiev. To avoid the annoying presence of Rosa, her long-time foe, Johanna went to France to visit her elderly mother.

On June 4, the Russian army, under General Alexei Brusilov, overwhelmed the Austrians, and Gino wrote that he was coming home. First, he stopped in Petrograd, where his father's poor color troubled him and his brother's apparent glow baffled him. Then he took the train to Pavlovsk. His mother and sister had only recently arrived, and he burst into the inn where they were staying, his mustache turned up, his hair shining mahogany, his eyes glistening with the victory which had exhilarated everyone connected with the Southwestern campaign staff. He lifted Sonia from her chaise longue, twirled her in the air, and deposited her, gasping for air, in a bed of pansies. Then he hugged his mother so that she thought the breath had been crushed out of her for good. He even succeeded in embracing his Aunt Rosa, who had never really noticed him before. Tania, holding the baby, gave him her cheek, and he thought: She is better disposed toward me, although her bloom has faded.

The young soldier admired everything around him at the agreeable resort. His eyes followed the women in their muslins and cottons, and when his cousin made a wry remark, he turned to her in all innocence, and said, "I had nearly forgotten what a lady looked like. Oh, sometimes we see milkmaids, in formless clothing. But never . . . such as this!" He motioned with his chin to a young woman with gay curls entering the lobby. But Tania stopped teasing when she noticed that the ladies, too, regarded Gino from lowered lids, surreptitiously admiring the man in uniform. He'd be perfect to be seen with, if only he were an officer, she thought.

When he entered the dining room and saw the tables with their white linen cloths, he nearly clapped with delight. "Oh, Mama!" he exclaimed. "Look at this! Can you imagine—being served upon this large clean sheet, in such luxury?"

His mother and sister started to laugh, and soon even Tania and Rosa were rocking back and forth in hilarity. "What have I said?" Gino cried.

"My love, you have been gone too long," Sonia declared. "Had you indeed forgotten that these 'sheets' are called 'tablecloths'?"

He kissed his mother, and said sheepishly, "You should eat in the trenches from a can. No, no, I did not really mean that. I would not wish it upon you, ever!" He blushed with embarrassment.

Sitting outside, in the warm sun, at a long table laden with freshly churned butter, loaves of newly baked bread, and jams and jellies, he told them of the campaigns, of his men, of Vassya in particular. He recounted how he had won the Cross of St. George, so proudly displayed upon his breast, suspended from a black and orange ribbon. "You know," he stated, munching with relish, "there must be something to faith." And he explained about the colonel who crossed himself before each battle, who had never been wounded.

But this brought grief to his young, ardent face. He pointed angrily to his sleeve, devoid of red stripes. "Look!" he exclaimed. "It would seem as though I were a coward. Men receive stripes each time that they are hit. But I— never! Yet I have participated in many battles, and have fought in the midst of the fray."

"I, for one, am gladdened by your virgin sleeve," his mother chided him. How he had filled out, how muscular, how healthy he looked. She smiled, and shook her head, remembering the day of his birth, almost twenty-one years before, at Mohilna.

"Tell us," Sonia demanded, leaning toward him, her gray eyes alive, "are you afraid, really, or is it true that brave men feel no fear?"

He laughed, gently. "My dear innocent," he replied. "Of course I am frightened! I am terrified, as is, I am certain, the greatest general. The fear comes when I jump upon my horse to go to the line of fire. But once caught up in the action, shots ringing about my ears, I cease to think of fear or of anything at all. I simply keep going."

One evening, in bitterness, he said, "My captain has attempted three times to have me promoted. But the order was rescinded each time, because of my religion." He did not see that his mother stiffened, that revulsion transformed her full, lovely face. She was thinking: Both my sons. Such waste, such hurt . . .

Another morning, he came downstairs for breakfast carrying a sheaf of music sheets, which he placed before Sonia. "These are for you," he told her. "I took them from an abandoned house in the outlands."

"But that is theft, Gino!" she cried in dismay.

His lips pressed to a grim line. "I merely retrieved them, because I knew you would appreciate and use them. But you should witness the pillage that occurs on both sides! Had I not saved these sheets, my men would have burned them, or used them for notepaper. In any case, you may be certain that they would not have left them alone."

He spoke with exuberance of the Russian army, which was being revitalized in strength and in supplies. "We shall defeat the Central Powers next year," he stated proudly.

But Mathilde's brow knit, and she asked, "What about the socialist conferences in Switzerland, the ones your father so often talks about? He claims that those men want an end to war . . . but not an honorable one."

Gino's face tightened with rage, and he hit the table with his fist. "They are maniacs, determined to undermine our nation!" he cried. "Anna has sent me letters. She says that all they care about is revolution."

"Revolution?" Sonia echoed, and her lips parted. Her cousin's eyes encountered hers, and there was fear in their blue irises. She looked at her aunt, nervously biting the inside of her cheek, and at her mother, whose features displayed vague shock. But her brother stared at her with fierce passion. "Let them only try!" he exclaimed.

The baby, Gorik, began to wail.

In the fall Sonia resumed her work for the prisoners of war, who had, in the meantime, greatly multiplied, as had the number of camps. She also continued to go to the Winter Palace to cut bandages. Petrograd, under gray skies, grimly attempted to deal with economic pressures and with the two million refugees which had to be relocated from the evacuated areas. Rumania had joined the Triple Entente, and suffered total defeat, and now Gino wrote that he was being sent to the Black Sea to help the Rumanians. The gallant warriors hardly paused from battle to battle, she thought proudly.

In December 1916, the illiterate peasant-monk, Rasputin, was murdered by three prominent men, of whom one, Prince Felix Yussupov, was a member of the Tzar's own family. For a long time now, able politicians such as Baron David had shaken their heads with disbelief at the thought that this strange, half-crazed, lecherous mujik wielded unlimited influence upon the Tzarina Alexandra, who was herself the power behind the Tzar. No political decision had been made without Rasputin's consultation over the past year. Now the horrible murder of this dreadful man shook the capital, and Mathilde whispered, "Has Russia gone mad?"

Baron David, his lips blue, went to his wife, and taking her plump hands in his own lean ones, said quietly, "I do not know what is going to happen. But you and Sonitchka must leave Petrograd, for if anything does happen, it will happen here. I am fine, and I have Ossip with me and Sasha nearby. We have survived the revolts of 1905, and we shall of course survive this, too. But look at our daughter: she weighs less than ninety pounds, and this time she will not wait till summer. She is about to collapse, Mathilde. Take her to the Crimea, where you can simply live off the revenues of our land until things quiet down and I can begin to send you money on a regular basis. And do not worry so about my heart. It has pumped for sixty years, and will continue to do so for many more."

Mathilde regarded the blue-veined hands that held her, and suddenly she bent to kiss them. "You are a good man, David," she murmured. Tears moistened her cheeks. "Make the arrangements for us. Give us two months, so that the estate manager, Zevin, can reserve rooms for us in a pleasant town, since we have no suitable house there. We can take our time, setting up the house here, for you and Ossip to get by in comfort during our absence. I do not want to leave in a hurry."

She announced her decision to Sonia, expecting opposition. But her daughter, her cheekbones drained of all color, simply sighed and shook her head. It was not a negation of her mother's words, but a negation of strength. She would make herself endure till February, for the sake of all those men who needed her services so desperately. But already, her right arm could hardly lift itself without nearly super-human effort. She certainly possessed no reserves with which to oppose her mother, or anybody, for that matter. Tania had left for Kiev in the fall, her cheeks their usual apricot hue, and Ossip was hardly home at all. She and Nina Abelson worked together, but there was no need to talk there either, for Nina, though more stalwart than her friend, was also weary to the bone. Sonia therefore had been living as an automaton, working, sleeping, working, sleeping, each day blurring into the next. Her only moments of life came with letters from Gino or Anna, or when she worried over her father.

During the two months that Mathilde took to put her house in order, Baron David came to a decision. He would sell the Judaica now. Life in Petrograd was becoming too complicated to put off the moment of resolution, and the war having cut off his communication with the University of Pennsylvania, he made up his mind to sell to Hillel Zlatopolsky, now residing in Moscow. "It is right," he stated, "for the Jews of Palestine to gain primary access to this collection, for it is their history that is recorded here. Hillel Israelovitch made a good point, one that is irrefutable. If the books must leave Russia, let them go to Palestine. Though I do not believe that the Jews shall ever need to create this special state to shield them from their foe . . ."

Hillel Zlatopolsky came alone this time, to sign the necessary papers. He had only one brief encounter with Sonia, as she was preparing to go to the Winter Palace. She was frailer than ever, her oval face drawn with lines of exhaustion, but her gray eyes regarded him with warmth. "I am trying to hang on," she told him, smiling in self-deprecation. "Silly of me, isn't it? I'm young, and should be working twice as hard. But always I seem to give out. Last summer, I was merely tired, but in Geneva I came down with enteritis. You must deem me a veritable Milquetoast, compared to your energetic daughter."

"You are possessed of different qualities, my dear," Hillel Zlatopolsky replied. "Strength is not measured by the loudness of one's orders nor by one's physical volume. You are like the geranium, which cannot be destroyed."

"Remember me to your son," she said, and as she mouthed the words a surge of heat flowed over her. Hillel Zlatopolsky bowed, and went into the sitting room to meet David. Sonia walked down the outer staircase, and shook her head as if to clear it. What an odd sensation had taken hold of her! But there was no time to analyze it, or anything else, for that matter. Baroness Sokolova was waiting.

"It is only necessary to pack old clothing," Mathilde said to Johanna de Mey. They were in her bedroom, folding gowns and shirts. "It is warm in the Crimea. Sonia will recuperate."

Sonia, Johanna thought. Always Sonia. She had returned to Petrograd during the fall, and the wretched girl had been busy all winter with her war relief work. Johanna had wanted to sob with joy. But the moments while Tatiana Halperin had hung between life and death had been dreadfully painful for the Dutchwoman, for they had separated her almost daily from Mathilde. Then, Rosa had altered her plans by coming with the Gunzburg women to Pavlovsk, and Mathilde had not discouraged her. She had even sent Johanna herself off with cheerful messages for her mother. But things were going to change. Away from David, away from this city with its brewing conflicts, away from his angina pectoris . . . and Mathilde's guilt. She smiled. "The Crimea must be a veritable dreamland," she said.

"Yes. But wait, do not bring your pearls, Johanna. I tell you, society is very simple there. Oh, Feodosia is a pleasant, civilized city, but very informal. Bring the comfortable corduroy suit. And your cameo, as single adornment."

"Surely you exaggerate, my sweet," Johanna demurred.

But Mathilde had ceased paying her attention. She had opened a large leather box filled with her jewels, and was lifting out a tiara from delicate tissue paper. "I wore this at the Coronation," she commented, almost to herself. She gazed with rapture at the rubies, diamonds, sapphires, and emeralds in her hands, and sighed. "It was in Moscow, in '96. But you remember that."

"Indeed," Johanna remarked acidly. She particularly remembered having had to remain in St. Petersburg to supervise those horrid children.

"I know, you were here," Mathilde stated gently, placing a fond hand upon the other's arm. Then, brightly, she announced: "We must wrap these for the safe, Johanna. David has too much on his mind to worry about what I have done with which pieces. So I shall lock them all away, except for the crab. You know—the diamond crab I'm so fond of. Though I can't see where I shall be wearing it!" She sighed. "We are growing old, Johanna. Don't you feel it, too?"

"The whole world is growing old," the Dutchwoman replied with asperity.

Sonia, Mathilde, and Johanna de Mey departed from Petrograd on the same day that the new session of the Duma opened, the twenty-seventh of February. David and Ossip came to the station to see them off. Sonia looked about her at the city she loved, where she had been born, and, as always, its spires and bulblike cupolas made her heart soar. Only this time, the emotion was ineffable sadness. She took her father's hand, caressed it softly, and began to weep. "I do not want to run away from you," she whispered softly, and dropped her head upon his shoulder.

"But you are going to the sun, and the fields, to rest. You are not running."

His face, so gaunt, so sallow, with its pale blue eyes, regarded her with tenderness that now, for some reason, she could not stand. "Oh, Papa!" she cried and burst into tears. He removed the fingers from her eyes, and gently kissed each eyelid. "My very little girl," he murmured.

Inexplicably, she could not erase the vision of her father's harried face from her consciousness. She wept and wept. Finally, Ossip took her aside, sat her down upon a suitcase, and kneeled before her. "What on earth is the matter?" he demanded.

Sonia threw her arms around her brother's neck, and wildly, without knowing why, she cried out, though he alone could hear: "You must find a way to tell him—now! About the boy. Something tells me that he must know. Do it, Ossip! I beg of you."

Bewilderment creased her brother's handsome features. "But Sonitchka," he declared, "you aren't making a bit of sense. What boy? And who's the one who should be told?"

A cold chill passed through her. "Oh, my God," she muttered. "It—it is nothing, Ossip. Simply that I don't want to go and leave you and Papa. But you're right—I wasn't making any sense. Forgive me?"

"Someday you must do me the favor of enlightening me," he teased her. He helped her to rise, and, arm in arm, they made their way back to her father and mother. Sonia said nothing more. She could not speak.

On the morning of March 11, 1917, Baron David said to his son at the breakfast table, "The Tzar has issued an order to stop the continuation of the Duma. I cannot understand this. Our Duma in no way interferes with his authority, as does the British Parliament, for example, which wields more power than the King. I am glad that your mother and sister have left town. General Ivanov is being sent here with a full battalion to quell an eventual mob, should the need arise."

Ossip blanched. He could not answer his father. He thought only of Natasha, who was coming to the apartment he had rented for them months before. She was coming at noon, when Sasha would be out of the offices. No one at the bank would miss Ossip, and he had begged Natasha to find a way to come to him for a stolen afternoon. Now, he considered the dangers she might encounter, and his blood ran cold. My God, he thought, how can I stop her? Send a note? But she is probably taking Lara to her mother's home, and will come from there . . . He covered his face briefly with trembling fingers, and his father exclaimed, "Ossip! Are you quite well?"

How can I tell him that I have brought a fine lady to shame, that the wife of one of our country's generals comes to my bed when he is gone, that she risks all for me, without thought of herself, her name, her daughter? Ossip said, "It's all right, Papa, I assure you." But as he smiled, he cringed with shame. His father, who had never committed adultery. Ossip felt nauseated. He was filled to the brim with self-loathing.

"You are not proposing to go to the bank, on such a day?" David demanded when his son rose abruptly from the table.

"It isn't that, Papa. I have some . . . other business, which cannot be put off." He thought of Natasha, her face brimming with love, and he was angry, insanely angry. They have done this to us! he thought bitterly, the old resentments surging up again. I wanted to marry her. I waited eight years. She had no wish to wed this other. And yes, he was part of it too, he, my beloved father, with his pious *shtadlanism*. To hell with them all, Tagantsevs and Gunzburgs alike!

He asked Vova to drive him to the city, and from a street corner he hailed a troika which he took to the discreet avenue where he had rented an apartment and hired a manservant. It was an elegant district, but not a fashionable one, as it had been in the days of his great-grandfather and namesake, the first Baron Ossip. Ossip stepped down from the troika, paid the coachman, and was about to ascend the stoop of the gray brick house when the man called out after him: "There are crowds gathering downtown, Excellency. How about an extra few kopecks to see me safely home?"

Pinpricks of annoyance assailed Ossip but he reached inside his vest and withdrew a purse, removing the requested coins. He nearly hurled them at the driver, then turned his back and ran up the three steps to the door. Once inside, he ran the remainder of the way to his second story apartment. His valet opened to his ring. "Monsieur is early today," the man commented. "Madame has not yet arrived."

"I didn't think she had. Fetch me a brandy, Pavel."

"The usual, sir?"

Ossip fell into an armchair and loosened his cravat.

"Yes, yes, be gone," he said, when he noticed the man, half-bowing, still awaiting his reply. He was filled with fear for Natasha, fear renewed by the anxious words of the coachman. Surely, surely she would not come, not if she would be in danger. Her father would keep her with the family, in spite of her protestations. He almost smiled: ah, yes, she would protest. In her heart, she would want to come, more than anything in the world . . . But of course she would be wise, and not risk it.

He sat and smoked, leaning forward tensely. He could not tell whether hours or only minutes went by. Pavel, tall and silent, passed by like a shadow, bearing trays of brandy and foodstuffs. Ossip waved him off distractedly, but gulped the liquor, and his nervousness began to abate with the slow warmth that was spreading through his body. He hardly realized that he dozed off, that night fell, that he awakened, startled to a new dawn. When her ring came, he jumped from his seat, perspiration beading beneath the waves of his black hair. He had slept upright in his clothes, and it was now morning.

He heard her voice, strained with agitation, and smelled her heady scent of wildflowers before he saw her. She rushed into the room, her day gown splotched with mud at the hem, tendrils escaping everywhere upon her neck, her cheeks scarlet. He tried to speak, but the sounds gurgled, caught in his throat, and she threw herself into Ossip's open arms.

"It was quite horrible?" he asked, sitting her down upon the sofa and rubbing her fingertips.

"Oh, my darling, it was dreadful! There are mobs everywhere. The carriage was jostled and nearly lost a wheel, and when I stepped out near Mama's house, we were splattered, Lara and I. But that was nothing—just minor discomfort! They've opened the Kresty prison and let everyone out, the reserve troops have joined in the fray, our court house is on fire—and they've arrested Papa!"

"What?"

"Yes! The members of the Duma met, and elected a kind of emergency group, and appointed commissars to keep the peace. But the people in revolt have seized the ministers, and when Papa left the house very early . . . I saw them . . . grab him! Oh, Ossip, I am so frightened, so terribly frightened! Is there nothing you can do?"

"I? But Natasha, my sweetest love, who am I but a bank employee? My own father would be a poor match for the revolutionaries. If the Duma people have named commissars, the mob will surely release your father within hours. Do not worry. He will be all right."

"He helped you once! Why can't you at least try to do something?" she cried, and her beautiful face became wracked with tears and grimaces of pain. She started to sob, pitiful small sobs of defeat, and he kissed her hands. But she pulled them away, wildly. "You are a coward, Ossip!" she exclaimed. "Even—yes, even my husband is braver than you, for he is at the front, and you do nothing!"

Her wide blue eyes, red-rimmed, met his, which clouded with sudden, profound shock. He moved away from her. "So it comes to this," he stated, and his calm tone of voice brought chills to her spine. "He is a better man than I. Have you ever thought, Princess, that you cheapen yourself each day that you come to me, for I am not a general, and merely a lower-tiered aristocrat whose title dates back a simple four generations? I am a Jew, Natasha. And to a Tagantsev, that is tantamount to being an ant upon the ground. The Tagantsevs wield the power to save Gunzburgs, but the opposite is not true. And to add insult to your demeaned situation, I am a virtual cripple, afraid for his back, who bears a white paper while your husband, beribboned, reviews his troops." His jaw muscles contracted, and he examined her with the utmost disdain. Then, suddenly, he cried out, "Why didn't you leave me alone, Natasha? Why did you come today? Why didn't you do the

honorable thing, at least this single time, and remain with
your mother, who is a decent woman, unlike her daughter,
and who is doubtless scared to the point of apoplexy? Why
didn't you stay to comfort her, to hold your Lara?"

"I couldn't stay away from you," she answered quietly,
lifting her small tear-stained face with its trembling chin.
"Yesterday I didn't come, because of the rumors—"

"But you are a fool! A Tagantsev, you know, can still be
a fool, in spite of his lineage. Coming here, when God only
knows how long we shall have to stay, cooped up like
frightened chickens. What have you told your mother?"

"And you? What did you say to your father?"

They regarded each other, sapphire eyes meeting in a
blaze of anger and fear and hatred and love. She looked
away first, tears streaming from her eyes. "I am so terrified," she whispered. "But also, you are right. I am a
shameless woman. For I am happy, Ossip. In the confusion
and the danger, we shall have to remain here, shan't we?
For the whole night perhaps?"

He turned to her and felt as though he were being pulled
by a magnet. She extended her hands to him, her face full
of hope, begging forgiveness, but he pushed them aside and
fell upon her with urgent passion. She uttered one small,
surprised cry, then fell back upon the cushions as he buried
his face in the crook of her neck. Her hat slid to the side,
and she mingled her fingers with strands of his hair. She
could feel his own tears on her soft skin, and she pulled his
face to hers, and kissed his eyelids. "Do not leave me," she
whispered. "Never go away from me, Ossip."

They did not notice that Pavel had discreetly closed the
thick velvet curtains of the small sitting room, that only a
corner lamp was lit. They had not forgotten Petrograd,
awash in chaos and fury. The passions of their city had
merely added fuel to their own, and their frenzied love-
making became tinged with the same hysteria that was
shaking the capital.

Ossip and Natasha remained together through the night, in the safety of their private enclave. They embraced in total abandonment as the Petrograd Soviet of Workers met in the Taurida Palace, without prior warning, in derisive indifference to the Temporary Committee of twelve elected Duma members. They drank giddily from champagne coupes the following day, while Tzar Nicholas left army headquarters in Mogilev and boarded the train for Tsarskoe Selo. But a quiet knock disturbed them on March 14, and while Natasha, her lovely face crimson with embarrassment, pulled up the silk coverlet to hide her alabaster limbs, Ossip, with annoyance, bade Pavel enter. "We are sick to death of pâté de foie gras!" he cried in disgust.

The valet, pale in his black frock coat, declared quietly, "I thought perhaps that Monsieur and Madame should know. The Tzar has abdicated."

Natasha turned to Ossip, and her face went suddenly white. He drew her protectively against him. "What else have you learned, Pavel?" he demanded.

"Just this, sir. The Temporary Committee has appointed a Provisional Government, under Prince Georgi Lvov. Its members are no surprise: Guchkov in charge of the War Department, Milyukov of Foreign—"

"My father!" Ossip cried.

"Yes, Monsieur. I said, no surprises. There is one: an Alexander Kerensky for Justice. He's the only socialist."

"My God," Natasha exclaimed, "now they will kill Papa!"

The two young people regarded each other, horror painted upon their features.

"No," Pavel demurred politely. "Let me reassure Madame. The mob has been quelled. Her father has been returned to safety."

"But you don't know . . . about my father!" Natasha gasped. Her teeth began to chatter.

"Madame needn't worry about anything," the valet

stated. He turned to leave, then apparently changed his mind and faced the lovers once more. "The Tzar," he said deferentially, "has also abdicated on behalf of his son, Tzarevitch Alexei. So now it's up to the Grand Duke Mikhail, the Tzar's brother."

"Thank you, Pavel," Ossip intoned emptily, as the servant noiselessly slipped out. He looked at Natasha, took her hands in his. But he too was trembling, and goose bumps had spread over his entire body. Her eyes stayed glued to his, seeking a guidance that he could not give. He said, softly, regretfully, "We must go home, my angel. It is time."

The first thing that Baron David said the next morning at breakfast to his son was strangely anticlimactic: "The Romanovs have reached the end of the line, my boy. The Grand Duke Mikhail has refused Tzardom, and has passed the governing power to the Provisional Government." He did not ask where Ossip had been until the previous afternoon, when he had entered the Gunzburg apartment with a haggard expression haunting his eyes. Too much had occurred for the mere comings and goings of his son to be of importance. Ossip wondered, his heart constricting with anguish, if Natasha had similarly escaped questioning. After all, she was a mother, and her own father had been held captive. More had been at stake in her case. But there was no way to find out. He could only hope, and now he wished he were a believer, so that he might pray.

Dear God, he thought, if you exist, which I doubt, please help Natasha through these days of confusion. And, he added tersely, help Russia . . .

Eighteen

Alexander Zevin managed the entire hundred and twenty-five thousand acres belonging to the Gunzburg clan in the Crimean peninsula. This was the property which the patriarch, Ossip Gunzburg, had purchased in disparate lots throughout the region, so that its yearly revenues should go to the Dynins, relatives of his wife, Rosa. He had been tired of their pleas for money, and had devised this plan to rid himself of the nuisance of their demands.

The lots were comprised of wheat, barley, and buckwheat fields, salt mines and fallow ground; some of the land was extremely fertile, while in other areas it was arid. And some of the estate was cultivated by peasants who reaped part of the profits, while other lots were worked by men and women who were paid wages by the season.

But no longer did the Dynins enjoy the proceeds of this land. Upon the death of Ossip, his children in France had allowed their brother in Russia, Baron Horace de Gunzburg, to buy their shares in the Crimean property, and when he in turn passed away in 1909, his own children had inherited a great deal of land.

Once a year, Zevin would come to Petrograd to bring the account books and the actual cash revenues to David and Sasha. But Sasha was a city man, without much interest in the country; and David was already the squire of Mohilna, in Podolia. There was no need for the brothers to concern themselves with this land, which to them meant only additional wealth, welcome but hardly essential. No family members had ever desired to live on their Crimean land, even for short periods of time to investigate this part of their bounty, so no manor had been constructed for them. Zevin possessed a small house on the estate, but spent most of his time traveling back and forth among his workers.

When Sonia's health had begun once again to show signs of deterioration, Baron David at first thought of sending his wife and daughter to Mohilna. But he wanted them to leave the city soon, for political reasons as well, and Mohilna, though beloved by Sonia, had never been a favorite spot of Mathilde's. It was too countrified, and Mathilde needed to be surrounded by civilized gentry, at the very least. He could not bear the thought of her alone with an ailing Sonia and Johanna de Mey, with her bright eyes that detested him and were constantly searching for new flaws in his character. Then, late one night, he had thought of the perfect solution: to have Zevin arrange for Mathilde, Sonia, and Johanna to rent a house in one of the jewel-like Crimean cities which he, as overseer to the Gunzburg estate, would know intimately. David's family could then live on the proceeds from the harvests of '17, and the Baron would not even have to worry about problems arising in the mail system, whereby checks could be lost and his wife's comfort might suffer.

Zevin's mother resided in Feodosia, an agreeable, comely town with a harbor, and it was there that the estate manager located the house which he rented for the Gunzburgs. It was on top of a hill, overlooking the Black Sea on the most elegant avenue of all, the Catherine Boulevard. Mowed grass sloped down from it to the street, then came

the railroad tracks, then the beach. The entryway was not
through the front; a road wound toward the courtyard in
back, leading to a garden and a porch, with an entrance to
the foyer. The magnificent living room looked out to the
sea, and before the street, a thick wall with an iron gate
closed off the property. Only Sonia's maid of many years,
Marfa, had come with them, and they had hired no other
servants. Mathilde proposed to live quietly. It was still
wartime, and in this community there would be no reason
to entertain. As it was, they knew very few people.

Feodosia was an old town with Greek relics, including a
fortress that had been erected by Mithridates. Sonia, who
was anemic and still quite weak, was not able to enjoy
many walks. But one day, after one of their own walks her
mother and Johanna arrived in time for tea and greeted
Sonia with lively faces. "We have met the most charming
girl," Mathilde exclaimed. "She will come to see you—we
have invited her. Her name is Olga Pomerantz, and !
mother is the leader of Jewish society here. Madam
Pomerantz owns a wheat exporting business, and they say
she runs it herself!"

"It hardly matters about the mother, my dear," Johanna
added quickly. "The daughter is a pretty child. She was a
student at the University of Kharkov, but because of the
troubled time, she has returned home, and has enrolled as
a day student at the nearby University of Simferopol for
the fall term."

Indeed, the following afternoon, Marfa announced a
Mademoiselle Olga Arkadievna Pomerantz, and a young
girl entered the living room. She was of medium height,
with short, waved strawberry blond hair arranged in curls.
She wore a suit trimmed with muted gold braid and her
elegant high boots glistened in the sunlight. Yet the small
round pink mouth was natural, the coral cheeks were un-
enhanced by rouge, and Sonia thought: She belies what
they say in Petrograd about provincial girls! Olga Pomer-

antz is most attractive, and fashionable, too. Yet she is very young! She touched her own thick hair in its traditional pompadour and topknot, and felt singularly spinsterly and old.

"Madame Zevina is acquainted with my mother," Olga said simply, taking a seat at Sonia's bidding. "I was so pleased when she told me of your presence. It was dreadful, what happened—the Tzar abdicating and all. Mama is the most strong-willed person I know—but still, I did not want to leave her alone here, and remain alone myself in Kharkov. Nevertheless, it has been rather lonesome."

"Your mother appears to be quite a legend in this town," Sonia commented with a smile.

"Oh, yes! Papa died most unexpectedly, while dressing one morning. And Mama simply took over. She always knew what Papa did: his dealings with the farmers, the estate owners, the shipping executives, the foreign clients . . . Now she goes to the offices, and turns a better profit than Papa ever did. We are great friends, Mama and I. But we have little time to spend together."

"I am sorry," Sonia said, her large gray eyes taking in the eager young girl before her. How old could she be? Nineteen, twenty—at most? Yet there was depth within her, Sonia thought. "You must come to visit us, then," she added, brightly. "I do not wish my mother to be so concerned over my welfare. I was ill some years ago, and weakened during some work that I was doing in Petrograd, for the war effort. Mama and Juanita—Johanna Ivanovna, her companion—should visit the sights, and go out more frequently. If you came for tea they would deem me in fine company, and everybody would be satisfied. Will you come?"

"Of course," Olga replied. Then, as Sonia paled as she began to rise, she held her in her chair with a swift movement of the arm. "I can pour tea as well as anyone in Feodosia," she declared, and the green sparks in her hazel eyes shone merrily.

The Pomerantzes owned the most luxurious mansion on the Catherine Boulevard, and soon the Gunzburgs and Johanna were invited there to suppers and teas. Madame Pomerantz, Nadezhda Igorovna, was tall and sinewy, with large gray eyes that peered shrewdly at those around her. Her black hair refused to stay tamed in curls and coils, and she absolutely abstained from wearing hats, even though this was not an accepted practice. She was vivacious and somewhat loud, her voice a tremulous alto, quite stirring. Feodosia permitted her her eccentricities, for she was an enfant terrible, frank, honest, disarmingly forthright. Her daughter Olga was as gentle as she was rough.

Nadezhda Igorovna took to Mathilde with instant affection, and brought her from room to room, pointing with mock horror at the lack of refinement of her furnishings, which were singularly devoid of personality. She did, however, possess the most remarkable Persian and Indian carpets that Mathilde had ever seen, but there were no vases, no flowers, no knickknacks, and no paintings or photographs upon the walls. "I cannot spend my energies decorating," she said, throwing her hands into the air in defeat.

"I could help you," Mathilde suggested, hesitantly. She felt drawn to this woman who ran her affairs like a man, and suddenly she felt proud of her own talents. "Perhaps my only gift lies in arranging rooms. It isn't much of a gift, like Johanna's in music, or yours, dear Nadezhda Igorovna, in business affairs. But I have always loved the feel of upholstery, the play of gentle colors one upon the other. I would not impose my taste on you, though."

"But you must! I insist! What good would you be as a friend, if you could not help me with this blessed house? Ah, I have asked Olga, but you know the young: they lead their own lives, and plan their own futures. You will help, then?"

"I should do so, gladly," Mathilde replied with a smile.

"Mama has never asked me to help her," Olga whispered to Sonia. "To tell you the truth, she laughed at the notion of spending money on what she calls 'the trimmings.' Even when Papa was alive, she hardly cared. But it appears that your mother's charm and excellent taste have changed her mind."

Sonia smiled, and the two young women, arm in arm, followed their elders into the living room. There, the maître d'hôtel served them an excellent tea. Only Johanna de Mey remained silent. But as soon as they had drained their cups, while Olga promised to pick up Sonia for a conference that evening at one of the lecture halls in town, the Dutchwoman hastened her farewells and insisted upon walking ahead of the Gunzburgs for the short trip from the Pomerantz house to their own. Mathilde called out to her once, and, more faintly, a second time. Then, shrugging slightly, she took her daughter's arm and strolled home, discussing with gentle laughter Nadezhda Igorovna, and with enthusiasm her daughter Olga. Once, Sonia thought with a pang of surprising envy, I was just like her: fresh, *moderne*, interested in everything. And Kolya loved me, and before him Volodia Tagantsev. But now, what is there to love in me? I am nearly twenty-seven, and my idealism has worn, like old silver. She said, "I never thought the Tzar would give up, did you, Mama?"

"Hush," her mother admonished, trying to retain her pleasant mood. "Do be a lady, Sonia, and leave politics alone . . ."

Once in their house, no sooner had her daughter gone into her bedroom than Johanna de Mey greeted Mathilde, her golden hair flecked with gray streaming down her back. She was already undressed, and in her peignoir, displayed a thin figure in apricot silk. "That woman is odious!" she cried, and clenched her hands together. "How *could* you, how could you, Mathilde?"

Shivering slightly, her friend replied, "How could I what, Johanna? What have I done?"

"What? You have encouraged the familiarity of a preposterous person, a person unfit for you! She is coarse and crass, and has no friends. No wonder she grovels so for your friendship!"

Mathilde raised her eyebrows and tilted her magnificent head to one side. "So," she stated calmly. "It is only the friendless who deign to care for me? Really, Johanna, your jealousy is most, most unbecoming. You resort to wounding me. But why? Because I have found the presence of somebody else agreeable to me? Can I no longer have other friends, Johanna?"

"You are cruel!" Johanna cried, and tears sprang from her eyes onto her meager cheeks. She rubbed her hands drily against each other. "Nadezhda Igorovna is not a lady."

"That is where you are mistaken, and fooled by the exterior," Mathilde countered. "She is admirably educated. I can tell that she has been speaking French from the cradle. She knows mathematics, poetry, what have you, far better than I. She seems tasteless only where she has not cared to give vent to her most excellent taste. And I like her. She is sophisticated but unworldly, and that is a rarity. Even my mother would enjoy her," she added, with a proud straightening of her back. "I shall accept her friendship with gratitude. We are not at home, Johanna. Her daughter has befriended mine, it is wartime, we are strangers. I will not reject one of the first ladies of Feodosia."

Johanna's almond-shaped eyes glistened and widened. "And if I reject her?" she whispered.

"You shall have to be discreet about it. I shall not lose this newfound friend because of you. Good night, my dear." Mathilde inclined her head, and turned toward her own bedroom. Johanna de Mey remained in the hallway, her shoulders slumped and her hands dangling at her sides.

Gino cast down his ration of dark bread and dried beef with a gesture of frustration. He had never been very facile with words. Now they failed him totally. He regarded little Vassya, the cowherd, his corporal, who had been promoted to sergeant, with irritability. "I am not against the Provisional Government," he finally said.

"Then it is the commissars you oppose," Vassya countered.

"Yes. Yes! What have they to do with this army? With this war?"

"We are tired of the war, Baron," Vassya smiled ironically. "Oh, I do not like the communists, this Lenin and his Presidium, which is no better for us than the Tzar. To me, the All-Russian Congress of Soviets simply means Lenin and Trotsky. And that's not even their right names, mind you. And the Presidium just wants to take my father's grain away to feed the Party, as they call themselves, without paying him in rubles and kopecks. No, we peasants do not like the Communist Party. But it looks as though your Kerensky—your Provisional Government—cannot do anything about them. Kerensky and Prince Lvov, they just ignore the communists. But they have ordered commissars for us, and that's what we have to check us from their side; and then the communists have given us our soldiers' committees, which are supposed to check the officers from our side. But tell me, Baron, what are we really to do if we're attacked? Go to Kerensky's commissars, or to the soldiers' committees? Who's to tell us what to do or where to fire? I want to go home, and tend my herd, and make sure my father won't be robbed by all of them put together! That's where we differ, you and me. You still want to fight."

It was the beginning of June 1917. Gino was infinitely demoralized. This was to have been Russia's moment of triumph. The troops were well supplied, and surely, he had thought, the Central Powers would be defeated this year— in the fall, at the latest. But then the March Revolution had taken place, deposing the Tzar and autocracy. Gino was not actually sorry. Nicholas II and his Tzarina Alexandra had not exactly handled their nation with finesse. He, a Baron, felt that the British system of Parliament was most suitable, allowing for the best of all sorts of people to rise and rule. But, as his father had always maintained, for a man to rule, he had to be suitably educated. Vassya, who was Gino's friend, could hope to make a good statesman, but only if taught the precepts of statesmanship and law.

The March Revolution disturbed many people more than it had Gino. The fact was that Gino believed that people were reasonable, that the Tzar had abdicated as a defeated nation surrenders, without bloodshed, because he had seen no other way out. So be it, thought the young man; now let us turn to the next step, the Provisional Government. But he had forgotten Lenin, and the Bolshevik element of the Social Democratic Party. They had become, with their own All-Russian Congress of Soviets, a sort of countergovernment that ran alongside Prince Lvov's and Alexander Kerensky's Provisional Government. At the heart of this Congress were Lenin, Trotsky, and a few other extremists who frankly bewildered Gino at first, and then infuriated him. It was they who advocated a separate peace tantamount to surrender, who wished to create havoc within the army. Soldiers' committees, indeed! Now little Kostya, the dim-witted, was telling him what to do and how to fight, while Kerensky's commissar, who knew nothing whatsoever about rifles and ammunition, got in the way when he sought to explain a maneuver to Gino's men. He did not need a sniffy bureaucrat to worry about, not in the middle of a war.

Milyukov, Pavel Milyukov, the man in charge of Foreign Affairs in Petrograd—a man that Gino remembered had once kindled the admiration of his sister Anna—now *there* was an honorable man, who had told the Allies that Russia would keep fighting for their cause, their common cause! But he had resigned in disgust, and Kerensky, Minister of War and the Navy, had issued a disclaimer, insisting that Russia would fight only a defensive war from then on. A defensive war! Those were fine words with which to conciliate the Congress of Soviets and Lenin. Gino spat and shook his head. "Do you know whom I found, laughing in his beer with the Austrians?" he demanded of his friend.

"Who, Baron?"

"Kostya. I had to shake him away. Singing bawdy songs, clear over in the enemy camp. There's total chaos, Vassya. Sometimes I do feel as you—I want to find my sister and mother in the Crimea, and have a civilized meal with them, and listen to my sister play the piano. But we can't just give up!" he cried, spilling some tea onto the ground in his excitement.

"Kerensky, for all he's said, is on the offensive, Baron," Vassya said gently. "Wait and see."

Gino munched on his bread and looked across the camp at the evening star, near the crescent of a moon that had risen. His heart swelled with yearning, but he was uncertain as to what he yearned for: warmth, love, victory? His sister had written him that she had made a new friend in Feodosia, a very young and attractive girl. How long it's been since I have danced, he mused. Then he chuckled. Was dancing to become outdated, too, like autocracy?

I wonder what she looks like, this Olga Pomerantz, he thought, and felt foolish. "Do you have a girl?" he asked Vassya.

"Me? Of course!" the soldier replied merrily, throwing back his head and laughing. In that moment, Gino felt loneliness such as he had never experienced.

"I have never had a girl," he said softly, almost with surprise.

The two men finished their supper, and Vassya wiped his grease-stained fingers on his trousers. A hoot owl emitted its nocturnal cry, crickets added their crissing noises. All at once, a shadow came between Gino and the moon, and a boot cracked a stick of dry wood. "May I join you?" a voice asked in courteous, measured tones.

Gino raised his head and encountered a civilian uniform. Damn! he thought, and his cheekbones suddenly splashed with vivid red. He bit his lower lip and regarded Vassya, who shrugged. "We may as well put up with this one. He's here, and that's all there is to it," the young peasant stated with disdain.

Gino cleared his throat. "Yes. Well. We are hardly gracious, Commissar. This is an army, in spite of its appearance, and most of us don't know what to do with our government supervisors. However—we are men, all of us, and Vassya's right. We may as well learn to live with one another."

"I did not choose to be sent here, Sergeant," the civilian replied with gentle irony. Gino scrutinized him in the dusk, and wondered, Have I not heard that voice before—and seen this man? Is he from Petrograd? He was momentarily baffled, and the other took that opportunity to sit down beside him and to extend his hand. "I am Ivan Berson," he declared.

A flood of sensations took over Gino's consciousness. Berson! He ignored the proffered hand and concentrated upon the longish, wispy white-blond hair, the eyes which shone green as emeralds. This man must have been somewhere in his mid-thirties. His fine-grained skin was etched with thin dry lines about the eyes and mouth. Gino shook his head in amazement. "So," he said.

"You know me?" Now it was the other who regarded him closely while Vassya, opposite them, stared at the two with open mouth.

"It was so long ago, I was just a boy of eight when you came to the house," Gino murmured, his brown eyes fastened upon the man beside him. "You would hardly know me. But yes, I remember you. My name is Gino de Gunzburg."

"Gino! For God's sake!" The green eyes lit with recognition, the thin mouth turned up in a broad smile. "Little Gino . . . But I should have known you. Do you recall a very fine portrait that . . . Anna . . . made of you, when you were a lad? She showed it to me, and that's when we became friends. I could not have forgotten you—never!"

Gino battled conflicting impulses, seeing Ivan Berson's hand outstretched in his direction. His hunger and loneliness propelled him to want to hug this unforeseen acquaintance from the past, the comfortable past of home; yet there were memories that thrust themselves between his desire to soothe his flesh and heart, and fulfillment of this desire. He saw his Grandfather Horace holding his father by the arm, the stern look on the old man's face, the tortured, ravaged appearance of his father. He saw his sister Anna before him, too: Anna, whose face had sagged except when he had come to tea, this Ivan Berson, and then his sister had been beautiful and radiant. But his sister had come home in the winter, and she had gone to sleep in the widows' quarters near the kitchens, and had not been allowed to sleep with Sonia. Ivan Berson . . . Terrible arguments with Juanita . . . Vanya?

"Vanya. It's good to see you," he said at last, extending his own hand to the other, his natural good humor eclipsing his doubts and torn family loyalties. There had definitely been more than a hint of scandal; yet, so long ago . . .

They shook hands, and starting to laugh like schoolboys, they embraced, pulled apart, and embraced again. "I'm going to see about the fellows," little Vassya muttered, rising. He shook his head at them, but they paid no attention, not even when he left. Gino felt joyful as a child, the child he had been when last he had seen Ivan Berson eating crumpets at the Gunzburg apartment.

"So?" Gino said. "You are a commissar for the Provisional Government. I shan't ask you what exactly you're supposed to do—but what about your family? Weren't they avowed Tzarists?"

Ivan Berson's face contracted. "I broke with them long

ago," he answered calmly. Then, bits of the puzzle fell somewhat more into place for Gino, who appeared embarrassed. "It's perfectly all right," Ivan smiled. "You were, as you say, still a child. I've been a socialist—a Social Revolutionary, like Kerensky, our War Minister—for many years. He appointed me. But the Bolshevik Congress of Soviets hampers us in Petrograd, and the soldiers' committees here think we're the enemy. But what about you . . . and your family?"

"Papa's in Petrograd, with my brother Ossip. My mother took my sister, Sonia, to Feodosia, because she was ill. My Grandfather Horace died in '09."

"Little Sofia Davidovna, the undaunted," Ivan said with a grin. "She . . . wasn't overly fond of me."

Anna hung between them, an unspoken barrier. At length, Ivan whispered, "Well? Tell me about her."

A strange compassion filled Gino's heart. Looking toward the distant evening star, he said, "I have not seen her for some time, you know. She lives in Switzerland, with a friend, a Persian lady who has a son. They paint. They live simply."

"She is happy?"

Gino's brown eyes rested upon the young commissar, and he said reflectively, "She's safe, isn't she?"

Ivan Berson rose, and buttoning his coat against a gust of wind, stated bitterly, as if to himself, "Safety! That was the last thing she ever hoped for!"

"And you?" Gino asked. "Are you happy? Is it"—and he smiled with irony—"truly fulfilling to be an envoy from the Provisional Government, which may or may not survive? Was this why you read law at the University, Vanya?"

Ivan Berson did not turn around. "Don't be a fool, Gino," he said. The younger man stood up, too, and walked toward his companion. The evening wind tossed dirt in their faces, and now Gino felt cold. Their steps took them toward the embankment where campfires were beginning to glow. Gino wished, with sudden fervor, that he had never met this old acquaintance, that he had been left in peace to finish his meal with little Vassya. When he made out his squad by the light of a flame, he placed a hesitant hand upon Vanya's sleeve, and said, "He's not so bad, your Kerensky."

"Neither are you. Good luck, Gino. And—" Ivan's green eyes pierced the night air, and the young sergeant waited. But the other did not pursue his words, and so, with a final wave of the hand, Gino broke into a run toward his men. I shall not write her, he decided. No, she has forgotten that he ever existed. Let her have peace.

Nineteen

The capital was in a state of confusion. Baron David no longer held any official position, for at the Ministry of Foreign Affairs translators and diplomats were hardly needed; nor were educational reforms at issue in a nation at war with outside enemies as well as inner ones. David read Gino's letters from the front with a measure of hope, for General Kornilov had become Commander in Chief after the offensive on the Austrian front had fizzled out because of internal disorders earlier in July. Kornilov, Gino said, wanted a stop to governmental intervention in army affairs; he was rebuilding his forces. And after a quick outburst from the Bolsheviks, Alexander Kerensky had officially assumed the Prime Ministry of the Provisional Government. "The only problem," David told his son Ossip at the start of the month of August, "is that each of these groups competes with the other two. Kornilov is backed by the conservatives, Lenin by the Bolsheviks, in spite of his flight to Finland, and Kerensky's government by the socialists. There is no true leadership in the nation."

Once, Ossip would have suggested immediate flight to Paris, but now he bided his time, for there was Natasha. He listened to his father with taut muscles, knowing that

Prince Kurdukov was one of Kornilov's generals. When, unable to withstand the strength of his opposition, Kerensky dismissed Kornilov in September, then had him arrested, Ossip went to the apartment and found Natasha awaiting him, her hair undone, her expression distracted. He took her into his arms, not knowing what to say, knowing only too well what she was thinking. If Kurdukov came home, what would become of them? And while she secretly hoped that matters would work out in her favor, she did not actually hate her husband. He was Lara's father, and did not deserve to die simply to avoid prolonging her anguish. "But I shall not live with him again," she declared, and Ossip felt as though he would never be delivered of the jealousy that he bore the absent general. He could only repeat to her his promise of faith, and his pledge to stay beside her. Nothing mattered but the two of them. No marriage on earth could be more binding.

David was busy trying to find homes and work for the Polish Jews brought to him by Ossip's convoys. With the fall of the Tzar, he had allowed more illegal refugees into his home, for the Secret Police did not operate the way they had under Nicholas II. So Ossip was accustomed to bumping into strange kerchiefed women in the hallways of the apartment, or to finding small children sitting around the kitchen table eating bowls of borscht. But his own anxieties were such that he hardly paid them any attention. He could think only of General Prince Kurdukov. He and Baron David passed each other with polite smiles and courteous inquiries, but each felt besieged by his own problems. They rarely had time to talk.

On November 7, Ossip washed, shaved, and came down to breakfast, preparing to go to the bank. The Baron greeted him dressed in a warm gray suit with matching silk cravat. Next to him stood a thin little man with a yarmulke and a woman, neither young nor old. "These are our guests, the Tchomskys," David announced. "I have promised to find work for Mendel Adolfovitch, who is a printer by profession. But the widows' rooms are filled, so I have told Stepan that the Tchomskys may occupy your sister's room."

"I am pleased to meet you," Ossip replied, and he held a chair out for the woman, who thanked him in Yiddish. Then the young man sat down, buttered a sweet roll, and began his meal. His father engaged the couple in conversation, and Ossip smiled, thinking of his mother and what she would have said to this little scene of hospitality. He missed her clear mind, so akin to his own, but for some reason he felt touched today by his father's behavior toward the refugees. For the thousandth time in his life, Ossip told himself that it was a pity that compassion, so strong and pure in David, was so filtered in himself; but he had long ago accepted his own detached nature. His father had been born and would die an idealist.

It was at the bank that morning that Ossip first learned that the Bolsheviks had seized most of the government buildings, that the Petrograd garrison had allowed them to enter the Winter Palace and had joined ranks with the insurgents.

"They want to prevent the elections to the Constituent Assembly from taking place," his Uncle Sasha stated, his blue eyes wide with horror. "So if their side doesn't win, they'll be in control anyway." But Ossip was hardly listening. Beads of perspiration coursed down his back, and he thought: My God, if Papa has ventured to a ministry, or to see anyone in government, on behalf of those Tchomskys . . . But he could not complete his thought. In cold fear, he went to the telephone and asked the central operator for the Gunzburg number. The lines had been cut. His uncle burst into his office, his eyes wild. "I'm going home," he said tersely. "Rosa is terrified. I could curse myself today, for having succumbed to her irrational preference for a household of female help. What good are they to her now?"

Ossip remained glued to his seat. What about Natasha? Her parents, the idiots, are still here, waiting with her for news of that husband which they had imposed upon her. What if insurgents once again seized the Count? But there was still Nicolai Nicolaievitch, Natasha's older brother, the one Ossip had never liked, who had served in the Senate with their father. He would protect his own mother, Maria Efimovna, and Natasha, and little Larissa. Ossip half-rose, thinking: To hell with them, Natasha is mine, and I shall go to her. And then he thought again: But Papa! I am the only one he can count on. Uncle Sasha will be with Aunt Rosa . . .

Maybe nothing will happen, just another of the many uprisings we've already gone through, Ossip murmured to himself. But he seized his hat and coat, grabbed his silver-studded cane, which he carried for effect alone, stopped only to withdraw a sheaf of banknotes from the family account, and hailed a passing coach. He would, he decided, go first to his father, simply to ease his mind. Then he would stop at the apartment to check with Pavel. Perhaps, if she needed him, she would send word through him, or even go to the apartment. He wanted to take care of her and of little Lara, and even of Maria Efimovna, if it were necessary. But first, his father.

The hired coach took Ossip to the front door of his house, but there, as he stepped down, his own Vova came hurtling toward him, his coat torn, his face haggard. "Ossip Davidovitch!" he cried, and in his frenzy grasped Ossip's waistcoat lapels in trembling fingers. "There're soldiers upstairs with your father, and those Jews! I was going for the police—"

"Soldiers?" Now Ossip felt goose bumps on his scalp, and he shook Vova roughly. "Who, and why?"

"Riots, that's why! Petrograd garrison's gone wild. Looting and beating. Do you want me to go for the police? Or will you go, and I'll stay to help?"

"No, you go!" Ossip cried. "I'm going upstairs right now."

"It's not safe," the coachman stammered. "You know, sir, your back—"

But the young man had pushed past him, racing blindly up the flights of stairs and arriving at the apartment disheveled and red. The door stood ajar, and Ossip pushed it open and entered the vestibule. He could hear voices in the sitting room, Stepan's and his father's, and the shrill cry of the Tchomsky wife. Then there were harsh, drunken voices which were totally unfamiliar to him. From the doorway he peered into the room, hearing his own heart-beat in his wrists and temples. His eyes were opened wide and he tried to breathe quietly, but gasped in spite of himself.

His father, blue marks around his pale lips, stood in front of Madame Tchomskaya. Stepan was next to him, standing erect in his black suit, like a dignified raven. The little Tchomsky man was not to be seen. But there were three soldiers in the room, and one of them brandished a bayonet at his father's throat and said, "A Baron and a Jew! What luck! But it's the woman I'll have, and now!" He seized Madame Tchomskaya by the arm and dragged her, screaming, to a corner. Then the soldier threw her into the wall and watched with laughter as she collapsed, whimpering, to the floor. He hurled himself on top of her, and she uttered the most frightful scream, a plaint in Yiddish, which appeared to die in her very throat. Ossip saw Stepan take an enormous step toward her, saw him raise a fist which held a glistening copper paperweight, saw him bring the fist down upon the head of the soldier who had thrown himself atop Madame Tchomskaya—and then saw Stepan himself crumple with a soft moan, as blood trickled from his neck. One of the other soldiers had gouged him with the tip of his bayonet.

Ossip stood as if mesmerized by the scene before him.

He could not think at all. The third soldier was yelling something, and he and the one who had struck Stepan now grabbed David by the arms, and began shouting something about the safe. Ossip saw them forcibly remove his father from the sitting room, leaving their unconscious companion still straddling Madame Tchomskaya, who had fainted. Ossip breathed deeply, again and again, until a purple rage seized hold of him, and he rushed into the room, moving toward the woman and disentangling her from her unmoving assailant whom he fiercely kicked. But he was not thinking about this woman, except in passing. Let them empty the safe! he thought wildly. It will give me time to find Papa's revolver, or else they will murder him, and me, and the lot of us. But as he tiptoed to his father's bedroom, neatly avoiding the study where he assumed that David was unlocking the family safe, he stopped for a brief instant by Stepan's body. Ossip kneeled, touched the servant's wrist, and quivered with hope: the pulse, though weak, was still present. He was miraculously alive! Ossip went to his father's bedside table and took out the small pearl-handled revolver that his brother Sasha had given Baron David as a precaution during the previous uprising. Now, Ossip praised the practical banker!

Armed, Ossip hastened noiselessly to the study, and found his father confronting the two inebriated soldiers, his face stark white. "You cannot take what has already been taken," Baron David was asserting calmly. "I have told you—two of your men were here earlier, and took everything. My wife's jewels, all our cash reserves—everything that was here! I have been wiped clean of my riches, gentlemen. You will have to look elsewhere to do your thieving."

David had not seen Ossip. Neither had the soldiers. Now one of them took the Baron by his shoulders and began to beat his head against the mantelpiece. Ossip's mouth parted, his breath stopped. Sheer horror convulsed his body. Without second thought, he cocked the pistol behind the back of the man who was holding his father, aimed and pulled the trigger. With a violent shout, half of surprise, the man fell sideways. On impulse Ossip fired at the other man as his lips opened in bewildered fury.

"Papa!" Ossip cried, running, but the Baron, gagging, clutched at his throat, choking and falling forward. Ossip reached him and turned him onto his back, loosening his cravat and holding his head. He could not understand what was happening.

Ossip, on the floor with his father, did not hear Madame Tchomskaya enter the study. He helped his father turn to his side, so that he might vomit. Madame Tchomskaya whispered, in Yiddish, "It's his heart, isn't it?"

"For God's sake, get a doctor!" Ossip cried. But the woman shook her head, tears streaming from her eyes. She mumbled something about "too long," and "day like today." Ossip wanted to grab her and kick her as he had kicked the man who had attacked her. "He was thinking of you, only of you!" he screamed at her. "Now do something for him!" But the woman stood still, crying softly, as Ossip wiped his father's mouth with his embroidered linen handkerchief. He had never felt so helpless in his entire life, not even during the years of his childhood, strapped to his crib.

"Your mother . . . respect her . . ." the Baron was whispering, and now Ossip stroked his face, his cheeks. and nodded, repeating his father's words. He knew that his own tears were falling on his father's chin, that he was sobbing like a boy. But he could not cease, even when Madame Tchomskaya moved him aside and insisted upon closing the Baron's eyes. It was unthinkable that his father would simply collapse like this, simply die! Yet his breathing had stopped, the woman was right, and only this body remained of what had been Baron David de Gunzburg. Ossip's shoulders rose and fell with wracking sobs. He could not leave the room.

At long last, Madame Tchomskaya said, "Your kind

servant is badly hurt. But he is alive, Ossip Davidovitch.
You must think of him. And of yourself. My husband had
gone to see about a job—I shall await him here, with the
other servants. But you must be gone. They will know who
fired the gun. You must think of leaving the city."

Dazed, Ossip rose and followed her to the sitting room,
where she had placed a crude bandage about Stepan's
head. Several scared chambermaids were clustered near the
wall. Suddenly Ossip's mind cleared. "Do you all have
places to go?" he demanded. They nodded. He cleared his
throat: "Then go. And somebody please take the Tchomskys. My father . . . would want them taken care of. Have
them go to my uncle, Baron Alexander. I shall take Stepan
with me, for he will have to leave this city too. The man he
hurt is not dead, and can come for him. I"—and he smiled
wryly—"have no more bullets left in the revolver. My father must have practiced, to have left me only two good
shots . . ." He thought: Yes, Uncle Sasha must have made
him learn to shoot, four times—but for what?

Tears stood once more in his eyes. He spoke again: "Is it
true, that others came this morning, and looted the safe?"

"Yes, Baron," one of the girls replied. "The funds from
the Judaica are gone, too."

Ossip sighed. "Here," he said, and handed her a purse
with some coins. "I shall keep some money for Stepan and
me, to see us through, but you will need this."

Vova and Madame Tchomskaya's husband came in together, and Ossip, his face suddenly paling, fell against the
wall and whispered that he wanted them to carry Stepan to
the landau. He wanted Vova to drive them somewhere in
the city. "I can no longer pay you," he said to Vova. "They
have taken all but what my father has invested in the bank.
My uncle will pay you, when I am gone. But I shall need
the landau for myself and Stepan."

Less than an hour later, feeling battered and unclean,
Ossip sat in his love nest, where Natasha had come to him

so often, smelling of wildflowers. Stepan lay upon the bed where his young master had made love to Natasha. Pavel had gone for medical supplies, and Ossip waited, wondering if the maître d'hôtel would live or die, as his father had. He, Ossip, had killed two men, and for what? His father had died anyway, and of a heart attack! He leaned forward and wept, bitterly. Suddenly he knew that for all their disagreements, he had loved David very deeply, had respected him although he'd never sought to emulate him. And Mama loved him too, he realized, and he wept for her also.

He did not know where he would go if Stepan survived. Nor did he know how to get word to Natasha, who was his life, his heart, his entire being. He did not think that he was ruined, for there was still plenty of Gunzburg money in the Maison Gunzburg. He simply thought that when all this was over, his uncle would wire him the funds, and later, when the furor would abate, he would be able to return to Petrograd. He had not committed murder, only attempted to save his father's life.

He was so exhausted that he fainted, like a paper doll flitting to the floor in a gust of wind. The gust of wind was the November Revolution.

The following day the Council of the People's Commissars established itself, with Lenin as President and Trotsky as his Commissar for Foreign Affairs. Alexander Kerensky left the city as quickly as possible. The Council issued two proclamations, the first that peace negotiations would be started at once on a separate basis, for the rest of the Allied forces were fighting more than ever for domination of the Central Powers; the second, that the gentry would be deprived of possession of their lands, which would be divided equally among all those who had worked them. Ossip sat, undone, in the little apartment, and sent Pavel with a hurried note to his Uncle Sasha at the bank. In it, he explained that his father had died and would need burial, that he himself would have to flee, that his maître d'hôtel, Stepan, was badly wounded, and that he planned to bring him along with him as soon as he could be moved without peril. He further explained about the looting of the Gunz- burg safe, about the Tchomskys, about the family servants. Then he sat on the sofa, unable to think or move. It was there that Natasha found him shortly afterward.

When he saw her, his first words were of concern for her and her daughter, but she sensed at once that something dreadful had happened and, sobbing in her arms, he told her of his father's death. "What a waste of a good man!" he cried repeatedly. "His heart had been weak for years! But he was strong. And then—I killed those two insane drunkards, and he simply collapsed before my eyes! There was nothing to be done. Now there will be no funeral for him as there was for my Grandfather Horace, no chance for the Jews of this city to walk behind the hearse to the cemetery. It was he who obtained the concession for the Jewish cemetery—he who cared for these people as his own family—"

"Do not torture yourself like this, my beloved," Natasha comforted, wringing her hands. Her own tears fell upon his hair, which she caressed. "You were very brave, Ossip. I am proud of you. Your father would have been proud. I'm sure that he *was* proud, for he saw what you accomplished to save him—"

"And now you must leave this accursed city!" Ossip interrupted, taking her face into his feverish hands. "Go— to the Tambov, anywhere! Come with us."

Her beautiful features softened, her eyes glowed under their veil of tears. "The Tambov property is no longer ours, nor is Mohilna yours, nor the estates in the Crimea. Didn't Pavel tell you about the Decree of Land issued today? Our property is gone, Ossip. At least for now. Papa believes things will quiet down, that the Bolsheviks will be quelled.

He wants to remain here, but Mama wants us to go to France while we still can. The safest way for me and Lara is . . . to try to find . . . my husband, at the front. The army will protect us. If we are ever to recapture Petrograd, the army shall have to do it for us."

"You would do that? Go to him?"

She could not speak. Tears blinded her. At length, she kissed his hands and said, "You must escape to guard your very life, my darling. Already, Stepan will be a burden. Do you honestly wish for Lara and me to add to that? A small child is difficult enough to handle in a large city. Think, Ossip. There is the future—"

"What future, if you go to him, and I go my way?" he exclaimed.

"I shall not live with him. I told you, Ossip, I shall not. After all this is finished, when the war ends, when Petrograd is ours again—"

"But that will never happen!" he cried fiercely.

"Then we shall have to keep in touch, somehow. If things are bad, if we are driven out, we shall go to France. And then we can be together—have our own children—" Her face twisted into a grimace of pain, and she turned away. "I want our own children," she repeated.

"I don't care! I only want you, you're all I've ever wanted. Until I met you I never cared for anyone except for my sister Sonia. But I lost you once, and that means more to me than having lost life, for I did not love life as I loved—love—you."

It was a strange sight that greeted Baron Alexander de Gunzburg when he followed Pavel into the apartment and saw his nephew, disheveled, with circles under his eyes, sobbing in the arms of a beautiful young woman whose mass of black hair would not remain in pins above her head. Sasha saw her rear her head proudly, meet his eyes with the brightest eyes he had ever encountered, and hold his gaze without flinching. To draw Ossip's attention, Pavel gently cleared his throat.

Ossip saw his uncle and jumped to his feet. He looked from Sasha to Natasha, pure horror etched upon his features. But it was she who spoke first. She said, calmly, "There is hardly need for protocol during moments such as these." Her delicate hand, with its long, tapered fingers, waved about the room. "I am Princess Kurdukova, Natalia Nicolaievna Kurdukova. And you . . . are Ossip's uncle?"

"Yes. Alexander Goratsievitch de Gunzburg. Under different circumstances, I would say that I am most honored to meet you, Princess. But there has been the tragedy, and my manners fail me." Sasha could not help thinking that his nephew had more in him than he would have assumed, ferreting away this extraordinary beauty, wife of a general and daughter of a well-known senator. For all of Petrograd had heard of this young noblewoman, of her illustrious connections. Then he vaguely recalled that a Tagantsev—wasn't her maiden name Tagantsev?—had been a bitter opponent of his brother, and of his father, and that there had been quite a to-do over the fact that Ossip's best friend at the gymnasium had been this Tagantsev's son. Apparently there had been further entanglements. He wet his lips, admiring Natasha's bravura, but thinking also of David, the brother he had spent a lifetime envying, but who was now dead. Sasha was much distressed at his own lack of ability to fit into this absurd situation, he, a man of the world.

"I must go now, my love," Natasha murmured. She wound her arms around Ossip's neck and buried her face in the lapels of his waistcoat. Briefly, her full red lips reached to his, and she clung to him with unrestrained passion. He attempted to hold her to him, but suddenly she broke loose and ran, holding up her skirt, her head bent down. She stopped in the doorway, her fingers eloquently placed upon her half-parted lips. Then she hastened down the stairs, out of sight.

"Well," Sasha stated dully. He sat down beside his nephew on the sofa. "You are not going to hold on to her?" But Ossip's eyes, blue-black, turned toward him with so much unspoken menace that he colored, and changed the position of his crossed legs. He said, "David. My God, Ossip! Why him? The most just of us all . . ."

"Perhaps because of that," the young man replied. "To spare him what's to come . . ."

"Where are you going to go?" his uncle demanded. "And Stepan?"

"Stepan is conscious now. We shall leave within the week, I suppose. I don't know where to go. If we go north, through Sweden, I shall end up in Berlin in the midst of the war. I suppose I can go to Odessa, and attempt to catch a ship to Marseilles. But I shall have to let you know. We will need money."

"Of course. I shall have to send money to your mother, too, for with this Decree of Land she has lost her Crimean estate. My share is gone too," he said, smiling wanly. He added, "Will you have sufficient funds for the trip—to Odessa?"

"I think so. If not, I can always pray. I wouldn't know to whom to address my prayers, though." Ossip smiled back at his uncle.

"You know the Ashkenasys of Odessa? They are relatives, and own a prosperous bank. Should we become cut off, call on them." Sasha examined his neatly manicured fingers, and bit his lower lip. "Why did David insist upon keeping all that Zionist money in his private safe?" he cried. "From the sale of the Judaica books? Why didn't it go to us, in the bank? Whoever thought of hoarding hundreds of thousands of rubles in his house, for God's sweet sake?"

"Papa was never a businessman, Uncle Sasha. He wanted access to large amounts of money to help the Jews from Poland. No wonder the soldiers came straight to our house! It could not have been hard for them to make some poor frightened Jew talk, and give them Papa's name. It makes sense, doesn't it?"

"Nothing really does, my boy. I only hope the Halperins take good care of Tania and Gorik, in Kiev. And you—be careful, Ossip. Rosa and I—have always cared about you, most of all. Now, with David gone—"

"I know, Uncle Sasha." He paused, his eyes downcast. "The funeral?"

The big man nodded, heavily. He placed a hand upon Ossip's shoulder, rested it there, and shook his head silently. Neither one could look into the eyes of the other. Here we are, the selfish ones, Ossip thought wryly, while the only one who truly cared is killed. He could not think of Natasha, nor of his mother and Sonia. If only he could go to Gino . . .

Pavel entered discreetly and spoke up: "The man, Stepan, Monsieur, he tells me that he feels much improved. Do you wish to go in to speak with him? I have changed the dressing on his wound."

"And I must go," his uncle declared, rising. The two men now faced each other, and silently embraced. At the door, Sasha called out, "God preserve you, Ossip!" Ossip watched his bulky shoulders disappear down the staircase, and he sighed. Everyone of meaning was gone. There was no haven now but from within. Yet what lay within but hollow sounds? I am a coward, he thought, only now there is no doubt remaining, no doubt to shield me from myself. I have a journey to plan . . .

Letters came irregularly to Feodosia, but reached their destination. So, almost at once, the Gunzburg women learned that the Bolsheviks had seized control of the capital, that David was dead, that the family safe had been robbed, and that Ossip had fled with a wounded Stepan to Odessa. Then they learned from Rosa that the banks had been taken in hand by the new government, and that she and Sasha, destitute (as were Mathilde and her children), had tried to flee the capital northward, but had been turned back at the Swedish border because their papers had not been properly signed by the new authorities. Sasha had been placed in jail, and had only been released when it was discovered that he possessed no hidden reserve of funds. They planned, Rosa wrote, to arrange to have their visas properly attested, and Tania would send them sufficient funds to join her in Kiev. Then they would all leave the country together, somehow. Ossip sent word that he had reached Odessa, not without adventures, but that he had run out of money, and knew that the Maison Gunzburg had been "nationalized" by the Bolsheviks in Petrograd; so he had gone to the family connection in Odessa, the Ashkenasys, and obtained a position in their bank. The Bolshevik system had not yet spread to Odessa.

Sonia read the account her brother had given of their father's death, and she sat down, holding her stomach as though someone had kicked her with brute strength. At first she felt nothing at all but this purely physical pain. She had left her mother and Johanna in the next room, wanting to be alone with her grief. But it was not sadness that filled her. It was a terrible, boiling anger that flared inside her stomach, like lye eating away at its lining. I knew it! she thought. I knew I should have stayed with him in Petrograd—I knew it because I loved him, more than the others did. Anna never forgave him for Vanya, and for not listening to the Union of Unions; Ossip always despised him, and was ashamed of being a Jew; yes, Gino loved him, but then again he was young and never knew our father, did not truly comprehend him in mind and soul, as I did. Mama? Oh, I do not want to think, I do not want to think! But Mama should never have married him. She had no understanding of his passions, nor did she want to have any; instead, she permitted Juanita to ridicule and scorn him. Uncle Sasha envied Papa, and Uncle Misha? Yes, he loved him, but from far away, as Gino did, for Misha was so much younger, and they lived apart . . . There was Grandfather Horace, then, and I. And I loved him more than any other man in my life, even more than Volodia, for when I had to choose between them, I chose Papa!

What could it possibly matter that they were ruined, apart from the remainder of the summer harvest money from the Crimean estates; that Rosa and Sasha were destitute and reduced to begging from their daughter's in-laws? She could work, her hands were good, her mind was clever. But she would never kiss her father again, never hear him call her his "little pigeon." She thought with a surge of passion that she had wanted him to know of Anna's boy. He would have understood, because he had loved Anna, and had wanted grandchildren.

Suddenly she felt two soft hands upon her, and in rebuff she jerked upright and was astounded to find Olga Pomerantz next to her. The young girl, with her fine blond curls, said, "I know that you mind my intrusion. But I came because, you see, I know what it feels like. My father died also, and left me with a hole this big in my chest." She made a vast gesture with her hands. "One morning, getting dressed. It was also . . . heart trouble." Her wide hazel eyes filled with tears. "And I was jealous of Mama. Such attention to the bereaved widow! I was certain that she had not loved Papa as much as I. Sometimes, I still wonder."

"With me," Sonia stated bitterly, "there is nothing to wonder about."

"But there are different kinds of love," Olga said tentatively. She was suddenly afraid of this beautiful girl who was older and wiser but also so harsh, so stark in her brutal anguish.

"Yes," Sonia agreed, and thought: Kolya, Kolya! Why isn't there someone to hold me?

"I came with a proposition," Olga stated. "Mita, the Rabbi's daughter, needs money, too. She wants to teach us stenography. I do not know how long our enterprise will belong to us, before the Reds will decide to come into the Crimea and 'nationalize' us, too. So—I shall need to learn a trade, Sonia. And, I thought you would, too."

Her eyes rested upon her friend's gray ones, and Sonia slowly came alive. Her chin trembled, then her mouth. She pressed Olga's arm with her frail fingers. "That would be perfect," she stammered. "We must think of ways to economize. We shall have to rent out part of this house, or move somewhere else. The harvest money will have to see us through an indefinite period of time. Thank you, Olga."

Finally she went to her mother, and placed her arms around Mathilde's shoulders. Olga left silently, but Johanna stood in a corner, watching with eyes that darted like quicksilver from woman to woman. Mathilde stood erect, dignified, her beautiful gray hair coiled elegantly atop her head, and her sapphire eyes moist but not overflowing. "Sonia," she said. "Sonia, I loved him . . . as much as it was possible for me to love him. I admired and revered him, and I gave him four unique children who helped fill his life. We all disappointed him, my daughter. He was better than each of us. But he loved us, and now we must treasure the bounty of that love. Condemnation, even self-condemnation, will not help either of us, remember that."

"I know, Mama," Sonia answered softly, kissing her mother on the cheek. "I have come to discuss our future with you, now that we are poor. I am certain that Ossip will earn enough for his passage to France, or England, at the Ashkenasy bank. Anna has some savings, and sells her work, and is safely out of this mess. Eventually Uncle Misha, whose fortune is intact, and our other relatives in Paris will be able to send us funds. But, in the meantime, all we have is from the last harvest. I am going to take stenography lessons with Olga, and we can look for board-

ers to share our rent here. It will be difficult for you,
Mama. Life will be simpler than you ever conceived . . ."

"Not so difficult," Mathilde retorted with a half-smile
that brought Ossip's image to Sonia's mind. "I would much
rather live in rags than beyond our income, as my father
did. You forget my childhood. For every diamond cufflink
he bought, Papa increased his ruin, and the ruin of his
children." Now tears glistened on the edge of her black
lashes. "Your father must have loved me very deeply,
Sonia. Not only did he choose a bride without a dowry, but
it was he, and his own father, who paid my father a price
for the honor of marrying me."

Sonia touched her mother's hand. "That is not hard to
believe," she remarked. She did not notice that her mother's smile faded, that an icy expression replaced it momentarily. Mathilde was thinking: But David was my cousin,
and had known me from birth! Who will take my Sonia,
now that there is no longer any dowry? She began to panic
but Sonia's voice brought her back to the problem at hand.
"We shall have to write this news to Gino," Sonia stated.
"He will want to be reassured that we are all right, although I'm certain Ossip will have let him know about . . .
Papa. Mama, I need your help now."

Johanna de Mey stood apart, wondering why this death,
so longed for by herself, was not changing her life as she
had hoped and expected. Mathilde was not guilty. She was
serene, poised. Why was she not coming to her? She turned
her face away, unable to watch her companion, unable to
bear her own acute misery. Tears of frustration flowed
down her cheeks, but the two women did not see them.
Mathilde and Sonia sat side by side upon the divan, composing a letter for their brave soldier, thinking of his suffer-
ings, and not at all of hers, which twisted through her
entrails like a sharply honed sickle. She thought: Nobody
has ever loved me, nobody at all, and if I have come to this
point in my life, stranded in a foreign nation in political
strife, with a destitute family, it was a sacrifice which

brought me nothing, nothing but humiliation. Suddenly, she regarded Mathilde with an expression of pure hatred.

Gino could not believe what was happening around him. On December 3, official negotiations for a separate peace treaty were begun between the Bolsheviks and the Central Powers, and the army began to disintegrate. Everything was happening so quickly, so haphazardly, it seemed. It was impossible to follow. In the south, where he was stationed, a counterrevolutionary movement was being organized, and his regiment was being transformed into what was called a "White" regiment. But the "Red," or Workers' and Peasants' Army, was now the official force of the nation, and was largely composed of the same officers as those who had served under Kornilov, and under whom he, as a sergeant, had served. So, Gino thought, our army now has two sides, and good men take part in civil war. This is not what we enlisted for! This is not noble fighting to defeat the Central Powers. He remembered Ivan Berson, Anna's lover, who was a Kerensky socialist. Yet he, Gino, had thought of him merely as an old Petrograd acquaintance from the old days. So men who had once served together proposed to slaughter one another—and all for political purposes which he did not as yet understand. He watched, baffled and outraged.

The officers were taking sides, but for many of the soldiers a joyride had begun. Officially, the nation was still at war, and all men wore the same khaki uniforms, with only small insignias on the cap, the shoulder, or the collar to differentiate among the various regiments. But the men, hearing of revolution, thought themselves free, and soon young soldiers were abandoning their posts and going home. Others, taking advantage of a wartime regulation that permitted members of the army first access, free of charge, on any train, hopped aboard and rode for days, changing trains as though they were merry-go-rounds at a fair. Gino realized that he would either have to sign up in the new White regiment, or leave the disintegrated army which was no longer fighting a war. He went to his captain, and, attempting to keep his voice firm, he declared: "I am a born Russian, and in good conscience, after much consideration, I cannot bear arms against a fellow Russian. I do not favor the Petrograd government. But I cannot kill my countrymen."

Besides, he wanted to go to his mother and sister at once, before the New Year, if possible. Feodosia was a port, and also had a railroad, and if the Reds came to the Crimea, they would reach the accessible cities first, and there would be street fights and destruction. Gino's heart was heavy with sorrow for his wounded country and for his father, whom he had loved devotedly. Unlike Ossip, he had never considered their father weak; he had found him a model of courageous dignity, of idealism pushed to the extreme. Gino did not find these traits ludicrous; he found them moving. He himself was a patriot, and could only sustain simpler passions. But he had admired David's character, and recalled their walks in Mohilna, their long talks of nature. Now he wept for the loss of this magnificent man, and for his mother and sister, who had lost so much as well. And on a cold winter's day, he too boarded a train, in his khaki uniform, knowing that no one would harm him, Red or White, for all soldiers looked alike. The thought was hardly a consolation.

She sat just underneath a staircase, on the deck that was crowded with howling refugees of all ages and backgrounds. She cradled her son in her arms, and crooned to him a song of her childhood. Her golden hair blew about her face in the wind, her cornflower-blue eyes glistening with memories of dances and gay moments, of the Mariinsky Theater, of a watch crafted by Fabergé. "But you, my love, are a Russian, don't you ever forget it," she said to the little boy, bouncing him precariously on her knee.

She had wanted to find Ossip, to take him with them all on this exodus. Her mother and father, impoverished, had told her he had gone to Odessa when last they had heard. Sioma had said, "Why not? We are already a crowd, and he is family." But the old man, the hideously miserly old man, her father-in-law, had shaken his head and propelled them all like a flock of sheep toward this ship. He could not wait, the Reds would catch up with them if they stopped to fetch this cousin of Tania. How she detested him, the old man, she thought, as she rocked her baby in her arms, and was jostled by another woman. Here she was, Baroness Tatiana Alexandrovna de Gunzburg, and she had been lucky to locate this tiny space beneath the staircase for herself and her son. Tears of rage came to her eyes.

But, she thought, it is this dreadful family, these ugly Kiev upstarts who are saving Mama and Papa today. Her father-in-law had hoarded a veritable fortune in a Swiss bank, and the Halperins were not ruined. She thought painfully of Jean, then dismissed the memory, and thought of Ossip, her companion-in-thoughts, her friend. Should she have married him? She licked her lips and mused. He would have enchanted her, given her passion of the flesh, made her collapse with hilarity. But he would never have amassed a fortune, would not have found a way to save her parents from ruin. Twenty years ago, Ossip would have made her a fine husband, with inherited wealth. Today, hard as it was to accept, she desperately needed Sioma Halperin.

"Honor thy father, partridge of mine," she said to the child, with an effort at light laughter. "Love him, sweetest. That is the least we can do, you and I. And I shall try, you'll see . . ."

The Red Army was coming to Feodosia. Newspapers no longer existed, only two-page leaflets filled with Bolshevik propaganda. The educated members of the town now attempted to refer to the Petrograd government as "the Bolsheviks" and to their army as "the Reds," so that they could speak more clearly of them. Russia was so vast that the Council of the People's Commissars, in the capital, could only spread its control through the individual soviets that were gradually forming in the towns, but not always in the smaller villages. Opposition to the Red takeover of government processes compelled Lenin to resort in December 1917 to the creation of the Extraordinary Commission for the Suppression of Counterrevolution, commonly called the Cheka. This body perpetrated such horrible deeds that it came to be known as the Red Terror. In addition, when members of the Red Army took over an area, executions and assassinations frequently took place as a matter of course. Gino had written his mother, "You must remember that civil war is the worst of all man's fights, and he turns most viciously on his own kind. White takeovers are bound to become equally bloody." But, he added, after the initial reprisals, life would probably resume its course.

When the Reds marched into Feodosia, the Gunzburgs were not at home, but at the house of the Pomerantzes, for it was New Year's Eve. Immediately, Nadezhda Igorovna and Olga took their guests to a back room where old furniture was being stored, and where there were no windows. Mathilde and Sonia, in mourning, had not wished to celebrate the New Year, but Nadezhda Igorovna, whom Mathilde now familiarly called "Nadia," had insisted that they come for a most simple supper, in order not to be alone with their grief. Johanna de Mey had refused to go along.

The four women and the Pomerantz servants huddled together in the dark, among the dusty crates and boxes. Sonia's hand remained on Mathilde's arm, as though to warn her mother to keep quiet. But Mathilde was far too terrified to scream. She leaned against Nadezhda Igorovna. Suddenly a noise, of glass splintering harshly, penetrated the musty room, and Sonia's lips parted on an intake of breath. Her heart was pounding in her throat. More noises followed, and Mathilde, who treasured peace, beauty, and wholeness, felt as though her own body were being violated along with the house. Then the looters departed, or so Sonia thought, hearing the shouts moving toward the street, and a horrid silence take over the house. She rose, and touched Olga on the shoulder. The two young women slipped out of the storage area and into the living room. Even in the darkness they could discern the damage, the broken tables and slashed Persian rugs. "Oh, my God!" Sonia cried.

But Nadia Pomerantz exclaimed, "They did not know about my lack of taste, did they, my friends? Aren't you pleased, Mathilde, that the paintings you selected for me had not yet arrived?" She began to laugh, the warmth of her resonant chuckles spreading to her daughter and two guests. Calmly, she requested her servants to attempt to make order in the house.

Only then did Mathilde suddenly clap her hand to her mouth, crying, "Johanna! She is alone with Marfa, the maid. Sonia, we must go at once. Will your valet accompany us, Nadia?" She thanked her hostess and left, Sonia pressing behind her with the Pomerantz servant. They nearly ran the short distance that spanned the two houses. There were no lights in the Gunzburg windows, and Sonia said, "I cannot tell if the panes are broken. Come, Mama, through the back."

They discovered upon entering their rented house that many beautiful carvings, oil canvases, and silver and crystal bibelots had been smashed and dented, while others had been stolen. Now they ran about the house, calling, "Johanna! Juanita!" and "Marfa, where are you hiding?" Naked terror filled them as they stepped over shards of glass in an effort to open all doors.

They found Johanna crouched in the kitchen broom

closet, her aquamarine eyes bloodshot and dilated, her thin hands scraping against her clothing, her hair, her face. Mathilde took a step back, bile rising to her mouth as if she had seen a wild animal. Then, as Sonia resolutely pulled the woman from between the brooms, Mathilde came to her, and extended her hands. But Johanna de Mey regarded her with enormous bulging eyes, and shook herself away. "You left me here for them to murder!" she cried, her voice rising shrilly.

"You must leave now," Sonia whispered with embarrassment to the curious Pomerantz valet. She walked with him to the front door, which had been pushed in, and he helped her to lift the heavy wood and replace it upon its hinges. In the kitchen, Mathilde, her face white, her eyes full of tears, was saying softly, "No, it was you who would not come to Nadia's. Remember, Johanna, it was your decision. She invited you. We . . . had no idea . . . they would come tonight."

"But you chose to be with her! You have stopped loving me, Mathilde. I can see everything; that woman has taken over, and it is her you love. Oh, if I had been replaced by a young girl, by a round plump girl, by a lithe sylph of a girl, then I might have understood, although it might still have killed me! But not this woman, this Nadia, who resembles a horse, yes, a horse! What solace can you possibly find in her caresses, the caresses of a woman every day as old as I, who have loved you more than twenty years?"

Johanna de Mey was now advancing upon Mathilde, her eyes wildly shining, her breath hot upon the face of the other woman, who backed away with sudden fear and loathing. Sonia, panting from her exertions with the door, entered, carrying a kerosene lamp. Her mother turned to her, her face agape, her body trembling. "Yes!" Johanna screamed. "Tell your sweet precious daughter about what we have done, you and I, during the years of your marriage to her sanctified father! Tell her, Mathilde, or I shall!"

Sonia stood like an ebony statue in her mourning gown, holding the lamp. Its flame lit the ceiling, then fell upon her mother's expression of sheer horror and fear. Startled, Sonia moved closer, then saw Johanna, her long body quivering, her face splotched with red, her nose etched like a knife against the background of darkness. "Sonia!" the Dutchwoman cried, her face coming alive. "Would you like me to tell you a story? About betrayal and abandonment, about lost faith, about kisses in the night—"

"I do not know what you are talking about," Sonia declared, her voice crisp and clear. "Here, you are hysterical with fright. Where's Marfa?"

"Marfa? Oh, the maid! That is another story of abandonment. God will punish you, Mathilde. The maid has vanished into the night air, wearing scarlet ribbons in her hair and proclaiming she wants to be free and join the Reds. She left, and now we have no servants at all."

"You're lying!" Sonia exclaimed, grabbing Johanna's arm and giving it a shake. "Marfa's been with us since I was a child! She wouldn't leave us. We've been good to her."

"But she has, nevertheless. She said: 'The Baroness has no money left, and I am tired of running errands.' And then she, a woman of forty, took the arm of the soldier who was here, and off she skipped, laughing. Bunch of hoodlums, the lot of them. Ossip was crazy to burden himself with Stepan—now he'll probably be knifed in the back, in Odessa, by that tall brute!"

"Shut up!" Sonia cried. She stepped directly in front of the Dutchwoman and glared at her from her large gray eyes. Her body was shaking, and she could hardly breathe, but she propelled the woman in front of her to the room which Johanna used as a bedroom. She pushed her roughly onto the bed, and stood over her, her white face taut. "You will remain here," she said with authority. "Mama will go to bed, and you will stay away from her, do you understand? I shall have to do some work to clean up this mess they have left us."

When she returned to the kitchen to fetch a dustpan and a mop, Mathilde still stood, transfixed, in the same spot. Sonia stated tersely, bending to pick up a piece of debris, "There is much work to be done. Windows to be covered up somehow, with pieces of wood or cardboard, or whatever I can find. Go to sleep, Mama." Then, without looking at her mother, she added, "Do you remember when I caught pneumonia, in '03? Looking for Anna? Well, you were never told the story of what happened that night. Not even Papa was told the truth. Actually—I alone know what happened. I did not even tell Anna, but Juanita had sent the Secret Police after her. Had it not been for our friendship with Lopukhin, Annushka might have been sent to the Fortress, on charges of high treason. Juanita tried to send Anna away, because of her insane hatred of her—of all of us. Don't you see that she's always hated us—Papa, Annushka, me?" She walked briskly into the living room, carrying her kitchen utensils.

Mathilde's sapphire eyes glowed like shiny new marbles, but they saw nothing. She could not speak.

As she swept broken windowpanes into a corner, Sonia remembered suddenly that it was the New Year, 1918, and that this marked the fifth anniversary of her engagement to Kolya Saxe. For the first New Year since 1913 she had failed to be overwhelmed by dejection and regret. She touched her hair, which was covered with dust, and thought: Could it be that finally I am over loving him? Or did all the things that happened tonight shadow my feelings? She waited, but the familiar, dull ache did not spread through her muscles and into her bones, and her throat did not constrict. So! she reflected, and resumed her activities.

Because of heavy fighting in the Ukraine, where White regiments had joined with the fierce separatist forces for an independent state, Gino was obliged to detour in his efforts to reach his mother and sister. Normally, trains were kept on schedule, and one could plot a voyage stop by stop; but now the young man realized that at every station the trains would halt indefinitely. He spent many nights stretched out on benches in waiting rooms, as had his mother on her honeymoon, during the Sabbath. And then, in Kursk, while watching for an approaching train, he found two urchins next to him, hovering over his bags. He turned around in time to see one of them making off with his knapsack, the other with a kit containing personal property and toilet articles.

"Hey!" Gino shouted, and he began to run after them, his sturdy, well-exercised legs pumping toward the thieves. There were many people at the station, and some now turned to stare with interest at the young soldier pursuing the boys. "They stole my bags! Stop them!" Gino cried, but in response he heard only a jeer. Nobody cared about personal property these days. At length he caught up with the one hoisting the knapsack, and he grabbed him from behind and forced him to drop the bundle. The boy began to scream, "Help! *Burshui!* Help!" but Gino, red with anger, was only interested in recovering his other bag. He clutched the knapsack, pushing the boy to the ground, and raced after the other youngster. But when he reached him, he himself felt dragged down to the hard cement quay of the station, and an enormous corporal stood above him, readying his fist.

"What is this?" Gino exclaimed. "They made off with my things, and now you're after me—"

He felt the blow, and fell forward, and as he fell he heard the whistle of the approaching train, for which he had been waiting almost twelve hours. Overwhelming nausea came over him, his head reeled, and then he was enveloped in darkness. When he came to, it was almost night. A freezing wind had started to blow, and there was a huge, bloody bump at the back of his head. His hand hurt, and looking down, he saw that the signet ring, inherited from his grandfather, Baron Yuri, was gone. The flesh around his knuckles was scraped raw. I have missed my train, he thought with dismay. And my bags . . .

A tremendous sense of defeat descended upon his emotions. Gino rose, and walked inside the station. He stopped one of the attendants, and asked, "The train south?"

"Gone, hours ago. But don't feel bad," the old man added, noticing Gino's downcast expression. "It can't have gotten too far. We've just heard that near Kharkov the rails have been removed for a very long stretch. Everyone going your way will be delayed for quite a few days. Might as well warm yourself with a glass of tea, boy."

Gino shook his head, bewildered, aghast, and finally amused. A year ago, though no officer's insignia adorned his uniform, this illiterate old station attendant would not have called him "boy." He would have bowed, and walked away backward, obsequiously, addressing him as "Excellency." Gino regarded him with sheepishness. "I've been robbed of my bags," he stated. "I have no money."

"Ah, well, then I can't help you," the old man muttered, shaking his head. "Tea's for the ones that can afford it, and a tip for me."

"We've lost all but one servant, too," Nadia Pomerantz said valiantly to Mathilde de Gunzburg. She dipped her spoon into the bowl of steaming soup. "And they've set about nationalizing my business. I have two Bolsheviks in the office, every day, peering over my shoulder. As soon as the girls finish that stenography course, we must go to Simferopol. It is a larger city, and it's not a port, and the Reds haven't taken it yet. Besides, Olga's signed up for some courses at the University . . ."

"But we've heard nothing from my son Gino," Mathilde said despondently.

"Ah! The soldier. That is true, my dear. Travel is so precarious these days, and if indeed he's left the army—"

"Yes, I must wait. But, if you go, will you take Sonia with you?"

"I shall wait beside you. Sonia would no sooner leave than would your friend, Johanna Ivanovna. Come now, rest a while, Mathilde."

But the mention of Johanna had made Mathilde perceptibly shiver. She said nothing, but hugged her shawl more tightly around her shoulders. "Simferopol, capital of the Crimea . . . Yes," she stated, "it makes sense. But what about your own funds?"

Nadia Pomerantz smiled. "They do not know it, but I possess a cache in a Simferopol bank. Most convenient."

"Indeed. We are so grateful to you, Nadia. What would we do without your counsel, and friendship?"

"Nonsense. You have a splendid, resourceful daughter. It's true, our houses are a shambles, but the girls, both of them, have kept them well. Although I'm tired of boiled barley—aren't you?"

The two women began to laugh. "Barley is about all we can afford, or this peasant soup," Mathilde sighed. "Sometimes, Sonia brings home beans. Creamy white beans. To think of pureed mushrooms, atop a bed of baby peas . . ."

"I never could waste time on such food," her friend cut in peremptorily. "But boiled barley . . . Olga burns the bottom of the pan. Sonia's soup seems a treat."

"Olga is a charming child," Mathilde stated. "How she would have enjoyed Petrograd. Was she never betrothed, Nadia?"

"Olga? No, she's only nineteen. Hardly had time for a proper debut. Yes, yes, don't look so at me—I gave her a most proper debut, with trimmings and all. She loved it. But she's adjusted. One of the young Bolshevik supervisors they've sent me at the offices has quite a crush on her, I dare say. She treats him as though he were scum. But who will marry her in this godforsaken country? And Sonia? What is to become of our fine young daughters, Mathilde?"

"Sonia tells me I must concentrate upon the essential task, which is remaining alive and in good health. Madame Zevina, our overseer's wife, lives in Simferopol. Perhaps the Zevins can help us find a place to live—inexpensively. We never did find boarders here, to help us with the rent, and it's created havoc with our savings. But I complain endlessly, my dear. Forgive me?"

"Complaining cleanses the soul," Nadia Pomerantz asserted. "Besides, it does no harm. It's better for the system than boiled barley."

Mathilde and Nadia were dining together in what had been the Gunzburg sewing room, but which had been clumsily converted into an all-purpose room by Sonia. Before going with Olga to a stenography lesson at the home of the Rabbi, she had prepared a pot of split pea soup with a hambone to flavor it for her mother and Nadia. There was so little time now, with the marketing and cleaning chores, to attend lessons during the afternoon. From an original class of five, the membership had dwindled to two: Olga Pomerantz and Sonia. But for Olga the necessity was not as pressing as for her friend. Nadia's careful management of her husband's business had included savings in Simferopol, while the Gunzburgs possessed only the remnants of the proceeds of the harvest of '17. Sonia attacked stenography as she had once attacked the difficult problem of Russian and French versology, and more recently, the problem of cooking. She had culled from her prodigious memory visions of the cooks at Mohilna preparing their own meals, which were simple but substantial. Soups and cereals, and thick bread, and milk. Anna had always enjoyed this food, heavily laced with garlic and lard (which the girls had not known was forbidden to them); Sonia had found it coarse. Now she found it quite bearable, and added the hambone without compunction: it was practically the only meat she could afford to buy, and her mother had never adhered to Kosher laws. God, Sonia reflected grimly, would simply have to forgive her. But she flinched at the notion of what her father would have said to her, his long, gaunt face saddened by disappointment. Papa, Papa, we must survive, she answered him in her mind.

Each day the single Pomerantz servant would take the coach with the young women to the Rabbi's house in a more modest part of town. But that evening, when they emerged with their books, the servant seemed more agitated than usual, and addressed his young mistress as soon as he saw her approaching. "Olga Arkadievna," he said hoarsely, "there is news of much danger. A ship is expected tomorrow from Trebizond, where people are dying of the plague. And another one is going to dock, bearing nihilists who have said that they will murder all the *burshuis* in Feodosia."

"Then we must go home at once and barricade ourselves," Sonia declared. "Come, Olga. Your mother is at our house. And you, Fedia. It will be better if we all remain together."

Her eyes, wide and gray, met Olga's, and Sonia squeezed the young girl's hand. The servant cracked his whip, and the coach started to move. Sonia said, "From the height of our hill, we should see the entire harbor. If the ship is carrying the plague victims, you may be certain that the soldiers on board will not go docilely into the quarantine building. They will more likely go on the rampage, and contaminate us all. Juanita has a medical book that I want to scan, for the plague is so uncommon these days that I cannot remember how the doctors handle it now."

"Johanna Ivanovna is a nurse, isn't she?" Olga asked. Sonia merely nodded. She was thinking of the nihilists and of New Year's Eve, so closely behind them. If only she could be reassured, at least, that Ossip was safe in Odessa, and that Gino was secure in one place, and not on the move . . . What with Mathilde's weakness and Johanna's hysteria, it was good to know that Nadezhda Pomerantz would be with them.

She and Olga and the servant, Fedia, went resolutely into the Gunzburg house, and called Johanna, who had been in her own quarters. It was Sonia who spoke, and as she did so, her eyes remained riveted to her mother's face, as if daring Mathilde to break down. But her mother merely uttered a single cry, and was silent. Johanna fetched her medical book, and she and Sonia flipped feverishly through its pages to the entry on bubonic plague. Sonia placed cold fingers upon Olga's arm, and sighed. "It's curable," she murmured, and she saw Nadia nod grimly at Mathilde, whose eyes were dark with fear. "Now please," she added, "it is essential that we keep our strength, and that you sleep as well as you can tonight. Olga, Fedia, and I shall work on the house. Tomorrow, we shall all need our wits about us."

Johanna de Mey regarded her with almond-shaped aquamarine eyes, which shone with complete detestation. But Nadia Pomerantz exclaimed, "I have two stalwart arms, and intend to help you. Do you small girls think to treat me like an old lady?" Mathilde half-rose, then sank once again into her chair. Her expression mirrored defeat and exhaustion. I would only be in the way, her eyes told Sonia, and her daughter nodded, uncharitably. They understood each other, and Sonia sighed.

The following evening, the five women and Fedia were as well prepared as they could be. They crouched uncomfortably in the darkness of the living room, fully clothed and ready for flight. They could see the porch before them, then the cultivated garden which had been untended since Marfa's departure, and at the bottom of the hill, the wall with its small gate. There were ten steps leading from the porch to the garden. Below the property stretched the haven. The garden wall was flanked by a wide path which led through the back courtyard to the rear door, which was the principal entrance. If the nihilists came through the garden, Fedia would quickly unbolt the back door, and the Gunzburgs and Pomerantzes could run out through the courtyard path; should the attackers make their way from the back, the women and their servant could escape through the porch and down the hill. Now they huddled together, in total silence, listening.

The panorama of the harbor stretched before their eyes. Late in the afternoon, they had seen a ship dock, and now it was lit up like a festival of lanterns below them. They heard cries, but in the distance. Then the cries came nearer, whoops of celebration common to sailors who had finally arrived in port. The cries died down. Mathilde sat still, her eyes shut to the sight, thinking of David's final moments, of her darling, Ossip, so cynical and delicate, killing the two soldiers. Sonia thought of nothing but the ship in port. Her fingers were laced together, her jaw tightly cemented. Nadia and Olga had their arms about each other, and Johanna de Mey stood near the back door, her body like the blade of a dagger, thin and sharp.

Far off, a church bell tolled, and in the dark living room every pair of ears made out ten chimes. One more hour had passed. Beads of perspiration rolled from Nadia's brow, and Olga touched it with her handkerchief. Then, the five women and the man were startled into suspended animation. Olga's hand remained in midair, poised before her mother's brow as the unmistakable sound of heavy boots reverberated from the porch. Without a word, they raced on tiptoes to the back door where Johanna had been keeping her vigil. But now the boots resounded here, and a knock pierced the sickening silence. Johanna cried out: "Who is there?"

The voice that replied was indistinct, blocked by the heavy wood of the door. "Gino," it said.

Wide-eyed, Sonia regarded her mother, whose mouth opened. But Johanna reiterated, tersely, "Gino? Gino, Who?"

Now a stranger sound came to their ears, the sound of joyful laughter. "Juanita!" the outdoor voice exclaimed. "Open quickly, it is cold!" Sonia grabbed her mother's arms and shook them, tears of relief and amazement streaming from her eyes. Mathilde uttered a sob, and rushed to the door, which she unbolted, and a young man with a mustache, in khaki uniform, stood before them, tall and broad and empty-handed. His mother threw herself into his arms, and his sister flung her slender form upon his side, clinging to him. He felt himself pushed inside, where no lamps were lit, and where a pretty young girl with short blond curls and an older woman with disheveled black hair were crouched near a middle-aged peasant.

"What on earth is going on?" Gino exclaimed, but his sister clamped her hand over his mouth, and dragged him down. She told him, in as few words as possible, about the ship from Trebizond and the other, full of nihilists, which they had been expecting. Gino shook his head. "But everything's all right," he told them. "I was in town. Yes, there is a shipload of sailors here, but they are not from where you think, and they are not nihilists. Haven't you noticed that your street is lit? I knew how to come, from your letters, and when I saw no lights in the house, I came to the back. Actually, this was the easy part of my journey. I had to make so many detours, it feels as though I have traveled throughout Russia. I was robbed of all I own, including Grandfather's ring, at the station in Kursk. Then, near Kharkov, the rails had been removed. But Mama, I am so desperately hungry and thirsty!"

"You mean—you are certain that we are safe?" Sonia demanded.

"Yes, yes. For today, at least. But please, I am so hungry, and dirty and smelly—" But his eyes had rested upon

Olga, and in his exhaustion he extended his hand to her. "I have forgotten my manners," he said. "I am Evgeni Davidovitch de Gunzburg."

"Gino!" Olga said. "We know all about you. My name is Olga Pomerantz, Olga Arkadievna, and this is my mother, Nadezhda Igorovna. We are friends, although naturally you would have no idea who we are."

"But I do!" Gino cried. "My sister has written of you." He turned now to Nadia, and bent politely over her sinewy hand. But it was the young girl who captivated his attention. His brown eyes looked her over from top to bottom, with obvious delight. "Friends . . ." he murmured. "I cannot believe it. After all those days and nights, I am home, and there are friends. But you have not heard—the Bolsheviks in Petrograd have disbanded the Constituent Assembly. Can you believe that it is now January 20, and that I left the army before the New Year? A week's journey has taken me three times that long."

As he spoke, his weariness giving way to a hysterical energy, Sonia brought him hot soup, and bread, and tea. He paid no further attention to protocol, but bit into the bread with relish, and even slurped his soup. His mother sat beside him, her large sapphire eyes full of mist. Sonia stood behind him, her hands upon his sturdy shoulders, and Olga Arkadievna sat on the floor, by his feet, casting her hazel eyes onto his animated, virile face. It was Nadia Pomerantz who turned the lights back on, one by one, in the Gunzburg house.

Twenty

———————————————•———————————————

The Ashkenasys of Odessa had always been the most important Jewish family of that city, which opened onto the Black Sea and was separated from Rumania by the Dniester River. They lived in a two-story house on the Boulevard, which was a large avenue bordered by tall trees and a park, and they had been renowned not only for their wealth but for centuries of eccentricities. Their house, a veritable manor, was the first building on the Boulevard, and it was there that Ossip and Stepan were given lodgings when they arrived, hungry and out of money, from Petrograd. Siegfried Ashkenasy owned a bank and was related to the Gunzburg family through his wife, a cousin to Baron David. As the Bolsheviks had not taken over Odessa, the Ashkenasy bank was still operating as an independent enterprise, and Ossip was given a position as assistant to his cousin Siegfried.

Odessa was actually the most southwest part of all the Russias, and one of the last regions to be reached by the Red Army. In March, Trotsky had signed a separate peace agreement with the Central Powers at Brest-Litovsk, and not long after that the Bolsheviks had begun to call themselves the Communist Party. Yet there were many groups that did not adhere to it. A volunteer army, the White Army, was gaining strength in the south. The independent Cossacks of the Don and Kuban areas opposed communist domination, and General Kornilov's most faithful officers were entirely dissatisfied with the peace terms of Brest-Litovsk; many former members of the disbanded Constituent Assembly, mostly Social Revolutionaries, felt that they had been illegally shunted aside when in fact the national electorate had actually selected them to rule the country. It was from these three groups that the White Army drew most of its fighting force. The ineffectual last months of the Romanov dynasty had shaken the faith of most Russians; they looked, rather, to a strong parliamentary system.

The Red Army encountered other difficulties apart from the resistance of the Whites. The peasants, it appeared, were not altogether pleased with communism either. Only the poorest found benefits to the new system, for the others did not want to give their hard-reaped produce and their livestock to city dwellers. The Red Army was not in a position to pay these wealthier peasants for their bounty; and so, frequently, to obtain food for the urban communities, the communists were forced to send the Cheka to the villages to collect meat and vegetables, fruit and grain. And nobody liked the Cheka, which murdered to obtain what it claimed to need.

By spring of 1918, therefore, the communists, who were also moving the nation's capital from Petrograd to Moscow, had many matters to deal with, and had been delayed in spreading their power all the way to their southwest border. But at the time when the thaws occurred, when buds began to appear on the trees facing the Ashkenasy manor on the Boulevard, a perceptible shiver began to ripple westward, so that the residents of Odessa looked with sudden fear over their shoulders, and started to pack their bags. One morning, Siegfried Ashkenasy appeared in

Ossip's office at the bank and announced that he, his wife, and their children had booked passage to Marseilles on a French ship, and were departing the next day. The young man regarded Siegfried with astonishment. No, I must not be surprised, he told himself. Why should they think of me, when they have never considered anyone outside their immediate family? Why should it occur to them to take me with them? They have already let me into their house, and they have offered me a paid position in their own establishment. So, courteously, Ossip wished his cousin a safe voyage, and thanked him for his generosity. He watched Siegfried withdraw all the Ashkenasy savings from the bank, and fill a deep trunk. Then his cousin said, "Take good care of our house, my boy. It's the best in town." Ossip thought: Yes, and that is why you feel so conspicuous in it, for if the Reds come, they will loot it first.

Ossip was very annoyed, and also frightened. He was a baron, and the house which he occupied now, alone with Stepan, was magnificent. The bank was all but dismantled, and the Ashkenasys had taken everything of value. The Reds would march into Odessa, head for the first house on the Boulevard, find there the older son of Baron David de Gunzburg, and not believe that he was nearly penniless. They would murder him in cold blood, especially if it was known that he had killed two members of the Petrograd garrison in his father's house. But what could he do? Where could he and Stepan go?

Ossip had learned that the most savage fighting was occurring between Red and White forces in the Ukraine, just midway between Odessa and Feodosia, where his mother and sister had taken refuge. He could not reach them or even get a message to them. Maybe they, too, have managed to escape to France, he said to himself. And what about Gino? Would he have joined them, or would he have thrown in his lot with the White Army? There was no way to know. Ossip felt totally disheartened. What had happened to Natasha? Was he alone, left to die at the hands of the Reds, with only Stepan as his friend? It is useless to hope, he thought. All that we had is gone. My family, my country, my wealth, my position—and most of all, my love. In his agony, he sat down and wept, his head in his hands.

Stepan had recovered, and was serving him, as always. It never occurred to the maître d'hôtel to ask any question whatsoever. He especially did not ask when and if he would be paid. Ossip accepted his sevices, but once or twice, in despair, he broke their unspoken pact of decorum and said, "I own nothing, Stepan. Please bear with me, if you can. But if you can find better . . ." He had not continued. Stepan's eyes, so proud and dignified, had quelled his words in his throat. He is a gentleman in his heart and in his manner, Ossip thought, whereas Siegfried, for all his wealth and status, was a boor.

Shortly after the departure of the Ashkenasys, Stepan appeared in the doorway of the immense hall where Ossip, alone, was drinking his morning coffee. "There is someone here to see you, Ossip Davidovitch," the maître d'hôtel said. "I beg your pardon, but although he did not give me a name, he regarded me in the most peculiar way, as if he knew me. And I felt certain that I had seen him before. But it is most bewildering. He asked for Siegfried Evgenievitch, and told me he came from the Provisional Government in Samara on the Volga."

"Those are mostly the representatives of the disbanded Constituent Assembly, who have set up some kind of headquarters there, I believe," Ossip commented. "But I know none of these men. Perhaps one of them knew Papa, when Milyukov was in charge of Foreign Affairs . . ."

"Shall I ask the gentleman to come in?" Stepan asked.

Ossip shrugged. "Why not?"

The man who entered the room took but one look at Ossip, and his face brightened at once. He was clothed modestly, not fashionably, but his hair was very fair and his eyes so green that they seemed to reach right inside Ossip's memory, so that he too sprang from his chair with a cry of recognition. "Vanya!" Ossip exclaimed. And the other said, "Ossip! What are you doing in Odessa?"

Stepan, in the process of respectfully removing himself, stopped, and regarded the newcomer with raised eyebrows. "Ivan Aronovitch Berson?" he asked softly.

"Indeed!" the green-eyed man stated. "Then . . . you are Stepan! I thought so, but . . ."

"I shall fetch you some tea, sir," the maître d'hôtel declared. "Or coffee? Ossip Davidovitch is having his morning coffee."

"I'll take whichever is already made. Coffee would be wonderful, Stepan."

The two young men sat next to each other at the table, and Ossip lit cigarettes for them both. Leaning forward, Ivan Berson said, "You know, I had no idea you were related to the Ashkenasys. I had come to ask your cousin to lend our organization some financial support. I've been sent to prepare the people of Odessa for the arrival of the Red Army, and to obtain what reinforcements I can get. Did you know that I had been elected to the Constituent Assembly, and would be serving now, if . . ." His sentence died in midair. "I saw Gino, a while back, at the front," he added.

"I didn't know! How did he look? Tell me, Vanya. I haven't seen my brother for so long."

"Gino was a fierce fighter, and well liked," Ivan replied. "He's a man! To me, this was amazing. Little Gino. But this was before the peace. The peace must have infuriated him. By the way, he didn't approve of me in the least. I don't know if he ever liked me, but he certainly didn't enjoy the commissars sent by Kerensky, and I was one of them. But—I liked him. He is a true Russian, as—"

"As Annushka was," Ossip said softly.

Ivan Berson flicked an ash away, and drank some coffee. "Yes," he said tersely.

"I haven't seen Anna in nearly as many years as you have," Ossip said, in the same gentle tone of voice. "And you know how apolitical I've always been . . . But I'm sure of one thing: she'd be proud of what you are doing."

"Perhaps. I wonder sometimes if we're not going to die as the Texans did in that fort, the Alamo—in a horrid way, but for a noble cause . . . You should leave, Ossip. If I knew you any less well, I'd ask you to join us. But, as you say, politics have never appealed to you. And with your back, you can't fight. Take the first ship out of here, my friend. In this house, you're offering yourself to those bastards for murder."

Ossip smiled. "I haven't a kopeck, Vanya. Stepan and I will leave, but not until I can find a way of getting some passage money. What do you say to a destitute Gunzburg? Probably, if I were you, I'd laugh. Serve 'em right! I'm sure you haven't wasted any love upon our family, after what they . . . we . . . did to you."

"I don't have time to hate," Ivan Berson said shortly. "But you were not a part of that affair. I never hated you."

They remained quiet for several minutes, smoking and sipping coffee. Then Berson said, "At least you escaped from Petrograd. It was dreadful there. A great many wealthy families were slaughtered. I'm sorry—I heard about your father, and I know how badly you must feel. I also heard that my dear parents and sisters went to Paris. I don't much care."

"Vanya—there is a family I'm concerned about in Petrograd." Ossip's bright blue eyes suddenly bored into Ivan's green ones.

"Go on—I'll tell you what I know, if I know. Who were you going to ask about? Old friends?"

"Yes . . . the Tagantsevs. Count and Countess Nicolai

Tagantsev, and their children. Their second son, Volodia, was a schoolmate of mine, and my dearest friend. He was killed, years ago, in Persia."

"I don't think I ever met him, but I knew he was your friend. I didn't realize you'd kept up with the family."

Ossip's eyes shone with insistent fervor. "Well?" he whispered. "Have you heard anything? Count Tagantsev was a well-known man. Surely someone must have heard something. His son-in-law was a general under Kornilov—"

"A Prince Andrei Kurdukov." Now Ivan tapped lightly on the table and looked toward the window. "I'm sorry, Ossip. The Tagantsevs are dead. Kurdukov is with us, heading up a White regiment. I know that the other son, the one who was a senator, was killed in Petrograd."

"And the daughter, Princess Kurdukova?"

"I don't see how she could have escaped. The palace was burned, the family decimated. We can't be certain, Ossip, for it's harder to keep track of women, people are always bringing news of men, the ones with whose names they are familiar—"

"But you say that her husband is alive. Couldn't she have joined him?"

Ivan turned back to Ossip, and sighed. He said nothing, but Ossip's bright blue gaze held him, mesmerized him, until all at once he was embarrassed by this naked vulnerability, by this silent grief. "Ossip," he began, but gave up and shook his head. "In this country, these days . . . Don't rely too heavily on what I say. Rumors are only that—not facts."

Ossip clasped his hands together, unseeing, his face white. He could picture the Count dead, even Maria Efimovna, who was a good woman. He made an effort to visualize little Lara, dismembered, but at the thought his features contracted in sorrow. He dared not think of *her*. "No," he said, and there was the wonder of a child in this statement. Ivan Berson twisted in his seat, not knowing what to do. Where had Stepan vanished? Ossip bit his lower lip, and repeated, "No." Then, oblivious of Ivan's presence, he rose and went to the window. At first he stood, perfectly still, a statue peering out toward the park below. Then he bent over, as if in pain, and rocked back and forth upon his haunches, moaning. Ivan could not help but stare at him, overwhelmed with compassion and helplessness. He called out: "Stepan! Stepan!"

It was the manservant who picked up Ossip, who literally dragged him to a sofa, who laid him down and brought compresses for his forehead. "I did not know he would take it so badly," Ivan said. "The Tagantsev boy died such a long time ago . . ." He searched through his pockets, thrust some bills into Stepan's hands. "Get yourselves out of here, on a ship to France or England," he said quickly. "Get him out of here! The Red Army is sure to come, and . . ."

"God be with you, Ivan Aronovitch." Stepan did not escort him to the door, but watched him walk rapidly away. Stepan remained with Ossip, and made a sign of the cross above his head. He counted the bills, and sighed. He thought of Anna, and of Natalia Tagantseva. They did not know, he thought, these two young men, how much they had in common . . . But Ivan Aronovitch is a survivor. If only I could be so sure about Ossip Davidovitch. Only God can help him now, though he does not believe in His bounty . . . And Stepan remembered the elegant little apartment where he had recuperated from his wound, and the voice of the Princess, so strong and lovely. It was no wonder that his master had loved her. He also remembered her as a young girl, when she and her mother had visited the Baroness. What a fine young woman she had been! No less fine, thought Stepan stubbornly, regarding the bills anew, than Anna Davidovna's young man.

It was Stepan who located the two rooms in a poorer section of Odessa, in a small house far from the center of the city. He packed his master's bags and his own, and

escorted Ossip to their new "home." "We must leave the
Ashkenasy house," he kept repeating to the dazed young
man, who followed him without expression, his features
frozen. When they moved in, they crossed the path of the
lady who lived in the small apartment upstairs, and Stepan
bowed, seeing her eyes widen as she regarded Ossip. She
was a tall, angular woman, impoverished to be sure, but
wearing her clothes with the elegance of a gentlewoman.
She was not pretty, with her short black hair and strong
features, her thin red lips and piercing ebony eyes. She
looked each one of her thirty years.

The following day Stepan saw a little girl with her, a
comely young child with blond hair and dimples. She said,
"Hello," and he answered her respectfully. Stepan mentioned the child to Ossip, to cheer him up. But the young
man seemed emptied of all emotion, and merely nodded
absently. When Ossip himself came face to face with the
black-haired woman, and she said, "I am Elizaveta Adolfovna Dietrich," he merely intoned his name, and went
rapidly into his own two rooms. She stood in the common
hallway, staring after his slender form, musing.

Several days later, Stepan knocked on Ossip's door and
declared, "There is a British ship due in tomorrow. I have
booked passage upon it, for us both." Ossip nodded, smiled
vaguely, and returned to his reverie. That day, the lady
from upstairs came to their apartment, bearing a tray of
home-baked cakes. She said to Stepan, "The Baron looks
very peaked. My daughter, Vera, baked these. I am afraid
they aren't very good, for the child is only eight, and our
ingredients aren't as excellent as they should be—but do
offer some to him."

"Thank you, Madame," Stepan replied. He was about to
close the door when she smiled and asked, "Please—let me
come in and chat with him, if he's up to it. We too are very
lonely, Vera and I. We came here from Tomsk, and have
few friends . . ."

He allowed her into the apartment, not wishing to affront a lady, yet certain that Ossip would send her politely away. But Ossip was in no mood to pay the slightest attention to this thin, bony woman, and he allowed her to talk in the way a weary mother permits her child to run rampant about a room. He regarded her without seeing her. Well, Stepan thought, she does possess a certain style, although she has no beauty . . . She insisted upon serving Ossip tea, and told him that she was a native of the Baltic provinces, a Protestant who had married an officer, named Tchernavin, of Eastern Orthodox faith, which was why her daughter was neither of the same faith nor of the same name as she. Elizaveta Adolfovna was divorced, and bore her maiden name of Dietrich. Ossip heard her, and he nodded courteously but didn't listen, all the while thinking only of Natasha, thinking that it was not true, that Natasha could not have died. "The Barons Gunzburg are well reputed," Elizaveta Adolfovna Dietrich said, as if to encourage him to bare his own past. But it was Stepan who was forced to reply in his stead, and the woman appeared annoyed. Then she sighed and returned upstairs, and Stepan finished the remainder of their packing.

The next morning, baggage in hand, Ossip and Stepan walked to the port, and joined the crowd of passengers who had booked places on the British ship. When it came time to board, one of the stewards came forward and, examining Ossip's papers, declared: "You are a Russian citizen. Why, then, are you not fighting with the White Army against the Bolsheviks?"

"The Baron suffers from the aftereffects of Pott's disease," Stepan replied for Ossip. He looked through their effects and brandished a white exemption paper. "See here," he exclaimed.

The steward shook his head doubtfully and went off to find the captain. Stepan, tall and erect, stood by his master, but Ossip looked vague and ill, and his eyes did not focus properly. The captain arrived, in his neat uniform, and his eyes softened as they rested upon the young man. "I'm sorry, Baron," he stated. "But I have my orders from my government. We are not to take any man of age to be serving. The British must consider you a traitor—a deserter."

"But what about his back? The Baron cannot fight, and the Red Army is coming! You must take us," Stepan cried.

"I cannot. But, sir, I can take you," the captain said to the maître d'hôtel.

"Yes," Ossip murmured vaguely. "Go, Stepan. I did not save you from those soldiers so that you would die here. You must go."

Stepan's eyes first scanned the captain, then his master. In his pupils shone the deepest indignation he could muster. "If you will not take the Baron, then you shall leave without me, too," he asserted. He picked up the luggage and turned around. Ossip followed docilely, and this time tears came to his eyes. It was surely his time to perish. He placed a trembling hand on Stepan's arm, unbearably moved. They walked back to the apartment, and there, suddenly, Ossip collapsed, all color drained from his face and lips. Stepan felt his forehead with alarm. The fever was so high that he put Ossip to bed and went up the stairs to Elizaveta Dietrich's rooms. When she admitted him, he said, "Forgive me this intrusion, but the Baron is ill, and I must fetch a doctor. Could you look in on him while I am gone, Madame?"

An expression of alarm passed over her angular features. "There is typhus in Odessa," she said. "Is his fever high?"

"At least 105 degrees," Stepan replied.

"Then it must be typhus. Wait. I know how to treat it. I have treated members of my family, in Estonia. But were you and the Baron not leaving this morning?"

"Yes, Madame. But we could not."

Elizaveta Adolfovna peered at the maître d'hôtel with

shrewd eyes, appraising him. "Go for the doctor, if indeed you can find one," she said peremptorily. "I shall be with your master. Verotchka! Come with Mama, my dear. And bring rags, clean rags, many rags. And vinegar and alcohol and pans."

Stepan watched her thin form move rapidly about and he went down the stairs. As he went out into the street, he heard the woman and her daughter go into Ossip's rooms. They may kill him with talk, but that is better than letting him die of the typhus, he thought with uncustomary irreverence. He could not help being reminded of someone in Elizaveta Adolfovna Dietrich, with her Teuton name. As he walked quickly in search of medical help, he nodded to himself. Yes, he thought, Johanna Ivanovna, although they don't look alike. Still, there are similarities . . .

Ossip was terribly sick with the typhus, so sick, indeed, that the physician summoned by Stepan and well paid from the remainder of Ivan's bills, declared that he would surely die. Elizaveta Dietrich and her daughter, Vera Tchernavina, stayed quietly by his bedside, and Stepan was forced to admire them. They appeared unafraid of the terrible possibility of contagion. Indeed, Stepan found it most unusual that this woman would permit her own small child to remain so close to someone afflicted with such illness. He thought: Johanna Ivanovna also nursed him, when he was but twenty.

During his moments of consciousness, which was only partial consciousness, Ossip saw a woman's face bending over him, and a vague outline of black hair. He tried to smile in his happiness. "Natasha . . ." he sighed.

"Yes, yes," the woman replied encouragingly. She touched his forehead with cool fingers.

"Don't . . . go," he pleaded.

"No," she answered.

"Never again . . ."

"Do not tire yourself," the woman said. Then, quickly, "No, don't try to rise. Never again."

He sighed once more. "Love," he whispered.

Another time he said rapidly, incoherently, "Divorce! Must . . . get . . . divorce!" His eyes shone with such intensity that the woman knew it signified more than mere fever.

"But I am already divorced," she stated gently. His features softened; he smiled, fell asleep.

Later he awakened abruptly, and saw the face of a child. "Lara?" he asked, breathlessly.

"Verotchka," the girl replied.

"Ah," he murmured, "then you must take another kopeck, and get another sweet roll." He could not understand what the child from the station in Poland was doing here with him, with Natasha. "Love!" he cried, and would rest only when the woman with the dark hair took his hand and stroked it. Then he slept fitfully.

One morning, when he was half awake, Ossip said to Verotchka, "You see? I am going to . . . marry your mother. Doesn't matter . . . about religion."

"Is he awake, Mama?" the child asked with disbelief.

"Enough to know what he is saying, sweetheart," her mother replied. "He is aware that I am Protestant, and he, of course, is a Jew."

Several days later, Ossip was able to sit up, and for the first time a coolness came over him. He said, "Where am I? Who are you?" He perceived a strange angular woman with jet black hair, cropped short, and a little girl of some eight years, blond and pretty.

"You've been very ill, with the typhus," Elizaveta Adolfovna Dietrich said.

But her daughter jumped up and clapped her hands, and cried out, "You're going to live! And then you're going to do what you promised, and marry Mama!"

"Where is Stepan?" Ossip asked. He felt that he was

dreaming. He stared at the odd child, clapping and spouting nonsense, and said, "Where's Natasha?"

"Stepan has gone for food," the woman stated softly.

"Who's Natasha?" the little girl asked.

"Hush, sweet. No one. No one important," her mother answered. Ossip had fallen asleep, resembling a cherub with a growth of beard, and she smiled at him. "Baroness Ossip de Gunzburg," she intoned in a singsong manner. Then she repeated, "No one at all."

But Ossip, asleep, was crying out, suddenly drenched with perspiration, "Don't die! Never go away again . . ."

"He's afraid of dying," Elizaveta Dietrich said to her daughter. "We all are, aren't we?"

When Ossip had sufficiently recovered, Stepan explained to him that the Red Army was approaching rapidly, and that the little money they still had would be sufficient to get them across the Dniester River and into Rumania. He cleared his throat, and added, averting his eyes, "Madame Dietrich and her daughter would like to travel with us, for protection. And besides, their funds have run out, too."

"Ah," Ossip stated. He chewed upon his lower lip, pensively. It was a miracle that he was still alive, and there was no doubt that the nursing of the lady from upstairs, Elizaveta Adolfovna, had made the crucial difference. She had stayed up nights to sponge off his brow, had exhausted herself to restore him to health. And yet, he had been a virtual stranger, and she did not seem to Ossip to be the sort of woman for selfless devotion. He was somewhat baffled. He owed her his life—and yet, why had she not remained outside the sphere of his existence, now that nothing remained for him to live for? A deep, dull anguish pervaded his body. Now he felt angry at the Dietrich woman for her interference. "Damn," he muttered. "I suppose it would be most ungenerous to refuse them, after all that they have done on my behalf. We owe them whatever we can offer, which is very little indeed." Oh, to indulge in pure cowardice, he thought, not to face this obligation . . . He sighed deeply and sank into the cushions of the old sofa.

"There is another matter, in regard to the ladies, which I must bring to your attention," Stepan said gently. "It appears that you . . . that when you were ill, you were delirious, and told the child that you were planning to . . . marry her mother. And Madame Dietrich . . . well, took this proposal seriously. It seemed to make her very happy, Ossip Davidovitch."

The young man bolted upright, his blue eyes blazing. "Is this an attempt at humor?" he demanded. When Stepan did not reply, he uttered a low moan and struck his forehead with his fist. "My God!" he cried. "Stepan—fetch Elizaveta Adolfovna for me, please. I must discuss it with her at once—explain that it is all a grave mistake, some kind of unconscious blabber—"

Deft on his feet, Stepan disappeared immediately and did not return. Moments later, the door swung open and a tall, thin form blew into the apartment. Ossip sat staring at Elizaveta Adolfovna, as if for the first time. She wore her hair short and straight, with bangs, and her lips were rouged—sensuous, perhaps. Her bony figure was anything but enticing, yet it touched him strangely. The meager breast was proud, showing its vulnerability, its poverty, yet demonstrating by the carriage of her shoulders that she was a lady of good breeding in spite of appearances. He shuddered slightly, finding her most unappealing—and yet, as an afterthought, he felt shame, for this was a woman who had sacrificed her own well-being to restore him to health. She stood before him, her prominent cheekbones with spots of color, her black eyes moist. He had found her hard; now, watching the smile that trembled on her thin lips, he was not so sure of his initial appraisal. "Sit down, please, Elizaveta Adolfovna," he said, courteously. "I beg you to forgive me for not rising. I still feel—weak."

She sat, not across from him on the chair to which he had beckoned somewhat carelessly, but right next to him on the battered sofa. He could smell clean skin, a female odor, rouge, perhaps pressed powder. She murmured in a low voice, "Do not call me 'Elizaveta Adolfovna.' Please, call me as my friends do: 'Lizette.' For—are we not friends, after what we've suffered through together?"

"I cannot express to you my gratitude. I . . . words . . ." Indeed, Ossip could not complete his sentence, so overwhelmed was he by solitude, and by the certain knowledge, suddenly, that Natasha was truly dead, that there was no hope. Tears came to his eyes, and he turned aside in embarrassment. Now that he was well, he finally understood all that her death entailed. This woman, here beside him, expressed his bereavement by her presence, which was Natasha's absence. He detested Lizette for not being Natasha, yet felt sorry for her because of his rudeness, because he did not like her in spite of her sacrifice.

But she simply took his hand, and brought it to her lips, and kissed his emaciated fingers. "My poor dear man," she said. "My poor dear Ossip. So tired, so alone. Stepan told me that you had lost touch with your entire family, that perhaps your mother and sister and brother have died. But surely, your relations in Paris will help you, and will do all they can to make you comfortable. Come, you must cheer up."

"Yes. Yes," he said, bewildered by her words, which had no bearing on the depths of his sorrow. Then, piteously, she began to weep. "I, too, am so desperately alone. My husband was—a horror. He—had other women, and deceived me ignobly. Poor Verotchka! She needed her father, and had to be deprived of him . . . Yes, I understand loneliness. It is worse than death."

He regarded her with widened eyes. "Yes," he said again, this time in true agreement. He thought of the small blond girl, Vera, who had helped nurse him. "How is your daughter?" he asked.

"Verotchka is so fond of you. That is why I am begging you to allow us to accompany you in your escape. We, too, must not be found by the Reds, for we are *burshuis*. But we would truly not be an encumbrance. We can make ourselves very tiny indeed."

Ossip looked at her and was touched. He had always detested himself for being a coward at heart. This was his chance to help another person, another lonely person. "Yes, we shall be glad to take you and Vera," he assented.

Then, the most extraordinary thing occurred. Lizette Dietrich threw her long, bony self at his feet, and laid her head upon his lap and kissed the cloth of his trousers at the knees. He attempted to end this silly gesture, to raise her, and she fell heavily into his arms, and began to kiss his face, his lips, his arms, his hair. He was so surprised that for an instant he could not breathe. But her lips pressed themselves against his, and her smell was in his nostrils, and he did not know how to be rid of her. He did what came most easily, for he was still weak and tired: he did not fight her, but allowed her to envelop him with her arms and hands and face and body. Blurred images passed through his mind. He saw her black hair, felt her warmth, remembered that Natasha was gone. Then, with a sob, he returned the kiss of this strange woman, drowning his sorrow in her embrace, clutching the memory of Natasha in the presence of this other woman. He made love to that unfamiliar, angular body, covered it with caresses meant for another, rounder, beloved form, one that would be his no longer. He paid this final tribute to the woman he loved, loving another in an effort not to release Natasha to the grave.

Hours later Lizette whispered, "Oh, Ossip, how I adore you! How we both adore you, my Vera and I. Stepan told me that you have often wished for a daughter, but one that would not have to be diapered, and breast-fed. Let Vera think of you as a . . . dear friend, a special protector."

He regarded her with momentary horror, suddenly aware of what had taken place, of what he had done. No, he would never marry this woman, who did not even appeal to him. Although, it was true, she was experienced in the art of giving pleasure to a man, this was undeniable. But he did not love her, not one bit! He wet his lips. Natasha was gone, and so was his purpose in living. This woman liked him, needed a protector for herself and her daughter. Did she love him? No, she could not possibly be in love with him. Stepan had told her of his family, of his title, of his rich relatives in Paris. Ossip thought: She is not stupid, this Lizette. Now I understand. But still, to have risked her life, when I could just as easily have left her behind, and contaminated her child . . . He looked at her, and her face softened, and she took his hand with infinite gentleness. "I do love you, my silly fool," she said, and kissed him. He drew back, wondering.

Then she burst into tears. "You have taken me lightly!" she cried. "You do not love me, will never marry me. And I took you for an honorable man, a gentleman, a fine human being . . ."

He recalled Natasha, angry with him for not helping her captured father, and then thought of how frequently he had detested himself for his pleasure with her, a married woman with a daughter. This woman, too, was a mother. She might mean it, she might not, but suddenly his sense of self-esteem was at stake, that much he knew for certain. She was a lady and could do him no harm—for who indeed could harm a dead man whose senses had been completely dulled? He felt infinitely sorry for this person who had risked so much for a man who could not offer love, who would never love again. Perhaps, because of this, he owed her the only thing he could offer, his name.

Oh, Natasha, he cried within his heart, I have never loved you more than now, never felt so incapable of making decisions, for you will never leave my being, my consciousness. And he looked at Lizette Dietrich, and thought: She is clever, more clever than Nina Tobias, whom I would have married but for that Abelson. And she is not a child, such as Tania was. She is a woman of substance, and there is no time to waste. The Reds are coming.

"Do not think so harshly of me," he murmured softly, touching Lizette's short, coarse hair. A deep feeling of protectiveness came over him, a feeling of importance such as he had felt when defending his father. Not even Natasha had been so dependent upon him: she had had a father, a husband. Silently, he looked at Lizette, saw the hurt in her eyes. Since I do not and cannot love you, since you will never be one with me because I am still one with *her*, then I shall do my utmost to make it up to you.

"Tell Verotchka that she will have to accept me as more than a 'friend,' " he said somewhat ironically. As she raised herself upon an elbow, he laughed tentatively. "Lizette," he intoned, saying her name for the first time. "Get dressed, Lizette. Russia has new laws now, communist laws, and we can be married at once, simply by placing both our signatures upon a sheet of paper in front of the first available official."

But he could not stand the sight of her face contracting into tears, and turned aside.

If Stepan was surprised at the sudden wedding, which was accomplished in five minutes at the City Hall of Odessa, not even a lift of his fine white eyebrows demonstrated this. He had already looked through Ossip's and Lizette's apartments and ascertained that since the Reds were already on the edge of town, it would not be worthwhile to burden their escape with unnecessary luggage. Lizette and Vera possessed nothing of value, and neither did Ossip.

So, papers in hand, they hastened to the house of a man known to ferry passengers across the Dniester River to the

Rumanian shore. Ossip paid him what he could, and the man brought them to a large cornfield, where he told them to stay hidden among the ripening ears while he surveyed the area and chose the proper moment for the trip. He left, and Stepan unwrapped the sandwiches which he had made before leaving the apartment. The Baron and his new Baroness sat on the bare earth with their daughter and servant, listening to rifle shots coming closer and closer. Lizette's black eyes gleamed with fear, and she pressed her spare body to her husband. Slowly, the sun began to go down, and then Lizette said, "He has gone off with our money, and will leave us here for the crows and the buzzards." The little blond girl patted her mother's hand, and Ossip murmured something reassuring which he did not believe. Only Stepan, white and dignified, was silent.

All at once, from somewhere near them, a burst of fire was heard, and the ferryman came toward them from out of nowhere, motioning wildly. "Quick!" he muttered under his breath. "The Bolsheviks have just fired at a small boat going to Rumania, and have killed the oarsman and his passengers, a father, a mother, and their baby. They never shoot twice in a row. This is our chance!" He pushed the Gunzburgs, Vera, and Stepan into his wooden boat. It was now night, and the man paddled furiously, dipping his oars expertly into the river without making a sound. Bats shrieked above them. A thud indicated that they had docked, and Stepan stepped out first, momentarily losing his footing. He leaned over, giving his hand to his new mistress. Then came the nimble child, and finally Ossip and the oarsman. Lizette threw herself upon her husband, moaning slightly, and quietly he held her to him while the ferryman spoke. "I have risked my life!" the ferryman was saying. "You have not paid me sufficiently. I need more money."

"But I told you earlier," Ossip stated succinctly, "that I have no more. I cannot help you any further."

"Then I can return, and alert the Reds," the man threatened, shaking his fist in Ossip's face.

"We cannot have that," the young man replied smoothly. He began to remove his jacket, and now his wife, Lizette, whispered angrily: "What are you doing? Are you mad? You will catch your death, Ossip!" But he quelled her hysteria with his blue gaze, and said simply; "There are many ways to die, my dear." He handed the ferryman his well-made jacket from Petrograd, and declared, "I have nothing left to offer you."

The four refugees began to walk through the night, until Lizette and Vera could no longer go on. Then, in a field, Stepan laid down his own coat and made a blanket of it for the ladies to sleep on. The following day, he produced raisins, and dried apricots, and lemons, and the family ate their breakfast. They stopped at a farm farther on and drank some hot milk they could not pay for. Then they resumed their journey, loaded down with some fresh fruits and vegetables that the farmer had graciously given them after their milk. They walked, Ossip wearing a hole in the sole of his shoe, and sharing the warmth of Stepan's coat, since he no longer had one. Lizette retained a grim silence as she walked, and Vera panted. But Ossip was proud of their resistance, and patted their shoulders amicably. After his bout with the typhus, his own head was swimming with the strain of endurance, and he knew that he stank of cold perspiration. They halted here and there at small farms, receiving crusts of bread and asking to sleep in haylofts or in barns. They headed for Kishinev, capital of Bessarabia. It was the nearest city, and from there, with hope, they could raise enough money to wire Ossip's Uncle Misha de Gunzburg in Paris.

On the outskirts of the city, at dusk, the bedraggled travelers spotted a rather large, well-kept farmhouse, and they directed their steps toward its front door. Lizette's hair clung in limp strands to her temples, and there were

circles under her eyes. She resembled a skeleton more than
she did a woman. Stepan, who was certainly sixty years of
age, appeared the freshest of all with his thick white hair
and his tall, elegant demeanor. Ossip was pale and haggard, his eyes bloodshot. Little Vera had lost weight and
was no longer red-cheeked and comely. To their knock, the
heavy wooden door opened to reveal a man of Stepan's
age, a leathery peasant with gray hair and beard, who
regarded them with astonishment. "What may I do for
you?" he asked. His Rumanian was heavily accented, and
in fact Ossip had found that everyone they had encountered on this side of the border spoke passable Russian,
since at one time this territory had been Russian soil. But
this man's accent was more familiar to him than that of
other farmers. He regarded the man with his sapphire
eyes, and wondered.

"What is it you want?" the man repeated. Suddenly
Ossip saw an old woman inside, a plump, neat old woman
with white hair, and in his mind he visualized her young,
with brown curls, in a large kitchen. "Are you Russians?"
he asked. When the old peasant nodded, startled, Ossip
examined him carefully and asked, "Podolians, by any
chance?"

Now the woman arrived, holding up a cotton skirt.
"Yes," she said, "we're Podolians. What of it? What d'you
want?" Her gaze, brown and round, grew slightly hostile
taking in their disheveled and dirty appearance.

Ossip stared at her, bemused, while his wife stood next
to him, knitting her brow. "Zina?" he asked, at length.

The old peasants regarded each other, their eyes widening. "I am Zina Tumarkina," she assented. "But—we don't
know you."

"Then—you must be Eusebe!" Ossip cried, joy lighting
his face as a candle shining upon the walls of a cavern.
"Eusebe, Eusebe, the water carrier, and Zina, the kitchen
maid. It's extraordinary! Don't you recognize me at all?"

Then, in his excitement, he began to laugh self-consciously. "Of course, you wouldn't. It's been ages, ages since Mohilna, and besides, I'm dirty and unshaven. But I am Ossip Davidovitch de Gunzburg. Mohilna, where you met and married, was my summer home! Don't you remember me at all?"

Now the two old people drew him inside, talking at once. "Yes, yes, Ossip Davidovitch! See, Zina, his blue eyes, so like his mother's?" the old peasant exclaimed, and she nodded, and beamed. "I can see the Gunzburg face, too," she said.

"We're starved, and cold, and exhausted. Will you take us in?" Ossip asked. "This is—my wife, Elizaveta Adolfovna, and our daughter Vera. And this is Stepan. Stepan was our maître d'hôtel in Petrograd; don't you remember how we all spoke of him so much? My sisters, my brother—"

The old woman took them all into the dining room with its high beamed ceiling, and sat them down at a large wooden table. She brought out sausages and bread and pickles and chicken and fresh vegetable soup. She passed her coarse fingers through Vera's hair, examined Lizette, and cried large round tears as she served Ossip. "What a family you have, Ossip Davidovitch, what a family," she murmured. "And you—how you have grown from the frail small boy we knew. Do you recall the night your brother was born, how happy we all were? How is he, the sweet cherub?"

"We don't know," Ossip answered. "We haven't been able to reach him. You see, Zina, Eusebe—we have no money. We cannot . . . pay you for your hospitality. My father is dead, and Mama and Sonia, the last I'd heard, were in Feodosia in the Crimea. Gino was in the Russian army, but then, that was before the peace treaty was signed, and Anna has been living in Switzerland—"

"Ah, yes, Anna Davidovna, my favorite child—I'm

sorry, Ossip Davidovitch, I did not mean to offend you. But I loved your sister—" Eusebe's words hung in midair, and his eyes were moist. Ossip patted his hand and said nothing. He was so infinitely tired, so drained, so empty.

The old water carrier had retired to this farm, he told them proudly, several years ago. The Baron—Baron David —had sent him a handsome sum to help him purchase this land. Now he escorted Ossip and his family to the bedroom where he and his wife usually slept, and settled them into it, bringing Stepan with him and Zina into the warm pantry. Tomorrow the Gunzburgs could sleep, and then, of course, Eusebe would drive Ossip to town and would give him the money to wire his uncle in France. It was understood.

Vera slept at the foot of the large bed, and breathed evenly, but Lizette twisted and turned restlessly next to her husband. Finally she whispered to him, "Oh, Ossip, isn't it dreadful? You, a Baron de Gunzburg, having to accept charity from your former servants. Don't you feel abused and violated?"

Softly rubbing her meager shoulder, Ossip remarked: "Why should I, my dear? The world is topsy turvy, and today it belongs to the Tumarkins. I wonder, actually, if it ever did belong to the likes of me . . ."

She stiffened, and retorted proudly: "It did, and it shall again. You aren't defeated, my love. Don't ever think it!"

In the darkness, under the soft quilt, he started to laugh. But she moved away from him, insulted. He kept on laughing, until Vera moaned in her sleep.

Twenty-One

———————————•———————————

Gino, like his sister Sonia, was fiercely loyal to his own ideals, and it took the spring of 1918, after his reunion with the family, for him to take a different view of this "civil war" to which he was so violently opposed. He wanted his mother, sister, and former governess to leave the dangerous port of Feodosia, but it was not so easy to find rooms in Simferopol, the Crimean capital. Alexander Zevin, who had managed the properties belonging to the Gunzburg dynasty for several decades, had promised to locate inexpensive quarters for them, as well as for his old mother's friend of long standing, Nadezhda Igorovna Pomerantz, and her daughter, Olga. In the meantime, the Gunzburgs and Pomerantzes continued their lives in Feodosia, now the scene of constant skirmishes between bands of Reds and partisan White groups that had formed in the area. Gino was invited to participate in the night watch of the city, and he observed that the Whites were unruly and untrained, and that they did not hesitate to loot and molest the population as much as did the Reds who sporadically vied with them for control of the city.

What occurred to change his sentiments was a sudden, mass execution of officers in Sevastopol by Reds who had taken matters into their own hands. The brutality, the senselessness of these murders spread like ripples over the south of the Crimean peninsula. Gino marched into his mother's room and declared, "When real regiments of White soldiers begin to form here, with a truly military attitude, I am going to enlist. Our country is no longer merely divided into two political groups whose struggles do not concern me. These Bolsheviks are brigands who must not be permitted to seize control of our proud Russia."

His mother regarded him with only a hint of a twinkle in her blue eyes. "So," she stated, "you have changed your mind. Very well, my son. But you will not be able to do anything right away. Even near Dzhankoi, in the north of our peninsula, the Whites who are attempting to hold back the bulk of the Red forces are nothing like the regiments you fought with against the Central Powers. And, like Sonia, you are an organized person who likes life divided into black and white. I'm afraid, Gino, that right now our world is in shades of gray."

He smiled sheepishly. How well she knew him, as did Ossip, his brilliant, cynical brother. They shook their heads over him, but he was aware of their pride in him, and even of a certain envy for his strong opinions and ideals. In a woman, such staunchness could sometimes be seen as rigidity—had he not often heard people speak thus of Sonia? Yet in him it constituted manliness. He blushed, thinking of Olga Pomerantz. He had begun to help her—and Sonia too, naturally—to try to improve her stenographic skills. The young woman could now decipher the symbols perfectly, but needed to increase her speed in the transcription of dictation. It had fallen upon Gino to read to her, and to Sonia, from articles and novels of his selection. One evening his sister remarked quite casually, "Why is it that we are now being deluged with passages of love scenes, while before you were intrigued by archaeology and chemistry?" Overcome by embarrassment, he had not replied. But he was finding it more and more difficult not to see, before his mind's eye, the pure hazel gaze and the yellow curls, that look of intense interest which so moved him, when Olga Arkadievna listened to his stories of the front, or to his dreams and hopes. Suddenly it occurred to him that she had become the personification of those dreams and hopes, that when he wished for the purification of Russia, he visualized his country as a woman resembling Olga. He was happy, but also frightened. What if, guessing at his feelings as his sister evidently had, she turned her beautiful eyes away from him completely?

In April, as if out of nowhere, a troop of Red soldiers came into Feodosia on the run, heading for the harbor. "The Germans are coming!" they cried. Gino said to his family, "That's absurd! Trotsky signed the peace treaty at Brest-Litovsk only last month"—and his handsome ruddy face brightened with shame—"and while the rest of the Allies are still fighting valiantly for their honor, we Russians are officially at peace." But in spite of his words, the following day two or three German soldiers straggled into Feodosia, then a few others, and, to the consternation not only of the resident population but also of the White and Red partisan groups, finally an entire battalion arrived. By then, the fleeing members of the Red Army who had alerted everyone had already escaped by ship. And, not two days later, Olga appeared at the Gunzburg house, her heart-shaped face full of tears, and knelt by Mathilde's chair. "They have taken over the Crimea, although in the capital their emissaries have recognized the communist state. Now they are in Mama's office confiscating her goods for their own people."

"My sweet, they cannot be worse than those Bolsheviks who were there before," Mathilde replied soothingly, patting the girl's thick curls. "Maybe they will even be better mannered. After all, these Germans are doing what they're told, as occupants do, but they will not kill us, as the Reds might have."

"Olga Arkadievna is right, Mama. No matter how disgracefully the communists behave, they are usurpers, not invaders. I shall go to your mother's office," Gino exclaimed. "I shall tell them that if they send one grain of your wheat to their accursed country, I shall fight them for it! Your mother may be an exceptional woman of business —yet still, she is a woman, and this is a man's affair. I have fought the Germans before—"

"Gino, don't be a fool," his mother stated. But the young man hastened to his room, ignoring her, and dressed in his discarded Russian uniform. Reemerging onto the porch where his mother and Olga sat huddled in apprehension, he noted, with a sudden surge of cockiness, that Olga's eyes were full of admiration and gratefulness. That was all that he had needed. He stood tall, defying his mother and rendering her helpless with his determination. He had fought many battles for the sake of his country's honor. This one was for Olga's sake alone.

Mathilde bit her lower lip, regarding Olga sideways. What chance was there for them, for those two comely, good young people, who were learning to find love in an atmosphere fraught with dangers and difficulties? Love. It had not occurred between her and David, not for her; and her three older children had suffered and lost. Tears rose to her eyes when she thought of Anna and little Riri, of Ossip and the Tagantsev girl, and Sonia's broken engagement . . . She wanted to say: Don't even try, Gino, Olga. But instead she sighed, her hand still on the girl's head.

Gino was not quite certain of what he would do, once in Nadezhda Igorovna's office. He knew only that he was outraged, that he had fought these people, and that they had broken a treaty. When he entered the wheat exporter's office, and saw two men bending over her account books, his anger rose. "Get out!" he said in short, clipped tones.

Two heads flew up, two common faces regarded him with open-eyed astonishment. He, Gino, did not choose to remember the son of General von Falkenhayn, who had died in his arms with such bravery, whom for nights he had imagined having shot from his own rifle. They stared with disbelief at the red-faced young sergeant before them, and when he withdrew a gun from his holster threateningly, the older man clutched his companion with fear, and exclaimed, *"Nein! Bitte!"* They were both dressed as civilians, and pointed at their garb to explain that they possessed no weapons.

At that moment voices broke out behind Gino, one of them the resonant alto of Nadezhda Igorovna Pomerantz, others harsh Teuton voices. Gino heard only Nadia, crying out, "Gino! For God's sake—" He felt something sharp prod him in the area of his ribs, and saw that he was flanked by two German officers with bayonets. "I told you, Frau Pomerantz, we wished for no trouble," one of them stated. Nadia shook her head, saying, "But this is merely our friend, who got carried away—" Her black hair, as always, was messy and badly pinned, and she appeared distraught and surprised by all this commotion. Gino looked at her, his clear brown eyes shining with both youthful abashment and courage. He saw that she seemed about to upbraid him, and talk to him as his mother had—and yet she was proud, for a young Russian had dared to come forward, no matter how foolishly. "Ach!" she spat out, and looked away. She was a strong, willful woman, but suddenly words failed her totally.

"We simply can't allow this," the senior officer declared. "We'll have to arrest him for disturbing the peace."

"You would dare?" Gino cried, in his perfect German. Now he turned to the colonel, and his eyes blazed with passion. "It is you who have broken the peace, the peace of Brest-Litovsk, the—" But he was being forcibly led away. His eyes encountered those of Olga's mother, who stood motionless in her office, her brow wrinkled with anguish. Her face was harsh, and as Gino was marched off, he could not help being pursued by that haunting look, which signified so much, and which would never have been leveled at him had this woman not known that her daughter cared for him. She understood the brashness of his action as a Russian and as the man who loved Olga.

He threw off his guards and walked away proudly, between them, to the Feodosia jailhouse. He had accomplished no good, had perhaps jeopardized Nadia Pomerantz's relationship with the Germans. He knew that he had appeared ridiculous in his bravado. But thinking of the heart-shaped face of Olga Arkadievna, he did not regret what he had done, any more than he had regretted his charity toward young Lieutenant von Falkenhayn. Gino de Gunzburg was not one to rehash a past action. What was done, was simply done with.

He was thrown into a large cell with a dozen other men of all classes and ages. He was the only one in uniform. Looking into the corridor through the bars, he thought of Olga, and wondered if she would come to see him, if she would be angry or worried. The glow which he had felt was now giving way to a more realistic annoyance, and apprehension. He remembered Sonia's letter about Ossip's imprisonment at the Fortress. Of couse, his mother had no money now, no influence, and he had threatened enemy civilians with a gun, whereas his brother had merely taken some photographs in a military zone. So absorbed was he in these reflections that he was unaware of his companions. But he could feel somebody tugging at his jacket from the back, and presently a voice inserted itself into his consciousness: "Baron! Baron, aren't you going to recognize me?"

That voice! He wheeled about, his face alert, and encountered a most shaggy young man whose expression, both shrewd and humorous, brought him back to the trenches. "Vassya?" he said doubtfully. The other shrugged lightly, as if to say: You should know me without confir-

mation, shaved or not, after all we've been through . . .
Gino began to laugh. "Vassya! What luck, finding you
here!"

"Luck indeed," he said ironically. "Baron, if our luck
persists, we'll share the same grave. Why'd they put you
here, the bastards? And—what're you doing in uniform?
Have you joined the Whites?"

"No, not yet. I . . . stormed the offices of a friend of my
mother, to get those Germans out of there. It was all very
dramatic—worthy of my brother Ossip, and not at all like
me. But—here I am. And you?"

"Came here to do some livestock trading, and they
grabbed my merchandise. Wouldn't stand for it. D'you
think they'll kill us, Baron?"

"I think they want to make sure that we feisty ones
remain out of the way while they do as they please," Gino
said with bitterness and anger. Then, more gently, almost
as if to a child, he said reassuringly, "But I don't think
death lies in our cards."

"Your Papa'd be right proud of you, standing up to
them," Vassya said warmly.

"I'm not so sure. He might find the entire matter absurd.
I suppose it is, too." Gino paused and shook his head,
memories flooding his mind. "Do you remember when I
asked you if you had a girl, and told you I'd never had one?
Well—I do now, sort of. If she ever considered me, she
probably won't, after this . . ."

But a third person had come up to them, and Gino
stopped, glancing at the stranger with quick appraisal. He
was a young man, under thirty, with powerful shoulders
and a massive head of black hair. His clothing was somewhat threadbare but well cut, and he possessed blue-green
eyes that Gino liked. "I beg your pardon," the stranger
now cut in, addressing Gino. "I must ask you—your friend
here calls you 'Baron,' and I couldn't help overhearing you
speak of a brother called 'Ossip.' You yourself are in a

sergeant's uniform. Are you, by any chance, a Baron Gunzburg, of Petrograd?"

Taken by surprise, Gino nodded. "Yes. I am Evgeni Davidovitch de Gunzburg. I was in the army, and Vassya here was one of my men, until he too became a sergeant. Now we are friends. But you? You know my brother? Have you seen him?"

"I have not seen him since the early months of 1916, when my father and I had the pleasure of dining at your home," the young man declared. "It was there that I met Ossip Davidovitch. I had met your sister before—Sofia Davidovna. The first time was in Kiev, when we were children; the next . . . when she visited there as a young woman. My name is Mossia Zlatopolsky—Moissei Gillelovitch Zlatopolsky. I have heard of you, and knew your cousin, Tatiana Alexandrovna Halperina, quite well."

"Then it was through your father that Papa sold the Judaica to the Palestinians," Gino said slowly. He smiled, shook the other's hand. "Vassya," he said, "this is a family friend, Mossia Zlatopolsky. A strange 'friend' to be sure, for his father is actually my uncle's friend, and but for your insistence upon still calling me 'Baron,' we might never have encountered each other. Are you living in Feodosia?"

"Not really," Mossia said. "My family had to leave Moscow rapidly, because of the troubles. The cases containing the Judaica barely had time to arrive, in fact, before we had to depart without them. They were confiscated by the Bolshoviks. We went first to Kiev, where we had lived so many years, and Papa picked up some of his best sugar beets. Then we went south, waiting to see whether the Reds would come this far, or whether we would be able to recuperate some of our enterprises. So far, the sugar beets are the only remnants of what was once a great wealth. Have the Gunzburgs suffered similar losses?"

Gino sighed. "My father is dead," he said simply.

Zlatopolsky regarded him thoughtfully, his blue-green eyes filled with compassion and understanding. "I am glad to have had the opportunity to meet him," he murmured. Gino felt a distinct liking for this man and saw that Vassya, who was naturally cautious, had confidently settled his small, sturdy form between them. Gino drew a measure of comfort from the presence of both men.

But now a strong, clear female voice reverberated in the passageway. "That's all right, we shall find him," Gino heard, and his features suddenly lit up with joy. He grabbed Mossia's arm, and cried, "It's her! My sister, Sonia! I wonder . . ." He did not finish his thought. He simply hoped that Olga would be with Sonia. But he looked at Mossia, and fancied that a strange green light had passed over his companion's eyes. Then he squinted to make out the people that were coming toward them.

They had come together, and the contrast between them struck Vassya most, for he had met neither girl before. The first was truly a girl, taller and stronger than her companion, like the sapling of a young oak. She must have been nineteen or twenty, with a heart-shaped face crested by blond curls, cut fashionably short. Her eyes were hazel, her nose uptilted, her color hearty and golden. She was clad in a sea-green afternoon suit, that revealed stockings and boots. The other was a lady, lovely and proud, with an oval face of pure white complexion, enormous gray eyes circled by thick black lashes, and pale lips below an elegant nose. Her hair was black and very thick, and probably, when she took it down at night, it came cascading to her knees. A timeless lady, dressed in black, to Vassya she was as beautiful as the carved face of a cameo brooch. Was she eighteen, or twenty-eight? He wondered. And then he thought: That isn't the Baron's girl. He'll be choosing the good strong blond, who is like him, made of the earth, not a woman as breakable as a china vase . . . I'd be afraid to touch her.

Gino, in his excitement, cried out: "Olga! You came!" and his brown eyes widened with joy. The girl came quickly to the bars of the cell, and took the hands that were offered to her. Her face, full of concern, eloquently conquered the last traces of reserve that remained between them. She raised one of his hands to her lips.

"Gino, Gino," she said, "we were sick with worry!" The basket of bread and cheese remained forgotten at her feet. She smiled, a trembling smile, and he knew then that she loved him as he loved her. They remained absorbed in each other, staring through the bars of the cell, and Sonia discreetly looked away from them. But as she turned, her wavering gaze landed upon Mossia Gillelovitch Zlatopolsky, and she was so surprised that her hand flew to her breast and her lips parted.

It was he, smiling quietly, who broke the spell by uttering a low chuckle. "I'm so sorry I gave you such a start, Sofia Davidovna," he announced. He did not seem to know exactly what to say, and she did not help him. A flood of color had risen to her cheeks, and she regarded him as though he were an apparition. "Is life very difficult for you?" he asked at last, softly, looking at the thinness of her. "I . . . heard about your father. I am so sorry, Sofia Davidovna." He realized that he had just uttered these very words, and shook his head at himself. "You look lovely," he added sincerely. "More so, in fact, than when I saw you in Kiev, and then you were resplendent in your Parisian finery. Anyone can look elegant at a reception. But at a jail . . ." His eyes twinkled at her.

"Why are you here?" she demanded in a low voice. "Is your family in Feodosia?"

For the first time since she had fastened her gaze upon him, at her Uncle Misha's mansion in Kiev in 1904, she saw him turn away from her entirely, as if in the throes of embarrassment. She was struck by a dreadful idea: perhaps his father, whom he loved so, had been killed, or had died, as her own had. Or had he committed a real crime, so that now he stood ashamed, he who had always seemed poised and self-possessed? Or . . . had something happened to Kolya Saxe, something he did not want to tell her? She cleared her throat, and smiled tentatively, and when he turned back he saw that this smile was joyful and proud, illuminating her translucent skin, brightening her eyes. Her haunting eyes . . .

"Mossia Gillelovitch," she whispered, "I must tell you that I have mended my broken heart, and that you needn't feel afraid that I shall fall apart again, as I did in Petrograd. That business is done with as far as I am concerned."

Her soft-spoken words were suddenly echoed from behind her, "What is this 'business' that is 'done with,' may I ask?" she heard, and, outraged that someone had overheard her private declaration, she wheeled lightly on her toes and stood face to face with a young woman. She opened her mouth, then closed it again, bewildered at the lack of good taste of this person. Her echo, so to speak, was tall and willowy, with hair of a most unusual color, a burnished amber surely helped by henna. It rippled down the woman's back, unpinned and unrestricted as a schoolgirl's. Her eyes were black, her complexion olive, her wide, full lips rouged. She looked thirty, possibly a year or two older. She was not beautiful, but she was striking and very impressive in a dress of soft red wool. Nothing about this woman was understated. Ignoring Sonia completely, she turned to Mossia and addressed him in a voice that was both low and raucous, not unlike that of Nadia Pomerantz. "And how is my beloved?" she asked archly.

He replied, quite easily, not looking at Sonia, "They're keeping me alive, if that's what you mean. And you? How are you managing?"

The woman raised finely penciled eyebrows: "I always manage, my dear, not exactly in the style to which you've accustomed me, but then again, survival is an instinct with me. Do you miss me?"

"I don't have time to," he replied rudely, his gentle blue-green eyes turning to ice-blue shards. The set of his jaw became more pronounced. Sonia's posture had grown rigid, her breath came in quick gasps. She felt the blood flowing once more to her cheekbones, and thought: It is not possible. But of course it's possible! Men have mistresses all the time. Tears rose to her eyes as she vividly recalled her conversation with him in her parents' home, when he had told her about Kolya's mistress.

The woman said, tauntingly, "Are you ashamed to introduce me to this pretty lady, with whom you were discussing such heated topics?"

"We were discussing nothing of the sort. Baroness Sofia de Gunzburg is an acquaintance of long standing." His face was set like stone, but he regarded Sonia, and his eyes softened, appealed to her—and held her. "Sofia Davidovna, may I present to you my wife, Elena Lvovna?"

Sonia had been prepared for anything but this. Yet, though her heart had leaped into her throat, she continued to stand upright, her features composed. She inclined her head, weighed down by her pompadour and topknot, and forced herself to smile, weak though it was. "How do you do," she stated.

She saw the stare of open admiration on Mossia's face, and all at once she felt terribly sorry for him. Why had he married her? Clearly, he did not love this woman. She felt certain of that. War made people do such stupid, senseless things . . .

"You must call me 'Lialia,' " Elena Lvovna said, placing a hand on Sonia's arm. "Lialia means 'doll' in Polish. It was my professional name. You see, I used to sing at a café-concert in Kiev. My mother sang operetta, and it was she whom Mossia met first. It was a strange story, really, but so typical of my husband," she said, glancing toward him. "He had won a fortune by being the only person at a horse race to bet on the winner. Naturally, this came about because of a mistake: Mossia had meant to place his bet on the favorite, as everyone else had. When his horse won he felt guilty, for this was money he had not earned. So he spent it on a magnificent house for all the actors and singers—and demimondaines, for there were many!—that he knew. He even hired servants. My mother went to live there, and so we met. Now I have become his own little doll, haven't I, sweet?" She eyed him with undisguised lust, as if to taunt him.

"I am certain that the Baroness had no desire to hear this long and ancient story," Mossia declared abruptly.

But Sonia regarded him with the pure straight gaze of her gray eyes, and smiled. "On the contrary—I found it quite touching."

"And did he tell you how he came to be put in prison? One of those Germans was drunk, and made improper advances toward me. Mossia didn't stand for it, of course. Isn't he . . . honorable?"

"Tomorrow I shall return with food for Gino," Sonia stated. "My mother will be most pleased to add some things for you, too, Mossia Gillelovitch," She nodded her head and placed her delicate fingers upon Olga's arm. "Come, my darling," she murmured. "Our mothers will be waiting." She took her brother's hand through the bars, and kissed it. Then she turned back to the Zlatopolskys. "Good evening," she said graciously.

Mossia watched sadly as Sonia disappeared.

During the period of Gino's imprisonment, Sonia went to the jail each day with a basket of food. She always brought enough to allow her brother to share with Mossia Zlatopolsky, and she would often stop to chat with the young man in an amiable way, never forgetting to inquire about his wife. Once or twice she saw the voluptuous, flamboyant Lialia in the streets of Feodosia, and she replied to her ostentatious greetings with utmost courtesy. When Mathilde commented with horror upon Mossia's choice of wife, her daughter stopped her. "Hillel Zlatopolsky did business with Papa, and knew Uncle Misha in

Kiev," she stated. "If his son, who is a gentleman, has married this woman, he has probably done so after mature consideration, knowing her qualities far better than we do. We owe her the same graciousness that we would give to any friendly acquaintance, Mama." She held her head high, undaunted by the fact that others of Feodosia society, such as the elder Madame Zevina, frowned upon her for speaking to this woman of dubious character.

One day, not long after Gino's arrest, Mathilde received a message from a distant relation, Hans Blumenfeld of Hamburg. Baroness Rosa de Gunzburg had been born a Warburg in Germany, and this young man was the son of one of Rosa's sisters. He was a lieutenant in the German army, however, and, as delicately as possible, was requesting permission to visit his relations in Feodosia.

"Gino is in prison because of the German occupants," Sonia objected. "We should not receive this young man, considering his nationality and what his people are doing to ours."

But Mathilde leveled her eyes at her daughter and replied, "He is a member of our family, and surely he is not responsible for Gino's predicament, Sonia. If we helped the Falkenhayns, why should we refuse Rosa's own flesh and blood? Had Gino been a soldier in Hamburg, I would have been most grateful to the Blumenfelds for inviting him to their home. He will have luncheon with us tomorrow."

When Sonia announced this to her brother, Gino's face flushed a deep purple and he grasped the cell bars with anger. "I have fought the Germans, risked my life!" he exclaimed. "The Falkenhayn episode was totally different. Blumenfeld is not dying. He is an enemy, and Mama is behaving outrageously. I am glad that I am here—or I should be obliged to go to Olga's house to eat, in order not to have to sit in front of him at the table. Mama shames me."

Sonia said nothing. Conflicting emotions were warring within her: loyalty to her country and brother on the one hand, family tradition and devotion to her mother on the other. But a plan was forming in her mind, although she would never have outlined it to Gino.

When young Blumenfeld appeared the next day, Sonia made him welcome, and served a beautifully presented meal which considerably stretched the Gunzburgs' budget. There was fresh salad, cold fish, and boiled potatoes sprinkled with parsley, and for dessert, apples and a cheese. The officer smiled, his light eyes brightening with pleasure, and he began to relax. He told Mathilde that he had heard that his Aunt Rosa and Uncle Sasha had reached France, that Tania and her in-laws had gone to Basel, Switzerland.

It was over coffee that Sonia cleared her throat, and said, "Hans, a grave situation has arisen on account of my young brother's—impulsiveness. You are a lieutenant, an officer. Might it be within your power to help a member of our own family, who has acted foolishly? Gino is in jail because of a girl, really." Then, without blushing, she began to recount Gino's actions, tempering them a bit, and smiling sweetly at the young man. "You see how overblown the case actually has been," she finished, gazing with her pure gray eyes at Hans Blumenfeld. "And isn't it romantic, really?"

And so it was that on the following day, a joyful Gino appeared at the Gunzburg house. "They released me!" he cried. "And I don't know why. Did Nadezhda Igorovna convince them that I was not a criminal?"

"I wouldn't know," his sister answered. "But some criminals are less dangerous than a fool in love." And she turned her back, seemingly annoyed at him. His mother raised her eyebrows and shook her head in Sonia's direction. Don't cross her today, her blue eyes told him.

Even after her brother's return to the family, Sonia continued her visits to the prison. She brought the same basket, filled with whatever food they could manage, and casually deposited it in the hands of Mossia Zlatopolsky. "I am sorry that we couldn't help you, too," she declared the first day. "But one favor was all that we thought we could curry from the enemy." When she departed, Mossia thoughtfully shared the food with Vassya, who was indeed grateful. For both of them realized that Sonia could ill afford her generosity and that, had she learned of Vassya's connection with Gino at the front, she would surely have sacrificed her own portion to add more to the basket. Mossia felt within his heart that no one in the Gunzburg household knew of her continued visits, nor of the tidbits she put aside for him. It was a gesture of personal honor that Mossia cherished.

But the two prisoners had another visitor each morning, one Sonia never knew about. Every day, Gino came to see Vassya and Mossia, also bearing whatever scraps he could save. In order to preserve the dignity of the siblings' selfless acts, the two men never revealed to either Gunzburg what the other was doing. It is the indomitable Gunzburg spirit which must at any cost be salvaged from this strife, Mossia determined. Even if Russia herself perishes, these two young people, the Baron's children, must fight to survive. They are his greatest legacy on earth.

Soon the Germans began to relax their hold on Feodosia, and could hardly be bothered with such harmless men as Vassya and Mossia Zlatopolsky. The two men were released from jail, Vassya returning to his nearby farm, and Mossia going in search of his wife, Lialia. It was old Madame Zevina who announced to Sonia, Mathilde, and Johanna that she had heard that the Zlatopolskys had gone to Yalta, where members of his family had been staying. "It is strange that he did not stop to say good-bye to us," Mathilde remarked, furrowing her brow. But Madame Zevina shrugged: "If he is indeed a gentleman, then he merely spared you a face-to-face encounter with his . . . vivid spouse."

Sonia simply smiled. She was thinking of a racehorse that had won, against all odds.

Twenty-Two

_____·_____

Sonia and Gino carefully perused the newspapers, which were not accurate, spouting German and communist propaganda. But these tabloids were all that were available to them, and they were eager to know what was occurring in the rest of the country. News of Ossip could not reach them, and if Hans Blumenfeld had not told them of Sasha, Rosa, and Tania, they might have thought them dead in Petrograd and Kiev. News from abroad was nonexistent, except to relate German exploits in the final throes of the world war—distorted exploits, naturally, for the Central Powers were, in fact, faring badly.

One event, however, did come through the propaganda, about a political murder which took place in July in Ekaterinburg, deep in Siberia. Brother and sister regarded each other, sick and frightened: the Tzar and his wife and four children had been shot and killed by the communists. "A purge," the tabloid had called it. Gino sat with his chin upon his clenched hands, thinking of his beloved country. He had been less of a Tzarist than his parents, brother, and sister Sonia. They had been true aristocrats. He thought of himself as a well-educated, simple man with the instincts of an intelligent peasant or soldier. He sat and pondered the fate of his Russia, and wept. The death of the Tzar signified the end of a truly Russian tradition, embedded in its land and in its people.

Cut off from everything that had given meaning to his existence, and fiercely set against fighting his own countrymen, Gino de Gunzburg felt as though a maelstrom were storming all around him. Chaos reigned, blood was shed, but at this particular place in the Crimea he was isolated from its direct effects. He might actually have been living in another nation. A logical, sensible young man, a young man imbued with strong principles, he could not sort out the confusion or his own part in it. He felt that the only ordered aspect of his life was centered around his mother and sister, and Olga, of course. She too was strangely at loose ends, not knowing how best to proceed with life.

Clutching at the first sign of safety, Olga and Gino felt that the best thing for them was simply to proceed with their lives, thereby lending a measure of sanity to their families too. After much discussion, therefore, the two young people resolved to enter the University of Simferopol in the fall. As soon as Alexander Zevin wrote that he had found lodgings for everyone, Gunzburgs and Pomerantzes made their way from Feodosia to the larger city, which was the capital of the Crimea. Zevin had rented a pleasant house for Nadezhda Igorovna and her daughter, who could afford it. But, knowing the tight straits in which the Gunzburgs now found themselves, with no resources but the small remains of the 1917 harvest, he took for them the living room and alcove of a large house which was being opened to boarders.

This residence belonged to a widow, Madame Solovéichik, who had once been of the wealthy gentry but whose income had greatly diminished. At one time, she had lived from the proceeds of her nearby farm in Beshterek, but now the communists were sending groups of the Cheka to collect much of her livestock and vegetables for the feeding of their own party members in the cities. Her income had therefore much declined, and she had begun to take in paying guests.

The house was large but had only a single story, and it already contained two families when the Gunzburgs arrived. Sonia and Gino cheered up their mother and ignored Johanna's complaints, converting the sitting room into a room for the three women, who would sleep on a couch and two cots, and preparing a third cot for Gino in the alcove, with a pinned-up sheet to separate him from the women, as a curtain.

Madame Solovéichik did not provide meals for her guests, but she allowed the Gunzburgs to use her kitchen facilities. Everyone ate together in the vast dining room, and the dinners were animated. Apart from her live-in boarders, Madame Solovéichik had with her an aged friend of ninety-two who, not wishing to accept charity, tended the enormous samovar all day long in a small storeroom; and also an impoverished lady of society who had become her housekeeper. Two schoolteachers came to supper, and an old poetess as well. Mathilde enjoyed these people and Sonia and Gino sometimes joined one of the boarder families, whose daughter played the piano and knew the youth of Simferopol. But the Gunzburgs were still in mourning for David, and did not dance. Besides, Gino spent most of his evening hours with Olga, working on their Greek or their history homework. And Sonia, after her household chores, was frequently tired.

Gino was serious about his studies, and, as his French and German were flawless, he took home translations for some of his professors to add small amounts of money to the family funds. Sonia, when there was time, occasionally accompanied her brother and Olga to a particularly intriguing lecture. But she had discovered that Alexander Zevin's wife owned a typewriter, and three or four times a week Sonia would walk to her house to practice on her machine.

The younger Madame Zevina was also an excellent pianist, and since Sonia had not had occasion to play for a long time, she would sit down with her hostess after her typing sessions and indulge in that pastime fraught with memories, four-handed piano. Together, Sonia and Ekaterina Zevina attacked classical symphonies, opera partitas, overtures, military marches, *Peer Gynt*, and many pieces by Schumann, Grieg, Saint-Saëns, and Tchaikovsky. They would play for two full hours, during which time Sonia forgot that she was poor, that her brother Ossip had disappeared, that her former governess did not miss a single chance to harass her. She forgot that the Solovéichik stove had only four burners for more than four boarders, and that each time she had to go to the bathroom she would return to find that one of the other ladies had substituted a pot of her own for Sonia's, and that the soup or barley which she had been boiling had been relegated to a cold corner of the stove, where it had begun to congeal.

It was to Ekaterina Zevina that Sonia admitted, one afternoon, "The last time that I played four-handed piano my heart very nearly broke." But she did not elaborate, and she spoke these words as if she had been discussing the weather. Madame Zevina sighed, and thought: For someone like Sonia, this is tantamount to a confession. She pressed Sonia's fingers expressively.

Madame Solovéichik had a small dog, Kaffa, who loved Sonia more than anyone and followed her around, sniffing nosily. Sonia would sometimes find upon arriving at the Zevins' that Kaffa was still at her heels. The two Zevin daughters would scoop her into their arms like a fuzzy ball, laughing. Sonia was grateful for their easy affection and acceptance of her, and to show her gratitude she began to teach the two girls stenography. So, on the days when she visited the Zevins' house, Sonia would seldom return until suppertime.

One winter day, upon awakening, Johanna de Mey discovered that she had caught a chill. She shivered and sneezed from her reddened nose, and within days seemed to become as thin as a wraith. It was Sonia who sat by her bed, nursing her.

Nadezhda Igorovna Pomerantz traveled a good bit between her rented house in Simferopol and her mansion in Feodosia, to make certain that some of the moneys from her business came to her after all, in spite of interference from the Germans and the Cheka. Of course, with the signing of the Armistice between the Allies and the Central Powers in November 1918, she no longer feared the enemy. But the Cheka sent members constantly to collect revenues. When she would go to Feodosia, Johanna's face would light with joy, and her aquamarine eyes, the only remnants of her once extraordinary beauty, would fill with moisture. Now that she was ill, she tossed upon her pillow, pulling strands of hair through nervous fingers, coughing for Mathilde. But Sonia said calmly, "Mama has gone to stay with Olga, for Nadezhda Igorovna is out of town. I did not want Mama to catch your cold, Juanita. She has been weak of late."

The sick woman sat up, her thin face distorted. "You?" she shrieked. "I might have known that you would separate us! If it isn't that ill-bred woman from Feodosia, then it is you, Miss Priss! Or are you in cahoots with the snake-haired Sappho, you ignoble girl?"

"You are echoing a tiresome refrain," Sonia replied. She plumped her governess's pillow and took up the book from which she had been reading aloud. But Johanna snatched it from her fingers, and hurled it across the room. Sonia raised her eyebrows questioningly, and folded her arms over her chest. "Now what is it?" she sighed.

"I'm not . . . going to allow Gino to marry that girl!" Johanna cried hysterically. "Mathilde will never permit it so long as I can prevent her." She smiled malevolently at Sonia. "Do you remember Kolya's mother, who was unsuitable? I showed your mother the foolishness of it, and you see? He did not marry you. Like Anna. I made Mathilde see how wrong it was for that Berson boy to keep calling, without openly declaring himself. He never *did* declare himself, did he? No, Gino will not have that girl, any more than you had your handsome Kolya Saxe. I shall see to it."

"We were all fools and weaklings," Sonia said as calmly as she could. "But Gino is strong, and he is a man. You never hurt Ossip, did you?"

"No," she replied. "Ossip was passive and obedient. There was no need for interference. But I hurt your father. Never forget it, little girl."

"I'm not about to," Sonia whispered. Her face was completely white, and there was not the slightest touch of red to her lips. She went to the fallen book, flipped through its pages, and found her place. She resumed her seat by Johanna's side and began to read: " 'So, Céline thought, depositing the brown chiffon scarf upon the sofa . . .' "

Her voice, clear and strong, rang through the small sitting room until the clock in Madame Solovéichik's kitchen struck twelve thirty. Sonia placed the book face down upon Johanna's cot, and rose to make luncheon. "Make sure not to burn my food," the sick woman said. Sonia nodded and left the room. In the hallway she leaned against the wall, rubbing her temples with tremulous fingers. No, she thought, I shall not cry. Never again for her. Clenching her fists, she walked quickly into the kitchen.

She had learned a new way of cooking oats. Instead of simply boiling the cereal, she whisked it in a dry pan over the fire for ten minutes, and only then poured it into the boiling water. This was Johanna's preferred method, and Sonia went through the steps of this more troublesome procedure, grilling the oats first. But when she brought the bowl to her governess, the woman rose on her elbow and began to shout, in her shrewish tones, "You have purposely done this, serving me what I detest above all, and preparing it in such an odious manner! You did this to be mean, because your mother is not here to protect me! You don't know what more to invent against me. One of these days, you will poison my food, I know it positively. There, you little monster, you plain little sparrow—see what I do with your meal!" She called Kaffa, the small dog, who had been, once again, at Sonia's heels. To the girl's humiliation, Johanna placed the bowl on the floor before the dog, gloating while Kaffa lapped up the oats. Sonia uttered not a word. She swallowed hard, and kept her eyes on the dog. When Kaffa had finished her snack, Sonia took the empty bowl and returned it to the kitchen. But, as she walked, she wept.

That evening, she took her brother aside and said, "Why don't you marry Olga, as soon as possible? She is so much in love with you."

"What's come over you?" Gino asked. "Are you all right?"

"I'm worried, that's all. I'm . . . afraid. I want to make certain that nothing prevents you from marrying Olga. You do want to, don't you?"

Her brother chuckled softly. "Olga is very young, Sonitchka, and we are in the midst of such bad times. I'm going to sign up with a White regiment, when a decent one forms here. I'd rather wait until all that's behind us before proposing to Olga. Besides, I have no money. I don't want her to think I want her because she still has some. Give us a little time, Sonia."

Inexplicably, his sister broke down and began to cry, and when he took her in his arms, he did not know why he was comforting her. Poor Sonitchka. What kind of existence was this for a society girl from Petrograd?

The Gunzburgs no longer were in official mourning for Baron David by the end of 1918. A year had elapsed since his death, but Sonia had no wish to wear bright clothing or to dance. She was too busy to fuss over pleasure or appearance. She felt that she deserved her moments at the Zevin piano, for they relaxed her taut nerves and enabled her to face each day as it came. In December she had discovered a new outlet for her passionate idealism. A battered White force had reclaimed Simferopol from the Red troops, and a canteen had been set up for the officers in the kitchen and dining room of the Hôtel de l'Europe, the largest such establishment in the city. Nadezhda Igorovna and Olga, Mathilde, Sonia and Johanna all signed up to help serve the men. Every woman was asked to serve at least one luncheon and one supper per week, but still Sonia thought that, compared to the rigors she had endured packaging food for the prisoners of war, this was a small thing indeed.

In the meantime, the young men had formed a night watch, as in Feodosia, and Gino took an active part in it. The guard was divided into two watches, the first from eleven at night until two in the morning, the second from two until six. The weather had grown cold and this duty was most arduous, frequently taking place in the snow or in glacial windstorms. Gino spoke to the officers in the city, and learned that a General Kutepov was recruiting White soldiers in the Isthmus of Perekop, where the fighting was fiercest and the Whites were attempting to hold off a new onslaught from the Reds in the north of the peninsula. He considered this carefully, then when he picked Olga up at the officers' canteen at seven one evening, he took her for a long walk in the dusk.

At first they said nothing, merely synchronizing their footsteps. She was clad in a tawny woolen coat with a fur collar and fur trim at the sleeves and hem, and she wore a toque of similar fur on her golden curls. He thought, absurdly, that his sister might never again possess a fur, and for a moment he felt disheartened. But Olga placed her hand upon his arm, and once again he was secure in the knowledge of her love for him. Not looking at her bright hazel eyes he said, "I have reached a decision, Olga. I am going to have to fight for my fellow Russians. I hope that if there is a God, He will forgive me."

She nodded. "Remember that a God who forgives man for killing a member of his own kind is a forgiving God, a God of nuances. Sometimes, Gino, you fail to think of nuances, of shades of gray. You would not engage in civil war, yet if Hans Blumenfeld had faced you in combat, your own cousin by marriage, you would have felt justified in killing him. You would have felt ennobled by your patriotism. Of course, you would have been unhappy at having had to kill—is that not so?"

"Absolutely," he murmured. "You know that I have never enjoyed this so-called 'heroism.' I did not deserve the Cross of St. George."

"Yes, you did. Enjoying is one matter, and believing is quite another. You believed you had no choice. And that is what you have decided now."

He stopped, and ran a tired finger over the smooth grain of her skin. "And when I return?" he asked softly.

"You needn't ask," she told him quietly.

"You are not afraid that I want you because you are still wealthy, Olga?"

She saw the pain, the humiliation on his face, in his eyes. She turned aside. "Perhaps I merely wish to wear your title," she replied. Then she looked back at him, and her eyes were full of tears. "I wish you didn't have to go so soon," she said, and she placed her hand in the palm of his, trustfully.

The next morning, Madame Solovéichik came to Gino at breakfast and said, "My farm manager in Beshterek is ill, my dear. He was to bring me the account books and some fresh produce. I wonder if I might impose upon you, Gino, to make the trip there and back, in his stead?" The young man readily accepted. He would take a buggy in the afternoon and enjoy the eight-mile drive. He needed fresh air to clear his mind and to fully accept his decision. It would do him good to have time to think.

On the way to the farm, Gino recalled the speech he, Sonia, and Olga had gone to hear at the University only days before. The lecturer had been a Conservative who had served in the Duma, and who had taken part in the assassination of the lecherous and self-seeking Rasputin, adviser to the deluded Tzarina Alexandra. An able speaker, this statesman of much controversy, Purishkevitch, had made good points. He had discussed the political situation in the south of Russia, which comprised the Crimea, the Ukraine, and Bessarabia; the German colonists, the Siberians, the hopes of the people, plans for various governments, duties of the White Army. To think that this man now fought for the same goals as Ivan Berson, Anna's beau, who had been a Kerensky socialist! Gino thought: How strange, I have been meaning for months to tell Mama and Sonitchka about my encounter with Vanya at the front. Why haven't I remembered to do so?

Yes, he thought, Purishkevitch, whom I had always considered somewhat extreme, like Ossip's friend's father, Senator Count Tagantsev—Purishkevitch is helping me to justify my stand against my own countrymen. Shaking the thought from his mind, Gino looked up and noticed that he was arriving at the farm. He stepped down from the carriage, tied up the horse, and went into the main house, where the manager, Feodor Rubashov, resided. His wife brought Gino to the ailing man, and together they began a thorough examination of the books.

But before they had gotten far a commotion was heard, and the front door of the house was pushed open. Gino left the books with the manager and rushed into the dining room, where he was confronted with the sight of all of the farm workers and peasants, including children, being shoved into the room by nine men with rifles and bayonets. One of the assailants seized Gino and pushed him roughly against a wall. "Your property is surrounded," he announced. "We are Red anarchists, and have come for the money. Are you the manager?"

"I have been sent by the owner," Gino replied carefully, afraid for the sick Feodor Rubashov. "What can I do for you?"

By now the rest of the band had bound the peasants and the children, and gagged them as well. "Bring the books," the leader ordered Gino. The young man went into the bedroom and returned with the ledgers, which he laid upon the dining room table. But the anarchists' leader was dissatisfied. "You will bring us all the money, or tell us where you are printing the counterfeit," he ordered.

Gino was very frightened. At any moment they might begin to shoot. Besides, he knew of no money beyond what was owed to the salaried peasants, and he felt that it was not his business to give away their pay. And counterfeit? That was preposterous. He said nothing. Then the leader, with a furious shout, bound Gino's hands behind his back and pushed him into the room where Feodor Rubashov lay in bed. They began to ransack the house, and, with yelps of delight, came to their leader with seven hundred rubles. "We wanted twenty thousand," he declared, pointing a bayonet under Gino's chin and watching one of his men similarly threaten the manager. But Feodor, trembling all over, stammered, "That is all we have! Take it, and be gone."

One of the bandits aimed his rifle at the ill man, who shook his head again and again, becoming gray with fear. "We have no more," he kept repeating. The bandit called out, "One! Two! Three!" and the gun went off. To Gino's horror, the pleasant face of Feodor Rubashov was transformed into a gaping red wound. The manager was dead. "If he could have told you, he would have, to save his life," Gino said, surprised that he could even utter the words. But, strange as it was, he felt calm, as though ready for whatever was going to happen now. Not even the raised bayonets frazzled him. "And I know nothing, either," he added. "I have come from Simferopol for the first time today."

"You will name the richest of the peasants," the leader said. But Gino shook his head, as Feodor Rubashov had done, and told them that he was not even familiar with anyone but the poor manager. Angered beyond reason, they began to beat him about the head and arms, until he fell unconscious to the floor.

When he came to, they reiterated their barrage of questions, and when he failed to give them replies they beat him a second time. Then they awakened him by throwing cold water on him, and propped his weak body against the wall. The man who had shot the manager shouldered his rifle again, took aim at Gino's head, and started to count. Gino felt his legs give way, saw swaying figures, and collapsed, wondering why the fellow had not fired. He heard laughter above him, and fainted with this bizarre sound in his ears. When he came to, this time, his first thought was: Yes, God forgives. But why have I been spared, and not Feodor Rubashov?

The bandits had untied him, and told him that it was six thirty in the evening. Only two hours had passed since his arrival. They pushed him into his buggy, and climbed in beside him. "Drive," they said, pointing a rifle to his right temple. Several miles beyond, near Dubky, they passed a carriage, and one man remained in the buggy with Gino while the others looted the vehicle and its passengers. Gino was ill, seeing spots before his eyes, unaware of the passage of time except to note that he had miraculously stayed alive until this point. He had met the devil, and survived. Nothing would ever be worse for him. When they had gone another mile, the Red attackers jumped out of the buggy and climbed into a stolen landau which they had left there on the roadside before arriving at the farm in Beshterek.

When they drove away, Gino fell forward, and the old horse made its way back to Simferopol without guidance.

It was after supper when Gino, pale and shaken, appeared before his mother and Madame Solovéichik. His clothing was in tatters, his hair on end, his eyes vague and staring. He opened his mouth and fell to his knees before the terrified, stricken women. Sonia dropped beside him and took him in her arms, peering at his face with terrified concern. She held him tightly and cried, "Call a doctor, for heaven's sake!" Keeping her own warmth close, she soothed him with tender whispers, crooning his name over and over. When at last the doctor arrived, they carried Gino to the cot in the alcove where he customarily slept.

The physician administered sedatives to Gino, and announced to his family that the young man had suffered a slight concussion and many contusions, but that, after several days of total rest, they might be assured of his health. "He has an iron constitution," the doctor said to Mathilde. "Many men would have died of the shock."

But Sonia stated proudly, "Gino is a survivor, Doctor."

It was in Olga's arms that Gino relived, at length, the murder of Feodor Rubashov and his own threatened death and cruel beatings. It was she who soothed him when he became hysterical, refusing to take his sedative, afraid to sleep for fear of reawakening in the midst of the killers. Olga spent that night by Gino's bed, holding his hand, and not even Johanna dared to utter the slightest word of criticism. But when it was time for another dosage of the medicine, it was she who insisted upon administering it to her former charge, and Olga, deferentially, moved aside in silence. They did not speak, but clearly, by her manner, Olga was saying: This man is pledged to me, and I am not afraid of anyone. Do what you will, you shall not separate us.

Several days later, Gino said to Olga, "Are the peasants all right at the farm? Did someone go to help them?"

"Yes, sweetest, it's been taken care of. Sonia and I reported all you told us to the Committee for Counterespionage. Would you like some tea?"

"No," he asserted. "I only want to go out and crush those monsters! You were right, of course. The Germans were not 'bad,' only political foes. But the Reds will massacre our entire country. I must go to Perekop, Olga, to join up."

She did not find it possible to answer him. But in her heart there was a terrible sadness, a weight that would not leave her. When he was well, Gino donned his old uniform and mounted a horse that he had been given by one of the White officers stationed in Simferopol. He bent down from his saddle and looked at Olga, and saw his love reflected in her hazel eyes. He smiled, and twisted the ends of his glossy mustache. Then he touched his spurs to the flanks of his horse and rode off at a gallop.

Sonia placed her hand on Olga's shoulder, and together, mutely, they watched him recede into the distance. Next to them, Mathilde felt another part of herself splintering away. First David, then Ossip, now her youngest child. And for what, dear God? she reflected bitterly. But this time, she knew. Gino had seen death and had not succumbed to it, and now he was going to crush those who had threatened him—just as Ossip had seen death, and fled. But we are all individuals, she thought with a surge of unusual passion, and there are no absolutes, no guidelines in terror. My sons are neither heroes nor cowards. They are men.

On March 19, 1919, the French took over the city of Odessa and began to send their own battalions against the Red Army. With the signing of the Armistice in November of 1918, the British and French had rallied, though somewhat haphazardly, to the cause of the Whites against the communists who had betrayed them with the treaty at

Brest-Litovsk. But the Red Cheka was not about to relinquish this major southern stronghold, which had already seen foreign occupation under the Central Powers the previous year.

The Red Army had become more cohesive, as had the White forces under Generals Denikin and Kolchak. Although the peasants did not for the most part like the role assigned to them, they could not resist the general conscription which had gone into effect in June of 1918. The Crimean and Moldavian peasantry was less harassed than that of central Russia, a stronghold of Red power. But as more young men such as Gino joined the White Army, and rendered it powerful in the south, the Reds were forced to become better organized themselves, as a retaliatory measure.

When the Reds realized that the French were taking over Odessa, they experienced a moment of panic. The Cheka began to seize citizens haphazardly from various parts of the city, herding them as hostages into makeshift camps. At the time, Hillel Zlatopolsky, his wife Fanny, his daughter Shoshana and her husband, and his son Mossia and Mossia's spouse, Elena, had taken refuge in a small house away from the center of the city. Hillel had succeeded in booking passage for everyone on board a French ship. Meanwhile, he and his son kept a close watch on their "fortune": five bags of sugar beets previously garnered from their Kiev plantations. But one day as Mossia was stepping out of the house, he was roughly grabbed by two members of the Cheka, and dispatched to an enclosed area outside Odessa. His wife and mother watched from the window, helpless.

Mossia found himself among other civilians inside an area bordered by rough wooden fences. His companions wore expressions of complete hopelessness. "Wait for nightfall," one of them muttered. Mossia was bewildered, but he was not quick to take fright. Later, when a black mist had enveloped the camp, a group of guards with searchlights came among the prisoners. "Clean-up duty for Raffalovitch, Kubelsky, Timoshenko, Lesnick!" one of the Cheka commissars announced. Mossia saw three men and one woman troop out behind the Reds. They did not return.

When dawn broke, the guards came back and propelled the prisoners to a nearby clearing filled with rocks and sand. They were given gruel and water to eat. It was then that Mossia saw the spot of brown at his feet. He kicked at it, horrified: it was caked blood. Mesmerized, his senses in abeyance, he started to walk among the rocks until he spotted the bits of bone and gristle. Mass murder would be difficult to conceal, but systematic shootings of small groups? He clenched his fists against the sides of his thick, strong body: somehow, some way, he would emerge from this place alive. But how?

Less than a week later, when the guards entered the enclosure in the middle of the night, his name was called among those summoned for clean-up detail. Then and there he decided what he must do. Unobtrusively, he removed the identification tag from his chest and stood his ground. "Go find the scum!" the commissar told one of his men, and the soldier, a short, lithe man, darted inside the group of hostages and began shining his light upon breast after breast.

Mossia stood totally still. At last the soldier reached his row. A horrid taste filled Mossia's mouth, and he closed his eyes. The light shone on his face, over his tagless breast—and he heard the soldier's breath below him. Then, miraculously, the man moved on! He heard him call out to the commissar, "I don't know where he could have gone, Excellency. I beg pardon—'Comrade.' "

It was this strange exchange that caught Mossia's attention. He had heard that voice before, somewhere—but where? And then he remembered! Vassya, Gino de Gunzburg's companion, at the jail in Feodosia. Little Vassya, with whom he had shared his food. At last he understood. In these days of tumult and danger, it was difficult for young men to evade the communists when they entered a village in search of conscripts. Or perhaps the young cowherd had at last become imbued with anger at the classes that had oppressed his kind for so long. Whatever the reason, Vassya had saved Mossia's life.

Somehow, when the French burst through the camp only hours later and liberated all the hostages, it was an anticlimax for Mossia Zlatopolsky. He returned to the house, and there his mother fell upon him with sobs of relief. Elena—Lialia—kissed him on the lips. But he could not concentrate his thoughts upon her. He was thinking of Vassya, and the Gunzburgs.

In Simferopol, the news had suddenly grown alarming. The Red Army was threatening to invade the peninsula, and the scant White troops were not strong enough to hold them off. Convoys of Red Cross workers began to evacuate the city toward Dzhankoi, an important railway point near Perekop. It was there that the road from the north branched off, its main trunk continuing due south toward Simferopol and Sevastopol, while a fork led to Kerch and Feodosia in the southeast.

On the sixth of April, which dawned clear and sunny after a night of spring showers, total confusion erupted in Simferopol. Various news bulletins made contradictory statements that found their way to the ears of Sonia, Mathilde, and Johanna. First they heard that Perekop had not fallen to the Reds; then that both Perekop and Dzhankoi were in enemy hands. The White officer who lived in the Solovéichik house panicked, and bundled his family into a cart, for the White headquarters and its military press were being evacuated. Then Olga burst in, disheveled: she had just come from the Hôtel de l'Europe where chaos reigned in the officers' canteen. All the ladies were gone, and the men were cutting their own bread and washing the dishes themselves. Her mother was in Feodosia and Olga had come to the Gunzburgs for advice and comfort. What were they to do?

They put Olga to bed, for she had become hysterical, and during the night Sonia watched over her, thinking of her brother. Before going to sleep, Olga had wanted to flee from Simferopol as fast as it could be arranged, but Sonia wished first to consult Alexander Zevin. The next morning, when she learned that the banks had closed down at two o'clock and that their managers had left town with all the money and the account books, she sent a small boy to the Zevin house with a note. "Please help us to make arrangements," she wrote. "Once again we need your wisdom and guidance." But when Olga heard about the defection of the bankers, she began to laugh. "It is nothing," she said, shaking with spasms of hysteria. "Only a joke between me and Gino. He still has his title, but we are ruined, you see."

The citizens were afraid that the communists of the city would form an uprising: they armed three hundred men and posted them in front of the prison and at other strategic points throughout the town with orders to kill any Red sympathizers on the rampage.

The streets were filled with vehicles. The families of White officers as well as some civilians were leaving in droves, bound for Sevastopol or Kerch. Coachmen demanded exorbitant prices to take frightened people to the station. In the midst of this, Zevin arrived, his features drawn, and explained that the communists had prepared a blacklist of all the suspect citizens of Simferopol, to be shot as soon as the Red troops entered the city. At the head of the list stood the names of the ladies who had served at the White canteen. "It is best for you three to flee," he urged them, "and take Olga Arkadievna with you."

But the young blond woman shook her head, claiming

that she had to remain for her mother and for Gino to find her. Sonia attempted to reason with her, but Olga, who the night before had wanted to escape at all cost, was now set against the plan, and her eyes blazed with determination. Johanna de Mey shrugged. Placing a firm and gentle hand upon Mathilde's shoulder, she insisted that a baroness would never survive the blacklist, that Alexander Zevin was a friend to whom they could turn.

"If you do not come with us," Sonia said somewhat roughly to Olga, "my brother will never forgive us. You are my sister. We are not cowards, who take the first flight. But we are not idiots either."

There were no newspapers that day, but word came that electricity would be left running the entire night, so that the streets could be lit until dawn, in case of trouble. Zevin told the Gunzburgs about a little town, actually a large village, to the west, inland from Feodosia, called Stary Krym. It was known for its pure air and there were many rooming houses there to accommodate the people who visited the town for health reasons. "Go there, for you shall surely find a place to stay, and you will be far from Simferopol," the former manager advised.

Stary Krym lay roughly sixty miles from Simferopol. The Tartar bootmaker, Saïd-Bekir, would take them there the following morning at five o'clock. Zevin brought the Gunzburgs some money, and took them, with Johanna and Olga, to the bootmaker's house after supper. Their driver would be their host for the night. His house was meticulously clean, but, as all Tartar homes, nearly devoid of furniture. A thick carpet covered the ground, and large cushions of velvet and silk lined the walls. Saïd-Bekir's wife brought mats and covers which she placed upon the floor of the large room. The women shook Zevin's hand, and he left them to lie down, fully clothed.

It was a most uncomfortable night. Fearing robbery on the way to Stary Krym, the women had put on many layers of clothing. Sonia wore two sets of undergarments, topped by two dresses, an overblouse, and two tailored suits. She could hardly breathe, and did not sleep much before Saïd-Bekir's wife awakened them before sunrise, with thick Turkish coffee. Her husband had gone to feed and hitch up the horses.

At the last minute, when she saw the vehicle that would take them away, Olga shook her head vehemently and clung to the young Tartar woman. "No," she murmured, "I can't go. Gino and Mama will come here to find me."

"Zevin will tell them where we are, and we'll try to leave word along the way," Sonia remonstrated, losing patience. "If you love my brother, you will protect yourself for his sake." She examined the *lineika* to which the horses were attached. It consisted of a large cushioned plank of wood set upon springs over the four wheels. She climbed on, and her mother sat beside her. Johanna de Mey took the third seat, her back touching Mathilde's. There were two strips of wood for their feet, and at one end of the *lineika* a small seat had been made for the driver, followed by the horses' beam. Sonia stretched her hand to Olga, and the young girl climbed next to the Dutchwoman. Saïd-Bekir took his own seat, and the journey began.

It was six in the morning. The sky was gray and the air was cold. Huddled together, the four women spoke little on the way to Beshterek. They traveled the same stretch of road that Gino had covered, half-dead from his beatings at the farm of Madame Solovéichik, and it felt as though his specter hung over them as they traced his path. Suddenly Olga said to Johanna, in a trembling voice, "But Sonia is right, Johanna Ivanovna. Gino would want me with his own people."

A gust of wind came up, blowing a wisp of hair into Sonia's face, and she did not quite make out the governess's reply. But Olga stammered, "There is nothing indecent about it. Gino considers me his fiancée."

Suddenly the *lineika* came upon a column of the White Army. There were battalions on foot, squadrons on horseback, cannons and supply carts. Saïd-Bekir methodically attempted to reach ahead of the column, driving alongside it, while the passengers ate their apples and raisins in the *lineika*, not stopping to eat at Zuia as they had planned. Instead, they waited for the larger city of Karasúbazar, where Saïd-Bekir left the ladies at the Café du Commerce to have another bite to eat and to order tea. The wind had grown stronger and, in spite of the layers of clothing, the four women needed to be revived by a hot beverage.

The bootmaker told them that he would not pick them up until two in the afternoon, and so Sonia and Olga took the time to write a short note each for Gino, should he pass through this city, and the younger girl wrote a similar one to her mother. It was highly likely that if either Gino or Nadezhda Igorovna learned from the Zevins of the Gunzburgs' destination, they would make a stop at the Hôtel de l'Ancre d'Or, a common stopping place. Olga took the notes to bring to the front desk of the hotel and the others awaited her return, savoring their tea.

Olga Arkadievna walked out into the cold street, drawing her coat tightly around her. As she walked, she thought of Johanna de Mey's cruel insinuations, and she shuddered with annoyance. Of course Gino means to marry me, she intoned reassuringly. But Johanna had told her that Gino was planning to marry a girl from Petrograd. Surely she was lying, Olga thought, remembering Gino, his face, his promises. But a new, nagging doubt filled her. She would have to speak with Sonia.

It is this war, it is his absence, and my worry about his safety, she reasoned, that are making me insecure, that are shaking my serenity. Breathing deeply to calm herself, she stepped into the lobby of the Hôtel de l'Ancre d'Or, and crossed the lobby to the desk. She handed the two envelopes to a young clerk. "These are for a Baron Evgeni de

Gunzburg," Olga said, and her voice shook slightly. She passed him the third letter, for her mother. "And this one is for Madame Nadezhda Pomerantz. I do not know for certain whether these two people shall stop here, on their way to Stary Krym or Simferopol—"

She did not continue, for his face, across the desk, peered at her with a rude insistence. She blushed, looked down at her boots. Suddenly she felt something at her elbow. "Mademoiselle," the clerk declared, and he was right next to her, "I'm sure that I can help you, but you will have to step in here and describe these people to me. They may not know that letters await them." He placed his hand upon her arm, and closed his fingers about her skin and bones. She turned to look into his face, saw the lewd glint in his black eyes, and drew back. His complexion was pockmarked, his breath slightly rank. She tried to shake him off with dignity, and his hand dropped down like a dead fly. Reassured, she almost laughed at her own lack of poise, and went ahead of him into the antechamber off the main lobby. She opened her mouth to begin a description of Gino, when she felt a hand clamp over her lips, and realized with horror that he had locked the door behind him.

Olga began to struggle, but the clerk, although lanky, was a strong man, and she could not move. The room was small and close and dark, and she felt him stuff a cloth into her mouth so that she could not even utter a cry for help. He was tying her hands behind her back, and a terrible panic seized her, a claustrophobia so great that beads of thick sweat clung to her hair and dripped into her eyes. "*Burshui* whore," he hissed. "I've had your kind tramp over me my entire life!" She shook her head: No, not I, I have never hurt you—but he was pulling at her stockings, parting her legs, and then, to her horror, he was undressing, fumbling with his trousers. It was the first time she had ever seen a naked man, and so deep was her mortification and her shock that she did not flinch from the awful searing pain, nor from the sight of her own blood. She thought only: Gino, Gino! But she could not cry, could not move.

All at once it was over, and he had buttoned his trousers and straightened his attire. He unlocked the door and stepped out, and she heard him say, "I beg your pardon, Monsieur? No, Madame Rykova has not left her room today." Olga fainted, her head falling sideways.

"I shall go find her," Sonia said to her mother. "Stay here. She may have gotten lost."

"I told you that those Pomerantzes are nothing but trouble," Johanna declared shrilly. "Why did you have to burden us with her? Getting lost! She's been a sorry mess since yesterday, my dear. Probably decided to return to Simferopol. Sit down, Sonia. I need a brisk walk. I shall fetch her." Johanna stood up before Sonia could stop her, and walked rapidly in the direction of the well-known hotel.

Johanna de Mey came into the lobby of the Hôtel de l'Ancre d'Or, and did not see anyone at the front desk. She frowned, looked about, then saw a hallway with a small door in front of her. Without hesitation, she pushed open the door, expecting to find the clerk. But instead, to her shock, she found Olga, unconscious upon the floor, her body violated, a cloth stuffed inside her mouth. Stunned, Johanna closed the door and leaned against it. Then she bent toward the young girl and took the cloth from her lips, untying her hands. She slapped the pale face until the eyelids began to flicker. "A sorry mess, indeed," she said harshly.

Olga, revived, was starting to sob, wild, loud sobs that shook her poor ravaged body, and Johanna, placing her pointed face in front of the girl's, whispered fiercely, "Shut up, you little idiot! You're lucky that it was I who came, and not his mother or his sister. When he learns of this, he will revile you."

"But I—it wasn't I who did anything," the young girl cried, tears streaming from her eyes. She looked sick with shame and anguish and physical pain. "He—"

But Johanna de Mey stood shaking with passion in front of Olga. "To let a man—a *vile, filthy man!*—do such a thing to you! Any woman who respects herself—and respects her fiancé—would die before allowing herself to be violated. And this man? A pig, no doubt, from the lowest classes! Gino will never be able to share your bed, not even if he tries to forget. You have dishonored him, his family, his belief in your virtue. Don't you understand? He will never be able to look at you without wondering what you did to provoke this man. How can you bring such *shame* to him? You cannot even be sure that there will be no consequence—that there will be no child as a result of this disgusting deed! Have you not had the brains to consider this? Then Gino would prefer to think that you had died! A man—a man such as he, a fine young man—would find your death the only bearable outcome. Even your own mother would disown you otherwise! If only the Reds had shot you in Simferopol!"

As she spoke, Johanna did not look at the stricken girl. Moving stealthily like a cat, she opened all the cupboards and drawers in the small room until she found a hard black object, which she tossed upon the floor without a word. It was a gun. Olga eyed it, her head reeling, and her fingers closed over the pistol. Then she regarded Johanna. Never before had the woman witnessed such total anguish. She turned her back upon the girl, opened the door, and walked out. Once in the lobby, she sat down smoothly and examined her nails, her heart beating rapidly, her face flushed and twitching.

When the shot rang out, another guest darted past her into the chamber, and yelled for help. In the confusion and the noise, Johanna de Mey stood paralyzed as she gazed upon the face of pretty young Olga, who had loved Gino. She did not hear the footsteps behind her, hardly heard the gasp of horror from the slender young woman with all the layers of clothes who had rushed in from the street and was bending close to the figure on the floor. Olga was not dead, not yet, and Sonia, who held her friend's head upon her own lap, heard her whisper, "She was right . . . Johanna Ivanovna. I couldn't let him live with . . . this indignity . . ."

Olga Arkadievna Pomerantz died in Sonia's arms, with a dozen people looking on. Nobody, it seemed, knew who could have done this. An old man commented that in these days of internal strife, morality had been suspended, that people killed and raped every day, as if it were natural. But something knotted itself inside Sonia's stomach. Her slender face registered no emotion, nothing but hardness. She touched her friend's delicate cheek, thought of her brother, shuddered—and regarded the tall, thin, angular figure of her former governess. Johanna, her face distorted, wringing her hands, refused to return her gaze. Sonia gently slipped the blond head from her lap, and advanced toward Johanna with measured steps. She stopped directly in front of her, her gray eyes shining like slate. "You were involved in this," she stated simply. "You are a demented woman. But you will not tell Mama, or Gino. He would surely kill you with his bare hands—"

Sonia did not know what to do. Common decency demanded a funeral, a Kaddish; but there was no time for this, not if she and her mother were to survive. She began to tremble. There was no choice. She said to the manager of the Hôtel de l'Ancre d'Or, "You shall have to arrange for the burial. Can you do this?" And holding his shocked gaze with a look of pure defiance, she pressed some coins into his hand.

"I am going to write a letter now," she said, attempting to control her voice. But when she took the pen, her hand shook violently. She sat down near the front desk and cleared her mind for the impossible task of explaining Olga's death to Nadezhda Igorovna. She wrote: "If I could make you understand how sick the world has become, your loss, and ours, would not be lessened. But at least you would have an idea of how unforeseen this tragedy was. I shall blame myself forever for not being with Olga every minute. She was alive one minute, gone the next. Perhaps when you receive this we too shall be no more."

"What did you tell her?" Johanna demanded, her breath hot upon Sonia's neck.

The young woman turned to her, her gray eyes narrowed to slits. "I told her that her daughter had been killed in a senseless accident. Period." She moved away, toward the manager. "This letter is for her mother, Madame Pomerantz. She will probably drive through here in search of news. Try to make it a funeral with dignity. And summon a Rabbi, if you can find one. That would have been important to her—to Olga."

Tears flowed freely down her face now, but she spoke mechanically, as though the dead girl were merely another obstacle to cross. Her pain was intense and tearing, and she thought: I must not think, I must not think about who she was. We must leave, or we shall be killed by the invading Reds. Nothing matters but the reality of our survival. She thanked the hotel manager, and departed, taking Johanna's arm and leading her toward the café and her mother.

Saïd-Bekir had come to pick up his charges, and found Mathilde alone at the café. He was pressed for time, and was displeased that the other ladies were making him wait. But soon they saw Johanna and Sonia approaching, both obviously disturbed.

When Mathilde asked, in bewilderment, where Olga was and what had happened, her daughter shook her head and bit her lower lip to keep from crying. Mathilde turned to Johanna de Mey, who avoided her eyes. Fear flowed into her as through a funnel, and she gripped her daughter's arm, repeating, "What's wrong?"

Breathing in short, staccato gasps, Sonia said, staring

straight ahead of her, "An accident occurred, Mama. Olga is dead." Then, as Mathilde's face slackened, and her mouth fell open, Sonia nearly pushed her mother into the *lineika.* She said, quite loudly and brutally, "But we're alive, Mama. Let's go, Saïd-Bekir."

Another military convoy was leaving Karasúbazar, and to avoid it the Tartar bootmaker took the old road out of the city. It was unpaved, unkempt, scarcely used any more. As they rode, Mathilde wept, her beautiful face distorted with grief, her thoughts incoherent. She did not understand. *Gino and Olga*—she wept, thinking of how she had hoped, how she had dreamed of happiness for them. But she was afraid to speak, afraid of her own daughter, Sonia, whose white, grim face gleamed hard beside her.

Suddenly, after they had driven some fifteen miles, Saïd-Bekir announced that he had not noticed the proper turnoff that should have brought them back to the new road ahead of the convoy. They would not be able to reach Stary Krym by nightfall, as planned. But after several more miles they arrived at a large farmhouse in Yushun, and the manager opened his doors to them, fed the ladies an omelette, and gave them cots to sleep on in the large living room. Saïd-Bekir slept in the horses' stable.

Sonia ate the eggs, in spite of her nausea. A tremendous anger seethed within her, and she thought: We shall not be defeated, we shall survive. When sleep would not come, she willed her mind to draw a blank over the events of the day. Somehow, she and her mother had to endure this, as well as anything else that came their way.

The next morning, Saïd-Bekir told them that his horses were exhausted and he would not be able to take the Gunzburgs and Johanna any farther. The horses had to rest at the farm. Before the women could argue, the farm manager kindly offered to have one of his workers drive them the remaining distance, which was another fifteen miles. Sonia paid him one hundred rubles on top of the three hundred that she had already paid Saïd-Bekir. She did not wait to be helped, but moved all their belongings into the small buggy. In a potato sack were the hard-boiled eggs, boiled potatoes, and meat pâté; in another was clothing; in a small suitcase was the household linen with the dry goods; in a basket was the china; the toiletries were disposed in a hat carton, and the three umbrellas were bound together with twill. Sonia did not stop to sentimentalize over Olga's umbrella, over the hatbox that belonged to her. She quickly asked her mother to climb in, and thanked the farm manager and the Tartar bootmaker.

It was drizzling when the driver reached the outskirts of the village of Stary Krym, more than two hours later. "There are soldiers here, who may requisition my horse," he told them. "You'll have to get out here, so they don't see me." Sonia helped her mother onto the wet pavement, and left her and Johanna with the baggage while she went to inquire about rooms to let. When she returned, she declared, "There is a widow, Aspasia Vassilievna Something—we'll have to find her. But I've been told that she has a small house to let, for two people, and another room in a second house where she herself lives. Mama and I shall take the first house together, and you, Juanita, can board with the widow."

She saw, but chose to ignore, the look of unadulterated hatred that Johanna de Mey directed at her. Instead, Sonia put an arm about her mother's shoulders, and whispered, "We're alive! Keep remembering that, and don't think about the rest. Do you understand me, Mama?"

Mutely, like a trustful but frightened child, Mathilde nodded.

Twenty-Three

The soldiers of the White column which Saïd-Bekir had bypassed were now strolling about the main thoroughfare of Stary Krym. Sonia and Mathilde found their way to the small house on the side of the road which belonged to the widow of the veterinarian, Aspasia Vassilievna, and found her inside, with fifteen officers who were eating in cramped positions on the floor of her living room. "Go with Juanita, Mama," Sonia directed, and when her mother had returned outside to where Johanna was sullenly waiting, Sonia produced false papers which the Zevins had obtained for them in Simferopol. "We should like to rent your house," she announced to the widow. "As you can see, my mother and I are Feodosians, and my father, who is deceased, was a schoolteacher there. We have a friend, who would like to take the spare room in the other house, with you. Our funds are low, but we are neat and clean."

The widow nodded. "Whatever you can offer me will help, I assure you," she said. "I live in my brother's house; he was murdered by some Red bandits passing through, before the armies were organized. Now it seems that people are safer, that even the communists, when they take over, establish a militia to prevent hooliganism . . ." She spoke in

———————— • ————————

the dull voice of one who had endured, and who did not care whether the Whites in her house heard her comments or not. She added, "These men will leave at four this afternoon. They have been on their feet since Sunday and already it is Thursday. They are bound for Kerch, and then for the Caucasus. Tonight the bedroom will be free."

That afternoon Sonia and Mathilde moved their belongings into the inconspicuous little house, and Johanna went to the other end of the village, with Aspasia Vassilievna. Sonia said tersely to her mother, "We are to trust no one. Our names are Gunzburg, no 'de,' and we are bourgeois of a lower order, provincials. If you can, avoid speaking to anyone."

Stary Krym was not fortified, had neither station nor port, but lay on the main thoroughfare that stretched from the east of the Crimea to the west. Each retreating troop had to pass through it, and the villagers could only rely upon blind faith to keep themselves from fearing each new arrival. Sonia went to the mayor and obtained bread ration cards, displaying her false identity papers to him. Then she fetched petrol for their lamp, but purchased a candle in order to avoid having to use the lamp for anything but reading and sewing. There was neither electricity nor running water in Stary Krym. She found some firewood and coal for the indispensable samovar. Then, biting her lip, she spared a few precious rubles to bribe a thin Jewish butcher to deliver milk to them each day. Two days a week, she was informed, there was an open market. Life could be managed, she asserted.

She discovered that bread was the most difficult to obtain. The lines were interminable in front of the main bakery, and it would frequently close before everyone had received his supply. Then Sonia would be forced to go to a bakery across town, and wait in a second line. She would buy two days' worth at a time, in order to simplify matters. The markets offered some dairy goods and vegetables, as well as pottery and shoes and caps, through which she had to wind her tired way.

The village spread over a length of several miles on the lower part of a cliff. Above stood a thick forest going to the top of the embankment, traversed by five or six roads. Beautiful villas with magnificent gardens lined these hillside paths, and far below the village gushed a spring. Across from Stary Krym rose another hill, and toward the south one could see the steppe; on the horizon, the mountains of the Tchatyr-Dag which hid the view of the sea. It was by this Black Sea that the Crimean Riviera lay crowned by Yalta, once the site of aristocratic summers.

All the woods around Stary Krym grew carpets of violets during the springtime. When the Gunzburgs arrived, the air itself was impregnated with their scent, and all had come abloom, violets, narcissi, hyacinths, and fruit trees. It was a glorious melting pot, populated by Russians, Greeks, Jews, Karaites, Armenians, Tartars, Germans, Turks, and Bulgarians. Only the Bulgarians dwelled in self-imposed segregation, weaving the bright cloth which they displayed on their lovely women, spinning their own pots. Actually, Stary Krym should have been termed a town, for it possessed both a city hall and a cathedral; but its roads were badly paved, and reminded Sonia of stories she had heard of Orsha, where her great-grandfather, the patriarch Ossip, had been born to the village clothmaker.

Sonia spoke little to the local inhabitants, but listened well, and learned that during these days of troubles the people frequently took refuge in the hills at night. Keeping this in mind, every two days she boiled a quantity of eggs, wrapped some firm tomatoes, and put them aside so that she and her mother might leave on a moment's notice. In the meantime, officers succeeded one another as unexpected guests in the houses of the townspeople, while most of the soldiers were sent to sleep in the barns.

Simferopol had been seized on April 11, neatly and

quickly. The Red general made his entrance at the head of his regiment, and no looting occurred. But they were not pursuing the White soldiers retreating toward the Caucasus. It was thought that they knew they were being followed by Denikin's troops, and would want to prepare themselves for this essential battle. The White retreat took place quietly and in orderly fashion, but the officers appeared demoralized. Orders and counterorders, arriving at a dizzying speed, bewildered them and impeded their progress, and Sonia thought of Gino. She dared not think of Olga.

The telegraph had been closed to civilians for a long time, but now it was not working at all, except toward Feodosia and Kerch, in the east. The army had no news of the west or the north, and knew what was occurring only by hearsay, as did the civilian population. Much of this news was wrong, and would be contradicted as quickly as it arrived. There were no newspapers at all.

On Monday, April 14, Sonia and her mother celebrated the Seder, simply by thinking about it. They had neither matzo nor a Haggadah from which to read. Both women thought of David. If not for the sharp, keen memory of her husband, Mathilde would have forgotten Passover. The holiday itself held no meaning for her. But Sonia said, "The Jews experienced the same despair that pervades us here, did they not? We do not need a holy book to remember their exodus, their fear of the morrow." But she grieved for the Seders of her childhood.

There was no question now of attempting to lead an everyday existence, as they had in Simferopol. At first, when tragedy had struck around them, Sonia had tried to shield her mother from it. Mathilde had become like a child. During moments of crisis, someone—her husband, Johanna—had always taken care of her. But now Sonia found that too much fast thinking was demanded of her: her mother would simply have to cope for herself. She herself could see to the preservation of their lives, but that was her limit.

On the morning of April 16, the women were awakened early by shattered glass. Sonia darted to the windows, in time to see four men running out of the house next door, carrying linens and silverware. "Mama," she cried, "I cannot believe it! One of them stole some soap! Of all things—soap!" The four thieves mounted their horses and rode off into the hills. Sonia said, "Mama, please help me. We need to round up our supplies, in case we have to flee to save ourselves. There may not be time later."

The following day, a young neighbor ran in to announce that the Reds were entering the town. Sonia followed her outside, into the street. A crowd had gathered. Her mouth a taut, bloodless line, Sonia hung on the outskirts of the crowd, hearing the beat of her heart above the roar of the fifty Red soldiers who marched down the road. Men and women in peasant garb threw salt upon them in welcome, and handed them loaves of thick rye bread. Some women ran up with colored Easter eggs, and Sonia saw that a few youths had donned sympathetic Red armbands. She longed to cry out against this insanity, but no words came to her lips.

How would her father have reacted? Sonia thought. Lately, her mind had frequently gone to him. His ideals had always loomed so high above the pettiness of life, and for him honor had reigned supreme among virtues. What would he have done in Sonia's place? Would he have left Olga's body with the hotel manager? Probably not; but then, he was dead and she was alive. This was no time for philosophy, nor even for goodness.

Several days later, waiting in line for bread, Sonia heard excited cries from the inn down the road. She debated whether to remain in her place, or to check on the disturbance. But if there was danger, she should learn about it, to protect her mother and herself. She did not even think about Johanna. Since Olga's death, Sonia had actually hoped that her mother's friend would die. Johanna had killed Gino's fiancée: somehow, Sonia was sure of it. There was no mercy for her now in Sonia's heart.

Lifting her thick skirt, Sonia ran in the direction of the commotion. Men and women blocked the doorway of the Omansky Inn but she slid between them, pushing her way through to the courtyard. Once there, her breathing stopped in a horrified gasp. The bodies of a man and a woman stretched down from the limbs of a tree, their limp necks tied to the branches by a heavy cord. Their faces were blue and very puffy. Sonia clenched her hands into fists, and swallowed back a spurt of bile. She had seen worse: she had seen Olga die.

That night she said to her mother, "Give me the diamond crab, Mama. It is no longer safe under the mattress. It is our last bargaining piece, should our lives hang in the balance." When Mathilde gave it to her, she pinned it unceremoniously to her bodice. Then she fetched a rusty axe: she had an idea.

On Easter morning, April 20, Stary Krym wore its holiday attire. The pear and plum trees exhaled a marvelous perfume, and the fields stretched in multicolored expanses of flowers. The forest was filled with violets, and in the villagers' gardens lilacs bloomed. The migratory birds had returned, and now cuckoos, hoopoes, bullfinches, skylarks, and nightingales added their hymns to the celebration of spring. Feodosia fell to the Reds the following day; and Mayor Slobodkin went there to fetch a commissar to prevent further outbreaks of murder in his little town. From a hillside promontory Sonia watched the billows of gray smoke in the harbor below: the long-awaited Allied ships were firing at last upon the Reds in Feodosia.

News of the fighting filtered in as various contingents of soldiers passed through Stary Krym. General Kolchak of the White Army had arrived at the Volga, his cohort Denikin now advanced on the Crimean peninsula, and the friendly Poles had taken Kiev. When the Reds learned that they were being crushed, Sonia thought, they would die like a struggling, wounded beast, wreaking bloody havoc. Communism would die like a bull in the ring. Life would resume, she and her mother would return to claim what was theirs in Petrograd . . . if they survived.

Troops passed through the village and men stopped to drink tea at the small house off the road, telling Sonia that Sevastopol had been taken by the Whites after a tremendous battle, during which the Reds had lost fifteen hundred men. There had been no fighting in Simferopol. In Karagoz the most savage band of Reds from the Caucasus, the Tchechians, had committed dreadful atrocities; they were feared everywhere, and were surnamed "the terrible infantry." Young women and wine, in particular, fed their inner fires. Sonia listened to the words, mulling them over as she went with her two buckets to the public fountain, to obtain water for brewing tea.

That evening, she told her mother of her decision. To the best of her ability, she had examined the foundations of the house and thought that a small cavity existed beneath the floor where she and Mathilde might take refuge in case of extreme danger. When darkness fell, she pried loose the boards of the bedroom floor, preparing for an emergency. She said to her mother, "On no account must Juanita learn of this hideaway. Our safety may depend upon your silence." But she did not elaborate and Mathilde had stared at her uncomprehendingly, with terror glazed upon her features.

Mathilde knew only that something had gone awry with Johanna, whom she had loved with total commitment. She had sacrificed Anna to her, and certainly David. She did not regret her betrayal of her husband, because she had not chosen to be his wife. He had known her well when he married her, the daughter of his dissipated gambling uncle, a girl reared in agnosticism, reared as a Frenchwoman. And he had wanted her nevertheless. But Anna had not chosen to be born, had only wanted freedom. Riri stung Mathilde's conscience as nothing else could. She had always felt most guilty about her lack of motherly love for her older daughter, whose appearance had displeased her maternal vanity. There had even been moments when she had blotted out Sonia's distinct features with Johanna's soothing comfort, willing herself to ignore the hurts piled upon her second daughter. Had there been other betrayals? Mathilde did not know. She knew only that Johanna had kindled her soft round body as no one ever had, that she had belonged to her body and soul, mind and will, from the start. Johanna had been salvation, a world beyond the world. But there had come a time for growing older and more thoughtful, perhaps less selfish. Mathilde had felt fewer moments of need for Johanna, and the result had been the destruction of their unity. An aging couple must grow old together, at the same pace, but she and Johanna had missed a step. They had met Nadia Pomerantz, and Johanna had treated her disgracefully and had never been the same since then. Mathilde lay down and wept, remembering the nights of soft kisses, the sweet-smelling golden hair. There were names for such as she and Johanna, and they were shameful names, but, Mathilde thought, those who name do not understand . . .

On April 24, a Red detachment of one hundred fifty carts and wagons appeared in Stary Krym, disgorging soldiers who proceeded to commandeer rooms for a week in the houses of the large village. It was this convoy which contained the two men who threw terror into Mathilde's life, and who made Sonia realize that she had planned wisely when she had pried loose the floorboards in their bedroom. The small, soft-spoken boy, Igor Plotkin, had been an actor before being drafted into the Red Army. No

————— • —————

one could guess what occupation might have been held by his companion, Pavel Antonov. Thickset and red-faced, with a wide, flattened nose, Antonov reminded Sonia of a large, uncouth ape. His bouts of drunkenness made her aware that his blood lust was demented, uncontrollable. She could not sleep while he was in the house. Hollows formed beneath her eyes, and her body twitched with nervousness.

Sonia had been so alert to the goings-on in town that Johanna de Mey's final plunge into madness was not noticed. She knew that her former governess had grown increasingly frenzied since Olga's death. But Sonia did not know that for Johanna the girl's suicide had brought about a swift justification against the seeping effects of guilt. Olga was a bad seed, Johanna insisted, and then, wringing her hands, she shrilly wept, overwhelmed by anger and pain at the idea of what Mathilde had seen in Olga's mother. No, Johanna thought, shaking her head back and forth rapidly: I merely evened the score. If I could not keep the mother, certainly the intruder's child should not have the son. It was justice.

But Mathilde had not made do with justice. She had not allowed herself to be cleansed by Olga's death and Nadia's absence. She stayed in her house, obeying Sonia, that most hateful of the Gunzburg children, David's true daughter. More than before, Johanna's loneliness ate away at her, ulcerlike. She had to effect the final purge. Mathilde could not be permitted to proceed with her life as though she, Johanna, had not spent her own lifetime pushing away the obstacles that had separated them. In anguish and despair, Johanna sought her revenge. She would expose the proud aristocrats from Petrograd.

Sonia stood in the market place by the dairy cart, watching absently. To her left was the fruit stand, and beyond, the vegetables. Mathilde was examining the tomatoes, her finely tapered fingers rough on the edges. The girl could see her from where she stood, but she could also see the soldiers straggling to their post, and the villagers bargaining for produce. Her black hair was tightly braided around her head, and her gray eyes picked over the crowd. Suddenly she froze. Her lips parted, her eyes widened. She had seen the soldier Antonov conversing with Johanna. Sonia watched as the woman turned and looked at Mathilde, then saw her furtive gaze travel until it met her own troubled stare. In an instant, Sonia turned and fled, leaving her eggs in the vendor's hand, and lifting her skirt so that she could run. She darted between the villagers, to the vegetable stand, and grabbed her mother's arm, startling her. "Come at once," she whispered under her breath.

"But—?"

"Never mind. Hurry!" She pushed the older woman ahead of her, out of the crowd and onto the street. When they had run a distance from the market, she said in low, tense tones, "We have been betrayed. Antonov knows about us."

Mathilde's sapphire eyes were enormous. "But—who?" she stammered.

The girl's face set itself into grim lines. When she spoke, bitterness seemed to slap the other woman across the cheek. "Who do you think?"

Sonia knew it would happen that night. When Johanna entered their house, hoping to cauterize her own wounds by watching the final vengeance as it took place, Sonia maneuvered her into the armoire so that she would not know about the hideaway that would protect Sonia and her mother. Then they waited, as if in a dream, for the inevitable sound of footsteps, for the awful, drunken sounds of the soldiers as they returned. It was after midnight when they heard Antonov's crude singing and felt the firm vibrations of his boots upon the floor above their heads. Sonia imagined the two men searching the small house . . . opening drawers . . . discovering Johanna's hiding place. And when she heard the shot, in her mind's eye she saw Olga, and a scarlet pain swallowed her consciousness, so that she did not realize for a moment that the drop that had fallen upon her was Johanna's blood. It was only then that her brain reeled, that she lost her hold on reality.

Sonia's mind flew like a frightened dove above herself, above the tiny space where she crouched with her unconscious mother. It flew up, up, into blue skies that offered hope and balm, the skies of her childhood. How could she die now, if she had become herself as a child of five, before Juanita had even entered their lives? She was at Mohilna, anticipating the birth of Gino, who would complete their family circle. She was Before. And then, as though a book were quickly flipping its own pages, her dove's mind flew over all the twenty-eight years of her existence, so rapidly that she glimpsed it all, all the joys and pain, beneath her like a plain crested with valleys and hillocks. All of her past, even the bad times, possessed the grace of life, and she clung to that grace, afraid of Now, when Antonov might kill her and push her headlong into oblivion. The Jews, her father had taught her, had no heaven for which to yearn. That was why survival meant everything to this race that had been threatened countless times, as she was threatened now, with extinction.

It was the acrid stench of the blood that brought her back to the urgent need for action in the present. The odor acted upon her like smelling salts, restoring her thoughts. She shuddered, wondering where she had been and if time had raced on or stopped altogether. Mathilde still leaned against her, heavily unconscious. Mama, the escapist, Sonia thought wryly. She looked around them. The tiny, cramped area seemed their last refuge, but Sonia felt a slight chill, as if there were a draft. She groped behind her: there was nothing but stone. Gently she pushed her hands behind her mother; and there, she had it!—an aperture.

She crawled to it and saw that there was an opening between the stone foundations, just large enough for a very small person to crawl through. Sonia's consciousness was all at once flooded with elation: here, then, was the way to safety, to fetch help for her mother.

Sonia allowed her mother to slump to the damp ground. Then she pushed herself between the stone pillars, on her knees. She edged her thin torso between them, panting, beads of perspiration streaming down her face. Dropping to her stomach, she propelled herself by the sheer force of her hands and elbows, slithering out of the hideaway into the blackness of the night. She could hear the two men, little Plotkin and Antonov, but they were probably on the road ahead. Sonia hesitated; she could go to the militia, but that would take time. Or they might not believe her, and accuse her of the murder. There were the hills. Without further consideration, Sonia ran, on the balls of her feet, in back of the rows of houses, behind the entire village until at last she reached the small house occupied by Aspasia Vassilievna, the veterinarian's widow. She did not know her well, but she recalled that she had said that her brother had been murdered by Red anarchists. Sonia reached her kitchen door and knocked on it, urgently, yet softly, so as not to alert neighbors.

When the woman came to the door, she stood back, agape at Sonia's appearance. "I don't have time to explain," the young woman said, panting. "But I need help. You are not young, it is not fair to ask you to exert yourself—but I cannot do this alone. Mama lies between the stone foundations of your other house—our house—and she is unconscious. I cannot tell you everything, only that the men who commandeered the house have killed your boarder, our friend. I must get Mama out! If you could go inside the house and find the ¬otato sack where I have stuffed eggs and tomatoes and a blanket, I can take Mama to the hills to hide for several days . . ."

Aspasia Vassilievna nodded. She was a silent, Greek woman with thick dark hair, and as she wrapped a black shawl about her shoulders, she reminded Sonia of a shrouded raven. But, for a woman well into middle age, she walked briskly, keeping up with Sonia as the young woman brought her along the backs of the houses, to escape detection. When they reached the Gunzburg house, Aspasia Vassilievna said, "There is no one here. They have probably gone to celebrate, God knows where."

"Then I shall go inside the house, and you can keep watch," Sonia stated. She had already decided that it would be easier to drag Mathilde up through the bedroom floor than between the foundation stones. She entered silently, and when she came to the bedroom she closed her eyes to prepare herself for the sight of Johanna, but it was even worse than she had imagined. Her mind reeling, she clung to the wall for support.

Mechanically, to keep from allowing the horror to overwhelm her, Sonia began to recite Hebrew psalms that David had taught her as a child. She muttered them, uncomprehending, in order not to see the dead body, the torn clothing, the face. She had to move all this in order to pry up the boards. Sickened, bile rising in her throat, Sonia repeated psalm after psalm, as Igor Plotkin had reiterated the Lord's Prayer to cushion his own shock at Antonov's deed. Sonia threw an old coat over the body, and mouthed the words that had once possessed deep significance for her, words about valleys and shepherds and green and God, but which now meant nothing at all. Then she rolled the body to the side, wondering with piercing clarity how such a thin, angular woman could have become so heavy to displace.

Then Sonia pulled up the boards, and bent down into the cavity where her mother was slumped. She took her mother's arms and began to pull. Mathilde's eyelids flickered, and she murmured something as she came to. "No," Sonia said. "You must not say a word." She brushed the dark strands of hair from her mother's face and once more tried to pull her up out of the hole. But Mathilde was too weak to help, and finally Sonia had to lower herself into the hiding place beside her mother, propping up the heavy wooden planks with her back. At last Mathilde managed to climb out. "Don't look," Sonia warned her. "Just run out the back door." Then she herself climbed up and let the boards fall askew. She could not straighten her back, but had to walk bent in two into the kitchen, where she gathered the potato sack from the pantry in preparation for flight into the hills.

She found her mother and Aspasia Vassilievna behind the house, and the widow came to her, agilely belying her years. "I could have helped," she remonstrated. Her face displayed concern as she saw Sonia, bent over from the strain of the plywood planks on her back. Sonia knew only that her legs possessed no further strength. But she willed them to move, taking her mother's arm and allowing Aspasia Vassilievna to take Mathilde's other arm. They walked, silently, three abreast, toward the hillside woods. Once there, Sonia collapsed, and the widow covered her with the blanket and helped Mathilde to lie down in the dirt, beneath a pine tree. Mathilde had not uttered a syllable since leaving the hiding place.

"I am going to tell the militia," Aspasia Vassilievna declared when she had settled them as best she could. "The Red Army is disciplined now, and punishes its men for looting and killing. They will hang Antonov for this." She turned resolutely to leave.

The pine tree exuded a fresh scent of strong resin, and the earth was moist. Sonia's body felt numb with agony, so numb that her brain could no longer function. But Mathilde's eyes, round and staring, kept filling with salt tears that spilled over and over from her thick black lashes. It was not until the next morning that she spoke. "Thank you," she said to Sonia, "for the coat."

"You shouldn't have looked," Sonia replied. She gazed

at the sun that was coming up between folds of hazy dawn, and added, "But we're alive." Her back still hurt, and she could barely turn, but her fingers clutched at a blade of grass and plucked it. It was green, and earth clung to its root. "We're alive," she repeated. Now the psalms returned to her, with meaning, and her father's voice, vibrating with his own love of God, echoed in her mind.

The Red militia, on the information given by Aspasia Vassilievna, arrested Antonov, and he and Igor Plotkin were immediately sent to the front. Mathilde felt somewhat sorry for Plotkin, but not Sonia. Her love of the noble, and her outright condemnation of baser human faculties, had returned to her in full force. She knew that the younger soldier had stood by and allowed atrocities to be perpetrated. Mathilde, on the other hand, was able to step outside herself and examine the breadth of a situation. She felt that Plotkin, young, weak, and small of stature, had done what he could to ensure his own survival. She comprehended his position and felt compassion.

"The Reds cannot afford to permit even the slightest plunder," Aspasia Vassiliena reiterated afterward. "Their army is strong now, and well organized, because the men are penalized for such actions. You can rest assured that after this other Red soldiers will be more careful, and the militia will be more watchful."

But still Sonia and Mathilde could not return to the little house where Johanna had betrayed them and had, in turn, been betrayed herself. The fact that she had expected it did not make Sonia accept her governess's actions, and for Mathilde the defection of her most beloved soulmate was a frightening shadow that threatened to engulf her forever. She wanted, above all, to forget, to obliterate. Sonia could not and would not: she carried Johanna's memory foremost in her mind, an open sore that she would not allow to heal. They moved into the house where Aspasia Vassilievna lived, and, after Sonia had vigorously cleaned and scoured the room that Johanna had occupied, took up residence there.

Their memories would not die, however, for the two women had to deal with Olga's survivors. Nadezhda Igorovna came at last to Stary Krym, driving her own buggy from Feodosia, during the dry hot summer. Her black hair was heavily streaked with white. Her lean face was more leathery, and her clothes hung limply over her big bones and sinews. She wanted to know the truth, which Mathilde herself did not know, and so she cornered Sonia, who told her, quickly and tersely, not allowing herself to relive the horror of Olga's death. Nadezhda Igorovna lowered her face into her large hands and sobbed dry, heaving sobs, until Sonia thought that she would tear herself apart with grief. But she was strong, and could look anew at Sonia after her cry. With a face bathed in tears, she said quietly, "You are good people. Olga would have liked to be part of this family."

"But she already was," Sonia replied gently.

Nadezhda Igorovna was silent, but nodded, expressionless. Then she went to find Mathilde, and the two women faced each other, their eyes speaking to each other. Neither was a passionate, overt individual, and so the words that were left unsaid meant the most. Mathilde took her friend by the shoulders and gave her a brief hug. "If Gino comes to you—" she said hesitantly. "He does not know that she is dead. Will you tell him?"

Nadezhda Pomerantz sighed. "He is stronger than you think. He can accept the truth."

But Sonia disagreed, though her brother Gino was not like Ossip, whom she had spared so carefully from learning of Volodia's death and Natasha's wedding, eons ago: a generation ago, she decided, touching the coils of her hair and wondering if any strands of gray had mingled yet with the soft black. Gino was able to deal with his own imminent death, even with their father's. He was earthy and almost peasantlike in his acceptance of what had to be. But he was also too much like herself, a man of principle and ideals. He had never accepted the treaty of Brest-Litovsk, for he had felt outraged by the indignity committed in the name of his beloved country. And he had loved Olga, somehow seeing her entwined with Russia in his ardent adoration. To know that she had killed herself because a man had defiled her would not be acceptable. He would turn his anger against himself, and what would happen then? Sonia realized that, for Gino's sake, Mathilde could no longer be shielded from the facts of Olga's death. She, as his mother, needed to know why it would be better just to tell him that she had died, and that was all. He would rebel, but he would finally accept the undeniable aspect of this simple truth, despite his grief. Sonia knew this because she knew that if Kolya Saxe had died in 1913, she would have recovered more quickly than she had from his cowardly abandonment. Volodia's memory stood out, in its purity, glowing in her heart, whereas now Kolya lurked there in shadows of disgrace and anger and lost hope. Gino would feel the guilt of Olga's unavenged death, her desperate action pointing to a lack of trust in him, in his ability to realize that there should be no question of forgiveness, for in her rape there was no shame to be forgiven. Olga had, by her suicide, doubted him.

Sonia and Mathilde had not received news of Gino for so long that when they saw him on their doorstep one morning, their first emotion was one of wild relief that he was alive and well. They had trained their minds not to think about unpleasant matters: too much had to be handled as it was, day by day. But every news bulletin that came created a bubble of questions in their minds: had he fought there? Had he survived? And then, by the sheer force of their will, they would make the bubble burst. An unspoken silence existed on this subject between mother and daughter; neither would have broken it for any reason.

But the young man appeared well, his cheeks ruddy and his eyes glowing. The front, apparently, agreed with him. He hugged his mother with vehemence and burst into the house as a fresh wind. "You've no idea how difficult it was to find you!" he exclaimed, his arm wound tightly around Sonia's thin shoulders. "They still had your letter in Karasúbazar. But that must have been written a century ago! We've been all over. When they finally gave us leave, I went to Simferopol. It was Zevin who sent me toward Karasúbazar. Something about a blacklist . . . Oh yes, you did mention it in the letter. I didn't read it properly. I just wanted to find you, to know you were all right! Is Olga with you?"

The innocence of that question hit Sonia in the stomach. She reeled from it. The idea of having to face Gino with this had always hovered in the back of her mind: how could it not have haunted her? But the relief at seeing him had momentarily pushed this preoccupation from its normal place. But no sooner had he uttered this than he came back with yet another question: "Where's Juanita?" he asked.

Mathilde's face contracted in a spasm of pain, and her lips parted. But her daughter said, "It's all right, Mama. I can tell Gino." She took her brother by the arm to the small sofa. He looked in shock from mother to sister— what was going on? "Juanita is dead," Sonia said softly. "She lost her mind, and did . . . something dreadful. She betrayed us to a Red soldier, who wanted to kill us, to rob us—and in the end it was she who was murdered. I'm sorry, Gino."

"Juanita? But Juanita loved Mama. It makes no sense!"

"Nothing makes any sense now," Sonia stated with cold bitterness.

"You still haven't told me where I can find Olga," Gino

said. "I bought her a small trinket, and I thought . . ." He blushed, and stopped. His sister's eyes had filled with tears, and her small face was crumpled in such total misery that he became speechless. An awful realization entered his brain. "Olga?"

"My darling, Olga caught a chill, shortly after we arrived here. She—"

"A chill? My God, it can't be!"

Seeing the expression of abject despair upon her brother's face, Sonia shook her head and took his hand. She began to speak in a low, trembling voice. The voyage from Simferopol had been fraught with dangers, she explained. Olga's chill had turned into pneumonia. There had been no adequate medical supplies . . . No, there was no tombstone. So many murders had taken place that the cemetery had fallen into disarray. But yes, the funeral had been properly performed. Nadezhda Igorovna knew. The need to keep speaking, to prevent Gino from losing touch with the present was so strong that she could not stop to feel her own pain, unexpressed for such a long time.

He sat, dumbfounded, unable to react. Then, slowly, tears rolled down his ruddy cheeks, and continued to fall. He said nothing: he had never been a speaker, unlike Sonia and Ossip. In this, he resembled most his sister Anna. He wept, and Sonia did not know what to do, so she took his hand and wept with him. Mathilde, framed silently in the doorway, watched them, and thought bitterly: All my children are cursed, because they have come through me, and my corruption, and from my father, who was the bad seed of this family. She surprised herself in her judgment, she who would not judge. But her children, in their pain, had been more than she could bear to regard with open, clear eyes.

When Gino returned to the front, Sonia felt as if a tremendous burden had been lifted from her shoulders. Her brother had seemed to accept Olga's death and appeared to be learning to cope with his grief. Yet he was not. She did not know, nor did anyone, that the young man's spirit was breaking. All the goodness of the world, all his simple faith, had been concentrated upon Olga. He felt disoriented, at odds. He wavered, and felt his own weakness and futility. *Why?* he asked himself, in bewilderment. Why am I being left behind in the tumult of the times? He returned to his unit, but in his deep brown eyes were questions that no one could answer. In losing Olga, Gino had lost his God, his true guiding spirit.

During the winter, Sonia decided that it was time to return to Simferopol. In October, the Reds had stopped Denikin's army at Orel, and what was left of his troops withdrew to Novorossiik, on the northeast shore of the Black Sea. Gino would be among them, might even be evacuated by the British. Sonia clung to the hope that the Allies of White Russia, who had taken such interest in overthrowing the communist government, would not abandon her country now that the White Army was performing so badly. But in January 1920, prompted by the British, the Allies yielded, ceasing their economic blockade of communist Russia. Sonia's soul let go like exhausted fingernails finally releasing their grip on a steep cliff: she sighed away the fierce hope that the Whites would triumph and restore the life that had been hers in Russia.

Forgive me, Papa, Sonia then thought, acquiescing to the inevitable. There is no other choice for us. It is one thing to be patriotic, but quite another to commit suicide. The Reds will never leave our beloved country, not now. And Mama has grown old. She needs peace. We are going to have to leave you, Papa, and leave you, my Russia. Surely Ossip, the realist, the cynic, has already departed. And Gino is a soldier: he will survive. What good can Mama and I possibly do him by remaining here?

Gino would want us to leave, to think of Mama's safety, she decided. He would not think that we were abandoning him. She wrote him a letter, explaining that she was going to try to put her own and their mother's papers in order from Simferopol, so that the two of them might sail to Constantinople from Sevastopol, the most important city in the south of Russia. Sevastopol was a mere three hours' drive from Simferopol, and it therefore made sense for the Gunzburgs to move there first. Alexander Zevin would be able to help them to prepare for their journey.

One of the peasants of Stary Krym offered to drive Mathilde and Sonia, with their potato sacks filled with dry goods, to the Crimean capital. So, in the cold, the two women made the journey, dragged in a wagon by two tired farm horses. They had to sleep in Karasúbazar, midway between the village and the city, to rest the horses. Mathilde fell asleep, exhaustion marking her face, but Sonia was kept awake by the ghosts of her past. She could not obliterate the memory of Olga's face as she had died in her arms. Close your eyes, Olga, Sonia said to the ghost. Juanita has paid for her share in your death. But the hazel eyes pursued her when she fell into fitful sleep. They were Olga's eyes, then browner ones, Gino's own. Was her brother reproaching her for leaving Russia, as he might have reproached her for not having guarded his beloved more carefully?

When they reached Madame Solovéichik's vast house, it was filled with boarders, but the woman did not have the heart to turn the Gunzburgs away. She arranged for a cot to be placed in the alcove where Gino had slept before, and now Mathilde slept there while Sonia made do with the sofa in the dining room.

That spring, the young woman began to make arrangements for their departure. Simferopol had changed, and the absence of Gino and the Pomerantz ladies made her heart ache dully. She was growing more discouraged than ever in her life of twenty-nine years. Always she had thought: Wait until tomorrow. But now she thought only to live through today. She wondered what would be best for her, and decided that when they reached Constantinople, she would wire her Uncle Misha for a visa to Switzerland for Mathilde, and one to France for herself. He had connections, and would be able to help her to find a position of some sort. She would work in Paris: there were bound to be more opportunities there than in Lausanne, and she desperately needed to earn her living. But at what? Stenography? The tutoring of languages? Misha would have to counsel her.

Mathilde did not suffer from Sonia's scruples. She thought of her elderly mother, of the hills of Switzerland, of her beloved Paris, and once again her face became the unlined face of a trustful child. Her home had never been in Russia. When Denikin resigned in March and General Wrangel was made Commander in Chief of the volunteer White Army, which now consisted of only seventy thousand men, she did not think of a dying Russia, nor of Gino's probable anguish over his country. She thought instead, as troops were sent to the Crimea from Novorossiik: I shall see my boy again, if not here, then in Constantinople. And we shall all escape together.

But one evening, after supper, Mathilde's face swelled into strange blotches. Sonia had never seen her mother like this, and when she touched her forehead it was burning. Quickly Madame Solovéichik helped Sonia to settle Mathilde in her bed and they sent for a doctor. Madame Solovéichik said, shaking her head, "I hear there's been an outbreak of cholera . . ."

Sonia would not listen. She sat by her mother, feeling the racing pulse. She could not die!

"You will be the first one to catch it," the concerned old woman said.

But Sonia glared at her with outraged eyes. "Leave if you will," she whispered. "If Mama is ill then I must help her to live through this. Mama cannot survive alone."

When at last the doctor arrived, he bent over Mathilde

and said, "Cholera isn't all that we've got here in Simferopol. I'm afraid there's also an epidemic of typhus.
Your mother has the typhus. She will need medication
three times a day"—he wrote down the name of the drug
for Sonia—"as well as fresh milk with every meal. The
problem is that we have no milk here in Simferopol. And
there is not sufficient medication for everyone; our patients
can only be given two doses a day."

Sonia did not know what to do. Mathilde's fever was so
high that she was sometimes delirious in the days that
followed the doctor's visit. The young woman would hear
her mumbling names: David, Anna, and then piteously,
"Johanna, Johanna . . ." It was unbearable.

Twice every day Sonia rushed to the pharmacy which
sold the drug. One morning she nearly collided with an
earnest young man who said, "My father has cholera."
That afternoon the pharmacist told her that the father had
died. One after another, victims of the diseases succumbed.
Meanwhile, there was Mathilde, writhing in her small cot
in full view of all the boarders at the house of Madame
Solovéichik.

When Sonia's hope was about to give out, Ekaterina
Zevina came to the rescue. It seemed that a farm delivered
a quart of milk a day to her family, because she did not
reside in the city proper. "I can give you one cup for
Mathilde Yureyevna," she offered kindly, and Sonia
thought: Now the worst is past. My mother will live.

But then the problems became worse. Sonia could not
come to fetch the milk until after she had stood in line for
fresh food, or there would be none left. By then it was nine
o'clock, and the hot Crimean sun beat ruthlessly upon the
young woman's head as she walked the twenty minutes to
the Zevins' house. She had to walk the same distance back,
and discovered that during the return trip the sun had
soured her milk. One tiny cup, so difficult to obtain, so
essential—wasted! Sonia sat down in the Solovéichik

kitchen and wept helplessly, too tired to feel angry. The next morning she wrapped the bottle in an old shawl, and it did not sour. But the fourth time the shawl was no help against the scorching sun. Mathilde could not drink the milk, and Sonia sank into despair.

On the tenth day, a crisis was to occur for which the doctor had prepared her. Mathilde's temperature would drop radically to far below normal, putting a strain on her heart. It was during this period that many people died: their hearts simply could not withstand the shock. That night, Sonia remained awake by her mother's side, watching her face. Oh, God, do not take her yet, not yet, she thought. She has lost so much, and I have failed her. I did not protect her with enough compassion. I was angry when she could not cope. I wanted her to be different, less good and gentle, more like me, hard and selfish . . . Oh, Mama, please, please . . .

A dreadful pallor came to Mathilde's face and her eyes opened for a second or two. She looked at her daughter without seeing her. In those pathetic blue eyes shone a plea, the same kind of plea that Sonia had seen whenever Mathilde would whisper, "David, David . . . Anna!" It was, Sonia knew, a plea for forgiveness, and she could not stand to think of its implications. She began to cry, sobs escaping her as she went to Mathilde and started the vigorous heart massage which was the only hope the doctor could offer for her mother's survival.

Sonia spent the night alternately administering cold compresses and rubbing her mother's chest until her arms ached. She had become an automaton battling against fate. When the first fingers of dawn stretched across the horizon, Mathilde still breathed. Sonia's back hurt so badly that she could not raise her neck to hold up her head. Her hands trembled so much that the wet cloth slipped from them onto the floor. The crisis was over.

That evening, Alexander Zevin came to Sonia and declared, "Your papers will be ready soon, and I have made arrangements for your departure from here to Sevastopol." Sonia stared at him, dully. He had expected tears, a sudden, emotional outburst. But the young woman merely nodded. She could not weep, could not speak. She would flow wherever the tides washed her up, from now on. Her mother had survived the ordeal. But the Russia of her bones, of her blood, had not. Everything would soon be over.

A wave of intense exhaustion passed over her delicate features, and Sonia closed her eyes. The room began to swim. She put out a hand toward Zevin, to steady herself. But the blackness, nevertheless, engulfed her. She fainted.

Because of the chaos which had spread throughout Russia, particularly in its southern regions, the Gunzburg women did not receive their final travel papers until August 1920. In fact, simultaneous with their departure from Simferopol came a diplomatic move from France which greatly reassured them about the possibility of going there from Constantinople. The French government, on August 12, recognized General Wrangel's troops as the de facto government of Russia. But the Whites were at their wits' end. The city of Sevastopol was in their hands, however, and it would be safe to leave from there as planned.

The final details of the voyage were left to Zevin. He arrived one evening at the house of Madame Solovéichik, and drew forth a large purse, from which tumbled onto the table a coin of twenty French francs, some German marks, Serbian and Rumanian change, several shillings, and a goodly amount of Turkish currency. "Our Russian money is worthless abroad," he explained. "But in Constantinople you will be able to change any foreign currency." He smiled modestly. "In preparation for your trip, I have been collecting any coin which came my way. I hope that these will be useful to you."

Then, stemming Sonia's flood of thanks, he told them that a ship was scheduled to leave from Sevastopol for Constantinople within the week. The exact date of departure was still unknown, but as soon as he learned it Zevin would arrange for someone to drive the Gunzburgs to the train station for the three-hour ride to Sevastopol. He advised them to leave Simferopol three days before the ship's departure, so that they might have two days in Sevastopol to see to any unfinished business with their papers.

It was not until the morning of the eighteenth of August that Zevin learned the date of the ship's departure. It was to leave on the twenty-third. Sonia purchased their tickets at once, thinking that she might be spending Russian currency for the last time. At noon, Zevin reappeared, announcing that a peasant would drive them to the station that very evening, and that he would accompany them on the train, to protect them. They would be able to rest in Sevastopol the next day. He had arranged for the two women to stay with a family he knew in the city.

During the afternoon Sonia packed their belongings and a supply of food for the train ride. She was grateful for the work, which kept her from thinking. After supper, a small thickset man arrived, saying that he was Zevin's man, the one who was to travel with them. He heaved their luggage onto his wagon, and the two women climbed aboard. The lone horse began the journey to the train station, as the moon glistened over the rooftops.

Mathilde recalled her wedding voyage in the winter of 1883, her first glimpse of this Russia which they were now abandoning, perhaps forever. She had loathed it then, in its immensity, in its grandiosity. Now it no longer cowed or terrified her. Too much had happened to her. She thought wryly: You are an old relative of whom I once was frightened, but now I am sorry to have to let you go. You have been part of me, even while I denied you.

At the station, the Zevins clustered around the two

women. But their driver was impatient and did not wish to tarry for farewells. Sonia embraced Ekaterina one last time, then went in search of their guide.

He had pushed their bags into a compartment, and in order not to lose him in the gathering crowd the two women hastily followed. After considerable effort, they joined him and took their seats astride their luggage. It was eight forty-five when the engines started in motion. Mathilde saw Sonia's sudden look of anguish as she turned to the window, and she laid a hand over her daughter's thin fingers. They did not speak.

The journey lasted ten hours instead of three. The Gunzburgs shared their boiled eggs and fruit with their companion, grateful for his presence which seemed to shield them against potential thieves. Nobody slept. At length, at three the next afternoon, the overcrowded train pulled into Sevastopol, and the uncomplaining peasant found a cart to take the women to the home of Zevin's friends.

They were a simple family whose house was already full, but they gave Mathilde a mattress and allowed Sonia to sleep on the dining room table. Their guide was set up with a sheet thrown over the balcony. But exhaustion had drained all three, and they slept on their makeshift beds as soon as they had eaten supper with their hosts.

Sonia rose early the next morning and cooked some food for their voyage by ship. Great numbers of White soldiers were in the city and she resolved to search for her brother Gino before they set sail. First, she took some papers to the necessary officials for signing, and there asked if anyone knew where General Kutepov's division was stationed. No one could answer her. She felt discouraged, but not defeated. After all they had suffered and survived, she would not be defeated, not now and not ever again.

She walked out into the sunshine, a diminutive woman weighing less than eighty pounds. She was totally unfamiliar with Sevastopol, but her footsteps took her along the harbor docks, and whenever she encountered a White officer, she would stop him with her question regarding Kutepov. She walked and walked, until her feet ached so that she could hardly continue to lift them. But if Gino were anywhere near the city, and they departed without making contact, she would never forgive herself.

Late in the afternoon, Sonia passed before a row of shops. In her weariness and disheartened condition, she nearly bumped into a lady strolling with a little girl. Sonia lifted her gray eyes to the woman's face, a hasty apology upon her lips. Instead, the words choked her. Her eyes took in the black hair with its loose tendrils, the high color, the regal yet graceful stance. She said, "Natalia Nicolaievna."

The woman blushed, hastily touched her forehead, and her deep blue eyes became sapphires, points of brilliance. "Sofia Davidovna," she replied. There was a softness in her voice, and yet embarrassment. She quickly motioned to the little girl, saying, "This is my daughter, Lara. Lara, this is Baroness de Gunzburg, a friend from Petrograd."

"How come we never saw you there?" the girl asked, with childish impudence. Then she blushed, resembling her mother, and added, "I am pleased to meet you."

"And I am pleased to meet you, too," Sonia replied, smiling at the girl. She could not look at the mother, but knew that for an inexplicable reason Natasha wished to hold her there. Surely not for the past? Finally she raised her gray eyes and said, "My mother and I are sailing for Constantinople on the twenty-third. I was searching for my brother, Gino, who is serving under General Kutepov. I had so hoped he might be right here, in Sevastopol . . ."

But Sonia realized that Natasha had stopped listening to her, that she had bitten her lower lip at the mention of the word "brother." It was a word that hung between them. Now Natasha murmured, "And . . . Ossip?"

"We haven't heard from him in several years. He had gone to Odessa—"

"Yes," Natasha said. Sonia stopped, and regarded her once more, wondering. Natasha hesitated, then added nothing. Sonia waited. For a moment, intense discomfort gnawed at both of them, and each stood on the verge of exchanging confidences, on the brink of understanding, but held back. Finally Natasha broke the awkward silence and said, with infinite gentleness, "My husband, Prince Kurdukov, is stationed here with his troops. I shall ask him about your . . . about Evgeni Davidovitch. If I hear any news, where shall I come?"

Sonia's austere, alabaster features relaxed, and a tint of pink rose to her cheekbones. "That is most generous of your time and effort, Natalia Nicolaievna," she replied. She gave the address of the family with whom the Gunzburgs were staying, and said good-bye to the woman and her daughter. When she returned home she could not shake off the odd sensation that had enveloped her and Natasha that afternoon. She kept fighting the desire to weep.

The evening before their scheduled departure, their hostess told them that a lady had come to speak with them, a Princess Kurdukova. Sonia's face lit up, and she clutched her mother's hand. "That is Natalia Nicolaievna," she said. "Perhaps she has located Gino!" The desperate hope in her voice filled the room.

But when Natasha entered, her lovely eyes were opaque, and she was not smiling. Sonia's heart plummeted. Natasha went toward Mathilde, took her hand, and said, "It is good to see you, Mathilde Yureyevna. But I have not found your son. However, my husband is on the lookout for him, and if we hear the slightest news . . ."

"You are so kind," Mathilde answered. She motioned for Natasha to take a seat on the small divan, and the young woman did so. The family had retired to other rooms in order to leave their guests alone with their visitor. Mathilde gazed upon Natasha and declared, "You are still as lovely as when we knew you. How are your parents? Maria Efimovna?"

Now Natasha's eyes filled with tears, which she brushed away quickly. "They are gone," she murmured. "It was a dreadful tragedy. My daughter and I are the only ones alive today—and my husband, of course." She looked away, then back to Mathilde, and said, intensely, "You do not know whether Ossip is safe?"

Sonia cleared her throat, and all at once her features glazed with frost. She was remembering Ossip before his baccalaureate exams, telling her that his life was over, that Natasha would not be his wife. She spoke, startling her mother with the curtness of her words. "Natalia Nicolaievna," she said, "why should it matter to you? Ossip has meant less than nothing to your existence. He was a despised Jew, to be hurt and eventually discarded."

The face that stared back at Sonia was red, and bathed in tears. "You have no idea," Natasha whispered. "No idea at all . . . How could you, Sofia Davidovna? I, at least, gave Ossip what I could. Small gifts indeed, compared to what he should have been given. But I did not let him kill himself in a reckless ambush, at the end of a crazy war. You may be able to live with your upright purity, but there are only venial sins on my own conscience. I am sorry that it was Jesus who said, 'He that is without sin among you, let him first cast a stone at her.' I wish it had been Moses or David. Then you would not accuse me of prejudice . . ."

"I did what I thought best, for both of us," Sonia replied quietly.

"Ah, yes. We each do what it is in our nature to let us do. It was Ossip who taught me to stop hating you, Sofia Davidovna. But I cannot hate you, for after all, you are his sister."

"This is no time for hatred, in any event," Sonia commented tersely. Her own eyes had filled with tears, and she clasped her hands in her lap.

"No. But . . . if you see him . . . when you see him . . .

would you give him a message? I want him to know—
that—" Natasha stood up suddenly, her face distorted. She
looked at Mathilde who sat uncomprehending of the scene
that had so shaken her daughter and the Princess, and now
Natasha could not continue. She went toward Mathilde,
took her hand once again, and whispered, "It was so good
to see you, to know that you are well. Good-bye, Mathilde
Yureyevna." She walked hastily to the door.

On the threshold, Sonia caught up with her, placing a
hand upon the other's arm. "What is the message?" she
murmured.

Natasha saw the earnest expression of the gray eyes, the
stillness of delicate features. She replied, her voice low, "I
am going to ask my husband to grant me a divorce, when
this is over. Even if it means that he will take Larissa from
me—"

But Sonia shook her head. "Wait," she said softly. "Let
us see where life takes you, where it may take Ossip, and
your husband. I would not raise my brother's hopes—nor
indeed should you raise your own. Good luck, Natalia
Nicolaievna."

Sonia did not speak to her mother after Natasha's departure. She finished the packing, and left Mathilde to wonder
at the cold, hard passion she had seen surface in her frail,
beautiful daughter, whose back seemed so fragile as she
bent over the luggage. And Mathilde thought: I do not
know my children. She thought of Riri, a searing vision;
then her mind lit upon Natasha, and she sighed. She remembered Johanna, and her agony in the end. Some of us
love forever, she reflected, and this love devours us until it
has decimated our existence. She worried about her sons.
Where were they now, and were they safe? Would their
lives ever be normal again?

"Sleep, Mama," Sonia told her, and obediently Mathilde
lay down and closed her eyes upon the pain and the lack of
answers.

On the following morning, the twenty-third of August, Zevin's peasant guide drove Sonia to the port, where she found their ship and climbed aboard to assume possession of the cabin she and her mother were to share with three other women. In the meantime, Mathilde made her rounds with the remnant of her Russian money, finishing with the peasant himself whom she tipped lavishly with their last rubles. He was now ready to return to Simferopol, his mission accomplished. In the late afternoon, he made his final stop, taking Mathilde to the ship with all the sacks of luggage. She found Sonia in the cabin, and then, together, they climbed on deck.

When the ship lifted anchor, it was early evening, and by the docks an immense crowd stood watching as the ship began to move. Dusk had settled over Sevastopol. Sonia watched as Russia receded to a thin line on the horizon. Salt spray tingled upon her face. A strange tranquility had seeped into her soul, had settled there as a thick quilt upon a bed. It seemed fitting that her last memory of Russia should be of the south, as was her first, of Mohilna. She was burying Russia, as once she had buried Volodia Tagantsev. "We each do what it is in our own nature to let us do." Or, thought Sonia, what must be done.

The next day the sea grew rough and rain came. Between the showers, bursts of sunshine appeared to relieve the darkness. The Gunzburgs ate their provisions. In the early morning the ship entered the Bosporus, and at noon it dropped anchor in a shaded cove between some wooded hills near Kavaca. Officials—Senegalese soldiers—stepped on board, rounded up the passengers, and divided the men and women. Each group was made to line up in twos, and the men went off in one direction while the women were sent off the ship into a hot waiting room with bars upon its windows.

Later, two Turkish women ordered the women to undress, and all but their hats, boots, corsets, coats, and change purses were taken out to be disinfected. Then, in groups of four, they were taken to four small shower stalls where, for the first time in days, Sonia and Mathilde washed away the soot and grime of their travels. In the next room they redressed, feeling rehabilitated by their cleansing, and at two thirty in the afternoon men and women were reunited and allowed to reboard the ship. It was time for the crew to be disinfected.

They arrived in Constantinople at four thirty. A commission of Allied representatives—French, English, Italian, Greek, and Turkish—came at once on board to examine the entrance visas. When they were done, dock officials arrived, offering to find rooms for those who were disembarking. But Sonia heard one of them telling a lady that he would obtain a room for "a mere twenty-five Turkish pounds" for her and her small son. Sonia turned to her mother, horror-struck. The two women only possessed a total of thirty pounds, with which they also needed to wire Misha de Gunzburg in Paris. Sonia could not move. They could hardly afford a porter, but if they left the ship without all their bags, they would never be permitted back on board to claim the rest at a later time. And Sonia intended to hold on to the few valued books and functional clothes which represented their only possessions. These bags, which now stood upon the deck, were Russia and their past, as well as their link with the future.

A dock official was telling Mathilde that they were the last ones, that they needed to disembark at once. Quickly Sonia stated, "Please. We are expecting friends. Give us a few more moments." When he moved away, doubtful, she whispered to her mother, "This will give me time to think up something. I don't know what, though . . ."

But the official had gone to fetch a companion, who said to Sonia, "We know how it is. You have very little money. Maybe we can help you. I know of a place where you can sleep for only three Turkish pounds a night. Come with me."

Three pounds! One-tenth the asking price of the other officials. As they followed the man off the ship, Sonia visualized a rat-infested cellar or a sordid attic. But they were almost beggars and had no choice. He had offered them their only way off the ship.

A truck came onto the pier, and the official helped the driver load the Gunzburg bags onto it. Then he helped the two women inside. Slowly the vehicle began to climb from Galata Avenue to Pera, the most elegant thorough-fare of Constantinople. To Sonia's astonishment, the driver halted in front of the once splendid Hôtel d'Angleterre. "Our hotels can no longer feed their guests," the official explained, helping them step down. "This one possesses an enormous dining room which is no longer in use. I know the manager. He will let you sleep there for only three pounds."

Sonia's eyes flew to the kind face of the stranger, and she placed a hand upon his arm. "However can we thank you?" she whispered tremulously. "God alone can under-stand how desperate our situation would be without your efforts!"

"It's quite all right," the official replied. He was clearly embarrassed by the intensity of Sonia's gratitude.

They were escorted to a large room where two iron beds had been set up in a corner. The women were told that they could place their clothing inside the sideboard drawers. The manager brought in a portable sink and a wooden table, and Sonia paid him for several days in advance and tipped the official. These transactions left the Gunzburgs with sufficient funds for frugal meals and their telegram.

Alone, mother and daughter looked around them, their odyssey ended, if only until Misha's response. Sonia's dark hair shone above her clear white brow, and her gray eyes were calm yet firm. Bolshevism was behind them, out of their life. Only the diamond crab had come with them from Petrograd, from another existence. As Sonia unpinned it from her undergarment to go to sleep, she said to her mother, "One day my daughter will wear this jewel, and imagine spires and cupolas that her eyes may never see. To think that a man nearly murdered us for it . . ."

But Mathilde was thinking of something quite different. She wondered at Sonia's absurd confidence that she would one day marry to produce such a daughter. Now that they had nothing, would there be a David to claim her?

Twenty-Four

———————————•———————————

Baron Mikhail de Gunzburg wired sufficient money to his niece and sister-in-law for them to make proper reservations to travel to Paris on the Orient Express. It would be their first time on this noted train, and Misha had sent them enough funds for a wagon-lit. This incredible luxury loomed magnificent in Mathilde's head, but Sonia had other reasons for rejoicing. Misha had made her a proposal, in answer to her request for help in finding a position in Paris. His son, Sergei, who knew little of Russia and was called by his French name of Serge, was now ten, and needed the firm hand of an excellent governess. Would Sonia consent to come to him and her Aunt Clara, in their mansion on rue de Lubeck, near the Place d'Iena, to care for Serge?

Sonia did not hesitate in accepting. Although her mother balked at the notion of her daughter's being placed "in a false situation," Sonia expressed astonishment. "Your best friend was a governess in your own household," she chided her mother.

But Mathilde thought of how Rosa had slighted Johanna, and of others who had treated her as hardly a step up from a servant. "Eight years ago you spent time with

Misha and Clara," she admonished her daughter, "and you were their guest. Now you would be returning, in a very different situation, as a salaried employee. Could you endure that, Sonia?"

"I endured the Crimea for three years, and I endured being rejected by Kolya for another woman," Sonia declared quietly. "I need to earn a living, and Uncle Misha is a good man. Also—I love children."

Ah, thought Mathilde, wincing. Anna too loved them, loved her own child, caring for him as though he were another woman's. Suddenly, the serene Mathilde was furious, furious with Kolya Saxe for what he had done: if he had not abandoned Sonia, she would not now be planning to serve in her uncle's house. But Sonia refused to reconsider her decision. Mathilde said, "You cannot accept without informing Misha of your condition. Your ribs are showing, Sonia. We shall need time, six or eight weeks' worth, to recuperate here."

Mikhail de Gunzburg replied that he and Clara were willing to wait. In the meanwhile, the two women walked about the city of Constantinople, meeting acquaintances from Petrograd and the Crimea who had similarly sought refuge there from the destructive forces of the Red Army. Then came a letter from Paris, and Sonia recognized the handwriting with a lurch of her heart: it came from Ossip! The first news in two years. She opened the envelope and scanned its contents, growing pale. "Mama," she said, "Ossip is married! He married a woman called Lizette Dietrich, from the Baltic provinces, and they are in Paris. Uncle Misha told him we were here. Ossip is working at the Franco-Asian Bank, which is owned by a cousin, and he is going to be sent to Tokyo. Lizette has a daughter by a former marriage—" She stopped, simply handing the missive to her mother, who awaited it with trembling hands. News of her favorite son. Stunned, hopeful, also frightened, Mathilde had let her daughter read the smooth handwriting first. But now she could not concentrate on Ossip's own words. Visions of Natalia Kurdukova printed themselves upon her memory, and she compressed her lips.

Sonia knew what was in her mother's mind, but she remembered more: those last few phrases uttered by Natasha about a divorce. Sonia knew her brother. But she did not sense joy in this letter, certainly no personal joy. She remembered Natasha in Ossip's arms, in the Tambov, by the lake. Fool, she thought suddenly, weak fool. But who was she to decide now in favor of Natasha, she who had so ardently sought to make her brother give her up?

While Sonia and Mathilde grew stronger in Constantinople, the White Army was dying, unsung, in the Crimean peninsula. General Wrangel, admitting defeat, began to send convoys of troops to the Bosporus, and to evacuate the wounded and the families of soldiers as well. The communists had finally, unquestionably, won, both in government and in strength of battle. The seventy thousand remaining Whites began to depart, on ships, though some had been retained for one last stand on the Isthmus of Perekop in the north of the Crimea.

Master Sergeant Gino de Gunzburg was given orders, in early October, to board the convoy ship *Don*, en route to Gallipoli. Eighty-five hundred others received the same command. The seventh regiment of the cavalry was being evacuated. The young man was cold and tired, especially in his heart. He and his companions were herded together in the third-story hold, where their horses were likewise accommodated. He was leaving his country for life, and, turning to Afanassiev, a young sergeant who had fought alongside him, Gino said, "This is truly exile and orphanage. I know only of one of my sisters, in Switzerland, who has survived. She is ten years my senior and I haven't seen her for a long time. My brother has disappeared, I have heard nothing of my mother and my other sister.

Papa is dead, our fortune is gone—and we are quitting Russia in abject defeat. Somehow, this seems too much to accept."

"I was counting on your customary heartiness to sweeten the dregs," Afanassiev remonstrated. But he knew that his friend had not been himself for many months.

Gino did not smile. He was feeling the weight of his youth, more strenuous to bear than old age. Regeneration had always taken place for him with a new dawn. Nothing that had occurred yesterday haunted Gino today. But since Olga's death, his beliefs had been, if not shattered, at least shaken loose. He did not feel self-pity, but rather the absence of hope.

There was a freezing wind moving through the troop carrier *Don*, and the men hugged their clothing tightly around them. A strong gust blew away Gino's cap, and he was not quick enough to retrieve it. He pressed his hands to his ears, aching with cold. Afanassiev said, "Put your head inside your cloak."

But try as he might, Gino could not hide from the icy wind of the Black Sea. Soon he was shivering, and his teeth chattered. His cheeks rapidly grew red with fever, and he lay down, breathing raspily. "It's going to be all right," Afanassiev soothed, lying down beside him. "They say we are to stop in Constantinople. We can disembark if we can find someone there to take us off the ship, officially. Your family was in the diplomatic corps—don't you have any connections in Constantinople?"

Huddling inside his coat, perspiring profusely, Gino replied, "Yes, the former Ambassador to Turkey, Tcharykov. His wife was a friend of my mother. She is deceased now, but he is still in Constantinople—as head of the Red Cross delegation. I have no idea of his address, however."

"Someone that important can always be found," Afanassiev said.

A storm had swept out of the sea, but Gino was hardly

aware of it, for a high fever shook him and made him delirious. Afanassiev bent over him, fearing pneumonia. But it had come on so suddenly! He covered Gino with his own coat, but soon he too began to shiver, and he crawled beside his friend, hoping to warm him with the heat of his own body. Hours passed. Finally there was an announcement that the ship was docking at Constantinople. It was the middle of the night. Afanassiev tapped Gino on the shoulder and said, "Tell me your message for this Tcharykov. I can write the letter for you."

"Thank you, Boris," Gino breathed. He knew now how the young German officer, von Falkenhayn, must have felt, dictating his last message. Such gloomy thoughts would normally have elicited mirth in himself, at his own absurdity. Now he merely allowed his head to clear before composing the words to the former Ambassador of the Tzar.

I am on the troop carrier *Don*, without funds, and I have become very ill. There is almost no food, and we are cramped. I may be taken from here by anyone who can officially vouch for me. We are headed for Gallipoli. Please help me. Thank you. Evgeni Davidovitch de Gunzburg.

He could not sign, for he had lost consciousness when Afanassiev finished writing on the small, creased notepaper which he found in Gino's coat pocket. He added himself, for the benefit of Tcharykov, "Baron de Gunzburg has lost his cap, and may have caught pneumonia resulting from a severe chill. I have written these words under his dictation. Sergeant Boris Ivanovitch Afanassiev, Seventh Regiment." He gave the note to one of the men going ashore, begging him to attempt to locate this well-known Russian in Constantinople.

Ex-Ambassador Anatoly Tcharykov was widowed, and lived in a sumptuous mansion on the Pera road. He felt, however, that the climate in Turkey was turning to sympathy with the communists, and had decided that since he could not reintegrate his own country, he would go to Rome. When the note arrived from Gino, he was in his study with his secretary, his wife's nephew Yenudinia, packing the remainder of his collection of books. Georgi Yenudinia had long known the Gunzburgs, and was of the same age as the Gunzburg children. He had danced with Sonia at balls, had spent many evenings playing chess with Ossip during their school days. He was older than Gino, but remembered him warmly. When his uncle read the dirty, weather-beaten note, and handed it to Yenudinia, the latter exclaimed, "We must fetch him right now. He must be very badly off to appeal to us in such manner."

But Anatoly Tcharykov shook his head. He had never particularly liked the Gunzburgs. His wife, Vera, had befriended Mathilde years ago, when Baron David had worked under Vera's father, Ivanov, at the Ministry of Education. Tcharykov had always felt excluded by the intimacy between his wife's family and the Gunzburgs. Now he declared, "It is the middle of the night, and you and I are planning a departure. There is much to do. Tomorrow morning, you can go to the boy's mother. She and his sister are residing in one of the hotels nearby. They can do more for Gino than we can."

"I could go to find them now," Yenudinia offered.

"I am paying you a salary," his uncle replied coldly, "and it is late. I want you here, with me, and not out in the streets. The ladies are sleeping now, in any event, and would not wish to be disturbed until the morning. What is the rush? He will not die overnight. We have numerous problems to contend with; Gino de Gunzburg is only one of many. Do not argue a moot point, my boy."

Georgi Yenudinia remembered the quiet evenings when Mathilde Yureyevna would calmly listen to his plans, would encourage his ambitions. He thought of pretty little

Sonia, a woman of thirty today, who would not even have considered him as a suitor, for his parents had not left him rich. He had gone to work for his Uncle Anatoly, and was accustomed to his sour moods and tightness of spirit. He missed the gentleness of his Aunt Vera, and of friends of hers such as the Gunzburgs, in whose house he had been treated graciously and kindly. But his uncle regarded him with his piercing black eyes, demanding submission. Yenudinia folded Gino's note and placed it neatly upon his uncle's desk, reminding himself to bring it to his uncle's attention right after breakfast. Then, sighing, he resumed his packing of the leatherbound volumes into padded crates.

In the troop carrier *Don*, filled with men and horses, Gino shivered and perspired, next to Afanassiev. During his moments of clear-headedness, the old glow of hope and life came to his brown eyes, and he would stir at each new sound, hoping that the soldier who had promised to deliver the message would be bringing back Tcharykov. At length, toward morning, the man did return, but alone. He told Gino that he had located Tcharykov's house and had brought him the note in person. Yet no one had ventured to come back with him to the transport. "He will come in the morning," the soldier said, afraid of the look in Gino's eyes. The rich mahogany tint had faded from them, and he stared at the messenger as though he were invisible.

When the sky became golden with the rising of the sun, an officer appeared among the men in the third hold, and announced that the *Don* was about to lift anchor toward Gallipoli. He made a tour of his passengers, and halted by the moaning form of Gino lying supine on the cold wooden planks, his breath a loud, troubled rasping. "This man needs immediate care," the officer declared, and sent for a gurney. They lifted Gino upon it, and the officer stated, "The *Dobrovòletz* is docked in this harbor, and is bearing Cossacks to the island of Lemnos. Take him there, and tell the authorities that he is to go to the French

Hospital at Lemnos. He suffers from pneumonia, and cannot survive in such cramped quarters, adjacent to beasts."

Afanassiev could not bid his friend farewell, for the young Baron was not sufficiently conscious of his surroundings. But Afanassiev thought, grimly, if that bastard Tcharykov arrives now, searching for him, he will know how to find me, because of the few words I added, identifying myself. But if he comes later, the *Don* will be gone. He looked at the sun, white gold in the sky of the Bosporus, as Gino's gurney was carried out of sight.

Georgi Yenudinia had not slept well, and as he drank his thick Turkish coffee with his uncle, he coughed and asked, "Don't you think that now is the time to attend to Gino de Gunzburg? I could fetch him myself, off the *Don* . . ."

"No," Charykov answered, crossly dismissing his nephew's pleading eyes. Georgi had always been such a homely lad, so sweaty and gangling and unappealing. A man to be crushed and disregarded. "You will go to the Hôtel d'Angleterre, where, I believe, Mesdames de Gunzburg are staying. Bring the note to them." He thought bitterly of his wife's father, Minister Ivanov, who had shown such familiarity to Baron David, the Jew in his fold, while regarding his own son-in-law, Anatoly Tcharykov, with relative lack of favor. The notion still galled the former Ambassador, and he glared at his wife's nephew with particular distaste. Sniffing audibly, he said, to quell the faint stirrings of his own conscience, "The young man has obviously survived two wars. A slight chill will not kill him. Was he not the most stalwart among the Baron's brood?"

"I believe so," Yenudinia said. He averted his eyes from his uncle and gulped the last swallow of coffee. "I am going now," he said, rising. He grabbed his hat and cane and ordered the landau. When it came to the front door, the young man stepped inside and said to the coachman, "The Hôtel d'Angleterre, quickly, please."

In the coach, Yenudinia felt guilty. He had heard of Mathilde's presence in Constantinople, yet he had not called upon her once, concentrating instead upon packing for his uncle. He had seen her and Sonia in a tea room, with another family from Petrograd whom he had vaguely known as a young man. He had stopped, shocked by Sonia's emaciation, at the grayness of Mathilde's hair. They had been dressed in long gowns, out of style and shiny with wear, and Sonia's hair had been discreetly knotted at the top in the fashion of 1908. Yet, strangely, this style became her, and her intense thinness served to emphasize the delicacy of her bone structure, the largeness of her clear gray eyes. He felt regret; once, as a student, he had thought that he loved her from afar. And, orphaned so early in life, he had found a serene solace in the person of Mathilde Yureyevna, his aunt's friend. To see them this way pained him, and he hid from them thereafter. His uncle had lunched with the two refugees following Yenudinia's encounter, but he had not repeated the courtesy. After all, the Tcharykov fortune was intact, the Gunzburgs destitute.

Yenudinia found Sonia alone in the dining room of the Hôtel d'Angleterre, and she rose, greeting him on the tip of her small toes, like a girl. She smiled, and a pink color flowed into her cheeks. "How delightful," she declared. He could not restrain his own answering smile, thinking that she had changed so little from their youth in Petrograd— Petersburg then—when she would greet all her guests thus, with the gracious head tilted becomingly in its topheavy coiffure. "Mama has gone for a breath of fresh air, with Madame Kholodny," she added. "Have you taken your breakfast, Georgi Petrovitch?"

"Yes, yes," he said, blushing, thinking of his mission. He could not look into her oval face, so unlined still, so alive with perception, or she would read his guilt. He fumbled with his breast pocket, and removed the crumpled note, clumsily. Sonia was watching him with narrowed eyes, wondering. He cleared his throat. "We have received news for you, Sofia Davidovna," he said. "It is extraordinary, actually. A true coincidence, your still being here at this time. You see—" And he could not continue under her gaze. He gave her the note, and watched her eyebrows quirk with mystification. He mopped his perspiring brow.

But she turned on him, blue sparks in her eyes, and cried, "This message is dated yesterday! What have you done about this, Georgi Petrovitch?"

He coughed delicately. "My uncle thought it best to wait till morning, so that we might consult you and Mathilde Yureyevna. We . . . I . . ."

"What kind of consultation did you expect? My brother is in dire straits, and you dared to wait and risk his life? You have wasted precious hours. But what am I saying? We must go at once." She rushed to the table, found a piece of writing paper, and scrawled a rapid note to her mother. Then she wrapped herself in a thick shawl, took her bag, running toward the door. She turned back and regarded Yenudinia. "Are you coming?" she demanded.

The young man followed, his large knuckles cracking as he bent his fingers inside each other in his nervousness. He was frightened of Sonia, of her white fury, of her determination. He ran ahead of her to the landau, tried to help her inside, but she pushed him off and climbed in by her own efforts. He did likewise. She said to the driver, "The Bosporus harbor, please. Leave us at one end, we shall find our way."

But at the port, they were confronted with a long line of transports, ship after ship of Russian Whites evacuating their country. Sonia clamped her fist to her mouth, and fought back tears of frustration. "There are caïques for rent," Yenudinia suggested lamely. "You know—Turkish rowboats. We can row past the ships, and go along the harbor, noting the names of the ships as we pass alongside them at the back."

She merely nodded, scanning the horizon. He helped her down, and they rented a caïque as he had suggested. She would not let him pay for the boat, but pressed her own coins into the hand of the man who pushed their vessel out into the Sea of Marmara. Yenudinia began to row, steadily, until he had gone beyond the length of the transports, and then he changed his route and paralleled the harbor, behind the ships. They rowed steadily for several hours, but none of the ships presently docked bore the name *Don*. Tears sprang from Sonia's eyes. "Take me back, Georgi Petrovitch," she asked. "And then go home to your uncle. I shall walk on the pier and question the soldiers. I do not need you anymore, and besides, your arms must ache. Anatoly Kirilovitch will wonder what has become of you." She smiled through her tears, and he was moved. All his life pretty women had made it known that they could live without him, but none more eloquently than Sonia, now.

He left her after they returned their caïque, although he lingered by his landau, half expecting her to backtrack in distress. But she had already forgotten his sorry existence. Her hair disheveled with the sea wind, she walked at a brisk, British pace, stopping one soldier after another. Each one shrugged, said he did not know, or told her that the *Don* had sailed earlier in the morning. At length she encountered a sympathetic dock official who confirmed this statement. The *Don* had left for Gallipoli, and she had missed it.

Now Sonia sat down on a large flat stone and began to weep. Oh, Gino! she cried, where are you? And can you ever forgive us, for what we failed to do? I failed to protect Olga, and now I have failed you again, when you called out so desperately . . .

She walked off the pier, wearily, her feet hurting inside the old boots. There was a carriage at the side, for passengers, and she hailed it and returned to her quarters at the Hôtel d'Angleterre. She entered just as Anatoly Tcharykov was departing, and she brushed past him rudely, her eyes glistening with tears. "Leave us alone!" she said to him. "For that is precisely what you did to Gino. Now he is God-knows-where, en route to Gallipoli, while you pack your precious books into cushioned boxes. Go away, Anatoly Kirilovitch. You are no longer our friend."

Her mother did not utter the words of polite retraction the former Ambassador was expecting. In her stern silence, she echoed her daughter's utter condemnation. Tcharykov replaced his hat upon his head, thinking: Those damned Jews. Thank God that something has happened to take them down a peg in their arrogance. He strode away in outrage.

On the island of Lemnos, chaos reigned, for the Russians were taking over control from the British. Some straggling members of the families of important officers of the White Army had been sent ahead of the convoys and troops, and some of the women had become nurses at the French Hospital, which needed assistance. But, after some strenuous weeks, many of them were now leaving the island at their husbands' insistence. Generals and their men were flooding the area, and needed to be reorganized after the massive evacuation from the Crimea. It was time for the women and children to think of a permanent move, and British and French ships were beginning to transport these branches of Russian families in exile to their own home ports. Although most of the White volunteer army had gone toward Gallipoli, troops were being disembarked each day along the way, adding to the frustration of the officials who attempted to keep track of all who entered as well as exited from the ports.

In Lemnos, a very sick Gino was transported to the French Hospital, where he was at once put into a clean, cool bed. He was barely conscious of the white-clad nurses who hovered over him, feeding him broth or taking his temperature. He could not breathe, and experienced panic each time he attempted to force his lungs to function. "Pleurisy," the French doctor said, shaking his head.

A young nurse, wiping her brow, sat down for a quick cup of tea with her companions. The oldest of the nurses, a robust Frenchwoman, asked, "So it's for tomorrow, my dear?"

"Yes," the young one said. She pushed strands of black hair behind her cap. "My daughter and I are taking the ship to France."

"And the general? Will he be following?"

"My husband will remain here with his troops, until he can join us," she replied. She looked tired, but her skin was remarkably rosy, the perfect background for her eyes, which shone like lapis lazuli, a deep blue. She smiled. "This training has been most useful, Madame Trévin. Perhaps I can find work in an infirmary of some sort in Paris. Andrei is not well. It will fall upon me to earn our living, and we gay flowers from Petersburg were singularly unprepared for adversity. You must despise us now that our regime has been torn down."

"No, my dear, we are only sorry. It is always sad to see whole lives crumbling, though we nurses have borne witness to that phenomenon since we nursed our first patients. Look at that helpless old man with both legs in splints. And the young Baron over there, for instance. Pleurisy. And such a fine-looking young man. We still can't predict if he'll pull through."

"Who is he?" the nurse asked curiously, sipping her tea.

Madame Trévin sighed. "He's a Russian, just as you are, Princess. His name is Baron Eugene—Evgeni, you would say, wouldn't you?—de Gunzburg. A strange Teuton name that, if you ask me."

Natasha Kurdukova uttered a small cry. "Gino?" she said. "Oh, dear God! How his mother and sister searched for him, in Sevastopol . . ."

"You knew the family, then?" Madame Trévin asked.

Natasha began to weep. She nodded. Swiftly, she rose, and walked to the bed where the young Russian soldier lay gasping for breath. She took his hand, and caressed it softly with her long, sensitive fingers. "Yes," she murmured gently, her tears falling upon the sheet. "Ossip was right when he told me you reminded him of Volodia. The world can only afford to lose one of you. Volodia is gone, Gino. You probably do not even remember him. But you must live, for all the Gunzburgs who love you. Listen to me through your fever, Gino. You can't let go."

She remained by his bedside, counting the labored breaths, sponging his brow, murmuring softly to him in his agony. It was only when the doctor sent her away that she remembered that she had to pack, that she and Lara were leaving for France the following day.

When the ship lifted anchor the next morning, Natasha Kurdukova waved to her husband with a little white handkerchief from her youth in Petrograd. As she listened with half an ear to Larissa's excited warblings, a sudden thought pierced her mind: She had left without checking on Gino. And she had promised his mother and sister. She felt the tears rise to her eyes, wiped them away. She had also promised Sonia something else, that night in Sevastopol . . .

"Why do you cry, Mamatchka?" Lara asked. "Is it because Papa has a hurt lung, and won't be himself anymore?"

"Yes," Natasha replied, tangling her fingers in her daughter's hair as she had done so often with Ossip's. "That, and the fact that none of us will ever be himself, or herself, again. Part of me lies strewn all over Russia, in Petrograd with your grandparents, in Sevastopol, perhaps in Odessa . . . And even beyond Russia, in Persia with your

Uncle Volodia, whom you never knew . . . and here, in Lemnos."

"With Papa," Lara declared, nodding her head. "But he'll come to us."

"Yes," Natasha whispered. "He'll come to us." She closed her magnificent eyes.

Twenty-Five

By the New Year of 1921, Sonia and Mathilde had settled into new lives. Mathilde had happily found the house of her parents, in Saint-Germain-en-Laye, and had made a large bedroom on the third story her own. Her mother, old Baroness Ida, resided permanently in Lausanne, and had rented out the two lower floors of her French manor, in order to add to her small income. Mathilde, after three years in the Crimea, after meals of boiled barley and abject poverty at the end, was at peace in this house, where so much had occurred. She did not think, in her room in Saint-Germain, of Johanna's betrayal, of the ugliness that had entered her friend's soul and had disfigured her blond loveliness. She remembered days of peace, moments that had been windbreakers in the gusts of life, and she was, if not happy, at least serene.

Misha had arranged for Mathilde to be paid a small income every year, enough for her to take several long trips to Switzerland, where the other half of her family lived. In this way she could share her time between Sonia in Paris and Baroness Ida, her daughter Anna, and the boy, Riri, all of whom lived in Lausanne. Riri was now fifteen. Mathilde found him the painful, living reminder of

Ivan Berson, but could never broach the subject with Anna; never could she have brought herself to discuss his illegitimate birth, this proof of what her daughter had meant to the son of the wanton Bersons. Yet she loved the boy, and thought him strangely beautiful, as only children of true love can be.

She had seemed to make peace with her older daughter. There was no Johanna to come between them, and, at thirty-six, Anna had mellowed and was able to regard her mother with compassion. Perhaps, thought Mathilde, wishing she could be open with Anna, her daughter had been a mother herself long enough now to have learned of parental frailties. Yet she went out of her way to treat her grandson as the child of Anna's friend. If Anna guessed at the subterfuge, she did not mention it either. And so the door, once left ajar by the error of two sisters, quietly closed between the mother and her daughter. Perhaps neither had the courage to throw aside the veil, or perhaps Anna loved the boy too deeply to risk his overhearing a damaging truth.

Upon arriving in Paris at the end of 1920, Sonia had asked her aunt and uncle for a few weeks more of rest, and had gone to Saint-Germain with her mother. Her emotions were in a state of upheaval. She could think only of her brothers—Gino, who had left no trace to follow, and Ossip, who was married to a stranger, and who was reportedly about to depart for Tokyo with the France-Asian Bank. She kept wetting her lips, wondering whether to discuss her encounters with Natasha Kurdukova in Sevastopol with Ossip. Natasha's words had left little doubt in Sonia's mind as to their relationship, but Sonia balked at the idea that so fine a lady as Natasha could have become anyone's—even Ossip's—mistress. Perhaps the two had merely run into each other in Petrograd, and become reacquainted and friendly. Perhaps, with a lack of discretion, they had even spoken of love. But the rest was unthinkable, and perhaps it was best for Sonia to leave well enough alone. Everybody had suffered enough.

Ossip did not waste time in calling upon them in Saint-Germain. When Sonia answered the door, and saw him, she uttered a short cry and threw her arms around his neck. He smelled of himself, his laughter in her ears was the same; he was here with her! "I've missed you so!" she cried, and for a moment it was as if they were adolescents again, before Natasha and Volodia had forever split the atom of their togetherness.

"My love, this is Vera," Ossip was saying, and Sonia found herself glancing toward a pretty blond girl much as her cousin Tania had been in her childhood. "Vera—this is my sister, Sofia Davidovna de Gunzburg."

"You must call me Sonia, for I am to be your aunt," the young woman said. "But come in—I am forgetting Mama! She has been so anxious to see you, my Ossip!"

Mathilde was waiting in the sitting room, for her legs had been causing her much pain since the Crimea. Ossip came to her quickly, and enveloped her in his arms, rocking her back and forth. Mathilde could not speak, so great was her emotion at once more being held by her favorite child. Too much had happened. When he finally broke away, laughing somewhat tremulously, he was motioning to the small girl. "Come, Verotchka. Meet your new grandmother."

But Mathilde was looking around the room. "Where is your wife, Ossip?" she asked.

Her son averted his face, and Sonia thought: How pencil thin he has grown, where before his fineness was etched in charcoal . . . And he is not himself, no indeed. He seems . . . ashamed. Ashamed, and emptied of spirit, that spirit that had returned after his imprisonment at the Fortress. Could it be that this woman was not making him happy? Suddenly she was angry.

"Lizette is not well today, Mama," Ossip explained. But he did not look at his mother.

"Is it serious?" Mathilde asked.

"It's a headache," Vera interposed. She seemed a bright child, well-mannered and attractive, and Sonia judged her to be ten or twelve.

"A headache? Indeed." Mathilde's blue eyes met Ossip's, and held them silently. Pride and outrage were contained in her magnificent chiseled face, the pride of an affronted mother-in-law, upon whom one has reversed the rules of etiquette. "I understand, Ossip. Do not bother with explanations." The words appeared to slap her son's cheek, and he blinked. Sonia saw pain upon his features, and pain too upon her mother's. Never before had Mathilde looked so rebuffed as now, by her son and his absent wife. And Sonia began to hate Lizette, who had made this reunion a humiliating occasion. How had Ossip allowed such disgraceful behavior?

"Yes, Mama is prone to headaches," Vera was saying in her trilling young voice. "When she goes to bed at night, Ossip and I have to sit by her side and hold her hand or she cannot fall asleep." She called her stepfather "Ossip" in adult fashion.

"Then your mother must be quite miserable right now," Mathilde commented. "You are both here."

Ossip, Lizette, and Vera, it was revealed, had lived in the house in Saint-Germain until a few days before the return of Mathilde and Sonia, when Baroness Ida had asked them to move. Lizette had been most resentful. This was explained by Misha and Clara de Gunzburg, who had kindly taken Ossip's family into their mansion in Paris for several days. Misha said, touching his upper lip with embarrassment, "Our Lizette thought that she had married into a royal family, it would appear. I do believe she'd hoped you had both perished at the hands of the Bolsheviks, so that she might be *the* Baroness de Gunzburg. Now, in Paris, she was faced with an entire clan of us; and her mother-in-law, to boot, is still alive and well. This did not sit nicely with her; nor did Aunt Ida's request that she move out of Saint-Germain to accommodate you, my dear Mathilde."

Sonia was outraged. How could Ossip have married that kind of person? She felt fiercely protective of her mother, and angrier than ever at her brother. Why had he allowed this woman to humiliate their mother by not coming at once to greet her, with him and Vera? But a full week later, Lizette did come, dressed soberly but with flair, in an inexpensive but elegant afternoon suit of navy blue, her black eyes piercing, her features sharp and angular, her carriage impeccable. She bent toward Mathilde and pecked at her cheek, accepted tea from Sonia, and spoke. She did not ask about their adventures in the Crimea, about their health. She talked, instead, of her devotion to her husband, of nursing him in Odessa, of their plans to go to the Orient, which had always been part of his dream. One could see the sparks which flew into her eyes whenever she spoke of "Ossip's brilliant career, which lies ahead of us like a road strewn with gemstones." Sonia thought: But my brother is not ambitious. She does not understand him at all!

During the days that preceded Ossip's departure, Lizette did not leave him any time alone with his mother or his sister. She clung to him, touching his sleeve, his hand, his elbow, almost as if to reassure herself that he had not left her side. She told sparkling anecdotes in her nervous manner, amusing the company around her. But Sonia and Mathilde were disquieted. Certainly this was not the marriage they had dreamed of for Ossip. Sonia thought, wryly: You have picked your Gentile, my brother, but if you had to go against the religion of your fathers, why did you not wait for the other? But the constant presence of Lizette prevented Sonia from having to decide whether or not to speak of Natasha to her brother.

Once, by the door, Ossip did succeed in retaining Sonia

for a brief minute. He bent toward her, and whispered, rapidly, "You see, my sweet, I owe my life to her. And I owe her more, because—well, because it is not within my power to give her what she needs: a man's true heart. Don't you understand? If I did not have Lizette, or Vera, why should I continue to push on, to live at all? They give me a reason to earn a living, to rise in the morning. I am grateful to them for that."

"But—why, Ossip? What has happened to bereave you so?" his sister demanded, searching his face for clues.

He brought his fingers to his eyes. "I cannot explain," he merely stated. But he added: "Did I tell you whom I saw in Odessa? Ivan Berson! He was a member of the government on the Volga. It was . . . an emotional encounter. He gave money to Stepan for us."

Sonia blanched. "And you told him, about Annushka?"

Her brother regarded her strangely. "What was there to tell? I did not want to dwell on what was obviously painful to him. I said that she was well, and in Switzerland." He scratched his chin: "Why? Should I have told him something else?"

"Of course not," Sonia replied. She knew now that she would not speak of Natasha. She herself felt no desire to learn what might have occurred to Kolya Saxe. The past was gone, forever. She kissed her brother, and let him out the door. Already Lizette's shrill voice was calling to him, impatiently.

Stepan had remained with Ossip and Lizette, but he did not appear happy. Sonia felt a flow of warmth and gratitude for this old man of more than sixty years, so tall and elegant, who had not forsaken their family. "Elizaveta Adolfovna is not easy, is she?" she asked of him one day, blushing at her own impudence. But he had not replied. Instead, he had tactfully commented upon the bloom that seemed restored to her own cheeks. When, in January, Ossip and his family departed for Japan, Stepan remained with Clara. She already possessed an excellent maître d'hôtel, but could, she said, employ Stepan as his assistant. It would mean a definite step down for him, but he was in no position to refuse. Mathilde simply did not have the funds with which to pay him, and besides, he would not feel quite so exiled if he could see Sonia, his little mistress of yore.

When Ossip left, Sonia heaved a sigh, partly in sadness that her beloved brother, after so long a separation, was going to be far from her again; but also partly in relief, for Lizette had put Sonia's nerves on edge. But Mathilde said, "Perhaps, although she is not our kind, she is good for him. She has protected him, and he needed that. He has given her his name, his care. Theirs is not a union made in heaven, but it may be a marriage to survive where others, created in the heart, have failed. At least my son has picked a lady born and bred."

Sonia smiled. She could say nothing, for she knew now that her mother too had married for comfort, and not for love. But she vowed within herself that when and if she pledged her troth again, it would be in a total commitment guided by her sentiments. Spinsterhood was no dishonor. Marriage could not include compromises; better to be alone and whole.

Rosa and Sasha de Gunzburg were no longer in Paris. A cousin of his and of Baron David, who owned many banks, had offered Sasha the management of the Amsterdam branch of his Bank of Paris and the Low Lands. But on February 21, Tatiana Halperina, who resided in Basel, Switzerland, with her husband's family, gave birth to twin sons, whom she named Jean and Vladimir, or Volodia. Sonia thought ruefully: In one blow she has surfaced our memories of youth, hers and mine together. And she thought: But Tania knew nothing of the business with the Tagantsevs. Her twins represent a coincidence in our lives, a strange harkening back to golden days in Petrograd . . . to other twins. . . .

She sent her cousin a warm letter of congratulations and wrote to her of Ossip's marriage, wondering whether Tania had ever really cared for her brother. Suddenly, at thirty, Sonia felt old. She had held out, hoping, hoping . . . for what? The realists had settled for less than what they had originally wanted, all of them, even her sweet friend Nina. She had found Nina again, with her husband and child, among the thousands of White Russian refugees in Paris. Even Nina had a child, a handsome boy.

Now it was time for Sonia to move into the three-story house of her Uncle Misha, time to assume her responsibilities. She took her single suitcase, filled with books and old clothing, and brought it to the luxurious rooms of the rue de Lubeck, in the elegant sixteenth *arondissement*, Paris's most aristocratic neighborhood. She crossed the vestibule, then entered the ground floor, passing the ballroom and salon, the dining room and the study. The carpets were soberly muted in color, fine Aubusson rugs which reflected quiet good taste. On the first floor were the master bedroom suite, several bathrooms, and boudoirs for guests, and on the top floor were smaller rooms, including Serge's lesson room, his playroom, and his bathroom, his bedroom and that intended for his governess, who was to share a bathroom with the nurse and the laundry girl.

An elevator took Sonia to these quarters, where Serge, bright-eyed, awaited her. He was ten, nearly eleven, and she remembered him with gladness. He had been a babe of two when she had gone to Kiev with Clara, and five when she had returned to Petrograd by way of Paris in 1915. She thought, without emotion: Eight years ago, before we went to Kiev, I slept on the second story, in the choicest guest apartment. Now I share a toilet with servants. But what does any of this matter? Of all our relations, of all the Gunzburgs who settled in France and whose fortunes are still intact, only Misha and Clara came to me with a concrete offer of help. She hugged the little boy, and questioned him about his favorite games.

In the morning, Sonia breakfasted with Serge in his lesson room, but she did not have to instruct him, as Johanna had her. Instead, she sent him to his school, a private one, with the chauffeur. Toward the end of the morning she would go and meet him there, and they would take a walk. One of his friends had a governess who followed the same routine, and so the two women with their charges would take walks to the Avenue du Bois or the Square Lamartine to play. In the afternoon a lady came to help Serge with his homework. Sonia had to watch him when he practiced his piano, take him to his gymnastics class and his drawing class, walk with him and bring him to and from the homes of his friends. She played with him, but his mother brought him herself to the dentist and the hairdresser, and the nurse took care of his clothes and put him to bed and awakened him in the morning. At seven in the evening a dumbwaiter would bring him his supper, and Sonia would sit with him, but she herself took her evening meal with her aunt and uncle downstairs, at seven thirty. She was free in the evenings. Compared with what Johanna had performed for her family, Sonia was amazed at the light work load. Misha employed so many specific servants that she had been relegated to a kind of supervisory status.

Sonia's Uncle Misha had loved her since her first visit to Kiev, in 1904, and would spend many evenings reading with her in his study. The servants, goaded by Stepan, adjusted quickly to this niece who played a dual role in their lives. When Sonia was with her pupil, they would say, "Monsieur Serge's car is waiting," or "Monsieur Serge's tea is served." But as soon as evening came, or if she was alone during the day, they spoke to her with reverence as to a Gunzburg, and called her "Mademoiselle Sonia."

The only problems arose in her dealings with Clara.

From the onset of their relationship, Sonia had been unsure of her feelings toward this dark, somewhat brooding
woman who had married her dashing uncle. There had
been mental illness in Clara's family, and during her pregnancy it had manifested itself in Clara. Although she had
treated Sonia perfectly during the social season in Kiev,
when Kolya had proposed marriage, Clara was known in
the Gunzburg circle as an eccentric; and now she seemed
abstracted, quickly irritated. She had a manner of greeting
people by tossing her chin upward and retracting her bust,
so that some felt rebuffed. She was not affectionate, except
slavishly to her son and husband. Her coldness toward
Sonia was so obvious that the young woman did not know
how to treat her.

Clara had resolved to pay Sonia every three months.
Once in a while she would offer her money for treats for
Serge, but when payment time came, Clara fussed over
every centime. Misha did not interfere; he never had with
the other governesses, and Sonia would have been shocked
if he had done so with her.

With her son, Clara was possessive in the extreme. One
day when the boy was ill, Sonia was sitting by his bed,
reading to him. His mother entered, and Sonia, tactfully,
rose and went to the window. Clara sat down in her place,
but would not take up the reading. Instead, red with anger,
she turned to Sonia and cried, "When I am with my son,
he needs no one else. Please leave the room, at once!"
From that day on, Sonia never remained present when
Clara came into a room where her son was playing, resting,
eating, or sleeping. She would exit quickly by a side door.

Clara would also insist, several times during the night,
upon checking on Serge. She opened his door and held a
candle to his face, and one time, a frightful cry awakened
Sonia. The little boy was screaming: "The devil, the devil!
Go away, you horrid devil!" She ran into his room and saw
her aunt in the doorway. Serge, clutching at Sonia, began

to sob. "Mama awakened me," he stammered. "I was dreaming, and I thought she was the devil, come to get me!" Sonia quieted him down with a cup of warm milk laced with honey, and she gently asked Clara to refrain from her nocturnal visits, for the child was impressionable. But her aunt replied crossly that she was nervous, and could not sleep herself until she knew that her baby was resting in peace. Sonia could think of nothing to reply. She had gone into this position with her eyes wide open; unlike Johanna de Mey, she had no intention of breaking her agreement with her employers by stepping beyond her allotted area of influence. She merely attempted to avoid her aunt whenever she could, and not to raise issues of controversy. But sometimes the woman's coldness would pain her, like a sudden, swift dagger to the side.

When her mother would question her, however, Sonia refrained from the mention of her humiliations. After all, a few rebuffs were nothing in contrast to what she had suffered in Stary Krym, or during Mathilde's illness in Simferopol. But the fact was that then she had possessed solace in the presence of Mathilde, or of Ekaterina Zevina. Now there was no one to turn to. Mathilde was so frequently absent, Ossip was in the Far East, Anna in Switzerland . . . and Gino, where was he now? God was the only one who could have answered that question. She thought of Tania, sometimes wistfully. For all their bad moments, Tania had been a companion, someone her own age. The expatriates, such as Nina, whom she had encountered in Paris, were all occupied with families of their own. Still, Sonia refused to succumb to self-pity—it went against her nature. To complain, when she was healthy and alive, would have been base, a dent in her strong pride.

Had she allowed herself to be sorry, she would have admitted a dreadful, tearing homesickness. But she attempted to divorce Russia from her bones and her blood, with that same determination with which she had decided, in the Crimea, that life was worth fighting for.

What spare time she possessed, between Serge's many activities, Sonia devoted to a cause which she could not abandon: the search for Gino. She and Mathilde had read the note appended by Afanassiev for Tcharykov, so they arranged for a small sum of money to be deposited each month at the Gilchrist Walker Bank in Gallipoli, for Master Sergeant Evgeni de Gunzburg. Mathilde wrote to the bank manager, asking him to get in touch with her son there and to notify him that his mother was sending him this amount. No news arrived in Paris from Gino, and by April the bank manager sent a disturbing message to Mathilde, telling her that no one had ever come to take out any money.

Extremely uneasy, Misha de Gunzburg asked his friend, Baron Felleisen, to telegraph the military authorities in Gallipoli. Sonia showed Afanassiev's note to the Baron, and shortly afterward Felleisen managed to discover that Gino had never disembarked at Gallipoli. Now Sonia and Mathilde became frantic, and Sonia wrote directly to General Kutepov, under whom her brother had served. She received a reply, not from the general, but from Boris Afanassiev, who explained to her that Gino, ill with pneumonia, had been transferred in the Bosporus harbor to another ship, the Cossack transport *Dobrovòletz,* bound for the island of Lemnos. Gino was to have been sent to the French Hospital there.

At once Sonia composed another letter, this time for the Chief of Staff of the French Hospital at Lemnos. But this man responded with confusion. So many sick men had been treated there during those chaotic days that he could find no record of Gino's presence. Sonia's heart contracted with fear. But she would not put a halt to her efforts. Gino was a survivor. She would not give up the thin thread that was bound to lead her to her brother.

Then, just before fall, Clara said to Sonia at the dinner table, "I went to my dentist today, Davenport. He has a new assistant, a pretty young Russian refugee, who was most interested in me when she learned my name. It seems that she knows you, my dear. Her name is Natalia Kurdukova—Princess Kurdukova. She gave me this address, begging me to ask you to come to see her. She said—and this truly amazed me—that she had something to tell you about Gino!"

The address was 37, rue de Rome. Amazed and apprehensive, Sonia excused herself and took the underground metro to the rue de Rome. She rang the doorbell at the stated apartment and was admitted by Natasha herself, a thinner Natasha with a slight pink tint beneath her blue eyes, a Natasha whose clothing was modest but trim, although not a single jewel adorned her. Sonia felt her customary sense of unease approach, then strangely recede. In its place a warmth pervaded her at the sight of the attractive dark-haired woman. She entered, and Natasha touched her shoulder. "I did not know you were in Paris," Sonia said, her voice low and guarded. Now she remembered Lizette, and momentarily balked.

She was standing in a pleasant living room that looked somewhat empty but for two magnificent candelabra. Natasha said, motioning toward them, "I did not arrive with much, but I have had to sell most of it—all my bibelots, the trinkets that make one's house a home. I am holding on to these for as long as I can last." She smiled. "But it is an old story, one you have surely heard before. How are you, Sofia Davidovna? Is your mother well?"

"Mama is in Lausanne with my sister Anna," Sonia replied. "And you, Natalia Nicolaievna? My aunt says you are working for her dentist."

"I was most lucky to find this position. I had some nurse's training, and Monsieur Davenport needed help with his files and his correspondence too. We are not destitute, but Lara is at the Lycée Racine and there is rent to pay and her expenses. My . . . husband recently passed away, and after the funeral expenses Lara and I took in a boarder. If we had not, we should have been obliged to move into one room together. This is better, but the other would not have been so bad. We are very close, she and I, and her presence is always a comfort."

Sonia accepted a cup of tea, and thought that Natasha had never appeared so beautiful, so striking, as now, in her pale mauve dress which was somewhat too large for her shoulders. It was an inexpensive dress, Sonia decided, noticing its cut. Sonia's own sewing expertise indicated details to her that would have escaped most women. She herself was dressed in one of her aunt's discarded suits, which she had retailored. She knew that the color, cerise, was completely wrong for her complexion and eye color. Suddenly she felt comfortable, a sister to this woman whose own life had entwined with hers in such convoluted ways.

Now Lara entered the room bearing a platter of butter cookies. She was eleven now, taller than when Sonia had seen her in Sevastopol, and with a hint of budding breasts. She would resemble her mother one day, Sonia thought. And then, almost wistfully, she mused: She could have been Ossip's own child . . . Sonia took a cookie from the platter and spoke to the girl, admiring her elegant fingers, so like Natasha's, and Lara laughed, her head thrown back. Emotion caught at Sonia's throat: the gesture brought back the summer in the Tambov in all its poignancy, the long walks with Volodia, Natasha's kiss, all that which could never be.

Natasha had bent toward her, her face earnest and somewhat somber. "If I had known you were in Paris, I should have come to you earlier," she said. "I asked your aunt about Evgeni Davidovitch, and she explained that no one had heard of his whereabouts since his arrival in Lemnos. Sofia Davidovna, I can confirm that he was there. I was a nurse at the French Hospital, and I saw your brother. He was very ill, with pleurisy."

"And?" Sonia asked. But she closed her eyes, afraid of the outcome.

"I do not know," Natasha said sadly. "Larissa and I

departed for France the very day after I found him at the hospital. I was never able to learn what had become of him, and he was unconscious when I was with him. But it seemed as though I knew him, although he was a child and only saw me once, ever so briefly, in Petrograd. I spoke to him—but naturally, my words did not reach him. I spoke mainly for my own benefit, actually . . . This is no help, is it?" she added softly. The room was quiet around the two women and the girl, echoing Natasha's tone of gentle appeal.

Sonia wiped her gray eyes quickly, raised them to the face of her hostess. "Yes," she asserted, "you have helped me. You are a good and generous person, Natalia Nicolaievna. I am sorry that we were never the friends we should have been."

"Perhaps," Natasha replied, "it is not too late yet?"

Sonia did not reply. She pressed the hand that Natasha had laid upon her arm, and rose. More than anything, she needed to be alone. Lizette gnawed at her memory, and her voice crept into Sonia's consciousness and scratched at its surface like pointed chalk upon a blackboard. Larissa followed both women to the door, and Sonia kissed her lightly on the forehead. Then she was in the darkness of Paris, enveloped in a chill dankness under a gaslight. She was confused. Nothing seemed under her control. She wondered whether Clara had informed Natasha of Ossip's marriage, and was supremely grateful that the child's presence had prevented any awkward questions.

Sonia had heard in the Russian community that Baroness Wrangel, wife of the Commander in Chief of the White Army, was in Paris at the Hôtel Marceau, and she wrote a letter to her, outlining the puzzlement of the Gunzburg family and seeking an interview. Baroness Wrangel promptly answered, inviting Sonia to call upon her during the week. Sonia brought with her all the papers pertaining to her brother, and was received in the Baroness's private salon. She found there a most gracious, sympathetic woman, who informed Sonia that she was about to join her husband in the Orient and would personally attempt to clear up the mystery. Sonia departed with a small weight removed from her shoulders: the sincerity and diligence of Baroness Wrangel reassured her. But there was apprehension, too. Mysteries had their veil of comfort: knowing could bring with it certainties which were better left undiscovered.

Several weeks later, Baroness Wrangel returned, and wrote to Sonia, asking her to tea. She told Sonia that she had gone through innumerable lists of disembarked Russian soldiers at Lemnos with the help of a capable colonel. Gino's name, in spite of Natasha's confirmation, had not appeared on any of them. But she explained that the Russians, during that time, had been taking the island over from the British, and that for some ten days confusion had prevailed and files had been misplaced. Camps had had to be set up, the evacuated men housed and fed. If Gino's name had not come up later, when order had been restored, it had to mean that in the meantime he had passed away. Baroness Wrangel could not look at Sonia as she said, "You must face reality, Sofia Davidovna. The colonel saw no other answer. I am truly sorry, my dear."

Sonia was too stunned to react. In a way, she had expected this news, but now it seemed impossible, a violation of her brother's spirit. Of course he was still alive! She thanked the Baroness, and left the hotel. Then she wrote a letter to the grave keeper of the cemetery in Lemnos, and sadly awaited his reply. She felt as though someone had hammered her forehead with a blunt instrument, and she could not touch food for three days. A dizzy pain slashed through her right temple.

When the answer arrived from the cemetery keeper, it relieved her misery. There was no tomb in Lemnos bearing Gino's name. Sonia thought: Then there is no proof that he is dead, and we can still hope. There was nothing more to be done, and she wished for no actual confirmation. She could more readily face a veiled truth than stark reality, in spite of the Baroness's words. But she was moved that so important a lady had gone through such pains to secure information for her, a total stranger. Exile and defeat had brought many together.

Some days later a bizarre letter came to Misha de Gunzburg from a friend in Leipzig. There was a man in that city claiming to be Baron Evgeni Davidovitch de Gunzburg, of Petrograd. He spoke French, Russian, and German fluently and was tall, with dark brown eyes and hair. Sonia's heart leapt with incredible hope, but her uncle said, "Read the rest, Sonia. This man claims to possess degrees in law and economics from the University of Petrograd, says that the Reds had seized him and sent him to Cheliabinsk, from which he escaped and came to Leipzig. He is forty-two, has lost all trace of his wife and child, has had no news of his mother and brother. He is without funds and wishes help in finding his family." Misha sent a telegram to his friend, asking him to obtain the signature and a photograph of this Gino. But the man disappeared before Misha's friend was able to prove that he was not the young Baron. The friend had already given him two hundred marks, which Mathilde insisted on reimbursing him.

When this story was revealed, the Gunzburgs' lawyer, Henri Sliosberg, who had been a great friend of both Baron Horace and Baron David, announced that another pseudo-Gino had appeared in Berlin, demanding money of the attorney. Sliosberg, who had known Gino since infancy, had sent the impostor packing, and had not told the family of this occurrence in order to spare them added pain; but now Mathilde, Sonia, and their relatives needed to know, in order not to waste their hopes in vain pursuits. It seemed that Natasha Kurdukova had been the last person known to have seen the real Gino before his probable demise. What other explanation was there?

None of the Gunzburgs acknowledged the death of the young soldier. They did not mourn him, or don dark clothing. Anna painted a large portrait of her brother, from a photograph of him in uniform right after he had been granted the Cross of Saint George. The face, flesh tinted, seemed as real as the deep brown eyes with their glow of mahogany, as the rippling brown hair and the khaki uniform. Mathilde kept this memento in her room in Saint-Germain-en-Laye, and when she traveled to Switzerland the painting went with her. But in Sonia's heart the small dark head of a baby in a cradle trimmed with Brussels lace remained uppermost when she thought of Gino. She would not brook defeat, nor yield him to eternity. Somewhere, she repeated to herself at night with passionate verve, he lives. To deny this would be an affront to Gino himself, the simplest, the best, the most courageous of the Gunzburgs.

While this drama was unfolding, leaf by curling leaf, Sonia's own existence had taken a turn that caused her great anxiety. True, it came about largely through her own doing, but Sonia had always placed duty above self-interest. She was very fond of young Serge, and noticed, early on in 1921, that he was frequently pale, grew quickly tired, and caught cold more than was the norm for boys of his age. She spoke to her Aunt Clara, and suggested that she consider placing her son in a Swiss boarding school, where the pure mountain air would strengthen his unsturdy health. During the summer, while visiting her mother and sister and grandmother in Lausanne, Sonia found the ideal school in nearby Rolle. Clara went there, approved of its setup, and decided that Serge could begin in the fall.

With her pupil gone, however, Sonia's job would disappear, and now she went to everyone with whom she was acquainted, asking whether they knew of any position for which she might apply. But Misha and her other relatives placed boundaries around her search. As a secretary in an office, she might be subject to rudeness and improprieties

from men; and she should not respond to newspaper adver-
tisements, for there had been incidents of white slavery,
young girls being kidnapped and sent to Brazil. Certain
offers to become governess to other children came her way,
but Sonia was advised to refuse, because of reputations of
miserliness or eccentricity on the part of the ladies, or of
lechery on the part of the gentlemen. Sonia did not know
what to do, and by summer she had grown frantic.

At that point, however, Mathilde's first cousin, Louise
Halphen, whose daughter Germaine had married Baron
Edouard de Rothschild, suggested that Sonia submit an
application to the Hebrew Consistory, which was situated
in the very building which housed the great Paris Synagogue, and which was, in effect, the synagogue's administrative annex. Sonia went for her interview with Albert
Manuel, Secretary General of the Consistory, and at once
admitted the negative aspects of her suitability. She had
never worked in an office, had only performed volunteer
work as a patroness. Monsieur Manuel smiled. "You shall
learn," he reassured her.

So, in the fall, she began her new employment, a bit
apprehensively. She would be the lowliest employee there,
earning a salary of five thousand francs per year. That came
to less than four hundred twenty francs per month. Where
to find a cheap room? But her Uncle Misha came to her
rescue. She could remain in the room she had been occupying as Serge's governess, eating breakfast and supper
with the family as before. Her measly salary would then
stretch much farther, and to Sonia, who had been econ-
omizing since the harvest of 1917, it then loomed as a
veritable fortune.

She found that the Consistory was a friendly place, and
that what was required of her varied from day to day. She
had been hired as assistant to the accountant, although she
had told him miserably, "But I know nothing of account-
ing . . ." She was, first off, seated at a large table and told

to copy receipts of donations for the Rothschild Hospital from a long ledger, yet later that morning she delivered papers to the cashier on the first floor: these were her main tasks on the first day. She also performed secretarial jobs for Monsieur Manuel, dealt with Rabbis, orphanages, and schools, and kept minutes for various meetings. She enjoyed what she was doing, and felt that as an infinitesimal cog in the large wheel of patronage to the Paris Jewry, she was performing a needed service.

She ate her luncheons in a small but clean restaurant on the rue Caumartin, a frugal meal to suit her budget. But she had been accustomed to taking tea with Serge, and had to bring with her a buttered roll to eat at four, so that she would not be hungry before closing time at six. She traveled to and from her work by underground subway, and sometimes it would be so crowded that she would have to stand all the way to her uncle's house, a distance of some forty minutes. She did not mind. It seemed a privilege to have found work at all, she who had never been trained except for her lessons in stenography and typing in Feodosia.

Although she ranked as the most unimportant person in the Consistory, the other staff members knew that she belonged to an illustrious family and that her father had been a well-known scholar and diplomat. They all called her, fondly, "Mademoiselle Sonia." In spite of her thirty-one years, she was the only unmarried person there under the age of forty.

She had heard from Clara that Aunt Guitele Brodsky and Maxik, who had once wished to make her his wife in 1912, had emigrated to Paris from Kiev, and she called upon the old lady in her hotel. They had not lost their money, having left Russia early enough to take it with them, and Max was unchanged. Sonia treated him with casual friendship, and when she departed, she wondered whether she might have found happiness with him after all.

It would be so easy to rekindle his interest . . . But, unlike her cousin Tania, Sonia did not consider marriage a practical matter when it reached the final consideration. She had not loved Max, and did not think that she ever would. When her Aunt Clara upbraided her roughly, exclaiming, "You would keep your petty job, remain a spinster forever, when a wealthy man might make a lady of you?" Sonia replied, simply and softly, "But I *am* a lady, Aunt Clara. My work does not devalue me in my own eyes."

"You were always a fool," her aunt retorted. "Once, you chose Kolya Saxe over Maxik Brodsky. He abandoned you shamefully, and I have heard that he has gone to North America, with no fortune to speak of, so that if you had become his wife after all, you would still be poor. One does not live on exalted principles when one has nothing, Sonia."

Hurt to the quick, the young woman did not reply. But tears came to her eyes, and she bit her lower lip. She had ceased to care for Kolya, but it had been gratuitous on Clara's part to bring up the humiliation of the past. She chose to ignore this unkind thrust. For more important than money or status was her own self-respect, which had remained intact. And equally essential was the fact that she was still a Gunzburg, impoverished though she was.

Twenty-Six

———————————•———————————

Among her many jobs at the Consistory, Sonia was in charge of donations to the poor. In her office were boxes of clothing, linens, shoes, toys, even canes and umbrellas, which the unfortunate would sort through to find whatever they might be able to use. The Consistory worked with volunteer organizations, but did not have a poor box, and Sonia herself possessed no money save her meager salary. But she took pride in being a Gunzburg, daughter and granddaughter of *shtadlanim* of renown, and could not have allowed a man in trouble to depart without having made a gesture to console him. She had three ways of helping such people: she could hand out used clothing, recommend a position, or send the person to someone or some institution which might better help him.

Having to deliver receipts for gifts and donations to the philanthropies of which the Consistory was in charge, Sonia frequently met with highly placed executives in the Rothschild, Rueff, Kohn, and Leven organizations, and sometimes with members of these exalted families themselves. She was received politely by all, for she was a Gunzburg, though destitute. So people, both rich and poor, came to learn that Sonia de Gunzburg was now an employee at the Hebrew Consistory.

So it was that still in 1921, Sonia received a letter at her office, and was amazed to discover that it came from Hillel Zlatopolsky. "Please forgive me for getting in touch with you at your place of employment, and not with Mathilde Yureyevna," he noted, "but I had no idea you were in Paris until recently, and did not know where to reach you at home. I would appreciate your coming to my place of business at your convenience, 63 rue de Rome." Sonia was much intrigued and went there. The offices were in a luxurious building on the corner of Boulevard Haussmann, and when she was admitted, she found herself in spacious rooms with tasteful furnishings. She waited, curious.

Soon Hillel Zlatopolsky, elegant as in Petrograd, appeared, and greeted her warmly. She did not want to ask about his apparent opulence, but he volunteered the information graciously. He and his son, Mossia, had succeeded in bringing to France five bags of sugar beets, and had sold some immediately upon their arrival more than two years ago. The Russian sugar beet was superior to the French, and with the profits from the sales, the Zlatopolskys had purchased sugar refineries in the Nord and the Oise sectors of the country. Hillel and Mossia's sugar was so much better than the French that Hillel had been awarded the Legion of Honor for having improved the quality of the French beet. Then, with these profits, father and son had founded a metallurgical factory, the Société des Travaux Métalliques, which built garages, depots, and hangars. Soon they bought a sardine cannery in Brittany, a factory that made foie gras near Bordeaux, a hosiery manufactory in Troyes, and a paper factory in yet another part of France. In two years they had become solidly settled, and, as in Russia, money now seemed to flow steadily in their direction. Hillel spoke softly, without boastfulness, almost in a self-deprecating manner. But he held Sonia captivated in her chair.

"However, I did not ask you to come simply to brag of

my success," the middle-aged businessman concluded. "There was a matter which deeply perturbed me concerning the Judaica. Among my papers, when I looked them over in Moscow before leaving for the south of Russia, I discovered that an error had been made in the payments to your family. I still owe your mother a small sum of money —not sufficient for her to have noticed the discrepancy at the time, but large enough to have caused my conscience to bother me. Please accept this check for five thousand francs outstanding in this transaction, on behalf of Mathilde Yureyevna."

Five thousand francs! Sonia was amazed, and thought: But that is an entire year's salary. She shook her head, uncomprehending, but Hillel Zlatopolsky was firm. "The books never even arrived in Palestine," Sonia demurred. "Therefore, you are paying us for something you will never be able to use."

"Nevertheless a deal was made, in good faith," Zlatopolsky insisted.

Sonia considered the matter, then accepted. But in her heart she thought: Something here is not right. Is Hillel Israelovitch attempting to help us, by telling us a complicated story of unfinished payments? Surely he knows that Mama and I are without funds. But if in fact there *had* been a debt, to refuse the money would be silly. She thanked him, and asked, "How is Mossia Gillelovitch, and his wife, Elena Lvovna?"

Hillel smiled. "Mossia is fine, fine. He manages most of my enterprises. And he is a bachelor again. Yes, his marriage to Lialia, the 'Polish doll,' has ended. Their divorce became final some months ago. My son succumbed to wartime foolishness, but since there was no child, no major damage was accomplished. Lialia and her mother are here, and Mossia feels obligated to support them. But that is the extent of his involvement."

"I see," Sonia replied, but she did not, and wondered

why such an elaborate answer had been necessary. Hillel rose and saw her to the door, and she left, somewhat bewildered by the entire interview. She wrote to her mother in Lausanne, enclosing the check. Then, in the flurry of her work, she forgot Hillel Zlatopolsky.

She was receiving many "clients" in her office at the Consistory, and they came to her as the Jewish petitioners had once come to her father in Petrograd. Generally they left quite satisfied, or at least with hope. But there was one man who was causing her no end of trouble. His name was Fuchs, a Russian Jew, and he was vigorous and well-bred. Once he had managed the largest metallurgical factory in Russia. Now he and his entire family had taken refuge in Paris, and not knowing French he was having problems obtaining employment. Sonia had already found him jobs as assistant gardener, salesman in a perfume shop, night watchman in a bank. But each time something occurred to prevent his taking these positions. She continued to try to locate something new, and he came frequently to hear whether she had made any progress. His small sum of savings had dwindled considerably, and matters had become drastic. His wife was knitting on commission, and this was their single source of income. Fuchs represented Sonia's only failure: she had even managed to find free hospital rooms for tuberculars, and sponsors to pay room and board for clients who were crippled. Only the Fuchs matter glared at her in its insoluble state.

During the final days of December 1921, Sonia received a letter addressed to Mathilde from a Rabbi Schneerson. She remembered that in 1909 there had been a Congress of Rabbis in Petersburg, to which her father had been invited. The young secretary of that convention had been named Rabbi Schneerson, and Baron David had brought him to their home several times. This letter was from the same Schneerson, who declared that he was no longer a Rabbi but now worked in metallurgy and resided in Paris, and wished to renew contact with his old acquaintances. He signed his letter after the phrase: "Always ready to be of service."

Sonia answered the letter in her mother's absence, but when she reached the end, she could not help adding a message concerning Fuchs. "Since you have so kindly offered to help us," she wrote mischievously, "I am going to put you to the test. You are now in the field of metal work. I know a Russian metallurgist who is starving. Could you not find him some form of employment?" She had been so young when she had met Schneerson, surely he did not remember her, and would be shocked at her nerve. But poor Monsieur Fuchs had a family to feed and was in dire straits.

Sonia waited, three days, a fourth. By that time she knew she had offended him. But on the third of January, Schneerson telephoned her at the Consistory: he had been absent over the holidays, but this evening, after work, he would pick her up and bring her home, and on the way they would discuss Fuchs. Sonia was overjoyed.

At six, his car was waiting for her. Schneerson was a middle-aged man, who politely explained to her that he was only the manager of the Travaux Métalliques, but that the owner's son, Mossia Zlatopolsky, would surely grant her an interview concerning Fuchs. "I know Mossia Gillelovitch," Sonia said in surprise, "although not well. I should have thought of it myself. Of course I shall go."

Thereupon, Schneerson asked her if she went often to the theater. He was waiting for his family to come to him from abroad, and wanted some recommendations for entertainment in the meantime. Sonia shook her head, smiling slightly. "I am afraid that my salary is too small to permit me such luxuries," she replied.

"Would you accept an invitation from me, in memory of the kind hospitality which your father extended to me, years ago?" the former Rabbi asked.

Sonia blushed. "Oh, no," she answered. "I may be very

free, but I could not go out in public with a man I do not know, alone."

"I assure you, my intentions are more than honorable," Schneerson demurred. "However, I understand. If there were several of us, would that make a difference?"

"Yes," Sonia declared. "That is a different matter altogether."

"Then, if you are free next Sunday, it is settled," Schneerson stated. "I shall also invite Mossia Zlatopolsky, who is my great friend, and another man, Vladimir Willner, who is dear to us both. Which play would you care to attend?"

Sonia's gray eyes suddenly sparkled. *"The Blue Bird,"* she replied without hesitation. "I have dreamed of seeing it for months."

She hardly had time to thank him before his chauffeur reached Misha's house. The next morning she made an appointment to see Mossia Zlatopolsky at his office after her workday ended.

Wearing a modest little suit of navy wool, Sonia was admitted to the small, comfortable room where Mossia Zlatopolsky met her. He came to her with an eager, brisk step, unusual for such a massive man, and she smiled, warmth spreading within her. They smiled with the knowledge of many small memories, the dinner at Misha's in Kiev, their encounters in the jail of Feodosia, his sister Shoshana's brusque manners. They also smiled in mutual embarrassment over the situation with his wife. But all this took place in less than a minute, and Sonia explained to him the reason she had come.

"Yes," he concluded, "I think that we can help Fuchs. We are building a factory in the Aisne department of France, and since this man is accustomed to leadership, we can place him in charge of the construction crew. This will be the perfect method to have him learn French, from his workers."

Sonia was astounded, and terribly grateful. She quickly sent a letter by special delivery to Fuchs, and the next day he came to see her at the Consistory. He was overjoyed. But a cloud seemed to pass over his happiness, and he suddenly asked, "How will I be able to work in the Aisne, if my house is in Paris? Will I have to pay rent for both places?" Sonia nodded. She would have to ask the question for him, make another appointment to see Zlatopolsky.

She deliberately wore the same suit that she had worn for her first interview, not wishing Mossia to think her arrogant or vain. Her visit was short, direct, and rapidly resolved. "Naturally we shall lodge him for free, and on Sundays he can see his family in Paris," Zlatopolsky stated.

She did not waste time in wiring Fuchs, who arrived promptly. But this time he bit his lip and murmured, "There is something else. I have no money left. If the Zlatopolskys pay me next month, how shall my family live these thirty days?"

Sonia knit her brow, disconcerted. She did not want to have to disturb Mossia again, despite his graciousness. But how could she fault Fuchs for thinking of his wife and children? Still, she was annoyed and rather embarrassed. She returned to the Zlatopolskys, once again in the same outfit, and explained the situation. It was becoming painful to sit under Mossia's scrutiny, to look into his blue-green eyes and reiterate her intercession for this third party. How had her father done it, day after day in some cases, with powerful ministers?

"I shall give him an advance of two months," Mossia declared, and Sonia felt a rivulet of perspiration moisten her back under her cotton blouse. Relief flooded her. She telegraphed Fuchs, for she knew that time was of the essence if he were to avoid eviction. This time, when he posed a fourth objection, she became angry, and stood up, tiny and frail. "I shall not plead for you!" she cried vehemently. "You are exaggerating, and will probably make

Mossia Gillelovitch rescind his kind offer. But I shall go to him and let him make his own decision." Sonia did not know why she added the latter, since she did not find Fuchs's last objection the least bit reasonable. Heat reddened her cheeks at the idea of returning to Zlatopolsky: why, then, go back to humiliate herself and risk his anger? Yet she found herself promising, and was surprised and none too pleased with herself.

She returned, and could hardly look at Mossia Zlatopolsky. But the young man said gently, "Of course I shall accommodate Monsieur Fuchs. And the trouble, Sofia Davidovna, was all yours, I'm afraid. You have brought us, I am sure, a valuable foreman. It is I who thank you."

She stared at him, her doe eyes widened with disbelief. He was amused, and laughed outright. She swallowed her confusion, and with dignity went home.

On Sunday morning, Sonia awakened with laryngitis, but she had a visit to pay in the afternoon to Brévannes, some hours from Paris, where one of her tubercular patients was hospitalized. No one else ever came to see this unfortunate man, and Sonia had "adopted" him. Her Aunt Clara declared that if she took this trip she would surely be too ill for the theater that evening. But Sonia had a dreadful thought: Neither Zlatopolsky nor Schneerson was listed at home in the telephone book, and she would be unable to reach them to cancel the date. And if she went to the country and to the theater, she would also have to go to work that morning, as Consistory employees were required to put in three hours on Sunday mornings. It was a point of honor not to miss work and then go out the same night. Deprived of her voice, she arrived at the office and insisted upon finishing a batch of correspondence that she had begun Friday. Albert Manuel was unable to convince her to return home.

She still felt duty bound to go to Brévannes, and so, sucking on honey lozenges, she took the train in the midst of a snowstorm, and then walked the twenty minutes from the station to the sanatorium. She was able to speak a few words because of the candies, and her patient friend was glad to see her. But when she returned to the house on rue de Lubeck, her aunt announced that under no circumstances would she permit Sonia to attend the performance of *The Blue Bird* that evening. The gentlemen would simply have to be told so when they arrived to pick her up.

Clara had not expected stubbornness, but she found that her niece, though voiceless, would not be put to bed. Instead, she selected an evening gown of muted gray which she had made herself, and wrapped a white rabbit stole, which had been passed down to her from Clara, around her shoulders. The three gentlemen came by car, and she gave them her hand, unable to utter a sound. Mossia Zlatopolsky was furious, exclaiming that she was placing her precious health in jeopardy. But, silent and beautiful, she entered their car.

She enjoyed the play, but during intermission refused to go out into the foyer, for in her condition she did not wish to change temperatures. Schneerson and Willner left, but Mossia remained in the box with her, although she was unable to converse. He told her about his escape from the Red camp in Odessa, and she listened intently, her gray eyes on him, a strange pulse beating in her throat. When the others returned, she was almost sorry. Then she remembered that Mossia was an avid smoker, and had sacrificed this pleasure to remain at her side. A deep flush spread over her cheeks, and she averted her eyes.

She could not rise the next morning. After the play, the three men had escorted her to Sirdar, an elegant establishment on the Champs-Elysées, and they had supped till midnight. She would have preferred to go to Weber, but the men had been strangely insistent on their choice of Sirdar. She was ill all Monday, and on Tuesday morning the florist delivered a dozen red roses, with a card from

Mossia Zlatopolsky: "Please get well," it said, "and remember that if you have any other poor to succor, my purse lies at your disposal." She smiled—he had certainly found her Achilles' heel. But she thought: Red roses—how lovely . . . A thrill of pleasure ran down her spine. She also thought: Perhaps I am imagining something which does not exist. Zlatopolsky is a man of generous impulse, a true Russian. Such gallantry may not mean more than gentle concern for a sick friend. Yet she did not want to believe it and was thoroughly delighted.

"Your mother is not here," Clara stated, "and you are a guest in my house. It falls upon me to make sure of the company you keep. Who is this gentleman who pays court to my niece in such a fashion?"

"But," Sonia replied with bewilderment, "you know him better than I! You are well acquainted with the Zlatopolsky family, and used to frequent them in Kiev."

"That was so long ago, and people can change," Clara retorted. "They left for Moscow, we for Paris. We lost touch. In fact, I doubt very much whether Misha and Hillel Israelovitch have even seen each other since their resettlement here after the Revolution. It was even said the boy made a disastrous marriage in the Crimea. Did you know of this?"

Sonia found that she was outraged. "Yes, I know all about it," she replied tartly, "and the divorce is final and clear. I do not associate with married men, nor do I believe that Mossia Gillelovitch would place a decent young woman in embarrassing straits. As for disastrous marriages, Ossip's is not one of which we Gunzburgs should boast."

"Still, you will invite him to tea on Friday," her aunt insisted with asperity. "Tell him to come at three, but that I need to go out at four. Then I can judge how he has turned out for myself."

Sonia gripped her blanket, shook her head. "He will not

come," she whispered miserably. "He is a businessman, and would have to interrupt his entire afternoon. At any rate, in Paris people take tea at five."

She wanted to weep, but all at once she determined to do as Clara had suggested. If indeed Mossia refused to come, she would know that his feelings for her were light, and not worth the trouble of postponing his business engagements. But if he accepted such a strange, disruptive, and actually rude invitation—for who in society told a guest when to leave?—there would remain few doubts as to his sentiments. She was seized with excitement, and composed the preposterous note to the young man. She asked Stepan to deliver it in person. Would he surmount her obstacles?

That afternoon Mossia sent a note back by his own messenger, agreeing to come; and that Friday, when the clock struck three, he was admitted to the home of her Aunt Clara. He bowed over Clara's hand and told her how sorry he was not to have called upon her before, then inquired after her family. To Sonia he spoke similar pleasantries. Clara laughed at his jokes and smiled at his easy compliments, while Sonia glowed, because he had passed her test and had come to her. At four he stood up, thanked the two ladies, and departed. Clara said, "He is everything he was as a very young man, only now he has matured and is even more attractive. That large lion's countenance fits a man of thirty so much more gracefully than it did that of a twenty-year-old. Don't you think so, Sonia?"

But Sonia was lost in her own reverie, and did not reply. She did not know whether she found him more handsome. She simply knew that as of this afternoon she was fully, totally in love with him, with Mossia Zlatopolsky of the sea-green eyes.

Shortly afterward, Mathilde returned to Paris, intrigued by Sonia's continued letters about the son of Hillel Zlatopolsky. Misha sat down with her, as he had done once before, and recounted what he knew of the Zlatopolsky family from Kiev days. Mathilde was already familiar with these facts, from David's research in his dealings with the Zionist leader. It disturbed her that Sonia might have acquired deep sentiments for someone of a Zionist background. But she knew that Sonia, unlike herself, was a true, proud Jewess, and of all her children the one least capable of any compromise. If her daughter was allowing this young man to pay her court, then he had to be a gentleman.

One morning, Hillel Zlatopolsky telephoned Mathilde in Saint-Germain, and asked if he and his son might come to tea there the next afternoon, a Saturday, after the Sabbath restrictions were over. She accepted, and said to Sonia, "Tomorrow, Mossia Gillelovitch will surely declare his intentions to us. Do you care for him, Sonitchka?"

Her daughter's wide eyes answered her, mutely, and Mathilde thought: Please, let him be sincere; let one of my children have a chance at happiness . . . She remembered the tall young man and his small, elegant father. She prepared a delicate tea, almost worthy of Petrograd days.

The two gentlemen came, and Hillel sat with Mathilde, while the two young people chatted amiably about new sugar refineries which the Zlatopolskys were building in the Nord, the Oise, and the Aisne departments. Sonia was fascinated, but she was bewildered at the lack of personal detail in their conversation. The father left with his son, and Sonia's face was gray: surely the young man had changed his mind, recalling the misery of his first marriage, and not wishing to reenter into matrimony after all. "But Hillel Israelovitch told me that he is leaving for London for ten days, and to make certain that you two are brought together," Mathilde said. "He must know that his son feels something special for you."

Mossia himself called upon them frequently while his father was away, inviting the two women to supper, picking Sonia up on Sundays from the Consistory and lunching with her at Noël Peters or Chez Laure. Her fellow workers said nothing, knowing that Sonia possessed a multitude of cousins and expatriate friends in Paris. To see her in the company of a young man was not unusual.

Nevertheless, people did begin to whisper. It was the first Sunday in March 1922. Mossia came to fetch Sonia from the Consistory, and brought her to the Trianon Palace in Versailles. After their luncheon he took her for a walk in the park, and they strolled past the magnificent gardens. During the meal they had shared stories of their youth: both had loved the south of Russia, both loved the countryside. He spoke now of his mother, and of his energetic sister, Shoshana Persitz, who was living in Homburg, a suburb of Frankfurt, Germany. Then he began to speak of his ideas about religion, about filial devotion, about the need for true understanding between spouses. He told her of his early youth, of his many friends, of his golden dawns in Moscow, of his sometimes reckless behavior. She listened, undisturbed. "You were wealthy and young, and you wasted no money but your own, and even then not too unwisely," she commented. "You are not shocking me."

"But my marriage did shock you, in Feodosia," he said.

Her footsteps stopped abruptly. Something constricted in her stomach. "It hurt me," she admitted, with surprise. "I did not know it then, but I do now. Elena Lvovna is flamboyant and beautiful, though not at all my type—I was jealous."

He murmured, "But I never loved her, Sofia Davidovna. I was young, as you say, and prided myself on being a man of honor. She had been . . . my companion. One day, in Yalta, during the days of the Bolsheviks, my sister saw us together, and in front of Lialia erupted into angry exhortations. You yourself know how thoughtless Shoshana can be! She humiliated Lialia and so, to spite Shoshana and to redress Lialia, I married her right away. It was the mistake of a child, but I wished to prove to Shoshana that I would not be bullied, that my life was my own. I saw myself as a knight in gleaming armor, saving a lady in distress. I doubt very much that Lialia ever felt distress, however, except from a desire to possess yet more gold or more jewels."

"So," Sonia whispered, "you did not love her. Not then, in Feodosia, when you were in jail?"

"Not ever," he replied. "I have never loved but a single woman, Sofia Davidovna."

She looked at him, her lips parted, and waited. But he seemed lost in thought, and began to walk again. Their footsteps synchronized, but they did not speak. She thought: How much more painful it can be at thirty-one, the worry and the waiting . . . But still, he did not say his piece, and she did not add any words of her own. She only stated: "Mama is expecting us for tea, in Saint-Germain."

"Tea?" he murmured. "Ah! Yes . . . Do you know, my mother and sister will be coming to Paris tomorrow, Monday. And my mother has invited you and Mathilde Yureyevna for supper."

"Tomorrow evening?" Sonia asked.

"Yes," he answered dreamily. Then he said, so strangely that she was jolted, "I am so happy that Lialia never gave me a child, though I do want a son above all else. I would not then have sought to divorce her."

Sonia thought of Ossip, and wondered whether Vera would stand in his way, though she was not his child. Then she was afraid. "What if you never have sons?" she asked him. "Then your fondest dream will not have come true."

"Not quite my fondest dream," he replied, hesitantly. He began to laugh. "If I were to have a daughter, I would love her as dearly. Men speak oddly at times, don't you think, Sofia Davidovna?"

"Yes and no," she said. But she sighed: Would he forever skirt the subject uppermost on her mind, and in her heart? All this skillful parrying had given her a migraine, and made her miserable. It had been delightful to play games at nineteen, to dally with love. But she wanted him to hold her, to anchor her within his life, never to let her go. She was a woman, not a girl, and she could not stand the insecurity which, in its suspense, had once been delicious. She wanted this tall, broad man, with his thick black hair, his sensitive eyes, his rough features. He seemed to her the perfect complement to her own chiseled frailty, and the sweep of his fierce male passions were the counterpart to her firm good reason. She wanted to cry out: We need each other, you and I—open your eyes! But instead, she said, "Mama will be worried, Mossia Gillelovitch."

Monday morning, at the Consistory, Albert Manuel brought Sonia into his office and asked her abruptly, "Well? Are you engaged yet? He is a fine young man. He and his father have acquired a vast fortune in only two years, but every sou has been earned honestly, and without speculation."

Sonia smiled. Folding her hands in her lap, she said quietly, "I am most touched, Monsieur Manuel, to see that you have taken the time and effort to research the background of this young businessman's family. But, to tell you the truth, had you discovered a bad strain there, or improper affairs, you could not have stopped the course of my feelings. No one can now: not even I, myself."

That evening she and her mother went to the apartment of Hillel and Fanny Zlatopolsky. The table was set with silver and crystal, with a magnificent centerpiece of spring flowers. Fanny Aronovna had donned a simple ankle-length skirt of blue raw silk, trimmed with fur at the hem, and her daughter, the formidable Shoshana Persitz of Homburg, was in deep navy. Mathilde's gown was her favorite mint green, a remake of an old gown that had once been Baroness Ida's. Sonia wore a sleeveless gown with a draped skirt of beige muslin, and no adornment whatsoever. She possessed none save the diamond crab which in fact belonged to her mother. Her hair was coiffed in the old-fashioned manner which became her so well, swept up into a demure topknot. She had made this dress with the help of Clara's maid, to save money. Fanny Aronovna admired it, and touched her arm with gentle familiarity, reminiscing about their meeting in Kiev in 1904; and Hillel beamed upon her, and placed her unquestioningly beside his son. But by the time Mathilde and Sonia were brought home to the foyer of Misha's mansion, there still had been no mention of marriage from the Zlatopolskys.

On Tuesday morning, Misha de Gunzburg asked his niece to meet him in his study, and closed the door. "Do you have any news for me?" he asked her. When she shook her head, he added, "Yet you have dined with his mother. He is not behaving properly toward you, Sonia. He should have declared his intentions. You are seeing him tonight, and if you do not return engaged, I shall close this house to you, little one. You can go live elsewhere." His eyes were twinkling at her, but Sonia was seized with a deep embarrassment.

She went to work and was met by Albert Manuel in the hallway. "So?" he asked, tilting his eyebrows quizzically. Sonia cast down her lids, and her manager declared teasingly: "Mademoiselle, if you are not betrothed this evening, do not bother to show yourself here tomorrow. One does not pull a young woman thus by the nose as this man does with you." He laughed and went into his own office.

He left her pensive. All this teasing was probably harmless, but she was no child of seventeen, who could be kept waiting. In their banter, Monsieur Manuel and her uncle had made her decision for her: this evening she would clinch her own destiny, once and for all, and put a stop to this emotional seesaw. She had no father to intercede on her behalf, and she was too mature to ask her uncle to do so, and too proud.

She was to sup with Mossia Zlatopolsky at Noël Peters, and then they were to see a play together, *The Chained*

Man. Very well, she thought, I shall see whether or not this particular man feels bound or free—the title is appropriate. She clothed herself very carefully in a narrow gown of utmost simplicity, a pearl-pink shade which matched the faint tint on her cheeks. Unlike the ladies of her day, she never wore rouge, and now she appeared particularly fresh and youthful and delicate, like a long-stemmed tea rose. The gown had been her New Year's gift from Clara and Misha, and she had never worn it, reserving it for a special occasion. When she met Mossia Zlatopolsky at the door, she was pleased to see the obvious admiration in his blue-green eyes.

He selected a small, intimate table, and ordered the supper: oysters on the half shell, potage Dubarry, duckling in wine, and a bottle of fine Bordeaux for himself, as Sonia did not enjoy alcohol. A string quartet was playing in a corner of the room.

Mossia ate in silence. Suddenly, her spoon midway between the soup plate and her mouth, Sonia regarded him and spoke, her voice clear above the beating of her heart in her throat. "Do you know," she asked, "that you are placing me in a compromising situation?"

"I?" he cried, his eyes widening.

"Yes," she continued mercilessly, "you compromise my reputation. Since the first time that you have taken me out, alone or with my mother, there been many occasions for you to speak. Yet you are silent, and now my friends have begun to ask why we are not engaged." Her gray eyes fastened on his large face, which had paled. "I need to know," she declared, leaning toward him, "whether the answer is 'yes' or 'no,' as to our future together."

"But," he asked in a low voice, "are you not afraid, after what I told you about my past, about my marriage?"

"No," she replied.

Her eyes, large and candid, remained upon his face, unabashed. He opened his mouth, shook his head, shrugged his massive shoulders—and looked at her with such unsuppressed ecstasy that Sonia could no longer doubt his feelings. "By God, of course it's 'yes'!" he exclaimed, taking her small hand and kissing it.

Sonia's lips parted and the blood rushed to her cheeks. She uttered a small cry of delighted laughter but she could not speak. The brilliant room seemed to whirl around her. Mossia motioned toward the waiter, who came at once. "Champagne!" he cried. "Champagne to toast my bride-to-be!" When the silver bucket was presented, Mossia said, "Forget the rest of the supper. Who can think of food?" But Sonia was still speechless with this magnificent joy that shook within her.

Then they became aware that the violinist had stopped by their table. After an elaborate bow, he began to play a gypsy song. Mossia laughed. "Do you know what this tune is?" he asked. "It's called 'Have Pity, Have Pity, My Darling.' How do you think he guessed at my sentiments?"

But Sonia raised his large fingers to her dainty lips. She was very moved. "My own darling, there is nothing in you to pity," she murmured. "Tell me, Mossia—was I really so frightening to you?"

"Perhaps more than you can imagine," he replied. "But my mind was made up from the first. When Schneerson, Willner, and I took you to supper at Sirdar, after seeing *The Blue Bird*, I had an ulterior motive for taking you to that particular restaurant. After Lialia, my mother did not trust my taste, and remembered you only as a girl of fourteen in Kiev. She knew that I had decided to marry you, and since Yosif Persitz, my brother-in-law, was in Paris on business, she asked that he look you over and report back to her, in Nice. You had never met him, for he always lived in Moscow, but he came to Sirdar by prearrangement and watched us. He found you utterly charming, perfect for me. And it seems that Papa has been in love with you since our first meeting, and rued my wayward ignorance of you when you visited Kiev in 1912. But how was I to know that another would declare himself right away, so quickly? It was the wrong moment for us. I was too callow, you would not even have noticed me. But I loved you truly when you first came to plead for Fuchs in your modest little blue suit."

"Yet you waited so long," she chided him, tears in her eyes.

"I was certain you would refuse me."

She could not resist then, and left her seat. She went to him and placed her arms about his neck, her laughter tumbling about him like joyous confetti. She kissed him. "You are a wonderful fool," she told him. "I want all that is you: your earnest look, your intense love of life, your generosity and impulsiveness, your loathsome past, even your domineering Zionist sister! I want to give you babies, to wake with you in the mornings. How could you have doubted me?"

"We must go at once to Saint-Germain," he interrupted her, "to tell your mother that I have ceased to bring you dishonor."

He stood and circled her frailty with his strong arm.

Sonia de Gunzburg sat at the outdoor café on the Champs Elysées, a string of the finest pearls around her neck, a matching pearl ring on the third finger of her left hand. "You would like him, Natalia Nicolaievna," she declared, and her gray eyes sparkled with small lights like diamond chips. "He is like Volodia—strong and steady, and yet he feels most deeply. He is completely Russian, a man of simple virtues and also of simple vices." She smiled. "You see, I already know him well."

Natasha said, "I am so pleased for you, Sofia Davidovna. You have suffered so, and deserve happiness. And I am glad that you compared him to Volodia—for my brother was very much in love with you, and would have sacrificed everything to become your husband."

Sonia bit her lower lip, pensively. The light spring breeze

kissed her cheeks and neck. Natasha sat opposite her, tall and graceful, wisps of black hair escaping at the nape of her slender neck. "Mossia would never want me to forget Volodia," Sonia said softly.

"Not if he truly understands you, which is apparent," Natasha replied. A sad smile painted itself over her lovely features. She said, "But I must forget Ossip, for I too understand him. He is a man who needs peace, which is one thing I cannot bring him. You must not tell him I am here, and a widow. Let him enjoy Japan with his new family. She deserves to try to make him happy. I have wrought sufficient havoc in his life. He is fragile, unlike you, Sofia Davidovna, and unlike myself. Do not blame her for her dominance of him: she is unsure of herself as his wife, as a Gunzburg. And if she loves him, she must know that Ossip will need guidance, that his own suffering has deprived him of a certain will. Forgive your brother, Sofia Davidovna."

"You will not attend my wedding?" Sonia asked.

"No," Natasha replied. "For many reasons." She smiled at the pretty girl her brother had loved, whose father had been her own father's fiercest opponent. She saw a girl who had alternately hated and liked her, who had lost and won and lost as she had. But Sofia Davidovna de Gunzburg was winning again. Volodia would have wanted that, she thought fondly, and then she sighed. Her own exile was more bitter, and she would win no more. She had to disappear from the lives of the Gunzburgs, forever. She did not belong to them. Regarding Sonia, she thought: But we have all changed, we are in our thirties. We shall never see Russia again. It is silly, and weak, to want to cling to the past. For it was the past that destroyed the Romanovs, when the present might have saved their dynasty . . .

Natasha rose, and behind her Sonia could see the Etoile, where her great-grandfather, the patriarch Ossip, had built his magnificent Parisian house, where her mother Mathilde had been born. There was great beauty in the sight of the noble Russian Princess outlined against the Arc de Triomphe. Sonia stood, too, and embraced Natasha wordlessly. No, she would not tell her brother.

After Natasha Tagantseva Kurdukova walked away, Sonia remained in place, feeling the sunshine upon her bare arms. Suddenly she knew that she had been right, long ago, to have questioned God's purpose in taking Kolya's love away from her. She had not understood it then, but now she did. God had known that, nine years later, she would find greater, more lasting happiness with Mossia Zlatopolsky. While she had grieved and sickened, God had planned. He had taken care of her, his daughter. She closed her eyes, overwhelmed with her joy, a joy she felt with every fiber of her body. She did not need to struggle any more, to wrestle with survival. She could afford to grow soft contours, to laugh freely. For she knew that she was loved.

Sonia de Gunzburg awakened on the day before her wedding with a calm feeling of plenitude. This was her last full day as an unmarried woman. She had never minded solitude and wondered sadly if she would miss it. She was marrying Mossia because she loved him, felt whole beside him; also because in many ways he represented all that she knew that she could never be: impulsive, generous to excess, a gambler. Still, she wondered. Her life had been as Sonia de Gunzburg, and it would be strange to become somebody's wife.

She did not want to speak with anyone that morning, wanting instead to be alone with her thoughts. This was one time in her life when she did not apologize for wishing to be selfish. Anna had arrived, and was staying in the house at Saint-Germain, along with Dalia and Riri. Now Sonia slipped noiselessly down the stairs and took the train into Paris.

First she had errands to take care of, going to various couturiers to try on items of a new wardrobe which Fanny Aronovna was purchasing for her as a wedding gift. At Dobbs on Avenue Victor Hugo there was a navy suit and several blouses; at Jeanne Lanvin a pink ball gown, its skirt composed of four floor-length pleats. Finally there was Worth, where she had her last fitting for her wedding gown. She departed carrying a large box in which lay a mantle of white velvet, trimmed with fur and lined with satin, for wearing to the synagogue. At a street corner Sonia undid the wrapping and removed the coat. It was sumptuous, a thing of true beauty, worthy . . . of St. Petersburg. Laughing, Sonia put the garment over her frail shoulders and walked off in the sunshine, a white princess among commoners, a snow queen among dribbles of rain. She felt good, wonderful in fact. And she was not ashamed. The Crimea was at last behind her.

Afterward, Sonia went to the temple for her ritual prenuptial bath. This was a ceremony which was important to Mossia's mother, and, strangely enough, to her own. At this crucial time Mathilde was holding onto rituals with ferocity. There was the bath, and also the matter of being married by the *Grand-Rabbin* of France. The *Grand-Rabbin* of Paris, a great friend of Sonia's, would simply not do for her mother: for since Mathilde's own wedding, all the Gunzburg women had been married by a Chief Rabbi of France, and anyone else would mar tradition.

When she arrived for supper at the home of her Aunt Clara, Sonia had spent the entire day walking and thinking, and was elated in her own quiet way. She went to bed early. Misha and Clara had thought it made more sense to have her sleep at their city residence the night before the great day, rather than let her return to Saint-Germain. But this time, when she slipped between the familiar covers, she was once again the young niece, the guest, and not the hired governess.

Before going to sleep, Sonia summoned two men from the past: her father, and Volodia Tagantsev. I have made a good decision, she said to them in her thoughts. You see, Volodia, I am too much a Jew to ever give up my faith. I am too much my father's daughter. But Mossia is real, as you were. He is of this earth, as I am. Somehow this make-believe conversation settled her last doubts. There was no pretense, no courtly dance about this wedding. Nobody would leave her at the altar.

But in the morning she awakened trembling. She was afraid. Kolya had thought fit to leave her. Had he not, too, loved her deeply? Was she meant not to marry, that one man should die and the other marry another woman? Mossia would not be there today; he would send her his excuses, and leave her standing alone, forever. Her heart was beating erratically, and there was a lump in her throat. All her ghosts had come rushing from their graves to invade her spirit.

With the enormous willpower upon which she could count to get her through the dire moments of her life, Sonia passed the time until ten thirty in the morning. Then her Uncle Misha came to take her to the city hall of the sixteenth district of Paris. She was going to be married there for the state, before her religious wedding. She donned a new champagne-colored dress, and put on her new hat, all of smart black osprey feathers. She was very pale. "What's the matter with you?" Misha teased her. But she felt so close to tears, so ridiculously afraid of rejection that she could not answer. She felt at once so foolish and so right that it would have been useless to discuss the black hole into which she had fallen that dawn. Not even Misha, whom she loved, would understand.

This was hardly an important ceremony for Sonia, and only Misha and his son, Serge, accompanied her. On the steps of city hall stood Mossia, with his two friends, Willner and Schneerson. When she saw him, Sonia nearly fainted. She saw her father-in-law, Hillel, waiting for them in a taxi, and began to laugh somewhat hysterically: whoever waited for the end of a wedding in a hired car? Sonia and Mossia were routinely married by the civil servant; and her uncle and small cousin, and Mossia's friends, signed the wedding forms as witnesses. In the street Misha's chauffeur jumped out to greet her: "Best wishes, Madame!" Then, and only then, did Sonia truly look into her new husband's face. He was laughing.

"Madame?" she repeated. "But we weren't really married yet, you know."

"No," Mossia said. "I suppose not. Although in the legal sense we are. We would have to divorce now to break our union."

Her gray eyes rested lightly on his mischievous features. But she did not respond. He might still leave her before the afternoon ceremony at the synagogue.

When Sonia returned to the house, the wedding gown had arrived from Worth, and now chaos reigned in the apartments of Clara de Gunzburg. Mathilde, in her pearl-gray gown, stood calmly by while seamstresses fussed around her daughter, and the hairdresser sent by Dondel, who had coiffed and curled the hair of every Gunzburg bride since Mathilde, combed and set the heads of Sonia's bridesmaids. There was Anna, in green; Tania, in pink, freshly arrived from Switzerland, and happily chatting to everyone; and Nina Abelson, in yellow. All three gowns had been made by Worth, and were cut in the same fashion, but Sonia had thought that the three women deserved to wear the color most suited to their hair and their complexions.

At last Sonia was dressed, and her magnificent black hair was loosely curled into a small chignon at the back, and coiled into two macaroons at the sides. The long white veil was pinned above the pompadour, and a small headband of orange flowers was placed over her forehead. Mossia had sent the bridal bouquet: three interwoven stems, the tallest a sprig of lilac, the second a fleur-de-lis, and the last a flurry of sweet-smelling lily-of-the-valley.

At the synagogue, Sonia saw Mossia, towering over his parents and his sister, Shoshana Persitz. Sonia took in her husband's gray striped trousers, black frock coat, and top hat. He was truly there, waiting to line up for the procession. His eyes held hers: I am here, they were saying. But she could not speak to him. They were being separated for the entrance. It was two o'clock.

As the organ music resounded in the Temple Chasseloup-Laubat, the various children, Gunzburg cousins and second cousins, walked in couples to the nuptial dais at the front. Serge was among them, and Riri. Then came the bridesmaids: Anna, Tatiana, Nina. Finally it was Sonia's turn. "Remember that I love you," Misha whispered. David would have said it just so. Sonia nodded, overcome; she stepped onto the heavy carpet, and behind her two tiny girls held her long trail. A suitable distance behind this billow of white, Mossia walked with his mother, Fanny; then Hillel with Mathilde.

The *Grand-Rabbin* of France spoke eloquently for twenty minutes. His discourse concerned the great Gunzburg name, allied as it was today with the Zlatopolskys. Sonia found herself listening to him with all her heart. It did matter, somehow, what was said at her own wedding. She had never thought to pay attention to the speeches at other weddings, but now she was hungry for the feeling of belonging to a venerable tradition. Someday a child of hers would want to know about the families from which he had come. A child. Hers and Mossia's . . .

She was so entranced by the magnificent words, by the mystical importance of the surroundings, by the music so noble in its strength, that when it came time for the vows she felt uplifted, above it all. Mossia placed the ring upon her finger, and said, "In the name of Abraham, Jacob,

Isaac, and Moses, you are my wife." The Rabbi had bent to whisper the sentence to him, but he already knew it by heart. She smiled then, a smile which radiated from her entire body.

They were married now, man and woman united. The Rabbi blessed them, read them the marriage act in Hebrew, and Sonia and her husband drank wine together from the silver chalice. Then a young boy brought Mossia the small glass to break. Sonia watched in dismay as her beloved, suddenly afraid to miss his throw, stepped back and, with all the force of his enormously powerful body, hurled the fragile object upon the floor. It shattered, its myriad shards flying in all directions, making the bridesmaids move back to avoid the glass. A noise bubbled, then grew in volume: and Sonia Zlatopolskaya turned to see the smiling, laughing faces of her friends and family. She looked at Mossia: helplessly, he made a charming gesture admitting his clumsiness. She pressed a gloved hand to her mouth and giggled, a girl again.

In high spirits, they proceeded to the reception at Clara's home. It was a moment for mirth and champagne. Mathilde, however, sat down on a small bench with Riri, and passed a hand through the fine gold of his hair. He was a young man now, and she said, seriously, "What plans do you have, Reza Hadjani? Tell me about them. You know, I have never known how to handle rebellion. But if you feel at odds with the world I shall listen. I think that I could learn to listen, to you."

In front of the fireplace, extinguished now because it was spring, Tatiana raised her periwinkle eyes to a face she had not seen for many years. Jean de Gunzburg had sought to avoid her at the synagogue, and she him. Now, by chance, as groups of wedding guests moved about, they found themselves side by side. "You are lovely," he said to her quietly, without preamble. "Maturity becomes you."

"But I don't always like it," she retorted. Weddings were not for tears of pain, only for tears of catharsis. She looked away, her throat constricting. "It is not fair," she said. "Leave me alone."

"You are not happy?"

Slowly then, with dignity, she met his gaze. "Who knows? But it's the way I am, anyway. I am happier than you, for I have three handsome sons, and you are alone."

"They told me that one of your children is called 'Jean,'" he said softly.

"Yes . . . I have always liked the name. Forgive me now, I must circulate among the guests." Casually, with the tips of her fingers, she brushed his cheek, then turned on her heel. He watched the small, voluptuous shape disappear into the crowd, and sighed. Somebody spoke to him. He looked up and smiled pleasantly. The music played all around him and he was alone, as she had said.

Enveloped in clouds of white lace, Sonia too heard the celebration of the string quartet. There were, she knew, no guarantees: perhaps the symphony of her life would not always retain the frenzied joy that was hers today, but there was a grandeur to the music, a grandeur to simply being alive. Sonia had survived, in her body and her heart. Pressing Mossia's arm, she whispered, "Why don't we leave now?"

That night, in the bridal suite of the Trianon Palace in Versailles, where he had bared his past to her, Sonia looked at her husband's reflection in the vast gilt mirror. She knew then why she had chosen to love him. He was broad and tall, like the vastness of Russia; poignant and vulnerable, a surging force like the four winds of heaven. In his sea-green eyes shone the soaring spires and onion-domed cupolas of her youth, a reflection of a paradise lost. There was no turning back, and perhaps there should be none; but she could never have shared her future with a man who did not, in himself, also contain her past. She smiled at him in the mirror, but her gray eyes were grave.

Before coming to him she went to the small table where

she had laid her bridal bouquet, and she extracted from it a small sprig of lilac. She inhaled its scent, then with strong fingers she opened her gilt-edged Bible, a Bible that had belonged to generations of Gunzburgs, to Baron David before her—and she carefully placed the white flower between two pages. "For Gino," she said. "When he returns he will know that we have waited for him, that this day did not go by without a thought of him."

When Mossia nodded, she walked to him on the tips of her toes, the better to reach him. She kissed him fully on the lips, and said, "This is my dowry, beloved."